MEMORY'S WAKE

Omnibus First Published October 2017
Paperback ISBN: 978-0-6480269-5-2
Hardcover ISBN: 978-0-9875635-8-3

THE MEMORY'S WAKE OMNIBUS
Book One - Memory's Wake
Book Two - Hope's Reign
Book Three - Providence Unveiled

www.memoryswake.com

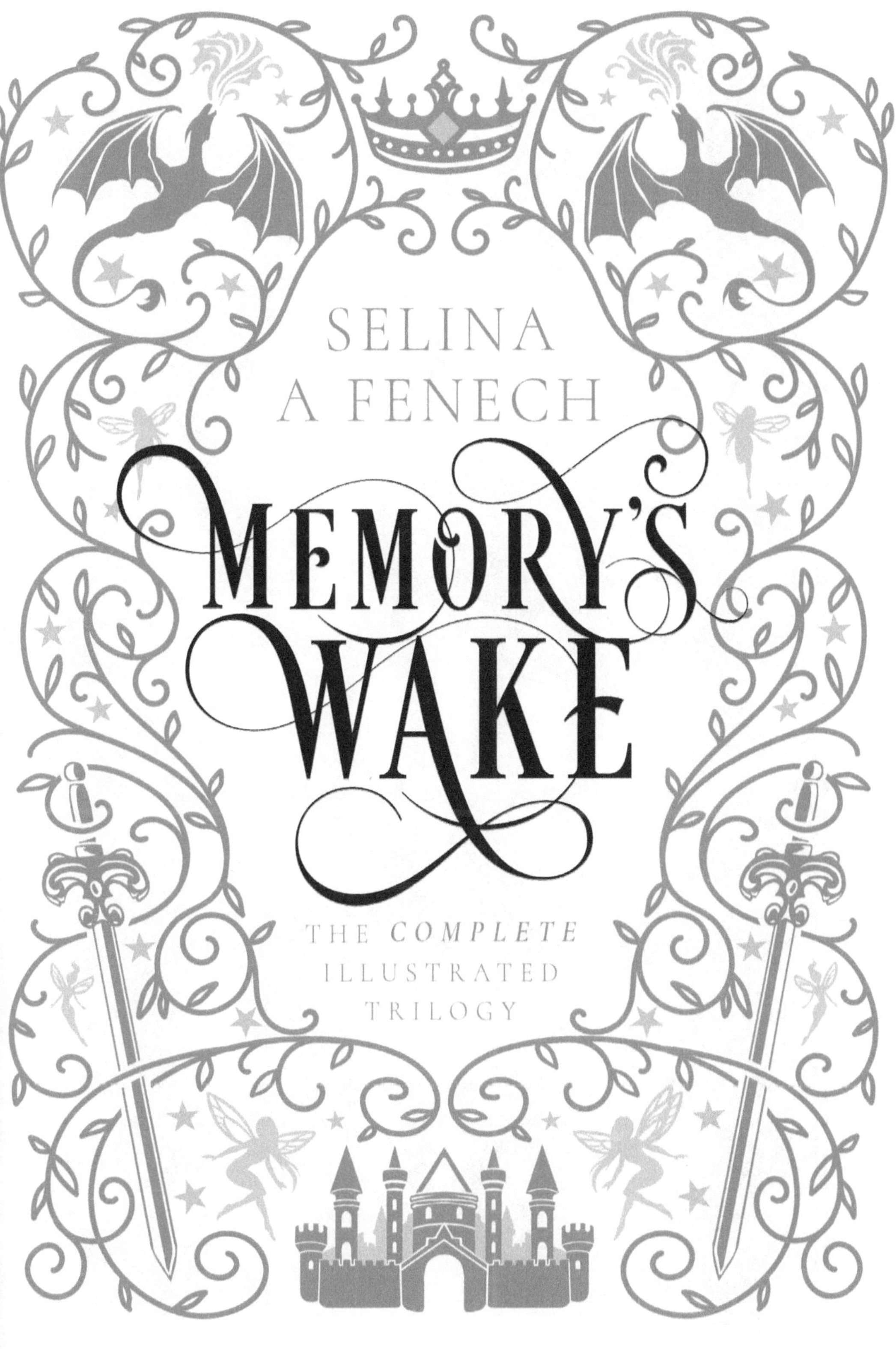
SELINA
A FENECH

MEMORY'S
WAKE

THE COMPLETE
ILLUSTRATED
TRILOGY

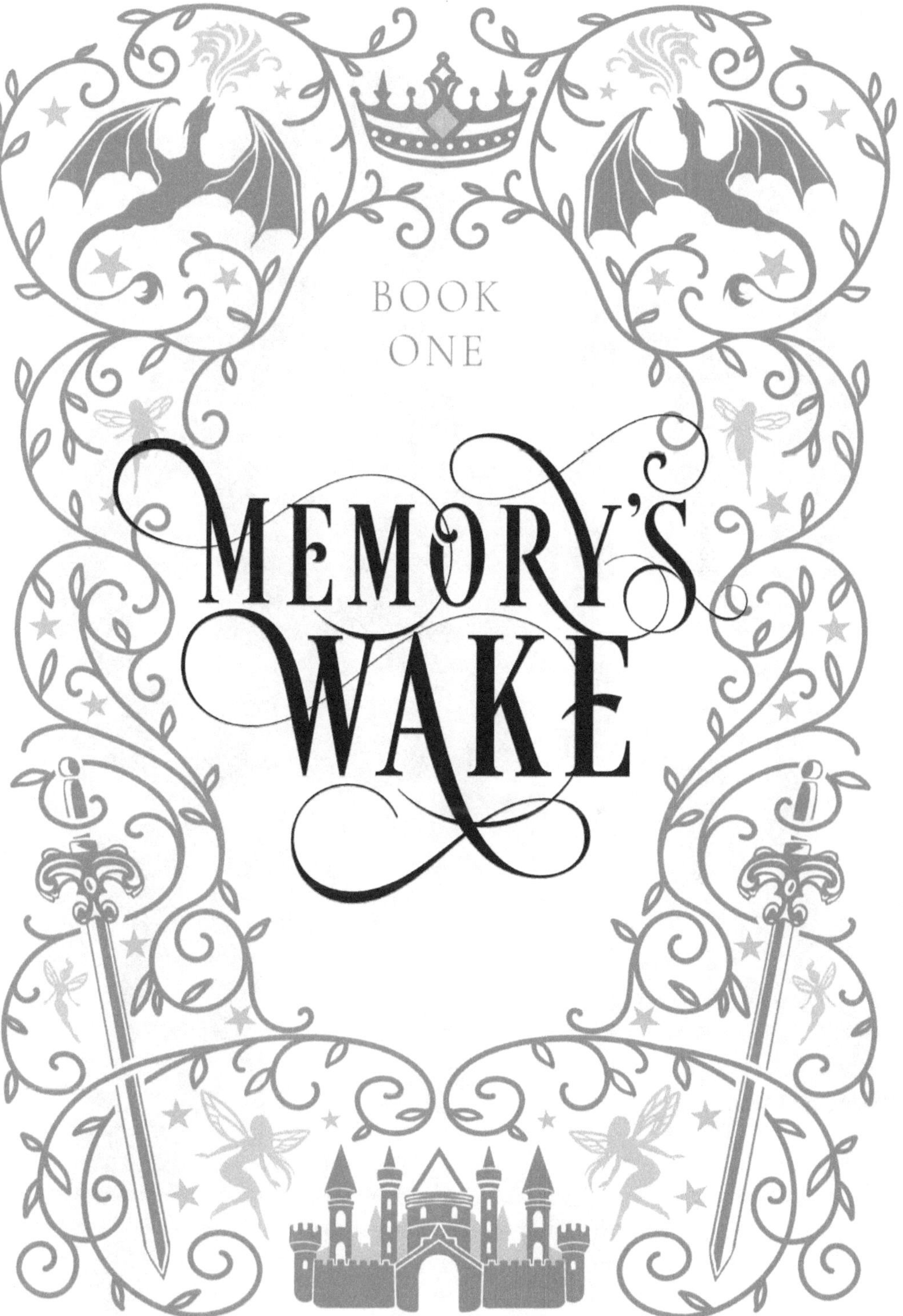

BOOK
ONE

MEMORY'S
WAKE

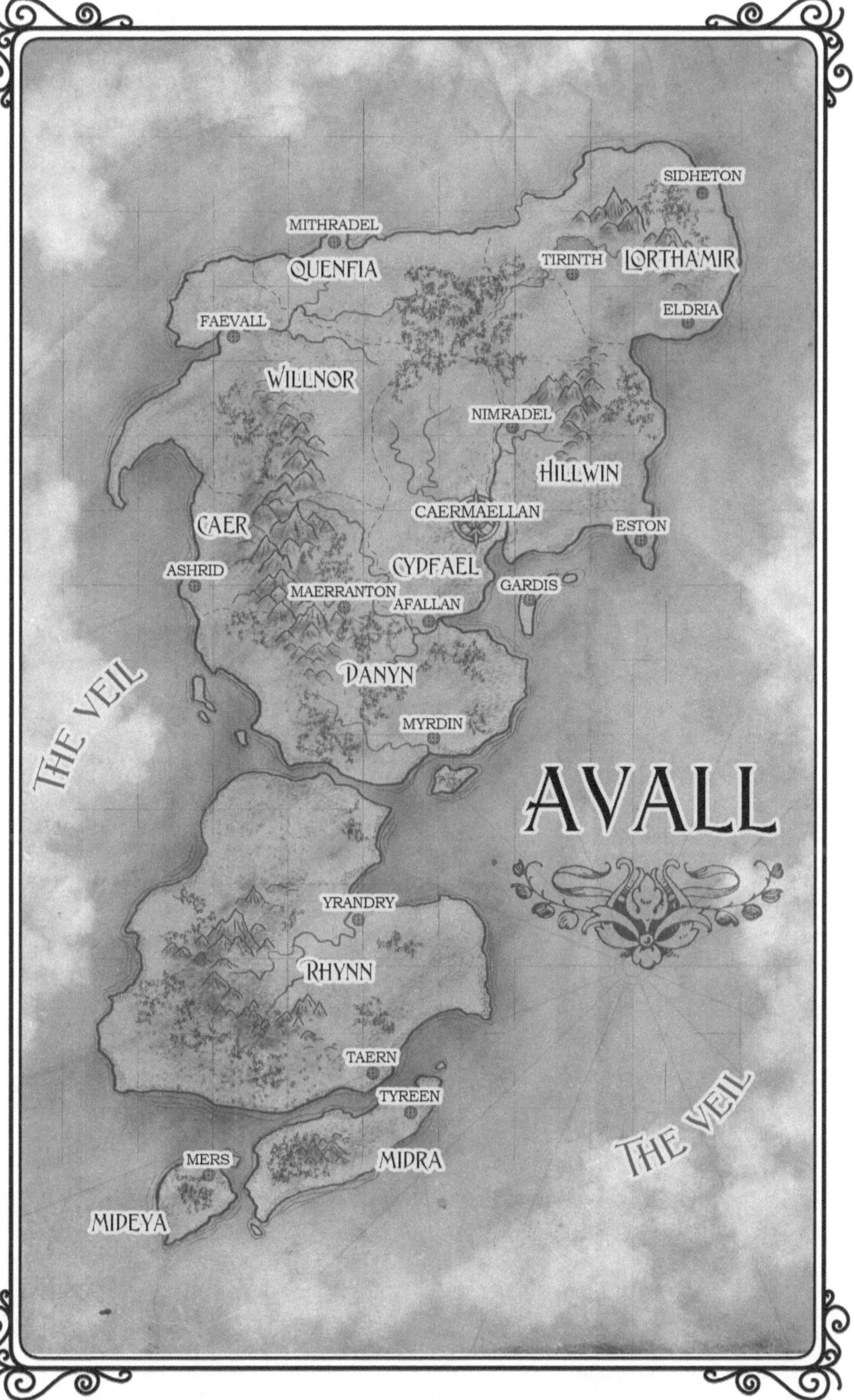

SIDHETON
MITHRADEL
QUENFIA
TIRINTH
LORTHAMIR
ELDRIA
FAEVALL
WILLNOR
NIMRADEL
HILLWIN
CAERMAELLAN
ESTON
CAER
ASHRID
CYDFAEL
GARDIS
MAERRANTON
AFALLAN
DANYN
MYRDIN
THE VEIL
AVALL
YRANDRY
RHYNN
TAERN
TYREEN
THE VEIL
MERS
MIDRA
MIDEYA

CHAPTER ONE

She knew only darkness and a horrible, hateful wind.

I'm falling.

She flailed, panicking.

Where am I?

All she remembered was a furious, bellowing rumble, like the call of a hungry dragon. It churned her insides as much as the sensation of falling.

As though woken from a nightmare, her senses felt muddled. Nothing made sense. She couldn't understand why she still heard that noise, why she still felt as though she plummeted into hell.

Some other sound teased her, unidentifiable, lost in the wind.

"What's happening? Is someone there?" Pain rampaged through her and the questions fell away.

The sound again. It was a voice. Hysterical, all static and unclear sounds.

The girl called out, tearing her throat raw with effort, trying to reach through the gusting void to whoever had spoken. "I can't hear. Help. It hurts!"

The talking stopped.

No, come back. Please.

The wailing wind and painful rumbling continued. Her insides

rattled as if her ribcage had been hollowed out and filled with marbles. She thought she might throw up.

Hands grabbed her.

The shock of that touch forced out a scream.

Then, like slamming a door on a windy day, the tearing air stopped. The world became solid. Her skin still tingled right to her fingertips but the pain had gone. Only a deep burning in her chest remained. Panic crawled up her back, tugging at her with icy fingers.

Stop. Look. Feel, she ordered herself, attempting slow breaths.

Dark hair hung around her face, curtaining her vision. She lay on the ground, face down.

Did I really fall? Her body hurt all over. Maybe she had.

Old blackened leaves spread in front of her eyes, and the smell of dirt and rot added to her lingering nausea. Sharp twigs poked through her jeans. She spat soil from her mouth.

That other voice spoke again. It was a girl's voice — young, like her own. A strange accent made it curiously elegant and musical. The tremor of fear in it only made it more so. "By the fae, what has happened? Can you hear me now?"

Fighting the weakness in her body, the dark-haired girl nodded to the voice and managed to roll over. She propped herself up on her elbows and looked out into a twilit forest of wild briars and giant trees. Beside her, another girl crouched on the ground, plump and strikingly pretty, with skin and hair so pale it was almost white against the shadowed woods. The long hair tumbled all around the stranger, making her look like a beautiful, scared ghost.

Their breathing matched each other's; fast, labored, scared out of their minds. An intense frown of thought and calculation marred Ghost-girl's face. The look of a mind weighing options, assessing risks, looking for answers. In her own head, the dark-haired girl could feel nothing but the fractures of stress upon her sanity.

She stared at Ghost-girl, hoping for some recognition. No name came to her, yet she felt a strange connection to the pale girl. She wondered what it could mean. Her thoughts scattered in all directions, racing frantically, searching for answers to the growing crowd of questions. Every query drew a blank. She felt completely lost.

"Alward?" Ghost-girl called out into the trees. "Alward? Oh no, he didn't make it through." Wide green eyes, shadowed and full of fear,

darted from the surrounding woods back onto her. "I'm not where I ought to be. Did you do this, did you bring me here? Was it magic of yours?"

The lost girl gaped at the blonde. *Magic? Is that why my skin's tingling like this? But magic's not real.*

She wasn't sure she could say just now what was or wasn't real, but the accusations confused and stung. She was sure she hadn't done any bringing. And certainly not with magic.

There must have been some kind of accident, she thought, feeling like the victim of something.

She worked hard to find her voice again. "What..." She paused. So many questions, where to start? "What happened?"

Ghost-girl wore a wary frown. "You don't know? Please, it is important you tell me the truth. If you are a caster of unauthorized magic, know I'm not an enemy." She made a complex hand gesture. When no response came, her frown turned from wary to scared. She gasped and spoke as though to herself. "Unless... no, you couldn't be one of Thayl's wizard hunters?"

"Whose what hunters?" The lost girl's words slurred, her head still spinning. "Was there an accident? Shouldn't we get help?" She sat up and brushed dirt from her face, wincing when she touched a tender area under her eye.

"You are hurt, but I don't know how, I don't..." Ghost-girl's voice worked up into the high pitch of panic. She visibly swallowed it down. "I need to find out where I am."

She turned away, reached down and dug her fingers into the earth, then spoke too quietly to hear. The ground trembled into a shiver, growing outwards, expanding quickly, up tree trunks, along branches, tickling the leaves at the treetops.

A thousand voices whispered.

Brilliant. I'm hallucinating. The lost girl put a hand to her forehead, dizzied by the disembodied voices. *How hurt am I? Concussion? Brain damage?*

The blonde was talking nonsense again, words flying. "...too close to home. The Veil door didn't take me far enough away. They've found me, already? The hunters, they're coming this way. We have to go! Please, I don't know how you came to be here, but listen. There are people chasing me. If they find you here, they'll think you're one of us. We have to run." She stood in a cascade of crumpled dress, face turned up toward the canopy of woven branches screening the dimming sky.

"They're almost here, and their beast… their dragon…"

Everything was on fast forward. With her face half hidden behind her black hair, the lost girl thought maybe she could let herself cry. This was too much, too many words, too much chaos, to still feel so empty inside.

"Slow down. I don't understand. Do I know you?"

"I do not know you, but I can't have you caught here when they are hunting me." She felt the touch of Ghost-girl's hand, plump and gentle on her own. Not a ghost after all. "Come with me. My name is Eloryn." She smiled, but the urgency in her features soured the expression.

The lost girl tried to respond. "I'm… My name is…"

Nothing. Nothing at all.

Her emptiness. It came into perfect, terrifying clarity. She knew nothing of who she was.

No name.

No home.

No memories.

Only a void where her life should have been.

The canopy above them shuddered as violently as her heart.

Leaves rained down. Through them, an impossible creature appeared. It crushed through the trees, talons reaching for Eloryn.

The hungry dragon from her dream.

Of course, I'm still dreaming. Ghosts, wizards, dragons, none of those are real. But the claws were so sharp, so vivid.

Squeezing Eloryn's hand tighter, the lost girl pulled her out of the way before the razor tips could strike. "Go!" she screamed, to herself, to Eloryn, or the dragon above them she didn't know, but they all began to move.

The dragon writhed, reaching for them from between the massive oaks above. Branches groaned and splintered against the beast's strength, creating a hailstorm of sharp twigs. Strong trunks held back the black mass and it hissed in frustration, talons swiping just above the girls' heads.

"This way!" Eloryn pulled her by the hand. The girls crashed through briars and stumbled over fallen logs slick with moss.

Through the grim grey trees, men in leather military jackets ran toward them. Orders were yelled, metal flashed, boots crushed ferns, thumping the ground with heavy feet. Wings beat in the sky above, blowing about dirt and dry leaves. Talons raked at the tree line.

The girls ran faster, hand in hand. The dragon roared.

Eloryn lead the way through the woods, her petticoats catching and pulling, slowing her down. In tight jeans, the lost girl had more freedom to move but her legs felt weak, wobbly. She barely kept up with Eloryn.

The hunters were so close.

To her left, a bear-sized man came within reach. She cried out, pushing her body to move faster. Her vision blurred from sweat running into her eyes. She cringed, expecting to feel rough hands locking around her arm, pulling her down.

Nothing came. She turned to see why. The man was gone.

She tried to look for her pursuer and still watch the treacherous ground under her feet. Trees flashed past. Shadows flashed between them, toward her.

Something struck another man, just to her right. A dark form dropped from the branches above, bringing him to the ground.

A cry of pain and the hunter was gone.

What fresh horror was that?

She had no time or desire to find out. The trees above cracked as the dragon plunged again. Lichen shook from the bark and fell like green snow.

Wake up. Wake up. This has to be a nightmare. Breathing burned her chest and rattled in her throat, but a deep inner dread kept her running hard. These men, that beast, chasing her, hungry for the hunt, boiled her emotions down to pure, distilled panic.

Eloryn still dragged her onwards by a hand and mumbled between her labored breaths.

Then the running became easier. Fewer branches blocked their path. Fewer brambles tore at them. The trees *moved*, bending away from her and Eloryn, then closing back in to hinder their pursuers. The lost girl blinked but the sureal images remained.

Reaching a sudden steep incline, Eloryn let go of her hand and ran toward a rocky outcrop. "In here!" she called and disappeared into a dark crack in the mountain side.

Moving to follow Eloryn, the girl slowed, faint from exhaustion. Her vision dimmed and starred.

Staring at that thin sliver of black, ringed by unwelcoming rocks, she shivered.

What, you're more scared of the dark than what's chasing you? Get in there.

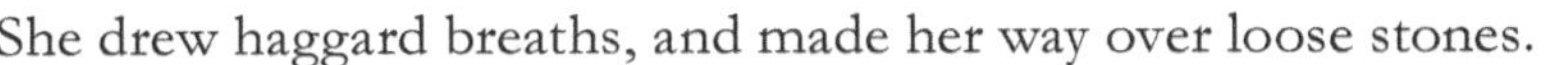

She drew haggard breaths, and made her way over loose stones.

Just a step away, a creature landed in front of her, blocking the cave entrance.

The shock stole her breath and her balance.

Scrambling backwards, she fell hard onto the forest floor.

No, not a creature, she realized, looking up from the ground.

The figure looked back at her with concerned human eyes. A young man, dirty and tattered and animal in nature, but a man. Soil darkened his skin and earth brown hair hung down bare shoulders in knotted locks.

His knuckles were reddened with blood.

She lay there, a deer in headlights, unable to move.

Then there were more men, pushing through the trees, yelling furiously as they battled against the forest itself.

Eloryn had left her, long gone into the slim crack in the mountainside. There was nowhere to go. Surrounded with the hunters behind and the beast-man blocking the way forward, she lay dumbfounded.

She wished her brain would work. Wished she'd just wake up.

The beast-man reached down for her.

"No, don't touch me!" She cowered but could see only worry in his features. Grabbing her arm, he lifted and threw her into the cave. She tumbled, barely missing Eloryn who crouched inside with her head against the stone, talking to herself.

Shaking with adrenaline, the lost girl looked out through the cave entrance.

The beast-man stared back in. His eyes shone piercing blue even in the fading light. His shoulders shifted as though he was about to follow, but with the deep growl of a hunting cat he turned away.

The hunters ran for the girls.

The ground shook. Stones scraped against each other, tumbling and falling in a dangerous tide, and the cave entrance sealed.

For the second time in the brief, harsh moments of her memory, all she knew was darkness.

CHAPTER TWO

She looked at me like I was some kind of animal.

Worse. A monster.

The terror in her eyes, her plea not to touch her, crushed him. It felt as though the rockslide that closed the cave entrance had also fallen on his chest.

Didn't she recognize me?

He had been waiting for her for so long. Then he heard the noise, that same gusting howl he remembered from his first night in this world, coming from the very same spot.

The night he would never forget.

Just how long had it been? The years felt longer for being unable to count them, but shorter for his time spent with the fae. So long, lost in that forest, doubting he'd ever see her again, wondering if his memories of her were even real.

But here she was, looking just the same. Same age, same hair, same clothes, even the same bruises as the day he had lost her. *How?*

The dust from the rockslide cleared, and the hunting men who had chased the girls still surrounded him. Them and the dragon. It circled above, waiting for something. To give the men their next order? He shifted his eyes upwards uneasily. He'd never seen a dragon before. They were legendary, even to the fae he knew, and scarce.

The men coughed and swore, wiping their eyes. They looked at him,

probably wondering how he fitted into their chase.

He'd been mistaken as an animal by hunters before. He didn't like hunters. A growl rumbled from his throat.

They were hunting her. He wouldn't let anyone hurt her. Not again. Not now that he was stronger. Getting out of this corner himself mightn't be so easy, but he had the advantage. This was *his* forest.

He sized up each of the men, picking the weakest of the herd. That bald one, who stood there puffing, winded from the chase.

He sprang at the man without warning. Landing on his rounded shoulders with both feet, he pushed off, using the man's height to launch higher. He burst through a spray of leaves and wrapped a hand onto a thick branch, swinging himself up onto another.

Behind him the men milled about, too busy yelling at each other over their lost prey.

Their voices grew dim behind him. He ran across branches as though they were solid ground.

His mind raced even faster. *Why didn't she recognize me? Have I changed that much?*

He couldn't remember the last time he'd seen a mirror. That sort of thing had lost its meaning out here in the woods. Until today. Seeing her again made him think of things he hadn't thought of for half a lifetime. Things like mirrors, showers, soap.

The hunters were far behind by the time he slowed and dropped back to the forest floor. He brought his hands up in front of his face. Black earth and muck painted his pale skin. *I'm filthy.*

He picked up his pace again, heading to the nearest stream. Then stopped abruptly. He wasn't thinking straight. He'd finally found her then lost her again within the same moment. Washing could wait. He had to go after her, and he would need help.

"Mina?" He didn't call loudly. She always heard him anyway. It was up to her if she came or not. He knelt down on a patch of moss between the vast trees and verdigris boulders, preparing himself to wait for her arrival.

"My sweet pet. You're here too?" Mina giggled behind him, her voice more familiar to him than his own.

He stood and turned to see her, and found her accompanied by a large host of other fairies.

What are they all doing here?

No matter how often he saw them, he never got over the sight of the fae. It made his heart ache and beat faster just to be in their presence. He'd learned names for some of the forms of fae he had seen in his life here. Names he knew from the myths of his childhood. Mina would have been a sprite. Her true form was tiny, glowing, a dazzling flicker of sparkling light. But she could take other forms, as could most of the seelie fae. Despite their names, their categories, they were each unique, changeable and perfect.

Before him now, Mina stood as tall as he did, able to look him straight in the eye, her clothes woven from strands of cobweb silk, blossoms and dew drops that drew delicate patterns across milky skin and hung in flowing waves. Her vibrant fiery hair lifted around her with a life of its own. She flashed a heart stopping grin at him. A dozen more sprites shimmered in the branches nearby. Watching from behind tree trunks, a few also took larger forms, some with skin tinted green or gold, some with wings, some without.

He recognized Yvainne amongst them, walking — gliding — toward him. "Something new has come to the forest. Something that will affect us all." Her voice tingled in his ears.

He knelt. "It's her. The one I waited for."

Mina scowled.

Met with silence, he continued. "Hunters were there too, and a dragon. They chased her and another girl into the caves." His heart lurched. Danger lurked in those caves. He'd planned to follow, keep her safe, but then the cave entrance crumbled, separating him from her again.

Yvainne's eyes fluttered, irritated maybe, or bored.

"I want to find her. Can I... Could you help me?" He bowed further, holding his breath.

"You should know she is changed. Within her there is something unnatural, something dangerous. She is not the way you remember her."

"Please."

Yvainne turned her back on him and glided away.

He jumped to his feet, taking a step after her. "Please!"

"We will be following her." Irritation clear in her voice, she didn't turn back to look at him. "She needs to be watched. Mina is coming with us, so I assume you will too."

She faded out of sight while her last words still rang through the air. Other sprites around her twinkled and vanished like stars disappearing

at dawn.

Mina remained standing next to him. "*Her.*"

He turned around with an apology on his lips, but Mina already grinned at him, her eyes sparkling. He was used to it now, how her moods shifted so fiercely. He smiled back at her. He couldn't help it.

"They know where she is. We'll follow later," Mina said, all chimes.

He itched to leave now. After so long, he didn't want to wait another moment. He started to wonder what he would do when he found her again. So long… and he'd never thought of that, only thought of finding her, making sure she was safe.

Could they go home? She didn't even recognize him… But those men chased her as though they knew her. And that dragon. Why?

Mina leant against him, toying with his arm, tracing the muscles and scars with a long finger.

"Do those men follow the dragon? Is that why they chase her?" he asked.

"Her! Can you think of nothing but *her*?" Anger flared in Mina's eyes, and her orange hair lifted in matching flames. She let his arm drop and stalked away from him. "And those men. They try to leash the dragon. They give him orders. How could they? Fool men! Better to leash fire or thunder! Using that desecrated flute, that abomination. They will burn for it one day." Mina growled, and a shower of glitter dust shook from her.

"The men control the dragon?" He knew the sort of power the fae had and even to them dragons were of unimaginable might. "Tell me how, I don't understand."

Something shifted in Mina's eyes. "Maybe later." She smiled again, bringing her hands up in front of her. Luscious berries of rainbow tones spilled from them. "Come and eat with me."

His flesh shivered over his bones, his whole body pulled with desire. He had no words to describe the flavors of fairy foods, the magic they made him feel. Mina stood in front of him like a picture straight from his memory. The very first time he'd met her, she stood just the same way, holding wondrous food when he had been so, so hungry.

With an almost painful effort he closed the hunger away. He tried to sound neutral when he replied. "I can catch my own food now. I'm not hungry."

Mina hissed, and threw the food on the ground. It grayed and rotted in an instant. In a flash and a blink, she was small enough to stand on the tip of a finger, and shot away into the forest like a shooting star.

"Mina, I'm sorry." No sign or sound of her returned. "Mina?"

A clammy sweat crept over his skin. He had to stay on her good side, or she could — she would — leave him behind. She'd left him on his own countless times before, for days, weeks, months, as punishments for the slightest affront. He didn't mind being on his own, but now he needed her help.

He looked around wildly for a sign of the fairy's trail, running after her, faster than he'd ever run in his life.

CHAPTER THREE

Earlier.

Why has it become so hard to keep my mind on a simple book? Focus, Eloryn ordered herself.

Her eyes skimmed over words without absorbing any meaning. She pinched her forehead and flicked back a page, trying to find the last information she'd actually retained from *The Principles and History of Infantry Warfare.* Alward no doubt had his reasons for making this dull book part of her syllabus but she couldn't see how it would ever be much use to her, either for her teaching or in practice.

If she was learning things she couldn't share with her own students, she'd prefer to be studying magic.

Learning used to be easy. As a child, Eloryn already knew everything Alward taught the farmers' children. She went to classes with them anyway, enjoying being with the other students. They stopped coming at age ten, schooled enough for their lives tending fields. She became a teacher herself after that while her own education continued. Now at sixteen, teaching felt repetitive, and she rarely saw anyone her own age.

Apart from her small clutch of young students she rarely saw anyone at all. They lived alone, just herself and Alward, here in the fortified old monastery high in the wooded hills, set apart even from the tiny rural hamlet.

It was a place where no one might recognize Alward, or herself, for

who they really were. A place they could be safe.

Eloryn brushed against the pink flowers that spilt over the garden wall where she sat. They released a syrupy fragrance and she breathed it deeply, hoping to quell the unnamed ache in her chest.

"Riddip."

Grateful for a distraction, Eloryn smiled to the speckled frog that hopped up onto her knee. "Kiss you? Why do you want me to kiss you?"

"Riddip."

Eloryn giggled. "Oh, a handsome prince under a curse, and just one kiss from a beautiful princess will set you free? I've known you since you were a tadpole, little fool." Eloryn poked him and imagined he smirked bashfully in return. But really, he always looked like that. "I shouldn't have read you that story." Eloryn sighed. Night approached, stealing away the friendly light. The high stone courtyard walls loomed over her. "I shouldn't have read me that story."

"Riddip."

"I don't know. There might be romance like that out there, and adventure and charming princes, but not here. Those things happen in places far, far away."

"Riddip."

"Shush! Really." Eloryn dropped her voice to a scandalized whisper. "Owain only comes by to deliver produce for us. I'm sure he's taken little notice of me."

But she couldn't say she hadn't noticed him, with his feathery brown hair and strong wide shoulders. Eloryn closed her eyes and turned her face into the sun, enjoying the last few warm rays. Rather than focusing on infantry warfare, Eloryn found herself developing tactics to be the one to greet Owain on his next visit. She wondered what it would be like to hold his work-worn hands, and the heat from the sun's touch spread through her whole body.

"Eloryn!"

She jumped, and a deep blush bloomed on her face.

Alward bellowed from his chamber window overlooking the courtyard. "In here. Quickly!"

The urgency in his tone made her bolt to her feet, dropping book and frog from her lap. She whispered a sorry to her friend and puffed her way up the stairwell to Alward's quarters.

Inside, Alward had shoved all the furniture aside to clear the space,

knocking precious books off shelves in the process. Shards of a broken porcelain cup lay ignored in a puddle of still steaming tea, and the floor mat had been lifted and thrown over an armchair.

Alward wore his normal grey suit, the top buttons now undone and sleeves rolled up. He hunched over the floor, scrawling magical symbols and words in charcoal. Eloryn recognized with excited fear what he was doing.

The workings of a Veil door.

"Ellie." Alward stood up to inspect his work. Pushing his glasses back up his nose he left a line of black soot behind. His graying blond hair, tied back in its usual ponytail, frayed and escaped from its bonds. "We have to go. We've been found. I don't know how. Someone in the village perhaps recognized me. I'm sorry child. Hurry, fetch the pack."

Eloryn's mouth turned dry. She always knew they could be found, but one thought stormed through her head, leaving her dazed. *Why now? Why have they found us now?* Her chest tightened. *Please don't let this be my fault.*

Forcing her body to move, she went to a large wooden chest and unlocked it with a spoken behest, pulling out a packed bag that had been prepared for just this day.

Alward still focused on the complex spell words, so to keep busy and calm her nerves, Eloryn took a fresh loaf from Alward's desk and tucked it into the top of the leather satchel.

Alward called her to his side and she skittered to him, stepping carefully within the wide ring of soot-black words and trying to hide her shaking. She tilted her head back to look up into his face, which had begun showing the deeper lines of age.

A crash rattled up from the monastery entrance, making Eloryn gasp. Alward's eyes darkened and he put a hand on her shoulder.

"It will all be well, my girl. The spell is set. Stay close to me. Be brave, the experience is not pleasant." His expression held sad secrets she often saw when their eyes met. It sometimes made her wonder if he was disappointed in her, in his responsibility to care for her. Her heart leaped about and she clung to the leather pack as though it were a stuffed doll.

The charcoal words hummed and glowed when Alward began incanting in his gravelly voice. The Veil door was a long and complicated spell that most would have to read from a page, but Alward knew the ancient words well from years of study. The spell markings on the floor

exploded into magical fire, and tendrils of smoke twisted around them, moving in unnatural ways.

The vapor enveloped them. Eloryn watched as her own body began to take on the likeness of the smoke, shimmering into the Veil. It was wondrous, terrifying and painful.

She turned to Alward for reassurance and saw a stranger standing in the doorway.

"Alward! They're here," Eloryn cried out.

Lost in his focus on the spell, Alward continued to chant.

The man at the doorway also called out and more men joined him, pouring into the room.

One man, with a scarred face and lion's mane hair, drew a fine crossbow. He shot a splinter-sized dart that lodged itself into Alward's chest.

Alward's form became solid.

Light exploded in the room, knocking back the other men. Magical fire and living smoke, no longer under control, sparked and hissed, shifting like violent shadows.

Whipping mists ripped into Eloryn, still caught within the Veil, barely there.

Alward strained toward Eloryn with charcoal blackened hands.

She reached back but her hand passed through his.

Then she was gone.

In the black of the cave, Eloryn took a moment to ease the burning in her throat and stifle the sob building in her chest.

She choked.

Asking the rocks to fall had seemed clever at first. Now she wasn't so sure. Dust hung in the air, thick and invisible in the darkness, clogging her throat with each breath.

At least I'm safe now. Safe until Alward can find me again. Eloryn pressed her bottom lip between her teeth. Safe, maybe, but she'd already made grave mistakes. The strange girl had even seen her using unauthorized magic.

Girl? Eloryn had taken her to be a boy at first, wearing what she did. Maybe it was a disguise? The girl even refused to share her name. She could be hiding something too.

Now Eloryn only needed to cast a simple behest, one of the few authorized spells every person in Avall knew. The behest for light. "Àlaich las."

Her request granted, the wisp appeared, creating a soft glow around Eloryn's hand and illuminating the girl across the tunnel. Her strangely trimmed hair, short, ragged and roughed up at the back and long at the front, was rich black and... pink? *Could hair be pink?* She cast her gaze over the girl's face and its odd metal pins and gems, pierced through nose, lips, eyebrows, sparkling against obvious bruising. The injuries weren't from their recent chase. The yellow swelling of the girl's jaw and purple around her eye had matured a good few hours. The hand the girl pressed to her forehead had fought some battle, with grated knuckles and blood around black fingernails. She moved with stiffness and hesitation that told of other pain throughout her body.

Worry nagged at Eloryn. Just moments out of his care and she already longed for Alward's guidance. She remembered tumbling through the Veil, turning to wait for Alward to follow, and instead seeing this girl. Screaming. Shimmering in and out of existence.

How, how could she possibly have appeared there, caught in our Veil door like that? None of this makes sense. How could I begin to guess her motives? Eloryn pulled her shoulders up to her ears to fight off a chilling shiver. *No, she's no older than me, just a girl, scared and lost. And it's my fault she's here.*

Eloryn smiled at the girl and tried to keep her voice level. "We should keep moving, if you are well enough to."

The girl didn't respond. She leant against the rough stones, half bent over, chanting under her breath. Eloryn listened closer, but the girl wasn't using the language of a behest. Shaking violently, she willed herself over and over to wake up, to wake up from this horrible dream.

"Let me help you." Eloryn reached out but the girl shied away and edged farther along the rock wall.

Her head flicked up. She glared at Eloryn with oddly familiar eyes rimmed in thick black that ran down her face in dried tears. "What have you done to me? Why can't I remember anything? Not anything! Have you used some kind of... magic on me?"

Eloryn backed away. *Did you do this, did you bring me here? Was it magic of yours?* She'd made similar accusations just moments ago. Now on the

receiving end, they hurt.

"It wasn't me, I, I didn't…" Eloryn said. "You don't remember anything at all?"

"No!" the girl snapped. The sharp word echoed against the rocks around them. A deep growl answered from the darkness, reverberating like distant thunder.

With a turn of her hand Eloryn shifted the light. They stood in a twisted crack of tunnel that opened into a large cavern. The rough ceiling hung with dry and broken stalactites, the floor scattered with their fallen remains like a rocky bone yard. Deep amid the shadows and gloom, she swore she saw movement.

"We have to go," said Eloryn. "We're not safe here."

The girl made no effort to leave. She put her hands over her ears and sank toward the ground.

"Please!" said Eloryn.

"I don't even know my name," the girl said, her words broken by a shiver.

"I'll give you a name," Eloryn promised in desperation. She'd never had anything she needed to name. Things spoke with her as she could speak with them. They already had their own names. Only one thought came to her. "Memory. Your name is Memory."

The girl looked both horrified and amused. "You're cruel."

"I'm sorry." Eloryn tried to think of an alternative, but the girl stood up.

"No, it's… it's okay. It's better than nothing." Her voice still shook as much as her hands, which she wedged under her armpits, but the glaze of confusion had left her eyes.

Eloryn nodded to the girl — Memory — then turned and took a tentative step forward, crunching twigs that had gathered at the mouth of the cave.

The scattering of pebbles echoed back. Something crawled toward them through the dark.

Eloryn mentally flicked through pages of her reference books. What lives like this? Animal or fairy-kind? What other clues did she have? She looked down and saw the sticks under her feet were in fact old, fragile bones. A slithering chatter of dark words ricocheted down the cavern walls. Eloryn realized what the creatures were before they came into view. She gasped.

"What is…?" Memory's question cut off as the monstrous shapes shambled into the light.

Flesh eaters, cave dwellers, unseelie fae. The illustrations didn't do them justice. Human in shape but larger and malformed, the creatures were long armed, with grey hanging skin that rippled underneath, as though they were made from dripping mud. Eyes like deep holes were set in their angled skulls, black and without shine. Their yellowed teeth, too big for their mouths, smelt of death.

Eloryn's first sight of trolls shook her to the core.

"I'm guessing they aren't your friends either?" Memory whispered.

"We should be protected by the Pact. They shouldn't hurt us."

"*Shouldn't* doesn't really do it for me right now. Like monsters *shouldn't* be real."

Eloryn took a deep breath, also finding no comfort in her words. They were in the trolls' territory. The Pact would give them no protection here. Eloryn could hear the twisted voices of the creatures, speaking of their desire to crunch small bones. Her stomach lurched. The trolls moved closer, but circled, keeping their distance, testing an invisible boundary. They hissed in frustration.

One repeated word reached Eloryn from the mess of whispers; *Forbidden.*

"This way." Eloryn stepped between the piles of bones, edging around the side of the cavern to another tunnel.

Memory followed closely, barely taking her wide eyes off the trolls. She picked up a large bone, holding its broken end outwards like a weapon. The trolls laughed in response; a harsh noise, like the bones crackling under their feet. They gathered at the edge of the light, coming to them from all the dark crevices of the cave, forming a wall of sharp toothed monsters.

Eloryn whispered, "When we reach that tunnel, run. It's small. They might fit but we'll move faster."

"What if we get stuck in there? What if we can't get out?"

"Please, trust me," Eloryn said.

One ambitious troll surged forward and Memory swung the bone blade. It crumbled against the troll like chalk across a stone. She dropped the useless bone, but the troll backed away, choking laughter again. Just a few more tricky steps from the tunnel entrance and more trolls tensed to lunge.

"Run, now!" Eloryn cried, then spoke her words of magic to the earth.

A trunk sized stalactite fell, crashing down between them and the trolls, shards and dust flying. Eloryn bolted into the tunnel. Memory tripped, stumbling into her. The tunnel floor dropped in front of them. Eloryn's knees gave way and they both fell forward, rolling down the uneven rocks and steep slope faster than they would have dared to run. Hips and elbows cracked into rocks. Eloryn's hands scraped raw as she reached out to slow her fall. The tunnel's descent smoothed and they washed up on top of a pile of broken pebbles and bones.

A blow to Eloryn's chest left her sucking breath back into flattened lungs. She was relieved she'd chosen not to wear a corset today.

She directed the glowing wisp back up the tunnel. Through the smallest gap between bends a few determined trolls could be seen making a less clumsy descent.

"Have to… keep going." She got to her feet too quickly and scraped her head, the tunnel roof too low to stand fully. Wincing from the sharp sting, she was too slow to warn Memory from doing the same.

The girl spat a word Eloryn didn't know. She guessed it was a curse.

They dashed over uneven ground, deeper into the mountain through the winding tunnel. Openings branched out on either side but Eloryn led on without hesitation, a clear direction whispered to her by the life in the earth.

The tunnel stayed tight by their shoulders, sometimes pressing in closer and making them squeeze sideways through the narrow gaps, sometimes dropping in height, making them crawl. The sound of the trolls' pursuit faded and the girls slowed to a tired stumble.

The strange girl blindly followed like a lost animal. Eloryn's heart ached for her almost as much as it ached for herself. Once enough stale air returned to her lungs, Eloryn gave answers to unspoken questions. She explained that the tunnel would lead them to Maerranton. The men chasing her might also head that way, it being the nearest major city, but the tunnel would be faster than travelling over the steep and heavily wooded mountain.

"Why are they chasing us?" Memory asked.

The very question Eloryn didn't want to answer. She couldn't tell the truth but it seemed wrong to lie to someone with no memory.

What if that was a lie, that Memory remembered nothing? Alward often chided her for being too trusting. *Just give the simplest details,* Eloryn told herself.

"My guardian is a wanted man. Those who associate with him are also considered to be criminals. They will no doubt believe you were with us too, having seen us together. I'm sorry. Please believe that he's a good man though, that we are no harm to anyone."

"You said 'Wizard Hunters' before. Is it not allowed, being a wizard? Doing that stuff you were doing?"

Eloryn cringed, and planned her words. "All but the simplest of behests have been outlawed." Eloryn shook her head, upset at herself. "Alward, he would be furious if he knew I had been casting in front of a stranger. You wouldn't... I hope..."

"Turn you in for it? No chance." Memory looked as if she could laugh. She waved a hand toward Eloryn's wisp that lit their way. "I feel crazy even talking about magic like it's real, but I'm seeing it right now so I guess I've gone crazy."

"The magic," Eloryn continued, "it could explain your memory loss. When a powerful spell goes wrong, it can often steal memories. A Veil door is a very powerful spell..."

"And it really went wrong? Ugh, just thinking about how that felt is all kinds of wrong, like the worst thing ever." Memory shuddered. "But worse."

Eloryn shook too, remembering reaching for Alward, her hand passing through his, leaving him behind. "It was interrupted. I went in and where I came out wasn't where we planned. It shouldn't have been possible, but you were there, caught part way, stuck between the world and the Veil. I helped pull you free."

"Thanks, for that. Damn lucky you didn't just leave me stuck there," Memory said.

Eloryn blushed. "It didn't occur to me to do so."

Memory did laugh this time. "It probably would have been the right decision by the sounds of things. I was a perfect escape goat for the slaughter."

Did she mean scapegoat? Eloryn's face flushed even more and she looked away. *Who would consider doing such a thing?*

"But thanks, anyway, for not," Memory added.

A loud grumble from Memory's stomach broke the awkward silence. They had been walking for what felt like hours, and Eloryn noticed her own stomach was also hollow and hurting.

"Will you share some food with me? I have enough for us both."

Eloryn tried to hide the pain in her voice. It should have been her and Alward sharing this bread.

She took it from where it sat upon the travelling cloaks that covered her and Alward's most precious belongings. She tore the loaf and handed half to Memory.

"God this is good. I don't know when I last ate. Literally," Memory said with a stuffed mouth.

"I wish I knew how you appeared, that I could give you more answers. Whether you were in the forest already, or the Veil brought you from somewhere else, or…" Eloryn let her musings fade out. She had read other explanations in Alward's research. Darker, scarier, more complicated alternatives she would keep to herself, not wanting to give more worry to her already confused companion.

"I wish even more I knew where I was before that. I mean, how am I supposed to find my way home?"

"Alward," Eloryn mumbled between nibbling on her bread. A flash fire of guilt passed through her to say his name. What would he say, when he found out it was her fault they were found? "He spent much of his life studying the Veil and doorway spells. He must know everything there is to know about them." Eloryn hesitated. She had to decide once and for all whether she would trust this girl. Her heart could find nothing to distrust, felt only warmth and sadness for her, empathy stronger than the warnings that came to her in Alward's voice. "We have another home in the south of Avall, on Rhynn island, that we were to go to if we were found here. That is where I am going and… You can come too, if you like. It is at least part my fault to have brought you into this danger, so I will help you as best I can, and I am sure Alward will too."

"If you think he can help me get my memories back, help me get home, I'm Team Magic all the way."

"I'm sure he can." Even though they were separated, Alward would come for her. And if he couldn't find her he would wait for her on Rhynn. Those men couldn't catch him, couldn't hold him. He was too clever, too powerful. And she needed him.

The two girls trudged onwards, dragging their tired bodies through the rough tunnel.

"Just one more question," Memory asked after a short silence. "Is life always like this?"

CHAPTER FOUR

"...and then the gnome said to the merchant, 'I'm sorry, I'm a bit short!'" The stall holder rumbled out the punch line. Around him, a huddle of corseted and bustled ladies giggled behind their gloved hands.

Observing as he strolled by, Roen wondered if they laughed at the man's humor or the man himself. Roen hadn't heard that joke since he was a boy and a few entrepreneurial little folk could still be seen trading on market day, bringing exotic imports and fairy goods. They rarely appeared any more and the fae had barely been importing for far longer. Funny to be joking about it now. The market suffered from their absence. One of the young ladies smiled at Roen, and he winked back, setting off another wave of giggles, quivering lace and ribbons. Shame he couldn't stay, he thought, letting his gaze linger on them. Unfortunately, he had to get to work.

Ambling along, Roen smiled to himself. Despite his reason for being here, he enjoyed the vital chaos of the market, now in its mid-morning peak of activity. Vendors spruiked from behind makeshift carts, boisterously laid out into a rough grid of narrow aisles. Children ran underfoot. Those with money bought sweet delights to nibble on. Those that couldn't buy bullied the sweets from those that could. *Innocent thieves,* thought Roen, envious.

Maerranton markets used to be legendary throughout Avall. It had been a rich city, a wealth still evident in the tall, handsome buildings of stone and sculpted bronze which stepped down the steep cobbled streets.

But these were harder times and much of the city fell into disrepair. It didn't mean much to Roen. He'd never known wealth. He did know every abandoned and derelict house, each broken and dry drainage tunnel. Hiding places. Secret routes.

Squeezing through a small gap between two men, Roen muttered polite apologies. *Decent weight, maybe some gold. I can easily do better.* He slipped the coin purse into a concealed pocket in his long coat and adjusted his cravat to cover the movement. His clothes were well suited to his career. He saw to that when they were tailored. Dark colored, neat but unremarkable, the suit had no frills or fancies such as some men wore. His sleeves and cuffs were designed to keep his hands free. The seam of his trousers hid a thin blade, the perfect tool for defeating locks, slicing straps of bags, or defending his life. Not that he'd ever let it come to that.

He wandered through the humming market, thick with the sounds and smells of people trading. A passing carriage disturbed a family of stray cats and one came closer to him, mewing for food. With a swift and casual movement, Roen lifted a strip of dried fish from a nearby stand and flicked it across to the kitten before continuing on.

He followed a man, clearly upper class, ridiculously dressed in startling turquoise-blue tails and top hat that oozed gaudy trims. He showed off his bad taste and bulging coin pouch to a lady whose bosom overflowed from her bodice. Roen idly browsed nearby stalls' wares, waiting for the best moment to move in and take his earnings. But despite the peacock man's flippant demeanor the opportunity never arose. His hands were always too tight around his money. Roen chuckled to himself at how the busty lady fawned over the miser, doubting she would get what she was after either. He could still have the man's money. He'd just have to work a little harder.

He rolled his shoulder in its socket, still stiff and sore, and turned away. It was too risky, even without an injury slowing him down. And risks he would not, could not, take. Last week's mess, the closest he'd ever been to capture, left him wary. He needed a new mark.

Roen headed back along the crowded aisle. Nonchalantly, he scrutinized the people around him. *There. Too easy. Almost a gift.* Spotting his next target, he couldn't help but give a tiny, wry grin.

The pair showed signs of poverty, with mud and scuffs of dirt covering their hooded cloaks, but were clumsily making a deal for some food with

an obscene amount of gold. Maybe thieves themselves, Roen thought, wondering who they'd rolled to get that sort of money. From their size he guessed they were younger boys, street rats, drifting through town, spending out a big take. After stumbling through the purchase of food the two moved along to a used clothing stall. They kept themselves well hidden under their travelling cloaks, but one struggled with his, his body obviously far too small for the garment. The clothing glimpsed underneath was bizarre even compared with the last man in his feathers and ruffs.

The boy in the out of place outfit fiddled with a small item of metal which flicked open into a sharp blade. He quickly fumbled it back into a pocket. Certainly fair marks, Roen decided. If anyone deserved to be victim of his crime, it was a criminal himself.

The other scamp placed his leather pack – if it even belonged to him - down on the table then turned away to trade with the merchant, picking up a plain heavy dress. Roen questioned the dress, but his mind was too fixed on the bag sitting unwatched on the table. *Surely not, could it be so easy?* Without a blink of hesitation he started into action. Strolling by he barely brushed the back of their cloaks as he passed, leaving no trace of the bag behind.

Roen kept his steady pace until he reached the end of the stalls and tucked himself into the shadow of a larger building. He might be finishing early today, after a take like that. He couldn't help but look back. He knew he should move on, away from the scene. It was poor form to remain and gloat on a take, and the large bag couldn't be hidden away like the smaller purses he took, but this intrigued him. The oddity of the pair he'd stolen from made his curiosity demand more. The inept thieves would be realizing their loss any moment now.

There.

The boy turned back to where he'd put the bag down. He froze, staring at the empty spot on the table. He looked to his companion, who shook his head under the heavy hood. They both searched around, on the ground, panic in their movements. They stepped away from the stall to continue their hunt, unthinking, still with unpaid goods in their hands.

Roen frowned. *Time to be gone.* A commotion seemed inevitable when the stallholder stepped out from his stall, raised his arms and started bellowing at the street rats. Roen turned away from the vendor's tantrum, when the large man, towering above, reached out and grabbed at the scamp, ripping back the hood of the cloak. Something caught Roen's eye, and he looked again.

Blonde hair spilled out from under the fallen hood, and a girl's face, soft like a petal, blushed pink with distress. Roen's forehead knitted. He breathed out hard, a lump forming in his chest. No wonder it was too easy, the girl was the very image of innocence.

The girl babbled to the vendor. He started yelling for city guards, shaking her in disgust by a fistful of her cloak. *The sort of disgust with which a thief should be treated.* Guilt heated Roen's face. The stallholder kept up his hollering, building a crowd of curious market-goers around him. The girl fell out of her cloak and she and her companion ducked back into the crowd, eluding the larger man amongst the mass of people. Too busy looking behind them, the pair scampered straight toward the city guards that had come, roused by the cries of "Thieves". He looked from the girl down to the bag he'd stolen, and swore under his breath.

"Excuse me, Miss," he called out when she passed within earshot.

They both eyed him suspiciously and continued to scurry forward, clinging together. Roen snorted out a breath and swore again. He held up the bag into clear view.

That got their attention, and the still hooded figure dragged the blonde toward him. Roen stepped back further into an alley, forcing them to come to him, out of sight of the approaching guards. Two girls, he saw with surprise now they stood before him. Maybe a couple of years younger than himself, which was still more boy than man. Both were attractive despite being exhausted and worn. He'd noticed before that they were dirty but could see now they were also damaged. One black-eyed and swollen, the other, the pretty blonde one, had a scratch clear across one of her cheeks, the ruby red of it contrasting starkly against her porcelain skin. They were both shaking and on edge, eyes darting, color drained from their faces.

The guards passed by without looking their way. Roen let out a loud and exaggerated puffing noise and gave his best smile.

"Nothing like a bit of excitement to start the morning! It must be your lucky day." He continued his faux-labored breath.

The two looked at him deer eyed and remained silent. He normally had an easier time getting a smile from a girl. *Not my lucky day,* he thought, and continued the show.

"Well, I saw it all happen. Some dirty purse cutter making off with your bag. I thought I'd see if I couldn't help out."

The blonde breathed out as though she'd been holding her breath since her bag vanished. "Thank you sir, so much. Thank you. You've no idea what this means... I...."

Something about her face seemed familiar in the way that made his palms clammy. She was beautiful, even on the verge of tears, but what was yet another pretty girl to him? Roen let his act fall, becoming somber again.

"It wasn't a trouble at all. When the thief saw me chasing him, he dropped the bag and bolted."

"Just a coward after all. Bloody bully," the dark-haired girl vented.

"What more would you expect from a thief?" he asked. He flashed a grin, but could not keep all the bitterness from his tone.

The girl turned and spoke to the blonde, shooting an awkward toothy smile back toward Roen as he watched. "Come on Eloryn, we should be clearing out."

Roen walked up to the blonde girl and stood close in front of her. She blushed vividly and looked down. He smiled a little at that. It was nice to feel like the champion sometimes. *Except that I'm the villain pretending to be a champion.* His smile faded.

"Eloryn, is it? Here, so you can be on your way. Do be more wary in the future, thieves aren't always so easily beaten."

As he placed the bag down into her open hands, his fingers brushed against hers and she twitched back bashfully. They both apologized and the bag thumped down between them onto the cobblestones. A small object wrapped in fine velvet fell out and rolled around, unwinding itself from the material as if with a will to be free, drawing Roen's eyes after it. It glittered where it came to a stop. Polished and precious.

The lump of guilt in his chest began to pound and he looked from the ornate amulet to the girl again. Her mouth just slightly open, she grabbed for the intricate medallion as he picked up her bag. Her effort to remain casual was ruined by her quivering lips. He could see her trying to judge his reaction, if he recognized the heirloom, if he made the connection.

He did.

A noise from the marketplace turned his attention the other way. The city guards returned, searching this time in a begrudging manner that made them all the more surly and determined. The vendor had certainly

scolded them straight to work. The guards walked right toward the alley he and the girls openly stood in. Any moment now the lawmen would see the girls they were searching for, and him standing with them. *Not good.*

Roen broke into movement, kicking in an old door. Grabbing the girls around their small shoulders, he pushed them through, both too surprised to stop him. All three fell down broken stairs into thick, pungent mud. The two girls landed flat on their backs, stunned and winded.

Roen spun around and pushed the door back into place. Her dress pinned under his knees, Eloryn tried to wriggle free. The other girl swore liberally at him. He turned back and dropped his body down on top of them, hoping the dark shade of his coat would hide them. He slapped a mud covered hand onto the swearing girl's mouth and gave a vehement shushing gesture to them both, pointing back through the holes in the door at the passing feet of the patrolmen.

The girls stilled. *Thank the fae.* Roen breathed out a silent sigh of relief. Another wriggle or scream would mean all sorts of difficult explaining to be done on his part and likely much worse for them.

The guards poked around in the alley way, making the appearance of a hunt. The dark haired girl glared at Roen. He removed his hand from her mouth and she wiped dirt from it angrily. Despite the buildup of rotting refuse, run off from the markets, this ancient, half-buried basement had been a hiding place for him on more than one occasion. Ignored by most people in the sprawling city, it even held an entrance to the city's large underground tunnel system through a half crumbled wall.

After he thought the guards had passed, Roen waited a few moments longer, just to be sure. Only then did he realize he pinned Eloryn's body down full length with his own. He could feel her pounding heart through the clothes between their chests. She stared at him with worried eyes in a haunting shade of green, probably planning how to get away from him. *What a way to make an introduction of this importance.*

Roen rose to his feet with steady movements in an attempt to not panic the girls further. The odd dark haired girl stood up next to him. She looked down at her freshly muddied clothes and swore again.

Roen reached down and helped Eloryn to her feet with as much care as he could offer. They kept their eyes on each other, waiting for the other to make a move. He knew he had to offer a sign of his allegiance.

Roen dropped down onto one knee in front of the girl, bowing low toward the unpleasant ground. "Princess, forgive me."

CHAPTER FIVE

Roen swallowed away the lump in his throat and waited for Eloryn's reaction.

Her mouth opened a little then closed again. She turned to her friend as though Roen weren't even there. "Memory, can you see, is our way clear? We have to leave now."

Memory blinked as if she'd missed something. "Huh? But he...? What did he mean?"

"She doesn't know?" Roen had assumed the princess to be in the care of this other girl. He hoped his assumption would not be the cause of more trouble to her.

"Know what?" Memory said.

"Nothing, I am not," Eloryn insisted to them both, flustered.

Roen pushed back to his feet, took hold of Eloryn's arm and moved her away from Memory. He placed Eloryn with her back to the furthest wall and bent down to whisper to her.

"Hey, let go of her!" Memory moved after them, but Roen gave her a warning look, stopping her in her tracks. He turned back to Eloryn who stared in alarm at where he held her. He pulled back his grasping hand and clenched his teeth. This was all going very wrong. For a moment that he, his parents and so many others had dreamt of for so long, to

find this person of such importance, and here he was, throwing the princess into rubbish and manhandling her.

"Please," Roen beseeched her. "Trust I am no enemy. Tell me it's so, that you are the heir. You're the right age. You're in possession of our late Queen's medallion," he swallowed, skin tingling with goose bumps, "and her appearance."

She looked from him to Memory with fear in her eyes. Roen dropped his voice to an even lower whisper. "This girl, Memory, who is she? Is she a threat? If she's a danger to you in any way, I can help."

"She's not, I'm not, she's..." Eloryn panted out the words then her knees gave way and she fell in a faint. Roen blinked in disbelief, just managing to catch the falling girl. Memory dashed across the room and took Eloryn's weight out of his arms, the two girls sinking to the floor together.

"What did you do to her?" she demanded. "What was that interrogation about?"

Roen stood above them, hand hovering near his mouth. *Could I be entirely wrong about this? No. Everything adds up to the same answer. She has to be.*

"You really don't know who this is?" he asked Memory.

"I just met her yesterday," she snapped at him. Eloryn's eyes fluttered back open and Memory loosened her bear hug hold of her. "We haven't slept. We've just... just been running."

The girls gave him matching glares. He didn't blame them. He couldn't believe in his desperation to know the truth he'd driven Eloryn - already injured, terrified and exhausted - to collapse. He felt sick to his stomach. Even if she wasn't who he believed her to be, he'd acted poorly. If she was, it was unforgivable.

"I'm sorry. Please forgive my behavior. Whoever you are, and it doesn't matter who that is, I can assume you've been running from someone, or something, terrible?" He dropped down next to them. Eloryn now kneeled unsupported, but swayed as she stared warily at him. Memory hesitated, then nodded for the both of them.

"You don't have to tell me what it is. Just let me help you. I can sneak you from the city, past anyone who might be watching, to somewhere safe. I give my word you will be safe."

No answer came. Roen bowed his head, unruly hair dropping over his face. "Forgive me, I only want to help," he whispered.

"You promise?" Memory asked with a pout, sounding very much

like a child.

He nodded with all the sincerity he could show.

"Will there... be food? And beds?"

Hope tweaked the corner of his mouth into a small smile. He stood and stretched a hand to her, which, after one false start, she took gingerly. He then offered a hand to Eloryn.

Looking defeated, Eloryn brought herself up to her feet with the wall as her aid, ignoring Roen's hand. "Memory, I don't... I don't want to go with him."

Roen put on his most charming, pleading look for Memory, who at least acknowledged his presence. He didn't know how she fitted into this situation, but if she could help persuade Eloryn to come with him, that was what mattered right now. No girl he'd ever known had been able to say no to that look.

"We need rest. We're a mess, Lory. I don't think either of us knows what we're doing. We might as well have had flashing lights on our heads out there. If he can help us get away from here then I vote we go with him." Memory's voice became a little kinder. "If he was going to rat us out, he had his chance before. He's helped us twice already. That has to count for something."

Eloryn gave the faintest nod.

Roen dug Eloryn's bag out of the debris pile where it had fallen and walked back to her.

"My name is Roen. Here." He did not pass the bag to her this time. Instead, he draped the large satchel by its strap over her shoulder and across her torso. His hand brushed her waist while he adjusted the strap and pressed the bag to her side. "Wear it like this. Keep it always close to your body." Letting the bag go, he stood the barest space away from her. "You should take more care of your belongings, and try not to be so tempting with thieves about."

"Oh, come on," said Memory. "You're going to make her faint again."

Memory walked beside Eloryn, following more than a few steps behind Roen. He led them through a system of tunnels under the town. Tunnels and caves were almost all Memory knew of life so far. Maybe that was why she didn't feel the discomfort that being down here seemed to bring

out in the other two. Maybe she was just too tired. No, she was definitely too tired. She felt like a visitor in her own body. It kept moving along of its own accord. She barely felt the ache anymore.

Earlier while they walked around the market, Memory had fished through all her pockets, trying to find out something about herself. Lots of things came to her naturally – words, actions, general knowledge - but still not a single memory of herself or her past had come back. She felt like she was learning everything from scratch again. *I don't even know what I look like.*

Her heart had sunk when she found a crumbled mess of multi-colored metal and plastic in her back pocket. She guessed it might have been a phone, before it was crushed some time during their hazardous journey the night before. Maybe earlier. When she asked Eloryn if she had a phone she could use, Eloryn looked at her as if she spoke a foreign language. Not that she knew any numbers or names of people to call anyway. But still, everything felt so strange. Magic. No phones. The fancy clothing everyone wore. Maybe she'd gotten lost at a LARP convention. Maybe she was just more messed up in the head than she thought.

That is *entirely likely,* she thought, glumly. She second guessed the reality of everything she'd seen so far. Dragons, moving trees and trolls were hard to believe after all. Even that beast man in the forest. She'd thought at first he was just another of the scary chasing men, but when he took hold of her, he threw her to safety, relatively anyway. She thought she saw recognition of some kind in his wild blue eyes, but in the riot of confusion that formed her first moments of consciousness she couldn't be sure of anything, not even his existence. How could she ever find him again anyway? She somehow doubted he'd have a phone number, even if she still had a working phone.

The only other things she found in her pockets were a piece of cherry gum and a knife. One look at the knife told her it wasn't the kind you take camping, it was the kind you threatened people with. *Is that who I am, the kind of person that threatens people?* She decided to keep the knife to herself. Eloryn already looked at her sometimes as if she was dangerous, and maybe she was, but that wasn't the sort of thing she wanted to find out about herself. Besides, she wasn't the only one keeping secrets and Eloryn's seemed much bigger than a knife in the back pocket.

Memory wiped her hands on her jeans, but gave up when it only made them dirtier. Resigned to eating even more dirt than she had already, she unwrapped the gum and popped it in her mouth. The candy cherry flavor rushed across her tongue, unfamiliar. She turned to Eloryn. "So, *Princess*, what was that all about?" Memory realized that she hadn't even known Avall was a monarchy. Then again, she only knew the name of the place because Eloryn told her.

"It meant nothing." Eloryn kept her eyes averted.

"It didn't look like nothing." The way Roen had grabbed Eloryn, moving her against her will, left Memory with a strange, ill feeling inside. She discarded it, filed away with all her other confusing emotions, and tried to judge Roen anew. She hated how handsome she found him, how she just wanted to touch that soft caramel hair, and how when he smiled, she couldn't help but like him. It made it hard to say no to him, and left her wondering if she'd made the choice to go with him for the right reasons. Why was everyone she'd met so far so damn *pretty!* Amnesia or not, Memory knew pretty people lied too. *Everyone lies,* her heart told her.

Wow, learned something new about myself. Turns out I'm a cynic. Surprise. She looked at Roen walking ahead of them. Not very tall, lightly built; Memory kept telling herself the two of them could overpower him if they needed to, but the way he moved revealed a casual, confident strength that made her worry.

"Really, I just felt faint, from exhaustion. That was all." Eloryn blushed so earnestly Memory had to suppress a giggle.

"I heard what he said, Lory. He said Princess. And with the kneeling and all."

Eloryn's eyes shifted as though looking for a way out of a trap.

Memory sighed. "Look, I'm working with nothing here, know nothing except what you tell me. Why the hell would you leave out a detail like being a princess? Seriously, if it's for reals it's kind of cool, right?"

"We're nearly there," Roen called back to them before Eloryn could give an answer.

So intent on needling Eloryn, Memory hadn't noticed the rich orange cast of light falling into the tunnel up ahead. They were at the tunnel's end, and it opened out onto an untended set of terraced fields. The sun had just begun to brush the sky with color as it fell toward night, and lit the dried crops to a burnished copper.

Eloryn and Memory caught up to him where he waited at the exit, haloed by the golden light. He pointed through the rambling reeds to

a small rundown cottage.

"That's where we are going." He gave a small cough and Memory thought he almost seemed embarrassed.

"My parents and I live out of town because, in a way, we are also running from something." He began walking forward again, but slowly this time, not letting them hang behind. He directed them straight through the web of unharvested corn stalks and twisting weeds, bending them out of the way. Dry stalks crunched satisfyingly under their feet, releasing wafts of musty mud fragrance.

"My parents, you see, are Grand Duke Brannon and Grand Duchess Isabeth Faerbaird. You may have heard of them?"

Despite Eloryn's studied indifference, her voice held an edge of suspicion. "I have. But if you were their son, you would be a prince, then?"

Memory swallowed her gum, coughing. "What, seriously?" She couldn't hide her surprise, but Roen didn't seem to care. He continued to watch Eloryn intently. Princes and princesses everywhere. She felt left out.

"I'm no kind of prince. If my parents were still ruling, then I may have had that title. But my parents were close friends of Queen Loredanna's, and our family loyal to the Maellan bloodline. When Thayl Vaircarn killed her and the King, my parents lost their titles, land and more, fighting him. It is his fault my parents have been forced to live poorly for so long."

"These are dangerous words," Eloryn said, her lips tight and stubborn.

"I believe I've already made my allegiances clear. If I'm endangered by that, can it be worse to explain why they are so?"

"Explaining is good," Memory said. "I like it when people explain things."

"Well," Roen continued, rewarding her with a lopsided smile, "I've plenty of stories to tell. My parents always believed Loredanna's newborn survived Thayl's slaughter. They and my brothers fought to remove Thayl, to find the lost heir, or at least assign a more worthy leader. Obviously to no avail. We went into hiding after that. We've still got a friend or two in the nobility who make sure we remain overlooked when needed. It's been hard for my parents, so I look after them now. They miss royal life, and it's risky even for them to be seen in town. So I work, and try and bring them things of value when I stumble across them."

"Things of value...?" *Like a missing princess?* Memory looked sidelong at

Eloryn. Could it be true? And if it was, what would it mean? She had no idea. She didn't get politics, and didn't know the first bit of this history.

Roen shrugged and grinned. "Although, most of my stories aren't nearly as exciting as the time I saved a couple of pretty girls from a thief and got to take them home. That one's my favorite."

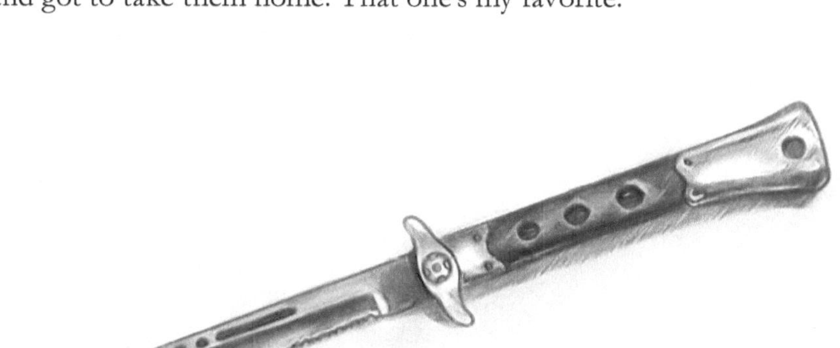

CHAPTER SIX

They pushed through a thicket of weeds into a small clearing. A neat garden of herbs, lettuce and pumpkins surrounded the cottage, hidden by the overgrown fields. Apart from the smoke that escaped the chimney, the house looked abandoned. Shutters hung off hinges. Windows were closed up with grayed, splintering planks. Grass and daisies grew from the roof. Memory dreaded going inside, in case the rickety structure fell on her.

Roen stepped forward, a small frown denting his forehead. He seemed to hesitate for a moment, then knocked. "Mother, Father, it's me."

A heavy bolt slid behind the door which squealed in protest as it swung open.

"I didn't expect you home 'til tomorrow." A graceful white-haired woman met Roen with a loving smile. The elaborate high-necked gown she wore contrasted starkly with the derelict cottage. Her smile fled the moment she saw Roen had brought guests.

"Who are they?"

"They were in need of help, and I offered it." Roen stepped aside, tilting his head to the girls.

Isabeth looked them over with her lips pursed. She placed her hand over her heart when she saw Eloryn and it rose up to her mouth when she looked at what Memory wore. Memory hated how different she looked to everyone else. They all wore long flowing gowns and there she was in a t-shirt and torn jeans. She felt even dirtier than before,

bloody, bruised, and unsteady on her feet. Eloryn wasn't much more presentable. She folded her arms into herself, and gave a closed-lipped, nervous smile.

Isabeth turned to the side, talking into the house instead of out toward her son. "Well. Well they are here now. I'll not be known for denying aid." She moved in, beckoning them after her.

Inside, only thin shafts of the setting sunlight broke through the blocked windows. Memory stepped in after Roen and Eloryn, seeing only gloom while her eyes adjusted to the darkness.

The door slammed behind them like a crack of thunder, shaking the cottage walls. Memory spun around and stepped backwards, running into Eloryn. Shadows shifted near the closed door and a figure loomed toward them.

"Mem, we shouldn't have come," Eloryn whispered over her shoulder. She clung to the back of Memory's shirt as though she stuck there when they bumped together.

Thanks for the told-you-so but we can't go anywhere now. Isabeth and Roen stood behind them in the small room. The man blocked the doorway, the dark silhouette of his features starting to clear in Memory's eyes. He stared down at the girls. Memory tensed. A shiver of terrified nausea crept up her back, and her hand moved itself toward her back pocket.

"What do you think you're doing?" He strode past them, straight at Roen, anger growling in his voice. He shook Roen by the shoulder with an outstretched arm. His only arm. Memory gasped. His right arm was missing from the elbow down, hidden by a rolled and pinned sleeve. Memory forced her mouth shut, trying to look anywhere but at his missing limb. Her eyes were inevitably drawn back.

Roen spoke calmly and looked the man in the eye. "Father, please, can we talk?"

"Brannon, love, they're just children," Isabeth said.

"No, they aren't. Look at the state of them. They... are trouble." Brannon kept a grip on Roen as though he would throw him back out of the house. He turned and glared at the girls. Memory cringed.

"We'll go. Let us go, please?" Eloryn's clutch on Memory's shirt tightened and her pitch rose.

"No," Roen cried, then his volume dropped again. "I mean, please stay, you are welcome here."

"You know they aren't. Get rid of them before their trouble follows them here."

"Father, please, they can't go. They still need help."

"Why would you bring them here? You should know better. You're free to come and go as you please. No one knows who you are. Has that made you forget what it's like for your mother and me? The danger we're in? You know what will happen if we're found."

Roen's composure cracked and his volume rose to meet his father's. "We weren't followed. They won't-"

"Do you even know what trouble they are in? Bringing a couple of strays home without any idea of the risk? What have you told them about us?"

Roen frowned, opening his mouth but not speaking.

Memory found words rushing out of her own mouth instead. "He really didn't tell us much – anything – nothing at all. We just needed some help."

Brannon scowled at her, the deep wrinkles in his face twisting around a grey-streaked beard. He pushed Roen out of his grasp. "I want them gone." He stormed across the room to a curtained off doorframe, and disappeared through it. A second later another door slammed.

Roen rolled the shoulder his father had grabbed. He turned to Eloryn and Memory with a strained smile and a shrug. "You don't have to go anywhere, really. Mother?" He gave Isabeth a pleading look and hurried through the same doorway as his father. The smell of bread wafted out, teasingly, and Memory glimpsed signs of a kitchen before the curtain fell closed again. Her stomach gurgled from the combination of hunger and stress.

Eloryn tugged at Memory's shirt and whispered, "We should go now."

Close behind them, Isabeth tutted. "I don't see the harm in letting you get cleaned up and fed. Don't mind my husband, he just worries."

Memory breathed in the scent of fresh bread again and closed her eyes. Whatever Eloryn's reasons to go, the lure of 'cleaned up and fed' overwhelmed Memory. She hoped Roen wouldn't be in more trouble if they stayed just a little longer.

Memory turned around to face Eloryn, who eyed the front door. "Roen promised we'll be safe. Let's just rest a little, then go."

Eloryn's lips pulled thin, but she gave a tiny nod.

"Take a seat and I'll see what I can find for you both," Isabeth muttered. "So dark in here. Àlaich las." A warm glow magically lit the room. Isabeth

walked out to the kitchen without looking back, as though it were the simplest thing to create light with her words. With the gloom cleared, the room suddenly seemed a lot more solid, even pretty. Furniture was sparse, but elegant and well cared for. Memory took a seat at a small dining table of carved dark wood. A thick curtain sectioned off the end of the room. Partly open, it showed behind it a simple single bed and a store of shelved belongings; books, clothing, and tools that she didn't think she'd know the uses for even if she did have any memories. Two curtains were draped across doorframes leading out, but Memory guessed there couldn't be much more to the cottage beyond them.

Eloryn sat beside her, head tilted, hiding behind her hair. Memory sighed and chipped black polish from her fingernails as her frustration rose. Her second day in the world for all she could remember, and she was left to make all the small talk. At least Eloryn wasn't making them run any more. It was nice to sit. So nice. Memory thought sitting might be her new favorite pastime.

Isabeth returned, carrying a tray of food, drink, and some small cloths. A steaming bowl of water balanced in the middle. The clatter of the crockery as she put the tray down on the table didn't cover the sound of Brannon yelling again from outside.

Isabeth dipped two cloths together into the water bowl and squeezed them out. She handed the girls one each. "Trouble indeed."

"Thank you, for letting us come in. And helping us. And stuff," Memory said. Her words became progressively more awkward but she kept tacking them onto her failed attempt at being polite. Roen and Brannon's voices hammering through the thin cottage walls didn't help her train of thought. She focused on wiping her hands clean.

The back door slammed again, and Brannon walked in. Roen followed, head low and jaw clenched.

Isabeth clicked her tongue. "These won't do." She picked the already muddied cloths out of the girls' hands. "Roen, fill the tub."

He went back into the kitchen without a word, emerging again a moment later with a large pot of water which he took into the other room. Brannon moved up and sat across from the girls at the table, staring at Eloryn who shyly looked down and away.

Isabeth lifted the pot of blackened water and rags off the table and took it away. "It may not be much, but please go ahead and eat. No formalities tonight, considering," she said and left the room again.

Memory mumbled thanks and looked nervously from the food to Brannon, not sure what formalities would have been anyway. Brannon reached out and tore off some crusty bread. He pushed the rest closer to them without a word. Her smile in return was ignored, so she took a filled ceramic cup and slunk back into her chair. Finding that the cup contained wine surprised her, but no one suggested she shouldn't drink it. The rich taste made her eyes droop and it added to the warmth that already burned in her chest. Had she been running on nothing but shock and adrenaline since she woke up? She was so tired she couldn't think straight, and now her body no longer moved, it was giving up any fight to stay awake. *Yes. Sitting. Good.*

Brannon fortunately had calmed down and had little to say to her. He tried to start conversations with Eloryn a couple of times. They led nowhere. Memory tried to chew on some food but her mouth refused to function. She watched Roen take pot after pot of water from kitchen to bedroom.

She didn't realize she'd fallen asleep in her chair until Isabeth came and shook her. "Dear, I hate to be waking you, but the bath is drawn, best to get cleaned up now."

Memory looked up and saw Eloryn gone. She couldn't see Roen or Brannon either. Somewhere deep inside panic burbled, but her body wouldn't respond. Isabeth steered her like a sleepwalker into the bedroom. A polished brass bath tub stood in a corner, half behind a dressing screen.

Memory noticed Eloryn lying on a bed canopied with red velvet. She was clean and asleep, a towel tucked under her still damp hair. The undercurrent of anxiety in Memory eased seeing Eloryn safe and still with her. If she knew Roen wasn't somewhere being bawled out by Brannon again it would be even better.

Isabeth moved as though to help Memory undress for her bath, looked her up and down and backed away. Memory sighed in relief when Isabeth left the room; she would have felt even more self conscious without privacy. Stepping behind the screen she pulled two t-shirts, worn short over long, off as one piece. She winced when she lifted her arms over her head, and looked down at a spot that had been hurting her. A multi-colored bruise covered half of her ribcage. Even worse, an old, large and twisted scar marked the middle of her chest. *Nasty,* she thought, wondering how she got it. *Do you even know what trouble they are in?* Brannon's words bothered her. *I don't even know myself. Could whoever did this to me follow me here?* Pulling down her pants, she forgot her shoes and wobbled about trying to extract them from the tight jeans. Peeling off a striped sock, she discovered blood around her toes. *Well, that could have happened anytime,* she thought, considering their chase through forest, cave and tunnel and the many hazards to toes they held.

Feeling cold and exposed in the open room, she quickly stripped off her underwear and stepped into the tub. The warm water came up to her shoulders when she sat down. It smelled of milk and honey, and soap suds made it almost opaque white. Memory breathed the syrupy steam and let the warmth seep into her. Finding a cloth hanging over one side, she washed it over her skin, soaking away the filth. She began seeking and removing clips from her hair. Feeling mud caked on the back of her head, she leaned back and dunked her hair into the water, massaging her fingers through. She closed her eyes and smiled.

This was the most content she'd ever felt, she thought wryly. She lay back in the warm water, letting the aches and tiredness seep out of her. She felt she could just sit in there for hours, until she remembered she wasn't alone in the room. She was in a house full of strangers where she wasn't welcome. She sighed and lifted her head back out of the water.

Her lazily opening eyes snapped wide with horror. Simple confusion blurred with possible nightmare. The white bath water had turned a sickening black. She screamed, she couldn't help herself. Eloryn woke with a start. Memory splashed about, trying to pull herself from the tub. She managed to slip over the side and fall onto the floor behind the bath just before Roen, Isabeth and Brannon ran into the room.

She cowered behind the bath while they stared at the water and then

at her. Isabeth rushed across and draped a blanket over her.

Memory stuttered, "The water, it just turned black. I don't know what happened."

Isabeth wiped some dripping water from Memory's shoulder and showed her the color. "Your hair has a dye in it, that's all. It's washed out in the tub."

Memory couldn't help but feel ashamed at the tone in which Isabeth told her this, as if she was a simple child. Her panic felt laughable. "I didn't know. I didn't know it was dyed."

"You two, out!" Isabeth snapped at her husband and son. Roen, who had been averting his eyes, moved quickly to hide a spreading grin. Brannon followed along at a slower pace, a war of glances shared between him and his wife.

Isabeth started drying Memory off, and she was too taken aback to protest. "How could you not know, child? It's your own hair."

Memory started to talk, but Eloryn shook her head at her. This wasn't missed by Isabeth, who briskly finished drying Memory and dropped a billowing chemise down over Memory's head, leaving her to find her own way through the expanse of fabric into the arm holes.

"I know it's not a noble thing to pry but I got barely a word out of this one," she said, sticking her chin out toward Eloryn. She rested fists on her thin hips, her voice scolding. "Roen told us who he thinks you are. True or not we could trust you both more and help you more if you would talk to us."

Eloryn didn't lift her eyes to meet Isabeth's as she asked, "And what do you think of what Roen believes?"

Isabeth softened a little, the slightest tilt to her head. "I think you are two hurt, frightened girls who need our help. It would be my greatest wish to see a child of Loredanna's alive and well. I've hoped it for the longest time but was never so foolish to imagine the heir would just walk through my door."

Eloryn choked on a tiny sob, her eyes still downcast. "I have."

CHAPTER SEVEN

Isabeth's hands rose to her mouth.

Tears flowed down Eloryn's cheeks, and she slumped forward where she sat on the edge of the bed. "I'm sorry. I'm sorry for sitting here silent while you've given us all your help. I couldn't even give you the honors of your rank. Grand Duchess, I've been so rude. You must know that I can't, I shouldn't tell anyone. Even my being here is putting you at risk, but I just don't know what to do. I don't know what to do on my own."

"Oh, child!" Isabeth wrapped her arms around Eloryn and held her as she sobbed.

The details fell into place in Memory's head. No joke, Eloryn really was a princess. A real goddamned princess on the run. Daughter of a King and Queen who were killed for their throne by some bad man who makes people poor and cuts their arms off. *Blah blah wars, blah blah Thayl, hunters, hiding and terror.* Had Eloryn lied to her about why those men chased them? What else had she lied about?

I don't know what to do on my own. Eloryn's words made her face burn. She didn't matter at all. The girl with no memories and no use to anyone. In competition with a princess, why would any of them help her?

Isabeth called out to Brannon and Roen. She nodded to them over Eloryn's head, stroking her hair.

"Hush child." Isabeth rocked Eloryn ever so slightly. "You are doing fine. By the fae, you are alive! That's a greater thing than many even

dared hope for."

"But how?" Brannon moved in closer, crouching on the floor in front of them.

"Wizard Councilor Alward saved me, raised me." Eloryn's sobbing slowed and she worked at wiping her face dry. "He was known before as Pellaine."

Isabeth and her husband nodded in comprehension. "We saw… Well, never mind what we saw just now. But we had reason to hope Pellaine had escaped, that Loredanna's baby had been saved."

Memory's nose wrinkled. She watched Isabeth fussing over the princess. Her heart ached, imagining a mother of her own out there somewhere, worrying about where she was and wanting to hold her while she bawled her eyes out like that. *I have to find my way back to my mother, my family, my home.*

No one flocked to help or console her. Why would they with a princess in the room? *Whatever, deal with her problems. I'll be fine on my own.* Like a ghost, she drifted out the doorway, through the kitchen, unbolted the small back door and walked out.

What the hell am I supposed to do now? She breathed deeply through a bout of panic, staring into the night. A forest backed the cottage, dark and imposing as though the house had been built in the open and the forest had marched right up to it like an army. A bitter vanilla fragrance wafted to her from a vine curling up around the back door, its white flowers still open at night.

A crisp cold settled on her skin. *Too cold to be sulking and smelling the flowers.* She swore at the pettiness that drove her out there alone, not even knowing where she'd go next. She pulled the chemise back up onto her shoulders where it didn't like staying, and hugged her arms around her chest. The cold bit at her and she considered going and sulking in the kitchen near the hearth.

Something moved high in the dark branches of the trees in front of her, catching her eye. Humming stars hovered still then zipped from place to place. She could see no detail, only beautiful, mesmerizing points of light. Each one glowed in vivid hues that shifted through a rainbow of color, blue into green, yellow into orange, red into purple. She took a step closer and they jumped away from her, a startled school of fish shimmering in the trees.

A voice shocked Memory, jolting her focus away from the lights.

"There must be something special about you."

She turned to see Roen had joined her outside. How long had he been there? She hadn't heard him come out.

"Making friends with a Princess and attracting sprites." He stepped up next to her, pointing into the trees. "They're so rare to see these days. It's like they've come here for you."

Memory snorted. "More like they came for Eloryn. She's the special one, right?"

Roen laughed an honest, easy laugh. "And you just met her yesterday! Had you ever imagined just stumbling upon the Maellan Princess?"

Memory sobered up quickly. He caught her mood and his laughing stopped.

"So nothing's been said then, about me?"

Roen frowned and shook his head.

"Not that I'd expect it, what with everything. I guess my problems aren't exactly the priority."

"No, not really," Roen said. She was about to tell him where to stick his priorities when he continued. "But you can tell me anyway."

Memory gaped, lost on where to start. "I can't… remember anything." She felt stupid now saying it out loud. "Before yesterday. Before waking up and meeting Eloryn and just running ever since, I have no memories."

Roen said nothing, only stared, his forehead furrowed crookedly. The intensity of his gaze brought an uncomfortable feeling rushing up through her chest. She kept talking to suppress the heat rising in her face. "Eloryn said it might be caused by this weird magic thing that happened. She said she'd help me, so I just went with her, but she never told me who she was…"

"And now you don't think she will help you?"

"Why would she? Why would any of you? I just need to find some way to get my memories back so I can go home."

Roen stood silent for a while, then said, "If I were you, right now, I'd stick close to the person who has offered you their help, despite their own troubles, whether they can help you or not."

"Are you talking about her, or you?"

Roen grinned.

"Thanks for that, by the way. I didn't realize it would be such a big deal with your parents. I hope you're not in too much trouble."

"Trouble? I just brought home the missing Maellan heir. They've

got nothing to complain about. Even just to know she's alive has given them so much hope. If we can get the news to the resistance, it might be what they need to make some real change, get back some of what's been lost."

"There's a resistance?"

"Oh, sorry. I'll need to explain everything won't I?" He laughed.

Memory opened her mouth wide and punched her fists onto her hips in exaggerated insult. "You can start by explaining why you're out here bugging me instead of your beloved princess."

Roen dropped his head. His caramel brown hair fell over matching tawny eyes. The colors in combination made him look like a statue made of gold. A sense of loneliness crept into his expression, hidden under the glossy facade.

Why would he be lonely? He has a home, a family. Memory's heart jittered, worried he might actually go back inside. She searched for something to say that would stop him from leaving her on her own again.

"You said about brothers before. They don't live here too?"

"None of them still live. The five eldest died in the wars, and the sixth, well, he's dead to us either way," Roen said through half his mouth.

"Oh god, why is everything so horrible? Every single thing that's happened."

"Except meeting me, right? That isn't turning out too bad," Roen looked back up, smiling again in a way that creased his eyes. "Don't worry for me, I barely knew my brothers. I was youngest of the lot by more than a few years. I don't even know what it's like to be a noble, except from what Mother and Father tell me." Roen leant toward her and whispered as though sharing a secret. "When I was younger, Mother used to train me in noble manners. One day she just stopped. I guess she gave up thinking I would ever be a prince."

Memory tried to smile in return, but her lips kept falling downwards.

Roen cleared his throat. "Enough about my family. I hope one day you can tell me about yours."

"Do you think… my memories could just come back on their own?"

"They might. But better to stay amongst friends all the same." Shaking his head, Roen leant on the wall near her and chuckled. "At least now I understand your odd name. Still don't understand what you were wearing before."

Memory turned away from him, staring at the strange magic of the tiny fairy creatures glowing in the trees. *How could they even be real? How could any of this?* Loss and confusion flooded over her. A sob shuddered up through her body and she caught it in her throat, swallowing it. She tensed to stop the tears that tried to escape.

"Hey, look here, what is that?" Roen stepped up in front of her. He stared at her ear, his face twisted in a strange half smile.

"What? What is what?" Memory released a worried giggle.

"Here, let me." Roen reached toward her and pulled a large white flower from behind her ear.

Memory's mouth opened wide again, this time in honest amazement. "How did you do that? How did that get there? Was that magic?"

Roen laughed so heartily it took a moment before he could talk again. "I can't believe that worked! You really have no memory at all?" He wiped his eyes. "I'm sorry, normally that only works on children."

His laughter was so good natured she couldn't begrudge him for it, but put on her best pout, and asked, "Show me how to do it?"

"All right. But only because you need something to fill that head of yours. It's simple really. Not magic at all. Just a bit of a distraction and a flick of the wrist." He showed her the flower tucked behind his fingers then pulled a funny face, pointing at it with his other hand. "That's the distraction."

"Oh," said Memory. "No wonder it only works on kids. Still, can I try?"

She picked a star shaped leaf from the ground and tucked it into her hand, trying the same movements he had used, reaching her hand up to his ear.

"Not bad. If I didn't already know what was happening."

"Yeah, yeah, be a smart ass. How about this?" Memory moved her arm again, fumbling the leaf. It slipped from her grasp and fell to the ground. Roen ducked down to pick it up for her at the same time that she did and they collided midway. They stood back up together and he held the leaf out for her.

"Poor." His mocking came gently with a smile.

"Really?" Memory said, raising an eyebrow. She giggled when he looked down and saw another large leaf poking from a buttonhole in his waistcoat.

He picked it out and looked at it, and then her, in amazement. "See I was right, you are special."

"Who would have thought?" Memory smiled and shrugged. The chemise slid off her shoulder again, revealing another dark bruise. She glared at it.

I'm going to have to start naming you blue bastards to keep track of you all. Roen frowned at it as well. He looked from the bruise on her shoulder to the one under her eye.

She suddenly became aware of just how close together they stood. "You've been attacked. So many bruises on you..."

His eyes darkened and a muscle twitched in his cheek. The look of concern only made his pretty face more charming. She could feel his warm breath on her, making the hair on her neck stand on end. Her heart drummed and she began to understand how Eloryn had fainted so easily.

"Oh, no. I mean, yes, we were attacked, or chased, yesterday. But we got away OK. I don't know where these came from. You know, the whole not remembering thing." She pulled the chemise back onto her shoulder, covering the bruise.

"Still, I do hope it was nothing too terrible." He brushed a finger across the purple under her eye. She flinched under his touch, even though it was too gentle to hurt.

A deep growl rumbled from the trees above them. Roen stepped in front of Memory, putting her between him and the flower-covered wall. She looked past his arm but saw nothing except the continued movement of sprites shimmering about, undisturbed by the noise.

"Just some wild animal in the woods. We should head back inside. It's too cold to be out anyway." Roen extended an arm, inviting her into the house in front of him.

The warmth of the kitchen made Memory's chilled skin tingle. She looked back past Roen for one final glimpse of the magical fairy lights. In the dark trees, a silhouetted figure moved amongst the twinkling, living stars. Moving into the kitchen she arched her neck for a better view and yelped when she walked straight into Brannon while looking the other way. Roen closed the door.

"Son, a word." He stepped back and opened the curtain to the main room, ushering them both through. Isabeth lay on Roen's thin bed, and another blanket had been laid out on the floor next to it.

Brannon led Roen across to the front door before looking back to Memory. "Eloryn is already asleep. You will be sharing the bed with her," he said.

Pulling back the curtain to the bedroom doorway, Memory lingered to watch, to make sure Roen really wasn't in any more trouble. Brannon talked to Roen in a whisper then slapped his hand on Roen's shoulder, giving it a small squeeze. Roen replied then turned and nodded a goodnight to Memory where she stood watching. His eyes drifted to her side and a smile tugged the corner of his mouth. Memory turned to follow his gaze and saw Eloryn sleeping on the bed, her hair draped like ivory silk over her small shoulders. The sound of the front door closing turned Memory back to find Roen gone. Only Brannon remained, watching her thoughtfully. She let the curtain fall closed between them.

Buried in a bundle of thick down quilt, Eloryn heard soft footsteps approaching the bed. Having just shared the biggest secret of her life, one she and Alward had kept for sixteen years, her insides churned under her skin. She feigned sleep to stop the eager questions and looks of Roen's parents. But when she lay down, despite her utter exhaustion, her mind would not quiet and let her get the rest she needed so dearly.

"All tuckered out from being a princess I suppose. Must be hard," Memory's whispering voice muttered from beside the bed. Her strange words made little sense. Eloryn hoped Memory would understand her words in return.

Eloryn sat up and looked to see they were alone. The double bed felt vast around her small form. Memory stared back for a second, her eyes red rimmed, making the green more vibrant in contrast. Then she turned away from Eloryn and sat on the other side of the bed.

"I'm sorry," Eloryn said to Memory's back.

She didn't respond.

"I'm sorry I didn't tell you, but you have to understand how important it was to remain secret." Eloryn gripped the quilt, wringing it in her hands.

"I get it OK," Memory said. "It's just on a serious level of suck. I don't even know what the hell is going on and you got me all caught up in it."

"I promised I would help you, and I will. We will still try to find Alward, find out what happened with the Veil door, and help you get home. My heritage changes nothing there."

"My ass it doesn't."

"You don't understand. You don't know-"

Memory turned and glared at her and her words cut off. *Of course she doesn't know. How could I have said that to her?* Her effort to apologize turned wrong rapidly. She hardly knew how to talk to someone her own age, even without the communication gap Memory suffered. She'd never been able to make friends, even when she was allowed to mix with children her age in class. Always too shy, too different. The weight of her secret always added an extra boundary.

With a look of exhaustion, Memory turned her back on Eloryn again. She pulled back the covers and wedged herself between them, as far to the edge of her side as she could.

I have to try again. Eloryn knew her title meant a lot more to everyone else but she only wanted simpler things, to be safe and happy with people she cared about. "I know I made things worse by hiding who I was from you. But maybe I can help you understand. I was raised by Alward, the man who saved me when my parents were killed." Goosebumps prickled her all over. How she'd dared to feel dissatisfied with her life before made guilt simmer inside. Their life together was good, comfortable, and safe. Alward did everything he could for her, to keep her safe and make her happy. He treated her as his daughter even though she wasn't, and she knew it meant he never had a chance to have his own children, his own life. If anything happened to him, it would be her fault. "It was hard, growing up, to understand why we lived how we did, the terrible things that had happened. Alward used to tell me a bedtime story..."

Memory made no movement, and Eloryn thought maybe she'd fallen asleep. Still, Eloryn pulled her knees up and put her chin on them, and spoke the words of the fairytale she knew by heart.

"Once upon a time in a beautiful land, surrounded by seas, man and fae lived side by side, peacefully, under the Pact. The Queen of this land was beautiful and young, and time came for her to take a King. Many tried for the place but only one could be chosen for her. One man, Thayl, became obsessed with the Queen. He swore vengeance on the Wizards' Council when they picked another man to be the Queen's husband. Then he disappeared, vanished without trace. The Queen married and grew large with her first child. The time came when the Queen went into labor, and on that night, Thayl returned."

Memory turned over and propped herself up on one elbow, wide

eyed and enthralled like the children in Eloryn's classes.

"Thayl stormed Caermaellan and slew all between himself and the Queen as he had vowed. The King, the council of wizards, the castle guard, all fell before him as he unleashed a terrifying new magic. One wizard escaped and ran to save the queen. Too weak from her labor, she ordered the wizard to take her newborn and flee, to only and most importantly keep her child safe. He did, and the Queen was left to her fate. Thayl took control of the kingdom, forever still hunting the few wizards that escaped him and seeking the heir he knew survived that night. Some tried to fight, but none could stand against him and his new powers.

"The wizard went into hiding and raised the Queen's daughter, caring for her and teaching her, and keeping her safe from all those he knew would be hunting her." Eloryn finished, and Alward's voice echoed in her head, the words he would speak each night before kissing her forehead and dousing the lights, *Always, always, keeping the princess safe.*

Memory stared unmoving for a long moment after Eloryn finished her tale. When nothing else came, Memory blustered, "But! What? He couldn't have her, so he killed her? That's crazy person logic! What kind of story was that?"

Eloryn cringed and wiped away a tear. "I thought it would help you to understand, to know what happened."

"He killed all those people? And this guy is still looking for you? Bloody hell." Memory put a hand over her mouth. "You were right, I didn't know. There's a lot that I don't know. But, it's a little bit less now."

Eloryn slid back under the covers, hiding her face and the tears that refused to stop. *Alward, where are you?* As her consciousness faded away into sleep, Memory whispered, "I hope your fairytale gets a happy ending one day."

CHAPTER EIGHT

She stood in an alley way. All grey.
Impossibly tall buildings, sharp and slick, bent over and watched.
She looked up, not into them but into a hand.
It glowed. It hurt her. It belonged to a man.
The hand, the man, the buildings spun.
She was losing herself.
Then found a young boy.
He yelled, punched, pushed the man and made him disappear.
One, two, three. They all fell into nothing.
An eternity of darkness.
They dissolved and swirled. Ran through trees.
Brambles tearing.
Talons and scales. Thundering, hungry roars.
She held his hand, he held hers back.
Their wrists matched.
They couldn't hold on.
She screamed.

She screamed. Strong hands held her down. She thrashed, clawed, bucked. Sweat and tears drenched her skin. Her eyelids felt glued. She tore them open.

Heart thundering and chest burning, Memory's eyes darted, trying to refocus in the morning light.

Where am I? How did I get here? I can't remember, I can't…
Oh… right. That amnesia thing.

Roen knelt on the bed next to her, holding her still by her shoulders. The feeling of his hands pushing her down kept her panic racing, and she pulled away, backing up against the carved headboard. The red velvet of the bed's canopy shook like blood dripping down from the ceiling.

Across the room, Isabeth had her arms wrapped protectively around Eloryn. Both had wide eyes and tangled hair, just awoken. A bathtub of black, cold water stood in the corner. Brannon watched from the foot of the bed.

"Sorry." Memory's voice cracked, sore from the screaming she'd done. "Nightmare."

She felt an awful disappointment that she hadn't woken up somewhere she recognized, with people she knew and memories of who she was. She wished that the few things she could remember were the nightmare that she could wake from.

Roen gave her a kind smile. "As long as you're all right." He looked tired and grim, and wore the same clothes he did yesterday. He got back up off the bed and seemed to be trying to catch his father's eye.

Brannon looked at Eloryn. "Are you sure she remembers nothing?"

"No, *she* doesn't," Memory cut in.

She wished she hadn't when Brannon turned on her, a hard line across his forehead. "Memories or not, you have to understand how strange you are, how risky it is for all of us to trust you here."

Roen choked. He apologized with his eyes before dropping his head away.

"I'd leave if I knew where to go!" Memory winced at the shrill tone in her voice and tried to calm it. "But I don't. I don't remember anything. I just want to go home and will as soon as I know where that is."

Tears from her nightmare still wet her face and she wiped it furiously. She felt like a two year old, sitting in bed crying while everyone stared at her. She wished she had somewhere else to go so she could leave right now.

Eloryn sat down on the bed next to her. "What did you dream? It might tell us something about where you're from, so we can help you get home."

Memory looked up just in time to see Isabeth and Brannon glance at each other with matching disapproval.

"There was a man. I think he did something...?" Acid rose in Memory's throat, startling her and stinging her eyes to tears. She paused, breathing deeply. *The hand, the man, the buildings spun.* Her head hurt. The images from her dream faded out of her grasp. "It was a mess of stuff, confusing. I don't know."

"It was probably just a dream, nothing real." Isabeth set her mouth rigidly. "One look at you says you've probably just had a knock on the head and gotten lost."

Memory pulled back the sleeve of her chemise and twisted her arm around to see the inside of her wrist. Obscured by a yet another bruise was a small tattoo in rough, dark ink. Like a symbol for eternity with a swirl through the middle. *Their wrists matched.*

Brannon turned his attention to his son. "Roen, all done?"

"I just got back when I heard screaming and came straight in here. I have news for you. I will tell you in a moment, needn't do it here." He gave a single nod to his father, and their eyes locked.

Eloryn stood back up. "News-?"

Isabeth spoke straight over the top of her. "Come then. Let's have you both dressed and fed. Then we can talk more." She flicked her head at Roen and Brannon, who turned to leave. On his way out, Roen gave Memory an apologetic smile. He started to smile at Eloryn, but then bowed shortly to her instead, making the rose in her cheeks turn bright.

"Have you any clean clothing?" said Isabeth.

"No, but I can clean what we wore." Eloryn continued to speak a string of musical nonsense. Their muddy clothes strewn around the tub wriggled to life. Dirt and filth shivered off them, shed onto the floor as though the fabric repelled it away. Torn holes in Eloryn's dress drew closed, threads weaving themselves back together.

"You couldn't have done that yesterday? We looked like we'd just left a mud wrestling tournament," Memory said.

"I didn't want anyone to see what I could do. I'm sorry."

"Right to be careful too," Isabeth said. "Few people could cast a behest that complex, and those are just the people Thayl is trying to find. My, you're good with your words though, just like your mother. But we'll still need a dress for Memory."

"I can't wear my own clothes?" Memory was dismayed. Her jeans and t-shirt felt way more comfortable than the tent she wore now.

Slipping into her dress, Eloryn looked at her with pity. "They stand out

too much; we already talked about this. But we'll keep them, of course."

Memory watched how natural Eloryn looked in her dress, with her long flowing hair and pretty rounded shape. She guessed that was what a princess should look like. She imagined herself in a dress - bony, bruised, boy haired - and shuddered. She grabbed a bristle brush from a side table and made an effort to smooth her teased hair.

Isabeth dug through an inlaid wood chest filled with clothing. "I may have something that will fit. Roen brings such lovely dresses for me, but not always just the right size. Still, it's the thought that's sweet. He's done so well to afford to look after us how he does, considering. Maybe… No that won't fit, scrap of a thing you are."

"I can just wear this," Memory offered, motioning to the gown she had on without enthusiasm.

Isabeth rolled her eyes, muttering in exasperation under her breath. "That is an under dress, dear. No, here, this is what I was looking for. We should be able to lace it down enough to fit you."

She pulled a simple rust-red dress from the depths, dusted it down and instructed that it should go *over* the *under* dress.

Grumbling to herself, Memory took the dress and struggled to make sense of the laces, layers and yards of fabric. While Isabeth was distracted brushing Eloryn's hair, Memory slipped the flick knife out of her jeans. She tucked it up into the binding sleeve of her dress, then stuffed her clothes into Eloryn's bag. She pulled on her skater shoes, glad the long skirt covered them, and stood back up.

Memory flinched, thinking there was a stranger in the room. It took a moment to realize she saw herself in the reflection of a gold framed mirror. There were things she'd gathered about her appearance, just from living within her body for the last couple of days, but seeing herself now struck her greatly. She was so little, slim-nearing-skeletal, smaller even than how she'd felt. She knew she was about the same height as Eloryn, but if Eloryn had an hourglass figure, she'd be a minute glass. She wished she had managed to eat something last night.

She frowned, seeing the fading black and pink color of her hair clearly for the first time. Of course it was dyed! And then there were the bruises. Despite having a pretty dress on, she still felt far from fairest of them all. She wondered if Isabeth had any eye liner then found herself thinking about Roen's eyes.

"Was Roen out all night?"

Working at braiding Eloryn's hair, Isabeth tutted. "Well, there was hardly enough room here for all of us. He often stays in town when he works late. Did he tell you he is assistant to one of the most successful businessmen in Maerranton? He's always been lucky, in his way. An unexpected gift he was, when we didn't intend to..." Isabeth cleared her throat. She shifted on her feet, pausing awkwardly. "You know, Roen was just a toddler when we heard Loredanna was with child. We had hoped it would be a girl for him to play with and look after. But then, well... Then we hoped there'd be a child alive at all."

Apart from her very first answer, Isabeth directed everything she said to the princess. *I might as well be invisible. She's been setting them up since before Eloryn was even born.*

"You said before, you had reason to believe I lived. Please tell me how?" asked Eloryn.

"It's not a pleasant story, love."

"I would still like to know, please."

Isabeth tugged at her thin fingers then sat down on the corner of the bed. "After Thayl struck Caermaellan castle, we had our wizard send us through a Veil door to your mother's estate, to warn her."

Eloryn slipped down onto the edge of the bed beside Isabeth, shaking her head. "Estate?"

"Lady Loredanna stayed at her country home, just across the mountains here, during the last months of her pregnancy. I don't know how much you know, but your mother wasn't happy after her marriage. She lived there as much as she could, isolated from the court, her husband, even her closest friends."

"I don't think Alward knew my mother much at all, not in person. But he said... are you sure she hadn't gone back to the castle?"

Isabeth's skin wrinkled around her face into a frown and her hand covered her mouth. "Oh, love. We found her at the estate. We were too late. She was already dead, surrounded by the bodies of every other man and woman from her staff. They must have tried to protect her. I don't know what happened. They were all out in the forest... But Loredanna was no longer with child and there was no baby among the dead. We knew there had been a younger member of the Wizards' Council at the estate, Pellaine - yes, Alward - who also couldn't be found. That is all we knew. That was enough to let us hope he got you away to safety."

Eloryn squinted as if she'd been slapped. "I know of the estate you

mean. The children from the village called it a ghost house. It was close to where we lived, within walking distance, but Alward never said... I thought she was with my father when..."

Memory watched silently. *Turns out I'm not the only one who didn't know everything.* Something seemed to pull from the inside of her chest like a magnet, as though she should do something - hug Eloryn, say some comforting words - but nothing she could think of seemed natural.

Isabeth patted Eloryn's hand consolingly. It looked as awkward as Memory felt. "I wish you could have known your mother. You are so much of her! In Faerbaird castle we had a portrait of Lady Loredanna from her coronation, when she wasn't much older than you are now. She wore the crested medallion in that portrait, the one you dropped in front of Roen. Mind you take better care of it from now on."

Eloryn moved her mouth, and it took a moment for her voice to find its way out. "Do you still have her portrait? I'd like to see my mother."

"I'm so sorry. There have been times we've had to run, and it was lost. Still it served its purpose." Isabeth gave her a knowing half smile. "Had Roen not grown up besotted with the lady in the painting, he might not have spotted the medallion so easily."

A clatter of plates brought their attention to the door. Roen's cheeks were noticeably red when he pushed through.

He brought in a silver tray laid out with bread and dry fruit and placed it on the dresser next to Memory. He seemed on edge and didn't even look at her.

Roen walked over and whispered to Isabeth, then bowed to Eloryn and backed out of the room. *Even if helping me isn't important to them, at least they're feeding me.* Without a thought to politeness, Memory grabbed a bread roll, stuffing large chunks in her mouth. Her stomach was a roaring pit of hunger. The absence of coffee dismayed her. She could really do with some coffee.

Isabeth excused herself and followed Roen.

"Are you going to eat any of this?" Memory asked Eloryn. There wasn't a lot of food, and while her stomach hurt less, she could easily keep eating. She eyed the entire platter with a lusting hunger.

"Please, quiet," Eloryn whispered. She stared intently at the curtain screen between the rooms. Over her chewing, Memory hadn't noticed the hushed, serious tones of the conversation coming from the living area.

"Are you eavesdropping?" Memory whispered back around a mouthful

of bread. "What are they saying? They aren't going to make me go, are they?"

Eloryn paled.

They are. They're going to kick me out. Memory couldn't make out any clear words, only quiet mumbling. It couldn't be worse than what she imagined they were saying. Looking at the green tint to Eloryn's skin, Memory bit her lip. *Nope, worse, and not even about me. When has anyone been that worried about me?*

"No," Eloryn gasped and bolted out into the living area. Memory followed on her heels, grabbing the last bread roll on the way past.

CHAPTER NINE

Roen's body shivered in an ongoing tremble he couldn't control. He was exhausted, but he often worked all night and it never left him like this. *Why am I so anxious?* His father looked grave, but smiled at Roen and patted him on the shoulder.

After the entire night spent listening in, seeking gossip and spying, Roen explained to his parents what he saw in town during the dark hours of morning. He'd finally managed to bring his parents something of such value it could change their hard lives. Pride mixed with bitter anxiety at the news he now delivered.

The princess burst through the curtain from the bedroom with a look on her face that made Roen shake harder. He gripped his hands together to still them.

Isabeth tried to herd the girls back into the bedroom. Eloryn ducked past her, straight to where Roen and his father were sitting at the table. They cut off their conversation.

"It's not true. He couldn't be," Eloryn insisted.

Roen turned to his father, not sure how to respond. Brannon shook his head in the smallest of movements.

Eloryn came to a stop in the middle of the room, her chest rising and falling from sharp breaths. "No secrets, please. I know what you said, but you must be wrong. They couldn't have caught him. Couldn't have!"

"Princess, I'm sorry. I saw him myself." Roen's muscles still ached

from the strain of moving unseen and unheard to get as close as he could to Alward's cell. But all he could do was watch, blocked by too many guards and gates locked by magic instead of mechanisms that would click open for his fingers.

"He is nearby? I have to go to him." Eloryn headed toward the front door.

With two huge steps Brannon moved in front of her. He held his only hand out in a calming gesture. "It is your safety that is most important, you know this."

Eloryn shook her head in a way that made her blonde hair shiver around her.

Roen forced his words out, wishing there were some other messenger for this news. "Alward is alive, but they have poisons that block his magic and he is heavily guarded. The wizard hunters also had a good view of you both," he said, looking from Eloryn to Memory. "They're already heading back out to continue searching for you. Fifteen of them, some heading back into the forest, others onto the roadways. The rest have begun searching houses and farms around Maerranton."

Isabeth dropped into a nearby seat as though her legs had been cut out from under her. "They won't be safe here, will they?"

Brannon shook his head. "We need to get Eloryn away from here, as fast as possible."

"And yourselves," Roen added. "They are Thayl's men. You can't risk them recognizing you if they come this way."

"No." Eloryn eyed the door, hysteria in her eyes. "No, I can't leave Alward."

Brannon stood as a barrier between her and the exit. "There's no doubt Thayl will come to see Alward himself, to be sure who it is. Once he is sure, he'll do everything he can to find you. Did Alward have somewhere else for you to go, to someone else he trusted?"

"He considered at times going to others from the Wizards' Council-"

"There are others still alive?"

"But we never did. I don't know where to find them on my own. We were meant to go to our other home on Rhynn together, to be safe there. What must I do to get him back? I have to do something to free him."

"Lory, that doesn't sound like a good idea. Not if that Thayl guy might be coming. Remember the part about him being a crazy person?" Memory mumbled from the back of the room.

Brannon's voice flooded over Memory's. "It's not what Alward would want, nor will we let you try. You're too precious to be lost taking such a risk."

Doubt and denial showed clear on Eloryn's face.

Brannon rubbed his eyebrows for a moment then spoke again, his voice smooth and comforting. "We will do everything we can to have Alward freed. There are local resistance fighters we can call on. They will be better fitted for the job, readier for such a task. Leave this to us."

Roen raised his eyebrows at his father's words. They hadn't been in contact with the resistance since the warring ended and they went into hiding, over a decade ago. "And what of Eloryn?"

"We'll send her to Lanval." Brannon nodded to his son, and Roen recognized the look of warning on his face. "If any of the Wizards' Council still survives, he'll be the best chance of finding them." Brannon turned to Eloryn, bending down to look her straight in the eye. "Duke Lanval is an old friend. He is trusted and well connected. It is wisest that you go to him now, understand?"

She nodded obediently, a tear dropping to the floor with the tilting of her head. Roen found himself on his feet, one hand wrapped tight around the backrest of the chair. His father had the sort of tone it was hard to say no to, the tone of a duke, last remnant of his lost nobility. To see it used on the Princess in this way lit a rebellious fire within Roen. He breathed deeply to cool it down. *After all, Father is right. We can't let Eloryn go after Alward. Who am I to judge his lies?* There was nothing they could do.

Brannon straightened back up. "Then you leave right away."

Eloryn turned so quickly to Memory it made her jump. "You'll come with me?"

"Err, yeah, of course," Memory muttered. Being included in the conversation left her looking dumbfounded.

"Can't we go with them?" said Isabeth.

"Too many of the wrong people in the Duke's court still know our faces," Brannon said.

"But the Princess…" Isabeth looked stricken.

"Roen visits the Duke often, he knows the way. He'll do his best to get her there safely." Brannon gave his decision without a look to his son for confirmation. His tone sounded more disappointed than trusting.

Roen cleared his throat, worried the tightness in it would taint his

voice. He handed his father a piece of paper. "You and Mother must leave as soon as possible too. Go to the inn at this address. Ask for Scarlett, she'll make sure you aren't found."

Brannon took the address and everyone began to move. Roen let out a lungful of air. He hadn't really expected a thank you. He was happy at least that Brannon had the grace not to ask who Scarlett was. Of all the sons in the family, he knew he wouldn't have been their choice to be the only one they had left. It was the simple fact of *what* he was that meant he could never be enough. *What they would think of me if they also knew what I did to make a living...*

Eloryn sniffled and drifted back into the bedroom. Memory hovered while Brannon and Isabeth rushed about preparing to leave. Roen threw a pack over his arm, stuffed it with a change of clothing and considered what else he might need. Still in his work clothes from the day before, he had most necessary items on him already and had few other belongings worth taking. It wouldn't take long to escort the Princess to Duke Lanval's. Once he got her there they would find someone fitter for the task of protecting the Maellan heir. Heading to the kitchen for food, he met his mother, who pressed a small jar of ointment into his hands.

He smiled at her from below pinched eyebrows. "Mother, my shoulder's fine now."

"You know you've got no healing behests to sort it out if it acts up on you again. Take it." Isabeth pushed it into his hands. "Look after her well. One day, maybe she'll be Queen, and remember the help we've given her." For a moment she looked over her son's face, her expression split between a frown and a smile. She left to join Eloryn and Brannon in the living room.

Ready to leave, Eloryn wore her satchel with the strap diagonally across her chest, tucked tight under one arm as he had shown her. Roen's lips twitched.

Shuffling out of the way, Memory backed into the kitchen and bumped into Roen. They both watched Isabeth wrap her arms around Eloryn in a strong embrace.

Memory tilted her head. "Don't you get one too?"

Roen whispered into Memory's ear. "I think we all know who is most important here."

Her eyes narrowed shiftily. "Me, right? Is it me? Yep. Definitely me." Memory lifted one corner of her lips into a cheeky smile which he returned.

His parents took their lightly packed bags and they all headed out the back doorway of the cottage. They knew how to pack for this risk, taking only essentials and a few identifying heirlooms and leaving their home so it didn't appear to have been fled in a hurry. With luck, the hunters would not come this way. Or if they did, they would find nothing suspicious and move on, and he could find his parents and bring them home in just a few days. *And return to...?* The question made his chest ache and he shook it off.

Brannon took Roen's hand and held it firmly. "Get her to the Duke's quickly. Don't let us down, son."

Isabeth fussed, brushing back Eloryn's hair from her face. "Be safe, and watch out for fairy rings."

Roen nodded a goodbye to his parents, and they headed separate ways.

Following Roen, Memory put on her best impersonation of hope. Lanval sounded like someone powerful, someone with connections who knew other wizards, so maybe he would be able to help her as well. *Because everyone's been falling over themselves to help me so far.*

Roen led them along a dirt track through the tall, untended crops. He turned his head continually, watching all around them.

Memory's legs ached and moved like rusty robotics, unhappy from their overuse. Beside her, Eloryn seemed to be struggling just as much with hers. She chewed on her bottom lip. Also failing at being hopeful, perhaps.

Memory nudged her with an elbow. "You 'K?"

"Sorry?"

"Don't worry. They'll sort things out, with Alward. Maybe the resistance guys will free him and he'll meet us at this Duke's place?"

Eloryn nodded and looked away.

"How far is it anyway?" Memory asked Roen.

"Normally, just a short trip through the city. His palace is actually that way." He pointed, and to Memory it looked as if he pointed back the way they came. "But it will be safer to travel out into the forest, avoiding the city and roadways, and coming back into the palace from the other side."

"Not safer for my legs," Memory whined.

"You won't have to walk far. Just down the hill from here is the Draper's farm. Good folk, lots of daughters. I know them well enough that they might lend us some horses."

Memory raised her hand. "Um, I don't know how to ride, I think."

"You seem like a fast learner to me." Roen winked at her.

Memory found herself blushing, and turned her focus toward the forest that followed the edge of the fields. She stared high into the red and yellow tapestry of leaves, hoping to see the little fairies she'd seen last night. In the morning sunlight she saw nothing but birds and insects humming through the treetops.

"Look forward to being well treated when we arrive at the palace. Duke Lanval is quite fond of me. He knew my parents well, and while he cannot safely host them, he lets me visit often. He has no children of his own, so I think he enjoys the company." Roen continued walking ahead, talking to them over his shoulder. The flow of his words seemed nervous. Eloryn had clammed up again and Memory had nothing much to say either, so she let him talk.

"Most think the Duke is loyal to Thayl, but the truth is more a loyalty to his wife. After my family and others refused to accept him as king, Thayl needed someone influential on his side. He tortured Lanval's wife to secure his compliance. Lanval won't risk his wife's safety again, but has no love for Thayl. He takes no action against Thayl himself, but has contacts in the resistance, whom he also funds. You can trust him, by my life."

Coming around a bend, the field ended and the path wound down a terraced slope. They were met with a view of a pretty farmstead at the bottom, and a scream that pierced through the air.

Roen pushed them back into the cornfield they'd just stepped out of. Down the hill, spooked horses jittered near a stable. From one of the buildings came the sound of someone yelling and a door slamming. A man stepped into view around the corner of the stables, dragging a young woman by her blonde hair. He threw her to the ground, and more men appeared from the other buildings, two younger girls in tow.

Roen grunted and stepped forward.

"They're looking for me, aren't they?" Eloryn whispered.

Roen clenched his fists, but didn't move any farther. The wizard hunters lined up the three girls. Kneeling in the mud, the sisters squirmed in confusion and the men pointed, stared and argued. One man ran his hands over the youngest girl's face, the one closest in age to Eloryn. He pushed her chin up, tilting her face for closer inspection and stroking his hand down her neck. A tangy taste filled Memory's mouth, and she realized she'd bitten into her tongue. Her feet were backing her away into the corn, but her gaze remained fixed on the farm below.

A man ran through the field toward the girls, their dad, Memory guessed. The hunters drew swords, and the man stopped. He held the hoe he carried up in front of him. The yelling between them echoed in the small valley, their sharp words barking back and forth. The farmer lunged and Memory shrieked. The daughters did the same, covering the sound. Their father slumped. The hunter he attacked stepped backwards, revealing a bloodied sword. The farmer fell face down.

Memory ran. Terror pumped her feet and she bolted back through the crisp dried corn stalks, out of the field, into the forest.

"Mem." Roen raced up behind her. He grabbed her arm, pulling her to a stop. Eloryn caught up.

Memory wrenched her arm away, stumbling against a tree. "He just stabbed that man." Memory's stomach cramped and she bent forward, sucking in deep breaths. "If they catch us, Lory, what's going to happen? Are they going to kill us? What are they going to do to me?"

Eloryn winced, looking green. "I don't know."

Roen glanced over his shoulder, fists still clenched. "It will be all right. I'll get you both to the Duke's safely. It'll just take longer."

Eloryn whimpered, tugging at the ends of her hair. "They were looking for me. I have to... I could help the farmer, heal him if he is still..."

Roen grabbed her shoulders, turning her to him, away from the direction of the farm. "It's not your fault. You didn't make the farmer challenge the hunters, and you didn't make the hunter use his sword. But yes, they're after you, and they'll catch you too if you go back there."

"He could die," said Eloryn.

"And so could we," said Memory. "We need to get gone. Now."

"If he's still alive his family will see to him. Memory's right, we have to go; we're already slowed for having to walk," said Roen.

Eloryn fumbled her words, starting three times before anything made sense. "I can get us some horses. I can ask with a behest and they will come to us here."

"Come to us? Can't you just abracadabra and make them appear? Instant horse?" Memory paced, chewing on her nails. She couldn't stand

the idea of waiting.

"Magic can only make requests from what is there, whether it's horses, the mud on our clothes, or the energies of nature. The farmer left the back field open. I don't think anyone will see the horses leave from there."

Roen looked over his shoulder again and nodded. "Bring them, but only if you're sure there's no risk. The faster we can be gone, the better."

Eloryn nodded and spoke another language into the surrounding woods, the lyrical words clipped between panted breaths. She stopped, and a short moment passed in silence. "They're coming; it won't be long."

"So, it's just pretty please, but in fancy magic words? How did they even hear you?" The whole concept seemed flimsy to Memory. Even having seen magic in use, the idea of relying on something she felt skeptical about when those hunters were so close left her stomach turning.

"The ancient words give the meaning, but it's the spark of connection that lets us communicate our behests. The internal connection to magic that you feel, in here," Eloryn put her hand to the centre of her chest. "The Pact has meant all people of Avall have the spark of connection within. Don't you feel it?"

Memory turned the concept around in her mind, wondering if she could connect to magic in any way. She looked down at her chest, feeling the warmth within her she'd known these last few days. She thought it was just panic-induced heartburn.

Three sleek horses trotted through the thin woods, crunching leaves under their hooves. One horse walked up to each of them, sniffing them in a friendly manner. Memory patted the brown horse beside her with a stiff and timid hand. She wanted to get away from here as fast as possible, but felt tiny next to the huge beast. What was she supposed to do with it?

Eloryn whispered to the dappled horse that nuzzled her. The horse knelt before her, allowing her to climb upon its bare back. "You don't need to know how to ride. They will look after us." Eloryn still looked nervous when the horse rose to its feet.

Memory patted her horse on the nose again and mumbled, "You're not going to do that for me are you? At least don't let me fall off and add to my bruise collection, OK?"

The horse whinnied. Memory took it as an affirmative, if a mischievous one.

"Quickly now, and keep your voices down," Roen said, and offered her a boost. She wanted to mount her horse gracefully, but in the end was happy just to drag herself on top of it. She clutched its mane with hesitation, afraid to either fall or annoy her ride.

Roen scanned the forest again and hopped up onto his pale tan steed with ease. *Well, he doesn't have a dress to contend with. I miss my jeans. I could run faster in jeans.*

The desire to run re-ignited the fire that burned in her chest since her first moments of memory when that demon dragon thing attacked them. *It must be somewhere, nearby, if the wizard hunters are here.* Her skin crawled as vivid flashes of the beast pulsed in her mind. She worried they would need something a lot faster than horses.

"So, you can't just want something and say, "bring me something to ride" unless you know… the… magic…?" Memory's chest flared hot like coals under bellows. Her mouth tasted of blood and the air around her bent in a way that made her seasick. She blinked, trying to shake the sense of vertigo that hit her, as though being up on the horse were suddenly higher than she could bear.

Eloryn gaped, her face twisted in confusion.

A hideous cry broke through the forest.

Darkness gathered around them. Living patches of ebony formed within snaking mist. A sucking wind and swirls of shadows met in a ball of heaving black.

The noise. The mist. The wind. Memory felt sick.

Something moved within the solid shadows, a shape, folding and emerging.

The huge form writhed and twisted. A jungle of powerful limbs lashed and tangled with smoky vines. Scales like black jewels sparkled dangerously on the flicking tail. With a final, louder cry, it tore from the tormenting mist, pushing itself through, still caught half way within.

It roared again. Angry. Hungry.

The dragon.

CHAPTER TEN

The dragon thrashed, trying to free itself. It screamed, vicious and guttural like murder and grief combined, clawing at the grey cobwebs of smoke that held it back like chains.

"No." Memory shuddered. The impossible creature matched her, shaking against the grip of the malformed Veil door. The very same torment she had experienced, the first horrors of her memory, the winds she thought would tear her apart. The magical gale gushed outwards, spinning leaves and dirt into the air. A high pitched hum filled Memory's ears and her eyes watered.

Closest to the beast, Eloryn cried out. Her horse wheeled on the spot. Its eyes rolled and froth dripped from its mouth.

Eloryn hugged it around the neck, and it steadied, pawing at the ground. She faced the dragon.

"Cuirdhùnadh fanhl," she called and waited, as though expecting something. The dragon's head swung to her words, flesh sliding back from its mouth. It hissed and twisted toward her in confused wrath.

"Princess, tell me you can make it leave." Roen grunted, pulling his skittish horse toward Eloryn by handfuls of mane. It whinnied and turned him back away.

"Fanhl," Eloryn cried again, her voice cracking.

"Lory, get away from it," Memory begged. Empty, wrung out, she sagged over her horse's neck. She couldn't think. Her mind had become chaos and body felt burnt out and charred.

Eloryn shot a look at Memory. Terrified, angry confusion twisted her lips back from her teeth. "You did this. How did you do this? How can I make it go?"

I did...? Memory gaped at the creature, the immense, inconceivable mass of muscle, talon and black diamond scales. Her thoughts split and twirled like a kaleidoscope. *Magic can only make requests from what is there.* She only wanted to run, a faster way to run. *Bring me something to ride.* Did saying the words make the request? A request that brought her the very thing she wanted to run from? *It's impossible, impossible...*

The dragon contorted, as though in pain. An armored claw burst free of the Veil. Eloryn's horse bucked in panic, throwing her off its bare back. She hit the ground hard and the dragon's talons lashed out, stripping skin from the horse's neck.

The horse cried a horrific scream, sounding too human, the scream of a child or woman more than that of a beast. Eloryn matched it. The horse crumpled and fell a fraction away from crushing Eloryn beneath its weight.

"Eloryn!" Roen struggled on his wild horse, close to being thrown off himself.

Memory's horse remained eerily still beneath her. She was just as petrified, fixated on the stream of blood running from the fallen animal's torn neck, and its motionless, turned back eyes. Roen yelled at her, trying to tell her something. It came through her ringing ears as crackling static. The dragon flailed, crying through an army of sharp teeth. Its ruby red claws flashed as it slashed away its misty bonds.

Roen's voice broke through. "Memory, ride, go!"

Memory squeezed her eyes closed. She was going to be ripped apart by this creature that had come for her, called by her. A demon she couldn't control. She opened her eyes and the nightmarish dragon was still there, glaring with thin slit cat eyes, judging her. It pushed another claw free of the Veil, its bonds dispersing into vapor.

Roen kicked his horse into movement. He tugged it by the mane to where Eloryn wobbled on her feet and scooped her up. Cradling her in his lap, he rode the horse back toward Memory.

"Hya!" he hollered, slapping her horse on the rump, startling it into movement. It jerked into a gallop and he herded it roughly ahead of him. Memory held on finger-achingly tight and they rode hard.

The dragon bellowed behind them. The sound of it thrashing and tearing itself free chased them through the forest.

Held in Roen's arms, her frightened face splattered with the horse's blood, Eloryn stared at Memory. Memory turned away, bent down close to her horse's neck and begged it to run faster.

Roen led them on a zigzagging chase across the landscape, across rocky crests and through sparse copses, out into untended fields, across roadways and back into forests again. Trees swam in Memory's eyes as they sped through them. On the verge of vomiting or passing out, she breathed deeply to avoid either.

Time blurred and night turned the world blue-grey. At times they stopped, stilled the horses and hid in the dark from the beating of vast wings in the sky above. Everyone kept utterly silent, as though a single word could bring the dragon to them. From their shared horse, Roen and Eloryn peered at Memory in a way that turned her stomach. The dragon could have torn them all open like that horse and they thought she summoned it. Her head and heart both pounded with painful ferocity. *How could I do that? Who am I?*

Finally they came within sight of a grand palace, standing at the edge of the other side of the city they had left when it was still morning.

Memory clung senselessly to her horse, her fingers chilled and knees locked. The neckline of her dress was soaked in tears and sweat. Uncontrollable shudders railroaded through her.

Riding up to a stone wall, Roen pulled up his horse, lowered Eloryn down and then dismounted. He pulled Memory's horse to a stop and calmed it, then pried Memory off, catching her as she slid to the ground.

Eloryn thanked the horses and consoled them for the loss of one of their herd. Memory watched the survivors gallop off. A pang of guilt started her tears flowing again.

Roen looked into the clear dark sky, scanning the horizon. He took her shivering hand, pulling her after him, Eloryn at his other side. They moved along the wall, ducked down, cut across through an arched gate, ran through an orchard and up to a small servants' door at the base of ancient stone walls.

Roen let go of her hand abruptly. He gave the door a push, tried to force it, lift it, but nothing moved. He grunted and hit the door with a fist. Pausing, he took a deep breath, then knocked loudly.

"Wipe your tears," he hissed at Memory. "And smile."

She did her best to obey, blotting at her face with her sleeves, wiping her nose. Just as she coughed her throat clear and put a shaky smile onto her face, a peephole in the door slid open and a pair of clouded eyes peered out.

"Roen, boy? Is that you?" The peephole closed, latches clicked in sequence and the door opened. A short but straight-backed old man met Roen with a wrinkled smile.

"Uther, thank the fae," Roen breathed out, smiling.

"Wherefore are you knocking here so late, hrm?" The way he spoke sounded as though he already knew the answer. He squinted past Roen at Memory and Eloryn.

Roen grinned and leant across the threshold, whispering to the old man. He tilted his head back, indicating the two girls. "Please, Uther, my man. You've not denied me before."

Uther winked and stepped clear of the doorway. He turned his head, pretending not to witness Roen and his ladies entering in the night.

Roen patted his friend on the back when he passed. He took both girls by the hand and led them at a brisk pace through the laundry room. The old man saw to re-barring the heavy door, chuckling behind them.

Roen pulled them around a few corners in a maze of narrow halls then stopped. He turned toward Memory so forcefully she backed up against a wall.

"What was that, back there?"

"I don't know, I don't," Memory stammered, unable to look at them.

Eloryn's voice came as a plea. "But it was you. I felt the power come from you. You brought a dragon, unwilling, through the Veil. That magic was... It shouldn't be possible."

"It wasn't me. I couldn't." Memory turned her face toward the wall, gripping her aching head in her hands. Her world, her small, short, confusing world fell apart with every step she took. She felt nauseous, the fire inside melting her away. She slumped and Roen grabbed her waist, supporting her.

"Is she going to be all right? Could she be damaged from what she did, by the magic?" Roen's voice blurred in her ears. Angry or concerned, Memory couldn't tell.

A silence, then Eloryn's voice came out trembling. "I don't know. This is... contrary to everything I... Even if she had the right words, what she did would be dangerous magic. She summoned *a dragon*."

Memory flinched, bringing her hands up in front of her face as though the words struck her physically.

Roen spoke again, this time more softly. "We'll work it out later. We need to get her to a room. Let her calm down. Make sure she's all right."

Someone had Memory's hand again, gently pulling her forward, off the wall and down the corridor. She didn't know who. She stumbled after them, blinded by tears. *Damaged? Nothing feels right in me already, and I might have just messed myself up even more.* The words, the desire, the flame that rushed through her like a blazing tornado... it was her. She'd brought the dragon. Magic, impossible magic. *Who am I?* Moving forward made everything blur into streaks. She pulled her hand free, to stand still and ease her pounding head, only to have her legs crumble away. Roen caught her just before she hit the hard, stone floor.

Roen carried Memory through the servant corridors and up into the more ornate halls of the castle. Still unconscious, she shivered in his arms. He wondered at how fragile and light she felt. *It's surprising she made it this far.*

Beside him, Eloryn trotted to keep up with his longer stride. He took them through the not-so-secret passageways to avoid servants and guards going about their night time duties. Designed for fast escape in case of a siege, they were used more often for romantic meetings and the staff gave them a wide berth at night. Roen had hoped to get inside without anyone seeing Eloryn, but if he could keep it to just Uther, that would have to do. Uther could barely see anyway.

Roen tried the sapphire suite, across the hall from his normal guest room. Marian had just finished redecorating and his guess it would be vacant paid off. Finding the door unlocked, he went inside and laid Memory onto a bed.

Eloryn hovered next to him. "What she did, I..."

Roen shook his head. "We have to go and tell Lanval what happened, now, in case we can't stay."

"Should we be waking him?"

"With this sort of news he needs to know right away. We'll be back to check on Memory soon."

Roen hurried Eloryn to the Duke's chambers, marked by a doorway

inlaid in gold with a design of a lion's face. He knocked gently. Putting his ear to the door, he listened then took a small step back to wait. Mumbling and shuffling soon turned into the creak of the door. It swung open wide, and a generously built man filled the frame, staring at them with sleep bleary eyes. He wore long rich bed robes, in a deep maroon that lit his whiskey colored beard from beneath.

"What is it, what is it? Roen, son? Why visiting so late?" Lanval held Roen's hands and patted them. He took a quick, second look at Eloryn's blood spattered face. "What's happened? Don't be bringing me bad news now."

"Good news, my Lord, great news. Maybe a little bad as well. I'm sorry it's so late, but we really must talk now." Roen bent forward in a shallow bow. Lanval put a finger to his lips and stepped out. The doorway through to the bedchamber stood open, and by the warm glow of dying embers, Roen saw Marian, tossing in her sleep on a massive, pillow-strewn bed. He frowned. *She still has nightmares.*

Lanval rubbed his eyes. "Never mind, I was awake. Come down the hall, we can talk there without disturbing Marian." He directed them to another room, a small meeting chamber with walls encrusted in carved flourishes that shone with gold leaf. It held a single elegant table, velvet padded chairs, and a woven tapestry of a captured unicorn.

Lanval took the largest chair at the end of the table, gesturing for the others to sit either side of him. Roen and Eloryn remained standing.

"Introductions, and then you can explain, what is this good news, great news, with a little bad, that is enough to drag me from my bed? News of a betrothal? That would fit the announcement." Lanval lifted an eyebrow.

"My lord, the news is in the form of an introduction. I fret my upbringing has not left me equipped for such an honor as this meeting. But still. Duke Lanval de Montredeur, this is Eloryn, daughter of Queen Loredanna and King Edmund. We have found the Maellan heir." Roen bowed his introduction with a small flourish to Eloryn.

Lanval blanched around his beard. He looked at Eloryn for a long moment, his face stern. "Found at last. Well met, Your Highness. It's good to see that Thayl wasn't able to destroy all things."

Eloryn curtseyed. "It is my honor to meet with you, Duke de Montredeur. I'm sorry for the late intrusion."

"Polite and lovely. Brought up well I see, wherever you've been hiding. Seems you've had some trouble finding your way here?"

Roen and Eloryn glanced at each other and Roen spoke again. "We have. Before anything else, we must know our trail has not been found leading here to you."

"There is a risk?"

Roen nodded.

Lanval stood and marched to the doorway, bellowing down the corridor. He turned back to Roen. "What else?"

"Wizard Councilor Pellaine, now by the name Alward. He has been captured and imprisoned here in your city. We hope for news of his escape, or chance for his release."

Lanval's fingers drummed against the door. "I've had no news. I'm to be informed when any wizard is captured within my borders. This is not well. What of your parents, Roen, are they safe?"

"Last I saw them." Roen swallowed.

Footsteps hurried up the corridor. Lanval stepped out, closing the door behind him so the small group wouldn't be seen. Orders were rushed out, the footsteps fled again and Lanval re-entered the room.

"Gawain, one of my trusted. He will look into these matters and let us know quickly if we've cause to worry." Lanval returned to the table. Grumbling out a breath he lowered himself into his seat. "Until then, sit. You make me weary just seeing you stand."

Roen pulled out a seat for Eloryn then sat down himself.

"So, how?" Lanval stared at Eloryn, rubbing his beard. "No, never mind that. Why, why come to me? I'm happy you're alive, no doubt, but I won't be able to shelter you. If you're not too proud to accept like Roen here, I can provide whatever money you need to find safety elsewhere. But I won't risk Marian's safety further than that. Not for anyone."

Eloryn hesitated, and Roen answered for her. "I would never ask of you what would risk you or the Duchess's safety."

"Then ask boy, what do you need?"

"We hope to know if you have contact with any remaining Wizards' Councilors, or with any who know how to reach them. We feel that until the Princess is able to rule again, she is best safe in their care."

"You believe so, do you?" Lanval bent forward on the table. It groaned under his weight. "They are hard to find, and for good reason. They're not only hunted by Thayl. I've heard the unseelie fae seek them as well. I don't know why. The fae have been causing more trouble all over Avall since Thayl has been in power. Would you find safety for your Princess with the most hunted people of this land?"

Lanval leant back in his chair again, gesturing to Eloryn. "And what of the Princess's wishes, how do her plans meet with yours and your parents, for returning her to the throne? Does she want that, considering she has done naught but hide these last sixteen years?"

"I do not," Eloryn said in a rush, then dropped her voice, embarrassed. "I only want to find Alward again, to be safe with him. I have no wish to rule, or way to remove Thayl so I could. Even if he were gone, I cannot say I would be the right choice to rule."

"Ah, a lady of little ambition, after my own heart," Lanval said with a fond smile.

Roen's shoulders tensed and he stared at the table. "A Maellan heir is the one hope the people of Avall have held onto during these hard times. We all have paths in our lives we don't want to take, but we must if it can help others. Your path could help the whole land, you cannot deny that."

"You speak well, son. And you, dear Princess, best heed him. The people want the Maellan line returned. So will the Wizards' Council, should you find them. Is this still where you wish to go?"

Eloryn, head bowed and silent, couldn't have looked more unsure.

Roen nodded firmly. "I still believe it is our best hope for the Princess. If they have managed to remain hidden so long with so many seeking them, then they will be able to keep her safe."

"Very well. I'll make inquiries." Lanval rose out of his chair and shuffled to the door. "Now, it is more morning than night, and for all your youth, you clearly need sleep even more than myself. I'll send word the moment I hear anything. Pray we don't hear the worst."

CHAPTER ELEVEN

"You... very good at that, you know. Should be... professional damsel catcher," Memory muttered, coming back to consciousness.

Warm, padded and covered, she opened her eyes and found herself alone and folded, not neatly, under sky blue covers of a single bed. Still fully clothed, less her shoes. A waft of sweat reached her nose, tainted by fear and turned pungent. She hoped she hadn't smelt like this last night. Roen and Eloryn were kind even to have removed her shoes.

The previous day came back to her and shame came with it, swallowed by outrage at the feeling. Why should she feel ashamed? She hadn't known what she was doing. It was an accident if anything. Apart from that poor horse, they were all OK. Or at least she hoped. Eloryn said she could have damaged herself somehow with the magic, but she felt fine, in fact, even better than she remembered. Although she still didn't remember much.

Memory stumbled out of bed. The sun burned bright lines around the edges of blue velvet drapes. Shades of blue and silver covered every surface of the room, in brocade designs across the walls and a trompe l'oeil ceiling of a cloudy sky. A mirror above a cornflower colored dressing table showed all her scrapes and swelling gone. She poked at the bruising on her ribs through layered clothing, but felt no pain. Her hair, however, was painful even to look at.

"Huh," she said aloud, wondering where Bill, Ben, Bob and Barry the Bruises had gone. The room echoed. Three doors stood in walls around the room, and Memory had no idea where any led. Door Number One already stood open, revealing an adjoining chamber – just as blue – with another bed, empty and unmade. She really was all alone. Memory stood in the middle of the vast blue room at a loss for what to do next. A latch clicked, making her jump. Roen peeked in through Door Number Two, and seeing her awake, strode in followed by Eloryn. They were both neat and clean, Roen dressed in a fresh white shirt, worn loosely, and Eloryn in her same grey and ivory lace dress that always managed to look perfect. Her hair was no less perfect. *Ambushed by the pretty people. Not fair damn it.*

Memory mumbled a curse and made a casual attempt to finger comb her hair, keeping her armpits wedged closed. "Um, morning guys. I just woke up."

"We were starting to wonder when you would. It's well into the day," Roen said, a line of worry across his forehead.

"Guess I needed the sleep. I feel much better though, in a few ways." Memory pointed to where she'd had a black eye the day before.

"After you fainted, I tried to heal you." Eloryn looked at her sheepishly. "Your surface injuries healed but there must be trust and consent for a stronger healing, and... I could not reach deeper and wake you. We were so worried for you. Still, I hoped if maybe the cause of your amnesia was more mundane that the healing magic might return some memories to you?"

"No change, but I think I'm OK, apart from desperately needing a shower."

"The bathroom is just through there," Roen said, indicating Door Number Three. He propped himself against a wall and raised an eyebrow. "Are you sure you haven't been here before?"

Memory shook her head and glared pure irony at Roen.

"Only that you would ask for a shower is curious. Castle de Montredeur is one of the few places in Avall that has such a luxury, thanks to the underground water system that supplies the estate. Still, if you were from around here, I'm sure I would remember you. You're not the type to go unnoticed," Roen said with a smirk.

"Not smelling like this anyway-"

A distant knocking made Roen interrupt her. "That sounds like my room." He opened the door again and leaned out. "Uther! Here, my man."

"Still not in your room, young sir?" The old servant spoke with laughter in his voice.

"Not the worst place you've found me now, is it? You've a message for me?" Roen asked.

"The Duke sends word that he requests your presence at the feast and ball this afternoon. That of yourself, and your two lady friends. A formal invitation." Uther handed Roen a wax sealed envelope.

"I'm not sure my companions have the energy for a social event. Not after last night," said Roen. Memory swore she saw him wink very unsubtly.

"The Duke thought that may be the case, but instructed that I assure you the ball is a masque, so you may all hide your faces, if you're feeling a little under the weather," Uther said, his battle to keep a straight face lost quickly.

"Is that so?" Roen clapped Uther on the shoulder with a returned laugh.

"He is sending the Duchess's very own handmaidens to see to the dressing of the ladies shortly." Uther, still grinning, bowed and whispered before he left, "Careful or you may find some competition for these two beauties."

When Roen closed the door and turned around, both Memory and Eloryn stared at him open mouthed.

"My deepest apologies Princess. It is only an act," Roen said, walking back into the room. Passing Memory he whispered just within her hearing, "As if there'd be any competition." With a hint of smile still on his lips, he took a seat at the end of the bed and cracked the seal of the envelope.

Memory, stunned, wondered more about who the two beauties were. Trying to be nonchalant she glanced at the mirror. Hair and clothes were as crumpled as each other; even a few visible wrinkles from her mummy-wrapped slumber still marked her skin.

Maybe being this disheveled would make the Duke more sympathetic to her when they met. She'd take her bruises back if it would mean he'd help her. "Are we going to see the Duke soon?"

Roen shook his head, looking over the letter. "We spoke to him already, last night."

"Oh, of course you did." *I bet I wasn't even mentioned.*

Roen read the note from Lanval aloud.

"Your arrival was well timed to match our grand Autumn Masque, which a well connected man within my trust will also attend. I believe him to be the source of the information you seek. Best he also meets the

subject of the required information, that he has strong enough reason to trust in sharing it." Roen closed his eyes for a short moment then smiled. "This is good news, Princess. You'll be in safe hands soon."

"Should we really be going out? If Lory looks so much like her mum, what if someone else recognizes her?"

Roen shook his head. "We're lucky the masque is tonight. I doubt we'll spend long at the ball, but it gives us freedom to move around the castle without anyone seeing either of your faces. The Duchess's handmaidens will have you not even recognizing yourselves. Clarice, Saoirse and Lily are the best."

"It says no more within the letter? No news of Alward?" Eloryn's voice lifted an octave.

"None, I regret. It also shares no bad news which is our luck, either of Alward or of us being tracked here after what happened yesterday."

And there it is again. I guess it was too much to hope they'd just let that whole summoning a dragon thing slip, Memory thought.

"So, whoever you are, Memory, you've got some talent in magic," Roen said. Memory thought he seemed too grateful to turn the topic away from Alward and shot him a glare telling him so.

Eloryn shook her head. She had never seemed more scared of Memory than she did now. "It's not only that. No one should be able to connect with magic in that way without the use of the magical language. There's only one other person ever known to be able to do that."

Roen and Eloryn looked at each other, drawing silent.

"Oh come on, who?" Memory asked, not sure why she needed to know another name that meant nothing to her.

"King Thayl Vaircarn."

Damn. She did know that name.

"That's probably not good, is it?" Memory asked, shaken. The few clues she had about herself kept leading to unwanted places.

"It's hard to say what it means, except that you need to be careful. Careful in what you say and how you say it," Eloryn told her. "When you cast that spell yesterday, at the same time you spoke, did you feel the connection to magic within you?"

Memory nodded, feeling her chest still toasting away.

"That is what you need to avoid. Better you try not to cast anything at all until we know what has happened to you," Eloryn said, her gaze turned away from Memory.

"But maybe it's better I try and learn what I'm doing, so I know how to control it?" Memory said, her voice husky, nearly breaking. "I mean, I did that yesterday completely by accident. I don't want to have another accident."

Eloryn frowned, shaking her head slightly.

"Please. It really scared me," Memory whispered.

"Perhaps just try something simple with her," Roen said.

Eloryn bit her bottom lip, but nodded. "Something simple then."

"The verbal light switch looks handy," Memory suggested.

"Very well, the behest for it is Àlaich las. First, just practice the words. Then focus on what you want to happen. The behest brings to you a wisp, a type of fae made of light, alive, but more a pure energy than a conscious being. Feel the spark of connection within you, and then say the words again," Eloryn instructed.

"Àlaich las." Nothing happened. *Fair enough, first try, and the pronunciation is a bit crazy,* Memory thought. She breathed in, trying to stoke the fires in her chest, to feel them burning this time. "OK. Àlaich las." Nothing again. "Àlaich las?" she whined. Still nothing.

"I suck," Memory said.

"Maybe something more physical that she can focus on," Roen suggested.

"Do you wish to demonstrate perhaps?" Eloryn asked.

"I'm sorry, please continue. You'll be a much better teacher for this than I." Roen got back to his feet and took a few steps away as if he'd been scolded to the corner by a teacher.

Eloryn took his place at the foot of the bed, and called Memory over next to her. "This is not as simple, and not authorized either, so be wary, if you learn it, not to use it where seen. But it is more *physical* in nature."

Roen cleared his throat. "Mind, what the Princess can do is somewhat more powerful than normal, and almost always less authorized."

Eloryn blushed in her usual, annoyingly cute way. "Not powerful, only, well, different. More complicated behests require more words, and it's more important that those words are correctly used. It's like speaking a contract. Alward taught me so much of the magical language and I can use it to ask what I need, without learning structured and proven behests. It is the talent of the Maellan line."

"So, if I pick this stuff up, how do I know what's authorized?"

Roen sniffed. "Nothing but fewer than a dozen household spells.

Light, Branding, warming water, some very basic healing. Metal workers, couriers and doctors can get permits for more but it's watched carefully and all very arbitrary. Most people realize the law is only there to flush out true wizards. It's made life harder, and generally better to use no magic at all."

"Well, if I can't pick this one up, using no magic at all will be my next choice. So what do we do, Lory?"

"See the hair brush on the dressing table there? Beirsinn fair nalldomh." Eloryn reached out a hand, and the hair brush flew into it.

Memory swore. "That's cool. Yeah, I wanna learn that one."

Eloryn replaced the brush on the dresser, and walked back to Memory, facing her where she sat on the edge of the bed. "You heard the words-beirsinn fair nalldomh. You should be able to easily focus on what you want here. Wisps can be contrary at times. Remember, work on feeling the connection to magic within you as you speak the words."

Memory repeated the words, again and then again, trying to find some connection inside her. Nothing happened, not a twitch, and she felt frustrated and foolish. "Oh just come here!" she snapped, reaching her arm forward in one last attempt.

Movement. The brush moved, but so did the dressing table. The wooden feet of the dresser cried as it scraped across the stone floor, speeding toward her and Eloryn. Memory pulled her legs up away from it. The dresser slammed into the foot of the bed. It spewed its drawers out onto the covers, wood splintering against the bed frame. Eloryn moved too slowly, saved only by Roen's speed, the professional damsel catcher in action. He grabbed and spun her out of its way.

As the dresser rocked on its feet, Roen held Eloryn in his arms a moment longer before he seemed willing to let her go. Memory could see a battle of color in her face, paling in fear, blushing in embarrassment.

Memory swore again. "Sorry."

"It's all right. She's safe," Roen said, only looking at Eloryn.

CHAPTER TWELVE

Three matching slim, raven-haired handmaidens arrived, introducing themselves with a row of curtseys.

Memory puffed a breath into her hair, thankful for the interruption. No one had been eager to speculate on her attempt at magic, and an awkward silence had grown long. Roen grinned at the ladies, and Saoirse and Lily chased him from the room with a spree of flirtatious giggling.

The handmaidens turned straight to fawning over Eloryn and Memory took the chance to slip into the bathroom.

It practically glowed blue. Above an aquamarine tub a brass showerhead shone like a small sun with two decorative taps like stars beneath. Memory glared at it, wondering what exactly was so amazing about a shower.

Memory struggled out of her dress and left it in a pile in the corner, tucking her knife out of sight underneath for safe keeping. Stepping gingerly across the cold tiles and into the tub, Memory spun the hot tap and a stream of steaming water soon sprayed down on her. It was a blessed relief to wash away the stink of the previous day. Showers were a luxury after all.

With a deep sigh and forced physical effort, Memory turned the shower off. As the sound of running water echoed away down the drain, she heard faint knocking from beyond. Not the bathroom door; the entrance door perhaps. No other sounds came from the main room, and the knocking persisted.

She wrapped a towel around her dripping torso, her hair still running dye-tinted streams down her back. Peeking out the bathroom door she saw the main room empty. Not sure what should be done, she tiptoed across the room and opened the entrance door just a crack.

Roen greeted her with a markedly amused expression. "I only wonder how you would have appeared had I knocked a moment earlier."

Memory dripped water into the carpet and tried to hide her embarrassment. "No one else was around to answer the door."

"I do hope this is what you're intending to wear to the ball. It's quite striking."

Memory smiled, hating that she couldn't hold it back. "You're not entirely dressed up yourself."

He wore the same simple shirt as before, its fine, nearly translucent silk overlaid with a plain and elegant satin coat in embroidered silver. It made his unkempt hair even more golden.

"Well, it'd be a crime to hide this face." He leant close to where she stood in the partly opened doorway.

"Is this how you talk to all girls?" *Except Eloryn,* she thought.

Roen looked both ashamed and audacious as he smiled back.

"And, it works for you?" Memory made herself sound so unimpressed that Roen actually looked hurt for a moment before she couldn't help but smile at him again. But by the time she did, Roen's eyes were elsewhere.

Memory turned to see Eloryn had emerged from the side chamber, fully dressed and done up. She looked like a porcelain doll, hair curled and pinned up on top of her head in ringlets of shining ivory. A silken gold dress clung around her bust and dropped in simple, shimmering waves.

Memory slumped. *I hope the mask that goes with that covers a lot of her face. Although I doubt any man will be looking at her face.*

"Does it not suit me?" Eloryn sounded nervous. Memory realized both she and Roen had been gawking at her since she walked in, albeit probably thinking different things.

Roen, dumbstruck for the first time Memory had seen, detached himself from the doorframe and straightened up as though about to speak, but said nothing.

"You look fine," Memory said, as kindly as she could manage.

Eloryn picked up the matching mask. It was quite large, after all — a butterfly design of filigree silver and gold that would cover most of her face.

The handmaidens buzzed back into the room and clucked when they saw Memory standing at the door with Roen, wet and wearing only a towel. Clarice, eldest of the three with a beauty mark that Memory didn't believe was real, walked right up to her and stared at her face judgmentally.

"There was no one else to answer the door!" Memory blurted.

"The jewels in your face; it will be easier when we begin your make up if you can remove them. Also, you may want to leave them out." Surely she meant it as kind fashion advice, but it still sounded just a little catty.

Roen winked at Clarice, stepped in and closed the door behind him. Shrugging, she smirked back and nudged Memory across to the dresser next to where Eloryn had been seated again for final touches.

Memory nodded thankfully to Clarice and started removing the piercings. What did she know about fashion anyway? She felt like an ugly duckling, even damp enough to be one. At this point, she would do whatever she could to fit in.

Sharing the short upholstered stool in front of the dressing table mirror, Memory and Eloryn were flanked by handmaidens. Lily cooed over their shoulder, "What handsome sisters you are, so much alike."

Memory snorted. The only thing they had in common was the color of their eyes, and even that Eloryn used to better advantage. But still, sitting together in front of a mirror, she could almost see what Lily meant. Both the same height, and without her black eye and swollen jaw line, her face looked a lot more delicate, like Eloryn's. It was... eerie.

Eloryn's skin had paled more than usual. She didn't seem pleased by the comparison. In fact, she looked downright skittish. Memory bit her lip. Even with her fading dye job and bony figure, was it really that insulting a comparison? Maybe Memory did have a sister out there somewhere. She had to find her real family, one way or another.

Memory turned back to Roen, on edge again. "So why were you knocking the door down anyway?"

Roen had taken a seat on the bed. "Duke Lanval wishes to introduce us to his friend who has arrived. They are waiting for us."

"The young lady is certainly not going anywhere until we have her dressed," Clarice muttered.

Roen lowered his gaze, shifting it between Eloryn and Memory. "Truth is, Lady Memory is not invited to this meeting. I am to escort Lady Eloryn only."

Memory paused half way into unscrewing her labret. She wasn't sure why the news surprised her, or hurt, but it did both. She couldn't even think of a valid reason to argue why she should be allowed to go. It had only been a matter of time before she was left behind. She looked to Eloryn, whose face showed a battle of emotions. When Eloryn saw Memory watching her she turned quickly away. Memory dragged out her last piercing and faux pouted at Roen. "I guess I'll have to entertain myself then."

"There will be plenty of entertainment at the feast. Some fun will do you well, and perhaps you will recognize someone? I'll even owe you a dance," Roen said, half smiling apologetically.

Saoirse finished tying Eloryn's mask into place around her elaborate hair-do and the three handmaidens turned their full attention to Memory. She shot Roen a look of terror as they backed her into the side room. He laughed in response and the door closed between them.

A range of ball gowns and accessories had been laid out to choose from. Despite her natural aversion to dresses, Memory actually got excited when she saw one, all black, amongst the pile of colorful gowns on offer. She picked it without hesitation.

The maids gossiped about people Memory didn't know while they approached her with the mounds of black fabric. Memory stood shivering, and just closed her eyes and tried not to wince as they went about their work lacing, tucking and stitching the dress into form. When they were done, Memory had to admit she felt a little bit kick ass. The dress was hot. Bodice all black lace over black satin, tight and low cut, only just high enough to cover the scar in the centre of her chest. The multi layered skirts combined both rolling ruffles and translucent gauze. Maybe in this, even next to Eloryn, she could be considered a beauty.

Directed back into the main room, Memory found Roen and Eloryn were gone. *They didn't even say goodbye before going to their fancy nobles-only meeting.* Memory coughed a short, insulted laugh. She wondered what part Roen had there, other than being there for the Princess. Who would be there for her in this big, unfamiliar castle?

Memory sat in front of the previously mobile dressing table. The handmaidens stood back discussing options with pinched mouths then got to work. For all that there were only three of them, at times Memory felt like there were a dozen hands on her, poking and primping. They managed to pull her hair up into an ornate design that made it look

like she had twice the hair she did. Her face was pinched and painted. She tried, between bursts of powder, to tell them to keep the make-up simple, worried about receiving stray beauty marks. Clarice tsked, but followed her wishes. When they were done, Memory looked at herself a moment then smiled an approval to them. As they turned away to gather up the unselected dresses, Memory grabbed a remaining kohl brush and added more black around her eyes.

"My lady, some guests are already gathering in the northern grounds. If you're happy with your presentation, we will take our leave. We'll have your clothes taken to the laundry so they will be fresh for you tomorrow."

Memory nodded thanks to them all, relieved that they were done with her before she remembered something. "Oh, just a moment!" Memory said, dashing into the bathroom. She grabbed her knife from under the pile of filthy dresses and slipped it down the secure front of her corset. No matter what it was for, the knife somehow made her feel better. She wanted to keep it close. She smiled at Lily who followed her in, and returned to the main chamber to find the others gone.

The remaining gowns and accessories had been taken and only a pair of crystal encrusted slippers remained.

Memory looked longingly for a moment at her sneakers, then grabbed the sparkling shoes and tugged them on. At least they weren't heels. Her stomach rolled with a tide of hunger and she focused on one word. Feast. If there was food out there somewhere, that is where she would go, even alone.

Memory picked up the mask that matched her dress, hurriedly tying its ribbons behind her head. She stepped out the entrance door and through the thin eyes of her mask the hallway seemed to stretch endlessly in either direction.

Lily caught up to her, laundry tied in a neat bundle on one hip. "Do you not know the way?"

Memory winced a no.

"Just down the hall that way. A left, down two floors, a right at the Duke's portrait, then out past the water channels, through the archway and into the grounds. You'll have no trouble." She bobbed a short curtsey and headed the other way up the hall.

Memory stood still a moment longer, repeating the instructions in her head while they were still fresh. She headed off at a brisk pace, mouth already watering at the idea of long missed sustenance.

A left, a right, oh hell. Left or right again? Memory quickly got lost. She wandered down long corridors, stopping to ask directions at every person she passed. Finding what she assumed to be the Duke's portrait, she smiled, glad to be heading the right way. *Jolly looking fellow, would have been nice to meet you.* Finally she saw an archway ahead through a large entry hall. The corridor ran straight through it, becoming a bridge bordered by knee-high stone walls carved with flowers. Rectangular pools of water ran the length of the hall on either side, burbling with deep undercurrents. She slowed, exhausted from the shallow breaths the corset forced her to take.

Out through the archway, the path led Memory into an emerald green paradise. Tall, well-trimmed hedges looped around the grounds, separating small and large areas full of flowers, statues and fruit trees. Running water sounded from everywhere. She could see, some way down the path, a large marquee posted amongst climbing roses and pine trees where people milled about. Looking back at the castle itself, Memory blew out a low whistle. *The place had goddamned towers.* The sun still shone, but dipped low. It had taken them some time to get ready, but she really must have slept most of the day for it to be this late. She had breakfast, lunch and dinner to make up for.

Part way down the path she froze, sure she had heard Eloryn's voice. Looking around, she couldn't see anyone down the long path to the grand tent. To both her sides, hedges stood tall and thick. But then there was Roen's voice too. She walked soft-footed, trying to trace them.

Soon she stood with her ear up against a hedge. They were on the other side of it, talking in hushed voices. What were they doing out here? They were supposed to be at their exclusive meeting. Had they lied to her? Betrayal burned in Memory, and she stilled herself to listen in.

"...your concern. It was right of you to mention this in private," Roen was saying.

"You see it too, the resemblance between us? I don't want to think it, but it explains too much." Eloryn sounded scared.

"I know she is strange in ways, but she hardly seems malevolent."

Memory sucked in her breath. *They're talking about me.*

"I've told you how she appeared, caught within the Veil door. What if she did not come from Avall?"

"There is no human land beyond the Veil anymore. There is only Avall, and the land of the fae. You don't think she is some type of fae?"

Feet shuffled. "A fairy changeling? I wondered so when we first met, but I shared bread with her and fae won't abide bread."

"But you still don't believe her to be human?"

"How she appeared, through the Veil as she did, how she looks so like me, how she has no memory or life of her own... Alward's research told of the hell beyond the Veil. He believed demons from there could find their way through. Doppelgangers that could cling to a traveler through a broken Veil door, taking their appearance so they can appear human..." Eloryn's voice faded out, distressed.

Ice shivered under the surface of Memory's skin.

They thought she was a *demon*.

CHAPTER THIRTEEN

Memory backed away from the hedge. She couldn't stand to hear any more.

A demon?

She sleep-walked along the path and into the grand tent. She'd thought she was just lost, confused, maybe even brain damaged. But she'd only been asking who she was, never *what* she was.

Memory passed by people in the tent. Some tried to speak to her, but she walked on. Wide gowns filled her vision with color, men dressed as admirals and highwaymen, women as peacocks and angels. Some of the guests hardly seemed human, in shape or sheer beauty. Their revelry only made the bitterness in Memory rise. The weight of betrayal dragged her down. She took the nearest seat, and glared through heavy eyes into the growing crowd. Other guests in the marquee stared back at her, gossiping behind lace gloved hands and enameled masks.

Fury burned Memory's eyelids and she huffed cooling air at them, refusing to let herself cry. Emotions did battle within her, taking all her energy and blocking out the surrounding festivities. It took her a while to realize she was being spoken to.

"Huh?" She turned to see a young man with shining black hair smiling at her. He wore no mask, just a well tailored black suit and a felt hat which he held in one hand against his chest.

"Perceval. My name. And if I might have the honor of knowing yours?" He smiled.

Memory hesitated. "Mem... Just Mem."

"It is a pleasure, Lady Mem."

He took her hand. She twitched, confused, but he kissed it gently, and returned it to her lap. She tried to smile at him and failed.

"You aren't enjoying yourself? It is a fine feast the Duke has put on this evening."

"Sorry, I'm just not..." *Human?* Memory swallowed bile. She was being ridiculous. She felt human, didn't she? She set her teeth against each other so firmly they hurt. *How dare Eloryn say I'm not human?*

"I haven't seen you before, have I?" Perceval didn't wait for her to answer. "You must be new to court. Everyone here has their eyes on you."

Like she needed the reminder. "I wish they wouldn't. I feel bad enough already."

"Bad? They only look at you either in desire or in jealousy. You're the most splendid lady here this eve."

Memory lost what she had been thinking and blushed in a way that would challenge Eloryn. She shook her head, unable to reply in any other way.

With her gaze locked on Perceval, she was startled by someone clearing their throat to her side. Roen had appeared out of the crowd in front of her.

"There you are. My Lady, the dress transforms you. Not that your previous attire didn't flatter as well."

Memory turned her face away from both men, her lips pulling into a sneer. She steeled herself then met Roen's eyes. He smiled but it didn't hide an expression too serious to be seen against the backdrop of giddy revelers.

When the silence dragged on, Roen frowned over his tawny eyes. "Have you eaten today? There is plenty of food about."

"Why aren't you with Eloryn?" Memory muttered.

A flash of hurt marred Roen's face then passed. "I was only to escort her to her meeting. I'm now free to enjoy myself."

"Right."

"And I do owe you that dance." Roen offered a hand to Memory and smiled again in a way that looked fake.

"Can't. Won't." Memory turned her back to him, unwilling to keep up any guise of conversation.

"You aren't being troubled here at all?" Roen eyed Perceval.

"Not by him." Memory smiled at Perceval, who gave Roen a victorious look that satisfied her.

"Well then, I wish you a pleasant evening." Roen walked away into the crowd, one final look over his shoulder which Memory pretended to ignore. He quickly found a flock of fawning ladies, and broke off into a dance with one wearing a devil mask.

Memory narrowed her eyes. "God, I could do with a drink."

Perceval eagerly signaled to a servant who brought filled goblets to them in an instant.

Memory laughed aloud, and lifted her cup to Perceval in appreciation. "Good service here."

"Indeed, a fine gathering. So I must ask, what could have made the heart of the most lovely lady here so shadowed?" Perceval clicked his goblet against hers and took a sip, his black-brown eyes never leaving her face.

Memory wasn't sure she liked the way he looked at her. It was nice to be the focus of attention, but it left an odd ill feeling in her gut. Still, she liked having someone to talk to who didn't care about the Princess, or whether she was human or not.

She took a large mouthful of mead from her goblet, enjoying the sweetness of it.

"I just want to go home," Memory said, staring into the honey liquid.

Perceval's shoulders dropped. "So early? Could nothing persuade you to stay?"

"No, I mean, I'm not going anywhere right now. But I sort of, can't get home. I'm kind of lost."

"Lost? Lucky then that I found you. I may be of assistance."

"You'd help me? I don't see any shining armor."

Perceval twisted his eyebrows at her comment, but smiled over his clear confusion. "In truth, I would help. See, you've not yet allowed me to tell you to whom I serve." Perceval flourished his hand. "For serving is what I do, and I do it very well indeed. If I am unable to help you, then he, of all people, is sure to have the power to help in any way needed."

Memory warmed to him. Or maybe it was the mead. She gave him a wry smile.

"It's really nice of you, but I'm not entirely sure anymore that anyone can help with the full scope of problems I have."

"Not even the King himself?" Perceval revealed under his breath.

"Indeed. I am in his personal escort, and he has come here tonight on an urgent matter."

Memory froze mid sip. The King… Thayl? Thayl who was chasing Eloryn, who killed her parents for the throne. Thayl, the only other person ever known to use magic like she did. The most powerful man around, both in magic and in title. Her mind sped through her index on this man, Thayl, until it caught up with her emotions. Thayl, who for all she knew, might not be all that bad, who might treat her like a human being. She had to find her family, people who really cared about her. The only person who had offered to help her so far also called her a demon. *If Eloryn thinks I'm a demon, how true can the rest of what she says be? Thayl's probably no more evil than me.*

"King Thayl, he's here, at the ball somewhere?"

"Hush now, his attendance is yet unannounced," Perceval said, looking pleased with himself. "He partakes in some business before coming to the feast."

"He's not meeting with anyone up in the palace just now, is he?" A small shiver of worry for Eloryn came to Memory unbidden. She searched her gaze over the crowd but couldn't see Roen. Both he and his buxom dance partner had vanished.

Her mood flipped back to dark. Why should she worry about them? She was obviously nothing to them, at best, and at worst she was a demon. The only thing Eloryn had done for her so far was give her something she could negotiate with to get help from Thayl.

She chewed her lip, considering her options.

"No, he is through the grounds here. I'd just passed a message of his arrival along to the Duke's staff when I saw you here, inexplicably alone, and was more than thankful my duties for the evening had ended." Perceval smiled at her with dark, half closed eyes. "And at the end of duties comes drinking," he raised his goblet to hers, "and dancing, if you…"

Memory interrupted him. "I want to meet him. I want to meet the King."

Roen excused himself to his dance partner as soon as he politely could. She turned away with a cute pout and flick of perfect ringlets. She could have been an amusing distraction, but Roen found himself in no mood to dance. He couldn't think why. He should be celebrating. He had brought the Princess here safely, and soon she'd be escorted to the Wizards' Council and under their protection. *It's for the best. She deserves better guardians. It's a good thing.* Roen repeated the words again in his mind, but he had to keep forcing the smile onto his face. After doing it all day, that smile wore thin.

Memory's hard tone lingered in his head, adding to his mood. She was normally so good humored her sudden coldness made him wonder if he'd stepped too far with his own words. He spoke so openly to her only because her wit matched his own. He enjoyed that.

Catching a glimpse of Memory laughing with the dark-haired man, Roen wondered again where he had seen him before. Roen skirted the feast, pacing through the crowd in a short lived attempt to kill time then found himself wandering back up into the castle, toward the private meeting room they had used with Lanval the night before.

He knew he wasn't welcome. Lanval made it clear his contact would see only the heir, no one else. Roen felt himself drawn back that way regardless.

He should at least find out when they planned to have Eloryn leave, to make sure he could see her on her way. He tried to play out the farewell in his mind. Should he have a gift of some kind for her? What did one do in a situation like this? Nothing seemed appropriate.

Even the thought of parting ways felt wrong.

Reaching the top of the stairs, he stuck his hands into the familiar pockets of his pants; his normal, plain but neat fitted trousers with concealed pockets for the tools of his trade. Maybe he should have dressed up more. Not that it mattered. He would be back to his normal life soon.

Coming around the corner into the corridor which held the meeting room, Roen almost ran straight into Duke Lanval. He came barreling past with a look of grim concern. He didn't slow down, but called back as he sped away. "Get her out of here Roen, just take her away!"

A message boy stood trembling at the open doorway to the meeting room. Roen increased his pace, and Eloryn met him in the hall. She looked as pale as the time she had fainted on him.

Before he could stop himself, he put his hands around her shoulders, holding her gently. "What happened? Are you all right?"

Eloryn seemed frozen for a moment, then jerked back to awareness. She stepped out of his hold and ran down the hall.

Roen looked at the quivering messenger and snapped louder at him than he meant. "What message did you deliver?"

"That King Thayl has arrived."

Roen bolted after Eloryn, catching up to her quickly. "That's not the right way. We have to get you out of the castle, keep you hidden."

She kept running. She shook her head and her voice came out as a panicked whisper. "She's out there all on her own."

Perceval's mouth hung open at Memory's request. "I'm not sure I can…"

"Oh please?" Memory pouted, rolling her shoulders back, allowing the corset to squeeze up what little cleavage she had. "You said you would help me. Maybe you can just walk me to him?" Memory wasn't sure if casually meeting the King was a done thing, but it was worth a try.

Perceval grinned as though sharing a secret and extended an arm to her. He hooked his elbow around hers and walked her away from the marquee, pulling her close beside him. Perceval continued his inane small talk and boasting and she tried to hide how uncomfortable she felt on his arm.

He led her around hedges formed like a maze, through smaller gardens, past larger trees to another part of the grounds, getting her thoroughly lost in the process. They emerged into a stone paved courtyard where a group of men in a range of armor and uniforms stood about in serious discussion. Perceval placed her against a hedge, winking at one of his friends who looked their way. Memory tried not to feel like a groupie.

"Which one is he?" She hoped she sounded innocently naïve. Her nerves jangled. She tried to calm them, but an odd sensation grew within her.

Perceval leant in and whispered into her ear, "Dark hair and dark purple coat."

Memory found him quickly. His hair was indeed dark, a tumbling shoulder length mass contrasted with a small and well trimmed beard. He wasn't as old as Memory expected, maybe thirty-five years, and she was shocked again to find he was actually gorgeous. All except for his eyes, which were dark and tired.

More surprising still, Memory felt as though she recognized him from somewhere.

The uneasy feeling within her swelled. *But I don't know anyone.* She

took in his features, trying to trace the fragments of familiarity within her barren brain. He seemed to share her discomfort. He shook his shoulders in an abrupt shiver, and reached up a gloved hand, stretching and clenching it before his face.

Memory's legs turned to chalk, ready to crumble. He was the man; the man with the hand. The glowing hand from her dream. She turned her face away from him.

"We should go. I don't want to interrupt him." Her voice wavered. *How could it be him? It was just a dream, wasn't it?*

"I'm sure I can make your introduction to King Thayl, Lady Mem. You no longer wish it?"

Right. Now *you're sure.* Memory shook her head, urgency panicking her. "No, let's go. Now. Let's go somewhere else. Private," she said, with a small smile and wink. A wide grin from Perceval told her she'd succeeded in speeding him up.

They turned to go.

"Do I know you?" A deep, smooth voice interrupted them. It had the tone of someone not interested in formalities, and not having need of them.

Thayl stood by her side, looking down at her. Memory reached up to touch her mask, comforting herself with its presence. "No, Your Highness." Was that even the correct way to address a king? Memory didn't know. She tried to force a blush to her chilled skin, tried to curtsey in the way she'd seen Eloryn do, low and formally. She wobbled, inelegantly righting herself. "No, I don't believe so."

"Remove your mask, girl," Thayl said.

Perceval's look told her to take this request seriously. She untied it with shaking fingers. The bow caught and pulled loose strands of hair, bringing tears to her eyes. With the mask off her face, Thayl's expression didn't change, showing indifferent confusion only.

"Your name, where are you from?" Thayl asked. "There is something about you..."

"This is Lady Mem, Your Majesty." Perceval took over for her when she hesitated too long. "I met her just moments afore. She requested to see you."

"You did? And why would you..." Thayl's face twisted with discomfort again. He tugged the glove off his right hand. Memory gaped at the mass of scars it held. Shapes and lines covered it to the wrist, carved

into the skin long ago and turned to puckered flesh by time. A faint glow built around it.

Thayl looked from his hand to her. His expression was still confused, but no longer indifferent. It was fierce, frightened. "You? How can it be? You've not even aged. Devil, how did you get here from that Hell?"

Thayl grabbed Memory with both hands. His fingers dug into her, wrapping fully around her slight arms with bruising strength.

Memory's heart stopped. His grasp made panic burn inside her. A blinding light burst around them, joining the glow from Thayl's hand. Her heart started again, thunder against the weakness of her body. Her vision back-flipped.

She stood in an alley. She looked down upon herself, mesmerized by the glow of light.

The life escaped from the other her, no longer wanting to be trapped within. It flowed into her outstretched hand, making her stronger.

She watched herself scream.

She blinked, back in the green castle grounds. She stumbled backwards in shock, free to stumble, with Thayl's hands no longer holding her. He stepped back too. She tripped on her own foot, her slipper left behind.

"Your Majesty." A booming voice broke through. "My apologies that I couldn't attend you sooner. Your presence tonight wasn't anticipated."

Thayl turned around in a stupor. Duke Lanval marched toward them with an entourage. Memory stood still, shell shocked. Rough hands grabbed her from behind. One forceful tug pulled her back into the scratching leaves of the hedge.

She tried to wriggle free, but strong arms pinned her against a body of firm muscles and furs. Dragged through the dense foliage, she closed her eyes to the twigs that rushed by. In a burst of leaves, she and her abductor emerged from the hedge. She looked up into blue eyes. Blue like the sea, they even made her feel sea-sick looking into them. Eyes she remembered from the forest.

She must have looked as though she would scream, because the young man put a finger across his lips. He grabbed her arm and pulled her forward. She drew a rough breath, unable to get enough air into her corseted chest. She wheezed and floundered. The savage man lifted her, threw her not too gently over a shoulder, and ran.

The savage's pace did not slow as he carried her through hedges and corners of the gardens shadowed by the coming night. The delicate

fabric of her sleeves tore and the fine work of the handmaidens on her hair was lost to passing branches.

The mad dash ended before she could decide whether to cling on or try to get free and he pushed her out onto an open pathway. She fell to her knees. *It's like he knew I needed saving even before I did, as if he knew Thayl would hurt me. Me, a king, a savage; how could we all know each other?* When she spun around, nothing but the rustle of hedge leaves remained of the man. She saw a familiar archway in the distance, and two familiar figures emerging from it. One ran to her.

"Memory, by the fae, what's happened?" Roen knelt beside her.

Memory couldn't force words out, her lungs still out of shape from being knocked against the beast man's shoulder. She coughed out a leaf.

"Was it that man from the ball? What did he do?" Roen's voice was slow and intense.

Memory shook her head. "Ran through bushes. Had to tell you. Have to go."

"Mem, are you all right?" Eloryn caught up to them, looking no less concerned.

Memory frowned. "Thayl. He's here."

"We know. We came to find you so we could leave," Roen said, helping her up.

Came to find me? If they knew Thayl was here, why didn't they just leave without me? They thought she was a demon, but here they were, looking at her with all the sympathy of someone on her deathbed. Memory's heart jittered.

A group of men led by Perceval, clutching the slipper she'd left behind, rounded the other end of the pathway. Perceval pointed, and the men ran for them.

Roen took both girls by a hand and ran back toward the palace. Gowns too long, corsets too tight, neither could move fast, but they had a head start against Thayl's men down the long garden pathway.

"We'll lose them in the secret passageways once we're in the castle." Roen sounded confident, but Memory felt his anxiety in the way his arm strained to pull her faster.

They passed through the archway. Across the pathway that bridged the pools of water, a tall man with lion's hair and a scarred face stopped in his tracks. He glared with wide eyed intensity.

Eloryn gasped a scream, stopping so suddenly she tore from Roen's

grasp. "He is the one who captured Alward."

Roen turned from the imposing man to the approaching group. They stood in the middle of the pathway bridge, blocked at both ends. Water rushed in deep channels to either side.

Memory looked to Eloryn. "Can you cast something? Help us get away?"

Eloryn rushed out words in the magical tongue, hesitated, shook her head, started again. Memory had no idea what she asked of what. The wizard hunter drew his crossbow and shot a tiny dart. It hit Eloryn's neck, and she fell, tumbling over the low wall. Roen reached an arm for her, this time too slowly. With a splash she disappeared beneath the churning water. One final glimpse of gold like a fish in the depths and she was gone.

"Princess?" he whispered. She did not resurface. "Eloryn!"

Roen dived into the deep channel without a second breath.

Left alone on the bridge, Memory looked from the dark water to the approaching men, terrified of both.

"Capture the demon," Perceval called out.

Memory took as deep a breath as her clothing allowed. She stepped over the wall and plunged into the water.

CHAPTER FOURTEEN

The ice of the water's touch burned Memory's skin. She could feel no bottom, no sides, just a rush of water pulling her down. The channel ran deep and fast. The fabric of her skirts tangled and lifted about, tying her limbs. She sank, breathless, reached the distant bottom then pushed up. Her cheek scraped against the rocky ceiling. She gasped air in the smallest pocket of space before being pulled under again. The channel narrowed around her, knocking her against rocks, finally expelling her into a great expanse of water.

Her chest ached and her mind lost focus. Ribbons of reeds twisted up from the ground, and she floated, still and suspended in the blue-green night. In the distance, Eloryn and Roen danced in the air. More figures joined them, lifting them into the sky; small, slender women with white skin and ridiculously long hair. Some flew around her, keeping their distance. She reached for them, wanting to touch these beautiful, flying angels. They scowled with large black eyes. The surreal moment ended and she realized they didn't fly. She was still underwater. They swam, and she could not breathe. Her lungs exploded and the last of her air burst out in bubbles around her. Her vision darkened at the edges.

Large hands pulled at her. Reaching the surface she filled her cracking lungs. The savage broke through the water next to her, droplets forming in his dark tangle of hair. Supporting her fabric-weighted mass with one arm, he made a slow journey across to the edge of the lake, dragging

her with him. They were alone on the bank where the savage crawled out of the water. She lay at its edge, unable to lift the waterlogged skirts any farther. He collapsed face down, gulping breaths.

Memory coughed out a stream of water, aching as though she'd been wrung out and wishing she was at least that dry. She wiped clinging hair from her eyes, trying to get a clear view of the strange man, wanting to be sure he was real. He still looked more like an animal than a man. He had a lean build with wide shoulders, every inch of bare skin muscled. She could just see the profile of his face, showing high cheekbones and long dark lashes that dripped water. He wasn't familiar to her in the slightest.

"Who are you?" Memory said.

Lying on his stomach, he lifted himself up onto his elbows and looked at her as though she'd just slapped him. His pale eyes flashed like lightning under heavy black brows.

In the distance, Roen called Memory's name.

"I'm here!" she yelled through a hurting throat.

The beast man's body tensed, and he stared in the direction of Roen's voice. When he turned back to her, his harsh expression caught her off guard. Anger, fear, accusation? She couldn't quite tell. He shifted to his knees, pulling himself up with a harsh breath.

"Don't go, they're my friends, they won't-" she begged, but he vanished in a rustle of leaves.

"Thank you," she whispered to the empty space he left.

Dragging the heavy gown from the water, she just managed to stand when Roen and Eloryn found her. Wet and bedraggled, Roen had Eloryn under one arm, supporting her protectively.

There were grim expressions all around, not helped by the lingering scent of swamp.

Memory couldn't meet their eyes. "I didn't know Thayl was there, I didn't know who he was until he spoke to me." The lies caught in her throat but she couldn't tell them the truth.

"He spoke to you? What did he say?" Eloryn asked.

"Nothing. Just an introduction." Over Eloryn's shoulder Memory saw the silhouette of the savage through the trees, watching her lie. The weight in her dress and her heart made her want to crumple to the ground. Thayl's words still rang in her ears. *Devil, how did you get here from that Hell?* Eloryn was right. She was some kind of demon.

Eloryn shivered. She'd never been so cold. Her home with Alward had always been warm and comfortable. Her teeth chattered and she tried to still her shivering, which just made her rattle harder. Roen must have noticed because he pulled her closer to him. His body felt warm against hers. He'd lost his silver coat in the lake somewhere, and she tried not to look where the translucent silk of his shirt clung to his skin.

"They will come straight to the lake to find us," Roen said. "The estate's water channels all flow down to here. Princess, is there any way you can make a behest to cover our path, so they can't track us? Let them believe we drowned."

"The dart was poisoned somehow. It's closed my connection to magic. I have nothing I can do. I'm sorry." *This is what they did to Alward, how they were able to catch him,* she thought. He would have felt just as useless, and he was all alone. She took a deep breath to hold off tears.

Roen let her go. He turned, eyes seeking landmarks on the lake shore. His hair sprinkled droplets of water over his face. "You two, head along the lake's edge this way. You'll soon come to a small inlet stream. Follow it. Stay in the water, leave no footprints. First bridge you come to, take the low road. It will lead you to an inn, Elders Bridge. Don't go in. Just wait and hide. Do you understand?"

"You're not coming with us?" Eloryn tried not to sound hurt. She could still feel the warmth where he'd held her, but it faded.

Roen looked at her with hooded eyes. "I will head away from the lake here. There's a main road not far through these woods. I will leave enough of a path for three people, then disappear when I reach the road. They may think we caught a passing wagon. I only hope it will be enough. I wish I could do this and also remain with you. But I will be at Elders Bridge, Princess, I promise you. Be safe."

Roen bowed to her and smiled to Memory as he always did. His departure left Eloryn with an ache inside. She didn't think he'd ever smiled at her.

"We should go quickly then, so his plan works," Memory said. She wrung water from her skirts, hitched them up, and began wobbling along the lake shore in ankle deep water. Eloryn thought she seemed agitated.

When she and Roen had taken the chance to discuss Memory in

private, the one thing they agreed was that her loss and confusion seemed nothing but honest. *Even suffering that pain, she's only tried to help me. No matter what she may be, or how frightening her magic, she's been a friend. And I still haven't been able to give any help in return.*

Sometimes Memory looked so much like her it chilled her bones. More often, she was so different – from her angular build to her blunt words – it seemed ridiculous trying to make comparisons. Eloryn wondered what Alward would have said. Had she over-reacted? She missed his guidance dearly. Still, despite Memory's sometimes ill temperament, Eloryn felt better having her nearby. *A friend.*

Travel was slow, and Memory wasn't talking. The night became thick around them, only a clouded moon lighting their way. The slippery rocks around the lake and up the small stream slowed them even more as they picked between them. Both girls fell into the water more than a few times and had to drag out and wring the heavy dresses before walking again.

The fifth time Memory fell in she actually laughed out loud, surprising Eloryn.

"Are you all right?" she asked, helping Memory out of the black water.

"I'm fine. I just lost my other bloody shoe." She sighed out the last of her laughter.

Eloryn didn't understand why this improved Memory's mood, but was glad for it. Memory continued to cling to Eloryn, and she clung back, unwilling to let go of the barest comforting warmth shared between them. By walking close together they also managed to avoid falling into the water again. Each time one slipped, the other held her up.

They were chilled through and aching by the time they reached a bridge. They hoped it was the right one, hoped they'd picked the right road, and hoped the inn wouldn't be far. Before long they were rewarded with a sign posting "Elders Bridge Inn" and a wide two storey building with a couple of smaller buildings close behind. The road continued along the front and thick forest surrounded every side. Golden light shone from the windows, radiating warmth. It looked so inviting it made Eloryn shiver harder.

"Sure we can't go in?" Memory whispered between knocking teeth.

"We were told to wait." Eloryn turned away from the light regretfully. They trudged a little farther behind some trees where undergrowth and darkness would hide them but they could still see the brightly lit inn.

The girls bundled up together in the embrace of a large buttressed tree root.

Memory glanced over her shoulder into the trees behind them, then whispered, "How's your magic going? Any better yet?"

Eloryn shook her head, unsure if Memory saw in the darkness, but unable to answer aloud. She felt miserable. She could not dry them, could not warm them. They had no other clothes. Everything Eloryn still owned in the world, even her mother's amulet, was left behind.

"I could maybe try something? Anything is better than freezing to death, right?" Memory said.

Eloryn hesitated, needing a moment to compose herself. Memory started muttering random words and phrases to do with heat and warmth. Eloryn turned to give her warning, but a flame already sparked in front of them, lighting the dry leaves at their feet on fire. Memory swore and smothered it with the wet bulk of her dress.

"OK, burning to death? Not better. Point taken."

Eloryn looked to the inn. There was no sign that they had been seen. People came and went, but not Roen. Before they were interrupted, Duke Lanval's contact had given her information and a token with which to contact the Wizards' Council. When she fumbled and dropped it in their flight from the castle, Roen took the token, keeping it safe, keeping her safe. *He should have been here by now. He could be captured as well.* Sudden tears filled her eyes and she winced to hold them in. Thayl had appeared at Duke Lanval's estate in such a rush. There could only be one reason for it: Alward. Thayl had him now, and she knew what became of any wizard Thayl captured.

The thought made her ache. That these people would risk so much for her, suffer so much hardship, just for a title she owned only in name. *No wonder Roen never smiles at me.*

Memory looked over her shoulder again.

"What are you looking at?" Eloryn asked, following her gaze, hoping to see Roen arriving.

"Nothing. I mean I can't see anything, but I was looking for something." Memory paused, then turned seriously to Eloryn. "OK, I don't want you to freak out, but there's this guy. I think he's following me, or us. I saw him in the forest when we ran into that troll cave. He helped me then. And again at the castle, well, he saved me in the lake I mean."

Eloryn blinked. "You think he helps you? Could he know you?"

"Don't know. It's weird. He's all Tarzan and stuff, like some sort of guardian-angel-cross-savage. I haven't even heard him talk, if he can. I can't think how I'd possibly know him."

"He sounds like a foundling child. There are lots of stories about them, children who become lost in the woods at a young age and are raised by animals or the fae themselves."

"He sure looks like an animal. You haven't seen him? At all? Maybe I've just really lost it."

"If you say he's out there then I believe you. There must be a reason he's following you. Alward says nothing is ever truly lost, everything goes somewhere..." Eloryn's voice faded out.

"Alward, he's like your family, isn't he?" Memory said. "We're going to meet a whole group of wizards, right? I'm sure they'll be able to rescue him. Maybe he's already free. Brannon said someone would try."

Eloryn just nodded. Saving Alward is what she should be doing, if only she could, if she only knew what to do. Instead, it was left in the hands of more capable strangers, still more people put in danger on her behalf. "I hope they will be able to help you too, to find out who you are and where you're from."

Memory shifted, hiding her face in shadow. "Yeah. Me too."

Eloryn turned back to the inn. The door opened, spilling warm light and a pair of bodies out into the night. "Is that Roen?"

Memory perked up.

Across at the inn, Roen stumbled down the steps, a pint glass in one hand and a red-headed barmaid tucked under his other arm. She stroked long fingers over his belt buckle, working it loose.

"If it is him, I may just need to kill him," Memory muttered through blue lips.

Roen whispered in the busty barmaid's ear, a huge grin on his face. He indicated with his hands. *You, me, two more.* The slap she gave him echoed out across the quiet night.

Roen laughed and rubbed his cheek. The red-head stormed back inside. As soon as the door closed, he sobered up, put the glass down on the stairs and pulled a key from his pocket. He scanned the area. Memory threw a rock at him, glancing off his shoulder. He winced and looked their way.

"Maybe not the best way to get his attention, but satisfying," she told Eloryn before he reached them.

When he did, Memory's voice became shrill. "Have you been in there the whole time? While we've been freezing our tits off?"

Eloryn stared between the two, confused and muted from overwhelming emotions- relief, shock at Memory's behavior and a strange cold pain in her chest.

Roen spoke urgently with his jaw set. "Hush. I'll explain it all. But let's get you both warm first. I got us a private room at the back. There's some food that will still be hot too, if we hurry to it." He ushered them through shadows to a door in one of the back buildings, unlocking it for them. He let them in, waiting outside.

"Strip your wet dresses, before you are ill from it. The fire is lit so you'll be warm inside. Knock for me when you're decent, then I promise I will explain everything."

Roen closed the door on them.

CHAPTER FIFTEEN

Inside the musty room at Elders Bridge Inn, Eloryn looked from the closed door to Memory, confused. Memory shrugged and skittered straight to the roaring fire.

"Oh. My. God. This is so good, you have to get over here." Memory tore her wet dress off and stepped out of it so all she wore was a scant black shift and petticoat. She turned herself around in front of the flames.

Eloryn fumbled to undo the clasps of her dress with cold, numb fingers, and soon dropped it to the floor. She tried to not feel self conscious so undressed. Her attire matched Memory's, only in ivory.

She looked around the small room for a space to hang the dresses so the fire would dry them. A modest sized bed with age-faded blankets filled one end of the room. A covered bowl on a table let out a small, tantalizing waft of steam, fragrant with thyme and pepper. It was surrounded by a stack of smaller pottery bowls, cups and a large flagon. Nothing to wear anywhere.

Memory peeled the top blanket off the bed and wrapped it around her shoulders. She tugged the next layer free and handed it to Eloryn when she joined her near the fire.

"Togas it is. Are we decent enough yet to let Roen in, or should we leave him waiting a bit longer?"

"I'm sure he had good reason to keep us waiting as he did." Eloryn muttered, remembering the way he had grinned when he pulled the

barmaid close to him, putting his face into her hair. "But maybe, maybe just a little longer." She felt wicked, but Memory gave an encouraging grin. She smiled back, and they jiggled the cold out in front of the fire, a haze of steam lifting from them as their petticoats dried.

Eloryn felt well and truly thawed before they invited Roen back inside. He made no comment at the time it had taken them, just took a seat by the food and served some creamy broth into bowls. He took none for himself. Memory and Eloryn sat on the bed, soup bowls cradled in their laps, looking at Roen with wry expectation. As his eyes passed over her, Eloryn shifted and pulling her sheet tightly closed.

"Princess, I am sorry you suffered so much waiting for me."

Memory cleared her throat.

"My apologies to you too, Memory. Once I'd entered the inn, there was reason I had to stay so long," Roen said, his voice low. "It is not what you think. I went in to book lodgings, and overheard men at the bar bragging. They said they were Thayl's men, hunters, who controlled a mighty dragon that does their bidding."

Fear stabbed at Eloryn, a feeling she hadn't grown used to no matter how often she'd felt it since leaving her safe home. "Could they have tracked us here already?"

"I worried the same thing. Having overheard them, I thought it wouldn't be wise to leave again too quickly. I didn't want to lead them to you, or appear more suspicious than I already did." Roen indicated to his torn and muddied clothing. "There were but three I saw at the bar. I didn't recognize them, nor they me. So I stayed, made pretence of being social and tried to find out what I could while I was there."

"And what information did Miss Frisky Fingers have for you?" Memory pouted through a mouth full of soup.

"She was nothing but my excuse to leave." A muscle jumped in Roen's jaw and he looked at the floor. "I'm sorry you had to see that. I spent my time inside listening in on the hunters and drinking with an older man, a traveler from Farwall in the north, who knew some lore about dragons."

"The dragon isn't here, is it?" Memory paused from eating for just a moment.

"I don't believe so, but the man from Farwall had opinion on how the hunters are able to give orders to the beast," Roen told them. "He said they use a magic flute. With it, even if the beast is far away they can call it."

Eloryn swallowed. The very men who knew her appearance and her connection to Alward, the men who were hunting for her, were right here, and could call the dragon to them at any moment. "Shouldn't we leave, be away from here before they find us?"

Roen put a hand out in a calming gesture. He met her eyes until she stilled, then looked away. "I think it better we stay. To flee a paid room at this hour would only arouse suspicions. It could put you in more danger. They know what you both look like, so we will keep you hidden in here until they have moved on. No one at the inn has seen you. I will keep you safe and keep watch on them."

"I don't know. Even if we are safe, any time we spend here lessens our chances to rescue Alward. Shouldn't we travel on to the Wizards' Council right away?" Eloryn tried to keep her voice steady.

Memory looked at her with an exaggerated frown. "But I just warmed up again! Also, no clothes."

"At least one night, Princess, so that we can recover and make better time travelling tomorrow," Roen said.

"It'll be OK." Memory bumped her shoulder against Eloryn's and wiped the last of the soup from her bowl with a finger. Eloryn looked down into hers and realized she hadn't even touched it. She put it back on the table. She didn't have the stomach for it. Memory grabbed the abandoned bowl and kept eating.

"If you think it's best, then we'll stay," Eloryn said.

Roen nodded grimly. He lifted the flagon and poured three cupfuls. "Here, I thought there might be some nerves that would need calming tonight."

"Understatement," said Memory, reaching for a cup.

"You know, sometimes what you say makes barely any sense. The rest of the time it makes none at all." Roen half smiled and tipped his cup to her.

Eloryn took a sip, her stomach still uneasy, and coughed when the first mouthful went down. "What is this?"

"What it is, is just what we need," Memory wheezed and passed her cup back for more. "Come on Lory, don't pretend you've got no worries to drink away."

Roen raised an eyebrow, tilting the flagon to her to see if she accepted Memory's challenge.

Between Roen, whom she believed knew a good many worldly things,

and Memory, who couldn't remember anything of the world, Eloryn wondered how, with all she'd learned, she always felt the one who knew the least. She downed the charring liquid and held out her empty cup with a restrained grimace.

Roen gave her a respectful nod, and poured more for them both.

Even the first cupful had Eloryn feeling dull and distracted. She wanted to ask why Roen wasn't finishing his, as he poured for them again, and then again. But she couldn't do it. Memory could have; she'd say anything, and frequently did. She was currently exchanging scar stories with Roen. Roen seemed to have some interesting anecdotes about his. They wafted in and out to her while the alcohol took effect. All of Memory's sounded the same-

"Check this one out, how do you reckon I got that?" Memory leaned forward, pulling her slip down and showing Roen right down the front of her chest. Eloryn turned away in shock.

Roen blew a low whistle, shook his head and chuckled. He leaned in conspiratorially to Memory. "A flagon to share, two girls in naught but shifts and sheets… any other night and this would have been interesting indeed."

Eloryn barely heard him, but even his tone made her blush pink. She wished she wasn't so prone to that, that she could keep her face under better control. She didn't feel she could control anything just now. Time seemed to be skipping forward in small jumps. Roen talked on with Memory but Eloryn kept catching him look toward her, small looks, so small she probably imagined them. She stared as the fire consumed logs greedily. Her mind drifted around, exploring dark places where she imagined Alward was held, hurt, or worse. Had he been saved? Was he now looking for her? Had he been tortured? Did he even still live? Was it all really her fault? She'd never meant to use her magic in front of the children, but she couldn't let them be hurt. Images jolted into her head of the heavy shelf toppling forward, books spinning and re-arranging themselves in mid-air, the wide eyed awe from the children caught underneath, unharmed in a protective space built by ancient tomes. *Lucky chance,* she had told her young students, *back to work and don't speak of it again.* She should have told Alward what happened, but was too scared of disappointing him. Barely more than a week later, the hunters came for them. A feeling of sickness blocked her throat.

Roen's laughter drew her attention. "Just devilish, you are!"

A cheeky smile on Memory's face disappeared. Her mouth clamped shut, bottom jaw sticking out. "I need some air," she said and wobbled for the door.

"You can't go out, someone may see you," Roen warned.

"What's wrong?" Eloryn stood up.

Memory waved limp-wristed at them. "I just, I… bah. My trains of thought are leaving the station too quickly," she slurred and pushed her way outside.

Eloryn took a step after her, but found herself going down instead of forwards. The world slipped around inside her skull. She awaited the ground's impact with numb clarity, but instead felt the hold of Roen's arms around her, lifting her back to her feet. Her sheet slipped down off her shoulders, and he reached to pull it back up. Her bare skin ached pleasantly where he brushed it. She'd never had this much to drink before, and wondered if it always had this effect.

"Careful there," Roen said. She continued to sway and he held her steady, just the barest space between them. He smelled of cloves and mossy stones, a scent that intoxicated her as much as the alcohol. She felt queasy with guilt. What had she been thinking about before? She couldn't remember.

"You've had well enough to drink, delicate thing you are. Time to rest. I need to bring Mem back in," Roen said, something worrying his expression.

"You do not enjoy my company." The words escaped Eloryn's mouth before she could make the distinction between speech and thought.

"That's not true." Roen's voice was gruff, as though caught off guard and choking out a lie. It hurt Eloryn more than logic could account for.

"I know I'm a cause of trouble for you. Is this why you don't like me? I see how you can be such easy friends with Memory, and it seems to me you enjoy the company of women, and yet I cannot even bring a smile to you." Eloryn's heart beat too hard, pushing all her blood up into her face. She dropped her head and let her hair fall to hide the shameful color.

Roen inhaled deeply. Eloryn didn't want to look, sure he'd be frowning at her again. One of his hands dropped to the side and curled into a tight fist. She felt every muscle in his other hand tense where it held her steady.

"I'm sorry if I've made you think that. All I can say to explain my behavior is that there are times when I feel no great value in myself. It is… easy for me to be with women, and take comfort in the value

they have of me. Memory, she is special, I must admit. But you, El," he breathed. The way he said her name made her shiver. "You are a princess."

Eloryn shook her head, confusion coming out in words. "I am hardly a princess. I've grown up in a small house by woods and never known a throne or kingdom, and that kingdom which was to be mine is not, even if I had want-"

Roen gently interrupted her rambling. "It's no matter. You are everything a princess should be: kind, clever, brave, beautiful. If I behave differently for you, it's only because whatever I was, whatever I am, I need to be better for you."

Eloryn lost her ability to breathe. A racing dizziness overwhelmed her. Her head bowed, she stared at his clenched fist. She wanted to say something in return, but had no words left in her.

Gently, she unwrapped his hand and held it with shaking fingers, lifting her head to give him a timid smile. Roen's eyes met hers, frowning and questioning. His mouth was set and troubled and a soft noise like a moan escaped from his throat.

Then the small distance between them vanished and he kissed her. His mouth closed around her bottom lip, firm and soft in the same moment. Her heart rushed and her eyes snapped wide open. Her hand squeezed around his and he kissed her harder.

One of his hands slid up her shoulder to the base of her neck, fingers twined into her hair. His other hand broke free of hers and moved behind her waist, pulling her body into his.

She brought both hands up and placed them against his flat stomach, some polite voice inside telling her she should push him away. Once there, feeling his smooth muscles beneath the thin silk fabric, she ached to think of the touch breaking.

She gasped breathlessly, lips parting, and he pulled her body up toward his with a strength that lifted her off her feet.

Memory sat on the steps of their room, staring out into the endless twisting trees around them. They swayed in her half closed eyes.

She tried to remember why she'd gotten angry. Her brain played over recent memories like a faulty video, all slow motion, slurring voices and skipping frames. *Devilish*, that was it. Why did he have to say something like that? They were all getting along so well, she'd almost forgotten she was probably a spawn of Hell.

The air was icy, but the alcohol provided enough fuel to keep her warm. Everything smelled of earthy wood smoke. Somewhere inside her she knew there was something she ought to be aware of, frightened of. She ignored the feeling, mentally filing it into her "Everything So Far" folder, and let her eyes glaze over.

"Don't try to use him," a hesitant voice said from nearby.

Memory turned around so quickly she slipped off the step down to the next with a bump.

A dark shape sat hunched on the small roof above the doorway. A flickering sprite hovered around, casting just enough light to show a body covered in animal furs.

"Ah, he speaks. Doesn't make much sense though," Memory slurred.

No reply.

The sprite had vanished and only the shadow of a hunched figure remained. Memory squinted to see if it really was her savage guardian,

and shook off a wave of nausea. "Ugh, is this real life?"

"The dragon." His voice sounded real, real enough to sound frustrated. "He's under a man's control. He can't do what he wants."

"If it catches and kills us, it doesn't matter to me if it wanted to do it or not," Memory said. "Were you eavesdropping?"

The savage's voice took a hard edge. "It's a living thing, not a weapon. The men use a flute-"

"Knew that."

"-made from bone of the dragon's soul mate, that they killed. You have to understand." The wild man's voice dropped back to a whisper. "They make him belong to them."

"That's…" Memory drew quiet, the smug smile falling off her face, "really sad."

The cold crept into Memory's skin. She watched the curling mist match the frost on the air that she breathed. With each breath, her frown deepened.

"Why do you keep helping me?" she asked after a while.

Nothing, again.

He was gone.

She stood up quickly, a little too quickly. She felt as if she left her head behind her, too heavy to follow that fast. She could only remember every second thing. Swearing, she fumbled her way back inside, swiftly plummeting into a woozy black sleep.

The sound of scratching at the door latch froze Roen and Eloryn in place, his nose still pressed against hers and uneven breath brushing over her lips.

"Pray pardon. It was wrong of me," Roen said. The frown had never left his face. He backed away from her and turned around as Memory stumbled inside.

Eloryn's legs conspired to collapse beneath her. She dropped in slow motion and found herself on the edge of the bed. Eyes closed in a slow blink and she filled her breathless lungs. She shook her head from the alcohol and emotions but could not clear it.

"Why the hell did I go outside? It's cold out there. You 'k Lory?" Memory flopped belly first onto the bed.

Eloryn put a palm to her forehead, blinking through her shock. "I don't… don't know."

Memory said something that was muffled by her face in the bed.

"Sleep well. I'll see you in the morning, hopefully with good news." Roen took the flagon and left the room without looking back.

Eloryn fell onto the bed next to Memory. Her heart beat hard enough to shake her whole body.

CHAPTER SIXTEEN

His knuckles split as he hit the rough bark of the tree. Leaves above rustled in protest.

A giggle rang out like the sound of chimes in a soft wind. "My sweet pet, come here, let me make it better for you."

"She was drunk," he growled low.

Mina appeared behind him. Her fingers stroked around his neck and she spun herself in a pirouette to his front. She bent into his chest with a smile. "Of course she was, blind drunk. Why else do you think I let you prattle on how you did?" Her voice lowered as she spoke, both sultry and cruel.

Prattle on. Saying even a word to her was the hardest thing he'd done for a long time. He wanted so badly to tell her everything, and when a chance finally came to speak to her without those others around, she was wasted. Absently, he pushed a hand up into Mina's fiery hair. The corner of his mouth pulled into a mockery of a smile. Never before had he been so aware of how little control he had over his own movements when close to Mina. Her hair felt like warm water between his fingers, and he bent his face toward hers.

A sharp thump-click sounded through the icy silent night, and he leant back into the shadow of a tree, pulling Mina in closer to him. She nuzzled into his shoulder and he turned to watch the thief boy slinking out of the room at the inn. Roen brought a large flagon up just away

from his lips and held it there for a few moments as though stopped in time, then tossed it angrily aside. Clear liquid spilled through the air and fell like rain, and the bottle thumped into nearby bushes.

The thief looked carefully around, and slipped into the shadows himself.

Standing next to Mina, the savage breathed deep through his nose. "He smells of her." Even from this far away, he could smell him, and her on him. And even in the dark, as well as the thief moved, it was easy to see where he went. His time spent with Mina and the other fae had its benefits. He was no longer what he once was, no longer weak.

"Enough about *Her!*" Mina's eyes glittered like sparking flint and her nails dug into his chest. Like the sun passing out from behind a cloud, her face shone with a smile again, but her nails remained clawed in his skin. "My sweet little boy. Who saved you when you were too lost and hungry to survive?"

"You did," he said, dropping his forehead onto hers.

"Who has shown you wonders greater than you could have ever imagined?"

He knew these words, knew the answers he had to give, but they hurt now, as they came through his mouth, more than they ever had before. "You."

"Who is the most beautiful thing you've ever seen?"

"You."

"Who do you love above all else, even your short mortal life?"

He looked across to the inn. The window to the small back room was now dark, and the thief boy worked his way into someone else's. Through the chilled night air, the familiar scent of cheap packet hair dye, blood and crushed flowers drifted to him. She still smelled just the way he remembered, the way she did back before they both came to this world. He breathed the fragrance deeply, holding it in his chest. His lips pressed hard against Mina's forehead and when he whispered they moved against her skin.

"You."

"You took your time. I started to think you had perished in the waters after all."

"I was just dreaming about this weird guy on a roof, telling me

things about soul mates or music or something. It's all fuzzed up and skippy." Memory talked to herself. She was nothingness, floating in a thick, comforting dark. Shapes were forming all around. A horse skeleton of rusted metal and chains swam past. Sprites fizzled like fireworks. Streams of golden light flowed in the distance.

"Sometimes we confuse dream for waking, and real for dream." The voice came from everywhere and nowhere, from inside herself, deep, sad and forceful.

"Am I asleep now, or awake?" Memory grew a hand, followed by the rest of her body, and reached out to pull a silk tasseled cord. It caused a ribbon of silver to fall which became a road paved in glass. She walked along it.

"You've only just begun dreaming, but I am real. We share this space as we did the dream yesterday morning. I mistook it as only a dream myself until I met you while waking." A tall figure strode out from amongst the condensing shapes.

"You?" Memory said, marching onwards. "I don't want you here."

"You have no choice. I was told we would remain connected, by time and space forever, but never thought I'd see you again for it to matter." Thayl drew a black velvet and ebony throne from the shadows and sat in front of Memory. He shimmered, his eyes less tired than in the real world, but still haunted. "Don't fret. I'm not here to harm you, and don't know if I could here, regardless. This is your mind, not mine."

She kept walking away from him but he remained right beside her in his throne. "That chair isn't mine."

"Well, it is somewhat sparsely furnished here." Thayl gestured to the black. "Where are you going?"

Memory stopped on the path. "It's all empty."

Thayl tilted his head toward a grey alleyway in the distance.

"I don't want to go there."

"Why?" His voice teased.

"Don't remember." Glass cobblestones rearranged under her motionless feet. They lifted and flew, a flock of invisible squares floating around her.

"You don't remember anything."

"I remember you said I was a devil."

"My mistake. Forgive that I startled you. I was simply shocked to see you after the dream we shared. I mistook you to have come alive from my nightmare. That is all. I think it must have scared you too."

"I'm not a devil?" She couldn't help sounding hopeful.

"Of course not. That first dream we shared was... just a mix of strange visions."

"But..." *Your hand,* she thought.

Thayl cut her off. "But I do know what is real. I even know who you really are and where you are from."

Memory floated, her path entirely gone from beneath her. Her stomach dropped away but she didn't fall.

"But..."

"But," he interrupted again, "you have something I want in return. The girl you were with at Palace de Montredeur."

"Ugh! Typical." Memory hissed and a swarm of tiny dancing gowns nearby caught on fire. "It's always about precious Eloryn! I'm so over it already!"

"Then let me have her and have all your problems solved," Thayl said, his voice as dark and velvet as his throne.

She wanted that. Wanted it so much.

"What will you do with her?" That wasn't what she meant to say.

"No wrong."

"What isn't wrong to a man who killed the woman he loved?"

A flame lit in Thayl's eyes and he arose in fury. He stormed toward her and Memory stumbled backwards.

Flashing shadows passed between them and when they cleared, the anger in Thayl had gone, replaced with simmering grief.

"Daring to say such things when you know nothing at all! I did not kill her. Never would have, never could have." His voice sounded too hurt to be a lie.

Memory fought the urge to back away further as Thayl glared down at her. "But everyone says."

"It's what everyone chooses to believe, that I am the evil to hate. Everyone can believe as they want, let them fear me more. But I want you to know the truth. I want you to see I'm not the one to distrust."

Thayl drew another, simpler chair from the black, offering it to Memory. His face had grown still, carved from wax and too cold to melt. "Sit; I will show you the truth. Once you have some knowledge in this empty head then you can make your judgment."

Thayl returned to his throne, and Memory took the second chair, lowering herself in with hesitation as though it might bite.

"Loredanna and I were in love..." Thayl began.

"You were a stalker," Memory interrupted with a whisper.

"We were in love, together," Thayl said, the corner of his lips turning down in irritation.

A scene lit in front of them. A woman in the finest of gowns with coifed cream hair sobbed uncontrollably, heartbreakingly, into the shoulder of a man; Thayl, when he was younger, straighter. The frown on his face was now fresh and not yet set in permanence.

"She looks just like Eloryn," Memory said.

"This is Loredanna, her mother."

"What did you do to her?"

Thayl raised an eyebrow. "You truly think me a monster? This is my memory, of when she was given news from the Wizards' Council that they had not allowed me to be her husband. My magical talent was considered too weak for the royal bloodline, so she was chosen another partner. She cried for weeks, and was never happy again, from that time till her death. I swore then that those who forced our love apart would hurt even more than she."

"So you killed the King and all those wizards?"

"I've never denied this. It was as they deserved, and I will continue until I see revenge on every wizard of the council who took her from me."

Alward, Memory thought, but it sounded louder than if she'd yelled, echoing through the black around them.

"*Pellaine.* Him most of all. He is mine now, and when I no longer need him I will see justice paid for his crime. He is the one who killed the most perfect being of this world." Thayl's voice dropped into a growling whisper, hissing through bared teeth.

Memory opened her mouth, needing the answer to a million questions.

"Just watch," Thayl murmured.

A new scene flashed by and Memory turned to it. Like a silent movie it played.

The beautiful Queen sat sad and alone, full with child in an unlit room. Through the open frame of a window she watched the moon fading into the sky around it, burnt to red by the earth's shadow. A sound startled her and a smile of hope lit her face when she saw it was Thayl who approached. He held her, and pleaded with her, and through tears she nodded agreement. Reaching up to her neck, she unclasped a chain and removed a heavy amulet, the same crested one Eloryn had owned.

She flung it onto the table with a look of disgust and triumph, then took Thayl's hand and not a single other thing and they left.

The vision flickered, cut and jumped, to a forest of grim trees and shadows. Thayl and Loredanna fled into the woods with a look of anxious, terrified hope.

Another jump, and Memory watched Loredanna, wet from the exhaustion of labor, being supported by Thayl. She reached out, crying for her child. A lanky blond man held a newborn baby, taking it away. "Pellaine," Thayl hissed.

The scene flickered, and Alward now held a scroll instead. A baby lay on the ground of the forest among dead bodies and dead leaves. Reading from the scroll, Alward shot a blast of red light from his hand which hit the young Queen fully where she stood just in front of Thayl, still reaching for her child.

The vision skipped again. Loredanna lay still and limp, held by Thayl. He knelt on the ground and screamed wrath and vengeance. Across the scene, Alward vanished like a ghost into smoke with the baby in his arms. The scene jumped, but did not change. A hooded figure flickered in and out of vision. Loredanna fell alone to the ground, the scene shifted, then she was again held in Thayl's arms.

Memory squinted through her tears. She wiped them quickly, but Thayl had already seen them. A shallow smile formed on his lips.

"These are my memories. Do you trust me yet that I will help return you yours?" His voice was clouded, his eyes unreadable and cold.

"Why would he do that? It didn't make sense!" Memory shook with outrage.

"You are like me, we are strong in emotion. The wizards know only logic and tradition. Loredanna and I broke those traditions when she fled to be with me. Both our lives meant nothing to them from that point on. They only needed her child to continue their ways."

The scene of Loredanna's death still flickered. Thayl watched the younger version of himself with his jaw clenched. The scene spluttered; again a faceless figure was silhouetted in the forest. Memory blinked and the vision had faded away.

"But Alward didn't, Eloryn doesn't..." Memory couldn't get her thoughts straight, something didn't add up, but a noise kept distracting her, breaking up thoughts she tried to form.

Someone was singing.

"Will you bring me the child of the woman I loved?" Thayl asked urgently.

Three voices roared in unison, another laughed.

"I don't... there are still things... don't make sense, but..." It became hard for Memory to focus. All her surroundings, even her own body, were crumbling away like wet cake. Only the rowdy song remained.

Losing sight of Thayl, she called out in a panic, "You really know who I am?"

Memory woke to the white light of early morning. Too early. *Ugh, my head.* She rubbed seedy eyes to get them working.

Singing floated into the room. Memory heard it as she did in her dream.

"When you catch 'em sneaking round,
You give their hide a tanning,
A kicking or a whipping, or a beating good and sound,
Cause thieves are only good for hanging!"

Visions from her dream washed over her. Her heart started up quickly but she couldn't tell if it was from guilt or exhilaration. If it could be; if only it were all true... She could hardly bear the hope. She remembered most of it, more clearly than she did the parts of the night before she fell asleep. Did her jungle man really come and talk to her? Why the hell did she drink so much? As soothing as it was to purge her thoughts of whether she was a demon, she cursed herself for it now. And Roen for keeping her cup so full.

She sat up gingerly and Eloryn continued to sleep beside her.

Roen wasn't there. Did he really stay out all night? *Wow. Either very chivalrous, or he found Miss Frisky Fingers again.*

Memory wanted badly to go back to sleep, but the singers continued.

"Thieves are thieves and that they'll always be,

No matter what you name 'em,

Cutpurse, dipper, footpad or a booter-free,

A thief's still only good for hanging!"

Fumbling out of bed she woke Eloryn, who winced and looked around the room.

"Where's Roen?" she asked.

"Good morning to you too."

Eloryn's face reddened and she mumbled in embarrassment.

"Hopefully Roen's getting us breakfast," Memory said and poked at her hanging gown. Only a few hot coals remained from the roaring fire of the night before. The morning air was crisp against her skin under the flimsy petticoat.

"Is someone singing?" Eloryn rubbed her eyes and cringed.

Memory chuckled, just a little pleased that Eloryn seemed to be suffering more than her.

"These are dry," she said, tossing the gold dress to Eloryn. She took a moment to analyze the black gown and realized it had a simpler underdress she could probably get on herself. The grander skirt, ruined now anyway, was left behind. And frankly she didn't care if the remaining dress was an undergarment or not. The fine sleeves were all but gone, so apart from having Eloryn help with her corset she was dressed and warmer in no time.

Helping Eloryn clasp the back of her dress, she wondered what Thayl, real or dream, would actually do with her. He loved her mother, so maybe he was going to let her be an actual Princess, as she should be, as if she was his own daughter? Memory shook her head to herself. Way too optimistic for her normal taste. She wiggled her toes, feeling them cold and bare, missing her shoes. Noticing her knife where it had fallen on the floor the night before, she slipped it back into her corset when Eloryn looked the other way.

Memory peeked through tattered curtains to see what the noise outside was all about. The daylight stabbed her tender eyes. Outside, a group of men lifted bottles and flasks, singing around a dirty bundle on the ground. During a rousing chorus, one of them threw his foot hard into the lump, which cried out and twisted out of the way, revealing a face.

Memory dropped the curtains back with a gasp.

"What is it?" Eloryn asked, moving toward the window.

Memory blocked her way. "How is your magic feeling this morning, any better yet?"

"Better, but perhaps not reliably so. Mem, what is it?"

"It's Roen. Some men have him all tied up, hurting him. Lory, he doesn't look very good." Memory wanted to look outside again, to find out more, but was too scared. All she could make out before were ropes, blood, and Roen's face.

"What do we do?" Eloryn squeaked a panicked whisper and the blood visibly drained from her complexion.

Memory felt the hard metal knife, a comforting presence against her skin. She had that, at least. Eloryn had her magic, maybe. That didn't feel like enough.

She held her breath and looked out the window again. The men were gone; Roen too. She could still hear singing, somewhere close. She swore. "Whatever we do, we have to hurry."

CHAPTER SEVENTEEN

"We'll sneak up, see what we can see and go from there." Peering out the doorway, Memory found the area empty. Dirty red painted a patch of ground behind the inn, and more blood marked the path where Roen had been dragged.

"That's your plan?"

"You have a better one?"

Eloryn shut her mouth and followed Memory out the door.

"Maybe they're done with him, and he'll be OK?" The sight of blood made Memory dizzy, made her want to run the other way.

"We have to help him. He has the token for contacting the Wizards' Council." Eloryn half sobbed. "We can't leave him behind too."

In her head Memory rattled through every swear word she knew. She could hear the singing again behind a thicket of trees.

"Is it the hunters who know us?" Eloryn whispered.

"Didn't get a good look, but there were no uniforms." Memory's mouth felt dry and her head ached out through her eyes. She tried to shake it off and concentrate as they crept toward the boisterous choir. The rough ground hurt her bare feet, already sore from river crawling the night before. Her eyes felt full of sand, no matter how much they watered to compensate, blurring her vision. She winced away from the bushes she pushed through and stumbled forward too quickly-

And she was suddenly being stared at by four large men. One was positively a giant.

Eloryn stumbled into her back.

Having already used all her others, Memory tried to invent a new swear word. *Frotz.*

The men gaped, sneered and laughed at their sudden appearance. Roen lay on the ground behind them, face down, his caramel hair matted with blood and dirt. He struggled to look up and see why the singing had ended mid chorus, and his expression filled with heartbreak and horror. He screamed for them to run, but only a rasping breath came out, mouthing the word.

A long rope hung over a branch above a man wearing a worn top hat. He paused, half way through tying a rough noose.

Another man wobbled forward, sloshing ale from his flask and smiling around protruding teeth. "Mornin' m'ladies, come for the show?"

"Look, they all shocked and proper." The man with the rope smirked and went back to tying the noose.

"If this isn't their flavor we could give them a different sort of show after," a handsome but greasy man slurred.

A couple of the men roared with laughter and clinked flasks.

Giant, Buck-tooth, Greasy and Top-hat; nope, they definitely weren't with the wizard hunters.

Eloryn stepped forward, setting her shaking shoulders square. "Sirs, show your respect. You address ladies of the court. What is happening here?"

Her voice was so formal and firm the men's laughter cut short. Memory also straightened up, desperately attempting to follow her example.

"Just dealing with a vermin problem milady, what we caught a-sneaking round."

"And we gave his hide a tanning!" Greasy sang, causing the others to break back into laughter.

"You are wrong. He's our friend." Eloryn shook her head at them, but her influence over them clearly waned. The girls' dirty and torn dresses didn't help their cause, and the men eyed them suspiciously.

"Then friends with a thief you are, 'cause we caught him right with his nose in our belongings."

"Did he actually take anything?" Memory asked.

"No doubt would have if we didn't catch him; tends to be how these things work, little girl." Greasy winked at her.

"It wasn't his fault, it was mine," Memory said before she could let herself decide against it. Roen shook his head into the ground. Memory licked rough lips and continued, looking to her side for the fragment of an idea that had come to her. "It was just a prank, a dare we made last night after we drank too much. I told him to steal something for me, from the toughest looking men at the inn, in return for..." Memory's imagination ran dry, but the men took her hesitation to have a different meaning, breaking into cheers again.

"I understand that well enough," said Greasy, running his gaze up and down the girls.

"Good. Let him go then." Memory tried to sound commanding but it came out too high pitched.

"Well, m'ladies." Top-hat swung the finished noose about in one hand. "Seems if he's worth something to your fine selves, then he's worth something to us as well."

"A thief like this would fetch a fine bounty I'm sure, should we take him into town," said Buck-tooth. Giant grunted agreement. Memory wondered if they'd bothered teaching the mammoth to talk.

"Oh no, we won't hurt him no more, but maybe you could offer us some compensation for our troubles, if the boy here's worth it to you."

"He is. If it's money you want, we'll pay." Memory could see Eloryn trying to catch her attention from the corner of her eye, and realized too late what she wanted to say. They had no money. They had nothing.

"Money will do just fine, being as you're both too little for my appetites anyhow," Top-hat said.

"Speak for yourself," Greasy said, and laughed when the girls squirmed in response.

"I speak for all of us. We have a deal, for a taste of gold." Top-hat dropped the noose, waiting. Memory hesitated, lost for what to do next.

"We have to check first you haven't beaten him past his use to us," Eloryn said, stepping forward.

"We've got all day, haven't we, boys?"

The men stepped back a respectful distance, letting the girls through.

Memory and Eloryn rushed over and knelt by Roen. He had been left lying on his stomach, arms bound behind his back. Memory rolled him onto his side with care. His face was split and torn in a few places and he groaned when she moved him. Most of the blood on him came from a gash on the side of his forehead, still slick and oozing. He looked up at them, eyes wild, then shifted away from Memory's hand.

"No, you have to go. Run before they have you too." His voice caught as he whispered. "The token is in my pocket. Take it and go."

"What the hell were you doing?" Memory whispered into his ear.

He turned his face from them. "Wanted to take the flute, have the dragon ourselves."

"It is not even them, thanks be. Just braggarts, pretending to be great with tales and lies." Eloryn reached out her hand, but withdrew it when Roen shifted away with a grunt.

"You idiot, why would you even try that?" Memory stared at her shaking hand, covered in his blood. She wanted to slap him, but figured he'd already had enough. She struggled to keep her voice low, out of hearing of the men who stood nearby, despite how she wanted to yell.

"Because it's what I do!" Roen closed his eyes, letting his forehead fall back onto the ground.

Eloryn's voice trembled. "I don't understand."

"There was no other thief than myself when I returned your bag that day we met. I only returned it because I... I don't even know why." His voice shook as he whispered into the ground, his shoulders tensed beneath a bloodstained shirt. "Just leave me."

Memory shook her head, confused. No other thief...? If he was a thief, what was that to her? Nothing but another lie, in any case. A thief pretending to be noble. A demon pretending to be human. She could guess what would be considered worse.

Eloryn choked out a few confused words before finding a sentence. "But they would kill you."

Memory pushed his shoulder again, forcing him to roll over and face them. "Stop sulking. Can you walk?"

He squinted away from her, but nodded.

"Lory, can you magic up so they think we paid them?"

Buck-tooth kicked a rock across the clearing, skimming it close by them. "Come on! When he said all day, you weren't supposed to take it!"

Eloryn scooped some pebbles into her hand, and bent forward as though speaking to Roen again but spoke to the rocks instead. She opened her hand again and gold coins shimmered. One faded back into a pebble, leaving only four.

"Quick as possible," she whispered and stood up.

Memory dug her small fingers into the knotted rope.

"This is all we have." Eloryn held out her hand. The men gathered forward to look and smirked at her. Giant grunted out a laugh from the back.

"It's just enough. A little less than value, but I guess we feel kindly today. Lucky lad," said Top-hat.

Memory had Roen out of his ropes and helped him up. She couldn't stand the smell of the blood, and staggered from it almost as much as Roen did from his injuries. Once on his feet, he let go of her and stood on his own. He looked at the ground, breathing roughly. Memory turned back and nodded to Eloryn, who handed over the money and the three of them hobbled as fast as they could toward the road.

They were just steps away when the thugs yelled in outrage.

"What is this? Think you can give us fairy gold?" Buck-tooth cried.

"Run?" Memory whispered.

"Can't," said Roen.

"Frotz," Memory said. She glanced back.

Top-hat squinted at her, his chin raised. "Get them. This is unauthorized magic. We'll have a bounty after all. Get them!"

Memory turned to Roen. He turned to Eloryn. Wavering on his feet, he begged her to run as he twisted the upper hem of his pants.

Eloryn stumbled back a few steps, slow and unsure. Top-hat caught up to her, grabbing her from behind. She shrieked and wriggled as he dragged her back. Roen went after them.

Giant came bearing down on Memory like a wall of flesh.

The sound of pounding feet came from behind her, and she turned, lifting her arms to protect herself from whatever approached. Her savage guardian angel ran toward her. His body blurred past and hit the mammoth man, knocking him down. They rolled out of sight behind bushes.

Greasy and Buck-tooth paused on their way to Roen, blinking, turning from Memory to their leader. He called back to them, "Get the skinny witch before she summons another beast. I've got the blonde, and the boy won't be any trouble."

Turning to approach Memory, Greasy smiled crookedly and her skin jumped.

A flash of light reflected into her eyes. Beside her, Roen drew a thin blade of flexible pale gold from the seam of his trousers. It snapped straight and sharp in his hands. He struck it against Top-hat's face. It was a clumsy movement, his arm visibly stiff and sore, but the shock made the man release his grip on Eloryn, and his top hat fall from his head.

Blood dripped around his mouth. He laughed and spat.

Eloryn ran to Roen's side. He stepped between her and the man, who drew a large bronze sword from his belt, spinning it in his hands. Roen rolled his shoulder, grimacing. He whispered to Eloryn behind his back.

Memory could read the words on his lips. "Just go."

A hand swiped the air in front of Memory and she dodged back, just out of Buck-tooth's reach. Greasy's fist flew in from her side, hitting her in the face. Her cheek split between his knuckles and her teeth. Her vision darkened and she fell onto her side.

Memory lifted herself on one wobbly hand, trying to will her pain away. She fumbled with her other hand down the front of her corset, grasping for the body-warmed knife.

A calloused hand grabbed her arm, bruising skin and making the handle slip from her fingers. Her eyes bulged. The crush of the man's hand made her faint with terror. She screamed with all her chest.

A flurry of feathers and claws descended from the branches above them. Ravens swooped through the clearing. The thugs swatted back at them. The birds tore at their hands and faces. Memory ducked back down to the ground, covering her head, but the birds left her alone. She could hear Eloryn's voice through the beat of wings, calling the birds to them. Memory reached again for her folded knife.

Top-hat sliced a raven out of the air with his sword. It fell bloody to the ground.

Eloryn cried out in matched pain. She called out more magical words, but a moment later the flock had cleared. Memory heard the sword swing again, and this time Roen grunted sharply.

Still on her stomach, Memory could see boots in front of her. She rolled up onto her feet, flicked her knife open and slashed it at Buck-tooth. He stepped back just out of the blade's arc. Grinning, he pulled a yellow hunting knife from his own belt, waggling it at her. It was two times larger than her flick blade.

He swung. She blocked with a cry, her eyes closed. The metals clashed. Her hand stung from the contact, but she held on.

His blade snapped an inch above the hilt. He cried out in honest shock and dropped the broken weapon.

Greasy laughed, right behind Memory. She tried to swing back at the man, but he slammed her in the shoulder, spinning her the other way. He locked his hands around her wrists, lifting her off the ground.

She kicked at him with bare feet.

He squeezed his hand around her wrist holding the knife. She squeezed harder, refusing to let go. She squealed and growled, twisted and wrenched but Greasy held tight. He pulled her toward him, running his nose up her neck. She pumped her legs uselessly in the air.

"Let me go! Don't touch me! Let me go or I'll hurt you!" she cried with a shredded voice.

Greasy threw her onto the ground, knocking the air from her lungs. He gripped both her wrists under one hand and knelt over her, crushing her hips.

He grinned hideously. "Got you."

A deep, primal terror took over, like a nightmare she couldn't remember but that still left her sick and scared. She screamed, and the fire in her lit, pulsing outwards.

The man's weight flew off her, blasted away.

Memory opened wincing eyes, and saw the greasy, horrible man lying bloody against a tree across the clearing. He was all the way over there, not moving, but she could still feel his hands on her. Still feel the force of his weight like a sickness inside her. She screamed again in fury, twitching on the ground where she lay, back arching. All sound left the world and her ears hummed.

She rolled onto her side, heaving air into a mouth that tasted of blood. Her head lolled up and she looked out through drunken eyes.

Buck-tooth stood next to her, fear and anger twisting his lips away from disfigured teeth. He ran the other way.

Roen knelt on the other side of the clearing, slouched forward. Fresh blood made the front of his shirt shine. Top-hat had Eloryn on the ground, a foot on her stomach, but he stared at Memory, angry and shocked.

Leaving Eloryn, the man ran at Memory, his sword held firm and angled straight at her, his eyes fixed and dangerous.

Clinging to her knife in one hand, Memory reached out with the other. Drawing power from the magical fire within her, she threw it at the man with a feral cry.

He skidded across the ground and fell to one knee. He coughed blood.

Through the ringing in her ears Memory heard sobbing, and distantly realized it was her own. The world spun like a mad-man's nightmare. Her skin still crawled. She wanted to tear it off. She put her feet under

her and stood, bent and slumped, stumbling toward Top-hat. She swiped at him again, her magic flinging out from her fingertips like an invisible whip, striking him. He fell onto his stomach. Still, still she could feel hands on her. She cried out, and beat the man over and over, bloodying him with the unseen, powerful force.

His grunts of pain were muffled. A movie with the sound too low. Screaming all around her grew louder as her hearing cleared.

"Mem, Memory, please stop."

She barely heard through her own fury. *There are! There are hands on me!* She spun around and swung her knife blindly behind her, meeting flesh.

The voice that gasped was a girl's. Her sight waved back into focus.

Eloryn stood in front of her. A thin scarlet line ran across the width of her chest below her collar bones. She drew short, hard breaths that shook her body.

"What are you doing?" Memory screamed.

"You were going to kill him," Eloryn whispered. Her lips and nose wrinkled as though she were about to cry.

"And he was going to kill me!" Memory yelled into Eloryn's face. Nervous energy filled her, running berserk through her body. Her grip around her knife left her knuckles white and aching.

Eloryn shook her head. Her mouth opened and closed without letting the words out.

"No? No what? What am I not supposed to do Eloryn?" Memory hissed. "How am I supposed to know? I'm not some perfect little princess that gets told what to do her whole life, with all these people around to look after me!" Memory jabbed her knife toward Roen who stumbled their way. "I don't know why I feel like this. I don't know what's wrong with me. Probably because I'm some sort of monster from Hell right? I know that's what you think! You don't even think I'm human!"

"Mem..." Eloryn breathed in anguish.

"Memory, that's enough!" Roen roared, setting himself between Eloryn and Memory's knife. He lifted his thin blade. Its tip was pointed down and defensive, but it sent a clear message.

Memory bellowed wordlessly at them. Her vision darkened, blocked by something. Confusion slapped the anger from her. She coughed out a breath she'd gasped in too quickly and gave her eyes a moment to work. Her vision was blocked by a body. The savage stood between her and Roen, his back to her. His knuckles were covered in blood. He growled.

Roen cried out in shock and Memory heard him stumble backwards.

Adrenaline still tingled in her fingertips. Reality rattled around in her skull, pounding into focus as her pulse steadied. She stepped to the side of the savage's back, unable to see past his wide shoulders. Roen lifted his blade at the animal man, who growled and coiled to pounce.

"Stop! Stop. I'm sorry." Memory's voice went from cry to whisper. She let her knife roll out of her numb fingers onto the ground. "Roen, stop, please."

Roen shook his head, his gaze fixed on the looming savage. Eloryn wrapped her fingers around his arm, making him lower his sword.

The savage stepped toward them again, growling.

"No! Please." Memory grabbed his bloodied hand in both of hers and pulled him back. She could feel his arm tense at her touch. Her chest contracted again into unwilling sobs. "I know you're trying to protect me, but I don't know why. Please don't hurt them."

Twisted strands of dark hair fell over his face but she could still see an expression of pain on it. He opened his mouth and his eyes shifted from her to the others. His lip twitched and he dropped his head away, struggling with something.

"You're not a monster," he whispered.

Memory felt his hand shaking in hers, and for a second, he squeezed her hands back then let go.

He glanced around the clearing at the fallen men. "One more." With one final growl at Roen, soft but no less threatening, he turned away and disappeared into the trees.

Memory fell on the ground and wept.

CHAPTER EIGHTEEN

Roen shifted on his feet in an attempt to steady himself. He breathed out and silently counted to ten.

The pain didn't ease.

Fair enough, it was the least he deserved, but he wished the wooziness would pass. His skull felt as if it swam slowly under his scalp. He struggled for clear thought. This mess was his fault, and the knowledge of that hurt more than the beating. He needed to sort it out and make sure the Princess was safe again. Above all else, they had to get away from here as fast as possible. Two thugs still lay unconscious nearby, but Roen had lost track of the other two and the commotion was surely heard from the inn. There could be more trouble at any moment.

And that savage man, what is his connection to Memory? Is he still nearby? Roen's hands shook. Roen just reached average in height and that savage dwarfed him and had the look of a predator. Even if he was hale he wouldn't have a chance against that beast. Somehow Memory trusted the animal, but after this he didn't know what that meant. Memory had barely blinked at his own confession, which he didn't take as a sign of best judgment of character. She had also hurt Eloryn.

Roen's squeezed his eyes shut. There was too much mess to deal with now, too many questions he didn't want to face. *Later, just start moving.*

"We have to go, now." Roen's voice cracked.

Eloryn jolted but didn't turn to him. She stared at Memory, still

crumpled on the ground. Memory's body shuddered, but if she cried it was silent. Eloryn knelt beside her, putting a hand on her shoulder. Memory twitched and pushed away.

"I'm so sorry. I never truly believed it, never believed you could be a monster. I was scared, and admit you scared me too, but I know you are a good person. A good friend," Eloryn said.

Memory mumbled into the dirt. "How could I not be a monster? Look at what I did to them, to you!"

"You didn't mean it. You were just scared and confused. That man, that came to protect you, is he the one who's been following you?"

Memory rolled her head in a vague nod.

"He seemed to know what... who you are. He said you're not a monster, and I believe him," Eloryn said.

Memory's chest convulsed in a final loud sob, then stilled. She rose to her knees, red eyes averted to the ground. A scowl twisted her mouth. "Whatever I am, something made me this way, even if I can't remember what. I'm... I can't help... I didn't..." Memory's jaw tensed. "Roen's right. We need to go."

Memory stood up, stepped to where she'd been staring and snatched her knife from the ground. She folded it closed and tucked it into her corset.

Eloryn's face changed when Memory picked up the knife. Roen couldn't imagine how scared she must have been, being cut like that. The thought of it made his breath shallow. But what he saw now wasn't fear, it was something else; the sort of intelligent confusion he often saw in her face that made him want to smile.

He had no smile in him now.

"Into the thick of the forest, and hope none follow. Go." Roen stood, pointing, and waited for them to walk past. He hesitated to move, his body ached so much. Eloryn stopped and turned back after taking a few steps that he didn't follow.

"Keep going, that way," he said. He made an effort to move casually after them. It hurt. He waited until Eloryn had turned away again before he let his teeth grit and eyes water. Blood still oozed from where the man had jabbed the short sword into his shoulder. It had only just broken skin before he managed to turn away from it, but it still pounded and burned.

They know who I am. They know what I am. The words repeated through his head to the beat of his pain. He'd only told them so they would

hate him, so they would leave, be out of danger. They were supposed to leave him to what he deserved. *My secret to the grave. But they know what I am, and I'm still here.*

He'd lived alone with this shame for so long, finding comfort for himself and his crimes in other ways that made him more ashamed. He'd only ever begun stealing out of necessity. No one would hire a seventh son of a seventh son. "Cursed and blessed," the saying told, but Roen so far only knew the curse. He did it for his parents, at the same time knowing it would kill them to discover the criminal their only remaining son had become in the common world they were forced into. What he did, how he did it had even helped the Princess. He would continue to do anything he could to protect her. But now he could never be anything more.

Roen ground his teeth. What more did he ever hope for? He was a thief and a fool, and from this point on his life was only here to protect the Princess.

A root clung to Roen's foot, sending him stumbling forward. Hands grabbed his arm and steadied him. He was further gone than he'd realized, not even noticing that Memory walked by his side.

Her mouth pulled tight, more a wince than a smile. "You're a mess," she said.

"Thanks. You too."

"Hmm," she nodded.

"You can let me go now."

"Nope. You need the help."

Against all odds, Roen found his mouth twitch into a smile. The strange girl never failed to surprise him. *They were supposed to hate me.* "Why?"

Memory stuck her chin toward Eloryn, walking ahead of them. "She's better than both of us combined. Us losers got to stick together if we're going to have any chance of helping her out."

"Hmm," he nodded.

They walked quietly for a moment.

"Don't ever tell her I said that."

Roen watched Eloryn's back, layered with her flowing blonde hair which had begun to show signs of the wear and danger it had seen these last days. She walked more slowly than a casual stroll, even in this time of flight. They were all moving too slowly. If anyone followed they'd be

caught up in no time, but he pushed himself as fast as his abused body could go. Eloryn should be running, but instead, she kept a carefully slow pace. Could she really be waiting for him, even now she knew his secret?

Memory cursed and hopped a few steps on one bare foot. Eloryn waited for the both of them.

The trees around them thinned, and Roen pushed harder to pick up his pace, breaking away from Memory's support. There were signs of a road ahead of them. *This isn't right,* he argued in his head, *there should be no road here.* He charged through a screen of wild hedge and saw it was true.

He collapsed onto one knee, a sheen of sweat dewing him. He could almost cry.

He'd sent them the wrong way.

Roen put his fist into the ground. The plan had been simple; if you can't run, you hide. He couldn't run, and he'd led them straight out into the open, to a main road, on which early morning travelers already moved about. Farmers on carts passed, and women with massive baskets balanced on hips walking produce into town. They couldn't go back; there might be people chasing after them. He wasn't even sure he could stand up again. He couldn't do it. He couldn't protect the Princess, not even that.

"Where are we?" Eloryn asked, walking toward the carved dirt road.

"Stay back in the forest, someone might see!" said Roen, struggling to control his emotions.

Roen licked broken lips, the tangy taste of blood focusing his mind as he got his bearings. He'd gone too far west, taking them straight back to the road and open woods instead of through the thick, concealing forest. Small consolation being it was the right road.

Eloryn and Memory remained waiting under the trees. Roen walked back to them, the pain from the decision he made engulfing the pain from his beating.

"This road will lead to Kenth, where you'll meet with the Wizards' Council. Take the token and run until you can no longer, then keep going as fast as you can. Watch the road for direction but keep hidden from it. Any help I can provide you is outweighed by the risk of my slowing your down. I'll stay, and if we're followed I'll do what I can to stop them reaching you." Roen pulled the silver disc from a concealed pocket and held it out to Eloryn.

"I can heal you," Eloryn said, without trying to take the coin.

"It will take too long."

"I'm not much faster being shoeless," Memory added.

"Try to be. She needs someone with her." Roen moved forward and pressed the coin into Eloryn's hand. The softness of her skin stung him. He pulled away as soon as she held the token.

"Screw that for a plan," Memory said, marching out onto the roadway.

"Mem?" called Eloryn.

"No, stop!" Roen saw what Memory had seen just a moment after her. A horse and covered wagon were being driven up the road from the south, and Memory jogged straight for it, arm waving. It was too late, the wagon pulled to a stop beside Memory.

When Roen caught up to her she already pleaded with the lady in the high driver's seat.

"…were attacked. They took all our money, but if you can give us a ride, anywhere close to Kenth, you can have his sword. It's made of gold or something."

"Can I see it?" The gaunt woman peered down, tucking bushy grey hair behind one ear. A second pair of big eyes and small hands poked out through a half closed window behind her.

"Sorry Roen, it's all we've got."

Roen frowned and slid the thin knife from his boot where he'd tucked it after the fight. She was right, it was the only thing of worth he had, but this blade was almost like a part of him, and indeed valuable; not just for what it was made of, but also for the quality in which it had been forged. It was the only thing of value he'd ever taken for himself.

He held it up to be seen.

"Electrum, nice, nice. All you have, hey? Look, I can see you're a fine type of folk, and can see you've had trouble. You put that away. No payment needed. We're heading past there regardless. Come in, be our guests," said the woman. Her face, more sun-worn than old, crinkled when she smiled at Memory. She knocked at the shutters behind her and they opened. "Let them in, Bonny. My daughter," she told them. A girl of seven or eight years old poked her head out and grinned through a set of lost front teeth. She disappeared again into the dark of the wagon only to pop back out eagerly at the larger back door.

"Lory, come on!" Memory called out.

"This is dangerous, for them as well as us," Roen whispered.

"Yeah and I don't like the alternatives, so let's go."

The wagon creaked as they climbed up onto the high first step and through the door.

It seemed bigger on the inside, awash with drifting fabrics. Bookshelf balanced over mantel which balanced over stove. Plush cushions made mountains on lounges upholstered on top of shelves and drawers. Everything impossibly stacked into the round roofed space. A bed of velveteen covers stood waist height at the end, beneath the peephole window to the driver's bench up front. Perched on top, Bonny grinned at them, bouncing on the mattress. Her patchwork dress was the perfect camouflage within the gaudy room.

Roen climbed in last. Memory squeezed up onto the bed next to the brown eyed child. Eloryn sat on a padded seat not quite big enough for two. He stayed standing and Bonny knocked on the wood between her and her mother. The wagon lurched forward. Roen swayed with the movement and thumped his shoulder against a bookshelf. He breathed through the moan of re-awakened pain.

"Please sit down." Eloryn shifted as far as she could to one side of the upholstered bench.

Bonny stuck her tongue between her missing teeth. "I love it when we get visitors. It's always so much fun."

The wagon knocked from side to side and Roen's legs refused to keep him up. He lowered himself next to Eloryn. His shoulder pressed against her no matter how he tried to shift his position. Eloryn pulled her arms into herself, and stared at the floor. The hair tumbling around her face didn't hide the red on her cheeks.

I can't believe I let myself kiss her. After purposely getting her drunk no less. They were just meant to have enough to stay asleep in the room while I got the flute. I wanted to make things better, and I only made them worse. She's not just some tavern wench I can have my way with, no matter how I feel. Roen dug his fingers into his thighs.

"By the Winter King, you look bad. Not very good at keeping yourself safe, huh?" Bonny's eyes glinted as she stared at Roen.

Roen opened his mouth, but Memory was already talking.

"Hey, how about I show you a trick?" Memory reached to the girl's ear and seamlessly pulled out a leaf. Roen wondered for a moment where she'd gotten it from, remembering the leaves on the ground behind his home that felt so far away. Then, through his pain bleary eyes he realized Memory still had dead leaves caught throughout her hair and

dress from her tussle on the forest floor.

Bonny snorted. "Oh, come on! You know, you smell bad."

A knock on the window shutters had the girl sighing. The mother's shrill voice called through, making Roen wince. "Bonny, come out here and leave our guests in peace."

"Fine." She gave Memory a skeptical look, and then slipped through the window on her belly, closing it behind her.

"Fun kid," said Memory, eyebrows raised. "But not a bad way to travel is it?"

"I still don't like this," said Roen.

"Better than leaving you behind. I just don't think we should leave anyone behind, for whatever reason." Memory pulled her legs up and wedged her back amongst the cushions, turning her face away.

"We have time, now," Eloryn said to Roen in a quiet voice.

"Time?"

"I can heal the damage those brutes did to you."

"No, don't. I'm all right." The wagon shook and Roen winced. Eloryn's eyes flicked up to his face, clear sympathy filling them.

"If you only don't wish me to because-"

"Too much risk of our hosts seeing," Roen whispered.

"I'll keep watch," Memory volunteered from amongst the pillows.

Beset, Roen gritted his teeth.

Eloryn's voice was quiet but firm. "If you're worried for my safety, then worry that without you well I would suffer more."

He didn't want her to have to do this for him. He was supposed to be helping her, not the other way around. But she was right. How he was now, he was useless to her. But it still hurt to hear her say it, to know that was the only reason she bore his company. "Very well, what do I do?"

"Just be still and relax," Eloryn said. She raised a hand to his forehead and his chest and placed them feather soft on his skin. Roen saw the color rise through her face and his body tensed.

Eloryn snatched her hands away, then looked at him with a pained expression before starting again. "Please try and relax."

"Is this what you did for me?" Memory asked sitting forward to watch.

Eloryn nodded, and began whispering magical words to Roen's body. Roen felt the air rush out of him and his eyes glazed.

A clattering bump bounced Roen's chin against his chest and he opened his eyes. He wondered why his body was numb, then realized

it was just the absence of pain. Eloryn watched him from close at his side. Her skin looked paler than normal, showing soft purple shadows under jade irises. The sympathy in her expression remained. His own eyes dropped away from hers, running down her neck and resting on the thin red line across her chest. The deep slash cut by Memory's knife had closed, but the blood it spilt still stained the gold front of Eloryn's dress. Eloryn shifted in her seat, and Roen looked back up to see her staring, mouth slightly open in a confused look. Roen cursed internally, realizing where he'd just been staring, and turned his gaze away into the rest of the cabin.

"Have I been asleep? How long?" Roen looked around, re-gathering information into a no longer woozy mind. The wagon interior was as he remembered, but now no light showed through the gaps around the wooden door.

"It took some hours. We weren't interrupted. Do you feel better?"

Roen rolled his shoulder, stretched out his back and nodded. He felt great, at least his body did, anyway. His clothing and mind were still in ruins. Roen looked to Memory, sleeping fitfully on the bed, woken when they hit another large bump in the road.

"Thank you. I'm glad you took a moment to heal yourself also." Roen's voice sounded rough even to his own ears. He tried to cover it by continuing to talk. "Can't be much farther till we're there if it's night already." Roen stood up, steadying himself with a hand on the ceiling. He opened the smaller window in the back door of the wagon and peered out.

It was past dusk. A blacker air surrounded them, helped by mammoth trees growing up on either side of the rough trail they rode. This wasn't the main road to Kenth. A wagon shouldn't even be driven on a track like this.

Roen took three stalking steps to the front of the wagon, pots and pans clattering on shelves beside him. He climbed up past Memory and opened the front window.

"How's the driving?" he asked in a cheery voice.

"Just taking a short cut. Not long now." The woman and her daughter sat side by side on the bench in front of him. The girl absently carved into the wood of the bench with a sharp fingernail. Roen smiled and nodded and closed the window again.

He swore under his breath.

"Mem, Eloryn, I think our ride should end here. I don't think they are taking us where we asked," he whispered.

Memory shrugged, groggy from sleep, but nodded to his suggestion as though she expected trouble as the norm. Eloryn looked drained but stood up right away.

Roen lifted his finger to his lips and silently unlatched and swung the back door. It opened to the darkness of the track growing smaller behind them. The wagon moved slowly, hindered by tree roots and rubble. He pointed out, and took Memory's hand as she stepped off.

She dropped out the moving doorway onto the ground and tumbled over herself. The sound of the wagon creaking and rattling covered her swearing. Roen lifted Eloryn down next, trying to judge the movement better this time. Eloryn wobbled when her feet hit the dirt, but didn't fall. Roen stepped off easily, took them each by a hand and started sneaking them back down the path in the woods.

The wagon came to an abrupt stop. Roen turned back, and saw Bonny perched like a grotesque on the rounded rooftop.

Her brown eyes had turned black to the edges. Her skin now gray; it darkened toward her mouth, now a gaping hole of sharp teeth.

"Don't go. We don't get our prize if you go," she howled in a disturbing imitation of the child's voice.

"Banshee?" Eloryn gasped to Roen.

"Unseelie fae, one way or another," he nodded. "Keep running."

The mother figure appeared in front of them. The magical glamour that hid her true form was gone as well. She seemed bonier than before, taller than any of them. Her eyes were also black, teeth menacing, and bushy hair knotted with tiny bones.

"Just stay back," Roen warned, drawing his pale golden blade against them. "You're not in your rights to hurt us. You would be breaking the Pact."

"Pact, ha! You agreed to come with us, agreed to be ours!" the woman sang at them with a thirsty smile, unworried by the sharp weapon aimed at her.

Roen knew electrum wasn't much use against the fae, that if he made a move before them, he'd be at fault under the Pact, at risk of being Branded, but he held the blade steady regardless. The banshee tricked and manipulated just like all the Unseelie, finding loopholes in the Pact that governed their behavior so that they could satisfy their dark cravings.

"We spoke no agreement." Eloryn stepped forward. "I will Brand you if I must."

"Can't Brand if we don't touch. Come with us! She just wants the magic ones. We're not going to bite, we're going to get a prize!" Bonny, or whatever her name truly was, bounced on the wagon's roof.

"Who?" Roen grunted, confused.

Bonny laughed in a tinkling, ear-piercing crescendo.

Roen heard the flick of Memory's knife opening and she moved beside him.

The mother leapt back.

"What is that? How do you have that?" she spat.

The knife shook in Memory's hand.

"Cold dead iron. I told you she smelled of it. But I'm not scared, I'm not scared!" The girl-like dark fae leapt from the wagon roof, imitating flight, and landed between Memory and banshee mother. Bonny thrust a grey-skinned hand at Memory, as though she meant to swat the blade from her hand. Yelping, Memory slashed the knife, tracing the smallest line across the girl's arm.

Bonny's eyes bulged. She howled. The point where the blade had touched her arm steamed and hissed and she threw herself onto the ground in fits, screaming vicious curses. The mother hunched over her.

"Pact? Pact! You are the ones who break the Pact!" she screamed wildly. She lunged at them, but the thrashing girl cried out and she stepped back beside her, baring her teeth.

Roen grabbed Memory and Eloryn again by the hands. Mournful howling filled the night as he dragged them away through the moonlit trees.

CHAPTER NINETEEN

They hobbled into Kenth under a cover of dismal clouds. A light wind lifted dry leaves in a dance around their feet. Eloryn had spoken with trees and earth in the forest to find their way, and they walked through the whole night. The effects of the poison in Eloryn had long passed, but pushing herself to heal Roen and lack of sleep left her spark of connection barely alight.

Her feet ached in her torn satin slippers. She wondered how Memory's, completely bare, must be feeling.

The small town huddled like a flock of sheep at the base of wooded hills. The houses were all half crumbled walls built of a dark stone from the nearby mountains, and thatched in patchy straw when they still had roofs. It was secluded, ghostly, and completely deserted.

"Sure this is the place?" Memory asked.

"Where better to hide than a dead town?" said Roen.

"Dead? Creepy much?"

"Dead of the fae. There are none here anymore."

"Isn't that a good thing? They seem sort of nasty," said Memory.

"Good or bad, the fae are what bring prosperity to the world. They leave, and you end up with land like this." Roen tilted his head to the cracked, empty fields and wilted trees. "We'll know soon if this is the right place."

Roen walked forward again, leaving the girls a few steps behind.

Tension strung his shoulders tight. Eloryn had traced over the strain there in her healing, feeling it like a weight he'd carried too long, one she couldn't heal but a burden she'd added to immeasurably.

He'd been silent almost the entire night.

Eloryn sighed and followed. They headed down the main street of the ghost town toward a well in the centre of a small square at the other end. Dark woods backed the view like an image from one of her fairytale books.

"What are we meant to do here?" Memory asked when Roen stopped at the well. She circled the ancient structure of moss covered stone and aged bronze woven in floral motifs.

"We make a wish. May I have your knife?" Roen held out his hand and pulled out the coin token with the other. Eloryn had given it back to him during the night, a gesture of her trust, but it didn't seem to please him at all. He took it like a further weight to carry.

Memory passed her knife over. "As long as I get it back."

Roen pulled it open and brought it up in front of his eyes, turning it around. Flicking the blade with his thumb, he glanced at Memory but said nothing, just started scratching into the back of the coin. The knife carved easily through the silver surface.

"Lanval's contact told me to write a message on the coin," Eloryn said, "and drop it in this well. Then the Council should come to us. It's a special coin made by the resistance, showing the Maellan crest, but minted after Thayl came to rule." She wondered what exact wording Roen used in the message, but didn't dare question him.

Memory sat down on the wide rim of the well with an odd look of satisfaction. Eloryn joined her.

"Mmm. Sitting," Memory said.

Roen tossed the coin down the well's mouth and they watched with held breaths. No sound came to tell them it had reached a bottom.

Eloryn smiled a little at the setup. "A magical interception. Coins dropped here must go straight to the Council."

"Wow, communication system and form of income in one. These guys are smart."

"Now you wait." Roen wiped off the blade and handed it back to Memory. She kept it in her hand, flicking and fidgeting with it.

He began walking away.

"Roen?" Eloryn stood up faster than she meant to.

"I won't be far," he called without looking back. She sat down again

and watched him go. He reached a mostly intact building half way down the road and sat against the shadowed wall, knees against his chest.

If this worked, he could go back to his parents, and no longer feel the responsibility of my presence. Eloryn remembered seeing a similar look of affliction in Alward's face growing up. Wherever he was now, it was her fault. If anyone else was hurt because of her...

"May I see your knife for a moment?" she asked Memory, looking for a distraction.

"Sure." Memory flicked it closed again and passed it to her.

As the knife came into her hands, Eloryn felt her spark of connection grow strong and a strange warmth in the metal. It wasn't silver, as she'd first thought. It was something harder. "Could this really be iron?"

"I don't know. Stainless steel or something." Memory shrugged.

"No, it's... this metal is poison to the fae. I don't know how you could have this. There should be no iron in Avall. It was all removed during the Purge, at the forming of the Pact."

"Is there anything that isn't to do with whatever this Pact thing is?"

Eloryn frowned. She often had to remind herself how little Memory knew. Things even a child of Avall knew. "The Pact was a deal made over 1500 years ago between the fae and humans, to benefit both sides. It brought magic and prosperity to the people of Avall, and Avall became a safe haven for the fae in return. Part of the pact is the peace treaty. If a fae hurts a human they can be magically Branded, and vice versa, unless under certain conditions. The Brand is a death sentence. I'm sorry. I should have told you these things before now. If you hadn't been acting in self defense when the banshee attacked, you could have been Branded. The iron itself isn't a crime as such. It simply shouldn't exist here any more."

"You don't think it means I could be from somewhere else, like Hell?" Memory asked, quiet and high pitched.

"I don't think you're a bad person Mem, or a demon." If only she knew more, if Alward had let her study the Veil with him. He had been obsessed with its research, even travelling into the woods where he could perform spells and experiments unnoticed. But he never shared that research with her, never explained why. She had stolen peeks into his work, but not enough for this.

"There are always other answers. I just don't have them for you, I'm sorry." Eloryn had always felt so clever in her home with Alward, able to answer any question. Now she was just lost. Her eyes turned back

down the street, searching for something, and found Roen gone. She looked to Memory, concerned.

"I saw him wander off just now. I'm sure he'll be back. Don't worry," Memory said, despite looking worried herself.

Eloryn lifted her bottom lip in the semblance of a smile and handed Memory her knife. Memory slid down to the ground so she could lean against the well, and closed her eyes. They sat in silence, and Eloryn held her hands tightly in her lap to keep them still. She stared at the sky, her mind racing in circles after any trace of calm she could catch.

Hours passed before Roen returned. He carried a scrap of hessian folded into a bundle. He handed Eloryn a small apple he held in his hand, blushed red only on one side, small and perfect.

"Found one tree still fruiting. They're small, but edible." He propped the makeshift bag against the well, showing a feast of green apples. "Sorry for taking so long."

"No apology needed when you bring food." Memory smiled and bit into one apple, already holding a second in her other hand.

Eloryn stared at the apple, but had trouble bringing herself to eat it.

"You need to eat," Roen told her in dull tone. "You're losing a lot of weight."

He turned back toward the road.

The world suddenly blinked out of Eloryn's eyes. Light and vision vanished, leaving only formless black. She shrieked, echoed by Memory.

"What's happening? I can't see!" Memory cried.

"Nor I!" Roen's voice.

Eloryn whispered a behest to let her eyes see again, and found they were surrounded by five old men in faded black and purple suits. They held knives in one hand, and scrolls in the other, held up ready to be read. When she looked them in the eye, no longer blinded, they turned to the youngest man for guidance.

"She can still see?"

"Look at her..." another muttered, dumbstruck.

The younger man with a narrow face and hooked nose unrolled his scroll. "It's a trick! Finish this."

"No! Stop please, we called for you!" Eloryn said, folding her fingers into the latticework triangle symbol of the Wizards' Council.

Another age-stooped man hesitated. "They're just children."

"You think they wouldn't appear in any way they could to trap us?

Remember how many died the last time we received a message from 'the heir'! Hesitate and how many will die this time?"

"Princess, what's happening?" Roen stood statue still, taut with distress. Memory sat frozen, gripping her knife behind her back with white fingers.

"I can prove it's who I am, let me prove it!" Eloryn cried.

This time four lowered their weapons.

The younger man, vocal against her already, sneered. "How?"

"She has the Maellan crested medallion," Roen said, turning blindly to the voices around him.

"No, it's still at Duke de Montredeur's," said Eloryn.

The man huffed at her.

"But I have the bloodline. I am Maellan!" Eloryn flicked through possibilities in her mind, looking down at the dead, bare ground around them. She spoke her words, a long string of pleading words, spoken loudly for the men to hear how she used them.

From the barren dirt, a meadow of grasses forced through, like green living hair. Wildflowers unfolded. Sprays of grass seeds and dander spread. The old men gasped audibly.

"No book, no scroll? She is Maellan! You cannot dispute that power, Hayes!" a bald, wide-bellied man said.

"You can see the Lady Loredanna clear in her behind the grime she wears," said another.

"Seems so. In which case we all need to be out of sight. We've been exposed too long already. Apologies, Highness." His lips twitched under his hooked nose, still skeptical. "You understand we must be cautious. These two are with you?" Hayes asked.

Eloryn nodded.

Hayes snapped his fingers to the aged man on his left, who began speaking words of annulment to the spell on Roen and Memory's eyes. As he did so, Hayes unrolled his scroll and began reading words that must have been intended to follow the blindness on them. The patch of ground Eloryn had brought to life blazed and shriveled into grey ash.

Eloryn cried out in alarm.

"It had to be done. Your proof was not exactly discreet," said Hayes.

The bald man tilted his head. "Common folk would just have thought it was the fae returned."

"It's not the common folk I'm worried about."

Memory already didn't like them. They were old. Really old. The kind of old that's misshapen with bitterness and arrogance. Hayes was the youngest – forties or fifties, Memory couldn't tell – but managed to be the nastiest of the lot. How she thought King Thayl would have been, the way people talked about him. She liked him way better than these guys.

The bald man, Waylan, wasn't so bad. Still old, but more friendly than the others. To her at least, anyway. They were all eager to be friendly with Eloryn. Memory itched and squirmed in her corset. If she'd known she would be wearing this dress for so long, she would have picked something more comfortable. She doubted this group of old men would have any clothes for her, even if they cared.

They marched under the cover of a spell to one of the houses they'd passed on the street, which now appeared much larger, and more solid than it had looked before.

Inside the building, the furnishing reminded Memory of Roen's home, with rich items in a small space, but these had not been well cared for. Dust lingered and mixed with a sweet smell of mildew.

They came to a room on the second floor laid out for meetings with mismatched chairs surrounding a wide square table.

"Summon Lucan," Hayes told Waylan.

"The others too?"

"Not yet, better not all be in the same place too soon." Hayes turned his gaze onto Memory.

Eloryn had walked with him through the house, telling him as much as she could of how she'd gotten here. He had no news for her of Alward, or any interest, as far as Memory could see. What little Eloryn had told him about Memory made Hayes's bottom eyelid twitch.

Lucan arrived. His back had the hunch of someone who tried not to be too tall and he clutched a thick tome with loose pages to his chest. He was younger than the others, more comparable to Thayl's age, but not at all comparable in looks.

"The heir, truly we've found her?" he asked, his voice friendly and eager.

"Almost entirely certain," Hayes said, indicating Eloryn. "Leave

the minutes book, we'll call council shortly."

Lucan stood motionless, staring at the Princess.

Hayes cleared his throat. "And bring us some refreshments. The heir has had a hard journey."

Lucan nodded, pushed the tome onto the table and slipped back out of the room.

Hayes, Waylan, and three more even older men, matching grey and bearded, sat across the table from Eloryn, Roen and Memory. Memory shifted in her seat.

"Thank you for coming to us," Waylan started with a sincere smile.

"Although you should have come much earlier. You may have saved yourself some hardship from Pellaine's follies," Hayes said. "We had heard from him, once or twice through the years. We suspected he had the heir with him, but he kept his location secret from us for some reason."

I wonder why, Memory thought. She shuddered to think what Eloryn would have been like if raised by these men.

Eloryn only nodded to them, politely stunned.

"Regardless, she's here now. This will mean big changes. Something to rouse the resistance. Finally, a return to rightful rule!" Waylan pounded the table enthusiastically.

Eloryn stuttered. "I'm sorry. I didn't come here for that. I only hoped you could help re-unite me with Alward. If anyone had the power to save him from his imprisonment, I hoped it would be the Wizards' Council."

Hayes shook his head and furrowed his brow, but the sympathy looked insincere. "Your Highness, I apologize, but we cannot risk ourselves for just one man. Not when your presence has given us some hope for the future. You must put him out of your mind. He's no longer your concern or ours."

"But he is my family."

"Are you the child born of Queen Loredanna and King Edmund Maellan, or do you deceive us? You have a responsibility to Avall and its people that is greater than Pellaine's fate."

Eloryn nodded, her eyes glossy. Memory snorted air through her nose, anger in her rising. She glared down the table at Roen who stared blankly at the wall opposite, the thinness of his lips showing the tension otherwise kept hidden.

Waylan spoke more kindly. "Thayl is like poison to this land. Since his rule we've seen the fae leaving or causing more trouble across Avall.

They were never such trouble with Maellan blood on the throne. Maellan blood signed the Pact. The fae honor that."

Hayes locked his gaze on Eloryn like a hawk onto a mouse. "Your Highness, for the sake of Avall, will you forget Pellaine and begin work toward your rightful path?"

Eloryn bowed her head.

Memory bolted to her feet. "Quit it already! Can't you see she's been through enough?"

"Ah yes." Hayes looked at her like he would a smudge on the wall that he was too arrogant to clean. "You're not needed here. You should leave."

Eloryn rose to her feet next to Memory. "Memory is with me. I had hoped someone here could help her with her problem."

"Her problem is not ours, or yours. Respectfully, Highness, you need to grow up and start dealing with issues of greater importance," Hayes said, moving calmly to his feet, his voice rising only a little, but still threatening.

"Fine. Let's start talking about whose problems are whose, shall we?" Memory snapped back. "Like who caused all your issues with Thayl in the first place? Wasn't it you wizards who made the Queen marry someone other than him? They were in love, and you knew it."

"Of course we did," said Hayes. "Thayl had no talent for magic when we chose the Queen's partner and was never right for the kingdom, I think that is clear. If you had a thought in your head, girl, you'd know marriages for the Maellan line have always been arranged, to preserve a strong magic ability."

"They were in love, and you destroyed them with that choice," Memory whispered, the realization hitting her hard. It was true, what Thayl had shown her in her dream. And if it was true, what about everything else?

Eloryn's face drained to white. "What? How did you-?"

"Just gossip, at the ball," Memory cut in, looking away.

"So, what of it?" Hayes moved his words slowly, fixing Eloryn in a stare. "You know this is the way of the royal bloodline, your Highness. It is not our fault, but Thayl's for bearing such villainous vengeance. Calm your guard dog here and show some pretence of your royal heritage, so we can do what is needed for the Kingdom."

Hayes sat back down. Eloryn looked at Memory, stricken, then nodded and sat down too.

Memory wanted to leap across the table, claw Hayes' tongue out and ram-

Lucan interrupted her thought, returning to the room carrying a tray of fine silver implements and pots for tea. Probably for the best. Hayes was a bastard, but she needed to start locking down her violent tendencies. If that was who she was before, she wasn't sure it was who she wanted to be now. She sat down again and satisfied herself with glaring.

Lucan placed the tray on the table in front of Hayes. He began arranging cups and Hayes put his hand out to stop him.

"Call the rest of the council. It's time we start making some serious plans."

Lucan straightened back up, as tall as his hunch allowed.

"Actually, I'll do it. You find the children somewhere to wait, outside the meeting room."

Memory threw one final glare at Hayes as they left.

Lucan let them into a room across the hall. It was someone's study, a table piled with parchment lit by a lonely, grimy window. With a shy smile and bow, Lucan left them alone.

"So much for getting some refreshments," Memory muttered.

Roen's face hung, pale and unreadable. His hair and shirt still stained with dry blood, he hardly looked alive. "Princess, I'm sorry for bringing you here."

"It's my fault, not yours," said Eloryn. "For not going to Alward right away, for trying to let others do it for me. A fault it's time I righted."

Roen shook his head. "Too dangerous."

"I have to try. No one else will."

"Lory, how well do you really know Alward? I mean, how much do you really trust about him?" Memory asked. *Do you know it was him who killed your mother? Would you still want to go to him?*

"What? He is all I ever had!" Eloryn gasped. "I will go to him. Alone, if I have to."

Memory and Roen shared glances of matching disapproval, then both agreed to go with her.

"Then we leave here now, and head back to Maerranton, where we last know he was held."

Eloryn eased the door open and led them out, tiptoeing down the empty hallway. At the top of the stairs they were stopped by a voice.

"Don't leave, please," Lucan said.

"We were just going outside for some air. It's stuffy in here," said

Memory.

"I was listening to what you said. I'm sorry." He shuffled closer to them. His eyes were pale and watery blue. Kind, if somewhat sad.

"Then you'll have to let us go, because we won't stay," said Eloryn.

"Please, just listen. I know Hayes can be harsh, but you do have friends here. I'm a friend. It's a miracle you're still alive, and I'm just happy to keep you that way, not force you into leadership. I could even help you be with Alward again, if you like."

Memory edged in front of Eloryn and looked the man up and down. "Why?"

"Pellaine... Alward was my friend too. We were invested into the council at the same time, same ages, only months before everything was destroyed. I was not even with the council when the Queen and King were married. All of this trouble, it's not mine. The council, they're old, they forget what is real and haven't much of a life left to change. And no one here takes me seriously."

"How could you help us?" Roen asked.

Lucan gave a weak, hopeful smile. "They give me all the tasks of book keeping and communications. I keep the Council's Speaking Mirror. I am in touch with leaders of the resistance in all regions. I know of some within Thayl's ranks, within his castle, even within his prisons."

CHAPTER TWENTY

Lucan hurried them down the street to another building that had appeared derelict before, but now revealed itself as solid and lived in. The council were using some very powerful glamour behests to keep themselves hidden.

Fumbling with his keys, Lucan opened the door and invited them into his home.

"Shouldn't we leave right away? If the rest of the council realize our intentions, they might make us stay." Eloryn asked.

Lucan replied with a crooked smile. "I'm sorry, Your Highness, but I doubt they'll even notice you missing for a while. They've called council. They'll be so wrapped up in debating plans they wouldn't notice if the house fell in around them. It could be days before they come to anything close to agreement or are likely to call on you again."

Lucan's house had been kept cleaner than the building Hayes had taken them to. An aroma of mulling spices awoke Eloryn's stomach. Lucan sat them in a windowless room he'd made both library and sleeping quarters- the only place with seating enough for all of them. "Just stay here while I speak with my contact, but you are free to leave at any time. If we can find out first where you..." Lucan kept talking as he left the room, his voice trailing down the hall.

Vibrating with nervous energy, Lucan buzzed back in again, bringing them a meal of wild grain porridge and herbal tea. "...exciting. You don't know what an honor it is that I could aid you in any way. The Maellan heir! Not to mention a chance of being free of those other men. I'm sure you can imagine it hasn't been fun living in hiding with no one but them..."

"Lucan, please," Eloryn called to him, stopping him floating out of the room again.

He stood still and blinked a couple of times before smiling with wobbly lips. "Sorry, sorry, I get a bit caught up sometimes. I'm going to try now and contact the resistance member I know who might have had a chance of seeing Alward. I regret, I sincerely apologize, Highness, but please stay here. I must contact him privately or he won't respond to my summons behest."

Eloryn nodded and tried to smooth the pace of her heartbeat. The hope she felt was almost too much to bear. Lucan fluttered at the door, hesitating, then closed it behind him.

Left alone in the full but neatly kept library, Eloryn took a deep breath and settled into a leather armchair.

Memory tried to get Roen talking to her. Her mutterings, out of hearing to Eloryn, managed to get the occasional coughed chuckle or bemused half smile from him, but nothing more. It was still more than Eloryn was able.

Roen met her eyes suddenly, and she looked away, embarrassed to have been staring. The atmosphere in this room made her chest tight. It was so much, too much, like Alward's library at home. Alward, like Lucan, had lovingly filled every space with books for them and their students. From ancient illuminated tomes to newer press printed collections and Alward's own studies, hand bound and hand written.

The monastery had an extensive library even before Alward arrived. She only had the faintest recollections of the people of the old religion who hid her in her earliest days. Their order valued secrecy on certain subjects, like that of men arriving with motherless children. The old men and women were faded memories by the time she was reading their books.

Eloryn closed her eyes. Leaning back into the armchair, she wondered if those books were still there. After the last of the priests passed away, it was only ever her, Alward, and the books. Often all three together, when she was still small enough to curl up in a chair with Alward and be read to.

I miss him. I miss those books. I even miss the high stone walls. Eloryn wished she had some token, some belonging of his. It didn't matter. Soon they would be together again, she just knew it. Maybe then, she could apologize for her error that brought the hunters to them, and hope he forgave her.

"Lory, wake up."

"No, shush, let her sleep."

Eloryn opened her eyes to see Memory and Lucan looking down at her.

He grinned, shivering. "Oh, she is awake! Good news, Your Highness, oh better than you could have hoped. Alward is already freed, already on his way here for you!"

Eloryn blinked, worried she really had fallen asleep and was dreaming. "How?"

"The greatest luck. Our man in the resistance was assigned to Alward's guard after Thayl met with him in Maerranton. He recognized Alward right away and helped him escape first chance he had."

Eloryn's head buzzed and her pulse built. She pulled herself up straight in the chair. "He's coming here, you said? Why would he come here? We were to go to another home on Rhynn island."

Lucan hesitated just a second. "He knows you're clever, and that with him gone you would seek us out. He's coming here for you. I'll watch for signal of when he arrives. It should be soon. Then we'll go to meet with him and we can all leave."

Eloryn's confusion washed away, and a smile broke across her face, aching unused muscles. She knew Alward would come for her, knew he would escape. He would be there for her again, to look after her.

Next to her, Memory chewed on her fingernails with intense concentration.

"He'll help you too Mem, don't worry. He's so kind, he'll do whatever he can for you." Eloryn smiled in divine happiness. "How long, do you think?"

Lucan's face turned blank. "Oh, well I say I hope soon, but I'm only guessing from the time of his escape. It could be any moment I'm sure, but be comfortable, it may be some wait yet."

Eloryn nodded, but still got to her feet and began pacing. Anxious joy spread through her.

Memory stole her plush armchair. She curled her legs up into herself and stared at a spot on the wall. Eloryn tried to avoid looking at Roen where he sat across the room on a solid wood bench. A sudden, tangible memory of his lips on hers made her trip in her pacing. Her first and

only kiss. She had no idea what it meant or why it happened, and didn't have the voice to ask. Since then, Roen barely seemed inclined to be within the same room as her. Owain came to her mind, followed by the children she taught. She wondered if they were still there in the village, still safe, or if her very presence in their lives had brought trouble to them as well.

Lucan brought in biscuits and mulled wine, and left them alone again, gone to wait for sign of Alward's arrival. None of them ate.

Eloryn moved from pacing, to sitting on the bed, to staring at books, to pacing. The others remained still and quiet. In the windowless room it was hard to tell how much time passed. Rain had been pattering against the roof for a while when Lucan's footsteps thumped up the hall again. She met him at the door.

"He's here," he said, wide eyed.

Memory and Roen got quickly to their feet behind Eloryn.

"No no, please, you two should wait. Alward won't know you. Only the Princess and I should go so he's not alarmed by strangers."

"Nah ah, we're coming too. He'll see we're with Lory and know it's OK," said Memory.

"No! You don't understand; he's careful, he'll be on guard. We need to explain to him alone first or he might think it's a trap. He could leave, or attack you. It must only be faces he knows," said Lucan.

"We won't be long," said Eloryn, not wanting anything to risk her chance of reuniting with Alward. "We'll be back for you right away, and we'll all leave together."

Eloryn nodded to Lucan, who bowed her exit in front of him. She looked back and smiled, to see Memory open-mouthed, and Roen frowning.

Lucan strode out of the building with her and down the street toward the square with the wishing well. His steps were long, and she trotted to keep up with him. She didn't think she could have walked anyway, she was about to burst. She hardly felt the icy rain that fell on her.

Her smile faded as they got closer. She couldn't see Alward. She'd expected he would stay out of sight, and yet apprehension crept in. The ground was uneven, more footprints than could be explained by their own movements marking the mud. A horse whinnied in the distance. Her excitement curdled.

She slowed her pace, and Lucan turned to see why.

"Something's not right," she said.

"Nonsense, come on, don't you want to see Alward?" Lucan grabbed her elbow and pulled her forward. His hand shook.

"Stop it, please. What are you doing?" Eloryn stumbled. She blinked raindrops from her eyes. He kept his grip tight around her arm, dragging her forward, hurting her. She cried out and tried to pull away. He put his other hand around her mouth, half carrying her into the town square.

Two streaks whistled through the air at them. Her arm stung. She clutched at it, tearing out the tiny metal dart. Lucan reached for his neck, grunting in surprise and dropped her. She fell on her hands and knees.

Eloryn felt the spark inside connecting her to magic close down as it had once before. Her head spun and she fought to stay conscious.

A league of men approached from behind the buildings around them, led by one man, devastatingly handsome with bitter eyes.

"My King, I did it, this is her," Lucan stuttered.

Thayl bent down, offering Eloryn a hand to help her up. The sadness in his face brought tears to her eyes. "Yes, I can see. It is her daughter. She is like Loredanna reborn."

CHAPTER TWENTY-ONE

No way, Memory thought. *No way was Eloryn going to leave me here after all we've been through.*

But she had. Alward was here now and she just left her and Roen behind. Sure she said she'd be back, but Memory didn't own the luxury of trust. She had to find out who she was, know that she wasn't some sort of devil. She had to find her family and get back home.

"I'm going after them. Are you coming?" she asked Roen.

Roen dropped his head in an unenthusiastic shake. "Don't want to ruin it for her."

"You're not worried they'll up and go without us?"

Roen huffed out a laugh.

"Fine. Sulk. I'm going to see what's happening." Memory marched out the room and Roen tried to call her back. By the time she reached the front door, he was walking with her.

"We better not be seen," he said.

"Good thing you're coming with me then."

Memory peeked out, seeing Eloryn and Lucan just within sight, nearing the square. They ducked out the door and behind the crumbling wall of the next house along.

Roen took the lead, dashing down the street behind low walls and unkempt shrubs, avoiding the growing puddles.

They were still far from the square when Roen stopped mid run,

skidding on the wet ground before he reached cover. He stood in open sight, staring down into the square.

A shrill cry broke through the patter of rain and Memory followed his gaze.

"Mem, hide," Roen grunted and broke into a direct run.

Memory hesitated, wiping rain from her face. She watched Thayl walk out from behind a building, followed by a group of armed men. Her brain whirred. Maybe this wasn't as bad as it looked. Maybe she could make it not as bad, if she just got a chance to talk to Thayl.

She ran after Roen.

Lucan tugged Eloryn back to her feet. Roen raced for her, leaving Memory behind.

A group of men uniformed in leather military jackets blocked his way. Their leader with his mane of hair and scarred face lunged. Roen twisted past him, sliding low along the ground, and continued to bolt toward Eloryn and Lucan.

Thayl lifted his arm and flicked his rune-covered hand. Light flashed, and Roen was flung the length of the town square. He hit the stone wall of a building with the sound of gravel crunching under boots. He lay still where he fell.

Memory and Eloryn both screamed for him. Memory wobbled to a stop at the edge of the town square, shocked out of movement.

"If your boy's alive, he will stay that way as long as you both stay calm," Thayl said, looking to her and then Eloryn. He nodded to the wizard hunters moving toward Memory and they broke away, circling wide around her instead, blocking off her escape.

Eloryn whimpered, "Where's Alward?"

"*Alward,*" Thayl said, a strange softness in his voice. "Alward was put to death for the crime of murdering Queen Loredanna."

"No. It was you who killed her. He can't be dead. You lie!" Eloryn sobbed out her words.

"I do not. I'm sorry for your loss, and your confusion. The help of Lucan here meant I no longer needed him or his knowledge to locate the rest of the council, and was able finally to see vengeance paid for his crime. He did kill your mother. If you don't believe me, ask her." Thayl pointed straight armed at Memory.

Memory stuttered as Eloryn looked at her with more pain than she could bear to see. "Thayl, he... he showed me things in a dream, showed me his memories of Alward killing Loredanna. I don't know what's true, but that's what I saw."

"It is true. Alward only ever took you in, kept you to himself because of the guilt he felt over what he had done. If he hadn't interfered Loredanna would still be alive. I would never have hurt her," Thayl bellowed.

Eloryn hung limp like a puppet in Lucan's unkind grasp.

"Where are the rest of the Wizards' Council?" Lucan asked.

Thayl smiled rigidly. "Already taken. You've nothing to fear of reprisals from them for your fine betrayal. After all this time, it was almost a shame there was not more of a fight. They were entirely unguarded and unaware, so wrapped up in their meeting. They are already under guarded escort on their way for formal execution, thanks to you."

Memory's throat grew tight. She didn't like the old wizards, but she just wanted to be away from them, not to have them executed. In her mind she remembered them as being so frail and grey.

Lucan looked about, an unsure smile on his face. "You said I would be rewarded, that you wouldn't hunt me any more if I did this."

"I did, and I honor my word. I will not hunt you any longer. Let the child go," Thayl said.

Lucan released Eloryn, and shockingly she did not fall. She stared blankly, all life leached from her, the rain soaking her through. She hardly blinked when Thayl put his hand on Lucan's shoulder, and Lucan dropped dead beside her.

Memory cried out loudly enough for the both of them. Her feet felt glued into the mud around her, her body tingling but unresponsive.

"Not one member of the Council can be allowed to live," Thayl said. He stared at the body on the ground, lips curling between a smile and a snarl.

Thayl pointed to Eloryn, and a man behind him moved forward with ropes to bind her. Eloryn's eyes snapped wide and she turned to Memory. "Mem, run, RUN!"

Eloryn struggled against the man, but was small in his hands, easy to hold.

Memory's eyes flickered between Eloryn, Lucan's body, and Roen, fallen loosely against the side of a wall, his shoulder pushed out at a horrifying angle. From this distance, she couldn't tell what blood on him might be new. Her own body was as still as his.

"You said you wouldn't hurt her. You said you would tell me who

I am," she whispered.

Thayl chuckled without humor. Approaching her, he dropped his voice to a tone meant only for her. "You still don't know? Interesting you could spend so long with her and not realize you are sisters, but maybe not so surprising. I'm sorry I left you this way, barely human," he said. He really did look sorry.

Eloryn... my sister? Memory's chest hammered like a mallet on a mattress.

He stopped an arm's reach from her and began pulling the fingers of his glove, loosening it, slipping it off his scarred hand. "I don't know how you've found your way back here from Hell, but it is fortunate. The ritual to steal your power was interrupted, leaving you like this, this shell. But I can end your suffering. I can finish taking the rest of your soul."

Memory jolted into movement. Her whole body screamed for flight and she spun to run away. The leader of the wizard hunters stood right behind her. He grabbed her by the throat, turning her face back to Thayl, pinning her against his body in an unyielding grip.

Thayl lifted his bare hand, twisted with carved runes. It began to glow.

He had done it, stolen all her life, her memories, her *soul*. Left her like this. She tore breaths through her crushed throat, her eyes wild. The fire inside her lit, burning her inside and out. A blazing pulse burst from her chest, ached down her limbs and tingled in the tips of her fingers and toes. She wouldn't let him take whatever she had left. She would use whatever magic she had to stop him. She screamed, expending all the air from her lungs, bellowing the force out with everything she had.

Silence followed. Dust and leaves lifted from the ground, floating upwards. Rain hung suspended in the air.

The world pounded and lit around her like a golden supernova.

All Memory could tell was that she was no longer held, and hoped the same for Eloryn. She screamed for her to run. Acrid smoke filled the air, and she choked on it. She lay on her stomach in the mud, falling again when she tried to get up, her body quivering. She could hear movement around her, men coughing and calling out in shock and pain. The slow rain barely swayed the blinding cloud around them.

Thayl bellowed from nearby, "Catch the girls. Don't let them get away!"

Memory heard fumbling behind her, and a shrill note whistled. Unable to lift herself up, she crawled along the ground. A hand grabbed

her ankle with vicious strength, dragging her back, then pulling her up to her feet by a fistful of her hair.

Massive wings beat above them, clearing away the smoke cloud. Men were sprawled throughout the square, dazed and muddy. Memory saw Eloryn on her feet, no one else around her, heading toward Memory instead of running the other way.

A pale shimmer of shadow in the dusk passed over Eloryn, and she froze. In a rush of movement she disappeared under a mountain of black scales and leathery skin. A sickly wet scraping sound could be heard through the square, and the dragon rose from its crumpled position, beating its wings and lifting from the ground. Inside a crushing claw it held Eloryn, talons slid deep into her flesh.

When its feet left the ground, it sprang its claw open and she dropped onto the dirt like a bloody, broken, porcelain doll. The dragon casually lifted back into the sky to circle above.

Eloryn lay still on the ground. Blood pooled around her, mixing with the mud.

"No!"

Memory's mouth hadn't moved, as much as she'd felt the cry tear through her chest.

It had been Thayl who screamed. "Loredanna, no!"

Thayl turned fiercely on the hunter with the scarred face who still held Memory. "You! What did you do?"

Oh God, Eloryn. Memory's eyes watered, her face pulled taut by the fist in her hair. She felt too weak to move, the rain freezing her skin. Thayl's fury terrified her. She twisted limply, trying to see Eloryn over the hunter's shoulder. He squeezed her tighter, and wincing at him, she noticed a thin silver chain running around his neck, and the glint of white bone.

The scarred hunter yelled back at Thayl, hurting her ears. "Only what you told me to!"

"I should never have allowed you to keep that beast. I said to catch them, not kill her!"

Wrenching her body around, Memory spat in the hunter's face, clawing vainly against him with her black nails. He turned to her in shock.

"Stupid bitch, this is your fault." He let her go and brought his hand down over the base of her neck. The blow chattered her teeth, and threw sparks of light into her eyes. She squeezed her hand closed.

Just a bit of a distraction and a flick of the wrist.

The man grabbed her by the hair again, pulling her back up. She looked him in the eye with a smile soaked in tears. Holding up her hand, she revealed the delicate finger sized flute.

"No!" the scarred man bellowed as though she'd ripped out his heart.

Every man in the square turned to stare at her, uncommon fear in their eyes. In the distance, she saw Roen stirring.

Time slowed.

The scarred hunter snatched for the flute.

Thayl blasted a bolt of violent magic at her.

She clenched her hand with a force that drew blood with her fingernails. The old, rigid bone within it broke into pieces.

The dragon roared.

And Memory waited to die.

Somehow, she felt nothing. The force of Thayl's magic flew at her, went straight through and killed the scarred wizard hunter behind her instantly. He fell forward, on top of Memory, pushing her down into the mud. His hand was still tangled in her hair. She cried out, pinned on her back beneath the dead hunter, staring up into the falling rain.

High above, little more than a spot in the sky, the dragon sang a deep, mournful cry that would be heard throughout Avall. Then it fell like a stone. It took down three men before the others knew what had happened.

Memory pushed at the dead weight on her with one arm, her other twisted beneath her. She pushed her feet at the ground and they slid in the mud.

Bloodcurdling terror screamed out all around. Roen moved toward her. She cried out for him but it was lost amongst the wailing of the dragon and men.

Roen stopped before he reached her, bending down to something she couldn't see. He bared his teeth, bent forward and scooped up Eloryn's body. He almost fell as he lifted her with one arm, the other hanging limp. He turned, stumbling, running, through the chaos around him, away from Memory, into the surrounding trees.

"Roen? Roen, no, I'm here!" Memory screamed. Her sanity tearing away in strips, she writhed like the possessed. Her consciousness faded out then in. Her insides boiled. The knife kept in her corset scorched her chest, heated to burning. She found herself free, the dead body of

the scarred hunter face down beside her.

She rolled onto all fours, panting. The dragon threw itself over and over at the men running through the square as they tried to find cover, help injured friends, make their escape. Blood covered the ground as though it were the rain that fell. A man in leather armor lay next to her, staring with dead, black-brown eyes. Perceval.

Illness overtook her like a knife in the stomach. Memory vomited wretchedly. She coughed it out, eyes and nose stinging raw. She wobbled and stood up on shaking feet, taking a step to follow Roen. A gust of wind from the dragon's wings threw her back on the ground.

She tried to stand again, and as she reached her feet, there were arms around her. They lifted her, cradling her, wrapping her chest, pulling her off her feet. She wrestled against them but the arms were like a vice around her, pushing her against a wild, scarred body as it ran. Taking her away from the slaughter of the men. Away into the forest. Away from Roen and Eloryn.

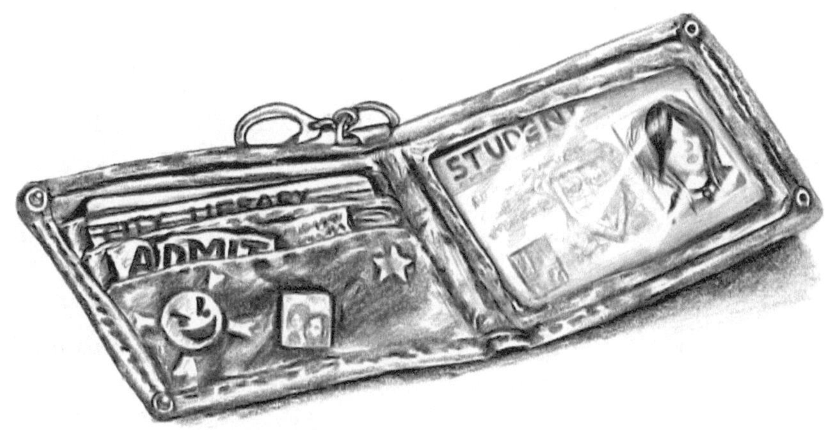

CHAPTER TWENTY-TWO

Under the cover of the trees the light rain barely penetrated through. Only the odd, heavy drop fell between the changing leaves, hitting him as he ran.

Memory swore and screamed in his arms, blending with the tortured howls of the men behind them. He hadn't been there to keep her safe. Mina had kept him away, kept him even though he wanted to go to Memory. He'd let her be hurt again.

Memory slammed her knee into his gut so suddenly he fell out of his run, dropping her.

She slipped forward, trying to run back toward the danger. He pounced, tackling her down. They skidded across slimy leaves. The ground opened up beneath them. He twisted around, pulling her on top of him, wrapping his body around hers. They tumbled down the slope of a gully in an avalanche of red and gold.

He landed hard on his back, and darkness took him.

Gasping, sobbing breaths woke him. His arms were still protectively wrapped around the small weight of her, her dark hair falling in his face.

She thrashed in his arms. "Let me go!" she squealed. "Don't touch me!"

I broke the rules again. But I had to, to save you. His arms went loose with guilt and she pushed out, bursting from their blanket of leaves and scrambling across the ground away from him. She hit the water-carved

earth of the steep gully wall and clawed against it.

He pulled himself up slowly, shaky from the fall.

"I need to get back to Lory and Roen," she said, not at all to him. She tried to climb the slope. Too weak. She tore her hands at the rocks and exposed roots, shrieking at them.

He reached out to her.

She beat his hand back, staring at him with ferocious red-rimmed eyes. "I said, don't touch me!"

She forced her back into the dripping dirt wall, cowering from him. "Who are you? Why are you following me? Was it you who hurt me?"

She didn't know him at all - he already knew this - but that she could think he was the one who hurt her like that opened him raw. He frowned, looking back toward the solace of the surrounding forest. Too hard to find the right words.

"What do you want from me?" she sobbed.

He knelt in front of her. What did he want? There'd only been one dream for so long.

"Hope," he said, shrugging as he forced his words to work, "just to find you again. Keep you safe, like I couldn't before."

An angry fire spread in him to say it. He knew what that man on the children's home staff did to her, and he could never do anything to stop it. He was too young, too weak back then. Perfect bully bait, a smaller than average boy who studied hard and had a talent for music. It was her that saved him from beatings from the older boys. He swore to her that he'd protect her one day. She had laughed at him in response. Kindly.

"How do you know me?" Tears still streamed down her face, but her sobbing lessened.

He nodded. "From the other world. You don't remember."

"Other world?" She buckled forward, clutching her stomach as though in pain. "I don't remember anything. Thayl took everything from me, my memories, my... everything."

"I know. I was there."

It was after she'd come back with that knife, shoplifted from somewhere. She looked at it like it was a thing of salvation. But when the man at the children's home had come for her again, the knife mustn't have helped, just as he had never helped. He didn't know what happened. She came back bloody, badly beaten, blind with panic. She'd never been beaten before.

"You ran away from the home. I followed you. When I caught up, that man, Thayl, had you. Don't even know what he was doing to you, but it looked bad and I… just pushed him."

"Oh God, I saw that in my dream. But it wasn't you. It was just a kid, some little boy."

He pulled his lips inward. *She does remember me. Just some little boy.* "It was me. Years ago, don't know how many. I don't get it how you look the same still, but things are different here, all magic and stuff. There was no magic there, only stories of it."

She shook her head at him, "I don't remember anything else before waking up here a few days ago. We were somewhere different? A different world? What does that even mean? It wasn't… hell?"

"Not hell. Just… our world." He shifted his legs, moving back away from her into a crouch. His throat felt tight. She asked so many questions, and he struggled to make his words work. Mina wasn't much for conversation. "I don't know. We were there, then I was here. They're different. The man grabbed me when I pushed him, pulled me back through his weird portal. You tried to catch me and we both fell. I lost my grip on you and you disappeared in the smoke." He swallowed and licked his lips. Sometimes he used to worry that she had never come through at all, that he would never find her. "Then I was in that forest, with all these dead people all around. Thayl tried to use his hand on me, but some woman started yelling at him like he'd done something wrong and I ran off. Been in the forest since."

"If you hadn't followed me, hadn't stopped Thayl…" Her voice broke.

"You ran off without your wallet. I was just taking it to you." He reached into the folded leathers at the side of his hip and pulled the wallet out, worn and tattered, and handed it to her.

She peeled it open, running shivering fingers over the contents. "Oh. Is that my name?"

He nodded. "Sorry it's dirty."

"I- I don't know yours."

"Will."

She reached out timidly for his arm and turned it over to show the wrist, holding hers up against it. Their wrists matched. Rough inked tattoos of the symbol for eternity with a swirl through the centre.

"Did them ourselves."

"Weren't you like, eight or something?"

"You were my best friend." Will's face heated. "And, kind of a bully."

"I'm sorry I don't remember you. I must be such a disappointment."

Will shook his head, but couldn't say what he wanted to; that she was the only thing from that world that he missed, after a while. Except maybe the internet. After he'd lost his parents, everything in that world seemed cruel except for her, no matter how tough she pretended to be. He knew she thought of him as a weedy younger brother, but he didn't care as long as she let him hang out with her. He always figured he'd make it up to her one day.

"Was I happy there?" she asked.

A frown chilled his face, and he looked away with a vague shrug.

She pried herself off the muddy wall, rivulets of water streaming down into the space she left. "Will, I need to find Eloryn and Roen. Can you help me?"

Will stilled himself and listened. No more screams, no more gusting of dragon wings. The smell of blood still lingered, reaching them on a gentle wind. Mina had left with the other sprites, back through the Veil to their homeland as they often did. There was no way to say how long they would be.

Until then, he could look after Memory.

He nodded, took her by the arms and swung her around onto his back. Memory's muscles jumped and tensed when he took hold of her and he cursed internally. In his time spent with Mina and the fae, touching was so natural that he kept forgetting the rules of his and Memory's once-upon-a-time friendship. He pursed his lips, waiting for retaliation, but she remained holding on.

He reached up for the strongest exposed tree roots, and began pulling himself up out of the gully with her holding tightly around his neck.

Roen slipped again. The increasing rain made the ground slick and his body burned.

His arm around Eloryn grew numb, his fingers locked in their grasp around her. His muscles screamed. He wasn't strong enough to carry her, not like this, but he had to get farther away. The trees in the direction he'd taken were thin and leafless, not providing enough cover from the deadly creature if it flew above. His other arm was useless, dislocated, possibly with bones broken. He wished it was numb too.

He floundered further into the woods. Sweat mixed with the dripping rain, running down his hair into his eyes. It stung, blinding him. Barely able to move, he saw a darker shadow, a thicker trunk. He gritted his teeth and dropped down to his knees. Lowering his shoulder, he let Eloryn slip down onto a bed of fallen leaves. He looked the other way.

Roen half walked, half fell into the wide trunk of the oak that covered them, its leaves not yet dropped. His shoulder muscles spasmed and he held back a moan, pulling his knife from his belt and biting down on it. He placed his shoulder up against the lichen encrusted bark and breathed out through his teeth. Then he pushed.

He couldn't believe it had been only a fortnight ago that he'd done this for the first time. He had become too complacent, too sure of his skills, too damn arrogant. The house guards at the estate he'd made a business call to heard him. They gathered secretly, silently, and surrounded him, cutting him off on the second floor. He'd jumped from a window, farther than he'd normally dare, before any of them could see his face. His shoulder tore then for the first time.

He'd relocated it himself before heading home. Somehow, his mother still knew, still saw the way he nursed it, and he had to lie to her even more. He remembered thinking that night that he could never live if anyone found out what he was, what he did. Now he knew there were worse things to lose.

If he'd never injured his shoulder, he would have picked a more challenging mark in Maerranton markets that day. He would never have met Eloryn. Lucky, his mother always told him; that was his blessing. If his *luck* hadn't brought him to her, would she have fallen into the care of someone more capable? Someone who could have saved her from this?

Tears ran into his mouth, mixing with the taste of metal. He pushed harder, and heard the pop as his joint was forced back into place. His knees withered and he bit hard into the knife, knowing he couldn't risk crying out, as much as he wanted to. He breathed through the pain.

Done, he pulled the knife from his mouth, absently noting the teeth marks, and forced himself to go back to Eloryn. He didn't want to know, didn't want to see, but some fool hope in him said there might still be time. Maybe he could save her.

Kneeling back beside her, Roen gently moved Eloryn's limp arms off her chest. Seeing her now clearly, he choked.

He ran his fingers over her neck, feeling for a pulse. His hands hammered to the beat of his own heart: useless. He bent in close over her face. Her normally alabaster skin was icy white. The warmth of a weak breath met his cheek.

"El." He frantically pulled his tattered shirt off his arms. Bundling the cloth, he held it against the torn flesh on her torso, trying to hold in her life. Blood welled up through the fabric, staining his hands. He tore strips off her skirt and tied them around her waist to pull closed the largest holes in her body.

Eloryn's mouth opened as though in pain, and spluttering a deep breath, she opened her eyes. They were dim and moved slowly, taking in her surroundings. Her eyes flickered over his shirtless chest and a trace of color made it to her cheeks.

"By the… Don't blush now, you haven't enough blood."

"Roen. Are you hurt? Where's Mem?" Eloryn's voice was the softest rasp of whisper.

Roen's emotions caught in his throat. Memory. He saw her fragile body fall under Thayl's deadly magic. No one could survive that. The Wizards' Council members were captured, awaiting execution. Alward was dead too. They were alone, and there was no comfort he could give her but more lies. Before he could answer she began to fade again. Roen squeezed her gently.

"Please, stay awake," he begged her. "Can you heal yourself, with your magic?"

Eloryn's eyelids fluttered. Roen knew it was no use.

"I'm sorry I can't… Is there nothing else I can do? Tell me what to do." He brushed his hand over her forehead, under her hair, feeling it cold under his flushed skin.

"Please don't leave me again," Eloryn murmured.

"Never, Princess. Just don't leave me."

Eloryn stilled. Roen lifted her shoulders, pulling her up into his lap.

Roen cradled Eloryn's body. He stared at her face, as still and silent as she, in too much pain to let tears fall. Hearing the sound of soft footsteps approaching he wrapped his hand around the hilt of his thin knife. His other arm remained around Eloryn. He barely looked up to see who approached.

"Roen! Oh God." Memory came to a stop just in front of him. "Oh God, oh God, oh God."

Roen tightened his hand around the knife hilt. "Spirit."

"It's me," she said, fighting the whine in her voice.

"It can't be. I saw you fall," he said.

"I'm fine. Tell me she's not dead, please." Memory moved closer, and he jumped in shock when she touched him, finally looking at her properly. He twitched again when he saw the tall shape of Will shadowing them. He pulled Eloryn's body closer to him and looked to Memory with a skeptical frown.

"He helped me find you," Memory said. "Roen, please, is she still alive?"

Roen's head dropped. He laid Eloryn flat on the ground so Memory could see.

Memory suppressed a dry heave. The dragon had messed Eloryn up badly. It took her three times to build the courage to feel for a pulse, but when she did, she found one, slow and fading.

Memory looked up into Roen's eyes. Red-rimmed, bloodshot, a question read in them clear for her to see. She nodded in slow motion.

"Do you think you can?" he asked.

No. "Yes. I summoned a dragon. I can do the goddamned impossible."

I can do this, Memory told herself. *God, I hope I can do this.*

Memory took her mind back, remembering how she felt the morning after Eloryn healed her, going over what happened between Eloryn and Roen in the wagon. The way Eloryn described the process. *There is magic in everything, an energy of life that can be spoken to. Our bodies remember what it is to be whole and healthy, and they want to be that way. The magic just gives the body the power to right itself. Reminding it how to be whole. Visiting the broken areas and helping to put them back together.*

Eloryn had spent hours putting Roen back together from just a bruising. Why the hell did she think she could do this? No magic she'd tried worked the way she expected. She was more likely to blast Eloryn away than to help her. Numbly, she realized at this point Eloryn couldn't be much worse off. Beneath thin bandaging, Eloryn still bled. Thayl's words to her repeated in her head, and she cast them away. If this didn't work, she didn't want to think about what she could be losing.

Memory put a shaking palm onto Eloryn's chest, tacky with blood, and one onto her forehead.

She took a deep breath. "Move back a bit, just in case."

Roen stayed and held Eloryn's hand.

This has to work. I hope you trust me, Lory.

She reached out to Eloryn with the furnace of magic within her.

It came faster and easier than she expected. The shock of the connection almost made her break away. Warmth, pulse, blood, muscle and bone. Pain. Surreal and abstract she sensed them. They engulfed her. She focused on the pain, feeling it herself, almost overwhelming. Willing it gone made it so. She imagined Eloryn's pale skin flawless and whole. She mended what she felt torn with a giddy omnipotence, spending energy without guard. She gave her own blood to replenish what Eloryn had lost. At the fringes of her perception, she could taste consciousness. A dreaming mind thick with emotions, memories and an ocean of painful guilt.

Memory gasped back into herself, needing a world worth of air.

She pulled her hands to her aching chest, pressing them against her burning skin. She struggled away from her body's demand to faint. Passing out could come later. She needed to know if it worked, first. The forest was still dusk lit and no one had moved. How long did that take? Did she do enough?

Roen stared, mouth opened, and Memory feebly clawed away the bandaging he'd done. She dug her hands underneath, feeling for skin,

finding it smooth and unbroken.

Roen squeezed Eloryn's hand, and Memory shook her gently, then harder, then roughly, calling her name.

Eloryn didn't move.

"I don't know, I thought I did something. Maybe I didn't do it right. Maybe I didn't get in far enough, like she couldn't with me?" Memory rocked on her knees.

Roen's head shook as if he was drunk. Knuckles cracked in a tightening fist.

"I can try again." Memory moved flimsy arms back toward Eloryn, but Roen lifted them away.

"You can't see yourself. You can't try again." Roen held her arms, and Memory found they were too weak to take from him.

Memory fell onto his bare chest, bridging Eloryn's body beneath them. She let out in long, painful breaths what she couldn't in tears. Roen brought his arms up around her, shaking from the cold, or something else.

"Mem?"

Memory and Roen jerked apart.

Eloryn stared up at Memory wide eyed. Fear, comprehension, and loss played across her face, taking her from relief to pain in seconds.

Eloryn flung herself around Memory, arms tight around her chest, face buried in her shoulder. Memory sat limp, arms hanging awkwardly, and Eloryn bawled.

"He's dead, Mem, he's dead. Alward's dead."

As Eloryn's sobbing quaked through Memory's body, empathy built like acid in her eyes. She wrapped her arms in a returned embrace and held as tightly as the weakness in her body allowed.

Eloryn wept wretchedly, and with the shared wetness of their faces, shared pain, and shuddering sobs shaking them both, Memory wasn't sure whether she wept as well.

"Thayl said such horrible things. They couldn't be true. I can't believe his words about Alward," Eloryn squeaked between gulping teary breaths.

Twice Memory had dreamt of Thayl. Twice she'd met him. Each time there had been things he'd said she also didn't want to believe, and others she hoped weren't lies. She could hardly tell which she wanted most. For now, for Eloryn, she would believe that he lied.

CHAPTER TWENTY-THREE

Eloryn felt more pain in her now than when the dragon had sunk its claws deep into her stomach.

A fury she had never known before overtook her pain. It burnt her tears away. It was her fault. Alward died because of her. If only she'd told him the mistake she made, instead of trying to hide it. Too scared of disappointing him, instead she'd got him killed when he'd done everything to keep her safe, had been everything to her.

Alward only ever took you in, kept you to himself because of the guilt he felt over what he had done. Liar. Why would Alward kill her mother? And if that wasn't true, could he have lied more? Could Alward still be alive?

Desperation ran riot through her with that small spark of hope. She had to know the truth.

"I have to see his body," Eloryn said, pulling away from Memory. "I have to know he is dead, and if he is I need to bury him. No matter what happened, I still love him. I can't just leave his body to whatever Thayl has planned."

"We don't even know where he is," Memory said.

Eloryn screwed up her face. Her body felt too healthy to be holding these dark feelings. The smell of wet leaves and her own blood on her dress were like the aftertaste of death. "If he is dead, he is only a body and no longer has will. He can be brought."

"No way. Lory, you can't be serious?"

Eloryn ignored Memory. Instead, she pleaded with the earth in timeless words of magic, trying to get it to listen, wishing for it. She spoke of Alward, the man who cared for her, taught her, kept her safe. She described every part of his face, his kind smile and ink stained fingers, and how she loved him like a father. She ended with the words she had not long ago taught to Memory. "Beirsinn fair nalldomh."

She felt no connection to the magic within or around her, that vile poison still blocking her. "Beirsinn fair nalldomh!"

Nothing. She screamed, digging her hands into the earth. "Bring him to me!"

She crumpled forwards, her forehead to the ground. "Bring him to me!"

"Magic may not hear you child, but we can. Screeching such vulgar pain." The voice held a regal level of distaste.

Finding herself surrounded by fae, Eloryn jumped to her feet.

At the same time, Memory's savage guardian dropped to his knees. "Yvainne, Mina."

Her body quivering from a whirlwind of emotion, Eloryn stared at him and the fae he knelt to. She couldn't remember anything from when the dragon sheathed its talons into her chest until she woke up and grief consumed her. She floundered, trying to regroup her thoughts. Memory must have healed her, and done it incredibly well. Impossibly so. A shot of panic turned Eloryn around to find Roen. He stood behind her, bloody but alive. Eloryn blinked a double take, wondering where his shirt had gone.

Memory stood up next to Eloryn and spoke to the savage. "Will, do you know them?"

Will nodded.

Eloryn hadn't even noticed his presence before, while anger and tears blurred her eyes. Had he come here for Memory again, or come with the fae? Up from his knees, he moved to stand with the sprites. A red-headed fairy with a young face leant into him and tangled a long fingered hand in his hair.

The gathered fae reflected the twilight tones in a shimmering silver glow. More than she could count, the wild gathering ranged in size and shape, from lithe seven-foot statures to tiny sparkling lights. A bizarre and twisted mix; some had animal eyes, some had antlers or claws, and more, with rough bark skin, glowing glitter, hooves or gossamer veins.

Although clothing and hair billowed with its own life, they did not move. They stood unthreatening, and some even nodded respectful bows as Eloryn passed her eyes over them. Seelie fae.

The only threatening movements were the glares and whispers directed toward Memory, who wobbled on her feet and looked more grey and ill than she had after calling the dragon through the Veil. Guilt edged in amongst Eloryn's other emotions.

"I'm sorry to have disturbed you," Eloryn said with downcast eyes. Seelie they may be, but no less dangerous to anger.

"Your call was loud, but not futile. We are pleased to know you have want. It means we can bargain. You may call me Yvainne. I know who you are." The tallest of the fae, waif thin, took an elegant step forward through a cloud of wafting silver hair.

"Bargain, for what do you wish to bargain with me?" Eloryn's voice wavered. There were lots of stories regarding fairy bargains. Few of them ended well for the human side.

"We will bring you the body of your Alward." Yvainne spoke like sweet chimes in a breeze.

So he is dead. Eloryn's heart shuddered. "And what in return?"

"You will take Thayl's place on the throne, and renew the failing Pact with Maellan blood."

"But if-" Memory started.

Yvainne cut Memory off, her voice turning hard. "Not you. Daring to carry cold iron." If she was the type to spit, Yvainne looked as though she would now. "No matter what you may think, you do not belong in Avall. You. A vessel too full. Liable to spill and spoil all around."

The fae hissed in unison.

Memory simply gaped.

Yvainne turned back to Eloryn. "That is our offer, Maellan. Do you take it?"

"No." Eloryn swore she heard audible sighs from Roen and Memory, but she focused on Yvainne. Pain and fury inside had been startled into submission, but still smoldered throughout. The word she sought came to her. Revenge. That is what she wanted, never having imagined before she could want it. Thayl had killed Alward, and she wanted it paid back. If she could do that, then it was a small step to take the throne after emptying it. "No, not as the offer stands. I will make a bargain though, for one more thing in return."

Yvainne smiled pleasantly, sending a tremor through Eloryn.

"Mem, you said Thayl showed you his memories of how my mother was killed?" Eloryn spoke over her shoulder, keeping her eyes on the fae. "I want to see Alward's memory of the same. Provide that, bring me his body, and I will take the throne and renew the Pact."

"Agreed." A chorus of birdsong and bell called from all the fae, covering the protests of the friends at her back.

"This is our binding deal." Yvainne suddenly stood with her hand on Eloryn's chest. Eloryn gasped to feel the spark of connection relight within her.

"We must go, and let the Summer Court know what has passed. The body will be brought." Yvainne turned, and sprites all around began blinking out of sight. Some sparkled away into tiny lights, and some skipped into the Veil.

Yvainne flicked her eyes to Will. "You stay. Keep watching that one."

"Keep watching?" Memory whispered.

The red headed fairy at Will's side glared hardest at Memory, and passed the glare briefly to Yvainne before vanishing.

"Wait, how is the memory shown?" Eloryn cried.

"With your blood on your hand, and the body of the man, know what you want in your heart and plunge that sinful blade into his." Yvainne pointed to Memory and faded away.

Eloryn's bones turned to wet rope. Binding deal made, she slumped back to the ground, waiting on what that would entail.

"What the hell, Lory?"

"Princess, you should not have."

Only Will did not yell at her. The strange young man crouched beside the ancient oak's trunk, blending into the shadows, watching with hurt eyes.

"It is done," she said. The biggest decision she'd ever made. Maybe the only one she had ever made, that wasn't just to follow another's. She hoped she would not regret it too much.

Memory put a hand on her shoulder, squatting down next to her. When she spoke, her voice was devastatingly tired. "Is this going to be worth it? I get the revenge thing. I so do. Thayl, he told me…"

Memory's words ended as Veil mist spread in curls below them, across the ground, leaving behind a man's body as it passed.

Eloryn's nose twitched, and her tears came again.

She found comfort that, in death, Alward looked at peace. Wavy graying blond hair he never managed to brush if she didn't remind him, a thin face with kind eyes, the face she knew better than any other. No outward signs of injury. No torture. No expression of pain carried with him to death. He seemed to be asleep, but was no less dead for that.

She gripped the shirt at his chest in both hands with tearing strength and wept into it.

"You died for me. And lived for me," she whispered into his cold body. "I'm sorry, I'm so sorry. What I am, my useless title that causes all this damage... I will make it mean something. I will own it. I will never, ever forget you."

Eloryn knew she was watched, knew they all listened to her and waited for her. She still let herself cry some more.

Sitting up, she looked down into her hands. Plenty of her blood on them still. They shook visibly.

"Memory, I need your knife."

"Are you sure you want to do this? Maybe sometimes it's better not to know," Memory stammered.

"Please, Mem."

Memory placed the folded iron blade into her hands.

Eloryn delicately, slowly, pulled it open and held it point down above Alward's no longer beating heart.

A silent snarl bared her teeth, and she rattled with erratic nerves, but could not push the blade.

Not only was her body stubborn, but her mind was in turmoil.

Roen knelt on her other side. "Are you sure?"

Eloryn nodded without really knowing.

From one side, Roen placed his hand onto hers. From the other, Memory did the same. And they pushed.

Eloryn cried out as though the blade pierced her own heart.

The three of them became ghosts; misty forms in a forest. Not this one, but another that they knew. The very place Eloryn and Memory had first met. Eloryn knew the trees well, having spoken to them, though here they were smaller, the brush thinner, making a small clearing. Alward ran toward them, more solid than them, or his dead body on the ground. He was young and fresh with the look of courageous purpose.

Wisp light filled the woods. A dozen men and women bearing weapons followed Alward through the dense trees.

He stopped and stared straight past Eloryn, Memory and Roen with a look of horror. All three followed his gaze.

A gruesome scene like an illustration from the books of blackest magic stood behind them.

Dark hooded figures circled Loredanna, turning on the forest floor in fits of hard labor. Young Thayl assisted anxiously as the baby came.

Behind them, blackest swirls of Veil mist tore the air, outlining a hooded shape that held aloft another newborn. Screaming and wet from birth, blood spilled from the baby's chest, a rune freshly carved into it.

"Stop. Stop this evil!" Alward yelled.

The leading figure loosed a disturbing chuckle from beneath the hood, and rolled the crying baby off long finger tips, letting it fall alone through the tumultuous Veil door.

Figures clashed around them, through them. Guards and chambermaids fought fiercely with those in hoods and cloaks, fighting for their Queen, and giving their lives.

Insubstantial as air, Eloryn, Roen and Memory stood back to back, watching the vision around them. Each swung sword or club made them flinch, only to pass harmlessly through.

Alward stood next to them, scroll in hand, reading words of power. As more fighters fell, between individual battles, glimpses could be seen.

Thayl pulled Loredanna to her feet. No longer torn by labor, blonde hair stuck to her cheeks with sweat. Another newborn lay on the forest floor, lying silent as bodies fell around it.

Thayl scooped Loredanna up into his arms, turning his back on the battleground and the newborn. Loredanna struggled, weak with exhaustion. She cried out, reaching desperately for her baby that was left behind.

She flailed. "No! Let me go. My babies, I won't leave them!"

Fingernails tore his cheek, and she ripped free of his hold, pushing past him, switching their places in the most fateful of moments.

Then she froze, arms still reaching toward her child, struck by a red bolt of magic. Thayl cried out, catching her falling body.

Next to them Alward also stood frozen, one arm outstretched. The scroll drifted to the ground, dropped from his other hand. Horror dawned on his face as the last of Loredanna's protectors were dispatched around him.

"Loredanna. No, no, no. Loredanna!" Thayl cried as her body gave

in, piece by piece in his arms.

She only had eyes for Alward, arm pointing to her child, as she breathed out words. "Save them. Keep her safe."

Watching through time and death, Eloryn could feel the tangible power of her words; words imbued with a force stronger than any behest.

Alward moved in an instant, snatching up the newborn, tucking her into his cloak.

Thayl dropped Loredanna to the ground, roaring into a charge at Alward who backed away with the tiny, precious bundle.

Behind Thayl, Loredanna's last breath passed through her lips, bringing with it final words of magic. Alward faded into the Veil, taking with him the newborn, just now starting to cry.

The vision faded away. Eloryn whispered some words, and watched Alward's body sink away into the earth. As the body sank, a pure white stone as large as Eloryn rose in its place. The knife, rejected, glinted on the freshly turned soil.

Eloryn placed her hand on the stone tenderly. A few more words and she dropped her hand away, but the impression of it remained, permanent in the smooth facing of marble.

"Goodbye."

CHAPTER TWENTY-FOUR

"That was-?" Eloryn began saying, turning away from Alward's grave.

"That was me." Memory bent down gingerly and reclaimed her knife. She wiped it on her already filthy skirt and put it away. "Look, I don't get all of it, not by half, but the baby with the cut chest; that was me. That was this," she said, tapping the front of the corset where it covered her disfiguring scar. "Thayl told me, just before the dragon got you; he said we were sisters. I didn't know then whether it was true, how it could have been true."

"Twins." Roen coughed a weak laugh. "To think we were worried that you looked so much like Eloryn. The resemblance is even clearer now the Princess has lost weight."

Memory fixed a glare on Roen. "You better not start calling me Princess."

"Alward never said a thing, nothing at all about a twin. But, there was always something he searched for, something he said was lost. His research into the Veil, his experiments in the woods... Are you sure it was you?" Eloryn asked.

Memory gave a wry laugh. "How the hell could I be sure? I'm just trying to add up what I've found out so far, and that's what it seems to come to."

Eloryn took a step forward, raising a hand. "May I see how you appear without the dye in your hair?"

"Uh, I guess?"

Eloryn whispered a few words, and Memory felt no change.

Roen however blew a soft whistle. "There's no question. Identical."

Memory reached and twirled a lock of hair in front of her eyes, finding it the same ivory blonde as Eloryn's. She wished for a mirror, to see if she really did look just like the beautiful, delicate creature Eloryn, whom she'd spent unconfessed time envying. It made sense, more than any other explanation had so far, but it just seemed surreal not only to now have a sister, but an identical twin. Whenever she imagined finding her family, she imagined happy smiles and hugs all around. Now, she stared at her twin, too awkward to move. Eloryn stared back mutely. Memory waited for some overwhelming joy or familial love to wash over her. It didn't come. She felt for Eloryn, undeniably, but was it the way a sister feels? Maybe she was in shock. Maybe the unanswered questions still blocked her.

She pounded her forehead with her palm. "But, but, but… We saw when we were born, but what happened next?"

A quiet voice came from the shadows nearby. "You always said you were found as a baby, right near the orphanage. All cut up with that wicked scar you like showing people."

Will, oh God, I completely forgot he was here. Still watching me from hiding, Memory thought, unsettled by the idea. Will told her he wanted to protect her, but his fairy friends didn't seem to have the same intent. She couldn't help wondering whose purpose he served first.

"And I grew up there? In some other world? How could there be another world?"

"There were other lands, once," Eloryn said. "Before the Pact. But the fae foresaw the end of days, which is why the Pact was made. Avall was separated into the Veil, to save the fae and the people of Avall from the hell that would swallow the rest of the world. Maybe, maybe some human life has survived beyond Avall?"

"Our world wasn't Hell." Will shifted in the shadows, his voice quiet and hard.

"I didn't mean…" Eloryn dropped her head, then looked back up at Memory. "I'm just saying what I know of Avall's history. To travel across the Veil into other lands simply isn't done. The fae used to, to bring back imports to trade, but even they haven't for centuries."

Memory paced short, shaky steps, putting together the pieces of her

lost life. Her body felt weak and wasted, but her mind ran on overdrive. "Thayl travelled through, Will saw him. Thayl came after me, to steal the magic from me, when I was like this, same age and everything. He took my memories, my powers, and all three of us fell back through."

She faintly saw Will nod in the darkness of the oak's shadow.

"You got there at the same time as Thayl. Dead bodies all around, you said, so it was before he took over, just after we were born? Oh God, that was sixteen years ago."

Memory ran out of direction for her mind and her feet. He'd waited for her, lost in the forest for sixteen years? How could she possibly have been a good enough friend to have deserved that? Her current record didn't feel up to scratch. She turned away, suddenly finding it hard to look at Will. Her next question came out in a whisper. "But I didn't get through. I was what, just gone all that time?"

"The place we first met, where you appeared in my Veil door, it was the very same clearing we were born," Eloryn told her. "It makes sense. If that is where you left this world from, that is where you would return into it. If you were lost in the Veil, time within it does not behave the same. You did not change, age, even think for all the years you were held by it. In magic, like calls to like. When I stumbled through, a troubled Veil door already, it pulled us both out there. It is all I can guess."

"Same DNA definitely falls in the alike category. And if you hadn't? I'd still be what? Nowhere? Forever?"

Eloryn bit her lower lip and shrugged.

"Uh, but I still don't get it! Thayl had no magic, right, only got it from me? The magic he used to kill the King-" *My father?* "and the wizards right after we were born, but he took it from me when I was this age? Thayl said we were connected, in space and time. Could he have travelled forward in time into the other world to find me even though it was right after we were born here?"

Roen cleared his throat. He stood next to Will, looking grave. "Memory, I know you still have questions but we've tarried here too long. I'm told by your tracker here we were far too easy to find," he said, tilting his head to Will. "We need to start moving again, now, before the trail of blood leads more to us. Most of Thayl's men were killed, but he lives. He could be anywhere."

"You're right. I'm sorry. Which way do we go?" Memory said, dragging her wandering mind back to her current problems, away from those of

her past. She felt half dead from the magic she'd used to heal Eloryn, and she hoped they wouldn't have to go far this time. She was so tired of running.

"Wherever we can hide."

"No," Eloryn said, more firmness in her voice than Memory had ever heard.

"Princess?" Roen turned back, having already taken a few steps.

"I can't keep running. There is only one place for me to go now. To Thayl, to do what must be done."

Memory had heard Eloryn use this tone before, times she pulled her shoulders back and acted the noble part. But in the past it never sounded true, as some wisp of doubt, some whine always tinged its color. Not any more. This was the voice of royalty, royalty with a purpose.

"There is nothing that must be done but keep you safe. Both of you, now more than ever, both equal as heirs and in Thayl's want of you," Roen said, his voice gruff and low.

"There is an unbreakable oath to the seelie fae. There is revenge."

"Revenge?" Roen lifted his hands, still red from her blood. His voice rose and he yelled, right at Eloryn. "You think of revenge when less than an hour ago you were lying bloody and dying? How do you think you can beat this man who's killed so many who tried? What could you possibly do?"

Eloryn blinked as though she would cry. Roen's words echoed in the tangible silence, but when Eloryn spoke again, her voice did not waver. "We know more about Thayl and his magic than anyone ever has. I can take his power from him. Take back all he stole from Memory, and take back my throne. Our throne. I will see revenge for the death of our father, for the Wizards' Council, for Alward and for our mother. And I know how I will do it all."

Silence again. Everyone stared at Eloryn.

Memory forced her tense shoulders down. "So what's the plan, Princess? As much as the idea of seeing Thayl again makes me want to barf out my happy thoughts, I'm with you. I want back what's mine." *I want back my soul. I don't want to feel like THIS any more. Without my soul, I might as well be a demon.*

Eloryn smiled in straight mouthed relief. "I do have a plan. Mostly," she admitted. "There is a clear connection between you and Thayl. Your rune scars, his runed hand, and his magic. Thayl is simply using magic

he stole from you. If we can separate him from that, he will be nothing more than a normal man. My hope is, given the nature of magic, that once freed the power and memories should also return where they belong."

"And his guards, his army, his wizard hunters and anti-magic poisons?" Roen growled.

"They will be suffering other distractions, and won't stop me reaching Thayl," Eloryn countered. "All I need is a way to get us into the castle."

Roen turned away, tearing a hand through his hair. Memory grabbed him by the shoulder and pulled him back. He winced at her, his eyes pleading.

"I can't do this, I can't keep you safe if you take this path," he said.

"It's not your responsibility to keep us safe, Roen," Memory said. "You don't even need to be here if you don't want to. We all look after each other, even if that's when facing our problems instead of hiding from them."

Roen shook his head, looking away into the black of silhouetted trees.

"You needn't stay any longer Roen. I will look after myself now, and I'd rather not see more trouble for you on my behalf," Eloryn said, a quiver finally breaking into her voice.

Roen stalked straight up to Eloryn with such ferocity it seemed he could hit her. Eloryn flinched but stood her ground.

He breathed deeply three times before he spoke, with each word separate and low. "I won't leave you again."

In the pause that followed, a gust of wind like a cool night breeze was their only warning.

Then the air rushed, blowing down so strong it knocked them off their feet, throwing them onto the forest floor. The strongest branches of the ancient oak that sheltered them screeched and split, a massive weight bending them down.

Memory gasped away from the wet dirt in front of her face. She spun onto her back, confused, and looked up to see that the sky had fallen. Pitch black and sparkling in stars, it draped over the tree above, and slithered off it, down around the branches to the ground in front of her. It snapped huge emerald cat eyes at her, sniffing then snorting hot air. Her now blonde hair gusted and fell.

Memory screamed. Eloryn next to her sat motionless in terror. Memory dragged her into a protective embrace, Roen backing in front of them. Will appeared by their side, growling like an animal. A clutch

of cornered mice awaiting the cat.

The dragon took a step forward with a claw still slick in Eloryn's blood, washed under that of many others.

"Quiet small ones." The creature lowered its glittering head down to their level. He spoke without movement, in a low growl that reverberated through their bodies. "I am not here to destroy."

They remained huddled together. The beast made no other action, just waited and watched.

"You won't hurt us?" Memory asked, confused.

"Indeed no." Words came slowly, an earthquake of sound. "I come to grant a boon for my release from imprisonment, in the last time I shall ever be in service to a human." Its last word held such distaste it made Memory squeeze Eloryn tighter.

"Thank you," Memory said in a squeak, feeling even more a mouse. "For not killing us."

The dragon's head gave a shallow nod. "What else would you have from me?"

"What the hell's a boon?" Memory hissed into Eloryn's ear.

"Anything I can offer that is within my power," the dragon answered through unmoving mouth, the sound growling through their bodies.

Memory gaped, wide eyed. "And what is within your power?"

A sound like autumn leaves, crumbling stones and crashing tides. The dragon laughing?

"We'll have no more debts with fae creatures," said Roen.

"This is no debt. You will be rid of me forever once my boon is given. Now think well on what you would have."

Eloryn stammered, still clinging to Memory. "Could you-?"

Huge green eyes fastened on hers. "Let the one to whom I'm indebted ask." The dragon raised its voice, enough for them to feel it like an ache inside.

Memory shivered under the weight of its gaze. What did she want most? "Can you bring back my memories?"

"Not while they are held by another."

Her mouth moved uselessly. She rolled her eyes, looking for inspiration. She needed her memories back. Without them how could she even know what she wanted? Thayl stole them from her and she had to find a way to get them back. "We need to get to the castle and deal with Thayl. Can you get us to Thayl? Fly us there?"

The dragon huffed. "I am no beast of burden. You think like those hunters, seeing me only as a predator and animal, never even considering my true power. So be it. You want to travel, then for your boon I will teach you how. I have seen how you fold the world and move across it. You have the power already, but random, limited, human."

"The Veil doors?" Eloryn breathed.

"Only that one will learn," the dragon boomed, pointing with a reaching claw at Memory. "Defying nature's laws as she does, yet it is still she that I owe."

With a lash of its tail, the dragon took Memory and vanished with her into the Veil.

CHAPTER TWENTY-FIVE

Within the Veil, time meant nothing. Neither did space, or self. Memory could see panic within her like watching from a distance, but a strange sense of calm kept it smothered. The very sensation, although disconcerting, made her grateful. It meant she could still think, still feel. She still existed. This time, unlike the last time she had spent within the Veil, she was aware. Even if it still felt only like a faded dream as she lived it.

In the presence of the dragon, the raging winds she remembered of the Veil were also calmed. Hollowness and pure power surrounded them. She could almost see it moving, a force of nature and life within the gusts and ribbons of wind that flowed out like a golden tide. It swarmed like particles around her chest, warming the fire within her.

The dragon whispered to her, its voice worming its way deep into her subconscious. The long pages of magical words any other person in Avall would need to behest a Veil door were distilled into basic theory. A concept rather than a contract, a way of understanding that Memory could use. The idea of using it horrified her. *What if I could be lost again?*

After a length of time that felt both instant and eternal, the dragon brought Memory back to her friends and the forest. The looks of outrage and horror she had seen on their faces when she was snatched away were still there. Not a moment had passed for them.

Memory breathed deeply, enjoying real air in her lungs until Eloryn latched onto her in a shaking embrace, squeezing the air back out again.

Over Eloryn's shoulder, Memory smiled to Roen and Will. Will flinched and turned away. Looking faint, he leaned suddenly against the trunk of the closest tree. *I could have been lost again.*

Eloryn let go, backed away and looked at her with a face full of questions. The dragon spoke as though in answer, all its focus on Memory. "You've been taught, now you must be tested, to know you can control what has been bestowed."

"Right now?" Memory gulped, filled with stage fright.

"I will watch over your first journey through the Veil. You will be safe."

Memory turned to Eloryn and Roen. "Where do we go from here? To Thayl?"

"Somewhere safe," said Roen. His jaw moved as though he had to force the words through. "If Eloryn has a plan, we will hear it, but we will hear it somewhere safe."

"I know where." Eloryn nodded, and took a long moment before she turned her eyes from Roen back to Memory. She spoke her words of magic that formed images of illustrations and maps.

Eyes closed, Memory filled her mind with the place Eloryn shared with her. The fire within her burned and she could feel the Veil all around her, how it hovered over and connected to the physical world like a shimmering net. She reached with her hands but touched nothing. She moved as though conducting an orchestra, pinching the Veil, bringing it together by two points of the world like folding a map, and tore it at that point. She opened her eyes to see the dark wisps of Veil door standing in front of them.

The fire inside her cooled and with the chill that followed she felt a rush of disappointment that she'd succeeded. Memory shook pins and needles out of her hands. It would have been better if she couldn't do it. She never wanted to step through a portal like that again. Just seeing this magical doorway - like the one from her very first memory, the one she summoned the dragon through, the one she was thrown through as a baby - made her chest ache as though it had been carved again.

The dragon waited.

Under his intimidating gaze, Eloryn stepped up to the doorway first. She nodded to Memory confidently, but the next step, the one that would take her into the Veil, didn't come.

"Do you not trust your sister, or do you not trust me?" the dragon rumbled. It almost sounded amused.

Eloryn paled. Memory didn't find it particularly funny either. She and Roen took their place on either side of Eloryn, and took a step.

Eloryn and Roen vanished, but a hand grabbed onto Memory, pulling her back. She looked up into Will's eyes.

Will shook his head in a brisk movement, his mouth formed "No" but no sound came out.

The dragon's shape loomed behind Will like a mound of black diamonds. Impatience oozed from him. Roen and Eloryn were already on the other side of Avall. "I have to go through. Come with me?"

Will slumped forward as if in pain. He reached a hand toward the smoky tendrils, then looked into her eyes. "This time I won't let go."

Memory crushed his hand in hers. She tried to be brave, for him, but still released a tiny, crying scream as she stepped through.

They arrived at a small cottage. It overlooked a sea that ended in a horizon of mist, lit by a near full moon. Lonely on a rocky bluff made barren by salty winds, a grove of malformed grey trees skirted the cottage, making it more sinister than cozy. Will vanished again into those trees the moment they arrived.

The dragon did not travel with them, and Memory knew she wasn't the only one to hope they wouldn't meet again.

Slowly, they shuffled indoors. Their grand scheme to stay up planning was laid to waste when they all passed out from exhaustion.

"That's it," Eloryn said.

"That's the plan?" asked Memory.

"That is the plan."

"Huh," Memory said. She sat on the very edge of a plush armchair, knees bouncing, chewing her lips. Blood red rays of the setting sun cast over waves below and through the wide open windows, dragging in the smell of rotting seaweed and sea foam. They had slept like the dead, and woken late. In the remaining hours of sunlight, Eloryn reviewed every last piece of information they had, every angle and advantage, until she finally explained her plan.

"It isn't any good?" Eloryn stood in front of the windows, backlit almost too brightly to look at, lips pulled into her mouth and frown forming.

"No, I mean, it's sort of brilliant. Free the Wizards' Council as a distraction, then some identical twin shenanigans to cat and mouse Thayl off on his own. Having the resistance help once Thayl is beaten is good. I reckon there'll be some unhappy people around."

"I won't ask the resistance to act until we've done our part, so they aren't exposed. I think they will agree to that. Alward has a Speaking Mirror here that he used to contact suppliers when setting up this home, and I saw that Lanval owns one, so we can send our messages through him." Eloryn drew in a deep breath. "I wasn't sure I could bring it all together, but the dragon giving Memory the knowledge of Veil doors was the final piece."

"Stupid dragon making me the important part," Memory muttered to herself.

Roen's head wobbled, somewhere between a nod and a shake. "I won't say I like it, but it could work, if your theories are right."

Eloryn turned a shade of pink that glowed in the setting sunlight. "All laws of nature and magic say they are. Like calls to like. Energy will channel to where it belongs."

"It still sounds dangerous," said Roen.

"I'll keep Mem and myself moving fast. I can behest our bodies to react quicker, keep us a step ahead of Thayl. He won't know which of us is which. I think we've a good chance of luring him away from the rest of his men with glimpses of us."

Roen leant forward in the matching armchair across from Memory. "And you say your behest can also help me fight better, to hold back any men with him until he's on his own? Will too, if he shows up again?"

Eloryn nodded, moved as if to pace, but instead fidgeted in place.

Memory leaned back into the upholstered comfort, pulling her knees up in an effort to stop their jittering.

This cottage had been set up by Alward, Eloryn had told them when they arrived. A home away from home in case their other was lost, bought and fully stocked with essentials by Alward's guidance from afar. Stocked and furnished but too sparse to be considered cozy. Memory now sat in a simple cotton dress, more grey brown than lilac, taken from a small supply in a room fitted for Eloryn. Inexpressible happiness filled her to be out of the destroyed black ball gown. Clean, dry, fed *and* sitting. All the good things in life. But a dark unease at what lay ahead continued to build.

"I don't know, isn't it risky though? He'll still have his magic the whole time. We know he hit me once and it did nothing, but the two of you... We're going to have to get so close to him. Maybe it should just be me. I can do it, lure him out by myself," Memory said past the fingers in her mouth, having graduated from chewing her lips to chewing on them.

"I can't let you take that risk on your own," Eloryn said firmly. "He could have any number of men with him even with the distractions. You need us there to help. Even if you're immune to his magic again, he could hurt you in other ways."

Roen rested his elbows on his thighs and bent his head down into his hands. "If anyone is to confront Thayl on their own it should be me. He doesn't know me, and I can probably sneak in close enough without being seen. Both your lives are too valuable."

"It needs to be all of us for the plan to work. Thayl needs to see Memory and me. I need to be there, close by, for my behests to work. Memory must be there for the chance to get her memories back."

"Then Roen at least can stay behind then, and Will; he doesn't need to be part of this either," Memory said, volume growing.

Eloryn paused with her mouth open, looking across to Roen.

"Not a chance." Roen's voice was barely below a yell as he stared at the two of them.

"But-" Memory said, her voice rising again to match.

"Mem, Roen, please, if we do this, we have to do it together. I won't let either of you do this without me, so you won't stop me. It is my plan. Now, do we follow it? Together?"

Roen nodded gravely then put his head down into his hands.

Memory tore off her last fingernail between her teeth and chewed on the rough fibers left behind. Her mind whirred, but all she could catch from the thoughts that flew past was a large amount of cursing.

She shrugged and nodded.

Eloryn sighed out enough air that she visibly decreased in size. "Then we do it tonight."

"I figure you heard all of that?" Memory said out loud to the copse of trees, feeling foolish.

With the faintest rustle of leaves, Will dropped down in front of

her, landing as easily and quietly as if he'd simply taken a step forward. She squeaked a gasp of shock at his arrival. At this point she could do without such surprises, and punched him in the arm in retribution. She thought she saw him smile in response, but it passed too quick for her to be sure.

Seeing him here now, so close in front of her, she realized she hadn't ever really looked at Will. William? William what? He had just been "that animal man". But he wasn't that. He was some normal boy whose life she'd ruined, lost in her own insane world of issues. Half the time she forgot he was even there, watching her from a distance. So many questions she hadn't asked him, things she hadn't seen. He seemed several years older than her now. On his bare chest large pale scars showed against the worn skin, silver in the moonlight. Clothing, if it could be called that, covered only parts of him. It was an odd mixture of finely made but worn garments and the furs that added to his animal appearance, all held together by strips of leather. He stood straighter than he normally did, making him even taller than she'd thought. She only just came to his biceps.

"Maybe you shouldn't go," he said.

"Don't you want me to get my memories back? Then, I would remember you too." She smiled, but her lips shook for some reason.

"Maybe. But others, maybe not. Maybe you shouldn't." He seemed uncomfortable, his eyes turning from edge to edge but not toward her.

Memory snorted. "Considering the grand memories I've made for myself so far this time around, really, what could be worse?"

No answer. Will's breath formed a shimmering haze as it shook from his mouth.

Memory lost the wry smile from her face. "I'm not talking about happy endings here. I honestly don't think that this will turn out the way Lory wants it to, but we have to do something."

"Then hide. I can keep you hidden, in the forests…"

"With your fairy friends? Maybe you haven't noticed, but they don't seem to like me at all."

"Somewhere, somehow I'd keep you safe."

He sounded so much like a child at that moment, so touchingly, that Memory breathed out a giggle. She instantly regretted it. He looked at her as though that laugh was something familiar and hurtful.

"I'm going to do this. One way or another," Memory muttered.

"What are you going to do?"

"Mina, Yvainne, the other fae... they won't help. But they're close. They're watching to see what happens. If it's done, after that, I don't know. But I will help. I'll follow you. As long as I can." He looked behind him into the trees, then finally brought his eyes onto her face. The corner of his mouth twitched. "I've never seen you without your hair dyed."

"You don't dig the blonde?" Memory folded her arms up into her chest, lifting her eyebrows. This was the one person in all Avall that knew the most of her life. His opinion suddenly seemed to matter a lot.

"Never in a dress either. You're different." The cool blue of his eyes remained fixed on hers, assessing her, making her heart jitter. "Everything is different here."

"I'm sorry. I don't know what I was like before."

Will huffed, mouth lifting slightly more, almost a smile. "You would never say sorry, before."

The faintest flicker of light caught the corner of Memory's eye, and Will turned away from her again.

"I have to go," he said.

"Oh, well, do you want to stay tonight in the house or...?"

Will had already taken three long strides, then stepped up into the trees and disappeared. Memory's words drifted to nothing.

She wished she could do that light spell, to light up the trees and see where he went. She just couldn't get it to work, a simple thing like that. If she couldn't even do that, why did she think she could do what she had to for Eloryn's plan? This wasn't going to work. The blood drained from her to think of what would happen if it didn't.

CHAPTER TWENTY-SIX

Roen watched Eloryn push the study door open and step out, looking grey and empty. She didn't notice him, sitting still and silent in the same armchair as before. He hadn't lit the room, finding no lamps or lighters in a wizard's home, and unable to do it himself any other way. Still just a thief hiding in the shadows.

A tiny wisp followed Eloryn and lit her face. Twin tears ran down and joined under her chin.

Roen cleared his throat.

She wiped frantically at her cheeks. "It's so dark in here. Sorry, you startled me."

"How went the messages?" he asked softly.

"I was able to speak with Duke Lanval. He won't be involved, as expected, but had information about the Wizards' Council. They still live, and I know where they are held. He also agreed to rush messages to his contacts in the resistance, so they can rally as many men as they can for this morning. He was more agreeable knowing that if we do not achieve our part, there is no risk to them. He said we were foolish, but wished us luck." Eloryn's voice had lost the regal edge it held before. She sounded tired, and more emotional than she wanted to show.

Roen leant forward out of the shadows, rose out of his chair and over to Eloryn's side before he knew why. Once there, he couldn't find reason enough to voice. He spoke awkwardly. "Are you all right?"

Eloryn nodded and smiled. Both looked false. "Where's Mem?"

Roen's hand, half lifted toward Eloryn, dropped and balled into a fist. "Gone outside to see that savage."

"I don't think he means harm, from what I understand happened to him," Eloryn said, her eyes following the line of his arm to his hand. He unclenched it, self conscious in the memory of her fingers wrapping his. Her innocent gesture that he took advantage of.

"Who's to say he's not also struck with vengeance, for his lifetime lost in the woods?" Roen turned and walked back to one of the two armchairs. Nerves jumping too hectically to sit again, he leant into the backrest from behind. One armchair meant for Alward, one for Eloryn, and nothing more. Even now he wore a shirt of Alward's, taken from what would have been his room. Eloryn had given it to him with a trembling smile, and as much as wearing it was necessary it made him uncomfortable. He pulled at the neckline of it, unbuttoning the collar that now felt too tight.

"Memory told me that when she healed me, I was bandaged in your shirt. I don't think I would have lasted, without what you did for me. I wanted to thank you," Eloryn said from across the room.

Thanking me for evidence of what I couldn't do. Bandages instead of behests, Roen thought, shaking his head. The image of Eloryn's gold dress, torn to shreds and bloodstained, came to him as a further reminder. Roen could see her in the new, clean and whole olive dress she now wore, and how it made her eyes and hair luminous, even though he didn't turn and look.

A sudden realization almost made Roen buckle over. He dug his fingers into the dusty upholstery of the armchair. Who Eloryn was, who he was… even after everything that had happened, everything she knew about him, some madness in him still clung to hope. The pain of that hope shredded his insides as he saw clearly. If their plan worked, restoring the Maellan line and the Wizards' Council to power, then he and Eloryn wouldn't be allowed together any more than Loredanna and Thayl were.

Roen covered a groan by clearing his throat again. "We don't have to do this. You're safe here, you could just… stay."

Eloryn moved to his side. "I know who I am is a burden to everyone around me. Understand, this is what I have to do to lift that. But my burden is not yours. You can be free of it at any time."

"I said I wouldn't leave you and I won't. Not until you're safe," Roen

said through unopened teeth. He glared into the fabric of the armchair, but still felt her next to him like the warmth of sunlight on bare skin.

"I don't want you to feel responsible for me. You saw what became of the last man who did."

"It's not just that."

"Would you still be here with me now, if I was never a princess?" Eloryn's tone became cold.

Roen's voice came up short, breaking before a word could come out. He forced the words through. "I didn't know you were a princess when I returned your bag that day."

Despite the words spoken being true, Roen cursed himself as a liar. He wouldn't have been here, now, if he hadn't seen that medallion, hadn't known with one look. He wouldn't have put himself at risk to hide them from the guards. And if that hadn't ended badly, he simply would have used her, like he did other women, and then forgotten her. That was the reality of who he was; criminal, philanderer, sparkless seventh son of a seventh son. A man who had no place by her side.

Eloryn only saw the lie, one that he'd been starting to believe himself. *It's time we were both reminded of the truth. There is no future here.*

"Thank you, for that also, that you returned me my belongings back then," Eloryn said softly.

Roen coughed a rasping laugh, and she took a step back when he looked up at her in anger. "Thanking me! That I stole the pack in the first place? You're too naïve for your own good. You have no idea who I really am."

Eloryn's lower lip trembled, and she stepped back again. "I'm… I need to get some sleep before we leave."

Roen dropped his head down onto the back of the armchair. After a few quiet moments, he noticed Eloryn hadn't moved.

"I don't regret that you stole from me. There is not one action I've seen you take that hasn't been of noble cause. That is who I know you are." And she left.

"Sweet dreams, El," Roen muttered once she was long gone from the room. He straightened back up, and went to fetch the bottle of fortified wine he had seen in the pantry stores when searching for lighting.

Memory threw an arm up over her head, trying to relieve the stuffy warmth of the feather quilting on top of her. The chill of the night air was even less comfortable and she pulled it into the bed again.

She rolled her tongue around her teeth, counting them, and wiggled her toes. Her eyes, unwilling to close, traced dark shadows on the exposed rafters of the ceiling.

She flung herself onto her side, knocking into Eloryn.

"Please, Mem. You should try to sleep."

Memory breathed deeply through her nose and stretched flat on her back again in her half of a small bed. It lasted a few seconds before she turned on her side facing Eloryn, propped up on an elbow.

"So, sisters huh?" Memory said through half her mouth. "It's kind of weird, right? Really. Very seriously. Weird."

Eloryn muttered under the covers just out of Memory's hearing.

"Did you just swear? No way." Memory poked Eloryn with her bare foot.

"Mem, we only have a few hours left." Eloryn tried to move out of Memory's reach but there was nowhere to go. She turned onto her back and sighed pointedly.

"Come on, you haven't thought about it at all? I mean, we're sisters, twins even. It's got to at least be better than me being some kind of demon doppelganger. Well, maybe not by much," said Memory. "I am already stealing your clothes."

"I don't know yet what to think. I thought I knew my past. I never imagined having a sister. Now please will you sleep, or at the least let me do so?"

"If I'm bothering you too much I could go share Roen's bed instead."

Eloryn's eyes snapped open and turned mechanically toward Memory. "His bed is smaller than this one."

Memory cradled her cheek in her hand, grinning at Eloryn. "But he's cute, huh? Seems like the kind of thing sisters would talk about. Nice body too. I mean, Will is way more built, but I can't say I was unhappy Roen lost his shirt for so long."

"I'm glad my almost being killed by a dragon had such a benefit for you."

"Ooh, she *has* got a sense of humor. Biting too. See, we are sisters after all." Memory could almost hear Eloryn roll her eyes.

"Mem, what is it you really want to talk about?"

Pursing her lips, Memory rolled onto her back, her shoulder up against Eloryn's.

She still felt the remnants of the need to get home she used to feel so devastatingly, but knew now she was as much at home here as anywhere. Any family she had sought was now right here beside her. And her stolen soul? Could she just live without the parts of it that were gone? The way her insides burned themselves away, the way she kept doing things that felt so wrong... No, probably not. Something had to be done. But this?

"I don't know if I can do what I have to do tomorrow," she said.

"I believe you can," Eloryn said with more confidence than Memory could stand.

"I don't know if I want to," she said with barely any sound at all.

Eloryn didn't respond, and Memory started to hope she hadn't heard.

"I know it's going to be difficult. I would trade places with you if I could," Eloryn finally whispered. "I don't know why your magic works how it does, whether it was your time in the other world or your time in the Veil that caused it. I'm sorry that and the dragon's boon mean so much of the plan relies on you. But if it helps, remember what Thayl has stolen from you."

"Yeah, about that..." Memory muttered. How could she tell Eloryn that it wasn't just her memories that were gone, that were at stake, but her very soul?

"He didn't just steal your memories, your magic. He stole your whole life; your throne, your father, your mother, your sister, your world." Eloryn found and squeezed Memory's hand under the covers.

"Yeah. All those things." Memory pulled her hand out of Eloryn's and rolled the covers back, stepping out of her side of the bed. "It's just that I feel like I've been looking for my family for so long, maybe even before I lost my memory. I'm not sure I can risk losing that again so soon."

Memory spoke quickly to cover any reply Eloryn may have formed. "I'll try and get some sleep, I promise. I just need some time."

Eloryn sat up in bed, looking in the moonlight like the Ghost-girl Memory first met. "Finding out you're my sister didn't change anything for me, because you already were in every way that mattered."

"Always with knowing the words." Memory paused at the doorway. "Can I take some of Alward's clothes, for Will? I want to give him something, you know, me not with the words and all."

Eloryn agreed. Memory tried to counteract the force of a shiver playing up her back and walked out. What she was going to do next would be harder than she first thought.

"Thayl? Thayl!"

The calling voice grew closer, and Thayl's eyes drew into small slits, annoyed by the interruption.

"Where the hell are you? Son of a…" A small figure popped onto the verdant horizon, seeming almost as surprised as he.

He smiled in recognition. His heart beat painfully. "Loredanna."

Rising from the wood and copper bench, Thayl strode quickly through the manicured rose garden. He met her with a wrapping embrace.

"Ew, gross, really?" She pushed him away violently.

Thayl froze, head tilted back, eyebrow twitching. "You?"

"Yeah me," the girl said in a defensive mumble.

"Not dead then?"

Thayl thought he saw her hesitate before she spoke again. "Just. Someone saved me, healed me."

"You've also changed." Thayl stared at her rough cropped hair, now a heartbreakingly familiar blonde.

"Not a lot."

Thayl dropped onto the garden bench, suddenly right behind him again. He rubbed his eyes, knowing he was dreaming. *You shouldn't be able to feel so tired in a dream.* He often dreamt of Loredanna amongst these roses. Beautiful, blessed moments of dream. Not tonight though. On every rose vine blossoms turned to ash and fell onto the ground as dust. "What do you want, demon? Why are you here?"

"Don't call me that. You know I'm not," Memory said, frowning at him.

"Tormentor, then."

She folded her arms across her chest and paced in front of him. "I came to make a deal."

"Why would you, now, knowing what I want from you?" Thayl blinked his eyes clear and leaned back, draping both arms along the

back of the bench.

"I'm kind of hoping you want other things more, and maybe we can forget about that whole sucking-my-remaining-soul-out thing?" Memory peeked from the corner of her eye and made another lap in front of him. "You've got the Wizards' Council, and with Alward dead too, I'm out of other options."

Thayl stared, waiting.

She licked her lips, and then blurted her words out under his still gaze. "Eloryn's alive."

Thayl jumped to his feet. Storm clouds doused rose bushes that now stood as big as ancient oaks, filling the air with the scent of rain. The shade of a bloodied dragon swooped overhead, making Memory flinch.

"You'd better not lie. What do you offer?" Thayl growled.

"Eloryn. I can bring her straight to you. But you have to promise you won't try and take more soul or memories from me. I don't even need the other ones back. I know I wasn't happy in that hell I was in." Memory's pace increased with the rapid flow of her words. "And also, I want to rule after you. I know you never married, that you have no heir. I want to be your heir. I should be anyway. I'm older than Eloryn, but everyone only ever wants her."

Thayl put out an arm, stopping the girl in her tracks. She stood pouting in front of him, all fire and unshed tears. As full of emotion as her mother.

"Those are your complete terms?" Thayl asked. "You bring me Eloryn, I take no more memories from you and make you my heir?"

"Will and Roen, they aren't anything to you. I want them too, alive," she said, her cheeks colored feverishly and shoulders shaking. "It has to be a promise."

The child was too terrified to know what she was doing. Thayl smiled.

"I agree. By the fae, our deal is binding, our oath unbreakable. Repeat what I just said." He pointed solemnly at her, waiting, and she fumbled out the words.

The garden returned to its original state. Warm sunlight shone from an unclouded sky above a field of thorned beauty. Thayl suppressed a joyous reel of laughter.

He dragged a finger through her hair, and smiled at the look of horror on her face as she shied away from him. "I didn't know you were identical twins. Even when I travelled through the Veil, right after

your birth and found you grown, magic matured and ready to steal, you looked not a thing like your mother. Not like now."

"How did you do it? How did you find me when I was sixteen, just after I was born?"

"You think I know?" Thayl's laughter boomed through the garden. "You think I planned it all? Think child, what magic did I have, before I stole yours? I had help."

"The one who dropped baby me through the veil door?"

"How do you know her?" Thayl looked around, alert, then calmed. He hadn't seen the witch in years, since the last time she appeared demanding he repay his debt. A debt he only owed when his revenge was complete. He knew when it was, she'd return, and that would be soon.

"I saw what really happened when I was born, what you didn't show me in our little memory lane excursion," she said.

"And how do you judge me now? What wouldn't you do for the people you love?" Thayl said, watching her expression.

"Probably not carve up their baby and throw it into Hell," she said through a twisted mouth.

"What do you know? You obviously have no people you love," Thayl mocked with a smile, but strain pulled it into a sneer. It didn't matter what this girl thought, he still knew the truth of his part, and she wouldn't be around much longer to torment him with her words and her face. His smile calmed and he watched her steadily.

"What are you going to do with Lory?" Memory asked. "I know you want her alive. You didn't want the dragon to hurt her."

"You bring her to me. That is our pact. What I do with her after that is whatever I wish. I am not too old yet to take a wife. I'm sure she'll be agreeable when death is her only other option."

Memory wobbled back a short step as though trying not to fall.

"Regretting the terms of our deal already?" he asked with melodramatic sympathy.

"You could say that," she whispered.

"Perhaps you should have considered them more carefully. But we are bound now," Thayl said. "Don't be glum. You get a kingdom and your two boys to play with. There is more I can show you too, about your past, after you've completed your side of the bargain. Which you intend to do, how?"

Memory's face lost all emotion and life. "It's happening soon, early this morning while it's still dark. Eloryn thinks we will be going to free the Wizards' Council, and with them as a distraction, we would come for you, but I'll bring her straight to you instead. I just need to see where to take her."

Thayl shifted the world around them to the castle with a blink. Flying by walls and doors of spectacular wealth, he led her to the main hall with a growing smile.

The room dripped with ivory and gold. Crystal chandeliers spun colored light throughout the room, lighting the blood-red carpet beneath.

This was the very place where the blood of King Edmund and many of the Wizards' Council went cold some sixteen years earlier. This would be the place his final revenge would be had.

"Bring her to me here."

This was the place every last member of the Wizards' Council and this cursed offspring of Loredanna and her forced husband would meet their ends. As the child faded out of his dream, he let laughter of relief and anticipation fill the grand hall.

CHAPTER TWENTY-SEVEN

Memory awoke covered in a thin sheen of sweat, still exhausted, anxious and restless. If it hadn't been for the dream she wouldn't believe she had slept at all. She'd never made it back to bed. Her limbs were locked into a crumpled form fitted to the armchair she slept in. Only moonlight showed through the wide windows of the sitting room. Early morning but still dark, it must almost be time to go.

The front door opened and Roen walked in from outside, covered in a damp layer of dew. He looked pale, his tawny eyes lined in red and smudged grey underneath. His face, still so charming, was marked by a frown that had become far too familiar. Thayl's face, with his tired, bitter eyes played into her mind.

"You shouldn't frown so much. Wind will change and you'll get stuck that way," Memory said and stood up beside him, groaning when she stretched her back. She paused and frowned as well. "Is that actually true? Is that some magic thing?"

"If it was, I don't think it would apply to me," Roen said, but his face softened.

"Look, I know it's not exactly kittens and circuses right now, but I hate to see you always sad. Isn't there anything that can make you smile?"

Roen looked at her through haphazardly ruffled hair. The golden color of it over his tired eyes made him look like a fallen angel. His eyes searched over her face and his lips turned upwards.

The smile that appeared slid away quickly when Eloryn joined them. They all stared at each other in silence for a few moments, until Eloryn spoke. "Ready?"

Memory nodded. *I should tell them. I should warn them. I shouldn't be doing this at all.* Memory struggled to hold their gaze and excused herself instead, leaving the cottage. *It's too late now.*

Outside, the air was thick and white, as though the Veil mist from the horizon had grown and rolled in like a tide. The mist caught and refracted the moonlight, making the night brighter than it should be, and formed cold droplets on her skin.

Memory knew she could create the Veil door inside, but the idea of it felt weird to her. It was somehow easier to grasp the concept out in the open, and at the moment, anything easier was better.

Her pulse fluttered behind her collar bone, echoing up through her throat like a feeling of sickness. She tried to imagine how this might play out. It felt as though all her other experiences until now hadn't ended very well. She struggled to picture the possibilities before her. If she had more experience, more memories to draw from in general, would she have made different choices? Would she have, if her soul weren't broken?

Roen stepped outside, Eloryn behind him. She smiled thinly. "This will work. We will get your memories back."

Memory chewed her lips, her face flickering between smile and frown. No matter how this ended, she just wanted to get it done.

On the low stone boundary wall, Memory saw the clothing she'd left out for Will the night before, now soggy from dew and sea breeze. He wasn't anywhere in sight. Memory sighed, not sure whether in sadness or relief.

"Mem, it's time," Eloryn said.

Memory caught her breath. The last chance to back down; unbreakable oaths aside. She wasn't sure whether creating this Veil door or what lay beyond it scared her more. She wondered what happened if you broke an unbreakable oath.

Memory tore a hole in the world, ready to lead them all to their fate.

"Ready?" Roen took them each by a trembling hand.

"Wait. Just, I need a moment." Memory pulled away. She flicked her eyes back and forth through the fog, seeking any movement. *It's for the best. He shouldn't have to be part of this.* Memory turned back to the Veil door.

The roof of the cottage creaked, and Will stepped down, standing

behind Memory almost as though her small form would hide him from the others.

"You don't have to come," she whispered, staring at the ground.

"I won't lose you again." He held out a hand. She took it and led them all through.

It took a moment for Memory to recover from passing through the Veil. It felt just as it had every time – like being pulled through a bastard hybrid of a vacuum cleaner and a smoke machine while having a bad hangover.

The big castle room wasn't as glowing and pretty as it had been in the dream, despite being brightly lit. A smell of decay filled the hall. The finely decorated walls were dusty and run down.

Memory squinted, her eyes still adjusting to the change in light.

Scores of guards in solemn military uniform didn't help the atmosphere. Between every few guards the old men of the Wizards' Council were held, subdued and shackled. At the end of the hall, Thayl towered, staring down at them from a raised dais.

"What happened? Why are we here?" Eloryn cried.

Memory turned and watched her friends with sad eyes. Guards grabbed them from behind, locking shackles around their wrists. Will threw his fists into one guard's gut, knocking him back three steps. A heavily gauntleted hand hit the back of his neck and he fell to his knees. Shaking off dizziness he tried to stand again. Memory shook her head at him, her expression full of warning.

The look he returned stung, but he stilled.

Memory's teeth clipped against each other, knocked by panicking nerves. No guard came to shackle her.

Comprehension showed on Roen's face first. He spoke slowly, dangerously. "Mem, what are you doing? What have you done?"

Eloryn said nothing, her face shaking with emotion.

I can do this, I can do this, Memory thought, playing the mantra on repeat.

Roen wrenched his hands in the manacles, testing their strength.

Thayl called down the hall to them, his voice echoing in the perfect acoustics. "Don't bother to fight. The shackles are runed to block any behests. Memory, why don't you come here and take your rightful place

to watch the executions?"

Memory, feet still bare, pushed slowly over the carpet toward Thayl. She winced her eyes shut and called back without looking behind her. "I'm sorry, Eloryn. This is the only way I can get what I want."

The gaze of every wizard and guard in the room followed her. The weight of judgment in their eyes rattled her, making each step she took a painful internal struggle. Hayes shook his head in disgust as though this was foreseen.

I can do this, I can do this.

Midway down the long hall she called to Thayl, "You said once I brought you Eloryn, you could tell me more that you knew about me."

Thayl barked a laugh. "Obviously I was lying. I just wanted to make sure you would come, so I could dispose of you."

Memory's stomach acid turned to steam, bubbling up through her body. But she was prepared for the worst. Thayl made no threatening move yet. He stood as confident and smug as she hoped he would, after finding just the loophole in her bargain she knew was there.

She continued toward him, projecting every bit of real pain and fear she felt into her words. "You can't, we made a deal!"

"You people and your deals. I learned long ago that when making a deal, you should be sure exactly what you will be getting. As you have yours, my side of our bargain is honored. You are my heir. Does everyone here understand that?"

A low chorus of agreement sounded through the ranks of guards as she progressed down the room.

"But that doesn't mean I can't kill you." The laughter fled from Thayl's voice. "If I can't have the rest of your power, I can't risk anyone else having it. As much as you look like Loredanna now, you're too damaged to be anything to me. Better to put you out of your misery." Thayl lifted his rune-scarred hand.

Not yet. Not close enough. Memory's mind found a new height of panic-fuelled overdrive. "There's something you don't know!" she cried out. "Something Alward knew, Eloryn knew, that you didn't. Something you need to know before you do anything to us."

Thayl sniffed, his eyes half shadowed by dark eyebrows. His hand relaxed. "Tell me if you will, but I'll make no more deals with you."

Just steps away, Memory said quietly, as earnestly as possible, "You're our father."

The impact was instant. Thayl's frown deepened, eyes widened, mouth gaped.

Memory stepped right up in front of him. *I can do this.* Eloryn's plan was too risky, putting too many people in Thayl's line of fire: Eloryn, Roen, Will. What she always wanted, since she could first remember. Her family. This way, they might be prisoners, but they were alive. This way, if she screwed up, it was all on her.

"Can it be?" Thayl whispered, his forehead scored with deep lines. Now. *I can do this.* "Of course it can't. Obviously, I was lying."

Fury screamed from him, shooting through his outstretched hand.

Memory screamed out at the same moment, focusing all her thought on the sharpest sword in the room. "Beirsinn fair nalldomh! Bring it to me!"

Thayl's magic passed harmlessly through her.

The sword now in Memory's hand passed through Thayl's wrist.

The world ended in blinding light.

Thayl's scream echoed down the hall to Eloryn. She saw his hand fall to the floor. It thumped in time with her heartbeat, and then the end of the hall lit as if a sun had been born within the room. She shielded her eyes with shackled hands, the light too painful to look upon.

A sandy-haired man stepped forward, peering into the glow. He turned around and raised an arm high in the air.

Guards loyal to Thayl stood dumbstruck by the violent amputation and explosion of magic. Those not loyal to Thayl were ready, waiting on the opportunity they had been promised. At the signal, they stepped forward and unlocked shackles down the line of wizards.

Eloryn's breath shook and she tried to comprehend what happened. This wasn't her plan, but the result was the same. *She did it. She really did it.* Thayl's rune-scarred hand was cut off, the source, the vessel of his power removed, leaving him powerless, a normal man and returning what he stole to Memory. *But we were supposed to be there with you Mem, helping you.*

The fluttering moment of peace broke. Cries of outrage marked the beginning of the battle when the actions of the resistance were seen and comprehended. Warring bodies scattered the hall and the eerie light show faded.

"Roen, please hurry," Eloryn whispered. The guards behind their back, apparently none on their side, were blinking out of their stupor. Roen forced a click from his shackles with a small strip of copper.

He left them hanging from his wrists and worked at Eloryn's. The fastest guard charged at his turned back. Will struck the man with his shackled hands, knocking him away in a spinning tumble.

Will growled. The guards hesitated, regrouped, drew weapons.

Roen pushed Eloryn's shackles off her wrists in revulsion. He caught her eye for a moment then turned to Will. Her heart felt as though it would tear out to follow him.

Another guard came running at them. Eloryn breathed out words in a flurry, speaking to the wood of the floorboards under the carpet. They rotted and splintered. The guard fell knee deep into the hole she made, sprawling under Roen's feet. Roen brought a boot down hard onto the base of the guard's neck. His attention turned away from Will's manacles, he couldn't turn back, as two more men charged, four coming behind.

"You need to get out of here. I can't hold back so many." Roen shook off his unlocked bonds and took a sword from the man on the floor.

"You can. I'll help." She knew there would be fighting, one way or another, and this was part of her plan that she could still do. Eloryn spoke more words of magic. Roen guided her behind him, backing her up against the nearest wall, parrying away blows from the men who followed.

"By the fae," Roen wheezed when her behest took effect. His next strike ripped the sword from his opponent's hand with enough force to lodge it into the wall where it flew.

Will smiled, teeth bared like a predator. Her words reached his body too, taking his strengths, making them stronger. He leapt across at the next wave of guards, pulling the first of them into a spinning tackle that tumbled the rest of the row.

The Wizards' Council stood between Eloryn and the chaos of fighting. Unprepared, they used simple magic, anything they had that didn't require being read. Roen and Will fought back those who made it through to threaten Eloryn. She kept a steady stream of words flowing, renewing the energy they spent.

A cacophony of painful cries, clashing weapons and rumbling magic filled the ornate hall, a hall made for dances of a less violent nature. Bodies fell, but the resistance won ground.

"This might actually work. I thought she... I can't believe Memory did that," Roen yelled over his shoulder, the confidence from the power Eloryn gave him clear in his voice. "Just up to the Council and resistance to get everything under control now."

Eloryn took a breath and a moment away from her words of behest. "Can you see her? Is she coming back to us?" The scarring white light that erupted from Thayl's severed wrist had gone, but the roaring battle now obscured that end of the hall.

"Can't see yet." Roen frowned, starting to lose the ease with which he kept more than one man at bay.

Eloryn raced her magic words back out again, keeping him strong. Will broke away from their side. Eloryn's eyes locked onto his back. He forced through a new surge of guards, cracking his still shackled hands against attacking swords.

"Will, come back!" Eloryn yelled between behests. He kept going, moving out of her reach of influence.

He pushed a man down, climbing him like a ladder. Stepping across other men's shoulders, he raced for the other end of the hall, clearing half the room before falling into the crowd again.

Eloryn followed his path with her eyes. Through a gap in the blurred motion of battle she saw a heart-shattering tableau.

Thayl still lived, still stood, wounded but awake. Memory lay beneath him, unmoving, collapsed on the dais.

Thayl tore a silk banner from the wall, pulling it with one hand and wrapping it around the bleeding stump where the other had been. Feral anger showed in every movement, in the twist of his face. He spoke words Eloryn couldn't hear and spat on Memory. Keeping hard eyes on her, he bent and picked up the sword still wet with his own blood.

Eloryn's pulse beat so fast it burned. *There's no one there to help her.* A line of guards held others back from the dais, protecting Thayl as the Wizard Council protected her. The resistance focused on blocking new waves of castle troops that headed toward the clearest enemies in the room – the Council, Roen, the defensive line around Eloryn. Everyone, everyone fought for her and no one fought for Memory.

Thayl examined the sword coldly. He stepped with menacing purpose over Memory's slumped body.

Eloryn's magic words faltered. She saw Will in the crowd, the only one fighting against the tide. He tore bodies out of his way, pushing through toward Memory. None of Eloryn's magic reached him any more. He fought with desperate strength as though it still did. Outnumbered, unarmed, already bleeding, the guards overwhelmed him, bringing him down.

Eloryn watched Roen fighting for her for a heartbreaking moment. *I'm sorry.* She changed the meaning of the ancient words she spoke.

Roen pushed a pair of disarmed men, knocking them back with the last burst of strength she gave him. In the second of time that bought him, he turned to Eloryn. The confusion and concern on his face wrenched her insides. *He knows I've abandoned him.*

Eloryn's knees folded, life seeping out of her. The sound of the battle dimmed.

Through clouded eyes she watched the two thrown down guards get back to their feet, pulling at Roen. He shook them off. He called out to her but she couldn't hear. Feather slow she drifted to the floor, sight flickering out like a finished wick. Four, five more men latched onto Roen and he thrashed to reach her. They forced him down onto his knees, stomach, pushing his face onto the floor, pinning down each limb. His fingertips outstretched in front of her face were the last thing she saw as her eyes closed.

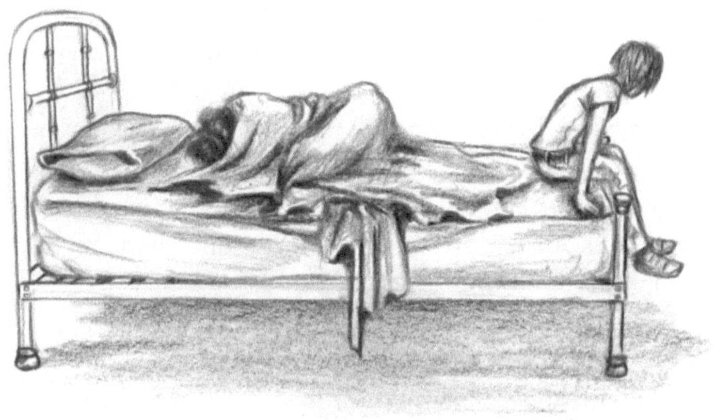

CHAPTER TWENTY-EIGHT

Eloryn found herself in a strange and horrifying world. She tried not to regret her decision as she blinked wide eyes and calmed her breathing.

This was not like a normal healing. Even for being out of her body she didn't expect this. She'd been channeled right into Memory's dreaming consciousness. *Like calls to like.*

A hard grey ground lay beneath her. Machines of grey metal lined the streets and grey buildings towered nightmarishly high up into a grey sky. Even the air tasted grey. A world full of metal and dust, all grey, everything grey.

It pounded like a ravaged heartbeat. The whole world pulsed, crumbled, being torn down and built up again with each beat, shaking and shifting. Eloryn put a hand to her mouth and fought the urge to be sick. She reminded herself she wasn't even in her physical body.

Images all around twisted and tore like burning paintings, blending the nightmare into a mess of malformed scenes. Streets led out in every direction further than she could see.

She screamed out for Memory.

The movement of people down one street caught Eloryn's eye. She broke into a run toward them. The street became an open park, appearing under her feet and before her eyes. Strange contraptions jutted from the ground that a group of children swung and stood on.

"Memory." Eloryn breathed out in relief.

The dark haired girl didn't react. She had Memory's face, but younger, a different hair cut, half black, half blue. She mouthed off at an older boy backed by a group of his friends. He called her something that almost made Eloryn faint to hear.

Memory broke his nose with her first punch. Then she kept hitting.

They vanished before Eloryn could blink or move.

She spun, disorientated, finding herself alone on the street again. She jogged back for the crossroads, calling out Memory's name every second step. Desperation burned in her.

Her next step brought her into a dark hallway.

A looming shadow stood in front of her. The wide-set man leant on a mop and grinned in a way that twisted Eloryn's insides. He stared right at her and she lost a shaking breath before a sound behind her spun her around. Memory, now with blood red hair, backed into the shadows against the wall and ran away.

Eloryn ran after her. She caught up with her in a new hallway lit with a strange crisp brightness. A different Memory, different age, different hair color. She stood by a door left slightly ajar, sneering and picking her nails. Words floated out from three adults within.

"I'm sorry. We thought we could handle it. But she's..." said a woman on one side of a desk.

"She's too much for us to deal with. She's just too old, too troubled," the man next to her said, holding her hand. An older man across the desk nodded and smiled as if he heard nothing new.

Eloryn reached for Memory. "Mem, please, can you hear me?"

A flash of a storeroom filled with brooms, mops and colored containers jumped in front of Eloryn, snagging the breath in her throat. A large silhouette approached her, making soothing noises.

Then Eloryn was alone in darkness. No, not alone. There was a bed next to her with someone in it. Body curled as tight as any could be. Suppressed whispers of sobbing came from the youngest Memory Eloryn had seen yet. Tiny and blonde, she looked just like Eloryn had when she was ten, except for the hair being cut short around her ears. The scene shifted before her eyes, but remained the same. Only Memory's age, Memory's hair changed. Then again, older still. A small boy with dark hair sat awkward and silent at the end of the bed. He reached a hand out toward the huddled, weeping Memory, but pulled it back without

touching her. Staring at his hand, he clenched it into a small fist.

Eloryn pressed both hands against her chest. She struggled a slow breath from the stabbing quick gasps that were overtaking her. The first time she'd tried to heal Memory, she couldn't get in at all, blocked by a barrier of distrust and fear. Now she understood why. These visions made no sense, but sheer grief overflowed from them. *Is this the suffering that made her what she is? We were born just moments apart. If I had been first instead...*

Eloryn's heart beat an erratic shiver through her body. She backed up against a wall, the next fragment of vision taking her completely off guard.

Memory, the Mem she knew. Sixteen years old, black and pink hair, wearing the very same clothes she first appeared to Eloryn in. Her open knife dropped on the floor. The wide-set man yelled and scowled and beat her and beat her and beat her until the world exploded around them.

Eloryn was back on the street.

She rolled forward and heaved terrified sobs. *This is no good. These aren't Memory, they're just visions of her past.* Caught up in these nightmares she wasn't going to reach Memory in time.

Again, a black and pink haired Memory appeared, running down the street with a wild look of glee on her face. Her pockets were filled and heavy. Eloryn didn't chase this time, but young Will did, struggling to keep up. A man came out of the doorway they'd run through, bellowing at them as the stallholder had in the markets where they met Roen.

She followed them with her gaze and saw a flash of strange blackness in an alleyway they passed.

Reaching for hope, she ran into the alley. She saw another Memory, backed into a corner, huddled into herself. Memory in a dress, hair flickering between blonde and black. Eyes achingly wide but lacking awareness. Shivering but not moving.

Eloryn raced to her. The world shook with another heaving beat, building and falling. A void of blackness pushed outwards from Memory. A nothingness, forcing the world away, forcing the visions away, forcing Eloryn away.

"Mem, please," Eloryn cried. "Please hear me, let me help you. You have to wake up. You have to get up or you'll die."

Memory remained unmoved, uncaring.

Eloryn had come looking for something she could heal, some wound

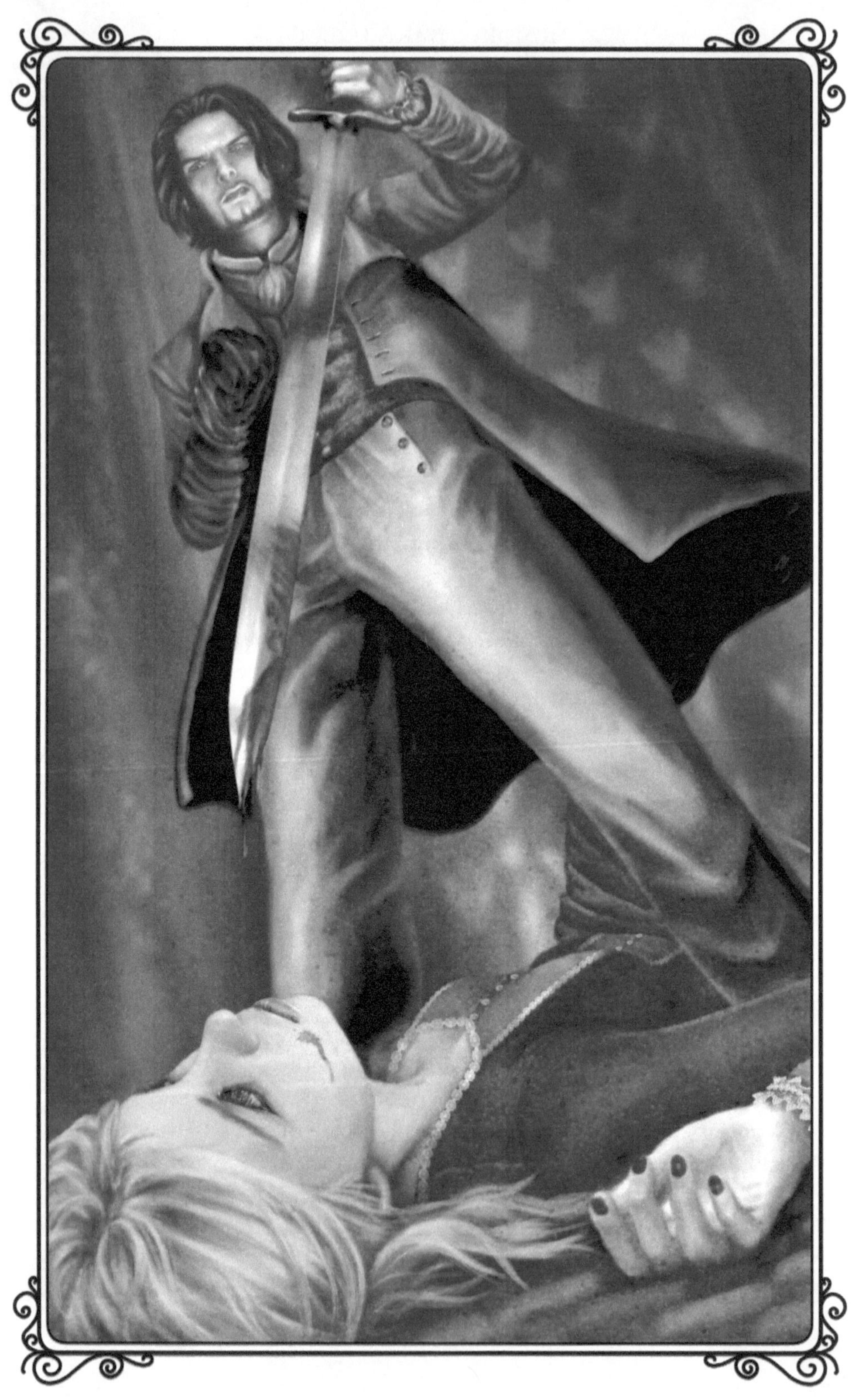

she could fix, to wake Memory up and save her; leaving her body behind since she wasn't able to reach her any other way. But there was nothing here she could repair. No wound, no physical blow had caused this.

Eloryn reached for her. The expanding darkness struck her back. Flung against the opposite wall, she slumped into piles of grey refuse. "Mem, I can't lose you too. I don't know what to do. I knew by coming here I couldn't leave again without your help. But I wouldn't leave you anyway, even if I could. Not to this. Not alone."

Memory's mouth opened a crack. Her bottom lip quivered. Eloryn tumbled on top of her and held her, no longer pushed away.

Squeaking, hysterical whispers flowed from Memory's mouth. "It's too much, too much, all at once, everything, it's too much, I can't, everything, I can't."

The memories. A lifetime of memories, all at once. Eloryn cursed herself that she hadn't realized, in all her theories and planning, what that would mean. But how could she have known the nightmare these memories held?

Squeezing Memory in her arms, she tore over options and outcomes, racing through them. She could not slow the intake of these memories, or help Memory accept them in some other way. Neither would be fast enough to save her body as well. Maybe she could force them all away again, but if she did, they might be lost forever.

"I'm so sorry. I promised you I would get your memories back, but more than that I want you to live," Eloryn said. Her tears dripped into her sister's hair.

Memory looked up at her with a shaking mouth. "I don't want to, I can't like this..."

Eloryn hesitated, even while knowing any moment could be their last, unsure how time flowed here or what happened outside. "I'll make it stop. But then you have to wake up, you have to wake up now!"

Something dripped on her face and she tasted the metal of blood. Memory's chest burned, inside and out, the knife she kept stashed there heated to scalding. Deafening sounds of battle smacked into her, thrumming through the floor she lay on and ringing in her ears. Memory's eyes snapped open. Her gaze raced up the wet sword pointed at her chest to an arm that lifted and tensed and a darkly handsome face torn with

a gruesome snarl.

She rolled across the floor and the sword stabbed down into the carpet. Thayl roared.

Throwing her legs off the edge of the dais, she stood from a crouch in time to duck again when Thayl swung the sword at her, screaming violently. She stumbled away from him.

"You lost it all. It was better left with me!"

Memory raced to fill confusing blanks in her mind propped between raging panic and anger. She'd cut off Thayl's hand, then only blind pain filled the next gap. *Did I faint? Likely. I did just sever someone's limb.* Blood drained from her so quickly she almost fainted again. *Oh my God I severed someone's limb.* Memory gritted her teeth. She did what she had to do, to stop Thayl, to get her memories and soul back. So where were they?

Something else was happening that she didn't understand. Her mouth spoke of its own accord, a language she didn't even know. She could feel a familiar presence inside her, another consciousness she'd tasted before. *Eloryn. My sister. How?*

"Soulless demon!" Thayl hissed at her. One of his arms ended in a bound and dripping stump, the other with the sword lunging into attack again. Memory did not step back.

His sword stabbed left and she shifted right, moving smoother and faster than she knew she could. Magic from Eloryn's words, spoken with her own mouth, flowed through her and made her stronger. She took Thayl by his sword hand with one of her own. Twisting the wrist, bones crunched under her fingers. The sword dropped. She forced her other palm up under his chin with teeth shattering strength. Thayl slammed onto his back.

She snarled and picked up the sword.

"Guards, guards to me!" Thayl screamed.

A dozen of his closest men scrambled toward their King. Memory's hand shifted, her mouth still moving rapidly. A solid rush of wind blew the soldiers back into the wreck of battle.

Memory choked on the words. Her own blank hole of pain was being filled, flooded. Eloryn's grief and rage poured in, overwhelming her. Her hand around the sword twitched and lifted mechanically. She stared at it open mouthed, not having willed the action herself. She could feel her face turn feral, fighting with her own emotions and Eloryn's.

"Lory, please stop."

He deserves this. The words screamed inside her, but weren't her own.

She shrieked so madly Thayl froze where he'd fallen, staring at her as though he saw a real demon.

The bronze sword swiped across as if drawn to a magnet within Thayl's neck. The tip pressed into the soft flesh. Thayl gagged, waiting with wild, terrified eyes.

You're not a murderer Lory, not you.

Her body shuddered, battling against a will not hers. She screamed aloud, "ELORYN!"

The sword fell from her hands.

Memory and Thayl stared at each other for a long moment. Thayl brought his bandaged stump up against his chest, grasping it with his hand.

Memory grimaced then forced her face still, staring down at him. "Game over."

His eyes flickered across to the sword that lay on the ground beside him.

"Don't think I can't take you out with this if I need to," Memory hissed, pulling her hand into a fist in front of him. She kicked the sword out of his reach.

Memory turned to the brawling chaos of the hall. Seeing their King lying prone on the dais, more castle guards rushed at her.

"Stop!" she bellowed, in a voice loud enough to crack plaster scrolling from the walls.

Throughout the hall, fighters stumbled in shock. Some turned from their battles and were taken advantage of by those not distracted by the loud interruption.

"I said stop. Now. Everyone!" Words continued to flow from her, from Eloryn, feeding on the fire within her. She crumbled every blade, every piece of armor and metal held by men in the room.

The fighting stopped.

Men stumbled out of motion, confused. Despite wary glances to others around them, all attention turned her way. The small girl, standing over the defeated king, looked out at the sea of blood-spattered faces. She didn't know which side was which. She didn't think half of them knew either.

What now, Lory?

You know.

Memory pulled herself up straight and called out into the hall. "Thayl is finished. The Maellan heir is back. If you're not happy with that you

better get the hell out of here now."

A brief moment of stillness passed then a third of the men in the hall turned and fled. They pushed away through the shell shocked crowd, running in blind panic. No one tried to stop them.

The remaining men turned to her with the look of awaiting their next order. A dozen or so pushed to the front, approaching her. She tensed, but they stopped below the dais and made the hand symbol she had seen Eloryn make. The resistance.

All eyes on her, Memory stuttered under the pressure. She pointed to Thayl. "Someone, come tie him up already."

A wiry man with sweat soaked sandy hair came forward, scooping a dropped pair of manacles from the ground on his way. He gave her a short bow. "If you serve the Maellan heir, then I serve you. I am Peirs. I'm what you might call the leader of this mob, if they've ever been enough to lead."

She nodded to the older man, swaying from the after-burn of adrenaline. "Thanks, for helping."

Peirs shackled Thayl's feet, shaking his head with an incredulous smile. "Thanks are all to you. A child who defeated this monster that no man could, and did it..." Peirs paused and his grin widened. "Single handed."

One of Piers' men threw him a tasseled rope from a nearby curtain. He tied it about Thayl's arms. Thayl sat slumped and silent, eyes turned so far down they were almost closed. His body quaked with visible tension. No longer a monster. Just a man now.

"It wasn't just me." Memory looked out into the unfamiliar crowd and stepped off the dais.

Peirs began calling out orders and all guards within the room looked to him. Faces all around, but no one she knew. The room was thick with people but they cleared a path for her, letting her through.

Through the murmurings and movement she heard Roen's voice, pleading. She picked up her pace. A crowd of wizards huddled in the back corner of the hall. She ran up to them but they didn't move for her as the rest of the room did.

She clawed through between them, pushing through despite their shocked exclamations.

In their midst, Roen knelt over the top of Eloryn. He bent down with his forehead on hers, hands on her shoulders, lifting and shaking her. "El, please," he whispered, his voice strangled.

Hayes knelt beside him, holding Eloryn's wrist, feeling for a pulse. He tried to move Roen out of the way and Roen pushed him back with a grunt, slamming the older man against the wall. He turned back to Eloryn, pulling her up into his arms.

"Stop this madness and let me see to her!" Hayes spat.

Memory knelt next to Roen and caught his eye. She put her hand on his, uncurled his fingers from a tight fist, and gave him a timid smile. His head tilted and he stared, all grief and confusion. He blinked, taking in who she was, and moved away from Eloryn without hesitation.

Hayes tried to take his place and Roen forced him back with his whole body. "Not you."

Eloryn was deathly white. Memory smiled wryly. "I hope you know what you're doing, sleeping beauty."

She lowered herself down. Her blonde hair draped into her sister's and she kissed her on the forehead.

A breathless moment stretched until Memory's chest ached. Eloryn's body gave a terrifying shudder. Green eyes opened. Eloryn blinked and her natural pink returned to her cheeks.

"There she is, back where she should be," Memory said.

"I knew you could do it," Eloryn propped herself onto her elbows. Her head hung weakly but she smiled.

"Smart ass," Memory muttered. She shifted back off her knees and helped Eloryn up. "We did it."

Memory heard a shaking breath pour out of Roen. She smiled at him with a pouting bottom lip. He stared back blankly.

Released by Roen, Hayes dusted his black and purple suit down emphatically and turned his attention to Eloryn.

"Waylan, Bors, Madoc, see to guarding Thayl. The rest of you help Peirs getting this rabble under control," Hayes said, taking Eloryn's hands out of Memory's as though she needed further support.

Eloryn straightened up, nodding to someone across the hall. Memory followed her gaze and saw Yvainne tipping her head in return. Her form already grew transparent. Her eyes turned to Memory in a cold glare like a warning before she disappeared.

The grey flock broke apart, each taking a moment to bow to Eloryn before moving away.

Throughout the room, order became visible again. Men grouped

into rows. Some rows moved across the floor, where bodies blended red with the carpet, aiding and clearing as they went.

Memory felt a dull weight form in her as she stared at the bodies. *Did I do right? Would more have died if the fighting began while Thayl still had magic?* A deep exhaustion filled her, every muscle spent and aching. She swallowed away the feeling and searched her gaze over every corner of the room.

"Where's Will?"

Roen's face had locked back into a frown. He lifted a hand to her face, and wiped his thumb gently beside her mouth, fingers lingering on her cheek. When he pulled it away it was red with blood. He spoke quietly. "Lost him for most of the fight, but when everything stopped I saw him drag himself out through a window."

"He didn't stay? Was he OK?" Memory asked in a squeak. Her own hand came up and cupped her cheek involuntarily. It didn't hurt. The blood wasn't hers.

"Injured, but didn't seem too badly. He's a strong one. Shackles gone with the rest of the metal." Roen's lips twisted to the side, not really a smile. "I don't think he likes to be seen by so many people."

Memory nodded unenthusiastically.

Hayes still held Eloryn by a hand, and put another in the middle of her back, leading her away. "It's a miracle you survived, your Highness. Such a reckless plan from that girl. But we finally have success against the tyrant Thayl. Now we can work together on ensuring our future and that of the kingdom."

Eloryn pulled away from him. "Wizard Councilor Hayes, I'm sorry I have left you uninformed, but that girl is my twin sister. Maellan heir as much as I."

Memory smiled at him when he turned to her in shock. She considered poking out her tongue, but decided against it.

"Her appearance; I thought it some magic ploy, a part of her plan. Her interaction with Thayl... Don't play tricks. Tell me how it can be so?"

Eloryn sighed, looking to Memory and Roen as she talked. "Hayes, we thank you for the help you've given us, and have trust in you for the help you'll continue to provide. I know this is only the beginning for what must be done for Avall, but please understand, we've been through more than you can imagine. Indulge us our whims a little longer. There will be time for it all later."

Hayes glowered for a moment, then bowed his head. "And what is it time for now, Your Highness?"

"Highnesses," Eloryn corrected.

"Highnesses."

"Mem, what is it time for now?"

Memory looked across the room to a wide arch window. Warm rays of morning light spilled in, bringing a contentment too overpowering to fight. She smiled at Eloryn. "It's time for bed."

Peirs gave priority to assigning the best of his men to the care of the twins. Ten men led Memory, Eloryn and Roen through the castle to their requested destination.

They walked silently down long corridors lined with suits of armor and tall stained glass windows. Memory gawked openly. She wished she had a camera then reminded herself this was her home now. *Home.* Servants gossiped together at a distance and stared at the passing escort. Some bowed and kneeled. No one gave them any trouble.

They reached wide double doors at the end of a corridor that had been chained closed. The largest guard dispatched the padlock with a sharp blow from the hilt of his sword. This part of the castle had been closed off, but they continued through the uncared for hallways over tattered carpets, up stairs with creaking, dusty banisters.

They stopped at a doorway carved with roses and painted ivory white. Memory ran her hand over the designs, feeling them smooth and glossy under her fingers. The paint here was not cracked or chipped. It smelled fresh. She put her hand around the cold brass handle and turned, clicking the latch.

The guards took up position, flanking either side of the door.

Memory motioned to Eloryn, who stepped through into Loredanna's chambers.

Memory followed her in. No dust settled on the fine pale furniture and silken upholstery. Nothing was torn or blemished. Jewelry and hairbrushes were laid out on the dresser as though their mother had used the room yesterday. It didn't have the appearance of a room recently

cleaned, but one that had always been well looked after.

Above a chaise lounge hung a life size portrait of Loredanna in a thick, ornate frame. It showed her not much older than her daughters, dressed for coronation in all finery, including the Maellan crested medallion.

The room smelt of soap and roses, and Memory brushed her hand over the petals of a fresh cut bunch beside the bed.

Memory thought back to how Thayl had held her when she walked into his dream rose-garden, when he thought she was her mother. Although the thought still made her skin crawl she suddenly wished she had reacted in some other, unknown way.

She coughed lightly. "At least it's clean in here."

Eloryn stood in the doorway, staring in only. She nodded, eyebrows pinched as she shared looks with her twin. Roen hadn't crossed the threshold.

Memory drifted back to them.

Roen shifted on his feet. He hadn't said a thing since telling her about Will, and he seemed to be having trouble again now. He leant in closer to them, whispering low, "I worry for trusting your safety to these strangers."

Memory giggled at him, tilting her head. "What would you worry for? We're safe now, we did it. The three of us are unbeatable, and everyone knows it." She raised her voice cheekily at the end.

Roen's mood didn't crack. "I won't be staying."

Memory's head snapped back up straight, and she furrowed her eyebrows deeply as though doing so would let her read his mind.

Eloryn stammered, "But, you said you wouldn't…"

"You're safe now. I'm going back to my parents, back to-" He faltered, and cleared his throat. "Maerranton. I don't belong here."

Roen turned his head down and to the side, caramel hair falling down over his eyes.

Memory opened her mouth in outrage, but Eloryn spoke first. "Of course you have a place here, you and your parents. Their titles will be reinstated. They will be returned to court with the highest honors for all of what they gave." She shook her head at him. "Even if you weren't already a Prince, you'd have earned the title."

Roen's shoulders shuddered, and a tear rolled off his cheek and splashed onto the floor.

Quicker than thought, Memory lashed her arms around him in a

crushing bear hug. He put his head down into her shoulder, soaking it silently, and squeezed her back with bruising strength.

Eloryn breathed raggedly next to them. Memory pried an arm off Roen and reached for her. One of Roen's arms loosed too, shaking, reaching out. Eloryn stepped into them and the three wrapped around each other tightly.

They held him until he stilled. And then a little longer.

He pulled away from them, hands lingering in theirs, his eyes red but dry.

"I will go. I want to see my parents returned safely. But I will come back." A small smile softened his face. "Memory. Eloryn." The smile continued to grow. He bowed deeply to both of them then departed.

Memory closed the door behind him. With mirrored movement she and Eloryn pulled back covers on each side of the bed and tucked themselves in. They lay face to face, holding hands between them like children in a fairytale.

Eloryn closed her eyes. "I'm so sorry you didn't get your memories back. They might be lost forever, but I won't stop trying to get them back for you, if you want."

Memory watched her sister's frowning face. "I'm not so worried. I found out my name, where I was, and know who I am. Found all the family and friends I dreamed of. Hell, I even got myself a castle. I'll make a new home, new memories."

Whatever else might still be wrong with me, wherever the lost parts of my broken soul are, for now at least I'm alive, can live, here with my family. She stared over Eloryn's shoulder, where daylight brightened the diamond cut glass window of the balcony doors. Outside a thorny vine grew around the balustrade. The silhouette of a wild young man perched on it in front of the sun. She smiled. "Besides, things never just disappear. They have to go somewhere, right?"

Eloryn's eyes fluttered back open again. She looked both shocked and accusing. "You found out your name? When? What is it? What am I to call you now?"

Memory smiled and closed her eyes. "Memory. Just call me Memory."

BOOK TWO
HOPE'S REIGN

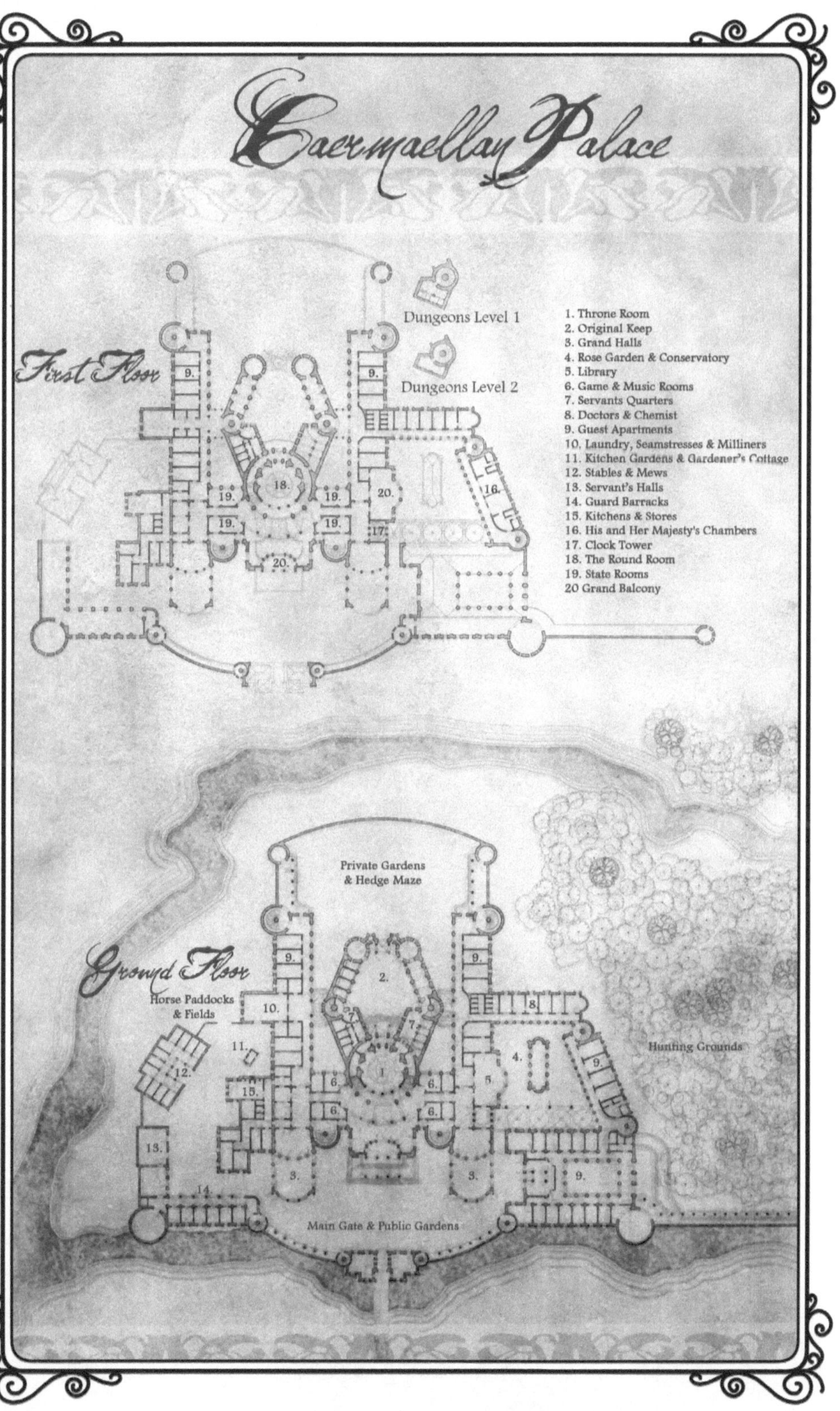

Caermaellan Palace
First Floor
Dungeons Level 1
Dungeons Level 2
1. Throne Room
2. Original Keep
3. Grand Halls
4. Rose Garden & Conservatory
5. Library
6. Game & Music Rooms
7. Servants Quarters
8. Doctors & Chemist
9. Guest Apartments
10. Laundry, Seamstresses & Milliners
11. Kitchen Gardens & Gardener's Cottage
12. Stables & Mews
13. Servant's Halls
14. Guard Barracks
15. Kitchens & Stores
16. His and Her Majesty's Chambers
17. Clock Tower
18. The Round Room
19. State Rooms
20 Grand Balcony
Ground Floor
Private Gardens & Hedge Maze
Horse Paddocks & Fields
Hunting Grounds
Main Gate & Public Gardens

CHAPTER ONE

Living in the castle with her friends wasn't turning out to be the Happily Ever After that Memory thought it would be. With skirts hitched up and heart fluttering with adrenaline, she bolted across the lawn and pushed through a gap between dense hedges and the garden wall. A final glance back showed a page, handmaiden, and guard stumbling down the palace steps, bewildered at her disappearance. Spying through the leaves, Memory grinned. If she knew it would be this easy to lose the entourage, she would have done it sooner.

Life had become an ongoing parade of public appearances, formal dress, legal documents, rehearsals, posing for portraits, fairy representatives, and the mighty task of rebuilding the kingdom of Avall. It gave Memory the distinct sensation of drowning. No time was left to just be herself. Whoever that was.

Moments ago, escorts had come to chaperone her to yet another meeting. *Yet another meeting. I couldn't stand another meeting!* Something snapped and she just dashed off when they were looking the other way. A tactic they obviously weren't expecting. And she'd become well practiced at running away from people since returning to Avall.

Memory slowed from a jog to a relaxed walk. Light rain misted the air, weighing down her pale hair and the wide-skirted gown better suited to a ballroom. A carpet of muddy leaves sloshed under foot, and the hem of the dress was already stained, but Memory didn't care. Water

beaded on soft ferns and she caressed the fronds, like wet velvet under her touch. *Silence.* She listened and smiled. *I've missed you.*

Memory wandered farther into the long strip of woodland that spread into the distance on the eastern side of the palace. Hunting grounds, left wild and ancient and full of life, including one new resident. Or at least Memory assumed Will now lived somewhere in these woods. Neck arched, she peered into the rain-blackened branches of the sturdy oaks but saw no sign of him. She frowned. *Mental note- must find out where and how Will lives.* Memory wondered if she'd come this way with the hope to see him, or just because being lost in a forest still seemed more familiar than the gold-leafed walls of the kingdom's finest castle. With Will, there was no pretense, no pandering. He was her only link to a forgotten past and distant life. She wished he'd visit more often.

Memory felt like the kingdom's newest toy, getting propped up next to Eloryn on display as the visible face of change for Avall, while behind the scenes Hayes and the Wizard's Council dealt with pulling the kingdom back together. The Council kept the information about where Memory had been on strict lockdown, letting people assume she had been with Eloryn and Alward the whole time, but rumors of how she defeated Thayl spread fast. The twin with the strange hair, name, and behavior was the hottest topic in Avall. The most people gossiped about Eloryn was to say "how lovely" she was.

Hayes and his cronies also treated Memory like some sort of arcane oddity to be studied. Her first visit with them, which had been advertised as being friendly and social, turned into a civilized interrogation full of questions she couldn't answer about things she didn't understand. Where did she get her powers, where had she been, what did Thayl's ritual do to her? They wanted her to use magic for them, to observe her. She didn't want anyone studying her too closely, worried about what they would see.

Memory swore as something sharp jammed into the side of her satin slipper. The stupidly big skirts prevented her from even seeing her own feet and the source of pain. Memory glared at the lacey gown, now woven with twigs and leaves. She was not dressed for this. *Run-away-and-plan-the-rest-later proves yet again to be a bad fallback strategy.*

Trying to settle the voluminous skirts, Memory sat on a nearby fallen trunk and brought the injured foot up into view. A sharp stick had wedged itself into the sole of her shoe. She pulled her knife from where it had been stashed in her corset, flicked the blade out, and levered the stick free with the point. *Eloryn would probably be able to just ask the stick to remove itself, not that she'd be hanging out with me in a forest anymore.* Memory sighed. Why did she think things would remain the way they were? Just her, Eloryn, Roen, and Will looking after each other. They'd bonded under extreme conditions, and now that they were safe, Memory could feel the group drifting separate ways.

The princesses' every minute was managed, and when Memory thought things couldn't get worse, Hayes sprung a new surprise on her. On top of the stress of the upcoming coronation ceremony, he insisted she had to go back to school. To that horrid land where bullies teased her hair colors and the only place to reliably skip class smelled like a urinal. She always hated school. She...

Chewing gum smooshed into the back of her head. The horrified disgust on her face when she turned around made the pointy faced boy behind her laugh. Gus. He was so getting unfriended.

"What's the problem? It's the same color as your hair anyway," he said.

Her hands became fists. "Nice one. By that logic I guess it means you won't notice when I stick your head in a toilet because you're just a piece of—"

Opening her eyes, Memory clutched at the rough bark of the log to steady herself. The flashback was far too vivid to have been only imagination. Gus's weasel-like features were still clear, and she could almost smell the dirty-sock scent of the school corridor. A shiver danced through her limbs simply by knowing what these were. Memories.

She replayed them like hitting the previous chapter button over and over on a remote, savoring them. She could remember something. School. Just a tiny fragment, but it was there, and it belonged to her. A low giggle started huffing its way out of her mouth, growing as excitement took over. She had to get back and tell Eloryn. A wide grin cracked her face. She closed the knife and jumped up to head back to the palace.

Memory skipped over woodland debris, ducking under dripping branches and trying not to slip in haste when she ran face first into something hard. A sharp sting shot through her nose, and she clutched at it with both hands. Eyes watering, she stumbled backward, only to hit something behind her. She blinked, trying to see what blocked the way, but found nothing. With arms outstretched, she tried all directions. The air seemed to spring back, like pushing on a firm mattress.

"Look what I caught," an ethereal voice whinnied through the cool air. "Pretty as a princess."

Creeping from behind some trees, a creature approached Memory. From a distance it looked like a little girl, but as it drew near Memory could see it wasn't human at all.

The creature moving forward twinkled from rain, which formed pearls on the fine layer of white fur that covered a feminine body. Bovine ears and curled horns protruded from a head of wooly hair, and long animal-like legs ended in cloven hooves. Was there even a little tail swishing to and fro? The creature stared straight at Memory with two nebulous black eyes and grinned.

Black eyes… does that mean unseelie fae? But she's so beautiful. It must have been some type of fae, something that had a classification, a name, a place in either the seelie or unseelie courts. Eloryn would know. Memory just knew the creature was gorgeous and terrifying.

She held her breath, remaining still as though movement would provoke it. Would the Pact protect her from this? Maybe it was time to start paying more attention to the politics of Avall.

"So, hi," Memory said. "Nice to meet you, I guess. I'm just heading off that way, as soon as I can move again. Are you causing that? Are you allowed to do that?"

The grin on the furry fae spread wider, and she tilted her head down to the ground. Memory's gaze followed.

Stupid skirts. She hadn't even noticed past all their ruffles that she'd walked directly into a fairy ring. She'd heard that wasn't a good thing to do. Memory pushed against the force that encircled her where the white-spotted red toadstools poked from the ground.

The fae giggled and danced around the circle. "My fairy ring, my territory. You're mine, mine, mine."

"Look, let me go, and I'm sure we can work something out. I'm, like, someone important here in Avall. And we're both reasonable," Memory paused, "people, right?"

The fae stopped and looked her up and down.

"I know who you are," the fawn sang like a nursery rhyme, "Little ticking time-bomb came home from Hell."

"What do you mean? And how do you even know what a time bomb is anyway?"

"We fae, we travel, see many things. Or we did, before the human plague poisoned the world." The fae grimaced. "Now, I could keep you as a pet," she began, stroking her furry chin, "but humans are so greedy and unclean."

The snowy fae poked Memory in the shoulder. Memory startled, flicking the knife in her hand open again and holding it up protectively.

The fae snorted. "Cold iron. You stink of it. That knife will get you into trouble, princess. Just try and use it on me, I'll Brand you faster than lickety-split. My territory means no Pact for you." The fae bent in close. Memory could see her face reflected in the creature's wide black eyes. "No, no, no. We'll find a use for you. You look like you could dance well. I could make you dance for eternity. Dance, dance, dance so beautifully."

Gulp. Time for an escape strategy. Memory took stock of her assets and disadvantages. Corset strung too tight. Skirts too big. Rights under the Pact lost. Unable to use her fae-burning knife or be Branded. No one actually knew where she was. Will hadn't seemed to have noticed his Memory-is-in-danger cue. Veil doors took too long to cast. Other magic was unpredictable and scary. *Assets, where are you?*

Memory made a display of putting her knife away.

"I'm sorry. I'm new here and don't know how things work yet. Is there any chance you can just let this one time slip, and if you ever catch me again I'll be yours for reals? What harm could there be in letting me go?"

"What harm?" the fawn cried, sounding like a whinny. "This from the girl child who pointed an *iron* knife at me? A jest! Stinky, ticking time-bomb means no harm!"

The fae straightened up to her full height, just taller than Memory's five-foot-nothing stature. "Perhaps, perhaps I will turn you into something harmless. That would be the best thing for everyone."

Okay, magic it is then. Memory hated using magic, the way it burned through her and left her empty and singed. But she had to get away. She prepared herself as the fae seemed to come to a decision.

"I'll turn you… into a flower!" The fae lunged forward, grabbing Memory's shoulders tight. She flinched backwards, lifting both fists as a shield. Releasing the flame of magic, she closed her eyes and hoped for the best, the only technique she'd mastered so far.

Magic exploded. Gusting winds and the disconcerting feel of the Veil pulled at her, but Memory kept her eyes squeezed closed. She waited, breath held, and after a few moments she couldn't feel the fae's grasp anymore. *And I don't think I feel like a flower, not that I'd know what being a flower felt like.* She peeled one eyelid open, and the sight made the other eyelid snap wide alongside it.

"What the…"

CHAPTER TWO

She was back in her room. Back in the castle.

Memory doubled over, breathing through the shock and pain of the instant, and unexpected, Veil transportation. *What in the holy horse balls was that?* That was not what she meant to do, but then her magic had always been as predictable as it had been explainable. The Veil door was something that she could do if she concentrated to control it, but to do it instinctively, or worse accidentally, made her stomach contract.

A shiver built in her back and shuddered out through her limbs, bringing with it a cold sweat. *Calm down. You're okay, you're still here,* she told herself firmly, but panic kept debating that with her. What if she wasn't? Was she even in the same time? What if she got lost in the Veil again for another sixteen years?

She straightened up and analyzed the room. *My room,* she reminded herself. It looked the same as it had that morning, still a total mess. Eloryn had ended up in Loredanna's well-maintained suite, and the pristine, ornate setting suited her, but Memory couldn't handle it. It felt like stepping right into the shoes of a mother she'd never known.

Instead, Memory took the adjoining chambers, which would have been the king's, her father's. She knew less about him than she did her mother. The royal bloodline was through Loredanna, and he was just some sorry soul whom the Wizard's Council picked to be her husband, and he only lived another nine months after that. His chambers had not

been well kept. Shards of broken vases covered the patchy rug and torn paintings, shrouded in cobwebs, sat where they'd fallen off the walls. This entire wing of the castle had been closed up during the sixteen years of Thayl's rule, with only Loredanna's chambers being cared for by Thayl himself.

The debris had been cleared out by servants, and the castle steward argued that room should be properly renovated before Memory moved in. She preferred it like this though, a clean slate. She intended to decorate the room with personal mementos, make it her own, but so far her only belonging was her old wallet that Will had returned to her.

No one had snuck in and renovated the room, or even made the bed, so she guessed she managed to come right back. But this was something that needed to be confirmed. She needed to see her sister and tell her what had happened, both the good news and the bad. How to share the news was another matter. *Hey, I remembered stuff, but then got caught by a furry fairy and Veil doored back to my room without meaning to! Yay?* Memory doubted her twin would take this new installment of weird very well.

She walked to the corner of the sitting room and heard muffled murmurings coming through the patchy wallpapered wall. She knocked hesitantly and the sound stopped. A second later Eloryn called her welcome. Her voice sounded tiny.

"Lory, you won't believe what I've got to tell you." Memory opened the doorway that looked like a section of wall, joining their chambers. It wasn't really secret, just designed to fit in. Nerves twinged as she thought how to share the news with her twin, but the sight in the room chased the idea out entirely.

Eloryn's neat and pretty chambers were now cluttered with wooden chests of all shapes and sizes. Some were open, showing folded clothing and books. Mostly books. Eloryn sat on the floor, surrounded by the boxes, her face splotchy red and wet.

"What happened?" Memory stood frozen for a second then managed to step through the boxes and kneel in front of her sister. Eloryn squinted through tears.

"Hayes arranged to have it all brought here. That's what the meeting you missed was about. All of our belongings, mine and Alward's." She held a man's shirt, hands like claws, gripping it tight.

"It's... a lot of books." Memory bit her tongue. She had to do better than that, be a better friend, a better sister, but felt so awkward.

"It's not even all of them. They kept everything that falls within the Council's legal domain - books on magic, the speaking mirror, and all of Alward's research into the Veil. I understand that the mirror and books had belonged to the Council to start with. Alward took them with him when he went into hiding. I'm not ungrateful. It's so moving that they went to such trouble to bring this all to me, but I would have liked to see Alward's research again. I wanted to see his handwriting again." Eloryn's small body shook as a loud sob ended her sentence. She covered her eyes with a forearm, blonde hair shimmering as she shook with silent sobs.

Memory had so many things to ask her twin about accidental magic, the fairy ring, and the black-eyed fae. She wanted to celebrate her memories returning. She paused for a moment and looked at her sister.

Memory leaned forward and wrapped Eloryn in a tight hug. The fabric of their skirts rustled against each other and puffed out like they were sitting in clouds. Eloryn put her head on Memory's shoulder and wept quietly.

"Mem, why is your dress all muddied? What did you want to tell me?" Eloryn mumbled.

"Nothing to worry about." Memory squeezed Eloryn and let her cry.

It was like some kind of cruel joke, but she was there, really there, standing right in front of Thayl's cell.

Memory's lip twitched in confused anger. She hadn't known where Thayl was being kept. She didn't want to know, as long as he was kept away from her. She had just been wandering the castle, and her traitorous feet led down the cold stone steps into the wisp-lit depths of the dungeons. Guards nodded as she walked by, unlocking gates, watching curiously but not daring to stop her. She just walked and found herself there.

She stood and glared. Thayl sat on a cot in the furthest corner of the room, back against the rough cut wall, hunched over, face hidden by dark wavy hair. Memory could see he'd been unable to shave. His right hand hung down on one side. *Right arm,* Memory corrected herself. Thanks to her, he no longer had a hand there. It was still bandaged, blackened by blood and dirt from the cell. A thick, rotting stench filled the space. His clothes, the same he'd worn the morning she'd cut off that

hand, looked grey now, not the rich blue and gold they once were. *Hadn't he been given anything else to wear?* She cringed off a feeling of sympathy, twitching it away like a spider crawling up her arm.

Thayl reacted to the movement, his head jerking up. He stared at her for a moment then rested his head again on his knees. "Come to gloat? I guess this was inevitable. Say your worst, demon."

Caught off guard, Memory rambled, "I'm not. I didn't come here for anything. I didn't mean to come here at all. I was looking for Roen."

"I don't think you'll find him down here."

"I mean, I went to try and see Roen, but Isabeth says he's not here, gone off on some trip all of a sudden without telling me. I couldn't find him and then I... I ended up here." *Why am I telling him this? What am I doing here? Why am I not leaving?* Memory looked to the stone stairwell then back to the cell. This was the only cell down these stairs, separate from the rest of the prison. A private high-security dungeon for the most hated man in Avall. Thick gridded copper squares let her see in clearly to the simple stone room. A wooden tray had been slid under a small gap at the front, with just one piece of bread the size of her small fist. She wondered if he'd eaten the rest, or if this was all he got.

Thayl sounded tired, any bait in his words overwhelmed, making him almost seem interested. "Surely you have other people to see. What about your sister? Or that savage pet of yours?"

"Will's not savage! And it's your fault how he is now. He wouldn't have had to grow up like that if it wasn't for you." Memory shivered. It wasn't only Thayl's fault. She couldn't help but feel guilty too. "He hasn't been around much. Being around too many people freaks him out."

She had thought of looking for Will, but it seemed he could only be found when he wanted to be. She knew he was still around, on guardian angel duty, but she hadn't exactly been in any danger lately, until the furry-fae encounter, and then he didn't show. He'd only visited a few times these last weeks and seemed to be getting more withdrawn. His sprite friends were also still hanging around, keeping an eye on her. Memory tried talking to them once, but they treated her like toxic waste. And Eloryn was always so busy, much like Memory should have been if she wasn't dodging handmaidens and duties. She needed someone to talk to, someone to share her big news, and found no one to turn to. But that didn't mean she wanted to talk to Thayl. She balled her hands into fists.

"Like you can talk anyway, you're not far from savage yourself.

Doing what you did to the woman you claimed to love."

Thayl half smiled, as though he were expecting this. The smile didn't reach his eyes, still as dark and sad as when she'd first seen them at Duke Lanval's estate. "Not just one."

"Not one... who what now?" Memory's raised voice faltered in confusion.

"Not just one woman I loved, but two." Thayl shook his head, the oily mess of his dark hair glossy in the low light of the cell. "It's not surprising you were drawn here. You don't know, but when you were born I had a sixteen-year-old sister. Another beautiful life sacrificed as part of the ritual to take your power. That bloody ritual. That's why you're here."

Memory shook her head, not understanding, not sure she wanted to understand.

"The ritual bound us together, you and I. I barely feel it now without my hand, but I know it's still there." Thayl tapped his chest. On the same place on Memory's body, a disfiguring scar twisted the skin. "Even if you won't acknowledge it, it's bringing you to me."

Memory stood frozen for a moment before a growling grunt of disgust burst out. "Connected to you? Make me want to barf my skin off. I wasn't drawn here, I just got lost! How could I be connected to someone who would kill his lover *and* his sister over revenge?" Memory breathed hard, snorting the anger out, but her feet remained planted.

Thayl spoke again after a long pause. "Does it help that I didn't know? I didn't kill either of them. And I didn't know they would die."

"Why should I believe you? Why are you even telling me this? You let them die. It was your fault. My mother died because of you, and you sent me away!" Memory screamed at the top of her lungs, not caring how far the words carried up the stone stairwell into the rest of the dungeon.

"It wasn't my fault!" Thayl's voice rose in return. "I made such a fool of myself in court, begging Loredanna to be with me. She refused me, in front of everyone. The Wizard's Council was so cruel. I vowed revenge on them all right there. That night the witch came to me, said she saw what happened, and that she could help. She promised me enough power to take my revenge on the Wizard's Council. Looking back, I don't know where I thought such power would come from. I should have known the cost would be so great, but I had no other way, not enough power to do anything on my own. I didn't know what my deal with her would entail. All I did was take Loredanna, my beautiful

Loredanna, to the witch, and then..." Thayl's last words shook from his mouth. He turned away.

"All you did? Then, killing my father, hunting the wizards, banning magic, and generally being evil for sixteen years, who was that? You won't even admit it, what you did to her, what you did to me! You screwed up my whole life. I hate you! I hate what you did to me!" *You stole my soul. You broke me. I'll always be broken!* Her mind kept screaming as her voice failed, and she turned away from the cell and dashed up the stairs and away from the man who took everything from her, making her as much a monster as him.

It took days for Memory to calm down after seeing Thayl. Her hands shook every time she thought about it. The worst part being that it was her own stupid fault for going there like that, talking to him. Saying she couldn't control her own actions, that it was some magical connection compelling her, made it both better and worse. She hated the idea that she wasn't in control, but being able to put the blame elsewhere brought some comfort. But the comfort had a bad aftertaste. Just like Thayl, not accepting the blame. She kept returning to what he said, wondering what was true, and denying the morbid desire to go back and learn more about the dark ritual that changed her life.

Memory thought through all of this instead of paying attention to the meeting currently underway. Her entourage had become wise to her escape tricks, and she hadn't managed to avoid this one. She sat beside Eloryn and did her best not to put her head down and fall asleep. Eloryn was engaged in the conversation, but Memory's mind roamed. The meeting room, which she'd heard called the Round Room, was part of the oldest section of the castle, the ancient stone keep the rest of the palace was built around. The high ceiling had a stained glass design of a glowing sword and light shone through, down onto the enormous ring shaped table they all currently sat around. She traced fingertips over the smooth, worn wood of the table where the colored light fell. The table looked like it had seen centuries of use.

Hayes shot her an unimpressed look at her blatant disinterest. He, Waylan, Madoc, Lambeth, Bors, and a bunch of other gray faces with names attached she hadn't managed to remember talked at her. They all

wore the same style of suit they wore when they'd first met. Rich black satin, floor-length coats with stiff collars, purple lining and trim, but the suits were new now, not aged and ragged as they had been before. They were saying something about school again. *Fantastic.*

They had explained that Thayl destroyed the university the Wizard's Council used to run in Caermaellan, Avall's capital. The university had been the place where they trained and taught future wizards, some of which became part of the Council, while others were assigned to townships to offer services throughout the islands. Other non-magical higher education was also offered there. The school was the only university of its kind in Avall before Thayl razed it to the ground as part of his hatred of all wizards.

Hayes had a strange, constipated look on his face as he announced that they would be reopening the university in the large Women's Finishing School that still operated in the city, taking over much of the grounds for their classes in magic, math, politics, and sciences.

"Your Highnesses." He nodded to Memory and Eloryn together, looking down at them over his hooked nose. "We hope to be ready for classes right after coronation. Your attendance at the school will be a sign to the populous of the return to normality and restored peace in Avall. And an opportunity to fill out any shortfalls in your own educations, of course."

Hayes didn't even try to be subtle in directing the last comment toward Memory.

"What about Will? Can he go as well?" Memory asked, trying to show interest.

"I'm not sure it would be the best place for him. The university is only open to those of noble blood," Hayes said.

Memory pursed her lips. "Will's not *NOT* noble. He's just, different. I think it would be good for him to be around more people again. He's been alone for so long. And maybe his parents where he came from were royalty? Huh? What then?"

"Mem," Eloryn spoke in her calm, quiet voice. "It would be lovely to see more of Will, but do you really think it is something he would want? We must encourage his reintegration into society but also be sensitive to his needs and undertake the process at his pace."

Memory sighed. *My sister, always right.*

"Fine, but if he wants to go, he should be allowed," Memory said.

"Same with anybody. Noble or not, shouldn't everyone have a chance to learn? Come on, guys. Thayl banned everything but really basic magic for all this time, right? Now he's gone you're still not going to let everyone use magic?"

"Respectfully, if everyone had access to higher forms of magic, what kind of world do you think this would be?" Hayes said in a mocking tone as though she could barely understand the concept.

"That's not the point. You're saying you want to limit the use of magic based on the title someone has. That's not right."

Eloryn spoke up again, and Memory hoped it would be to take her side. "It's not only about title. It's in honor of the heritage of magic. Noble families are the ones with the right to the education because it is their families who established the studies of magic, who did the hard research to confirm the wording of behests throughout history."

Memory's mouth hung wide. "I can't believe you're with them on this. It's not exactly like we've been brought up noble. I wasn't even brought up in Avall!"

"It's still in your blood. You should be eager to begin learning again. Eloryn at least had some education from Pellaine," Hayes said. Eloryn cringed slightly as Hayes continued to use Alward's old name. "It will serve her well after her coronation as queen."

"You mean Memory's coronation," Eloryn said.

Around the table, everyone froze so still it seemed as though time had stopped, apart from eyes darting from person to person, blinking through the silence.

"Memory is to be crowned queen, is she not?" Eloryn asked the room.

Hayes frowned sympathetically. "We thought it was an obvious outcome, considering your pasts. You will be crowned queen, and you will be a fine queen."

Eloryn paled, clearly shocked.

"It's okay," Memory spilled out, directing her words to Eloryn and ignoring the prickle of tears. "I don't mind. I mean, I'm not exactly queen material. I know Eloryn's got her head screwed on better than me." She should have known. It was an obvious decision. Not even a decision. It's just how things were. *What kind of queen would I be anyway? Lory already sounds like a queen.*

Eloryn shook her head and spoke firmly. "Memory is the legal heir before me. She was born first, is the elder, and was Thayl's stated heir as well."

Hayes took over again. "Memory may be legal heir for all our human reasons, but do not forget your deal with the fae, Princess Eloryn. You are required to rule, and renew the pact with them, or the consequences could be dire for all of Avall."

Eloryn dropped her head. Memory could see she hadn't thought of that.

"It is important now more than ever to maintain peace with the fae," Hayes said. "So many are leaving Avall, and those remaining are stirring, upsetting the order, acting out. They will not accept Memory as the ruler of Avall. Not the way she is."

"Then could we not both rule? We're twins. We should be together. We can do it, rule equally." Eloryn turned to face Memory, a strange desperation in her expression. *Is she scared to do it alone?*

Hayes's eyes shifted side to side, seeking his words. *Oh,* Memory thought. *They really, really don't want me as queen.*

"Of course we considered this," Waylan spoke up, kindness in his voice instantly more sincere than Hayes's. He rested his hands on his round belly as he talked. "Never before has such a thing happened, and with reason. Having two figureheads essentially divides the power, weakens the throne. Power needs to lie within one hand, a strong, unilateral decision maker who the people believe in." Waylan looked apologetically towards Memory as though the words were harsher than he'd meant. He offered her a small smile. "Memory will still be crowned and recognized officially as princess of the realm at the coronation ceremony. She can be with you and help you when you need her. This would also officially place her as heir to the throne, until as queen you have your own children as heirs, of course."

Nods around the table marked the end of the meeting, and the Wizard's Council departed. Hayes left last. Although he was the youngest of all the wizards, he carried a dragon-headed walking cane that he didn't seem to need, other than to thump on the ground as he disappeared down the hall. Eloryn and Memory remained in their chairs for a while after, silent together. Eloryn seemed to be trying to say something, but after a while she left Memory alone in the room.

Memory ran her hands over the ancient table's surface, wondering how something she didn't even want hurt so much for being taken away. *It's because no one believes I can do it. Not even me.*

CHAPTER THREE

Eloryn stood next to Roen, trying to be as quiet as possible. They'd just sent for Memory and waited in Eloryn's sitting room, watching the door. She felt more nervous than she had need to and kept glancing over at Roen for reassurance. He'd just returned from his trip and hadn't changed out of riding clothes, knee-high boots and tight leggings slightly marked with mud and caramel hair still windblown. The loose-fitting shirt he wore revealed his collarbones and strong angle of his shoulders. Eloryn's heart beat faster, and she quickly turned back to look at the door. It opened and Memory walked in.

"Happy birthday!" Eloryn and Roen shouted together, enjoying the shocked look on Memory's face.

"Happy what the... what?"

"It's our birthday." Eloryn smiled.

"Surprise," Roen added.

Memory raised her eyebrows. "Surprise the amnesiac. Fun game."

"We thought we could celebrate tonight, just the three of us. It's actually our birthday tomorrow, but tomorrow is also a day of mourning because, well..." Eloryn trailed off, not sure how to finish the sentence.

"Oh right. The whole massacre thing," Memory said.

Between Memory's lukewarm reception and the reminder of the past tragedy, there wasn't much celebrating occurring. Eloryn really wanted to do this for Memory, do something to make her happy and

feel wanted. The recent meeting with the Wizard's Council was awful, and Eloryn hated that Memory had been denied so much in her life. She wanted to give her sister something, even something small. Eloryn tried to stay positive.

"There are presents!" she said cheerfully.

Roen gave Memory a quick hug and laughed. "Just a couple of small gifts. You get the rest tomorrow. I don't know how you've missed the river of presents flowing into the castle. Still avoiding your staff, I assume?"

"Like they were itty bitty plague rats," Memory said.

Eloryn bit her lip. It was obvious Memory hadn't had any handmaidens or staff around to help her. Her pale hair was loose and barely brushed and her gown's fastenings hadn't been done up properly at the back. She was worried about how well Memory was adjusting to this world that should be her home. *Although considering I had handmaidens spend three hours this morning using hot irons to set my hair into perfect ringlets and cycle me through three gowns each day, I can understand the allure of keeping them away.* The plum velvet off the shoulder gown they had picked for her evening attire stood out as far too formal compared to Memory or Roen's outfits.

Memory kicked Roen softly in the shin. "When did you get back, anyway?"

"Only moments ago. I didn't mean to be gone so long. I went to Duke Lanval's, and he insisted I stay and travel with him when he came to Caermaellan."

"Lanval's here too? I never know anything! And don't you tell me it's my fault because I don't want a million maids fussing around me all day." Memory jabbed a finger at him.

Roen held out a large silk-covered box to her like a peace offering. She stared at it like it might bite her, but soon reached for it and a grin split across her face.

"Well, hopefully you at least know what to do with that box." Roen smirked.

Memory made a scrunched nose grin and headed over to the lounge. She sat down with the gift on her lap, tugging at the satin bow that imprisoned the box.

After pulling the lid open, an audible gasp wheezed through Memory. "My stuff? My stuff! You found my stuff!" She plunged her hands into the open box, dragged out her strange shirt, and rattled through the jewelry she used to wear in her face. She bounced a little on the edge of the seat, and looked like she could leap up and hug Roen, but became too engrossed in rediscovering her belongings. "I have stuff! That's mine!"

"Even Isabeth's dress she lent you is in there, not that you have a shortage of fine dresses now, but she wanted you to have it. I thought you might want your belongings back and was sure Lanval would have kept them safe somewhere after what happened that night."

Memory's bouncing stopped. Some dark emotion past over her face then cleared quickly. A smile returned, but the bouncing energy didn't.

Memory's words came out raspy and quiet. "Thank you."

"You're most welcome." Roen put his hands in his pockets and leaned on the wall, a bashful look on his face. Eloryn watched the whole exchange between the two of them, wishing she could have the easy friendship they had.

"He also brought back my bag I left there, and my mother's, I mean, our mother's medallion." Eloryn stumbled over the words. She'd barely had a month to get used to having a sister after a lifetime of thinking all her family were dead.

"Oh. Of course he did." Memory's face dropped again.

Eloryn fidgeted her fingers. She'd said the wrong thing. She looked across the room where the medallion of gold and rubies sat on velvet in a glass jewelry case, a priceless artifact of the Maellan family. "I'm sorry. It is ours, and if you wish for it, I'd not hesitate to let it be yours."

Memory rolled her eyes. "No, it's yours. I know it is. Always has been."

"Well, I have a gift for you, something new that can be yours," Eloryn said, biting her lower lip. She reached behind the chair and brought out another pretty box.

Memory's mouth flickered into only a slight smile this time. "Damn. I'm an idiot. We're twins. It's your birthday too, and I don't have anything for you."

"What more could I need than my friend and sister to celebrate with? Open your present, I hope you like it."

Memory pulled a well-worn book as large as her chest from the box and flicked through the pages with raised eyebrows.

"It's a history of Avall." Eloryn paused, seeing her present wasn't getting the excited reaction Roen's had. *She doesn't like it.* "I thought you may be interested to read about our history and family, and learn some more about how the kingdom operates."

"Yeah. It's good," Memory said. "All the better to not keep embarrassing

myself, right?"

Eloryn tried to stay enthusiastic, but an awkward silence descended over them.

Memory stood up and shrugged. She didn't appear to have enjoyed herself. In fact she looked sadder than Eloryn had seen for a while.

"So, I have this thing. A headache, kind of thing happening. Thanks for the birthday surprise, but I'm going to take an early night. Sorry." Memory sat the book on top of the box of her old belongings and left, apologizing again on the way out.

Eloryn sighed and looked at Roen who offered a sympathetic smile. He reached for something in his pocket.

"I have another present for you," Roen said.

"You shouldn't have. You went so far to collect our possessions back for us."

"Well, I thought Mem would be excited by her present. Her clothing is part of who she was." Roen paused, hand still in his pocket, half smiling. "Close your eyes."

Eloryn took a deep breath and let her eyelids drop. She could hear Roen approach as he kept talking. He sounded nervous, words running fast.

"It was no trouble to collect your items from Lanval's as well. And I knew the Council was bringing you your other belongings, but I believe many of your possessions have sad pasts. So I wanted to get you something new." Roen's voice caught at the end.

Eloryn felt the warmth of his hands on hers, bringing them up and placing something soft onto them. Her eyes opened and saw a gold embroidered pouch. With a nod from Roen, she tugged the drawstring open, fingers shaky from her pounding heart.

A small teardrop of rare jade on a thin strand of silver poured from the pouch into her palm. It was still warm from being kept close to Roen's body.

Roen shrugged. "Just a small token. It reminded me of your eyes."

Eloryn looked from the pendant up at him with her lower lip between her teeth. "It's beautiful."

Roen cleared his throat, looking across at the fist-sized medallion of gold. "I understand it's not a grand piece as fitting a lady of your rank, but I hope I chose something you may find occasion to wear."

Eloryn shook her head. "I'll wear it all the time."

She undid the clasp and brought the chain up around her neck, her

hair getting caught as she tried to do it up.

"May I...?" Roen moved forward, reaching to help pull her hair back. Eloryn scolded herself internally when the clasp clicked closed and he moved back away again. Frustration bloomed red in her cheeks.

The long silver chain was like a strand of hair, glimmering when the light hit, but almost invisible otherwise. Roen's eyes followed it down, the pendant disappearing down into her chest. He quickly looked the other way. Eloryn saw a faint glow of red on his high cheekbones, which made her blush more.

"Thank you for inviting me to share gifts with you and Memory tonight. I will take my leave. My parents will wish to see me now I've returned."

Eloryn grasped for more to say, wanting the conversation, her time with Roen, to continue. "Are your parents well? I've not seen them lately. Silly I know, since they are so close in quarters."

"Yes, both well." Roen hovered for a moment then bowed stiffly, pausing at the bottom. Eloryn heard him curse softly before he straightened up. She'd requested he wouldn't bow to her anymore, at least in private. She frowned, knowing how much trouble he went to for her.

Roen left and Eloryn curled up in an armchair, holding the pendant in her hand. She spoke words of magic to it, asking it to hold onto the warmth it had drawn from Roen's body, to keep it always, the way she wished she could but knew she couldn't.

Roen leaned on the closed door to Eloryn's chambers, grinding his teeth. The evening had not played out well. It was significantly easier getting along with either of the twins when they were running for their lives. He constantly fought down feelings for Eloryn. He couldn't be with her, nor did he deserve to be. But he now worried even for the friendship they'd tied between them. He could feel those bonds slipping loose.

Out of habit he felt for the edge of the blade he used to keep within the seam of his work pants and found it missing. He no longer carried the tools of his old trade.

How life has changed. Memory and Eloryn never once brought up the subject, that they were the only people to know the truth of the criminal he used to be. He never raised it either, never asking for their silence

or secrecy. He wasn't sure whether it was because he trusted them or some guilty part of him hoped they told.

It was enough that they knew. No matter that they didn't seem to care. He could never outrun the shame of that.

Roen rubbed his forehead. And that silly gift he got for Eloryn. He had almost said out loud how he wanted to buy it for her properly. He could have stolen her something that would have taken her breath away. His family had no real income while they were being housed here in the castle, with no estate or lands of their own anymore. They were given most of what they needed, but Roen spent some of his time at Lanval's working. Honest work. Earning money rather than taking it. Funny, given his new reputation as friend to the Maellan twins, he found a job much more easily than in his days as a sparkless nobody. It was enough to buy the small pendant for Eloryn, but he couldn't tell her any of that, without reminding her again of what he had been.

Tonight, seeing Eloryn dressed so finely, she reminded him of the portrait of her mother, Loredanna, that he'd seen as a child. She somehow seemed so fragile, even though she wasn't nearly as brittle thin as her identical twin. Was it just who she was, the pureness in her? Or was it a hangover from the trauma they'd suffered just weeks before? Everything about Eloryn made him want to protect her, from everything. Even himself.

Roen brushed back the fall of hair from his face and looked down the hallway to see a shadowed shape slip suspiciously around the corner. Roen straightened up, shifting from discomfort to worry. His need to protect Eloryn took control.

Muscles running up the backs of his legs worked hard as he moved silently down the length of the hallway. He closed the distance quickly. The man he'd seen didn't look like a servant. Servants in this castle didn't skulk. It was prestigious work, and they were almost as arrogant as the nobles. He reached the corner so quietly that the man had no idea he was there, which was evident when he peered around the corner again to spy down the hall, finding himself face to face with Roen.

Roen moved fast, grabbing the front of the man's shirt and pinning him against the wall. "What are you doing?"

The man stuttered, and Roen saw he looked familiar, wearing the black and purple of the Wizard's Council.

"Bors? Why were you spying on the princesses' chambers?" Roen growled at the man, who stared back at him with as much outrage in

return. No guilt showed in his features at all, and Roen released his tight grip on his shirt, worried he'd over-reacted.

Bors straightened out his clothing and re-buttoned his coat. "It is important to know the virtue of the princesses isn't being compromised."

Roen took a step back as though he'd been struck.

"I would never..." Roen's words ran to nothing, knowing full well he'd once taken advantage of Eloryn, after he'd gotten her drunk no less. Even with how bashful Eloryn could be, the three of them felt so familiar together with everything they'd been through. Now life had reclaimed some normality he'd never realized how improper his behavior had been. He shouldn't even be seeing them like this, these private, unchaperoned visits to their very chambers. What if he had been wrong about everything? What if the reason Eloryn was so uncomfortable around him was because of what he'd done when they were alone together at Elders Bridge Inn? Roen stepped back again, and the man smiled.

"The Council understands you have some relationship with the princesses, but these inappropriate evening meetings won't be tolerated. Don't think we haven't checked on your past. We know of your exploits with more common women. The princesses are no common women." The man stepped forward, so close Roen could smell his stale breath. "Know you've been warned."

Memory found her chambers empty. A week ago they would have been swarming with maids, turning down the bed, fluffing pillows, trying to help her change clothing. She'd been so standoffish, to the point of actually hiding from them, that they had stopped showing up.

Memory pushed aside her newly tailored gowns and squeezed the box of old clothes into the bottom of the wardrobe. Thinking about what had happened the night of the masquerade ball stole all happiness from the gift. Not that she'd be allowed to wear any of her old things anyway. Jeans and t-shirts didn't seem to go down very well in Avall, and she'd been trying to fit in. Guilt weighed on her. She had considered at times trying to tell the others what she'd done that night at Lanval's castle, how her actions got them so close to being captured, that she considered selling Eloryn out to Thayl. But fear gave her excuses. Why should she tell them? She didn't actually do anything. They're all okay.

It all worked out fine. It was all just a mistake. Excuses on excuses.

Memory gave the box a swift kick, denting the silk covered side. A noise distracted her and she turned around.

The diamond glass doors to the balcony stood open as always, Memory's way of letting Will know he was welcome. A peach-tinted sky changing to night over the forest silhouetted Will as he climbed easily over the balustrade. The fires inside her already burned, and when she saw him there, they sizzled more, fueled by guilt. He tried to save her as a boy, and for that he got sucked into another world where he lost his whole life growing up like an animal in the woods, waiting for her. She only wished she could do more for him, but he hadn't even accepted a room here in the castle. The weather had started to grow icy, moving from autumn into winter, but Will still wore the strange collection of old torn clothing and furs, lashed on with leather strapping. Most of his back and chest were still bare. The thick layer of dirt that darkened his skin when she first saw him in the forest, confusing him for an animal, had been cleaned away. His skin was a lot paler than she'd thought, making his lightning blue eyes glow against dark brows and hair.

"Hope." He smiled at her, remaining perched on the balustrade where overgrown ivy and rose vines tumbled over and curled onto the balcony.

Will was the only one who knew her real name and hearing it made her feel odd, a remnant of a past self that she could barely recall.

Memory rolled her eyes. "Please don't call me that. So typical for people to give such a lame name to an orphan. I'm Mem now."

"Sorry." Will looked like a struck puppy.

"Crap, no I'm sorry. I'm not in a great mood. And it's good to see you no matter what you call me. But don't take that as an invitation to go name crazy."

He mumbled, turning away so she could barely hear him, "Why didn't you tell me it was your birthday?"

"Geez, learn to eavesdrop better why don't you? I didn't know myself!" Memory's voice became shrill. She dumped herself down onto the bed, and the book Eloryn got her poked into her backside. She pushed it angrily out of the way. "You probably know more than me with my whole month worth of memories. And if you want to know something you should just come and ask me instead of lurking around listening in like that. Not like I could tell you anyway since you're never around!"

Memory glared at the book, and when she turned back to the balcony,

Will was gone. *Right, first time all week he shows up and I yell at him and scare him off.* Memory cursed seven times and hurled the heavy book at the wall. It made a satisfying thump, dislodging some old wallpaper before it fluttered down onto the floor.

Memory stared at the ceiling and took a deep breath. *Calm.* She'd been so worked up ever since seeing Thayl, as though seeing him again flared up every wound inside her. She could still hear the words he said to her that day in Kenth: *The ritual to steal your power was interrupted, leaving you like this, this shell. But I can end your suffering. I can finish taking the rest of your soul.*

No one but Thayl and her knew. The others knew he took her memories and magic, but nothing else. Memory wondered how it could work, how she could still live, breath, talk, and move with only part of a soul. Maybe she couldn't, not well anyway. No wonder she couldn't keep her friends, why she kept being such a monster to everyone.

The tantrum slipped straight into a dull depression. She stepped across to the wall and squatted down to pick up the book, wondering if Eloryn would notice the new dent in the cover.

The book lay open on the floor, its ruffled pages showing an intricate illustration of a majestic sword. *Oh, pretty.*

Memory picked the book up and drifted across to the armchair in the corner, staring at the sword. The caption called it Caliburn, sword of Arthur Maellan. Memory wondered if he might be one of her ancestors. Memory flicked to the next page, skimming over the text, looking for more information.

She couldn't believe she'd never shown a proper interest in the history of Avall, when that meant the history of her family. She tended to take a lot for granted and not ask questions because after a while it just became easier not to know when the sheer number of questions overwhelmed her.

Memory turned another three pages, absorbing information about Avall before she turned the weighty tome back to page one with a thud, ready to start at the beginning. *Damn it, Eloryn, this* is *interesting.* Memory pulled her knees up onto the chair and balanced the book on top of them, her mind swimming with the words.

And how Avall suffered through those darkest of times. The beginning parts of the book were sparse, indicating a history rooted in despair. Stories about people starving to death, invasions, and slavery; horrors from some 1500 years ago from what Memory could tell from the timeline.

And the magical creatures from beyond the Veil didst warn mankind of the approach of a greater Hell that would consume all.

Arthur Maellan appeared again in the text, and Memory read on to discover whether he was related to her. He was a commoner from Avall who had "a talent for tongues." Able to speak with the fae, he had a friend called Myrddin who was half human and half unseelie fae.

It was through Myrddin that both courts of the fae approached Arthur with a deal. The fae would save Avall, removing it from the rest of the world, bringing it into the Veil to become a safe haven for man and fae alike. In order to make Avall a sanctuary for the fae, all iron would have to be removed and in return the fae would bestow upon the humans of Avall the Spark of Connection, allowing them to use magic.

Lo, Avall was saved and the rest of the world thus lost. Arthur took this offer to the king, Uther Aurelianus, who accepted and the Pact was formed.

Memory frowned. *So Avall was separated from the world way back then and progressed on its own ever since?* According to everyone she had met in Avall, no other land outside Avall still held life. They only spoke of Hell beyond Avall or the land of the fae beyond the Veil. But the rest of the world must still be there. She'd grown up there. Will too. The land of big buildings and cars and grimy old orphanages. Memory shook her head, not understanding. She read on.

The great Purge was begun, the great sword Caliburn drawn from the stones of Avall. The fae were serious about removing iron from Avall. Not only did they have the humans ship every piece of forged iron off the

islands before the separation, but to guarantee no more iron could ever be forged, Arthur and Myrddin worked magically to draw all iron ore from the land. The ore was smelted into an enchanted sword – the one from the illustration – which became a symbol of the human rulers' solidarity and strength, the one tolerated item of forged iron in the land.

The very presence of the fae in Avall made the land fertile and prosperous. Uther Aurelianus had no heir of his own, and so made Arthur Maellan his heir as reward for saving Avall. Memory whistled. The Maellan bloodline went back so far.

Memory considered her knife. If such effort had been taken to remove iron from the land, it only seemed right that she respected it. She pulled the knife from her corset and held it like a pet.

"I understand you want to leave," a voice in Memory's head echoed.

She was in an office with the blinds pulled down. In front of her was a figure that she couldn't quite make out.

"But what do you expect me to do, Hope?" the man said. "We tried to get your fostered, Jesus, we tried. But you always end up back here." The figure stood up and paced, silhouetted by what little light came through the blinds. "Same old story. We find a nice family for you, get you settled, and then there's a fire. The cops say there were no signs of arson, but these accidents just keep following you around."

The front door opened with a quiet creak, and Memory looked up with a start, drawn out of the vision from her past. No one had knocked, but a tall figure walked in. The room was dark and the fire had all but died, leaving just a spluttering candle to light the room. The serving staff treated her request for candles very oddly. Surely a Maellan heir could create their own light? Memory squinted from her chair at the approaching figure.

The person stopped in the middle of the room, looking her way. They seemed as shocked as Memory.

"Your Highness, forgive me. I expected you slept," said a breathy female voice.

"What time is it?" Memory looked around. The sky outside was pitch black, and the moon had risen high. The doors to the balcony were still open, rushing icy air inside. *How long was I reading for?*

"It is well past midnight. As you're awake, do you mind if I light the room?"

"Sure."

"Àlaich las."

The serving girl stood awkwardly next to a light fitting that now glowed with a soft golden light. Tall and buxom, she had wavy red hair and a peachy complexion. She wore the neat gray maid's uniform of the castle and carried a copper tub with cleaning tools hanging around the edge. She curtseyed deeply. "I can see to my duties another time if I am disturbing you."

"No, it's okay. You just surprised me. I thought I'd scared all my staff off."

The girl almost smiled at the joke, but stopped, looking unsure as how to react. "I'm newly assigned to your keeping, Highness. The other servants warned... I mean... told... I mean..."

The girl blushed and winced. Memory smiled to try and comfort her. "Yeah, whatever they said was probably true. So you do this work at this time of night?"

"We must keep the fire warmed for you during the night as winter closes on us, it would be poor form to have our royalty waking to a cold room." The girl eyed the dying embers and wide open bay doors. She briskly swung the doors shut and locked them, drawing the heavy curtains. The room felt instantly warmer, and Memory reminded herself to unlock the door next chance she had.

Memory detected a hint of scolding in the maid's tone. "I'm sorry. Is there anything I can help with?" Memory left her book and knelt next to the girl who had put her tub down near the fireplace. She was sifting through the embers with a poker, drawing up the still glowing few and speaking behest words to them that brought them to greater light.

The girl stopped, rigid for a moment. "I'm new to the castle, but I am capable in my duties, Highness."

"It's no problem. I'm wide awake anyway."

The girl paused again, midway to putting a log onto the coals. She gave Memory a look that though friendly, bordered comically quizzical. "That's not... You really wish to help?"

"I'm not exactly great with this stuff, but if you just tell me what to do I pick things up quick. Sorry, what's your name?"

The girl looked completely dumbfounded. "Clara, your Highness. But your Highness, this is not clean work. It wouldn't be well for your Highness—"

"Less of the Highnesses already!" Memory rushed her words out in an exasperated sigh. "Just call me Hope."

Memory's brain froze in confusion. "No, I didn't mean that. I meant..." Memory frowned. She stood back up, moving towards the bedroom. "Don't worry about the fire. I'm fine, I don't need it. The room is fine how it is."

"But your... Hope—"

"Clara, please, just go."

CHAPTER FOUR

The next morning, the shock of getting her name wrong still affected Memory. She sleepwalked through the birthday-celebrations-cross-remembrance-day, her thoughts too busy to pay attention to the lines of visitors offering gifts and condolences. Sleep deprived and confused, she couldn't understand how she could slip up on something so fundamental as her name. With some of her past returning, was she becoming Hope again? And if so, what would happen to Memory? Did she even want to be Hope again? Both of them had been pretty rude to people lately.

Memory added Clara to her list of people to apologize to, along with Eloryn and Roen for ditching them despite their birthday plans.

Will made the top of her list, and she hoped he'd also have some advice on how she could get rid of her knife appropriately, since he was in with the fae. Actually finding Will was the challenge. She grew hoarse calling his name in the forest, carefully avoiding fairy rings, until he showed up.

Memory apologized and then asked if he'd help her find a place to hide her knife, and the very next day she found herself with Will again. He led her into the hunting grounds to a spot just out of sight of the hedges that marked the end of the manicured palace gardens.

"Are you serious?" Memory looked skeptically at the subsided well he had brought her to. In front of her, the ground buckled and sunk into a black pit, the stones that once formed the well lay strewn like a

breadcrumb path down into the darkness.

Will nodded from where he leant against the mossy trunk of a tree. "I'll go with you."

"Of course you bloody will. I'm not going down there on my own." Memory felt for the purse at her side and the hard weight of her switchblade inside.

"It's what you asked for. A good place to hide your knife. The only place I know that the fae never go."

"I'm not surprised. I don't know why anyone would go down there, except maybe the insane, like me." Memory sighed. This had to be done, but she didn't like it. Being someone important in the hierarchy of Avall meant she simply couldn't be in possession of something as controversial as cold iron. She had to get rid of it, in a way that wouldn't further insult the fae who already seemed to hate her.

She moved toward the sink hole, and Will stepped in front of her, going first. Ahead of them, the ground sloped down then quickly dropped away into a black rip in the earth.

"Is it even safe? How far does it go?"

"Not far. I checked yesterday. We should leave the knife at the end. Don't worry, I won't let anything happen—"

"I know, I know." Memory hitched up the rust red skirts of Isabeth's old dress. She had almost worn her jeans for this expedition, but didn't want to be so conspicuous since she had to get away on her own again. Isabeth's dress proved to be a good disguise since it was less formal than her new princess wardrobe. It was the plainest gown she had, no bustles, frills, or hooped petticoats. Still, it wouldn't be easy scrambling down into a cave in floor-length fabric. At least she got away with wearing her skater shoes. They felt like old friends on her feet.

Will squatted down at the edge of the hole then stepped off into the darkness. Memory panicked when she didn't hear him land, worried he'd fallen into a bottomless pit, and knelt down to look over the edge. His face was right in front of her, an arm out to offer her help. *Silent bastard.*

Memory wriggled around so her feet dangled off the edge, then slid down over it into the hole. Will caught her around the waist and eased her descent. She put her hands on his shoulders to balance and felt the tight chords of muscle moving under his skin. The instant her feet hit the ground he let go of her, acting like he'd done something wrong. He paused for a moment, looking concerned.

"I can do this without you. Let me take it," he said.

Memory shook her head. "This knife almost feels like part of me. I feel weaker without it. I know it's dumb, but I have to say goodbye to it properly." *What an odd, morbid funeral this will be*, Memory thought, *crawling into the depths of the earth for a little piece of metal.*

Memory surveyed the tunnel, a dirty crevice hanging with tree roots lead down, back in the direction of the castle. Dark brown and blue fungi grew on the walls, and a thin layer of mucus gave the rock a slick sheen. It sounded like water was running in the distance. It looked like a fairly smooth descent, and she'd hardly have to duck. Will, on the other hand, stood nearly two feet taller than her and twice as wide. He turned toward the tunnel, pushing through sideways. Memory winced and hoped he wouldn't get stuck, but looking at the powerful shape of his back, she figured he could probably dig his way out if he did. She would still feel guilty since he was only doing this for her. But at least he was talking to her again, interacting with something other than Mina and the trees.

The tunnel quickly became claustrophobic. Memory drew deep breaths of the cool earth-flavored air.

"Are we there yet?" Memory joked. They were running out of natural light, and she wondered how far they would go, how deep the tunnel led, when she ran into Will's back.

"Yes," Will said. Memory thought he was smirking, but there was barely enough light to tell. Ahead of them was a dead end. "This is as far as it goes."

A strange sensation passed through Memory. Something warm and welcoming.

"There's something…"

Memory pushed past Will, and he squeezed awkwardly out of her way. She didn't put down the knife. Something drew her forward. She put her hands against the end of the tunnel. It shifted under her fingers. Memory looked to Will and without a word he moved to help, pushing at the dirt wall. Earth and stones crumbled out of the way leaving a dark hole of a tunnel that led much farther, deeper than expected.

"We shouldn't go in. I haven't checked it's safe past here, and it's too dark," Will said.

"Scaredy cat. I want to keep going. Look at this wall, these were bricks. Besides, I came prepared."

Memory pulled a candle from her purse and struck a match against a nearby rock. It hissed alight with the smell of sulfur. "I don't suppose you can cast that light behest?" Memory asked, lighting the candle with the scarily spluttering match.

"Only people born here get magic. That's what Mina says," Will said. "What does it feel like? Having the connection to magic?"

"Like a bonfire burning me away from the inside."

Will frowned.

"And not good for much when I can't even cast the light spell. You know I saw a three-year old cast it the other day." Maybe she should wait until Eloryn could come with them, but crawling into dirty holes somehow seemed below her majesty these days. Memory took another candle from the purse, lit it with the first, and handed it to Will.

Memory looked at Will, the candlelight reflecting in his eyes. "Did I ever use magic back in our world?"

"I never saw it." Will hesitated then took the candle and stepped through into their discovered tunnel.

Memory blinked as his candle light disappeared to the side, then realized the tunnel had opened wide, wide enough for him to stand to full height and step out of her way. She crept through the last of the earthen tunnel, pushed through a web of tree roots, and tripped over a brick on the ground. Will grabbed her arm, and she pivoted around and ran into his chest. Memory felt a jagged scar, smooth and raised, under her fingertips. Her heart ached. *So many scars…* Will stepped back, running into the wall, and half way through an apology he hissed as hot candle wax spilled on his hand.

Memory turned away to see where they were and to hide the blush on her cheeks. They had stepped through the broken-down wall into a manmade tunnel. Rough-cut square stones of mismatched sizes formed the ancient walls. Will used his candle to light a crumbling torch on the wall, and its light illuminated a long hallway sloping down, disappearing again into darkness at one end, and the signs of a spiral stairwell at the other leading up.

"Do you think we're under the castle? Could this be part of the castle?" Memory muttered, her voice low as though someone might hear.

"Maybe, close at least. Up or down?"

The warmth Memory felt grew strong, coming from the downwards direction, pulling at her. "Down. That way. We have to go that way."

The stone hallway was only just wide enough for them to walk side by side, and Will seemed to be making an effort not to brush his arm against hers. Memory wondered what problem he had with her, knowing how touchy feely he was with his sprite girlfriend Mina. Not that she wanted to be all touchy feely with Will, but she didn't want to feel like an untouchable. Memory's teeth ached from being clenched, and she shook off the frustration and tried to get her mind onto a different subject. She had important questions to ask Will after all, and what better time than when he couldn't dash off into the trees.

"So I was reading this book," Memory started.

"Since when do you read books?"

"Since shut up."

That quiet smirk in reply again. The tunnel took them a long way, down slippery stairs covered in slime where moisture dripped in from above. A thin glaze of limestone coated the walls like milk where the water ran.

"I was reading this book," Memory started again. "About the Pact, and how the fairies said the rest of the world was going to become Hell, and so they just took Avall off the map, like poof, gone. That's why everyone here thinks the rest of the world was Hell. But it wasn't, was it?"

Will huffed, almost a laugh. "Not Hell. Hell wouldn't have the internet. But different from here. Normal, not all old fashioned. No magic or fairies. Do you remember..." Will paused. Memory could almost hear his teeth grinding in the silent subterranean pathway. "Back in our world, there were lots of stories of lost lands. Whole cities, islands, or countries that disappeared. Like Atlantis. Things are different here, but a lot is the same, even the language. When I ended up here, for a while I thought I'd just gotten lost, until I saw fairies. Might make sense if it used to be part of our world."

"So we're in Atlantis or whatever, and the rest of the world is still okay out there too, so what's the deal? Why did old King Arthur make the pact with the fairies?"

Will stopped walking. "King Arthur? Like King Arthur and the Knights of the Round Table?"

"I dunno. I just know Arthur Maellan was my ancestor who made the Pact. But you know the castle totally has a round table, I kid you not."

Will shook his head. "Avall isn't Atlantis. It must be Avalon. From what I remember of the stories it fits, even the name. And Caermaellan,

it's like Camelot."

"There are really stories about Avall you remember from the other world? Could you tell me more about them? The more we can understand about this place, the better, right? We might work something out between the two of us."

Will's voice grew quiet. "I used to think maybe this was an alternate Earth. Like there could be infinite Earths, and you could be in any of them, lost anywhere."

Memory bumped his shoulder with hers, a small gesture of comfort. "Sounds to me like it's just Avall and the rest of the world."

"And the fairy world. It's different again, very different to here."

Memory's jaw dropped. "You've been to the fairy world? Get out! What's it like?"

Will just shrugged then started walking again. "You're descended from King Arthur. I can believe that."

Memory was about to question him some more, since this was the most words she'd gotten out of Will, ever, but the sensation she'd been feeling spiked.

The last flight of stairs opened into a room so large the dim light of the candles didn't show the ends of it. Memory saw another old torch and lit it.

The ground wobbled in front of them, sparkling with gold flecks of the torch light. Memory took a step toward it before seeing that it was water, some kind of underground lake. The manmade tunnel had come to an end, and they were in a massive underground cavern.

"Hope," Will said from behind her as she stared out across the midnight water.

Memory spun around, glaring, but saw what Will pointed at and refrained from complaining about her name. A stack of wooden crates and chests stood against the wall, on top of which sat a silver-colored metal dagger.

"Is that iron?" she asked.

Will picked up the dagger and hit it against the stone wall. Sparks flew. "Too hard to be silver."

"What are these doing here? Is this why the fae don't come here?" Memory brushed her hand over one of the boxes and cracked it open, finding what looked like the head of a hoe lying on a bed of velvet. *Weird.*

"No way they'd come close to this much iron."

"Maybe when they got rid of all the iron from Avall, they missed some and stashed it here?" Memory puffed out a long breath. She put her hand into her purse and pulled out her own small knife. "I should leave my knife here then, too. I guess this is goodbye."

Memory placed it on the top of the boxes.

The buzz of hot energy rushed through her, and she could feel her eyes closing.

"Hope?" she heard Will ask, his voice different, high and clear. "Hope?"

"It'll be so cool," she said. She sat at the head of an unmade bed, on yellowed pillows. In front of her sat Will, but much younger, wearing flannel PJs, his hair cut short and neat. He was hiding how scared he was in the completely obvious way that little boys do.

"Won't it hurt?" he asked.

"Well, yeah!" she said. "But once it's done it'll be forever. That's what it means. Friends forever." Memory held out the paper with the draft design on it, tracing the symbol of eternity with a swirl through the middle. Next to the bed was a small table that had a lamp, a ballpoint pen, a needle, and a lighter on it. The room was dim, grey. A wisp of moonlight shone through thin curtains.

"Forever?" he asked.

"Yeah. You and me against the world. Together forever." Memory examined her wrist. "I think we should do them here. It's okay, I'll go first. Scaredy cat."

"Hope?"

She had completely zoned out. Will called her name a few times, but got no reply. She just stood there, eyes closed, with a hand still on the knife on top of the boxes. Will reached to touch her, to see if she'd respond but decided against it.

"Memory?" he tried. He struggled to think of her by a different name.

"What?" She opened her eyes and looked at him, blinking a couple of times. "Sorry, wow, I spaced, huh?"

"We should get out of here. You probably need fresh air."

A frown pinched her eyebrows, and she reached out and took his hand, turning it palm up to see the tattoo they shared. Her hands were so small around his, cold fingertips sending thrills up his arm. Will tensed and Memory let go, clearing her throat.

"Yeah, some fresh air would be good, but can we check out where

the rest of the tunnel goes? I bet you it goes into the castle. Could be a short cut."

Will looked around for Mina out of habit, but knew she would never come for him here with all the iron. He had plenty of time. "Okay, we'll go up."

The passageway up proved to be slow going, with narrow stone tunnels and winding stairs. Memory began complaining that she'd neglected to bring food with her.

Will smiled. It was nice seeing her eat. She was still so thin, but at least she ate now. Eating seemed to be one of her new favorite things.

Hunger crept up on Will as well, urged on by Memory's descriptions of what she planned to eat the moment she got back to the castle.

"They even have two chefs just for making cakes. Can you believe that?" She puffed as she talked, sentences broken up by heavy breathing. The stairs were steep and unevenly cut, each step often as high as Memory's knees. *It must be hard for her.* Will almost offered to carry her, but decided against it. He'd broken the rules enough. He would only make exceptions when it was necessary to keep her safe.

Will worried more about the lifespan of their candles. He tried to carry one of the old torches, but it broke apart when he pulled it from the wall, too fragile to be moved. The tunnels must have been ancient.

Up ahead, the hall ended in a heavy wooden doorway. It looked solid, and no sound or light travelled through it. To the best of his judgment, they should be in the castle, somewhere, but he lost most of his ability to track distance and direction when not under the open sky.

"This had better be the way out, or I might have to just eat the door instead," Memory said, peeking over his shoulder as he carefully pulled at the handle, worried it might break like the torch had.

The wood of the door felt solid, newer than anything they'd passed so far. Will stopped with the handle half turned, pausing to think. Everything except the boxes of iron objects, he realized. Many of those seemed new, not covered in dust or the grime of centuries.

"Any time now," Memory said.

Will pulled at the door, sensing the weight of it, but it glided open smooth and silently. On the opposite side, the door was rendered in stonework to match the walls around it.

Memory followed him through into another long, skinny corridor where enough natural light fell to let them douse their remaining candles.

"We're in the servant runs. I used these yesterday to lose my shadows but ended up getting caught out by Clara. She said they're for the servants to get around the castle fast without bothering the nobles, which seems silly to me. The halls out there are wide enough for everyone."

There were slits in the wall every dozen paces that showed the main hallway running parallel to them. Memory turned back and closed the secret doorway behind them and wedged her small stump of a candle into a gap in the rocks next to it. "I don't know if anyone else knows about that tunnel, but I want to be able to find it again."

Will heard voices and put a finger to his lips, not wanting to be found there. Along with the men's voices, the rhythmic thump of a walking cane could be heard.

Memory pushed past him to look through one of the peep holes. She always was the game one, breaking rules, daring risks.

She said in a breathy whisper, "That's Hayes. I want to hear what he's saying."

Memory stood close to Will in the small space, so she could press her ear to the hole. He put his back up against the wall, shivering as he inhaled the scent of her, rising from her hair. Blood and crushed flowers. The scent of hair dye she used to always carry had left now that her hair was its natural pale blonde again. She had changed in so many ways; the loss of a whole life's memories did a lot to her. But in others, she was still Hope. Impulsive, brash, and fragile. He breathed her fragrance again, and let it take him back to when he was young and idolized her, and never dreamed she'd ever see him as anything other than a little boy. Now he towered over her, and she seemed so delicate as she brushed against him in the confined space. The desire to wrap her in his arms, bury his nose in her hair, press his lips onto the soft skin of her neck, rolled over him with knee weakening force. He denied the desire. Even if he wasn't a boy anymore, he still remembered the rules.

Will could hear the conversation clearly through the wall without moving closer. His time with the fae had improved all his senses.

"Plans for coronation and surrounding celebrations are going well. Princess Eloryn has undertaken her rehearsals with diligence."

"That's Bors, too," Memory whispered.

"She is perfectly amenable, is she not? What of the other one? That scamp can't even be kept track of half the time."

"She does as she wishes, sir, completely wild. We're no closer to understanding her in any way, not her upbringing or her magic."

Memory grunted. "Yep. That's me they're talking about."

Hayes continued. "I had hoped schooling would add some needed structure to her life, but she's already resistant to that concept. We simply need something to keep her entertained to which she agrees, and once occupied she will stay out of our way and out of trouble. I have a thought or two on that matter."

Their voices carried out of range as they left that area of the corridor.

"Pfft, I doubt I'd find anything they chose for me entertaining," Memory said. She looked through the peephole again. "I think we're in the old keep, near the Round Room. Oh, do you want to see it?" Memory asked.

Will looked through the hole above her head. A number of nobles in well-tailored and spotless suits were wandering through. Will looked down at his fraying clothing and furs. "Can you find your own way through the castle from here? I think I'll go back out the tunnel, the way we came in."

Memory also seemed to be assessing how he looked, then looked down at her dress, spotted all over with powdery dirt and slime.

"Okay, maybe it's not the best time for a tour, but I hate that you feel like you can't be in the castle." Memory folded her arms tight around her chest. "We can probably make it most of the way to the gardens in these servant halls, then if you want you can leave from there. But my rooms are pretty close too. We could do a runner and no one will see us. I mean, if you didn't mind. I'd like to spend some more time with you."

Will enjoyed these times he had with Memory, getting to know who she had become, but the more time he spent with her, the more terrified he became. He knew how easily, how quickly, everything in his life could be taken away, his parents and whole family lost in one tragic natural disaster and then his whole world in an entirely unnatural way. *I only just got Hope back. Not Hope, Memory,* he reminded himself, trying to get her new name right. He'd only been able to be with her while Mina wasn't demanding his company, something she had been demanding more and more often lately. Mina had always been possessive, but the more time he tried to spend with Memory, the more possessive she became.

Memory put her hands together like she was praying and made a puppy dog face.

Will smiled. "Okay, let's go."

Memory dashed into her chambers, startling Clara as she tidied up.

"I don't even want to know where you've been." Clara raised an eyebrow at Memory's dirt-covered dress. Then something cheeky flashed in her eyes. "Or maybe I do? Did it involve a man?"

Memory had managed to apologize to Clara the night before, and Clara had received the apology as an invitation to take over all of Memory's maid's duties. She'd become downright feisty since Memory gave the order to be free with her words and opinions.

"Clara, could you come back later? I'm expecting company."

Will chose that moment to emerge over the top of the vines on the balcony. He'd refused to come through the last small stretch of palace with Memory, so she agreed to meet him there.

Clara studied Will up and down.

"Oh my. Now I understand why you leave your windows open," she said. Memory's cheeks flooded with hot blood, and she imagined she must match Clara's hair. Will looked ready to bolt, but too stunned to move.

"Clara, this is Will. He is my friend, from when we were kids. It's a long story. Clara, since you busted us anyway, would you mind helping us get cleaned up?"

Memory still found it hard asking for help for everyday tasks. But she had to be honest. She had so much trouble getting changed and looking after the antiquated chambers on her own, she needed someone. She couldn't even take a hot bath on her own. Water came out cold, and people expected her to use a behest to warm it.

"Anything, Hope."

"How about calling me Memory now?"

Clara smiled and answered as she went to draw the bath. "Unless you're taking back your order to let me speak my mind, I'll stick with Hope. It's such a pretty name, and I can't be changing what I call you every time you ask."

Memory had no other response than to stick her tongue out, so she went and dragged Will in from the balcony.

Clara eyed him again. "Would you like me to fetch some clothing for Master Will?"

Memory thought back to the last time she'd offered clothes to Will,

and they were left untouched. "Okay. Maybe between the two of us we can wrestle him into wearing something clean."

"Oh, I like the sound of that." Clara giggled and left the chambers to find something for him.

"And bring us some food!" Memory yelled after her.

Will was giving Memory a look.

"What? I should have said please, right?"

"Maybe I should go." He looked catastrophically uncomfortable.

"You said you'd stay for a while. Come on. Let me do this for you. Everyone likes a bit of pampering, right?"

"Just worried about your idea of pampering. You painted my nails hot pink once. Got me picked on for months."

"Just a hot bath and some clean clothes this time, promise," she said, swiping an X over her heart.

"A hot bath… that would be nice." Will half-smiled.

Memory put her hands on her hips, appraising him. "And a haircut. Let me cut your hair, please?"

There was a lot of grumbling, but Memory soon had Will on a chair and worked at removing the largest of knots from his hair. She had a plan to make Will more presentable, so he'd fit in at the castle, but with scissors in hand, she realized how much she liked his hair how it was and became scared of doing something that changed it. She didn't take much off, just trimmed the roughest parts out to make it a bit more manageable.

Clara returned with clothes for Will and sent him into the bathroom where the tub had filled and warmed. She put down a tray of neat sandwiches in a range of cut shapes and rolls, and Memory grabbed three.

Stuffing them in her mouth, Memory took the chance to kick off her muddy shoes, leaving them in the middle of the floor while she went to the closet for a clean dress.

Clara picked them up, pouting. "I'm happy to assist you in whatever way I can, but that's no excuse to be a slovenly. Watch out, or I'll have to call in extra help again."

Memory smiled at the motherly tone. "And I sure don't want that."

Clara inspected the muddy shoes. "You two look like you've been on quite an adventure."

"You know me, anything to get out of the castle."

"Funny when so many people would do anything to get into this castle."

Memory pawed through her current selection of dresses. Only a dozen or so filled the wardrobe, but these were exchanged and refreshed every few days so she was never seen in the same dress twice. Each one looked like it would take a month to create, with delicate beading and embroidery, and so many layers of fine fabric folded to create bows and roses. "That's just the thing, Clara. Look at this stuff. This isn't me. Or maybe it is, but the point is I don't know yet. I'm a diary full of blank pages. I went from nothing, to forests and fear for my life, to crazy opulence. I feel like I've missed a few steps in between. I want to know more about the normal people of Avall, what their lives are like."

"It's a fine sentiment. But after all you've been through you may find us quite dull."

"If everyone else is anything like you, I doubt it. Is there any chance… Could we go out somewhere? Into the city, just for a night?"

Clara pouted a cheeky smile. "You know the whole of Avall has been celebrating. It's a shame you're stuck in here on your own while the celebration is so much for you. You have me scheming now. I think we could do it. Oh, partying with the princess! My sisters will be so jealous when they hear!"

It will be good for Will too, to get out with some normal people, Memory thought. "Can we go tonight? Will isn't around much, and I want him to come with."

"We'd better get you changed then. One of the coachmen is a friend, but his shift ends soon."

In just moments, Memory leaned against the thick carved post of her four-poster bed as Clara tugged at the lacings of her corset. "Oof, really? Aren't I skinny enough?"

"Might as well flaunt it," Clara said.

"Skinny is over-rated. I want curves like Lory. Do you think I'll get boobs if I eat enough, or have I permanently stunted my growth?"

Memory reached for the silk bolero to match the gown Clara had chosen for her. The smoky purple skirts fell in a neat bell shape with a small bustle, and the shrug jacket buttoned over a simple square topped corset. Classy but unassuming, Memory liked it.

After she was dressed, Clara set to work on Memory's hair while Memory threw on some make up. Memory flinched and twitched as Clara poked through her hair with fingers, combs and pins. She was growing fond of Clara but still not keen on having other people dress

her, touch her. But her hair was one of her most recognizable features, and there was no way she could do something with it herself to disguise the modern cut. She'd been trying to let it grow out, but a month hadn't gotten it much longer.

Clara managed to create a style that completely hid her ragged haircut. With a few strategically placed braids and curls, it looked like her hair was a lot longer than it really was.

Just as they finished with Memory's hair, the bathroom door opened slightly. They turned around, but Will didn't immediately emerge.

"What's up? Come on, I've got a surprise for you!"

The door opened fully and Will stepped out. Memory got her own surprise. She fumbled behind her for a chair but found nothing, so put extra energy into her legs to make them keep holding her up. *Oh dear god, he's gorgeous.*

Will had been a bit cleaner lately than the day she first saw him, but she'd never seen him like this. His hair, Memory saw with relief, looked great. Still wet, he must have finger combed it back from his face, and it fell in neat waves to around chin length. There was nothing animal about him anymore, the furs and skins replaced with a neat pair of trousers, a black shirt and vest and a deep blue knee length overcoat that his shoulders were just a bit too wide for.

He held a tie of some kind in his hand. "I don't know what to do with this."

"Oh my, I could volunteer a few ideas," Clara muttered, fanning herself with a hand. Memory elbowed her.

"You look great, really." Memory beamed. Her comment caused an obvious blush on Will's high cheekbones. Or maybe it had been Clara's comment. "We're all ready then. We better get going!"

"Going where?" Will asked.

"That's the surprise."

CHAPTER FIVE

Clara left them briefly to get changed from her maid's uniform and arrange for their exit from the castle. Memory spent the time convincing Will that he looked good enough to go out in public.

As the three of them climbed into the carriage, Clara gave the coachman a sly grin. He tipped his cap in return, and the horses broke into a trot.

The cool night air blew softly in through the windows as the carriage clattered along the road, and a sense of freedom exhilarated Memory. Caermaellan castle lay just on the outskirts of the city and before long they were being driven through narrow cobbled streets, full of revelers and the subtle smell of wood-smoke. It had been explained to Clara that Memory suffered a form of amnesia and was relearning everything about Avall, and Clara took pride in offering as much information as she could. She pointed out various important buildings they passed, including the finishing school the twins would soon be attending, and sprinkled her information with juicy bits of gossip.

Memory asked if they could stop, to get out of the carriage and continue on foot. The coachman pulled up near a watering fountain for the horses and agreed to wait for them there. Memory hopped down from the carriage, wanting to run off in every direction at once. The city was so enticing, full of misty secrets and winding pathways to explore.

The lively sounds of a busking fiddler filled the air. Men in top hats and waist coats and women in dresses much like hers surrounded them.

Clara had chosen her outfit well. The utter volume of people passing by made Memory feel completely anonymous. She found comfort in that. The pebbled pavement under her feet felt real compared to the silky marble floors of the palace. She kept checking on Will to see how he was managing the crowds, and he seemed more intent on keeping an eye on her than worrying about himself. She smiled. *He's doing fine.*

To cater the city-wide street party, food vendors had set up on nearly every corner. Some roasted chestnuts and whole potatoes in small ovens. Others offered boiled sweets and candy apples. The sweet smell intoxicated Memory, but she could see that not everyone was benefiting from the business taking place on the streets. Next to nearly every stall that sold food there was a child or teenager begging. And where there weren't stalls there were yet more people hunched together, either sleeping or pleading for alms.

"Who are these people? Are they homeless?" Memory asked Clara.

Clara grimaced unpleasantly. "I guess you could say that. They've nowhere else to be. They're beggars."

"Why are there beggars? I thought Avall was supposed to be all prosperous and rich."

"Oh, it is," Clara said. "But I've heard some of the older folks say that things are changing. That there are less fae in the world these days, and it is the fae that turn Avall from barren to abundant. There are stories of some land becoming infertile and dead like in the olden times."

"Like Kenth?" Memory shocked herself in having information to offer the conversation.

Clara nodded. "And when a township cannot grow food any more, folk must look for work elsewhere and often go missing, and the children who are left behind find their way here, looking for help."

"Are they not finding it? Why isn't anyone helping them?"

"I'm not sure anyone knows quite what to do with them. This has never been a problem before. Some say it was Thayl the fae disagreed with, but others say it started earlier. Anything I know is just gossip and rumors of course, I mean there has even been wild talk of beggars being found drained of every drop of their blood. Vampires, some say it is, but I don't prescribe to such superstition."

Superstition? In a world full of dragons and fairies?

"Well this is a terribly depressing topic of conversation for your night out on the town. Shall we find something more entertaining to do?"

"How about we go there? It looks good." Memory indicated a busy looking tavern across the road from them called "Beyond the Veil."

"Oh fun! They welcome the fae there, and boy do the fae know how to have a good time!" Clara grinned.

Will had been following along a step or two behind the girls as they chatted, but moved up close beside Memory now. "I'm not sure that's a good idea."

Memory hesitated. "Yeah, isn't that dangerous?"

"Dangerous? Pish. It's all fine as long as one adheres to the usual precautions when dealing with fae."

"What, like don't piss them off?"

"Indeed. Also remember that although they may sometimes appear human, always be on guard," Clara warned. "Never accept food or drinks lest they've been spiked with fae-food. Always purchase at the bar. And certainly don't agree to do anything for anyone. If in doubt about whether someone is really a human, offer to share some bread or some salted food. They won't touch the stuff. That's a sure way of telling whether or not they're fae. Just follow my lead, you'll be fine."

Memory looked up at Will for confirmation. He frowned, but shrugged and nodded.

Inside, the tavern was alive with energy. The décor was lush, with red velvet furnishings and dark, oaken walls. Memory could see fae mingling with humans throughout the room. A lithe woman with green skin and leaves sprouting throughout her white hair lounged in an oversized armchair and a circle of entranced men surrounded her. Smaller sprites, bright as stars, socialized in the rafters and a couple sat on a chandelier, making the crystals shoot bright spots of light around the room. From what Memory could see, none of them had fully black eyes. That made her a little more comfortable.

As she moved through the room, the fae watched Memory suspiciously. She almost walked straight into the bare chest of a tall fae man with elk horns, and he hissed and pushed through the crowd to get clear of her.

"The fae keep such a distance from you," Clara observed.

Memory shrugged. "Yeah, they don't like me very much. Vessel too full, gonna spill and spoil everything or some fairy nonsense. Guess we didn't need to worry about avoiding them after all."

Most of the fae and human patrons were engrossed in some sort of play being acted out in the center of the room. A large table formed a

makeshift stage, but nothing else about the performance seemed makeshift. It all looked far too fancy for being performed on a table in a pub.

Clara must have noticed Memory's disbelief. "The fae use their glamour to change the player's appearance and dress the stage. Looks wonderful, doesn't it? I love these. We can watch it, if you wish?"

Without responding, Memory sat down at a table, with Clara and Will following suit.

Clara pouted and stood back up. "Oh, I've seen this one. And it's nearly over. You watch. I'll get some drinks."

Nearly over? To Memory, the play seemed in full swing. Arthur Maellan was locked in armed combat with another man. Or at least, some actor glamored to look exactly like Arthur from the illustrations Memory had seen.

"Ooh, he's using Caliburn." Memory told Will, recognizing it also from her book. "You know he and his fairy friend Myrddin drew up all of the iron ore in Avall to make it with?"

Will looked thoughtful, his eyes on the play. "In the stories I know, Arthur drew a sword from a stone, but it was way more literal."

The swordplay intensified, and the men lunged upon each other, swords bloodied, piercing through each other's torso. Memory gasped. It looked too real.

The men fell apart, both lying still when they hit the ground. Another man ran onto the stage, distraught. He looked human, but his eyes were solid black orbs. He tried to revive Arthur, and cried beside him when he could not. With a look of resolve, he stood, took Caliburn from the ground, and vanished into thin air.

The dead men on the ground lay still, as dirt and grass grew up over them. A creature of powerful beauty walked in, calling for Myrddin. Tall and built like an Amazon goddess, this fae woman wasn't waif-thin like sprites Memory had seen. She had the all-black eyes of the unseelie fae and matching black hair that was not so much hair as swirls of pure darkness that caressed her figure, flowing down to her heels. She wore regal gowns, but where her skin showed it rippled like tree bark and shone silver with the scales of a serpent.

She continued to walk, calling Myrddin's name, as the graves beside her feet turned white, covered in snow, then sprouted fresh blossoms which withered into dust and blew from the stage. She fell onto her knees, called out for Myrddin one last time, and then collapsed into tears.

The audience stood in applause. The fae glamour faded, revealing a cast of normal human actors who looked nothing like the roles they played. Even the female fae was played by a man. They stood and took their bows.

Clara returned with glass goblets that held some kind of pink-blushed cocktail in them, and Memory thanked her. She had got one for Will too, who accepted it but sniffed it suspiciously.

"Did you enjoy the play?"

Memory grunted. "Damn spoilers. I hadn't gotten that far in my book yet. I didn't know how Arthur had died."

Clara waved off the comment with her hand. "This is just one version of events, a dramatization. King Arthur and his nephew Mordred were indeed found dead together, and Myrddin, who had been King Arthur's closest companion, was not seen ever again after that time. Playwrights have come up with the rest on their own."

"Who was the fairy woman, at the end?"

"Lady Nyneve. She was Myrddin's lover. Some say she still looks for him and still mourns him. It's a sad tale, but they love to show it in taverns. I think it makes people drink more," Clara said, taking a swig as proof.

Memory brought her own goblet up to drink from, glancing around as though she could still get in trouble for drinking alcohol. She was the youngest person in the tavern. Even Will and Clara were older than her. She guessed Clara might be twenty. She had done the math and worked out that Will should be eight years older than her, but he looked much younger than that, closer to her age. Must be a lifestyle thing.

"You're not drinking. Don't you like it?" Clara asked Will, pouting slightly.

"It's very sweet. And pink," Will said. He still acted so much like a boy, too.

"Not man enough to drink a girly drink, huh?" Memory challenged, hammering her own drink on the table with a slosh.

"I'm sorry," Clara said. "I'm not used to buying drinks for men. Normally it's the other way around. I have to head back to the bar anyway as I appear to have finished mine. I'll get you something else." Clara stood back up. "Do you have a request?"

Will shook his head. Memory doubted he went out drinking much.

Memory offered Clara some of the money she'd brought, but Clara refused.

"No, this is my treat! In return for getting to party with the *you-know-who*."

With a very conspicuous wink Clara headed to the bar. Memory watched as she went. She seemed so natural, talking to people on the way and giving the occasional flirty smile to men. After a few moments, she returned with drinks on a copper tray. Two more pink cocktails and a monstrous jug-sized mug filled with something brown and frothy. She heaved the mug onto the table and pushed it towards Will.

"Here is something you might like better," she said.

"Clara, are you trying to get Will drunk?" Memory said.

"Me? Why never," Clara said in her breathy voice that made everything sound sexy.

The three of them continued to drink and enjoyed some of the music that was being played. It was a mixture of human and fae musicians, with two human fiddlers and a flautist and the fairies singing in voices that reminded Memory of birdsong. Clara dragged Memory up to dance, showing her a set of moves where they clapped hands and spun each other around. Memory got the sequence wrong half the time, turning the wrong direction and laughing all the while. Some men approached the girls on the dance floor to request a dance, but the girls both refused through giggles, having far too much fun together.

Memory and Clara returned to the table rosy cheeked and all smiles. They each took Will by a hand, trying to drag him up to dance. They couldn't budge him, but a smile broke on his face at their efforts. The girls gave up and returned to their seats. Memory was happy Will seemed to be fitting in. He wasn't doing much more than sitting and watching, but that was a big step up from hiding in nearby bushes and watching.

"How about I get this round?" Memory offered after looking into an empty glass. She left Clara and Will together, a little worried of what Clara would do with the opportunity. Memory would have to break it to Clara later on that Will already had a girlfriend. Or girlfae. Or whatever he called Mina.

As she waited to be served at the busy bar, a thin man with slicked back hair and oiled moustache approached and stood far too close to her. A friend hovered behind him, looking over his shoulder with a dopey smile.

"My lady," the thin man said, holding a cup in a spidery hand and pausing for a sip. "That was a fine display of dancing you gifted us with

before."

"Yeah, right. Me and my two left feet don't know much about dancing."

"Would you be interested perhaps in some private dance sessions?" he suggested with a smarmy smile.

Oh gross. Memory held up a hand between her and the man. "Sorry, mister, not interested."

"Come now, don't be like that. This is a time of celebration and free spirits."

The man ran his finger down the length of Memory's lifted arm.

Memory recoiled in disgust, but before she could react more, something hit the skinny man. His head hit the bar, his arm twisted behind his back, held down by Will.

"Will, stop!" Memory shouted. Everyone nearby fell silent, and Will withdrew his grasp. The thin man took his wrist in his other hand and rubbed it. His friend fawned over him. Another group of men hurried to their side.

"You brute. I was just speaking with the lady."

Will growled.

The thin man shivered, but his voice rose in outrage. "You've made a big mistake. Don't you know who I am? I'm Count Delaney, you fool! And I'll see to it that you hang for this."

Clara pushed through to the middle of the confrontation, wobbling slightly and red faced. "Don't you know who this is? Do you not recognize your princess when you see her?"

"Clara, shush!" Memory said, too late.

Clara's voice was only a little raised, but the entire tavern stilled, everyone looking their way.

Count Delaney looked amused for a moment, but his eyebrows started twitching as he looked at Memory again. He quickly took to a knee. Half the tavern followed him, the other half whispering and gossiping. Memory was glad no one here had camera phones, but already knew how fast gossip in Avall could spread.

"Hayes pulled me up in front of the whole Council for what had happened at the pub. Talking to me like I was a little kid, like they could ground me or something."

Memory ranted, pacing back and forth. The space was small with grimy beige walls, spotted with old sticky tape, and a single bed made of metal framework that looked like a flattened cage. She could hear the noise of cars and a busy street outside. Thayl stood near the small window and looked out through the bars that covered it.

"Where are we? I feel I'm still in my prison cell."

"This is where I grew up. Where you sent me. Trust me, it gives me the creeps too." Memory folded her arms and dumped herself down on the bed with a huff. The mattress springs screeched.

Thayl assessed the dreamscape with a serious expression. "I'm sorry," he said, simply.

"Sure you are." This was the first dream they shared since she'd cut off his hand, which, she noticed, he had grown back in dream form. Until now she wasn't sure it was still possible to share dreams, but whatever was linking them together had brought him into her head again, into her dream. They were still connected, just like he said. She wasn't sure why it happened now, but he proved to be a sympathetic ear for complaining about the Wizard's Council.

Disembodied voices carried through the room.

"This is not behavior befitting a princess of the Maellan line."

"It is an embarrassment to your sister, the queen to be. We cannot have this sort of scandal on our hands while we try and reestablish a trusted ruler for Avall."

"You can't play dress up with him and think he's a man. That boy is an animal, and the sooner you realize it the better. He is not proper company for a princess."

Memory swatted at the air like the voices were flies that she could bat away. She grunted. "They don't want me to see Will anymore. They have no right to tell me who I can and can't be friends with."

"They would disagree. They think meddling in other's relationships is exactly their duty when it comes to the Maellan bloodline."

"Right. You and Loredanna," Memory said. "Wow, they haven't changed at all. Talk about learning nothing from past experience."

Thayl nodded grimly but kept his eyes on the cars passing by on the street below. Memory wondered what he must think of them.

"Would you laugh were I to say I have learned? You know, I told Loredanna we were running away together, that night, but instead I lured her to the witch, so her unborn child could be part of the ritual. I have learned, and could I have my time again I would have run away with Loredanna as I promised and forgotten my revenge. But my mistakes

have all been made and paid for."

"You knew I'd be part of the ritual? You would sacrifice a newborn baby for your revenge, but you expect sympathy from me that things went wrong for you?"

Memory gripped the edge of the bed, anger rising. The smell of smoldering plastics filled the room and small wisps of smoke rose around her, forming the shapes of carved runes.

"To me, back then, the offspring Loredanna carried were nothing but another man's spawn. How could you know what it feels like to have another man's children grow within your beloved? I despised what you were and fooled myself into thinking that justified the terrible ritual." Thayl turned away from the window and looked at Memory, right into her eyes. "But now, I see you not as another man's, but as Loredanna's. You are so clearly the daughter of the woman I loved. In you I see her fire, her spirit, her natural compassion. You are a constant reminder of what I lost, the mistakes I made." Thayl held his ghost hand up in front of his face. It flickered in and out of existence.

"Just because I'm blonde now," Memory muttered.

An awkward silence spread between them, broken only by the dull roars of a dragon, competing with emergency sirens in the distance. The dragon often haunted her dreams.

The smoke cleared. The urge that came to Memory to comfort Thayl irritated her. He deserved whatever he got, and she reminded herself of how he ruined her life, her soul. She was the one who deserved comfort and answers.

"And you're a reminder of what I've lost," Memory said. "I need to know more, about what you did to me. Like how, or why, are some of my memories coming back now? Could my soul be coming back, too? I have to find some answers. Can you tell me more about what happened, how the ritual worked?"

"I could. But why would you believe me?"

"Because I'm asking you, because you owe me. You owe Loredanna. You've got a lot to make up for and not much else to lose."

Thayl laughed wryly. "You are right there. But you might be disappointed in what I can tell you. I know nothing of magic. In my youth I never studied the lore. I was never a talent. The only power I ever had was what I stole from you through Providence's ritual, and I used it like a weapon. Your raw power was all I required. I didn't try to understand it."

"You've got nothing for me? What about Providence? Would she know? Where is she?"

"You don't want to meet her. At first I thought her just an old woman," Thayl scoffed. "I could not conceive she could hold such evil. It took me a very long time to realize that she was more than she seemed."

"Then show me. Do your flashback thing and show me what happened," Memory demanded, not sure if she really wanted to see.

Thayl turned back to the window, head shaking slightly. "So be it."

A scene emerged in front of Memory, but Thayl kept his back to the vision. It showed the forest clearing the ritual took place in. Bodies lay scattered on the ground, including her mother's. It must have been just after Memory had been dropped through the Veil and Alward and baby Eloryn had fled. A young Thayl knelt with his hands clasped around his face. Behind him stood a hunched figure, covered in robes so nothing showed but undulating skeletal fingers spotted with blood.

"You still thirst for revenge? You would do anything for it?" An old woman's voice came from under the robe's heavy hood. The witch, Providence.

"I would do anything, give anything. My need for vengeance is now tenfold." The young Thayl lifted his head from his hands, stood and looked squarely at her.

"With this knife," Providence drew a blade. Memory felt a pang of pain in her chest. The serrated edge was still wet with blood. *My blood.* "We do sacrifice."

A girl was brought out. She was tied and blindfolded, being hauled by two men wearing cloaks like Providence. The girl looked similar to Thayl with bundles of wild dark hair and handsome face.

"No," Thayl shouted. "No, I will not!"

Providence raised the knife. More of her men moved to hold Thayl back. "It has already begun. You have given your permission and made your bargain."

"But why? Why her? There must be another way."

"No other way. No other chance. She is the only link that will enable you to venture into Hell and steal the power of the mature Maellan girl. The power you'll need to gain your revenge."

Thayl sobbed, looking over at his sister. The girl, blindfolded, recognized his voice and was begging him for help. Providence uttered words that Memory didn't understand, like the words Eloryn used for her magic, before slitting the throat of the young girl in one smooth, brutal motion. Blood flowed from the gaping wound as she choked and the men held her upright. Memory had to look away. When she looked back, young Thayl sat staring blankly at the girl's limp body as Providence carved symbols into his hand with the twice bloodied blade.

She spoke technically, as though the explanation would console him. "The doorway must be tied to the Maellan child. We cannot tie it to a place. We do not know what the hellish lands beyond Avall look like to do so. With the child's blood, your blood and your sister's blood all tied, we can focus the doorway to find the Maellan child when she is older, the age of your sister, when her magic has grown strong, ready to steal."

The doorway opened, and the young Thayl, feral in his loss and anger, stepped through with determination.

The older Thayl finally spoke again and let the vision fade. "When I stepped through that Veil door, I didn't know what I would find. I barely trusted the witch's words and hoped I would die myself. I welcomed Hell. But instead, I found you as promised. My hand was drawn to you and the feeling of the flow of power as I stole your essence, I cannot explain it. Then your boy showed up."

"Will. He stopped you, before you could take all of... me."

"If he hadn't, I wonder if I would have been more powerful. I may have been able to defeat all of the Wizard's Council much sooner. There would have been more death, more destruction, and I am sure that I would have achieved my goal. Then have had that power set to Providence's goal."

"What was her goal? What did she get out of all this effort and bloodshed?"

"There was a covenant, a debt," Thayl said. "She would help me destroy all of the Wizard's Council for my revenge, and then I would repay the debt to her."

"Repay it? How?"

"I never discovered what I was to do for her. Some of the Wizard's Council still lived, so she had not fulfilled her side, so I had no reason to follow through with mine."

Memory tried exercising her dream control skills and summoned a vision of the witch back into the room. She stood frozen like a mannequin and Memory walked around her, trying to peak under the hood to see who was underneath. The shadowed face just revealed a normal-looking

old woman, with a spatter of blood on her wrinkled lips.

"She's one scary old lady that's for sure. I bet she would have answers for me, but I'll be damned if I want to be in the same room as her."

Thayl looked from Memory to the frozen vision of Providence with a frown. "I am sorry that I don't have answers for you. Though there is one thing Providence told me that you should know. If you travel through to Hell, there is no guaranteed way to return. She would say it is easy to get from here to there, but not the other way around. The only way I managed to come back was because Providence maintained the gateway at this end."

Memory shrugged. "I haven't really thought of going back since I don't really remember it there. My home, family, friends – they're all here now."

"Just keep in mind, if you ever change your decision about going back to this world you grew up in," Thayl gestured to the room around them, "Be sure it is what you want, as you might not be able to return to Avall."

CHAPTER SIX

"Mem, it's *Bron-marbh Ai-leadh*." Eloryn enunciated each syllable carefully. She knew the Branding spell would have no effect unless used in a situation where the Pact rightly allowed it, but saying it aloud still made her uncomfortable.

"Bron-marf Allalee. Oh pfft." Memory sputtered out, obviously aware how far off her pronunciation was. Eloryn frowned at Memory's inability to articulate the behest. She should have learned the Branding spell by now, and Eloryn felt neglectful that it had taken this long to find time to teach her. Hearing about Memory's recent run in with an unseelie fawn made the lesson more urgent. She'd only just told Eloryn about being trapped in a fairy ring. The thought of losing her sister to an unseelie fae terrified Eloryn almost as much as the fact that Memory had taken so long to tell her about it.

Both Memory and Eloryn's guards and handlers trailed a few feet behind as they made their way to the Round Room, acting as though they couldn't hear or had no interest in the girls' conversation. Memory kept glancing at them like she was embarrassed to be getting this lesson here. She folded her arms childishly. "Damn it. I can't get it. I don't even understand how it's meant to work anyway."

"That's all right. I've never used it myself and hope neither of us ever need to. To be honest, the Brand is more of a punishment than a defense. It can only be used if a fae has already acted unjustly toward you, even

a small act of violence. And you must remember it's a death sentence. Not only does the Brand itself kill the branded within twenty-four hours, but the Brand is also a sign that the fae, or human, has violated the pact and can be hunted and killed by anyone. But it's important to at least know the words, so you have the option of threatening its use as a deterrent. Try one last time? Bronmarbh Aileadh."

"Bron-marv Allay-ay," Memory repeated.

"Almost." *Not quite.*

"Why do I have to come to this meeting anyway?" Memory moaned. "It's not like I was invited."

"I want you to be there. It's important to me." Eloryn felt like she hadn't seen much of Memory recently. The growing gulf between them made her stomach ache. Her time had been almost completely consumed with rehearsals and planning for the upcoming coronation. She'd been hearing rumors of how her sister had been spending time without her, from fairy rings to public taverns, and it increasingly concerned her. She refused to admit it also made her jealous. At least Memory was accepting some help from palace staff now. Her new handmaiden was doing a good job of keeping Memory presentable, looking like the princess she was. Her hair was almost always up now in a style that disguised the short cut, and she wore elegant gowns Eloryn was sure Memory wouldn't have picked herself, like the shimmering aqua dress with a giant bow for a bustle she had on now. Eloryn knew how some people talked about Memory and was happy to see her fitting in even a little bit more. "I want to help you to understand magic and your connection with it. I'm sorry I haven't been able to do that yet."

"I'd love a chance to talk to you about that stuff too. There are things I have to tell you and haven't had a chance. But we're not going to get to do that at Hayes's dumb meeting, or here," Memory said, glaring back at the following guards again.

As the twins approached the entrance to the Round Room, they heard angry shouting. Their bodyguards reacted swiftly, breaking from their position behind the girls to run forward and create a wall in front of them. Peeking between the bulk of their guards, Eloryn saw Hayes in heated conversation with a red-faced man who she didn't recognize. The rest of the Council surrounded them, muttering amongst themselves.

"It can't be allowed. The kingdom shouldn't be ruled by some little girl who's been who-knows-where for who-knows-how-long! Not at

such a fragile and crucial time," the man shouted, each word a short, sharp bark.

"I don't like this guy already," Memory whispered.

Hayes lifted his hands in a calming gesture. "We have invited you here to allow a reasonable discussion. If you will not be reasonable then there is no more to discuss. Should you calm yourself you could meet with Princess Eloryn and see what a fine young lady she is, and you should have confidence that we the Council and our knowledge and experience stand behind her."

"In a role that is not yours. Running the government is not the role of wizards." The man waved away Hayes's gesture. "I don't need to remind you how powerful my family name is. We are the ones who should be ruling, and I'm willing to fight for that right should the need arise."

"Quiet yourself and think twice before making such rash threats. Perhaps if you spent some time with the girls. They are, after all, family and becoming close to them could prove beneficial, providing you with the power that you desire."

"From what I hear those girls are nothing but harlots. I want nothing to do with them. At least my family maintains its dignity."

"Then might I remind you, Sir Ewain, that you in fact have no rightful claim to the throne? You may quip about the pedigree of the sisters, but unlike you they are of Maellan blood and are therefore the heirs. Be warned you speak of treason."

Eloryn thought to her studies on the family trees of Avall nobility. From the name Ewain and the crest he bore on his vest, Eloryn made a swift guess at who this man was.

Eloryn pushed through her bodyguards, ordering them from her path and strode in to join the conversation.

"Dear Uncle," she began.

The man snorted in disgust and pushed past both Memory and Eloryn on his way out. Their guards stepped in and moved to apprehend the man for the insult, but Eloryn waved the order to free him, and he stormed off down the corridor.

"Uncle?" Memory asked. She and Eloryn moved into the Round Room where the tension of the argument had everyone on their feet.

"Yes. Your father's brother." Hayes moved over to the table where he took a seat, motioning for the sisters and the rest of the Council to do the same. He ran a hand over his short cropped salt and pepper

hair. He seemed tired, making him look as old as some of the other Councilors. "He's hotheaded and believes that his family has a right to the throne. Whilst there's no legality to it, they could still pose a threat should they gain popular support."

"First I've heard of any uncle," Memory said. "Do I have more family I don't know about?"

"None of Maellan blood," Eloryn answered. "Yet there are some on our father's side. I'd hoped to welcome them as beloved family. I had no comprehension they had such ill feelings toward us."

"I'm sorry they are not the family you've hoped for, princess," Hayes said. "I've been in talks with them to try and settle the matter, but it seems they resent your family's bloodline for what happened to their son and their brother, King Edmund."

"That's not exactly fair," Memory said. "It's not as though Loredanna was the one who picked him as her husband."

Hayes, who already looked worn from the argument with Ewain, glared at Memory. Eloryn wished Memory wasn't so blunt sometimes.

Waylan spoke up from across the table. "I would have to agree with Princess Memory in this case. We the Council do have much to atone for, and our taking on so many roles in rebuilding Avall is clearly agitating people. I understand the need for our guidance at this time, but we need to start putting the normal order of government in place. Ours is the role of guardians and teachers of magic in the land, not of ruling and politics. Seeing the Council step back from that may placate Ewain and his family."

"And when should I step back, Waylan, now? While rash families are hovering the throne awaiting any mistake by our young princesses?" Hayes said.

"Their rage is misdirected. Perhaps the execution of Thayl will calm their boiling blood," a Councilor from the far end of the table suggested. Lambeth, Eloryn reminded herself, still teaching herself the names of all the Councilors "After all, he is in fact the one to blame."

Memory rose to her feet in an abrupt movement.

"Whoa, whoa, whoa, what are you guys talking about? What execution?" she asked.

"Having been found guilty of high treason, murder, and numerous other crimes, Thayl is to be publically executed not long after coronation as part of ongoing celebrations," Hayes explained.

Memory shook her head. "You're using the words executed and celebrations in the same sentence here. Have I just gone to crazy land? You're not really talking about killing Thayl in public?"

Lambeth spoke up again, his voice crackly and dry with age. "The sentence for Thayl's crimes is to be hung, drawn, and quartered. Crime in our lands is treated very seriously, perhaps unlike in the lands where you have been."

Memory glared at him, mouth hanging open.

Eloryn stood up by her sister's side. "I must admit, Council, the sentence does seem ghastly. Avall suffered many years of such terrors under Thayl's rule. Perhaps we should reconsider, so that Avall's new beginning is free from such bloodshed."

"What would you have us do? Have him go unpunished?" Bors scoffed from the other side of the table.

"You think having your hand cut off and rotting in a cell for the rest of your life is 'unpunished'?" Memory replied.

Eloryn felt torn. The man had been the cause of great sorrow for her, but she couldn't find it in her anymore to wish for his death. She had once, and when sharing her sister's body, she almost took his life herself. She was glad she did not, and it felt odd to have spared his life then only to see him executed now.

"I agree with Memory. I do not need to see this man's blood on display," Eloryn said.

Bors stood to respond and Hayes stood as well, giving him a firm look which quieted him. "I understand that executions aren't a pleasant idea for a heart as gentle as your own, but the people of Avall expect this. Why should the murderer of your mother be treated differently than any other criminal?"

Memory huffed. "But he didn't kill our mother. That was an accident."

Eloryn winced. The man who raised her like she was his own daughter was the one who committed the deadly accident.

Memory looked at Eloryn as though she were sorry to have reminded everyone of it and then continued. "Besides, Thayl was being manipulated by someone else, a powerful witch called Providence. She was the one who gave him the power and encouragement to do what he did. It wasn't all his fault."

"Princess, we can see you are concerned, but your sympathy for this man is unhealthy. The bailiff informed me of your visits to Thayl's cell.

Undoubtedly, you have become emotionally attached to this murderer, and he is manipulating your sympathies for this very purpose of trying to spare his life."

"Memory?" Eloryn looked at her sister. Memory's face turned pink, and she looked away. Eloryn felt ill. "Memory, you've been visiting Thayl?"

"So what? I was looking for some answers. That's no crime," Memory snapped.

"What is more," Hayes said, looking down at Memory, "we've no knowledge of this woman 'Providence.' Indeed, no women have a high enough learning or understanding of magic to do what she is said to have done, except, perhaps, those of Maellan blood. Princess Memory, these are nothing but the tales of a man attempting to shift the blame.

"The public expect, no, *need* Thayl to be executed. They need to know he is gone for good. Your highness," Hayes said, pushing a piece of paper towards Eloryn. "I implore you to sign his death warrant. It is the only way that we can secure the safety of the kingdom. He could still be a threat."

"He's not a threat. He's just a poor man in a cell. He can't do anything." Memory looked from the paper to Eloryn. "Lory, please, you can't do this."

"Mem," Eloryn said quietly. "You didn't have to experience it. The things he did. You escaped it all. The murders, the torturing, the decay of the land. The banning of magic put a strain on everyone, you can't imagine. Something as simple as sending a message to a friend was almost impossible, and there was no magic to heal the sick. Thousands died. You can't imagine the suffering this man caused."

"I escaped it all?" Memory's face scrunched up. "How can you say that after what I've been through?"

"It's for the best." Eloryn held her breath and signed the death warrant. Her chest pounded. She felt faint. Hayes took the paper from the table.

Memory looked at her sister in disbelief then turned and ran out of the room.

"And that is why you will make a far better queen than your sister," Hayes said.

Eloryn could tell that he was trying to be nice, but she wasn't sure she believed him. *What have I done?* Her legs wobbled beneath her. She fell onto the chair, put her head on the table, and started to cry. Hayes

knelt beside her and excused the rest of the Council from the room, leaving him and Eloryn alone.

"My dear, my dear, I know it is difficult. But it takes a true queen to do what you have done today."

"I can't do this," Eloryn implored. "I can't say who lives and who dies."

"I understand. Your role is not an easy one. But know we of the Council are here to advise and assist you in any way. It is traditional for a monarch to delegate their duties, for to carry every responsibility alone would be a weight enough to crush any man."

Eloryn wiped her eyes and looked up at Hayes. "Could you? Would you take this horrible task from me?"

Hayes paused, as if considering, then nodded. "By granting me the power of court legislature you won't have to sign another piece of paper like this again. Perhaps it would be more appropriate for me to see to the matter of death sentences. Living through what I have, I am more equipped to deal with such dreadful decisions. Such matters should not be the realm of children."

But they are the realm of a monarch. How can I be that person? Eloryn shook her head. Maybe she couldn't be that person because she couldn't put her name on a piece of paper like that again. "Yes. Please have the appropriate documents written up to transfer this role to you. Thank you, Hayes. Thank you for being here for me."

Memory ran all the way from the Round Room to the dungeon, her dress swishing around her like an aqua tide. Her heart hammered. Her face burned in anger at her sister and the Council. Her anger also turned inward. Maybe she did she have an unhealthy connection to Thayl. But she still thought everything about an execution was wrong, no matter who was being executed or why.

Memory stormed past the bailiff, giving him a filthy look for ratting her out. She wondered if as a princess she had any hiring and firing powers. After passing the first floor of cells, she took the final flight of stairs to Thayl's solitary confinement.

On her approach, she heard the sound of hushed conversation, but as she stepped in front of the bars she saw only Thayl, sitting alone,

chained up as before.

"They're going to kill you," she stated. Her face turned redder, embarrassment mixing with her rage for the fragile and desperate tone of her voice.

"Of course," Thayl responded. "You didn't know till now?"

Memory shook her head. The cell was cold, but Memory burned inside and out, the flames inside her threatening to burst through her skin, kindled by her emotions. She leaned against the damp stone walls in an attempt to cool herself down. "I tried to stop the execution, but no one will listen to me. Hung, drawn, and quartered. Does that mean what it sounds like?"

Thayl nodded slowly. "It is the traditional punishment for treason. What would the people think if they changed it for the likes of me?"

Memory's stomach clenched at the thought of the punishment and she bent forward.

"Why does this matter so much to you?" Thayl said. "After all I did to you I thought you would be pleased to see me gone."

"Not everyone thinks blood for blood is cool. It's wrong to kill people like this. And there's got to be more you can tell me, about Providence, or my mother, or..." *Or I'm making excuses. I just don't want him to die. Could I have gotten that close to this monster? What does that make me?*

"I often think on it, how much you took from me, and I from you, and yet I cannot ignore the fact you have saved my life once and again attempt to do so." Thayl stood and moved as close to the bars of his cell as his shackles allowed. He looked broken, gaunt, not at all the way he used to look. "I do appreciate it, but I think I'm beyond help."

Memory's eyes watered. "They can't kill you."

Thayl looked blankly at her, but then gave a smile with the corner of his mouth.

"Do you remember that trick you played on me, when you told me that you were my daughter?"

Memory just nodded.

"I'm glad that you're not," he said.

Appalled, Memory fled the room.

CHAPTER SEVEN

"I don't even know what this thing is," Memory said, lifting a strange golden utensil from a silk-lined box. Clara giggled and showed her the finely crafted tea set it accompanied, making the item some kind of tea strainer. Memory sat by her dresser while Clara worked on her hair, incorporating stuffing and wirework into the structure to build volume, and lacing strands of pearls into twirling braids. They were up before the sun had risen, and the elaborate hair style was almost complete, but Memory still sat in her bed-clothes. The flowing chemise was light and draped in silky falls over her body, but a roaring fire across the room kept her warm. Clara had already mentioned three times how much faster she could prepare Memory for this day with some extra help, and how she'd gone out of her way to convince the designer to let her prepare Memory on her own. Apparently dressing up for a coronation was even more of a big deal than normal. Memory couldn't bear the idea of more people buzzing around, touching her. She'd been dreading this day since it was announced. Not only did it mean suffering the embarrassment of being paraded around the city streets like a carnival float, but it was also the day before the execution of Thayl, the bloodbath her twin had sanctioned.

"We've got plenty of time," Memory said again, secretly hoping they would be late. She pushed the boxes with the tea set and implements of tea making over into the Do Not Want pile. It was already much larger than the Want pile.

Clara put a bobby pin back in her mouth and shifted the set into the Want pile. "Those are from Duke Lanval and Duchess Marian de Montredeur. You may want to keep them for when they visit you. You really should read the cards."

Memory rolled her eyes. A knock on the door and four servants entered with more stacked presents. She'd already been through this for her birthday, and here she was again, getting buried in finery.

"Just put it all over there," she told the servants, indicating the Do Not Want pile.

Clara tsked and put a new box in front of Memory to open. "Can we at least see what's in them? It's so exciting."

"It will be more exciting to see all this stuff go to a good cause. When I told Hayes I wanted to help those homeless kids, he allocated me some 'promotional funds.'" Memory dropped her voice to a mock imitation of Hayes's. "A handful of coins to give out on the street, smiling and patting babies on the head. He said it was a good idea, good for improving my image. It was nice, but I didn't have enough to give all of them. Not even close. Hayes won't increase the funds. He's got no idea of what's going on out there, so I figure I'd make some money myself, right? I just hope this crap sells for lots." Memory lifted a vase, decorated with a sculpted scene of lilies and frolicking otters. It looked made of gold, but was almost transparent and icy to touch.

Wide eyed, Clara took the vase carefully from Memory like she cradled a priceless newborn. "This one will fetch a fine price indeed. True fairy gold!"

"I thought fairy gold was a bad thing?"

"The broken scraps of it are worthless since humans can't work it. Only the fae can, creating masterpieces like this, or weapons. It is almost as brittle as glass, but makes deadly sharp blades. A beautiful thing."

"Beautiful and useless. Over with the rest."

Clara pouted, but put the vase carefully back in its padded box and onto the Do Not Want pile. "You might not understand it, but the people do love you, Hope. You are the one who defeated Thayl. They want you to have these fine things."

"Yeah, I'm sure those orphans want me having golden strainers while they are begging for food."

Clara paused and smiled. "You have a good soul, highness."

If I even have a soul. Memory shrugged. Soul or not, it was just common sense.

A racket of marching feet and clattering weapons came from the hall and the door burst open. Peirs rushed in followed by a huddle of guards among which Memory could barely see Eloryn and Roen. Eloryn, already in her dress for the big day, barely fit through the door with the sheer volume of her skirts and oversized lace collar fanning out behind her.

Memory knew that Peirs, who previously led the resistance against Thayl, had been made Captain of the Guard at Caermaellan castle, but the place was so big she hadn't seen him since the morning they defeated Thayl. Peirs did a quick check of the rooms, and the guards averted their eyes from Memory when they saw she still only wore her silky undergarments.

"Okay. What's going on? You lose something?"

Roen squeezed through the crowd filling Memory's sitting room. He hugged her briefly. "Thank the fae, you're all right."

"It's Thayl." Eloryn ran up to her sister and held her as well, shaking. "He's escaped."

Clara did a dramatic cross between a gasp and a squeal. Roen took and squeezed Memory's hand.

Peirs returned from checking her bedroom and offered a brisk salute and bow, followed by the lopsided smile she remembered. "Sorry for the intrusion. We feared he may try to come after you. It's good to see you're safe."

People kept talking around her. Peirs arranged soldiers to stand inside and out of Memory's chambers, and Eloryn explained how they hadn't been able to track Thayl through magical or non-magical means and had no idea how he had got out of his cell.

Memory's head was shaking softly from side to side and she chewed her bottom lip, the news sinking in. She mumbled, mostly to herself, "He won't come here. That would be crazy. He hasn't got any power anymore. He must be trying to get away, but where could he hide?" Her words were lost under the other conversations.

Roen kept looking to Eloryn, the worry on his face clear. A plan formed in Memory's mind. *They'll be safe here. But this might be the only chance to avoid the execution.*

Memory raised her voice over the crowd. "I'm just going to chuck some clothes on."

Approaching the bedroom, she gave the guards in there a look. "A

little privacy please? And, Clara, I'll manage by myself, thanks."

Memory smiled in a way to indicate she was calm and coping and closed the double doors to her sitting room, leaving her alone in the bedroom. She dashed across to the wardrobe and yanked out the box she'd stuffed in the bottom. A minute later, she'd wriggled into jeans and pulled on the t-shirt and shoes.

She stepped out onto the balcony and scooted up onto the balustrade. Looking down, she swallowed. It was a long way, but the only way she could get out of here alone was Will style.

She began to lower herself, taking care to hold tightly onto the vines. Thick, ancient ivy intertwined with woody rose stems. She inched her way down, managing to grab the thorny option more than once and her hands bled by the time she had her feet on the grass below. Memory cursed at her stinging hands. *Will makes it look so easy.*

The palace grounds were clear of people except the occasional group of guards. Memory waited behind some bushes for a patrol to pass and tried to work out what to do next. She only had one option, walk, and hope whatever connection she had with Thayl led her to him, or vice versa.

She ended up heading into the northern wing where Thayl had lived during his reign. The area had been closed up since his defeat, as there hadn't been time yet to properly dispose of his belongings, and no one was keen to move into the same rooms as he'd been in anyway, as though they were tainted. The rooms she wandered into were small, more the size of the castle's guest rooms than the sort of chambers made for the monarchs, which Memory and Eloryn now inhabited.

A wardrobe had been raided, and the old, gray rags Thayl had worn in prison lay on the ground. This was the right place. Memory could hear Thayl up ahead, arguing with someone about debts. Memory reached the stairs to the far tower and crept up them. The tower was large, with round rooms between the spiraling flights of stairs. Memory went up two stories, trying to listen in to the conversation above her, but her rubber-sole sneakers squeaked on the marble steps, and the conversation ended.

"Memory?" Thayl's voice bellowed. "I know it's you."

"Who are you talking to?" Memory called back from halfway up the flight. "Is Providence there with you?"

"She's gone. You can come up. I won't hurt you."

Memory stepped up into the tower's highest room. It seemed to have been turned into storage, mostly full of disused furniture, a pile of old

mattresses, and gold framed paintings stacked against the wall. Thayl wore clean clothes, standing by an open window. Memory almost fled again when she saw his remaining hand had been freshly cut, covered in the runes and markings like the one she had dismembered.

"What are you doing?" Memory pointed at his hand, keeping her distance, circling Thayl in the round space. A pigeon fluttered in the conical roof above them and Memory jumped.

Thayl raised his hand, examining it as though he'd forgotten what it meant. "Don't worry. I'm not going to be part of that witch's plan any longer, although letting her help me escape will serve a purpose."

"I wanted to help you, let you get away, but that hand, how can I trust you?"

"You don't have to. Thank you, but I don't need your help. I hadn't even expected to see you again." Thayl seemed so eerily calm, it scared Memory more than if he were angry. "But I guess that is good too. I can tell you now that I fear you misunderstood what I last said to you, when I said that I was glad you aren't my daughter."

Memory scrunched her nose, angry at the sting there threatening to cause tears.

"What I meant in truth was that I am glad you didn't have me as a father. I'm not worthy to be father to someone like you."

Memory moved closer to him, but he motioned for her to keep her distance, stepping back so he pressed against the small balcony outside the open full length window. From this height, Memory could see the hedge maze, garden wall, the river that encircled the castle, and green pastures spreading into the distance. It felt like she could see half of Avall.

"Thayl, the execution doesn't have to happen. We can get you away from here," Memory said. "I could open a Veil door to where I came from. You can escape for good, start a new life."

Thayl shook his head. "I am still such a problem for you. You don't wish me killed, but you must know I have to die. There is nothing else left for me."

Memory refused to listen. Instead she tried to focus her energy, to concentrate on the room in the orphanage she now remembered clearly and open a door to it, but nothing happened. A force pressed back at her as she tried to open the Veil, like pressing against stretched fabric.

She grunted at the failure. "No, there's got to be another way."

Memory started pacing, trying to think but was distracted by a

strange sight. On the path she'd walked to reach where she stood now, glowing footsteps lit up like made of sunlight, following her trail. *Some kind of magic, some spell?* Memory drew a sharp breath. A spell to track her.

"Memory!" Eloryn's voice echoed up the stairs, and Memory could hear the approach of armored men. Her sister, Roen, and a small division of soldiers in bronze armor ran up into the room, immediately surrounding Thayl and forcing him against the low balcony wall at weapon point.

"Leave him alone!" Memory rushed forward, but Peirs and another guard held her back. "Let go! Lory, Roen, stop this! They're going to kill him!" Memory yelled as the guards lifted her by her arms.

"Memory, please, it's all right," Thayl spoke calmly. He looked into her eyes as he stepped backwards, elegantly raising himself onto the balustrade.

"Remain still!"

"Not another step!"

The soldiers yelled, and the sound of more people charging up the stairs filled Memory's ears.

"What are you doing?" she mouthed, barely a whisper.

"Removing a problem," Thayl replied. His soft words reached her clearly over the shouting men.

"No!" Memory screamed.

There was no grief in Thayl's face, merely resolve. Only his brow suggested that he felt anything at all, curled and pained. He stood up straight, almost appearing as his former self, darkly handsome and charismatic, and looked around at those in front of him. Then he let himself fall backwards from the tower and to his death.

The guards ran to the edge to peer down. Peirs sent men to ensure Thayl's demise. Roen blocked Memory from looking herself. Eloryn tried to hold her, but she wouldn't be held. Memory's head swam and she felt about to explode, her insides boiling. It seemed like the tower trembled. Old frames clattered beside her.

The Wizard's Council arrived, armed with scrolls and loose leaf pages of spells at the ready.

The guards beckoned them over to the edge and Hayes looked down.

"What happened here?" he asked. He approached Memory and began to shake her. "What happened?"

Memory put her arms up, clawing away his grasp on her. Eloryn stepped between them. "Memory had nothing to do with this. She merely tracked Thayl down."

"The people are robbed of their execution," someone said.

The world blurred and Memory realized she was crying. She couldn't deny it or make excuses anymore. She'd grown close to Thayl. No matter what he was or what he'd done. Maybe because they were both broken and wrong inside. Memory couldn't believe what she heard, disgusted that this death meant nothing to anyone else but the loss of their bloody execution. How could a life mean so little to these people, any life?

She pushed everyone away, stumbling toward the stairs. Eloryn called after her, but no one followed.

Memory stopped running only when she neared her room. Someone was up ahead, staring down the stairs. The figure stood in shadows, obscured, blurry, but familiar.

"Eloryn?" Memory called out, wiping her eyes clear.

"It's your fault, all your fault," was the hissed reply.

Memory charged forward but found no one there. She turned to look back the way she'd come but found herself alone.

A tap on her shoulder sent Memory jumping back against a wall. Clara, who had tapped her also jumped about a foot with a squeal.

"Highness!" she gasped like it was a curse word. "Are you all right? I was told what happened and sent to find you."

Memory gave a hollow laugh. "Am I all right?"

"No, I suppose not by the look of you. Such a horrible thing, and you, young lady, running off like that! What were you thinking? Come, let's get you cleaned up and into your dress. At least your hair is still decent."

"Decent enough to curl up and sleep for the rest of the week?"

"Oh, Hope, no. I've been instructed to prepare you for the coronation. It's going ahead."

CHAPTER EIGHT

A set of eight white horses pulled Memory and Eloryn along in a gilded, open-top carriage. They drove through the streets of the city lined with billowing pennants, accompanied close behind by another open carriage carrying Hayes and key Wizard Council members, followed by battalions of soldiers and dignitaries. Massive crowds lined the streets and rooftops, trying to get a glimpse of the Maellan twins. The people of Avall had hoped for an heir of the Maellan line to return for so long, and now they had a matching pair. Her whole life had become a surreal side show in which the twin sisters were the biggest crowd pleaser, and folk from every corner of the known world came to watch. The people were so jubilant. Maybe Clara was right, and Memory just didn't understand how much this meant to them and the hardships they had gone through under Thayl.

Despite the crisp coolness of late autumn, the sun shone warmly, making the carriage and her over the top coronation dress sparkle. It was a beautiful day, but Memory couldn't focus on more than keeping her tears in. She struggled to breathe in her - she could hardly call it a dress, it was more like some kind of bizarre artwork. Folds and frills wrapped and tied into place so tight she couldn't move or bend her back, the silver fabric covered in so many fine gemstones it weighed more than she did, and a huge filigree collar fanning out behind her.

Memory couldn't believe what had just happened on the castle tower,

and that this supposedly joyful scene could happen straight afterwards. She tried to take a deep breath and it came out more like a sob.

Eloryn, her dress matching but in rich gold tones, took Memory's hand and gripped it tightly as she waved to the crowds with her other. Memory could feel her shaking. Eloryn kept smiling to the people around them, but it looked strained.

"I'm sorry for what happened with Thayl," she said, while still looking out at the crowds, keeping up the happy monarch impression.

"For how you were going to have him killed, or how you didn't get to because he killed himself?"

"I didn't want for either outcome." Eloryn gave Memory a pitiful look before quickly returning to the smiles and waves.

"It doesn't matter. It's over now." As much as she wanted to, Memory couldn't blame Eloryn. She could only blame herself for caring too much for a man that everyone else thought of as a monster.

"Look at them all, Mem. Look how happy they are. We owe it to them to do our best by Avall." Eloryn obviously had the coronation on her mind. As much as Memory didn't care for the day, it was a much bigger deal for her sister, about to become queen. She sounded so nervous that Memory squeezed her hand back.

Occasionally amongst the exuberant crowds Memory saw small faces she recognized. The homeless children she had given coins. When she saw that they were cheering just as hard as the more well off people on the streets, she found herself actually smiling back. She spent the rest of the parade making her plans to visit them again soon with more alms and whatever she could get selling off her presents.

Eventually the cavalcade returned to the palace. The massive front yard leading to the castle was also crowded, filled with the nobility of Avall. As Memory and Eloryn were driven up to the front steps, fireworks streamed into the sky, hissing and exploding in the twilight. *Is it that late already?* Memory thought, looking blearily at the multicolored lights blazing like living flame in the sky, enhanced with behests to form sparkling representations of the twins and Maellan crest.

The carriage stopped, and Hayes helped Eloryn dismount, leading her up the palace steps that had been lined with red carpet. Another Councilor that Memory couldn't name did the same for her. This wizard looked like the oldest of the Councilors, and Memory took baby steps to help him keep up pace with her.

The entrance hall and the public throne room that it led into had been decorated for the coronation. Banners hung from the ceiling and massive floral arrangements spread like gardens across tables. Wisp-lights hovered throughout the room, dancing around crystal chandeliers, casting a golden glow. Near the furthest wall, a grand throne stood the height of three men with a smaller throne beside it. They would have been the king and queen's throne, but for now would be the queen's and princess's.

Eloryn and Memory took their seats. Clara appeared at Memory's side, standing half hidden behind the throne. She offered a supportive smile as she did a quick adjustment of Memory's hair. Memory tried to get comfortable, but the torturous dress didn't allow it. It didn't look like the night would come to an end any time soon and Memory groaned.

Following Memory and Eloryn into the room were delegates and representatives from all over Avall. Dukes, counts, earls, and the monarchs of the fae courts queued up to pay their respects to Eloryn. Clara indicated to Memory who was who, whispering in her ear as the guests greeted Eloryn, so by the time they turned to recognize Memory beside her she knew who they were.

The first to approach the throne was Aine, the seelie queen. She appeared as everything Memory expected a fairy to be. Her translucent skin emanated a comforting glow. Auburn hair that ran down the entire length of her back and a few feet along the floor behind her was woven with flowers and framed a too perfect face and eyes that shone like stars.

Next to Aine was Lugh, a handsome man, all in shades of bronze, who carried a golden spear twice his height. *Fairy gold*, Memory noted. He appeared human, and Clara confirmed as much with her gossip.

"Aine took a human lover, and just look at him, you can see why! He's been with her for decades, some say nearly a century, but doesn't show it. They say it's the fairy food and spending time in the land of the fae, it makes a human ageless like the fae. Wouldn't mind some of that medicine myself."

Memory thought of Will, wondering how his time with Mina had affected him, but she didn't have long to think on it before the procession continued and two creatures with the all black eyes of the unseelie fae approached.

"It's her, the one from the play," Memory whispered to Clara.

"Lady Nyneve, yes, she's daughter to King Finvarra of the unseelie court."

Memory stared at the raven-haired Amazon goddess. She was as stunning as in the play, but there was something unsettling about her. Her hands were delicately clasped together, and she wore a dress woven from black cobwebs, as though she were still in mourning. A huge sword hung from an ornate belt about her waist, as though it were jewelry. It seemed the fashion for the fae to be seen with fairy gold weapons. Memory wondered if they were just status symbols or actually put to use.

Nyneve and her father bowed to Eloryn. Where Aine was the picture of feminine beauty, Finvarra was a skeletal mess of geriatric masculinity, hunched and angular. He appeared withered like a dead tree and his fingers looked more like talons. When he opened his mouth a set of gleaming sharp teeth could be seen. His mouth held a permanent scowl, which seemed to stretch into a more grotesque anger when he turned to Memory. Nyneve put a hand on his shoulder and it seemed to calm him enough to continue on, muttering under his breath.

After the fae came the nobility of Avall, starting with Duke Lanval and Duchess Marian, followed close behind by Roen and his parents, Isabeth and Brannon. Seeing them brought a brighter moment in a long and difficult night. Both groups expressed great joy for the twins, but could only speak for a moment before the seemingly never ending stream of people had to continue. The twins' uncle was conspicuously absent.

The rest of the ceremony became a boring blur of speeches, etiquette, and a lot of standing up and sitting down. At some point Eloryn was crowned queen, but Memory couldn't be sure when since it seemed to be mentioned so many times. The solid gold masculine crown just seemed to appear on Eloryn's head at some point when Memory wasn't looking. It appeared to be the very same one Arthur Maellan once wore, and she wondered if it was a replica or the real thing.

The girls were herded from their thrones into the ball room. The center of the room remained clear and some folk were already dancing to a softly playing string quartet. Around the edges of the room, great tables stood, piled with towers of food. Memory longed to go to them, desperately needing to eat, but Hayes interrupted her by handing her a sheet of paper.

"What is this? This had better be something I can eat." She waved it vaguely.

"You will be speaking after Eloryn. Don't worry. We kept your speech short."

Public speaking? Kill me now. Memory wondered why she hadn't been told about this earlier or given a chance to read what she was meant to say, but she probably would have if she'd actually attended the rehearsals. Memory glared at Hayes as he herded her back to another dais and two smaller ceremonial thrones to sit beside Eloryn. Hayes drew the attention of the room. Clara had followed and took her place again just behind Memory's seat and explained to Memory that Eloryn now had to read out and confirm the renewing of the Pact, which is something that every new ruler must do.

"It's really more out of tradition than anything else." Clara kept gossiping to Memory straight over the important words Eloryn spoke. "The only real way the Pact could be broken was if an act of war was committed, and even then, only if the offended monarch wished for it."

Memory tried to listen to both Clara and Eloryn, and it sounded like Eloryn was doing a good job. Her voice seemed so small and shy, but she spoke every word perfectly, having memorized the whole thing. At the end of the speech, Aine and Lugh both nodded their heads, and Finvarra just sneered.

Hayes took over again. In his speech, he explained that ordinarily the various representatives of local governments and regions would confirm recognition of the new monarch, but as the Wizard's Council was temporarily overseeing all governmental functions at this time the re-establishment of the government would be unfortunately delayed. This caused a few murmurs in the crowd, and Hayes thumped his cane on the ground to silence them and smiled gleefully.

"I also wish to share some good news. By the wishes of our Queen, Thayl Vaircarn was put to death in a private ceremony earlier this week."

Memory's head swung around in slow motion to stare at Hayes in disbelief. *He's really going to lie to everyone about how Thayl died and pretend it was all their plan?*

"Her majesty rightly felt that the tyrant needed no fanfare to his death, and the sooner he was removed from the land the better. We were, of course, happy to carry out that request." He chuckled, as if he had made a joke. The crowd joined in, applause building through the laughter.

Memory's inner fire raged. The sum of the day's events caught up with her. She tasted bile. Memory didn't think puking on the dais would make a good impression and stood to make her exit. Hayes smiled at her as she did and opened for her to begin her speech. Memory stood stunned for a moment, blinking at the roomful of people staring at her. So many expectant faces. Her gaze settled on Eloryn, who looked at her with an encouraging smile. *Crapness. I'm really going to have to do this damn speech.*

Memory cleared her throat and stared at the written notes. Her hands sweated, smudging the ink, and trembled so much she could barely read the words.

"People of Avall," she stammered. There were a few claps and cheers. "I speak to you today not just as a princess, but as one of you. A daughter of Avall, joyous to once again be free, delivered from the blight on our land." Memory skimmed over the script. *What is this bullshit?* She'd never say these things. Making it sound like she'd grown up in Avall and that she was ecstatic that Thayl was dead. More lies from Hayes. Memory crumpled the paper in her hands. If she was going to say anything they would be her words, and something meaningful. Something she believed in. *And if it pissed off Hayes at the same time? One stone, twice the value.*

"And as princess of Avall, I want to announce that the new Wizard's University won't be restricted to just nobles. The study of magic will be open to anyone, no matter who they are."

Memory swore she heard crickets. Some muted applause from a few individuals was covered by Hayes, stepping beside her quick as anything and laughing over her announcement.

"Of course commoners are welcome to join the university," he said. "If they can afford the entrance fee!"

The room roared with laughter again, as though they were putting on a funny skit together. Memory looked at Eloryn for support, but Eloryn just looked embarrassed for her.

Memory stepped off the dais, pushing angrily through the gaudy crowd. These were the people she was expected to live around? People that laughed at jokes about people being killed and the poor being unable to pay for their education? Memory dug fingernails into her palms to distract herself from imminent tears.

Clara trotted after her. "I think what you said up there was amazing."
Your fault.
Memory turned on the spot, looking for the source of the voice.

Clara smiled back sympathetically. "Although I think you chose the wrong crowd for such an announcement, being as everyone here was eligible to go to the university anyway and probably don't want the likes of commoners attending beside them."

Unnatural.

From behind her again.

"Did you hear that?" Memory pushed through the crowd haphazardly. Her head ached. Her whole body ached. She was so exhausted she was probably delirious. Hissing whispers came from all around her in the crowd, dizzying her. She searched for their source, grabbing people as she went. Some laughed, others were diplomatically shocked, all were confused.

"Hope, are you all right? You're white as a ghost." Clara kept after her but was swallowed up by the crowd, unable to keep up with Memory's wild rush.

Murderer.

The word hit her like a freight train to the chest. She pushed her way out of the ballroom and ran.

Memory was an emotional wrecking ball. She stumbled down long hallways, each step shaking under her and a sound like distant thunder filling her ears. Decorative suits of armor along the wall rattled as she passed them. She felt unstable, her insides steaming out. In her mind she kept seeing Thayl step backwards off the ledge and disappear. Over and over. She was far from the celebrations now but still heard the voices whispering. *Your fault. Murderer.*

Memory tugged at her hair, pulling it free from its cage of bobby pins. *Did I drive him to kill himself by making him talk about the ritual so much? Did he do it for me, so I didn't have to see him executed?*

Her body jolted, faded. She was slipping, the Veil tugging at her. Passing a stairwell, she clutched onto the banister as though holding on to it would keep her anchored. The banister shuddered.

Someone walked past, a shadowed shape. Memory caught a look at the face.

"Lory? Help me, please." Memory reached out, but the figure continued without pausing.

Memory let go of the banister, stumbling after. The person's body was blurry, shadowed, but Memory saw small glimpses of the figure's face, reflected in darkened windows as it walked ahead. It was her sister's

face, for sure.

"Eloryn? Stop it, this isn't funny."

The figure turned a corner up ahead, and Memory broke into a wobbly jog. The rattling of armor and light fittings around her became more intense and curtains swirled and fluttered unnaturally.

Memory turned the corner and gasped. Herself, she saw herself, face to face in a full length mirror framed on the wall. And standing next to her, right behind her, reflected in the mirror was a second Memory. Not Eloryn at all, but her, Hope, how she used to look, complete with the dyed hair and piercings. She even wore the same clothes that Memory had on when she had arrived in Avall, the same striped long-sleeved shirt, broken heart tee over the top, and torn jeans.

Memory stared at this other self. Her other self smiled back.

Holding her breath, Memory turned around. Horror ran like ice water in her bones.

The other her wasn't just a reflection. She was there.

Memory stepped back.

"Don't be afraid," the other version of herself said.

"Who are you?" Memory asked, her lips quivering.

"Hope."

But I'm Hope. No, I'm Memory. This is not real. I'm losing my mind.

"I'm you. And you're me. The broken pieces of our self." Hope looked at Memory, a vacant, sad look in her eyes. "I'm here to be with you. Nobody can ever like us and nobody else will ever understand. Those idiots won't take long to figure out you're not a whole, *real* person. What do you think they'll do when they realize the monster you are? Still pretend to be your friend?" Hope spoke vehemently, but then softened her tone. "But I'm here now. *We* can be together, you and me, like we should be, and I'll make things better for you."

"No, you're not real. Not real!" Memory screamed out loud, shutting her eyes tight. The rattling intensified and a great cracking sound came from the mirror at her back. Shards of glass shot out around her, in every direction as though projected out from her own body, which remained untouched. The sound of smashing glass was only overpowered by her shattering scream.

CHAPTER NINE

Will could hear her screaming. Over the fireworks and oohs and aahs and giggles of nobles wandering the castle grounds enjoying the celebrations, he could hear her.

He ran over the soft grass of the gardens, keeping himself within the shadows cast by tall hedges. He still wore the shirt, vest, and pants Clara had given him but knew he wasn't presentable compared to the standards of those around him. He looked through an open door and quickly ducked inside.

The long halls of this part of the palace were fortunately quiet. His bare feet padding on the cold marble echoed back to him. He broke into a full run, no longer keeping to shadows, only worried about getting to Memory as fast as possible.

He found her curled against a wall, surrounded by broken mirror.

He wanted to go to her, scoop her up, and keep her safe in his arms. His first step brought a bright burn of pain. A small sliver of mirror cutting into his heel.

Will growled in frustration. His feet would be cut to shreds to reach her. He almost went anyway. After a deep breath to calm himself, he took off his vest and used it to clear a path to Memory, pushing the sharp shards away.

Memory turned her head, acknowledging his presence.

"Are we alone?" she asked.

Will frowned and nodded. "You can get past the glass now," he said, indicating the path he'd made. "Are you okay? How did it break?"

"It's okay. It wasn't real." Memory mumbled and made little sense. Tears still wet her cheeks and her makeup ran. He hadn't seen her this bad since back in the other world.

Memory stood up and stared at the path, making little effort to move.

Will coaxed her. "Come on. I've got something I want to show you. Come with me?"

Memory looked up at his face and after a moment a tiny smile appeared, and she walked clear of the broken mirror. "I'm sorry. God, I must be such a mess. I've had a pretty rough day." A sob broke the end of her sentence.

"It's all right. We can have our own celebration, just us, okay?" Will nodded for her to follow him. Memory dried her eyes with her wrists and followed.

Will had been wanting for a while to show her the place he'd found while roaming the palace grounds, but there'd never been a good time. Now also didn't seem good, but he needed something to distract Memory with and maybe make her happy. He led Memory through the quiet halls, up towards her rooms. Then he detoured, taking her up the spiral stairs of the tower at the eastern end of the palace. He hoped this way would work. Normally he'd come here from the outside of the building.

After reaching a window on the second landing, he opened it. Memory gasped and shook her head, but he smiled and stepped out onto an old section of the castle walls. It looked like it had been abandoned and built around at some stage when the palace was expanded. As she followed him out the window, he held Memory's hand, so she wouldn't fall due to the monstrous dress she wore. He would break the rules to make sure she stayed safe. She didn't seem to mind, and held his hand back tightly, and he could feel her shaking despite that she'd calmed down and no longer cried. She gave him a wry smile like she agreed how ridiculous her dress was for climbing around like this.

Ahead of them a massive mound of overgrown ivy sprawled like a sea monster, leafy tendrils like tentacles reaching out in every direction. Memory had told Will how this wing had been closed off during the sixteen years of Thayl's rule. The plants had completely grown over this end of the roof.

Parting a section of vines, Will revealed a secluded entrance and motioned for her to go inside.

He gestured to the room they were standing in. "It's sort of a late birthday present," he said. "A secret place, where you can just be yourself."

The room must have been an old lookout or birdhouse. No longer part of the main castle walls and without easy access, it had become disused and forgotten. It was small, with just enough room for two stone benches that sat under windows without glass but screened by ivy, letting in just a little moonlight and the flashes of fireworks. Across the courtyard they could see the clock tower lit up, about to strike midnight.

"Thank you, it's amazing," she struggled to speak. "A place to be myself. Hopefully not to be with myself."

Memory laughed strangely then seemed to notice they were still holding hands and let go. She stared at his wrist where he had the tattoo they did together.

"Will," Memory's lip trembled a little. "Something is happening to me. I've started to… remember things."

Will's heart jarred. Too many painful things for her to remember, things he wished she wouldn't ever have to know again. Like so often, he wanted to hold her, comfort every pain she had. He wanted to protect her from her own memories.

He made the mistake of moving forward, his body drawn to her.

Memory made a half cough, half laugh embarrassed noise and moved away. Will stepped back too, cursing silently.

"Don't look like I'm dying or something. Getting my memories back is good, right?" Memory hugged her arms around herself.

"I'm sorry," he said. "And I'm sorry that I haven't always been able to help, that I can't always be here for you."

Memory perked up. "Hello bright idea! How about we spend some time together here, every day? How does that sound?"

"Sounds great," Will said.

"Right, we'll meet here at six every day. Spit promise!" Memory hocked into her hand and held it up to him. The way she used to, when he was a kid and she wore jeans and they sat in the dirt together throwing rocks. Seeing her do it now when she wore something fancier than any wedding dress he'd ever seen made him smile broadly.

"Promise," Will said. He would try, for her, but he knew that this was a promise that he couldn't keep.

CHAPTER TEN

In the school's dining hall, a long table had been laid out with crisp white linen, silver cutlery, and an arrangement of arum lilies, lending a feeling of elegance to what was otherwise a mess hall playing dress-up. Ladies' classes now only occupied a small portion of the large finishing school grounds since the Wizard's Council had requisitioned the rest of the space for their displaced university.

Memory sat at the table, wondering why she and Eloryn had been sent into the finishing school section, rather than the university classes run by the Council. Her first day here and she'd already sat through a morning of lengthy lectures about the proper way to curtsy, stitch tiny flowers, and other 'womanly arts.' Memory thought it was fair to say she could do with improving her manners, but Eloryn was meant to be queen. Surely there were more important things for them to be learning than how to bend perfectly at the waist. It felt insulting to them both, and there was also the fact Memory was bored out of her mind. And hungry. *This is ridiculous.* Memory looked at the plate of rapidly cooling crepes in front of her. She was starving but hadn't been given the all clear to begin eating.

Memory glared in disbelief at Mistress Ursula, the teacher instructing her on the intricacies of how to eat, something she thought that she

could do pretty well already. The way Mistress Ursula's waist had been cinched in so small under her all black, high-necked dress, Memory doubted her expertise on the subject.

Memory wore a plain gown and jacket combo similar to the one she'd worn out with Clara that night, but something about the cut or quality of the fabric still made her stand out compared to the other girls' simple lacey frocks. Around the room almost all the girls stared dumbstruck at Memory, Eloryn, and the crowd of Eloryn's bodyguards standing at attention in the background.

Ursula tapped what looked like a conductor's baton on the table and asked, "Can anyone tell me the correct amount of food that a lady should consume?"

"As much as possible?" Memory smirked at the girls around the table. A few smiled politely back, but the slight look of confusion in their eyes kept the tone flat.

"That is incorrect, your highness," Ursula said, her voice flat. "A lady should only consume a portion the size of which would befit a child. The correct amount is one-third of what is on your plate – and not a bite more!"

"Any chance we could get bigger plates, then?" Memory asked.

Beside her, Eloryn snorted, covering the laugh by coughing politely into a napkin and giving Memory a small kick under the table.

"Wouldn't bigger plates be lovely?" A girl with a mop of auburn ringlets piped up, looking so cheerfully at Memory and Eloryn it made Memory's teeth ache. *Suck up.* "They would make us look so charmingly petite in contrast."

Ursula's head twitched, shaking her mound of perfectly piled gray curls, but her face remained impassive.

"The size of the plates is more than sufficient." Ursula sat at the head of the table and brandished her own knife and fork in demonstration. "Remember that each forkful must be no larger than the end of your little finger, and you will place the food in your mouth, place the cutlery back on the table, and chew slowly and swallow before cutting your next piece."

Memory sighed, staring at her plate of food. *Dear crepes, you smelled fantastic and look so cheesy, but if I have to eat you under these conditions I shall go insane. We were not meant to be, my love, so I bid you farewell.*

Memory took her napkin from her lap and folded it with as much sarcasm as she could muster. "Mistress Ursula, I require the use of doth little girl's facilities yonder and was wondering, per chance, if I could be excused temporarily forth hence?"

The openly mocking tone appeared to be lost on the teacher. "Certainly, your highness. But don't be too long. We have to discuss desserts and the correct way to use a spoon." She smiled as if the prospect was exciting.

"Can't wait." Memory gave two thumbs up, tucked in her chair and left the dining area, breathing a huge sigh of relief.

A cartoon escape sound effect played in her head as she slipped out the door and off to find an interesting place to kill time. The room was on the ground floor of the hollow rectangular building, and Memory looked longingly through the windows at a group of boys in the central courtyard. They were lined up, performing some matching exercise routine that Memory didn't know the purpose of. Whether it was spell casting or aerobics, it seemed way more interesting than her classes. Down the hall Memory caught sight of Hayes, who was making his way around the building with the finishing school's headmistress. Memory felt the need to express her concern over the nature of her education. Surely, as a princess, she shouldn't have to go to school if she didn't want to? She knew she'd hate school, even before she realized that it included such bizarre forms of torture as sitting her in front of food that she wasn't allowed to eat.

Memory waited until Hayes and the headmistress had finished and approached him.

Hayes's eyes narrowed when he saw her, but his expression quickly changed to a welcoming smile. "Your highness, how are you finding your first day of school?"

He says like it's the only time I've been to school ever.

Memory matched his agreeable tone, trying to stay on his good side. "That's kind of what I was hoping to talk to you about. Do you have a minute?"

The corridor had a few passersby who nodded or bowed to them both. Hayes indicated a nearby vacant office which they entered. He pushed the door closed behind them with the end of his walking stick.

"You have some problem with your classes?" Hayes snapped, rubbing the bridge of his hooked nose. He stared down at her, making her nervous and Memory felt a ramble coming on.

"Well, yeah. Are they really necessary? I mean, it just seems a bit

silly learning how to sip soup when I'm meant to be heir to a kingdom. There's just so much other stuff I don't know that I could be learning. And Eloryn too, although she already knows lots."

"Are your etiquette classes necessary? Well, that depends, *your highness*," Hayes's voice became a grumbling hiss. "Are you ready to conduct yourself accordingly? As a princess? It's clear you don't even know how. We know that your background is… questionable, but it's high time you started learning how things work around here and stopped behaving like a wild girl."

Hayes stepped forward, looming over Memory with barely any space between them. Hayes glanced at the closed door then back at her with a sneer. The close proximity shot a disgusted shudder through Memory's body, and she tensed at the ill feeling in her stomach. Memory wished they weren't alone. He'd never speak to her like this in front of Eloryn. Her face heated with shame, and she bit back at him in outrage.

"I do want to learn how things work here, that's my whole point. But not all this girly rubbish. Real things about how to run the kingdom."

"The Council and I are managing all of the affairs of the kingdom. These are not duties for women or girls. If you can't carry out the simplest task of attending *charm lessons*, why should I think you deserve to study subjects that are of the realm of men? The fact is, *princess*, that you may not think that what you're learning is fun or interesting, but you will do what you're told if it has any chance to prevent you from causing further embarrassment to the throne."

Hayes yanked the door open and left, obviously finished taking advantage of the privacy for his tirade.

Memory was stunned into silence. Yeah, she'd made some mistakes, but she wasn't wrong about this. *Realm of men, my ass.* Memory kicked a cabinet and one of its glass doors swung open. It caught her reflection, and the reflection of Hope, just beside her.

Stumbling back out of the office into the hall, Memory tried to straighten up and act normal when she drew the attention of a group of passing students.

Great. Hayes was right. I'm embarrassing myself again already.

Memory found a seat on the low windowsill across from the dining hall and waited for the class to end. She didn't have anywhere else to go, but refused to go back inside as her own form of protest. She also needed a moment to recover after seeing Hope again. The glass was cold

against her back, and she let it calm her boiling insides. She wondered if witnessing Thayl's death could really have tipped her over the edge into full-blown psychosis. The first time she saw Hope she was emotionally and physically exhausted, delirious, so she could write it off as a mental hiccup. She had no excuses for this time.

The lesson ended and Eloryn was first out, escorted by her intimidating entourage. Memory imagined that it must be difficult to constantly have a small battalion of soldiers trailing you around. The girls that followed looked torn between a bursting desire to befriend the young queen and white-faced terror at the prospect of doing it in front of heavily armed men.

Memory stood up and started walking beside Eloryn. "I miss much?"

"No. It got even more boring after you left." Eloryn gave Memory a sideways smile and blushed as if she had said too much.

"I bet you knew all that stuff already anyway, right?"

Eloryn's blush deepened. Memory figured that was a yes.

"Can we go eat some food like real people now?"

Eloryn gave her head a small shake. "I don't think we can fit it in before our next class- Posture and Perambulating."

"Perambu-what?" Memory grunted. "Maybe I should attend that one. I don't think I even know how to perambulate."

Eloryn giggled, and the sisters continued to walk. The long corridors were lined with arched windows showing the inner courtyard on one side, and along the other side, portraits of past school headmistresses were spaced between the classrooms. Memory didn't appreciate the sour-faced glares most of the women held, staring down at her like she was offending them just by being there. They passed by open double doors, revealing a large hall where two men fenced before a substantial crowd of girls.

Memory bounced on the spot. "Let's watch, let's watch, let's watch!"

Eloryn frowned. "We'll be late for class."

"We can learn to perbamuwhatever any old time, come on."

Memory pushed Eloryn into the room, and the two struggled to see over a crowd they were mostly shorter than. As the girls around them started to realize who the newcomers were, they hastily moved aside and Eloryn and Memory ended up with a front-row view.

The two men in matching padded jackets and mesh masks lunged and parried, moving backwards and forwards like crabs. One of the men moved very formally, and the other fenced with a swift fluidity that won

him more gasps of admiration from the watching girls.

The formal fencer struck at his opponent, but in an effortless twirl the blow was dodged. The other man continued the graceful move and struck back in return. The point of his sword embedded into the padded jacket above the first man's heart and flexed into an arch.

That seemed to mark the end of the fight, and the combatants bowed to each other with their swords to their chests. The girls in the audience sighed and giggled when the winner took off his mesh mask and shook out his ruffled tawny hair.

Roen.

Memory grinned and gave a loud wolf whistle which drew a little more attention than she intended.

Roen noticed and smiled at the twins. He gave his sparring partner a solid handshake and a few words Memory couldn't hear.

"He's pretty good, hey?" Memory asked Eloryn.

Eloryn's cheeks had lost all their color. Her whole face paled. With a small nod, she took a step back. "We'd better get to class."

"I'm going to go say hi. Come with, I'm sure he wants to see you too."

Eloryn's mouth twisted and her head dropped. With a small shake of her head, she ducked back through the crowd and left the hall, surrounded by her handlers.

Roen was already headed their way, and Memory noticed the hurt look on his face when he saw Eloryn leave.

"She has a class now," Memory covered, more to save Roen's feelings than whatever was going on with Eloryn.

"You don't?" He smiled warmly, but a small frown still marred his expression.

"Nope. Free as a thing that's free," Memory lied. "That kicked ass, by the way. You were like a fancy ninja."

"Thanks, I think." Roen started heading out to a side door and motioned for Memory to follow. Around them, girls stared with open jealousy and gossiped to each other. Memory wondered what they thought Roen's relationship with her was, which made her wonder what it was as well. She felt a little satisfied to be walking out with him while he barely acknowledged the throng of smitten girls he left behind.

"What's up with the adoring fans?" she asked with a sly grin.

"Didn't you hear? I'm a great big hero. Rescued a couple of princesses and helped save the kingdom, they say. The ladies are practically throwing

themselves at me." Roen smiled roguishly. "It's lucky I'm so used to it. Otherwise, I might let it go to my head."

They stopped at some wooden lockers, and he put away his fencing mask and sword. Memory stared at the roll of his shoulders as he pulled the jacket off and put it away as well. He ruffled his hair again and Memory found herself needing to catch her breath. *Yeah, I can understand the fan club.*

"Those masks make my hair feel awful," he explained, noticing her watching.

"Girl."

Roen laughed loudly. "I'm finished for the day, how about you? Want to ride back to the castle with me?"

"Best suggestion ever. Let's get the hell out of here."

A line of carriages awaited their passengers beside the school grounds and like a true gentlemen, Roen helped Memory into one marked with the royal crest. He tapped on the front to the driver, and the carriage started to rumble and bump about as they made their way back to the castle.

"The fencing, was it for something particular or just to show off your moves to the ladies?" Memory leaned back and put her feet up on the seat across from her, next to Roen.

"A friend offered to catch me up on proper technique, as I haven't had many formal lessons. I don't want to be too behind when fencing classes begin." Roen tilted his head. "And maybe just a little to show off."

"You have classes for *sword fighting*? This is so unfair! Men get to do all the cool stuff. I hate to talk down on my kingdom, but there are some funny ideas here about the positions men and women should have."

"Don't look at me, I think women should be able to take any position they want." Roen paused a moment then laughed. "That was a little risqué even for me."

Memory made an exaggerated kissy face. "You're just ahead of your time, ladies' man. Meanwhile in Memoryland, I'm seriously considering magically changing myself into a boy just so I can get into some politics lessons."

"You know, if you really want to do some classes outside of the finishing school curriculum, I have an idea for an easier way to go about it." Roen leaned toward her like they were sharing secrets. "It's not the sort of thing a girl of Avall would normally do, but then, you're no normal girl, are you?"

CHAPTER ELEVEN

Eloryn hadn't seen Memory since they stopped to watch the fencing. She'd missed all of the afternoon's classes. Eloryn sat through them alone feeling an equal share of anger and worry. The gossip that Memory had left the school early with Roen reached her as she boarded her carriage to return to the castle. Her stomach ached every time she hypothesized on why they left early together, and so after walking to Memory's door three times only to return to her seat again, she finally knocked.

"What's the secret password?" came the reply, followed by giggling.

Eloryn frowned. "I don't know the secret password, but I am your sister. Who else would be knocking at our adjoining door?"

"The correct answer was 'Not by the hair of my chinny-chin-chin,' but come in anyway."

All anger fled Eloryn when she walked in on her sister trying on clothes in the middle of her sitting room. She looked as if she had been struggling to put on a pair of boy's trousers that were still around her ankles, the rest of her covered in a shirt that was far too large. Clara lounged in a nearby arm-chair, red-faced from barely suppressed laughter.

"Mem," Eloryn began, slowly stepping into the room. "What in Avall are you doing?"

Memory paused for a moment and then laughed.

"Clara got them for me. Ugh, so many buttons." Memory did a twirl when she finished putting the trousers on. "What do you think?"

"I think I'm confused and a little concerned for my sister?"

"It's an idea me and Roen came up with. I was all 'I'm gonna zap myself into a boy,' and he was all 'it'd be easier to just dress like one' and I was all 'duh, Mem!' and then here we are!"

Eloryn tilted her head. "You… want to be a boy?"

"Sort of, yeah. Just so I can attend the classes that I want, and not attend the ones I don't. Roen's enrolling me as one of his brothers, Tristan. He said he had so many brothers people would assume one had just come out of the woodwork. As *Tristan* I'll be able to learn whatever I want." Memory looked genuinely enthusiastic as she worked on tucking her shirt in. "And *Memory* will be unwell for a while and unable to attend her lame girly classes."

Clara wheezed a squeaky laugh. "You should tell the teachers you're having women's problems."

Is this all just a joke to them? Eloryn wanted to be supportive of her sister, but Memory was making it hard. Eloryn had no way out, no freedom to skip the classes she'd been assigned. Even if she wouldn't be missed, she had a duty to make her appearance, to do and be seen to do her part. Who was being supportive to her, the sacrifices she was making? Her next words took on a spiteful tone that she didn't like. "And why are you getting dressed out here? If you did so in your bath or bed chamber where there are some mirrors you'd see you've got that shirt on inside out."

Clara burst into tearful laughter and hid her head in a cushion, as though she'd just been waiting for someone else to notice.

Memory frowned and shrugged. "I'm a bit over seeing myself at the moment."

Memory pulled off the shirt and mock-whipped Clara with it while standing in just a bodice and trousers. "You, Giggles McLaughsalot, these shirts are way oversized. How big do you think I am?"

"You're just a teeny tiny little thing." Clara got up and headed to the door, still chuckling. "I'll go and see if I can find something smaller, but I'm really not sure any of the men I know are quite that small. Alack, now she's making me steal clothing from boys!"

Memory pointed sternly at the exit. "Just walk away before I make a comeback so awesome it will explode you."

The door closed after Clara and Memory looked at Eloryn, her expression changing from mirth to concern.

"Okay. What's up, Lory? We were just having a bit of fun, but I am serious about doing this. I should be able to learn what I want to learn." Memory sat down in front of her and Eloryn took a seat as well.

"I know. I'm sorry." She paused, lowering her head. "I'm simply tired and upset. It's been such a long day, and I just bumped into Hayes. He told me he's received intelligence that our uncle is plotting to amass an army against us, to make his claim on Caermaellan."

Memory stood back up again. "What? No way! Why would somebody do that? After all this place has been through?"

"Power is the worst kind of motivator. There is no sense to what it makes people do." Eloryn stood up as well and started pacing, fidgeting her fingers. "I just… I feel like if I could speak with our uncle I could make things right, but Hayes says he's refusing to even see me. He says we need to act aggressively to show a firm hand and stop any voices of dissent against us or the Council."

Memory looked as overwhelmed as Eloryn felt. "I'm sorry. I had no idea you were dealing with stuff like this. What are you going to do?"

"For now, I'm going to keep sending requests for a meeting. But everyone is pushing me to take a firmer stance. There are just so many decisions to make and changes to oversee." She'd been queen for not even a week and it already wore her down more than she wanted to admit. "I appreciate everyone's opinions and advice, and Hayes has been so helpful to me, but I worry that he's too aggressive when it comes to diplomatic policy. He wants to have more control over the courts and sentencing, to catch and question conspirators and stop issues like this from arising."

Memory frowned as she picked up another shirt and started buttoning it on. It was slightly smaller than the last men's shirt, but masses of excess fabric still draped over her small frame.

"Hayes seems to be taking on a hell of a lot of responsibilities. You know, I don't trust the guy. He outright said to me that ruling isn't a woman's job. I feel like you're giving away too much power to a man we don't actually know that much about."

"He's just trying to ease my burdens."

"Then why is it taking so long for him to establish the proper government instead of taking all those burdens on himself? Hayes might seem like he's looking after you, but he's not Alward. It's like Hayes is trying to step in and take Alward's place, but you can't assume Hayes

has your best interests at heart."

Alward's name felt like a slap to Eloryn's face. Hayes could never replace Alward. They were nothing alike. But that didn't mean she couldn't look to him for guidance. Eloryn straightened her back and stopped pacing. "I have to trust Hayes and my other advisors to take on some responsibilities. I have to delegate to get things done. And who would you rather have in power? Some noble who we've never even met? Neither of us know who we can truly trust in this time, but at least with the Council we know that they support us for rule and are doing as much as they can to help us, even if Hayes's behavior may seem firm at times."

"And you're not worried at all about the Council running *everything*?" Memory kept pushing, but Eloryn had run out of any energy. Her reply had no attitude, just honest curiosity.

"Do you think you could do a better job, Mem?"

Memory pouted, looking at the ceiling. "Not right now. But maybe one day, if I learned about the right things. That's what this is all about," she said, tugging at her trousers. "They don't even want me to have the chance to be able to do it."

"That may be so, but I've had all the training and teaching I'll need for a lifetime from Alward, but only experience can teach me who I can actually trust. That isn't something you can learn at school."

"Maybe you're right," Memory conceded, standing to leave. "But at least I can admit that I do have a lot more to learn, and I'm doing something about it. There's also something to be said for instinct, and it sounds like you're ignoring the heck out of yours." Memory grabbed a bag from a table and strapped it across herself, then loaded it with bread rolls from a tray nearby. "I'm going to see Will."

Eloryn raised an eyebrow. "Dressed like that?"

Memory looked down at herself. "Sure. Will doesn't care what I wear." She paused, as if considering something. "I might pop by to see Roen on the way, to get his approval on my costume. Want to come? I think he was sad you didn't stay after the fencing."

Eloryn's hand went to her neckline and wrapped around her jade pendant. She took a moment to compose herself, to give the answer she should instead of the one she wanted. "No, that's probably not a good idea."

Memory sighed audibly. "When will it be a good idea? Why are you avoiding him?"

"It's just… easier this way."

"Look, Lory, I know you're shy, but you have to get over it." Memory paused at the door on her way out, thoughtful for a moment. She put a bowler hat on then turned back again. "I can tell you two make each other giddy around the knees, but do you really think he's going to wait forever? You saw the girls at fencing. I don't see how it's going to be easier for you when you see him in the arms of someone else."

Grateful to be in pants instead of a massive gown, Memory climbed out the tower window onto the old castle walls. She looked forward to seeing Will. They'd dubbed their meeting place the Ivy Room. *Our secret place. My safe place.* The thought made her smile. She gazed out over the battlements at the view of the city in the distance, a grey forest of steeples and smoking chimneys. Swallows swooped around her chasing tiny insects in the waning light. The temperature chilled quickly as the sun dropped. It was fresh, and despite having an emotionally draining day, Memory was in a good mood.

Until her path was blocked by Hope, standing right in front of her.

Memory stopped and blinked a couple of times, trying to rid herself of this vision of how she used to be. When it refused to vanish, she forged on ahead, hoping it would just fade away. It didn't.

Hope followed closely beside Memory as she marched along the ramparts.

"I wouldn't bother. He's not there."

Memory ignored her.

"I said Will's not showing. He's off with his fairy friends."

Memory put her fingers in her ears and hummed, looking the other way. Hope grabbed her hands and tugged them out, shocking Memory at her tangible touch.

"Stop being so childish!"

"You're not real, go away."

"Yeah, I am real."

"I know the clothes you're wearing are put away in my cupboard, so they're not real at least."

Hope gave an exasperated groan. "Really? My clothes are probably

the least weird thing about my existence."

"Fine, I'll bite. What is the whole thing with your existence?" *I ask a figment of my insanity. Break with reality - complete!*

"I told you, I'm you. Not Memory you. I'm who you used to be."

Memory shook her head. "Still not getting it."

"It's crazy, I know. The best I can figure is that I'm the missing parts of you. The bits that got lost when you cut off Thayl's hand."

"Right. So his brand new stump gave birth to you?"

"Of course it's going to sound dumb when you say it like that. But all my, your, memories and soul, were caught up in all that magic, and ta-da, here I am."

They arrived at the Ivy Room, and Memory lifted the leafy screen that concealed it.

And Hope was right. Will wasn't there. This was the third day he'd missed meeting up already, and he had only dodged Memory's questions about why.

"I'm not going to say 'I told you so,'" Hope said.

"Just did."

Memory sat down on one of the small benches and blew a raspberry. Hope sat on the seat opposite, her legs crossed the same way, looking so similar but different. The two watched each other, like sitting in front of a twisted carnival mirror. Memory realized the whole scene was creepy, but somehow it comforted her. If a magical ghost of her past self insisted on following her around, she might as well take advantage of the company. Part of her longed for Hope to be real, desperately curious to get to know who she used to be.

"I really wanted him to see," Memory said softly.

"To see what? You dressed as a boy?" Hope scoffed.

"No, I wanted him to see you. For one thing it'd prove you're real. And also, I thought that maybe he'd be happy to see you, to see the girl he waited so long for. He must be so disappointed. He finally found me, and I'm not that girl anymore. Not you. He doesn't talk to me much, and he avoids touching me like I'm a leper or something. But if he saw you-"

"He can't see me. You can't let anybody know about me. Promise me you won't tell." Hope stood up, agitated, staring Memory in the eyes. "If you do, they'll work out that your soul is broken. We don't want that, do we? I want to be with you, and I bet you want to be with me too. We're meant to be together, but it has to be our secret, just the two of us. Secret best friends, okay?"

Memory looked up at Hope. She was right. She couldn't let anyone know how broken she was. "Okay."

Come back, I can't keep up.

Will ran ahead of her. Scrawny little boy version Will. So small, she should be able to keep up. Her legs glided in place, aching from effort, not moving anywhere.

Wait for me. Don't leave me.

Wind gusted and slammed against her chest. Will got farther away, running down a long corridor of squeaky Formica and grimy beige walls. Memory called out again and realized her voice wasn't working. The words just jangled in her head. Will was big now. Bare-chested, beast-like. How could such a small boy grow so big? The hallway stretched on forever, and Will ran out of view, so far away.

She checked in each of the small rooms she ran by, looking for him. All the rooms were the same. Her room from the children's home. Wind swirled again, and her feet smacked the ground, finally able to move again, bare feet slapping on the artificial coating, slippery with water. She wasn't alone.

The man up ahead of her now wasn't Will.

He carried a mop and grinned at her. Memory reversed, smacking her back against a cart full of cleaning equipment. The janitor dropped the mop and came after her, saying something she couldn't hear over the sound of rushing wind in her ears. Her feet skidded on the wet floor. Her body exploded with panic as she broke into a sprint, pushing past dangling tree roots, stumbling down stairs and around dark cavernous turns. The wide-set man remained just steps behind her, no matter the breakneck speed she moved at.

The janitor's cart blocked her way, and she wondered how she'd done a complete loop. She slipped past it and came to a dead end, dark and rocky. Fumbling through the cart, all her instincts turned to self-preservation. She grabbed a box cutter and held it out.

The figure loomed in front of her like a giant made of nothing but shadow.

Memory awoke, sweating, half fallen out of her bed. She struggled

to extract herself from tangled sheets, and her hand pressed against something sharp and stung fiercely.

Her knife lay on the sheets, spotted with blood dripping from the gash on her hand. The knife she'd left at the underground lake.

Did I really leave it there? Sleep hazed her thoughts. Maybe she didn't. Maybe she just remembered wrong, and the knife had been here all along. Either that or some of the dream was real, and she'd Veil doored again without meaning to, this time in her sleep. But if some of the dream was real, how much of it and which parts?

Memory closed her knife and tucked it carefully under her pillow like it used to be. Wide eyed and sleepless, she slouched out of bed and into her bathroom. She washed her bleeding hand down in the sink with a sigh then looked up at herself in the mirror. Her shoulders shook as the image startled her. Some blonde girl in a lace-edged sleeping gown.

That's me now, Memory reminded herself. She stared at the mirror, trying to hold onto what was real. But the lines between real and dream, new and old, tangled in her head.

CHAPTER TWELVE

"I'm not sure I'm fooling anyone," Memory said, walking out of her first class as Tristan. She felt at home in pants, but the stiff-collared coat, hat, and tie felt clunky and uncomfortable. Clara had even found her a wig of bowl-cut mousy brown hair for the disguise.

Roen walked beside her down the second floor hallway of the finishing school. The sun shone warmly in through the arched windows, disguising the fact the wind that buffeted the glass was brisk and chilled.

Roen stopped walking for a moment and made a show of eyeing her up and down. "I don't know. I think you make a fairly convincing boy, albeit a twelve-year-old one."

Memory punched him playfully in the stomach. "Yeah and you'd make one pretty lady."

"Watch it, Tristan. Don't you know it's wrong to hit girls?"

Memory started walking again, grinning back at Roen. The sunlight hit him from behind, making his golden hair glow. *He really can be beautiful sometimes.*

"Are you sure you don't mind me using your brother's name? I feel like I'm somehow shaming his legacy."

"Not at all. It's an honor, and I'm sure if Tristan were alive he'd be very fond of you. He was my closest brother, not in age, but in every other way."

"Which one was closest in age?"

Roen looked away from her, out the windows at the treetops swaying in the wind, rasping against the glass. "We… don't talk about him."

"Oh, that one."

Roen shook his head and when he looked at her again he was still smiling. He stopped at a door and bowed to her in a flourish. "Delivered safely to your next class."

"You're coming in with me, right?"

"Sorry, you're on your own for this one. I'm not enrolled for magic classes."

Memory looked at the floor. "Can you come in anyway? I'd really like someone I trust to be there. Given my history with magic, I'm…" Memory took a deep breath, her nerves shaking her up. Her magic was explosive at best. Even the only spell she could really cast, the Veil door, was going wonky on her. "I'm scared," she admitted.

"You'll be fine. Tristan is tough," he said, reaching out for her hand and giving it a squeeze. "But Memory is even tougher."

A group of girls walked past, giggling hysterically to see what appeared to be two boys holding hands in the hall. Roen and Memory looked at one another and laughed as well.

"I don't think you can hold my hand while I'm being Tristan. People will begin to talk, and I genuinely think that Avall isn't ready for it if it's not even up to women's liberation yet."

"That's a shame."

Memory smiled as Roen loosened his grip, but instead of letting go completely he quickly, and surreptitiously, kissed her hand.

Memory blushed. Roen didn't let go of her hand.

"So, what are you going to do now?" Memory asked, pretending everything was normal and her heart wasn't racing. "Oh! You should totally dress up as a girl and go to my etiquette classes for me."

"I should. I agree, I'd make a good-looking girl." Grinning wickedly, Roen looked down at himself and nodded as though he liked what he saw. "I'd call myself Roena. She and Tristan could court."

Memory laughed loudly in reply. *He's just joking, right?* She and Roen always joked around, but she started to wonder if it was something more. The way he looked at her was warm, his eyelids half closed, smiling widely.

Then he let go of her hand as though she'd burnt him.

Memory turned around to see Waylan, Hayes, and Eloryn heading their way. Eloryn looked stunningly feminine in an A-line, dusty pink gown

with her long hair loose and set in neat curls. Memory felt increasingly self-conscious in boy's clothes. *I really am just one of the boys to Roen, compared to her.*

Eloryn blushed and stared at Memory and Roen, but Waylan and Hayes were engaged in an argument and didn't notice them.

Waylan puffed as he waddled, the effort of debating and walking at the same time clear from his flushed round cheeks and beads of sweat on his bald head.

"I think all this talk of Sir Ewain building an army is drummed-up nonsense," he said.

"Are you questioning the reliability of my intelligence contacts?" Hayes replied.

"Yes, frankly," Waylan said with confidence.

Memory smiled. Waylan had been one of the few people to back her up in meetings, and she loved seeing someone stand up to Hayes.

"From what I've heard," he continued after a pause for breath. "He's just gathering support to get the Wizard's Council back to their normal role and hasten the reestablishment of proper government."

"A proper government with himself on the throne. My contacts are reliable, Waylan."

The trio reached the doorway Roen and Memory stood beside. Hayes barely glanced at Memory, not recognizing who she was enough to care, and instead scrutinized Roen and the look he shared with Eloryn. Memory whispered a goodbye to Roen and ducked into the classroom before Hayes could work out who she was.

"So you say." Waylan stopped and gave a short bow to Eloryn. "I want to talk to you more on this, but have a class to run now. Your Majesty. Councilor Hayes."

Waylan followed Memory into the room, and she could see Hayes lead Eloryn away without a word to Roen who left in the other direction.

There were already a dozen students sitting quietly in the classroom. They ranged in age from about thirteen to twenty-five from what Memory could tell and were all finely dressed. Even the youngest of them wore neat suits with stiff-collared shirts, ties, and tailored coats. Everyone sat at attention and seemed keen to be there. She imagined it must be a big deal to be allowed into this level of education after having it unavailable for so long. There was something snooty about their manner, and Memory wondered if she just thought that because she knew they were all from noble families. Some of the boys whispered and stared at her as she

entered. She took a seat at the back with a sense of satisfaction. *Even if I'm not fooling anyone, they're all too chicken to do anything about it.*

The room shared the same pale limestone walls seen in most of the university. Waylan had made his way to the front of the classroom where a grand wooden desk was piled in a large collection of weighty books. A few crates were stacked to the side, full to the brim with more age-yellowed texts, but a seamstress dummy still stood in the corner as a reminder of the room's previous assignment.

Waylan put on some glasses that pressed into the chubby sides of his face, then looked over a note on his desk. "I see we have a new student, Tristan Faerbaird." He looked up, pulling the glasses down his button nose to inspect the room and nodded briefly when he confirmed his new addition. Memory gave a timid smile back, but he barely glanced at her. The glasses went back up and he started talking, scrawling illegible words on a blackboard as he did.

"We'll continue on from where we were, Tristan. We can catch you up if needed, but this is all very basic theory thus far. We're starting simple, considering the last sixteen years, you understand."

Waylan underlined something on the board that looked like "The Spork of Cowchicken."

"This Spark of Connection-" Waylan said.

Oh, that makes more sense, thought Memory.

"-was granted to those in Avall at the time of the Pact and has been passed down ever since, becoming a hereditary trait of humankind so that everyone in Avall can connect to magic."

A boy in the row in front of Memory whispered to his friend, "Not *everyone.*"

Waylan didn't seem to notice and continued drawing a rough body shape on the board with a star in the center, then energetically scribbled lines directing out from the person. Memory smiled to herself at the comparison between his artistic merit and his enthusiasm. "The Spark of Connection doesn't give a person power unto themselves. It simply allows a man – or woman – to become a conduit for magical energy. We all understand behests, that the words of the magical language must be correctly spoken to make requests from a required object or natural force. But the request isn't always enough. An object can have a will to fulfill your request, but not the power to do so. I can say the words to ask this desk to shatter into a thousand pieces, but it needs something more. The Spark of Connection becomes a channel for pure magic to enable these requests."

Memory thought over the times she'd seen Eloryn use magic. A body may want to be healed and respond to the request, but of course it would need something more, something to give it the power to do so. Same with clothes shaking themselves clean or objects flying through the air.

"But where does that magic come from?" she muttered to herself.

"Good question!" Waylan barked, surprising her that he heard. He looked overly pleased at having a student interacting with him.

"There is an energy that flows through us all, the energy of life. It moves through the blood of all living things, through the blood of the very earth. It is a powerful force and that is what is channeled to harness the behests we speak. It is also the lifeblood of the fae. It is speculated that this energy does not exist in the fae realm, Tearnahn-Ohg, which is why they require an earthly home."

Waylan looked at her expectantly like she should respond to his answer. "So magic is from living energy, and it channels through blood, but isn't blood also full of iron? Wouldn't that be poisonous to the fae?"

The same boy in front that had talked before spoke up. "Only *forged* iron, pure iron changed by the hand of man, is poison to the fae. Everyone knows that." He didn't turn around completely to speak to her, and she figured he had no idea who she was. Some of the other students looked at him shocked, like a battalion of guards was about to appear and arrest him for being sassy to the princess.

"That's right." The prospect of a class debate had Waylan grinning ear to ear. "Otherwise we would not be able to call a wisp for our lights, as they are beings of fae energy. They would not come close to forged iron, although that point is purely theoretical since the Purge."

Yeah, theoretical. Memory did a mental face palm. So many times she'd tried in vain to cast the light spell, all the while having her iron knife nearby.

"Any more questions before we continue?"

Memory raised her hand hesitantly. She felt like she was taking over the lesson, but had so much she wanted to know, and Waylan nodded for her to speak up so she asked her question.

"Behests are just meant to be requests, right, and requests that can be denied. So how can behests that kill people work?"

Some of the boys at the back who were chatting shut up. Everyone stared

at her. Waylan looked at Memory, more with concern than anything else.

"And why would you ask that, young man?"

"I don't want to know how to do it. I just want to understand how it's possible. I mean, it's not like you could use a behest that would *ask* someone to die."

"Yes, clever of you to realize that." Waylan didn't look pleased and answered through thin lips. "No, one could not ask another's body to simply die. But your body is not all your own, you understand. There is a behest that calls upon disease, bacteria, and life forms on and within the body to attack and kill the host. They rapidly degrade internal organs and shut them down, causing the person to die almost instantly. Such magic exists, but only members of the Wizard's Council are allowed to learn that behest, and then it's only to be used in extreme and dire situations."

Waylan took no more questions, and instead read aloud from one of his books for the rest of the lesson. Dull was an understatement of the quality of the text, but Memory already felt as though she understood magic far more than she had before.

When the class finished and the boys left, Memory hung back to speak with Waylan, another question nagging at her that she hoped Waylan could answer, a question she couldn't ask as Memory. As Memory she felt like an anomaly to be studied, but as Tristan she was just a normal Avall student, eager to learn. It surprised her just how eager she was. She wandered to the front of the classroom.

"Thanks, that was an awesome lesson," Memory opened with, wincing at how stupid she sounded.

"I'm glad you enjoyed it." Waylan nodded as he cleaned the blackboard, small clouds of chalk puffing under his hand. "I can tell from your constant questioning in class that you're going to be a clever and challenging student."

"I actually have another question, is that okay? I was wondering if there was some way that something, like some spell, could change a person's Spark of Connection?"

Waylan stopped clearing up and peered down at her over his glasses. "Princess Memory, there's no need to keep up this pretense."

"Oh." *Busted.*

"Don't worry. I'm not going to turn you in. It is a sincere pleasure to have you as a student. I am already impressed by your insight and curiosity."

A strange sensation struck Memory. *Is that what pride feels like?* Memory looked at her feet.

"Rest assured, young princess, you are always welcome in my classroom. It's wonderful that you're making an effort to learn more, regardless of where some may consider your place to be."

"Right? Man, I thought I was only one to think Hayes is getting a bit pushy about where a princess's place should be."

Waylan shook his head. "Hayes may seem harsh sometimes, but we do follow him for a reason. It was his diligent leadership that saved us and kept us hidden all those years. But I must admit, I do have my concerns with how he is running things. I find myself challenging him more and more during Council meetings, and not just over matters pertaining to the school. I'm afraid that it goes far deeper than that."

Fired up by finding a co-conspirator against Hayes, Memory had to cut off her next comment regarding things that go far deeper and Hayes's ass when another Councilor walked in.

Waylan stood and gave the man a hearty embrace. They looked similar, both bald and wearing glasses, but while Waylan was round and chubby, the other Councilor was stocky, solid, and tall enough to make his weight intimidating rather than endearing. She'd seen him at some Council meetings but didn't know his name. He always stayed quiet and looked grumpy.

The wizard glanced at her and bowed briskly. "Princess."

"I'm really not convincing anyone, am I?"

"Memory, this is my brother, Bedevere."

"Taking some interest in exploring your magic ability?" Bedevere said. By his tone, Memory didn't think he expected an answer, and he continued too quickly for her to give one. "If you've become amenable to investigating your powers and past, I would be very interested to assist. I've many questions I'd love the chance to direct to you."

And there it is, back to being the lab rat. Memory tried to keep the groan out of her reply. "What kind of questions?"

"I know you must be keen to study your own powers, but to be honest I'm more interested in learning about the technology of the lands you grew up in. I'm in possession of some fantastic schematics, brought in as imports from a fae supplier last century. My colleagues tell me they are fakes I paid too highly for and that there couldn't be such fantastical devices existing outside Avall, but I feel theoretically

they should work."

Memory blinked a few times as she tried to understand the stream of information.

Waylan cleared his throat. "My brother has somewhat of a fascination with the world that we left behind. He has some rather... controversial views on the matter."

"Like maybe I didn't grow up in Hell after all?"

Bedevere smiled for the first time. "Indeed."

Memory smiled back.

Eloryn and Memory took the aerial walkway that connected the newer palace to the old keep on their way to the Round Room, trailed by Eloryn's usual entourage. Eloryn had read all about Caermaellan Castle as she grew up, studying its floor plans and dreaming about what it really looked like. She knew all its history and admired how her family and architects had worked to preserve the ancient stone keep at the heart of the palace when they came to expansions. The gray slabs of stone were at odds with the decorative grandeur built up around it, but somehow it worked.

Rain washed the windows on both sides of them, making the view streaked and blurry. Barely mid-afternoon, Eloryn felt ready for bed rather than her fifth meeting for the day. The crinoline cage under her scarlet gown felt too heavy and her bodice too tight. She rubbed her eyes and tried to keep pace with Memory, who skipped ahead, full of energy.

"The meeting isn't even to start for a while yet. I never thought I'd see you so keen to be there," Eloryn said.

"I don't care about the meeting," Memory laughed like the idea was crazy. "Waylan said he'd be there early, and I wanted a chance to talk to him."

The twins stepped out of the walkway into a hall that lead up to the Round Room. Roen was walking toward them and Memory ran up to meet him. They whispered together, and Eloryn didn't catch what they said as she caught up.

At the end of the hall, Waylan could be seen through the entryway into the Round Room. Memory waved to him. She gave Roen a soft punch in the shoulder. "You two kids stop and have a chat. I'm going ahead to see—"

A thunder crack of sound shook through Eloryn's skull.

A powerful explosion blew outwards from the Round Room. The rumble of flame deafened Eloryn as her mind caught up with the situation around her. Shards of exploded furniture and stone shot toward them.

"Beirsinn fair nalldomh!" Eloryn yelled, unable to hear her voice over the ringing in her ears. Tapestries flew off the walls, creating a barrier that the projectiles thudded against like hail. Small, sharper fragments of wood and glass cut against the fabric, some pieces piercing through. Air rushed past the barrier, hot and pungent, filled with chokingly thick smoke.

One of her guards grabbed Eloryn from behind and tackled her to the ground softly. Others shouted around her.

"I'm fine. Off me," Eloryn ordered, but the smoke made her voice raspy. She cleared the vapor from the air with a behest and the guard helped her to her feet.

Beside her, Roen had Memory shielded in an embrace. A rage of jealousy fired through Eloryn, until she realized that Memory was forcing herself forward, trying to push past Roen who was holding her tight to keep her from running into the Round Room, or what remained of it.

"Is everyone all right?" Eloryn called out, her voice muffled in her ears.

"We have to help Waylan," Memory said, desperately trying to get out of Roen's grasp.

"I don't think you can," he said.

The guards tore down the tapestry barrier and hobbled over the crumbled landscape to assess the damage. Red splashed the stone entryway to the room, and Eloryn looked the other way.

When she did, she met the gaze of a man watching from further up the hallway. He wore a servant's uniform and had terror all over his face. The man backed away, breaking into a run. His escape was blocked by Hayes marching toward them, walking cane held out like a weapon in front of him. She heard the words of Hayes's spell with a grim realization.

"Guidhe beag lugha ob ciorram greim-bàis..."

"Stop, hold your words," she cried.

Eloryn dashed toward them. The shining bolt of Hayes's behest hit the man as he ran and he fell to his knees, then face, his life twitching away.

Eloryn stopped, stunned at the action. Hayes reached her and gave her a firm embrace.

"Your majesty. Thank the fae you're unhurt!"

"Hayes, what have you done? Who was this man?"

"A traitor against you. I was informed of a plot – an assassination attempt. I tried to come as quickly as I could." Hayes stared at the damage down the hallway. "Evidently not quickly enough."

Hayes knelt beside the corpse, patting the man down and searching pockets. He produced a piece of paper folded into a small square. He stood and read it, glaring at the note.

"This man was just a tool, and here is the proof of the man who wielded him. This is a writ, your majesty. A payment letter, signed by your uncle."

Eloryn's head drifted slowly side to side. Her ears still hummed, and a weight of sadness settled on her, making the whole world feel underwater. "He would do this?"

"Forgive me, Majesty, but I warned you he was dangerous. Still, you are safe. It's a mercy that the room was not occupied."

"Waylan. He was in the room." Eloryn looked back up the hall. Memory was hunched down against the wall with her head in her hands. Roen sat next to her. The ground shook slightly, and Eloryn worried the building had become unstable, but it passed quickly.

Hayes ran a hand over his mouth, face taut with grief. "There will be justice for this."

Eloryn noted that Peirs and more soldiers had arrived. Peirs jogged up beside her and bowed. "Your Majesty, I vow I will discover the cause of this."

Hayes sneered. "We already know who caused this. That you don't is an added sign of your incompetence at this position, along with even letting this occur to begin with, right in the heart of Caermaellan castle."

Peirs stepped toward Hayes, squaring up his shoulders. "I'm confident the guard has done everything warranted to protect the Queen. We could not have foreseen this."

"I've told you numerous times of the threats being made. I instructed you to increase patrols."

"It is not in your power, respectfully, to order an increase in patrols."

"Please stop," Eloryn said. "This is not the time for bickering. This is a time for mourning, for the loss of a good man, and that one I call

family felt driven to such extreme action."

Peirs lowered his head deferentially. "I cannot believe that Sir Ewain is the cause of this, but I will investigate every lead to discover the truth here."

"We already have proof," Hayes said, thrusting the writ at Peirs. "Had you acted sooner on my information this wouldn't have happened."

"Or if I had. Have I handled this so poorly?" Eloryn asked Hayes. She should have dealt with the threat from her uncle. Instead she delayed the process because she didn't want to make a difficult decision. It felt like the only decisions she had been making were to delay making decisions. In times like this, they needed someone who could make a decision at the right time. Waylan had died on account of her inertia. She blushed from grief.

Hayes put his hand on her shoulder. "Any hesitation on your part was only brought by your tender, if misguided, feelings for your family, your Majesty. But now is the time for action, swift justice for this crime."

"I need to see the damage." Eloryn turned away from Hayes and made her way slowly into the Round Room.

Peirs stepped in ahead of her, taking one of the torn tapestries from the ground. He laid it over Waylan's body before she could see and gave her a solemn nod, which she returned as a thank you.

The room itself was in passable condition. Ancient walls of stone built to withstand sieges had been charred and scratched, but not broken. The furnishings, however, had been torn asunder. The leadlight above had shattered and fallen, creating a multicolored carpet of razor-edged jewels. The wide round table where important decisions had been made for centuries had been reduced to kindling by a single act. Even Thayl hadn't dared touch these treasures of Avall history. *Perhaps they could be repaired over time. Even if I have to spend every day speaking behests to splinters, I will repair this.*

"Gunpowder," Peirs said, sifting through the debris.

"Obviously. Set up by a paid off servant and triggered by a simple behest." Hayes studied the scene further, turning over broken furniture. He looked over to Waylan with deep regret. "Though it is tragic indeed, it is fortunate that Waylan was the only one in the room. The assassin must have panicked at your approach and set off the blast too early. Imagine had this occurred mid-meeting. This is what I warned of earlier. This is why we need greater power to investigate, imprison and sentence anyone who threatens us and the stability of Avall. The current system is too slow. If the roles of Grand Bailiff and Legate of Civil Defense were held by a single dignitary, the process would be greatly expedited."

Eloryn felt like crying but held it back. Her hair had come loose from its pins. She pushed the blonde strands from her face and turned to Hayes.

"You're right. I need someone in those positions who can prevent tragedies like this from occurring. Someone I trust. Councilor Hayes, will you take the ranks of Grand Bailiff and Legate of Civil Defense?"

Hayes bowed briefly. "I would be honored to take these roles, your majesty, if you see fit to bestow them upon me."

"I should have done so sooner." Eloryn felt defeated, as if she had failed by handing more of her responsibilities to Hayes, but she knew someone had to take action. Actions she was loath to take.

"Your majesty, you have made a wise decision," Hayes bowed low. He straightened back up, then turned and pointed at Peirs. "And as my first act, you are to be stripped of your rank as Captain of the Royal Guard on the grounds of your complete incompetence and negligence of duty."

Peirs's jaw worked, but he made no reply. He bowed low to Eloryn and paused, looking at her for a moment with a worried frown, before being escorted from the castle. Eloryn turned away, unable to watch him go, or look anyone in the eye.

CHAPTER THIRTEEN

Memory sat on her pillows with her head against the quilted backboard of the bed. She ran her hands through her hair over and over, trying to soothe herself to sleep. Too many thoughts rushed through her head. *So much death.* Her balcony doors were open, and she stared out into the night but no-one came.

I'm never going to get to sleep if I keep staring at the forest, waiting. Memory pushed herself off the bed and went to close the doors.

She looked out across the tree tops. The rain had stopped, but the trees still sparkled in the moonlight. Flashes of darting sprites matched the shining leaves. She thought she could hear singing, somewhere distant, mingling with the sounds of night. A bittersweet song with a strange melody, somehow familiar.

"It's embarrassing," Will said. He wore old army pants and a dirty t-shirt that said "Not It" and they sat together in a vacant lot, down the street from the children's home.

"I know it is, that's why I want to see you do it." Memory cackled. "Look if I'm going to protect you from the other boys, I at least want to know why they love to beat on you so hard."

"Fine, just, close your eyes, okay?"

Memory groaned dramatically and made a point of rolling her eyes as she closed them.

Will began to sing. Something classical, in another language. Something Memory had never heard before. It was strange how her heart reacted to the sound, aching

sweetly and beating just slightly faster. His voice was so beautiful. He was still a boy, but his voice was deeper than she'd expected.

Memory's eyes opened to watch him sing. He quickly stopped.

He frowned and stabbed an empty drink can with a stick. "My parents made me take lessons."

A gust of wind rattled the balcony doors and swirled Memory's ivory nightgown and hair about her. She grabbed the doors and pulled them closed. When she turned around, Hope had taken her spot on her pillow.

A small smile appeared involuntarily on Memory's lips. "Hey."

"Hey. Need someone to talk to?" Hope patted the pillow next to her.

"Really do." Memory sat at the foot of the bed, face to face with her other self.

"I know about the explosion."

Memory looked away for a moment, getting her emotions under control. "Waylan died. He was nice to me, and I thought he could help me with my magic, and now he's just gone."

"Who cares about him? What about you? You could have died, too."

Memory shrugged. "I guess the prospect of not existing isn't so scary for me since I only feel like I've existed at all for a couple of months. What I can't handle is how everyone I grow close to is taken away from me."

"I'm not going anywhere. I'm the only one you can trust to stay by you."

Hope's intensity made Memory feel strange, knowing that was her, how she used to be. *Is that the friend Will knew? That he'd waited so long for?*

Memory tilted her head and glanced back at the balcony doors.

"Thinking about Will?"

"Yeah. I didn't make it to the Ivy Room today, with everything. I'm worried about him. Usually his 'Mem is in danger' sense tingles, and he's here like a flash, but he didn't come. Again."

Hope rolled her eyes. "Will is probably too busy with Mina. You can't rely on him. He's not that little boy anymore, following you like a puppy. I think you should spend more time with Roen. He doesn't hang around with slutty sprites. He's there for you and, well, he makes you happy, right?"

"Yeah, but Roen likes Lory. Fact."

"Maybe, but he *could* like you more. I mean, you're basically the same thing as Eloryn on the outside, and as for the inside, you guys get along great. Eloryn doesn't want him anyway, right?"

"I don't know." Memory leaned against one of the bed's posts and played with the tassel that tied the canopy back. "Do you think that you being around is what's bringing back my memories? Is that how it works? Do we share them or something?"

Hope stared at Memory for a moment. "Would you want them back if you could have them?"

"For sure. I would have got them back before, but Eloryn had to reject them to save me from Thayl."

"Did she? Did she *have* to? Think about it. What if Eloryn did that because she wanted to keep you confused and unsure about yourself, keep you unable to know or control yourself? I mean, that is what she did, after all."

Memory frowned skeptically.

"Don't look at me like that. When Eloryn connected with you, when your spirits joined she must have seen that your soul had bits missing. She *knows*. She can never really treat you as family. Why do you think everything's played out like it has? Her becoming queen instead of you?"

Memory focused on the tassel again, unwinding the weave of the threads. "No. That just… made more sense."

Hope crawled down the bed and took the tassel from Memory, making her pay attention. "Did it? The only sense it made was keeping you from power, from the title that should be yours. Hayes and the others treat you like garbage. You were meant to be queen, you should be queen. Just imagine how people would treat you if you were."

"I don't want to be queen. I just want my friends…" Friends she already barely saw. *I see Eloryn so rarely maybe she is avoiding me on purpose. Could this really be why?*

Hope threw the dismantled remains of the tassel onto the floor. "You think you're making friends here. You think you're starting a new life. But eventually they'll all turn on you or leave you. Every last one. Trust me. I'm the only one here for you. You think they like you? How could they? They don't know you. *You* don't know you. You're not even a whole person."

The morning after the assassination attempt, Memory found herself on complete lockdown. No school and no way out of the castle, not even

with Clara's help. Hayes had ordered a new guard detail to keep an eye on Memory. These guys treated the job like they were imprisoning Memory, rather than stopping others from getting to her. Memory glared at them from the window seat in the palace library.

Memory had been moaning to Clara about missing lessons when Clara pointed out the palace had its own library that she could keep studying in. Memory decided to check it out and quickly ended up walled into the window seat by piles of books on history, law, and economics. She'd hoped to continue reading up on magic as well, but apparently all of those books were kept by the Wizard's Council.

Memory wriggled her legs around trying to find some comfort amongst her layered skirts. She ended up taking her slippers off, hitching the skirts up and sitting cross legged on the velvet-covered cushions. Some of the guards looked at her funny, and she hitched her skirts up higher in response - daring to show her thighs - until they turned away in shock.

Memory smiled, satisfied and picked up a fistful of small pastries from the tray beside her, popping them into her mouth as she read.

"Look at you. One week of school and you're already burying yourself in texts and tomes." Roen walked up to her, carrying the Avall history book that Eloryn had given Memory for her birthday.

"I sent Clara to get that for me. What have you done with her, you scoundrel?" Memory said with dramatically widened eyes. She wiped the pastry crumbs off her hands onto her skirt so she could take the book off him. The flakes showed starkly against the black velvet.

Roen held his hands up innocently. "I ran into her up at your chambers and gave her the rest of the day off. You've got the poor girl working triple shifts."

"Oh, she loves it. Besides, it keeps her out of trouble with the guards."

"She's in trouble with the guards?"

Memory wriggled her eyebrows.

Roen laughed. "I see. But you do have servants you could call on other than her, you know."

Memory looked up with a sinister smile. "Nope. I finally got rid of all of them."

"Mem, what did you do? Also, remind me not to get on your bad side."

Memory shrugged innocently. "They kept buzzing around, like it was my job to find work for them—"

"It is," Roen interrupted.

"So I did. I've sent them down into the city. I figured I could find better use for them than tightening my corsets and brushing my dresses, because seriously, why do dresses need brushing? They are helping out with the homeless kids I've been taking alms to, while I'm on lockdown and can't do it myself. It's pretty exciting actually. Maeve has found a building to set up base in."

"And Maeve is?"

"One of the older orphans. She's helping me get things organized since she knows a lot of the kids on the street. She's awesome. You've got to meet her. I just wish I could get away from this goon squad and go check the place out. But I'm just going to have to buy it unseen. Apparently I can do stuff like that because I'm some rich princess."

Roen laughed and sat down on the window seat next to Memory, his shoulder up against hers and head back on the glass. "Look at you."

"What?"

"Never mind."

Memory took another fistful of the delicate bite-sized pastries. Pushing them into her mouth, she pointed at a book across the seat from them with her bare foot.

"Can you chuck that one over here for me?" Memory said through a spray of pastry flakes.

Roen laughed as he passed the book to her. "When you're allowed back to school, perhaps you should reconsider skipping your etiquette classes. You could stand to learn to be a little more ladylike."

"Ladylike your face."

Roen grinned and reached for some of her pastries. Memory play-swatted his hand then let him have some.

He popped them into his mouth one at a time, and Memory couldn't help but stare at his lips. Between bites he said, "Honestly, though, I prefer your current schooling arrangement. It means we get to spend more time together. I feel like I'm getting to know you all over again, and it's amazing seeing you get to know yourself."

Memory shrugged bashfully. She could feel the warmth of Roen's arm up against hers. He smelled like soap and cookie spices. Next to him, she felt comfortable, content, and at home, but she hadn't thought she really wanted Roen in a more than friends way. He was funny, handsome, brave... Why shouldn't she want that? Maybe she was just

stopping herself because of some notion of Eloryn's feelings, but all Eloryn did these days was avoid Roen. Maybe Hope was right.

"It's been nice getting to know you more, too," Memory said softly, unable to make eye contact.

"Roen, Memory, good morning to you." Eloryn's voice made them both jump. Memory shifted away from Roen, so they were no longer sitting against each other, then wondered why she felt so guilty. *We weren't doing anything wrong.*

"Lory, what's up?" she asked, as innocently as possible.

Eloryn stood in front of them, clutching her hands together and clearly trying hard to seem cheerful. She also wore all black in mourning, and the stark shade played up the pale quality of her skin and hair. Behind her were twice as many guards as she normally had following her around.

"I had some spare time and thought we could all lunch together."

Roen stood up, brushing crumbs off his pants. "I'm afraid I have to pass."

Memory pouted and Roen gave her a smile. "Some of us are considered expendable enough to still be expected in classes."

Roen's smile dropped when he turned to Eloryn. He seemed about to say something, but then left awkwardly without saying anything else.

Eloryn flinched a little then turned to Memory with a smile. "Just you and I then? I've barely seen you since the incident. And I wanted to say I'm sorry about Waylan. I know that you'd grown close to him and enjoyed his classes."

Memory nodded, looking over her shoulder. The window looked out onto a rose garden, one she found familiar from a dream she once shared with Thayl. The roses bloomed in a rainbow of shades throughout the courtyard. The world outside seemed too bright for this topic.

"You know, I finally managed to cast that damn light behest thanks to Waylan. I thought he could teach me so much. But now he's not here anymore."

"It was a great loss. He'll be missed by a lot of people. I really hope that you can get back to magic classes soon."

There was something in Eloryn's tone that didn't sit right with Memory. It sounded more like a warning than an encouragement. "What do you mean?"

"Just that I know there's a lot we still need to understand about your magic and what Thayl did to you." Eloryn's sympathy sounded strained. She was overdoing it.

Memory felt her lips curl, defensiveness building. "What do you know about what Thayl did to me?"

"No more than our existing theories. The Council has tried to decipher the rune scars on Thayl's hand, but it's an ancient language, the very basis of the magical language we use today."

"I'm sorry, *what*? They kept *his hand*? You didn't think that would be important for me to know? How could you keep something like that from me?"

"I hardly kept it from you. Had you been at all co-operative with the Council I'm sure you'd have known. I don't have time to tell you every little detail myself." Eloryn became flustered. "You know how full my time is. It must be nice spending your time frivolously, dressing up like a boy and lounging about eating pastries, but some of us have duties that must be performed."

"Duties my ass. Don't go getting angry at me because you're jealous I'm spending more time with Roen. It's not your duties stopping you spending time with him, it's you."

Eloryn's mouth shut, and her back straightened like she'd taken a huge breath and held it.

Memory made a show of picking the last pastry from her plate and popping it in her mouth as she stood to leave. "I'll skip lunch, thanks. I've already eaten."

Memory paced in her chambers. A grandfather clock in the corner read a quarter past six, and she fretted that she wasn't going to make it to the Ivy Room for a second time. Not that Will hadn't missed more than his fair share of meet ups.

Memory knew the minute she stepped out of her chambers her new guard escort would be on her heels again, and she didn't exactly want to take all of them with her to her secret place. She briefly considered opening a Veil door to get there, but it seemed like overkill, and scary, especially when her magic still felt so unstable.

Memory opened her balcony doors, hoping Will would just come to her. But he hadn't, not since her birthday, not even when she missed their meet up for the first time last night. He probably didn't make it

himself and hadn't even noticed.

The sun was setting, and being on the eastern side of the castle, the shadows were already dark and cold. Memory brushed a hand over a blood-red rose bud on the vines around the balcony. The tower that led to the Ivy Room was right near her chambers, and one of the windows on her side was open. The vines grew across to it, but much more thinly than the way they rambled up to her window.

Memory knew it was dangerous, but something inside her didn't care, almost dared her to try. She quickly changed into her jeans and t-shirt and stepped onto the balcony edge. A brief glimpse down at the ground shook her, and coldly she wondered how Thayl must have felt, as he fell.

She reached across and grabbed a strong ivy vine stuck on the wall, grateful that the ivy had grown further and faster than the roses, so her hands wouldn't get cut up this time. Clinging to the vine, she stepped out onto the small ledge that ran from her balustrade across to the tower window. Edging along it, she kept herself stable and upright with the vines. It was easier than she thought it would be.

The vines grew thinner as she went. Just a few steps from the window, one of them tore under her hand. The vine pulled off the wall like tape, tearing a long strip off before it snapped. Memory swung backwards, her other hand slipping from where it still held a vine. Her center of gravity pulled away from the wall. She tumbled.

With a push of her legs, she jumped through the open window and landed inside the tower.

Memory sat on the floor in the Ivy Room. She was barely aware of how she'd made it there from where she'd landed on the tower steps. She still felt in shock, replaying what would have happened if anything had gone differently, if she fell. No one would have known what happened. She wondered how long it would have taken for her to be found, or missed, or who would miss her first.

Memory rubbed the goose-bumps on her arms and her breath blew puffs of mist. Will hadn't shown up yet. She stood up to see how long she'd been waiting. The clock tower across the courtyard read nine o'clock. Memory blinked. She could tell she'd been sitting there a while based on how numb her legs had gone, but hadn't realized it was so late. Will wasn't coming. He'd broken their promise, again. He'd probably be the last person to miss her if she was gone. She was about to leave when the vines rustled.

Will pushed through and half stumbled into a dark corner. Even in the low light, he looked dirty, and the shirt she had got for him was missing.

He shifted, and seemed surprised to see her standing there, staring at him.

"I didn't think you were coming. Do you know what time it is? I know you haven't got a watch, but there's this ginormous clock, like, right there," Memory said, flinging an arm out to point at the clock tower.

"Sorry," he said. He stayed curled in the corner, seeming shyer than usual.

Memory's gaze kept returning to Will's bare chest, and the ripples of muscle just visible in the darkness. She should be used to him being topless by now, but the act of having seen him in a shirt seemed to highlight the bareness now it was gone.

"And what happened to your shirt?" she asked.

"Got ruined."

"If you didn't want it in the first place you should have just said." *Just like our promise for meeting here every day,* Memory thought. He'd probably made that promise thinking of how she used to be, wanting to see the old her, not who she was now.

Memory sat down again across from Will and sighed.

"I'm sorry I'm being snippy. There's just so much going on, and I feel like I'm losing it. Seriously, seeing things style losing it. It's hard enough trying to fit in around here without being crazy."

"It's okay. You're not snippy. You're honest." Will spoke softly, barely a mumble. "You can tell me what's happening."

You can't let anybody know about me. Promise me you won't tell. Memory bit her lip. She couldn't tell him about Hope. The bombing, Waylan, even what happened on her way there tonight, it all felt like too much to put into words.

"It's just confusing, all this crap with me and Roen and Lory. I mean, I'm just friends with Roen, and Eloryn barely even acknowledges the poor guy's existence anymore, but I'm supposed to feel bad for spending time with him? We're just good friends."

Will grunted but said nothing else. It was so dark Memory couldn't see any expression on his face. She could barely see him at all in the dark corner he sat in. She might as well be telling her woes to the empty corner.

"Oh hey, check out my new mojo." Memory spoke the words to the light behest, remembering she could actually do that now. "Àlaich las."

A small wisp cast a glow in the room, its light shining off the glossy leaves that enclosed them.

The light also reflected off wet blood on Will's arm, which he kept pressure on with his other hand.

"Jeezus. What happened? Why didn't you say something?"

"It's nothing." Will turned his head away, like he was embarrassed to have been seen.

Memory crawled across the floor to him. Up close, she saw there were also fresh scratches on his chest, torn over much older scars.

"Is it bad? Damn, it looks bad."

Will didn't reply or move. Memory grabbed his chin in her hand and turned his face back toward her.

"I'm not kidding around, Will. Tell me what happened."

Will growled. "Just hunters, in the forest. An accident."

"Hunters in the forest?" Memory lifted a hand to her face in disbelief. "It's the royal goddamn hunting grounds. Why didn't I realize there would be hunting? Will, you shouldn't be out there. I'm going to put a ban on hunting, but you've got to move into the palace. I know I've asked before, but maybe now you've been shot by a damn arrow you might have to admit I'm right."

"Can't."

"Of course you can."

"No," he said firmly.

"Why? So you can stay closer to Mina? Is she why you won't live in the castle?"

Will didn't answer. His eyebrows were low over his eyes and his jaw set.

Memory moaned in frustration. "At least, let me heal you? You can't be running around in the dirt with a hole in your arm."

Will shook his head. "Better not."

Memory poked his arm, right above the wound. "Really?"

Will flinched away. She poked him again.

"All right!"

"I thought so."

Memory moved in closer to Will. He kept his eyes on her and remained still. Memory could smell the blood on him, mixed with mossy earth.

She placed one hand on his forehead and one on his muscled chest. Her heart hiccupped.

Memory cleared her throat, but her voice still cracked. "Okay, here we go."

Memory tried to make a connection like she had when she healed Eloryn. In her mind she ran through the theory of healing, but nothing happened. She took her hands back and shook them, then rubbed them together like they needed charging up. Trying again, still nothing worked. The only person she'd ever healed before was Eloryn, her twin. In magic, like calls to like, so healing her twin was easy. Maybe she wasn't skilled enough or focused enough to heal anyone else.

"I don't think I can do it."

"I thought you were supposed to be all powerful at this stuff?"

Will's tone was gentle, joking, but in Memory's fragile state the words stung.

"Why don't you just go back to your fairy lover and get her to fix it for you? And while you're there you can report back to her about me and my lack of ability. That's what you're supposed to do, isn't it? Spy on me and tell her what I'm up to?"

"Do you really think that's why I'm here?" Will's voice remained stable and soft, infuriating Memory even more. "I don't report back to them. They don't need me to. They keep track of what you do themselves."

"Then why are you here? You only show up when you feel like it."

Will pushed to his feet and Memory backed up, out of his way and stood up as well. He looked hurt, but he still didn't raise his voice. "You haven't tried to understand what my life is like, has been like. You just expect me to fit into yours. You're here a month, and you're a *princess*. I've been here a lot longer, and some things… can't just change. It's too complicated. It's easy for you, but I can't be what you want."

"You think things have been easy for me? If you were around you'd know they aren't." Memory was nearly crying, but the reckless energy of her sadness found its way to her voice instead and she screamed at Will. "How am I supposed to understand your life when you're never around, never tell me anything. You didn't even tell me you'd been shot by hunters! You haven't even tried. Just go back to your fairies."

Memory tore the vines away and ran along the old castle wall back to the tower, not caring how close she came to the edge.

She sprinted down the tower steps, round and round, grazing her

elbow against the wall in her rush, trying to expend all of her emotions in physical form. The fires in her chest burned bright hot. A rumble built within her. She ran hard, trying to escape herself.

She stumbled out into the eastern entrance yard, having blindly made wrong turns and run too far. She bent over, her hands on her knees, to catch her breath.

Hayes's voice reached her, and she ducked back through the doorway again. She loathed the idea of him seeing her like this, running wild and dressed in otherworld clothes. Marching feet and another man's voice, crying accusations and pleas, passed by right in front of her. Peering out, she saw her uncle, Ewain, being lead bound and under armed escort toward the main keep. The guards wore a strange uniform, something new that Memory hadn't seen before. The symbol of the Wizard's Council, a stylized mouth with a star inside, was embroidered on the sleeves.

"I did nothing. These are lies." Ewain spoke to Hayes, to the guards around him, trying to get the attention of anyone but no one responded. "I wanted the twins off the throne, of course I did. But I have no army in my control, and I'd be a fool to attempt their assassination! I only voiced my wish to remove them from power because it is the right thing to do. They're an abomination, a corruption of the Maellan line. My brother and Loredanna never consummated their marriage."

Memory found herself running toward the small group, and she skidded to a stop on the gravel right in front of her uncle. "What are you talking about?"

Hayes stepped between them, putting his hands on Memory's shoulders. She flung them away.

"Princess, what are you doing out here at this hour? This is no time-" he began.

"What is he talking about? Tell me."

Memory couldn't see Ewain behind Hayes blocking her way, but she could hear him.

"My brother wasn't your father. He told me your whore mother never opened to him."

Hayes turned and hit Ewain across the face with the back of his hand. "How dare you speak of the beloved Loredanna like that. For such disrespect, I'll make what is ahead for you all the more worse."

Hayes clicked his fingers and the guards picked the man up, dragging him up the stairs into the building.

Memory chased after them, half jogging to keep pace. "Then who? Who was my father?"

"As if you don't know." The prisoner spat at her feet.

Thayl? The burning inside her, already alight, roared and her vision blurred, the world flashing grey. The idea crumpled Memory's heart. So much was wrong, everything about their lives broken from start to end. She thought Thayl had just been some sick father-figure in her life. *Did I watch my real father die? Did I cause it?*

"No, you have to tell me more, I need to know for sure." Memory tripped as she tried to keep up and keep talking to Ewain. She yelled at the guards. "Stop. Stop walking. I order you to stop!"

They continued. Hayes paused briefly to look down his hooked nose at her. "You have no authority here. These men are under my orders, as Grand Bailiff I am in control. Do not listen to this lunatic. He is lying, trying to sow the seeds of mistrust to weaken you and your sister. You must not tell anyone of this fabrication. Go back to bed, princess. The truth will be revealed under duress."

Memory shook her head, incredulous, and followed the group down the stairs into the dungeon. The rooms on the first level looked different to the last time Memory had been through there. Vicious contraptions filled the space, and the tables were laid out with all manner of unkind tools. Memory clutched her chest, wringing her t-shirt in her hands, the heat inside her torso unbearable. The room shifted, contorted. It became beige walls in a small space, tall shelves on either side filled with plastic chemical bottles. Shelves with knives, pliers, hooks. The back wall had mops propped up in a messy pile. The back wall had chains hanging down, manacles on the ends. The floor was wet and smelled of detergent. The floor was stone, rough, spotted red.

Memory didn't know what was happening.

She didn't know where she was.

She ran.

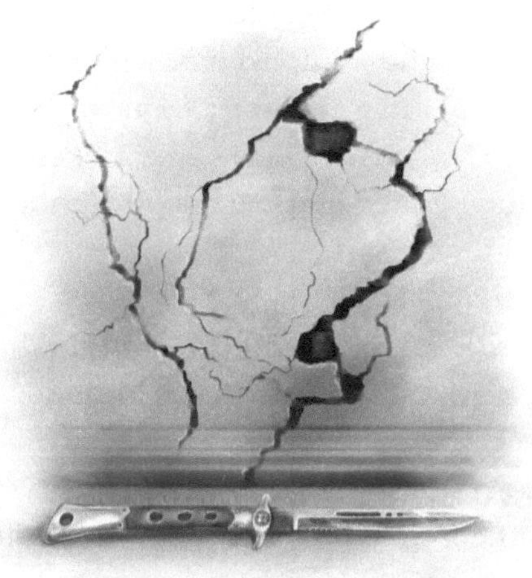

CHAPTER FOURTEEN

Roen sat up in bed and rubbed his face. He could have sworn he just saw Memory step through his room. The way she used to look, in her strange otherworldly clothes, but her hair was its current natural blonde. She seemed distressed, careening past then blinking out of existence.

He pushed the covers back and grabbed the pants and shirt he'd worn that day. He tugged them on, not bothering with shoes in his rush to leave the room. He might have just been imagining things, but it shook him up so much he thought he better check on Memory to be sure. He hadn't been able to sleep anyway.

The chambers he and his parents had been housed in were smaller guest quarters just downstairs from the old royal chambers Memory and Eloryn were in. Given the time of night Roen was grateful it wasn't far to go.

Up the stairs in the corridor leading to the twin's rooms, Roen was surprised at the complete absence of guards. He assumed Eloryn was working late in the queen's office as she often did. Maybe Memory also wasn't in her room, but he still went to check. No guards meant no gossip, for which he was grateful.

Roen knocked at Memory's door and heard whimpering and the rattling of furniture. He pushed the handle and it clicked open, so he slid inside. Armchairs and desks were tipped over throughout the sitting room, and the floor seemed to tremble under him. He pushed through urgently into Memory's bedchamber.

The room was dark, but he could see Memory curled against the far wall, between her bed and a knocked down wardrobe. Tussled gowns tumbled out around her like she was a castaway in a sea of lace.

She muttered to herself, shivering. She flickered in and out of sight.

The wall behind her had cracked and grout shook from it when the room trembled again.

By the fae, what is happening?

Roen knelt beside Memory and brought her into his arms. At first she pushed back, her hands in fists, rigid around her folded iron knife. He held her tighter.

"Mem, it's me, it's okay," he said, using the word she'd taught him.

She dropped the knife and grasped at him, pulling in close.

The tremors stopped. *Was she causing them?*

Memory cried hard in his arms. She mumbled into his shoulder, the words jumbled and incomprehensible. Memory always seemed on the verge of both laughter and tears at any moment, but he'd never seen her like this. He could make no sense of what was happening.

Roen ran his hand over her hair, trying to calm her, reassure her. He kissed her softly on the forehead.

Memory jerked away and looked up at him. Her eyes were fierce and questioning. With a sob, she leaned in and kissed him hard on the lips. She pressed her body into his and he tasted the salt of her tears.

The kiss was so desperate Roen didn't dare push her away, and it stirred confusing feelings in him.

Roen knew he loved Eloryn. He knew it since the morning in his family's old ramshackle home, when she'd charged in, interrupting his father, demanding to know the fate of her guardian. Seeing so much affection and bravery changed something in his heart, and he was hers. He still longed for her, dreamed of her, but he had no hope to ever be with her.

Memory meant so much to him. She was a summer storm, with passion and intensity that awed him and at the same time she was the flower caught within that storm. He would do anything for her.

Memory's lips broke away from Roen's, and she buried her face in his chest. He held her on his lap until she fell asleep, leaving him with nothing but questions.

Memory's whole body ached. She woke slowly, hating the idea of moving, doing anything other than lying still, half-conscious.

She'd gone right off the deep end last night and a dark apathy spread within her. Even opening her eyes was more effort than she liked.

Hope sat on the end of her bed and poked her feet through the blankets. She smiled widely.

Memory pulled one of her pillows over her face and mumbled through it. "What are you happy about?"

"This time I will say it. I told you so. Didn't I say you could have him?"

Memory bolted upright, her heart kicking into life again. *Roen. Frotz.*

"Don't freak out. This is a good thing. Forget about Eloryn, you and Roen can be happy."

Memory's head spun like a killer hangover. Still in her old jeans and t-shirt, she tripped out of bed, her feet getting caught in the sheets. She wobbled to the doors to her sitting room.

"I need some water. I need to think this out."

Swinging the doors open, she saw Roen, looking disheveled in one of her armchairs, his caramel hair falling over his face. Memory cringed and hoped he was asleep but didn't get lucky. He stood up and walked to her, looking her over as if checking for injuries.

"Morning. I thought I heard you talking to someone?" he said.

Memory glanced over her shoulder, her bedroom empty. "Just myself."

They stared at each other, both unmoving.

Roen coughed quietly. "About last night-"

"Assbuckets." Memory covered her face with her hands. "I am so sorry. I was freaking out and not myself and it was just a mistake. I didn't mean it. It didn't mean anything. We can just forget it ever—"

Roen put his arms around Memory, gently pulling her in and kissing her lips over her rambling. Memory froze, stunned, then softened into him. He lingered just a moment before pulling away, his arms running from her shoulders down her arms to hold onto her hands. He stared at their joined hands instead of looking in her eyes.

"If this is what you want, then it is what I want."

"It's what I keep telling myself I want. Maybe I should start listening."

Roen smiled, but somehow it looked sad. "What I was going to say, however, was about last night and the scary magical cracking of walls and flashing out of existence business."

"Oh. That." Memory sat down on a turned over desk. Books and

papers littered the floor under her feet. The whole room looked like a tornado hit it. Clara was going to kill her.

"Was that… you?" Roen asked.

Memory nodded. Roen was the closest friend she had at the moment, other than Hope. Maybe she could talk to him. "Things have been happening to me. Some of my memories are coming back, but other bad things are happening too, like the Memory-localized-tremors when I get upset. I'm also kinda slipping through Veil doors without meaning to."

Outrage spread over Roen's face. "You haven't told anyone about this? Mem, you need help and this is far from my field of expertise."

Memory kicked at the papers on the floor. "I wanted to work it out on my own. Promise me you won't tell Lory, okay? She's just too busy right now. I don't want to worry her any more with this."

"Mem," Roen shook his head.

"No, I don't want her to know. I just can't trust her right now, to not freak out I mean, with all the other stress she's under. I'll work this out on my own."

"All right. But you don't need to keep secrets, not from me at least." Roen shrugged and sat on the tipped over desk next to her. He pulled her iron knife from his pocket and handed it to her. "You dropped this last night. I thought you'd purged it."

Memory cradled the knife in her palm. "Yeah, I thought so too. I should probably get rid of it again. Speaking of secrets, do you want to see something cool?"

"I suppose?"

Memory grinned. "Can you give me some time to clean up and meet up again after lunch?"

Roen gave her a deadpan look. "It's already past midday."

"So I slept in!" Memory pouted. "You were in here all night? I don't think our reputations can take that."

"It's all right. No one saw me come in. I don't know where your guards were, but they are back at your door again now," Roen said.

Memory thought back to her climb to the tower and encounter with Hayes. The guards must have known she wasn't in her room and been looking for her. "Okay, new plan. You hang out until I'm decent again, then I'll leave first and draw the stooges off. You can get out when the coast is clear. Then we'll go and get rid of this nasty iron again."

Memory stood up, wafting her t-shirt and longing to get into clean clothes. Roen grabbed her hand and pulled her back to him, kissing her temple. He frowned as he looked at her.

"Last night, it wasn't a mistake, at all, but we should still keep this between ourselves. There's just too much politics involved. You understand, right?"

"Yeah. Of course."

Memory slipped into her bedroom and closed the door between them. She took a deep breath to steady herself.

The kisses made her feel wanted, warm and real. Alive again. But Memory kept spiraling to the same black thought. *He doesn't really want me. He's just taking the look-a-like runner-up prize.*

Hope's voice came from over her shoulder, whispering, echoing her thoughts. "He just doesn't want precious Eloryn to find out and be upset. If you don't do something, you'll always be second to her."

Memory wore the dress Isabeth gave her, since it had managed the journey well last time. Her bodyguards followed close behind when she left her chambers, and Memory realized her own escape would be trickier than Roen's. She strolled the halls as boringly as possible, hoping they'd leave her be, but they remained diligent. Trying a new tactic, she took a seat and hitched her skirts up to sit cross-legged. When they turned away as they had before, Memory jumped back up and slipped unseen into the servant runs.

Roen waited there for her, and met her with a light kiss on her cheek.

Memory put her finger to her lips and motioned for Roen to follow her. She ran her hand along the stone wall in the narrow tunnel until she felt the waxy lump of her candle stub that she'd left as a marker. Feeling for the door, she tugged and it swung open. Roen followed her in, and when the door closed, she lit a candle for both of them.

"I thought you could cast the light spell now?"

Memory patted the purse at her side. "Not with my knife on me. And for other reasons, you'll see."

"What is this place?" he asked.

Memory led the way, skipping down the stone steps. "Something Will and me found. I don't know if anyone else knows about it. Just wait till we get to the bottom."

The permanently damp state of the tunnel made the steps slippery

and Memory's foot skidded. Roen caught her hand and held it tight. "Slow down, you'll fall and break your neck."

Memory blew a raspberry back at him, but kept holding his hand. It made her feel strange, both comfortable and wrong, adding to the reckless emotions that had grown inside her. Like there was a voice telling her to break rules and take risks and that didn't care about the consequences. *What does it matter if I'm not even a whole person?*

Roen lifted their joined hands and held his candle near to look at her wrist.

"What is that hideous thing you're wearing?"

"It's not hideous! It's cute." Memory defended the bracelet of splintery, chunky, wooden beads she wore.

"I'm a little worried about your taste now. You don't consider me cute, do you?"

"Not at all. If I had to describe you, pretty is the word I'd pick. And this *is* cute," Memory said, shaking her wrist and making it rattle. "Little Edele gave it to me last time I visited the orphans in town, just before the bombing. She made it herself. I can't wait to get back into town and see them all again."

Roen laughed softly. "That's really sweet. I'm not surprised they like you so much."

Memory smiled wryly. "Yeah, it's because I hand out cash."

Roen laughed and squeezed her hand, but Memory didn't feel like she was joking. It felt like there was always some reason that people liked her that wasn't anything to do with who she really was.

They walked in silence until they reached the bottom of the tunnels. With a grand flourish of her arms Memory showed Roen the stacked crates and artifacts.

Roen let go of her hand and lifted the lids of a couple of boxes. "This is all…"

"Iron, yep. A dirty little secret under the capital of Avall. I figure some items missed the Purge and they've been collected here, but I haven't found any official records or acknowledgements of anyone doing that. Will says the fairies have avoided these tunnels since the days of the Pact, so it must have been happening a long time."

Roen ran his hand over the crates. "Have you told anyone about this? Have you told Eloryn?"

"No, if I tell her, she'll tell Hayes, and the Council will be all over

it. I think this place is secret for a reason." Memory took her knife and added it to the collection again. "Hey, do you think you can find your own way back? I'm not ready to go just yet. Being down here helps to shake a few memories free."

"I can stay with you if you like."

Memory stared out over the glittering black water that seemed to go forever. "No, I'd like to be alone."

Roen frowned, but nodded. He paused, then kissed her forehead and walked away.

Memory sat down on a wooden crate and played with a dented spearhead with a hole in its base. She wondered if any other memories would come to her, or how long it might take, when warmth rushed through her.

The frail boy stood in front of her, a tiny soldier at attention. Unrecognizable otherwise, his wide blue eyes told her it was Will. The children were never officially informed of how others ended up in the home, but the gossip always managed to get around. She heard that this kid lost his parents and rest of his close relatives in a landslide while they were all on a family vacation together. He was the only one to survive. Some kids said he was stuck under rubble with dead bodies for days before he was dug out. Maybe that was why he was so scrawny.

It had been a week since she'd stepped in and stopped some of the kids beating on him. It wasn't the first time he'd been in fights. It was his fault, taking arty classes and reading books in public. The kid had no survival instincts. She'd ignored it like she ignored what happened to everyone else, but that time the bullies went too far, drawing blood, so she drew a bit of their blood back and warned them off the boy.

He'd been trailing at her heels ever since, saying she'd saved his life, that he owed her.

She tried to shake him off, but as much as she hated to admit it, she liked having him around. Her little minion. He did anything she asked.

Will stood silent, waiting for her to speak.

"Okay, kid," Memory said. "If you're going to keep following me about, then we need to establish some ground rules."

Will nodded. She leaned in close to him, staring him right in the eyes, almost cruelly.

"First rule — no touching. Break that rule and I break your wrists."

He nodded again.

"Second rule — That thing that happens? No talking about it. Ever. Nothing happens. So there's nothing to talk about."

"Third rule—"

Memory found her face wet, tears spilling down her cheeks. Will

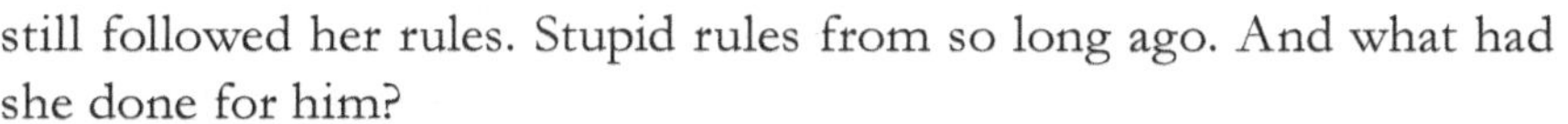

still followed her rules. Stupid rules from so long ago. And what had she done for him?

She had to find him. She had to apologize. Again.

Memory took the other exit from the tunnels and ventured up through the dried-up well and into the hunting grounds.

The late afternoon sun was a rich orange tone, shafts of light shining through the last few blood-red leaves clinging to branches above. Memory called Will's name, and a flock of birds startled and flew from a tree nearby, up into the golden sky.

But Will didn't come.

She wandered farther into the forest, meandering slowly, watching her footing for pesky toadstools. She called his name again, and he didn't come.

The forest grew dark and Memory came to a small pool, lush with ferns and water lilies, the flowers all closed for the night. Her eyes felt sticky from her earlier tears, so she wet her hands and wiped her face. When she stood up from the water's edge, Mina appeared in front of her.

Memory had never been so close to Mina before. The sprite hovered just above the water, her pointed toes occasionally dipping in and causing ripples. There was an almost faded quality to the way that she looked, translucent and glowing like milky glass lit from behind. Her flame red hair, the one splash of color on her, lifted and swirled around a pretty face marred by a scowl.

"Stop looking for him," Mina ordered.

"Why? Doesn't he want to see me?"

"You can't be with him. He doesn't belong to you." Mina flew up closer to Memory, bobbing from side to side. Her wings, like tattered dragonfly wings, fluttered and shimmered.

"Listen, lady, I know Will doesn't belong to me. I'm not trying to take your boyfriend off you. I'm just trying to find him to talk to him."

"No. I said you can't be with him!"

Mina lashed out, swiping at her, scratching her arm, tearing through cloth and skin. Memory recoiled in pain and shock. "You did not just do that!"

Mina hissed, "Stay away from my boy."

Before Memory could respond, Mina vanished.

Memory touched her arm. She was bleeding. The pattern of the scratches was familiar, similar to the ones on Will's chest the last time she saw him.

An angry worry filled Memory. She thought Will actually liked Mina, that they were together with whatever mutual emotions that involved, but now she was concerned. *Just what kind of relationship do they have?*

Whatever it was, it was Memory's fault. It was her fault he was here at all. If only she could send him home, back to the other world. She'd tried for Thayl and couldn't, but there must be a way. She just had to try harder, learn more. She hadn't even asked Will what he wanted. She shook her head. *Of course he wants to go home.*

Memory dropped to the mossy ground with a thud. "I have to make this right," she said aloud.

Hope squatted down next to her, plucking leaves off a fern stem. In the darkness of the forest, the bright pink heart on her t-shirt seemed to glow.

"Did you see that?" Memory asked her, fuming.

"Jealous fairy attack? Yeah. All the more reason to keep away from that lot."

Memory groaned and threw a pebble into the pond. "There's got to be a way to get home. To help Will go home, away from that she-beast."

Hope dropped the fern and put her hands on Memory's knees, looking into her eyes. "You're not thinking of going back too, are you? You can't. You have to stay here with me. You don't remember what it was like there."

"No. But Will deserves a chance to choose." Moisture had started wicking through Memory's dress from the damp ground, chilling her. She stood up, feeling like she should go back to the castle, but not really wanting to. "I guess I don't really have any home. There, here, nothing feels right anymore."

"You can make here work. I'm here with you, and if you were queen everything would be better. You wouldn't have to be second to Eloryn anymore. You'd have the power to make everything how you wanted it."

"It wouldn't give me the power to help Will. Are all fairies so horrible? And Mina is a seelie fae. I thought they were the good guys." Memory's breathing became ragged. The encounter had upset her more than she knew why. "I don't like the idea of Will being around her."

"From what I've seen, all the fae are nasty, untrustworthy and better off extinct." Hope stood up and looked in the direction of the old well. "I don't think you should have gotten rid of your knife."

CHAPTER FIFTEEN

At Memory's instruction, the chef placed the top of the bun on the stack of food. She picked up one of the creations and took a bite.

"It's close, but still missing something. Probably the special sauce."

Memory had woken up that morning craving something she hadn't remembered until now. A burger. She'd come with Clara to the kitchens and commandeered one of the chefs to help with the process, and they ended up with a large tray full of burgers. Apparently making just one of something wasn't the way they worked in here.

A small creature crept up the edge of the marble-topped bench. It looked like it was made of twigs and had huge aqua blue cat eyes. It made a grab for some leftover mince.

The chef shooed it away. "Cheeky boggart."

The kitchens were hot and busy, filled with gusts of smoke and steam, sizzles and clanging pots. Memory's bodyguards remained outside, unable to fit into the chaos, which made the experience more enjoyable for her. She sat up on the kitchen bench overseeing the chef's work and Clara leant next to her. They'd taken over a small worksite, but the rest of the kitchen still bustled with staff preparing meals for an entire castle of nobles, servants, and guards. Even the pets had meals prepared here, Memory learned, when she questioned where a plate of raw meat was being taken and learned it was for the falcons in the mews. *Mews,* thought Memory. *Sounds like something a cat does, not a house for birds.*

Although Memory had managed to find most of the necessary ingredients for her burgers, the cheese wasn't the same sort of rubbery processed slice she remembered, the ketchup was fresh and chunky, and the bread was heartier and crustier than the sponge soft bun she wanted.

Clara took a bite of one. "I think they're brilliant. These are sure to become popular in Avall. I'm going to see that my favorite tavern starts serving these. If I tell them the princess invented them they will have no hesitation adding them to the menu."

"That would look great in the history books. Princess Memory Maellan, Inventor of Hamburgers." Memory smiled as she chewed her burger. It wasn't how she remembered them, just close enough to tease her senses.

A large man approached through a gust of steam, kitchen workers scurrying out of the way of his imposing presence. His suit was black and purple. Memory smiled when she saw who it was.

Bedevere stopped in front of Memory and bowed. "Your Highness, I was told I would find you here. I'm sorry to disturb your meal." He held out a folded piece of paper, without seal or envelope.

"No probs. Is that for me?" Memory wiped her hands on her apron. It had been forced on her by Clara and seeing the sauce smear she'd just made across it she was thankful she hadn't just done that to her ice-blue dress.

"Yes. From my late brother." Bedevere kept his usual steadfast expression, but Memory could see that Waylan's death was still too fresh for him, just as it was for her. "I discovered it on his desk. It was addressed to you, but he hadn't yet sealed it before his untimely death."

Bedevere looked at the row of burgers with interest. "What are these?"

Memory lifted the tray for him. "Something from the other world. Try one."

"Then there will be less for me," Clara said with a playful sad tone.

"No way you could eat that many," Memory scoffed.

"True indeed. That is something you would do." Clara poked Memory's stomach. "Councilor Bedevere, ignore my poor humor. Do try one. They are delicious."

Bedevere, who had been holding a key in his free hand, placed it down on the kitchen bench next to Memory.

"I will take that offer indeed." He reached for a knife and fork.

"That's not how you eat a burger. This is how you eat a burger," Memory said, and demonstrated grabbing a burger in both hands and stuffing it into her mouth. Juices ran down her wrist.

Bedevere raised an eyebrow, but picked a burger up as directed. He didn't begin eating right away. "It is nice to be away from the meeting chambers for an intermission. So much organization still to do for security concerns. The Council fails to agree upon a proper magical security system for the Council's most important works. We're storing such important books and documents in an archaic safe room that uses mundane keys of all things. Very primitive, if you ask me. The only failsafe is that the door requires two keys."

He glanced at Memory with a serious expression then took a bite of the burger. As he chewed, Memory thought she almost saw him crack a smile before his normal dour expression returned. "Yes, delicious. Since the fae ceased bringing imports of food and technology into Avall over a century ago, I fear there must be much we are missing out on. If you don't believe, as most do, the reason they ceased importing was the complete fall of the rest of the world into Hell. At some point, your highness, I'd be appreciative of your co-operation in mapping and comparing timelines, from what you may remember, of course."

Bedevere placed the burger back on the plate, having only eaten one mouthful, and gave Memory another swift bow. "I had better be back to work. Thank you for sharing some of the other world with me. I hope to learn more from you soon."

Bedevere's gaze dropped for a split second to the key beside Memory then back to meet her gaze before he nodded and left.

Understanding the message but not entirely sure why, Memory tucked his key into the palm of her hand before anyone else noticed it.

"What an odd gentleman," Clara said.

"Yeah." Memory looked at the letter he'd given her. For her from Waylan, not long before he was killed. She looked up at the ceiling until her eyes stopped watering.

"Are you having any more of these? I'd like to take the rest to some friends around the palace," Clara asked. Memory took the one she'd already started off the tray then shook her head. Clara took the tray and left.

Memory opened the letter and read while eating the rest of her burger.

The letter was, as Bedevere had said, addressed to her. It explained that Alward's magic books, which had been prohibited from going to Eloryn under the grounds of them being Council property, had already been catalogued and dispersed into the Wizard Council's library. However, the filing of Alward's personal research had been delayed due to short

staffing and the time it was taking to catalogue the rambling studies. It had fallen to Waylan to catalogue the work, and while examining the notes he realized much of it was pertinent to Memory. Waylan noted that he had set these papers aside in the storage safe, out of the way on the back table beside other unsorted documents. In the letter he expressed that he believed these studies should belong to Memory and that he would be lobbying the Council to release them.

Then he died before he could.

Memory took a deep breath, a small smile shaking onto her mouth. She realized Bedevere had read the letter before handing it to her. His dead brother's intent was for her to have Alward's research, and Bedevere had left her with information on their security and a key to the safe they were kept.

Memory didn't need to think too much about stealing the documents. In her mind they belonged to Eloryn, and if there was anything in them to help her understand her magic better, then she needed them. She just had to get another key.

Her first thought was of Roen, but asking him to help her steal seemed cruel, given the way he felt about his past. She'd just have to wait for another opportunity.

The window seat in the library was piled in soft pillows and lush upholstery, and made the perfect refuge from the gray weather surrounding the palace. It was becoming one of Memory's favorite places, and the sound of rain on the glass helped keep her calm when thoughts confused her and emotions became dark and volatile, as they did too frequently these days.

She had just wriggled into a comfortable position when Eloryn approached. Her ever-present guard duty kept a distance, planting themselves like suits of armor along the walls.

"Might I join you?" Eloryn's voice wavered. Memory hadn't seen her sister since their argument the last time here at the window seat. She looked perfect as ever, and Memory wondered how her hair always looked so stunning. Rivers of jealousy inducing pale gold. *Does she say her magic words to it and make it do what she wants? Seems like cheating, but then, who'd want a hair straightener when you have magic?*

"You're reading the book I gave you?" Eloryn asked, sounding even more nervous and making Memory realize she hadn't replied.

Memory had the Avall history book balanced on her lap. She offered her sister a small smile. "It's pretty good actually." She tilted her head to the vacant opposite end of the window seat. Eloryn sat down with a look of relief.

Eloryn clutched a couple of books against her chest, but didn't immediately start reading any. Memory wondered if they were for study, or for an excuse. She smiled a little more. She regretted the words she'd said to Eloryn when they'd fought. Memory wasn't entirely sure what to think about Eloryn right now, but could tell Eloryn was trying to mend their relationship. Memory decided to try as well.

"This book has taught me a lot. Also, the pictures are really pretty." Memory demonstrated by flicking to a portrait of a white-haired wizard, surrounded by archaic chemistry equipment.

Eloryn leaned forward a little and smiled "Lauphmer the Wise, one of the most powerful wizards of Avall history. It always was one of my favorite books of Alward's collection when growing up."

Memory ran a hand down the slightly worn but well cared for binding. "This was one of Alward's books? I didn't realize. Are you sure it's okay for me to have?"

"Of course, that's why I gave it to you."

Memory couldn't look her sister in the face. She'd been so ungrateful when she'd first received the book as a present. She stared at the illustration instead. Something caught her eye, and she frowned in recognition.

"Just how accurate would you say these pictures are?" she asked.

"Quite. Most are portraits the wizards would have sat for personally."

In the portrait, a small object hung from a chain about the wizard's neck. An arrowhead, the same she'd seen in the iron stash beneath the castle.

Memory started flicking through pages, back to other portraits, examining them.

Eloryn moved closer to see what she was looking at. Memory poked the page hard, pointing to another powerful wizard from Avall history who sat beside the hoe she'd also seen in the stash.

"This is iron."

She flicked back to Lauphmer and pointed out the arrowhead. "This too."

Something twigged in Memory's head and she turned the book right to the front.

"And, of course…"

Arthur with Caliburn.

"Mem, how do you know? They could be silver, or bronze. Caliburn is the only cold iron artifact."

Memory shook her head and chewed her fingers. "No. No, this makes sense. Is it possible?"

"I'm afraid you've lost me," Eloryn said with a confused giggle.

"All these great wizards with their iron tidbits. Me with my magic and my knife. That's not a coincidence."

"If indeed these wizards did carry cold iron, which I doubt they would have as there should be no iron in Avall."

Memory looked up from staring at the illustration of Arthur. "Why do they call it *cold* iron? It always feels warm to me. Doesn't it feel warm to you?"

"That's what the fae call it — cold iron. And yes, the one time I have held your knife it did warm me. In fact it relit my Spark of Connection after it had been shut down." Eloryn bit her lip, staring intently at Memory, her eyes and eyebrows twitching with thought and the edge of a smile on her lips. "It's only forged iron that harms the fae. Raw iron is like a conductor of magic, of life, in our blood and the composition of our earth. What if when iron is worked by man, it somehow becomes affiliated to man, and becomes a magnet for magic?"

Memory's eyes grew wide. "Drawing magic into humans?"

Eloryn nodded in return. "And out of the fae. Magic is their life force. And if forged iron also steals that from them, that's why it hurts them."

"So I've had my knife for who knows how long, just soaking up all this magic?"

Eloryn's eyes sparkled as she paused to think. "For at least sixteen years within the Veil. That we know."

Memory smiled, enjoying bouncing ideas back and forth. They were getting somewhere, assuming they were right, and Memory was happy to assume.

"And that's why my magic's all messed up. I'm not accessing magic like others by using the Spark of Connection. I just use the magic within me that I'm full of." *A vessel too full, ready to spill and spoil everything.* Memory scowled. *The damn fairies already knew.* "What if it wasn't just my knife? There might be more iron in the rest of the world. Why wasn't everyone over there all magicked up? Will said there was no magic there."

"No Spark of Connection. Maybe you need that, to attract the magic

into you through the iron, like calling to like." Eloryn looked away for a moment then back to Memory. She'd grown serious. "If this is the case, it explains the ritual. Thayl sent you to the otherworld, to build up all that power, so he could steal it and use it for himself. That's why he had to twist time to find you when you were sixteen, when you'd had those years to absorb so much power."

The air huffed out of Memory and she stared out the window. The rain splashed onto the roses, knocking loose petals to the ground. "It was never about me. I was just a tool, a battery to charge up and steal the power from. And with the magic, my memories." *My soul.* "Why? Why did I lose them too?"

It was Eloryn's turn to shrug.

Memory kept pondering out loud. "What if it all just gets jumbled up together?" *Like Hope, created from my magic and memories and soul all messed up.* "When he took all that magic out of me, it took everything else? Then why don't I lose memories now when I use my magic?" Memory clutched the book on her lap, pulling it up like a shield. "What if I am and I just don't know it?"

Eloryn shifted closer to her, putting a hand on Memory's knee. "If Thayl took nearly everything you had, we could surmise all the magic you have now was channeled into you while you were within the Veil, when you formed no new memories for the magic to become attached to. But I'd have to say it might be best to be careful when and for what reasons you use your magic, just in case. As you form new memories now, we aren't to know the magic within you won't become tangled with those, and be lost as you expend it."

Memory put her head back into the pile of pillows with a prolonged groan. "Yeah, like I can control when and for what reasons my magic splurts out. You've got so much control and power. You can ask anything of anything and just, bam, done. My magic is more bam, HAHAHA DID SOMETHING YOU WEREN'T EXPECTING LOLZ."

Eloryn blushed. It was all too easy to make her blush. "It's not really that powerful. I can talk to animals or speed up natural processes, but not a lot more. To be honest, the most exciting thing I ever did was have some wood rot and break under a guard's foot when fighting Thayl."

"But that's cool. That was being creative. I bet if you thought about it, you'd have the power to do almost anything if you're creative with it. Like doing your hair." Memory eye-balled Eloryn but didn't get a

reaction to prove her suspicions so she continued. "Me and Thayl, we're just human-shaped blaster-guns. Okay smart girl, here's one for you. How come Thayl didn't run out of magic after all those years blasting stuff?"

Eloryn looked like a kid who finished her exam before everyone else. "The basic rule. Like calls to like. Having that much magic within may have made him a powerful magnet for more. The growth would be exponential, almost uncontrollable at times."

I know that feeling. All the information swirled in Memory's head, picking up more and more details as it went, a tornado sweeping up debris. Each time she'd had a memory come back to her she'd been near iron or holding iron. If her magic and memories were out in the world, lost when she cut off Thayl's hand, tangled together still, maybe some were coming back into her through the iron? *But aren't they in Hope now? Or is Hope just made from my soul?* Memory's theories started colliding and getting confused, and she started to lose confidence in them.

Eloryn sighed and half smiled. "But this is all really just theory, based on your wild notion that those items were all iron."

Memory opened her mouth and almost told Eloryn everything, but something held her back. Not quite her own voice, the voice of Hope, warning and whispering. She'd gotten so caught up exchanging ideas with Eloryn, but even now what was Eloryn doing? Telling her not to use her magic.

She closed the book and stood up, the desire to leave taking her. "I guess we all believe what works best for us, right?"

Eloryn stood up right after her. "We have made a start though. The theories are promising. I swore to you once I would help get your memories back, and I still wish to uphold that. But only if it is what you still want."

"Of course it's what I want," Memory snapped. She rubbed the bridge of her nose and looked away. Eloryn genuinely seemed to want to help, but Memory's defenses had gone back up. She felt like a wild dog, at once ready to snarl and attack and yet desperately wanting affection, unsure which direction to run. "Is it what you want? Do you even want me to get my memories back?"

"If I had the power I'd have done so already, I would give you back everything that was taken from you."

Memory's eyes narrowed, and she walked away without another word. *Everything that was taken from me. Everything... She knows. She does know my soul is broken.*

CHAPTER SIXTEEN

When Roen opened his door, his hair was tussled like he'd just woken up. He squinted at Memory and tugged a shirt on.

"Did I wake you up?" she said.

Roen panted like he'd run to the door. "What's happened? Are you all right?"

"I just came to ask a favor."

Roen winced, looked into his room and back at Memory. "At two in the morning?"

"What? Really? Sorry, I haven't been sleeping much lately. I didn't realize." Memory wondered if that was why all the bodyguards that followed her down from her chambers were looking so amused. *They could have said something.* She glared back at them where they stood out of earshot down the hall.

Roen shook his head and chuckled. "I thought there was some danger, or, at the very least, hoped for a more entertaining night call."

Memory stuck her tongue out at him. The joke made her feel awkward, but the favor she was about to ask felt even worse. She'd decided to ask for Roen's help to steal after all since she'd made no progress on the heist on her own. With her recent breakthroughs about her magic, she needed to know more and felt Alward's notes might hold more clues.

Memory took a deep breath and spilled out all her words with the next. "I want to get Alward's notes off the Wizard's Council, but to do it I need two keys and two people to turn the keys, and I have one key but still need to get another one and I'm just not as good at that stuff, you know, as you are."

Roen frowned as he buttoned up his shirt. "Alward's notes? They're important to Eloryn aren't they?"

"Well yes, and to me. A lot of the research was about trying to find me through the Veil. I'd try and get it myself, but I haven't seen the inside of the safe room, so I can't Veil door in, and if I try and use my magic some other way I'd probably just blow everything up. I know it's asking a lot from you, and I didn't want to—"

"I'll do it, Mem," he said, cutting her off with a warm smile. "For you."

Memory nodded, looking at her feet. *For me, or for her?*

"I've got a plan and it shouldn't be difficult. But, um, maybe I'll tell it to you when it's not two in the morning?"

"I wouldn't mind, if you wanted to come in." Roen opened his door a little more.

To hear my plan, or...

Roen's shirt was still only half buttoned, his hair mussed, and a sleepy smile on his lips. The whole look was undeniably sexy, and a flush of warmth ran down Memory's back. Even if it started with planning, she didn't think it would end there.

Memory gave herself a mental cold shower and pointed with a thumb at the guards watching from down the hall. "The walls have ears, and eyes, and great big gossipy mouths."

"Your faithful protectors. I didn't see them down there." Roen nodded solemnly. Then a smirk cracked the expression and he grabbed Memory around the waist and pulled her two steps back into his room. Out of sight of the guards, he bent and gave her a long kiss on the corner of her lips, then let her go again.

"Sweet dreams, princess," he said, and smiling cheekily, closed the door between them.

Memory touched the place he kissed her with her fingertips. *He always used to call Eloryn 'princess.'* Even without the risk of a scandal, Memory wasn't sure she'd have gone in. She wasn't sure what she wanted at all.

Late in the evening Memory left her quarters, telling her bodyguards that she wanted to go to the kitchens again for another culinary experiment.

"I'm going to cook up some doughnuts even if it takes me all night."

Memory strolled into the hazy, clanging kitchens and frowned when one of her guards followed her in. A chef soon chased him back out again to wait at the entrance as he had last time. Memory smiled wickedly.

Dodging the cooks and kitchen hands, she made her way into one of the larger pantries and pulled the door closed behind her. On a shelf lay her boy's clothes, delivered there earlier by Clara. Memory quickly wriggled out of her night gown and tailored robe and dressed in her Tristan disguise.

Memory stepped back out and grabbed a cupcake decorated in delicate sugar roses. She winked at one of the chefs who watched her, the one who'd helped her make burgers. He winked back in return and went on with his work. A couple of servants were leaving with silver trays of food and Memory slipped out of the kitchens with them, straight past her bodyguards who didn't look at her twice.

The plan is rocking so far.

Memory had to resist the urge to skip, she felt so free. It was the first time for a while she wasn't being trailed by burly soldiers. But skipping while dressed as a boy would probably draw too much attention.

When she reached the meeting point, Roen was there waiting for her.

He held up his hand, dangling a key on display.

Memory high-fived him. "Nice work. I hope it wasn't too hard to get."

"For me? It was a piece of cake." Roen said, ducking past Memory and revealing her half-eaten cupcake stolen in his hands. She grabbed for it, but he popped it in his mouth.

Memory smiled, relieved Roen was in a good mood. She always thought his skills were something to be proud of. Maybe he didn't mind so much anymore.

"The hardest part is next though. The old safe room is at the top of the western tower, but there's a guard at the bottom of the stairs." Memory pointed with her thumb around the corner to the arched doorway down the hall, blocked by its sentinel.

Roen looked quickly. "I could probably sneak through while he's looking the other way. But getting us both through without a distraction could be difficult."

Memory put a finger on her chin, pretending to think. "A distraction you say?"

Giggling fluttered down the hall to them, and they both peeked around the corner again. Clara leaned against the wall next to the guard. The maid's uniform she wore was a size smaller than usual and the guard leaned in toward her. He stepped out of the doorway, sliding an arm around her waist.

Memory whispered dramatically, "The dove has taken position! Go, go, go!"

She dashed down the hallway, keeping as quiet as she could. She grimaced whenever her feet hit the ground, still sounding so loud. She expected the guard to hear her at any moment and started to reconsider her tactic. Memory couldn't even hear Roen behind her and was worried he hadn't followed when she made a run for it.

Roen's hands wrapped around Memory's waist and lifted her. She silently squealed. Carrying her, Roen slipped passed the guard without a sound. He put her down just up the stairs, out of sight around the spiraling column.

Standing a step up from him, they were nose to nose. Her heart raced and her face felt flushed.

Roen lifted his chin and looked up the stairwell. Memory nodded and they continued to the top. A small antechamber opened up, revealing a massive door of solid metal, bronze banding and studs reinforcing its strength. To each side, further apart than a normal human could reach, were two keyholes.

Memory pulled Bedevere's key from her pocket and Roen took his, and they turned them in the lock simultaneously.

Gears clicked and rolled, and with a push, the door swung open. The room was small, just enough to fit a couple of tight rows of bookshelves and tables which overflowed with badly sorted and stacked volumes.

Memory punched the air with a silent woot. "That all went surprisingly easily! Let's grab these notes and get back out before that poor guard proposes to Clara and has his heart broken."

Roen pushed the door closed until it was just slightly ajar. He threw Memory the second key, and she pocketed them together, then they went seeking Alward's documents where Waylan's letter had said he left them.

"Which ones are they?" Roen asked, stepping over stacks of books on the ground. The room smelled of powdery paper.

Memory had made her way to the back and stared dumbfounded at the table there. *Papers*, Waylan had called them. *Notes*. What she had

imagined as a journal or two to snatch and run with turned out to be crates full of hand-bound tomes stacked one atop another amid mountains of loose leaf parchment and scrolls.

Memory blew out a sigh. "We might have a problem."

"They can't all be his, surely," Roen suggested, whispering.

Memory checked through some of the unsorted papers and books that were strewn amongst the more regimented ones. All had the same handwriting, the same topics, same style to the scratchy diagrams. Sixteen years' worth of research.

He must have been trying so hard to get me back. Memory felt guilty about assuming there would be so little.

Memory kicked the table leg. "We're screwed! We can't exactly do multiple trips to carry all this out."

"I'm sorry. I know this was important to you." Roen moved next to her and put his hand on her shoulder. "Could we remove it all some other way? Could you use a Veil door?"

Memory twitched, the thought of using her magic giving her goosebumps. She wasn't sure whether this research would have any of the information she really needed, but if it did, it was worth the try. She had to, for her, and for Will.

"You'll have to do the heavy lifting, Roen. I need to concentrate." Memory imagined her own chambers, and pinched the fabric of reality with her fingers, opening a door through the Veil. "I'll keep it open. You take everything through."

Roen nodded and moved fast, loading up an armful of books and carrying them through. Even this way, only moving the books a few steps, it would take a lot of trips.

As Roen went back and forth through the door, he took a moment to catch his breath and balance. He started to look gray from the effects of the Veil. The books weren't so much placed as dropped onto the floor in Memory's living room.

Memory focused on keeping the door open and tried to shuffle the remaining books around on the desk to hide what had been taken.

Roen gathered up the last few books when they heard men's voices on the stairwell.

"I hear movement. Someone is in there," one man cried.

Roen froze, a look of terror on his face. Memory looked from him to the door as the footsteps grew closer. The agitation in the approaching

voices was clear. Memory and Roen were going to be caught. They could both go through the Veil door, but then there would be no answer to what had occurred there. There might be an investigation, and the Wizards had magical ways of finding out who did what and where. Memory had dragged Roen into this, and the prospect of being caught here, stealing, had left him looking shattered.

Memory charged him, pushing him through the Veil door into her room. She let the door close between them. Grabbing the nearest book, she hopped up onto the desk and shook herself into a casual expression just as Hayes burst in, followed by Bedevere and another Councilor.

"And here we have our culprit," Hayes declared.

Memory looked up from the book she pretended to read. "What brings you all up here? I was just doing bit of light reading, myself."

Hayes marched up to her. "Madoc here discovered his key missing, and when we checked around it turned out Bedevere's had also gone astray. And here we discover – 'Tristan,' is it? – at the scene of the crime."

Hayes pulled her cap off her head, throwing it to the floor. Her blonde hair that had been tucked up in it tumbled down around her face. Memory jerked back away from him and sneered.

"If I weren't locked away in the castle, if you actually let me go to school, and I mean *real* school, with magic classes, maybe I wouldn't have to sneak around to read this stuff myself. Or dress as a boy."

"Nothing excuses your outrageous behavior. I thought you'd been keeping your nose clean, and then you pull this stunt? How on earth did you manage to acquire the keys?"

Memory looked at Madoc, red faced and seething, and then to Bedevere who watched the proceedings with the same lack of expression he always showed. He met her eye, and she was surprised by a tenderness there that seemed to invite her to give him up.

Memory stood up and reached for Hayes's ear. "You mean this key?"

She made a show of pulling a key from his ear, then reached with her other hand to his other ear and pulled out the second key. "Or this key?"

Hayes swiped his walking cane across her arms, knocking the keys from her hands. Madoc skittered forward and chased after them, picking them up.

"Childish games. You have broken the law, and we must administer a suitable punishment. *Tristan* will be expelled from lessons. When you return to school, you return as Memory only. You need to understand that acting out like this is no way to get what you want."

No more Tristan? Memory had only used the excuse of needing to attend magic lessons as a boy to cover up what she'd really been doing. But to have that taken away from her hit her hard. She leaned back against the desk, needing its support.

"But I need to go to magic class. I need to learn more," she said, her head shaking side to side.

"To do what? Cause even more trouble than you currently do by adding magic into the mix?" Hayes scoffed.

In just one class with Waylan, so much understanding had opened up in Memory. She had been looking forward to little else like she had returning to magic class, even without Waylan teaching. She couldn't lose that. She just couldn't. She had to do something.

"I have to because I'm scared." Memory let all defenses drop. She addressed Hayes, but then turned to Bedevere, finding his calm gaze more comforting. "I'm losing control, of whatever is happening within me. I've Veil doored without meaning to. I'm worried about what else could happen. I need to learn about this stuff."

Bedevere's expression changed ever so slightly, a bend of the eyebrows, a softening of the eyes.

Hayes spoke first. "If you would just let us examine you as requested—"

Bedevere spoke over him, his deep voice easily covering Hayes's. "How about this: rather than attending classes with the male students, which is of course unseemly for a girl of the royal family, I can offer to privately teach the princess. As a tutor."

Memory stood up straight again, leaning forward hopefully. "You'd really do that for me?"

Bedevere grunted softly. "I can probably work my schedule around to find the time."

Memory tried hard to act chastised still and not let loose a toothy grin. She looked to Hayes for approval.

"Fine, so be it. If Bedevere has time to waste on such pursuits, he is free to do so. But this leniency is on the understanding that there will be no further incidents from you. If you step wrong again, a much more dire punishment will need to be found."

Memory jogged briskly all the way back to her chambers. Running in, she found Roen still there, biting his thumbnail and pacing back and forth around the stack of Alward's research. When he saw her he stopped short then strode up to her, grabbing her hands tight. "Are you all right? Why did you do something so foolish?"

Memory rolled her eyes and smiled. "I'm fine. A little slap on the wrist was all. And I threw them off the scent. I doubt they even noticed this stuff was gone or that I had an accomplice."

"I can't believe you took the blame like that. If I were found, if…" Roen's words stuttered away to nothing.

Memory could see it on his face. It would kill him. It almost did in the past. He was more willing to be hung than be known as a thief. *I was stupid for asking him to help me with this, thinking he'd be okay with it.*

"Forget about it. Tristan took the brunt of it, but things worked out okay. And hey, check out our haul," Memory said.

Roen didn't turn to look. He stared at Memory intensely and bent in to kiss her lips.

Memory shied away and cleared her throat.

Roen remained still, his cheek beside hers. "Thank you," he whispered.

Memory slid her hands free of his and crouched down beside the sprawling papers, beginning work sorting and stacking them. She remembered sitting surrounded by books in Eloryn's room, holding her sister as she wept from the pain of missing her guardian, wishing for something so small as to just see his handwriting again.

These belong to her, Memory thought. *Just like Roen does, and I'm taking both from her.*

"Change of plan," Memory said, standing back up. "Let's give these to Lory. Don't you think she'll like them?"

Roen just nodded, staring at Memory. She stared back and an awkwardness rose.

"I know you like her," Memory blurted. "I mean, I know you like her more than me. And that's okay. This thing, you and me, I'm not so sure it's working."

Roen's lips moved into a very small smile. "To be honest, I'm not sure either. It was nice, to try, but I would not risk our friendship by forcing something that doesn't want to grow. I love you, Memory. You are the best friend I've ever had, and could I have anyone as a sister, it would be you."

"Or brother, right?" Memory joked, waving at her clothing.

Roen chuckled and gave her a tight hug. "You're truly something special."

"Just not quite as special as Lory?" she said into his shoulder.

Roen pushed her away again and dipped his head a little to look seriously into her eyes. "You and El, for all your similarities, are very different. Don't forget that."

"I know. It's just difficult with her being so perfect all the damn time," Memory admitted.

"That she is. Unobtainably perfect. I want to be better for her, to deserve her, but whenever I try to act up it makes me feel worse." Roen moved back and looked down at their steal. He bent to start clearing it up, but Memory waved him away.

"Leave it. I'll deal with it all in the morning." Memory took Roen's hand and led him from the room. She paused at the door and gave him a stern look. "Roen, take my advice. Just be yourself around her. Your flirtatious, sexy self."

Roen smiled back but his brow was furrowed. "And what if she doesn't like that me?"

"Terrifying, isn't it?" Memory grinned wryly as she let him out the door. "Maybe it's not best to take any of my advice. I wouldn't know how to be myself if I tried. But it's important to be loved for who you really are, right?"

CHAPTER SEVENTEEN

Eloryn sat on a garden bench in the center of the rose garden. Entering her office for the day had caused an abrupt anxiety attack, so she made an excuse that she wanted to spend some time outside and would do her work there instead. A wooden desk and a lacy white canopy had been carried out by servants, and she flipped through her paperwork in the wan sunlight. With a sigh she noted that it was the job itself she wished to escape, not just the office.

She focused on her surroundings and a small wistful smile grew on her lips. Pebbled pathways ran between neat rows of well cared for roses, blooming in shades of peaches, pinks, and behested purples, within a courtyard framed by the tall palace. Something about the space reminded Eloryn of the high-walled courtyard in the home she'd shared with Alward and her time stealing slips of sunlight there. The sweet smell of the roses hung in the air. With the aid of magic, the roses there were always in bloom, even now when the weather grew steadily worse.

Eloryn's usual guard detail accompanied her, some manning the perimeters of the courtyard, with one always standing directly beside her. She was distracted from her work when another soldier arrived and with a few quiet words, dismissed the soldier closest to her and took his place.

He nodded to her meaningfully. His sandy-colored hair and densely freckled skin highlighted bright blue eyes.

She gave a polite smile and nodded back, meaning to return to her paperwork, when he cleared his throat.

"Your majesty," he said in a boyish voice and bowed to her. "My name is Erec. I am here to protect you."

"Thank you." Eloryn tried to sound grateful and hide the truth that having these bodyguards around smothered her every breath. Despite knowing the reality of the situation, she couldn't help but be nostalgic about her time in the forests with just Roen and Memory, running for their lives.

Erec cleared his throat again, and Eloryn raised an eyebrow at him. He looked around as if to check for listeners and leaned in slightly.

"Majesty, I am the younger brother of Peirs. My brother is concerned about your safety, even though he's no longer captain of the guard. So he has sent me to watch over you."

"Peirs? Why is he so concerned as to my safety? As you can see my safety is being managed," Eloryn said, gesturing to the other guards.

"With respect, my brother feels the guard isn't being properly managed."

Eloryn's eyebrows squeezed toward each other and she forced them apart. "I know I have little experience in this role, but it should no longer affect the guard as it is now under Hayes's control."

Erec's head dropped and he spoke quietly. "It is Hayes's management that concerns my brother. Hayes is removing many good men from important positions, saying they were in league with your uncle's plots. The people he is replacing them with have little to nothing to recommend them, save their complete loyalty to Hayes himself. I'm not sure that—"

Erec immediately fell silent and at attention beside Eloryn as Memory and Roen approached. Memory had her arms behind her back and a smirk on her face.

Eloryn stood to greet them, smiling warmly and taking a deep breath to fight the painful shivers she seemed to get every time she saw Roen.

"Your Majesty," Memory said, giggling slightly as she did a terrible impression of a curtsy while keeping her arms hidden. "I have been feeling bad that I missed getting you something for your birthday," she continued, with an exaggerated shrug. "But what could I possibly get this girl who has it all? Well, dun-uh!" Memory revealed the wad of papers she held and waved them in front of Eloryn.

Eloryn took them, her first thought being to the prospect of more paperwork, until she saw the handwriting on the top sheet and knew it

instantly. "Are these...?"

Memory grinned. "They're all yours. Happy late birthday, sis."

Eloryn grasped the notes to her chest. Her voice was small and choked. "Thank you so much. I can't express how much this means to me."

"And there's more. Lots more. Like, 'you'd better come and get it all out of my living room because it's blocking the whole place up' more," said Memory.

Eloryn's heartbeat grew strong, warming her through. She'd felt horribly at odds with Memory lately. And Roen, what he must think of her, how she's behaved. But here they were bringing her this gift, this amazing gift. She pulled them both into a tight hug, not caring if it wasn't a proper thing to do.

She whispered into the gap between the three of them, "I definitely won't ask how you managed to acquire these."

Roen bowed his head and his hair fell over his face, but Eloryn could see he smiled. "That is indeed very wise."

Pulling away from the group embrace, Eloryn grinned at her sister. "Mem, I hope Alward's notes will have usefulness for you, too. I will study them to help you, like I promised."

Memory tilted her head and smiled softly. "Sounds great. Well, you two have some catching up to do so I'm off!"

Memory dashed away too quickly for either of them to object.

Eloryn and Roen both turned and looked at each other, then at their feet.

Memory left her bodyguards in the hallway and ducked into a bathroom with a window. She stood up on a white pedestal basin in order to peek out the small window and spy on Roen and Eloryn. After an embarrassing start, they sat down together and seemed to be having not the most awkward conversation ever. The small smiles they shared now and then made Memory feel both fluttery and sad. She scrunched her nose up and fanned it with a hand to cool her emotions.

"I can't believe he chose her over you. What was he thinking? You are so the better catch." Hope stood in front of a mirror and picked at a floral arrangement on the side table. The effect of seeing them both

in the mirror, like there was four of her, dizzied Memory. She hopped down off the basin.

The deep grimace on Hope's face made Memory smile. It touched her that Hope was so defensive of her feelings. "I just didn't feel that way about Roen after all."

Hope pulled petals off the flowers and flicked them into the air. "Why the hell not? I'm you, and I'd wife him straight up."

A petal landed on Memory's nose, tickling her. She batted it away. "I guess I've known him longer. He's just a good friend."

"Sure he is. He was probably just trying you out while he built up the courage to go for the real thing. And her, with that innocent-little-me act. She's just a tease, stringing him along, and you're just going to let her?"

Hope's words were like every guilty thought Memory couldn't bring herself to say, even when she prided herself on being blunt. Were those dark thoughts true? They didn't feel right. Her sister, hugging her and Roen among the roses. That felt right. She wanted her friends and wanted to shut away her nasty paranoia.

"Hope, enough. Try to be happy for them. I just want things back to how they used to be. Me and Lory and Roen and Will as friends. I feel like we're getting there again. Except for Will." *I miss Will.*

"And what cost has this regained friendship been to them. Admit it. Everybody else gets what they want and you just get spurned. You shouldn't have let him go. You shouldn't have let Alward's notes go." Hope pulled the whole arrangement from the crystal vase and threw it on the floor. Water and green stems splattered on the tiles. "We'll see soon, what kind of friend Lory really is. She has all that research now, knowledge you could have kept, that you needed. We'll find out how genuine she is about helping you when she provides you no help at all."

"You're wrong." Memory had to trust Eloryn would help her if she found anything in Alward's studies relevant to her. She had to trust that Roen and Eloryn were a better match than Roen and herself. If she started to doubt, she had to face tough realizations. That maybe Roen didn't want her because he sensed something wrong within her. Something broken and lost, and at the same time so overfull it could explode.

"Eloryn has helped. I already understand more, about myself, about magic, and iron."

Memory stared at the piercings around Hope's face, the silver-colored buckle and studs on her belt, on her jeans, on the cuffs and bracelets she wore.

"In the world we grew up in, just how much iron was there?"

Hope rolled her eyes. "I told you to forget about that place."

Memory continued, her voice strong. "Tell me. There was a lot, wasn't there?"

"Yes. A whole stinking world of iron."

CHAPTER EIGHTEEN

After three sleepless nights, Roen found himself waiting outside the Council's chambers for an audience. *If I dare to try for her, I have to do it properly.*

It took some time before he was ushered in, and only Hayes and a small handful of Councilors were in attendance, but it was enough to make a decision.

None of the Council members seemed happy to see him. They put down the paperwork that they had been seeing to.

Roen swallowed hard and bowed deeply.

"How can we help you, your grace?" Hayes asked. "I'm afraid that we're very busy, please be brief."

Roen still wasn't used to the title, now that he was the son of a duke once again in good standing. He wasn't sure he'd ever feel worthy of it.

Standing tall, Roen delivered the speech that had chewed away his ability to sleep through its repetition in his head. "Esteemed Council, I have asked for your time today in the hope that you will sanction my courtship of her majesty, Queen Eloryn."

The Council said nothing at first, merely looking at one another. One of them smirked before correcting himself.

"For what reason would we grant such sanction?" Hayes asked, his eyelids lowered.

Roen bowed again, and spoke from his bent position, the words too

hard to speak to these stern men face to face. "Because you can trust me to always be there for her. To protect her as I have done and to love her truly as I forever will do."

Roen stood up straight again, awaiting their answer.

Hayes paused, his face hardened and eyes twinkling, as though he relished what he was about to say. "In short, the answer is no. Did you seriously believe we could allow such a thing? Negating the fact that you have been dashing court protocol by seeing both the queen and the princess whenever you so desire, and putting aside your questionable behavior in general, you are the seventh son of a seventh son. Your connection to magic is null, and your offspring will have the chance to carry the same burden. What good would you be to our queen? What semblance of an heir could you provide?"

Hayes stood, walking down the long table toward Roen, thumping his walking cane with each step.

"Hayes, if you would—" Roen attempted to interrupt, but wasn't sure what argument he could give. It was all true, and he had known this would be the outcome. His mouth spoke of its own accord, trying to give some miracle reasoning in his defense that his brain couldn't find.

Hayes reached Roen and looked down his nose at him. His voice had grown soft, a friendliness in it that mocked him. "No, Roen. No. You're young, handsome, and I know you do well with the ladies. Forget these foolish feelings for the queen and find someone else. And do it soon. Need I remind you where an obsession with someone you cannot have can lead? Of Thayl's path to revenge over someone he was never worthy to possess?"

Roen lifted his chin. "No matter what I am, I am not Thayl, and would never take an action against the queen or the Wizard's Council."

"Or the man we choose to be her king?" Hayes's voice dropped lower, threatening. "Remove yourself from the queen's company. That is not a suggestion. It is an order."

Roen turned and left the room, unable to say or hear any more.

He made it back to his chambers where he sunk into a seat, his hands shaking.

At least now he knew that nothing could ever be. Even if he were lucky enough to woo her to love him in return, it could never be. But at least this way, knowing that was the case before declaring his feelings to Eloryn, it would only be him who suffered.

Between the blast and the clean-up, the Round Room looked like it had an inch of stone-work scrubbed off its walls. What had been ancient grey rock had been sheered away, leaving pale limestone. All the original furniture had been removed, replaced with one long, straight table. Hayes sat at one end and Eloryn at the other, with the rest of the Council spread along the length.

Memory had the seat closest to Eloryn and shot her sister a smile.

"You're excited to be here?" Eloryn observed.

"You can tell?" Memory whispered back while the rest of the Wizard's Council arrived for the meeting.

"You are bouncing in your seat."

Memory chuckled. "This is my first official invite to a meeting I've received since longer than a lying puppet's nose. And I actually know some things now. I might be able to contribute, worthy member of society like!"

Bedevere arrived and took his seat, and Memory smiled warmly to him. He appeared to be the last of them, and Hayes began the meeting.

"Thank you for attending," Hayes said, indicating Memory particularly. "We have a number of important agenda items to discuss, beginning with the matters of marriage for the queen and princess."

Memory's seat felt suddenly unsteady. "Matters of ma-what?"

Eloryn had turned pale beside her and looked down at her lap.

Hayes continued as though Memory's outburst hadn't happened. "Both of you are of a suitable age to be married, and given the current political climate, it's been decided that the process be given a high priority."

"Okay, slowing down here." With all the reading and studying Memory had been doing, marriage had not been anywhere on her radar. "For one thing, some might not agree that seventeen is an appropriate age to get married. And what the hell process are you talking about?"

Eloryn spoke softly from beside her. "Memory, for hundreds of years it has been the responsibility of the Wizard's Council to select a suitable partner and arrange marriages for the Maellan line."

Memory spoke mostly to Eloryn, wanting her guidance and not wanting the rest of the room to hear her ignorance on the subject. "I thought that was just some weird thing with Loredanna and Thayl

because those guys didn't like him? You mean they pick the husband for every Maellan woman?"

"And man. The royal line flows through Maellan blood whether it be a male or female heir. It has simply been the case that there have only been female heirs for the last few generations. And it is the role of the Wizard's Council to…" Eloryn's voice grew scratchy and she stopped, paused, then looked up at Hayes at the other end of the table. "I knew this was coming, but I hadn't expected it so soon."

Memory shook her head, staring at everyone around the table. "I hadn't expected it at all. I want it known that I am not cool with the idea of arranged marriages. Not cool at all."

Hayes quirked an eyebrow up. "Your temperature is duly noted. Understand, while we want to begin taking action on this straight away, we will not force you hurriedly into anything. Taking into consideration your unique circumstances, and the considerate upheaval of both your lives recently, we have made a plan that we believe to be acceptable. We're providing unprecedented leniency in allowing you to court and select from a list of pre-approved candidates."

A few of the Councilors nodded like this was some kind of grand charity on their behalf.

"Thank you for this considerate clemency, Hayes. Council," Eloryn said.

Memory hissed, "Don't thank them! You're encouraging their backwards ways."

"Mem, please don't," Eloryn whispered. There was something desperate in her tone, something exhausted. She knew this was coming. The way she'd been avoiding Roen made sense now to Memory. She doubted she was going to find Roen's name on this list of approved dates. But even if the list was filled with steamy hotness, it didn't sit right with her.

"Why should I have to date who you say? What if I don't want to get married at all?" Memory challenged Hayes with a stare.

"The reason this needs to be done, your majesty and princess, is because after all they've been through, the people of Avall need assurance that the royal line will be stable and ongoing. There has already been an increase in civil unrest, with the flurry of vagrancy and the amount of beggars ever increasing." Hayes scowled at the notion. "This, in itself, is a massive risk. Our political opponents will rally the poor and the discontent and they will target the queen — she is unmarried, female, and inexperienced as a ruler." He motioned to Eloryn who listened

with a blank face. "That is what they will say. Marriage is merely a way to smooth this all over."

Memory shook her head. "If you're worried about the discontent rising up against you then maybe try and make them, you know, content? I don't think a wedding is going to do that. What they need is assistance to get their lives back together."

Hayes thumped his walking cane on the floor. "What we really require is to increase the town's police force and clear out the undesirables. We should be establishing a stronger, more robust militia under the control of the Wizard's Council throughout the city in order to resolve this issue. The middle and upper classes who support us will think better of Eloryn should we clear the streets of the poor."

"The poor need help, not clearing off the streets!" Memory said.

"Some action needs to be taken, whether it be the wedding of our queen or a display of military force." Hayes turned his attention to Eloryn. "Your majesty, would you put this issue to rest and give the Council authority to build a militia, so that we may handle it for you?"

Eloryn seemed to think for a moment and her brow twitched. When she spoke, her voice was empty. "At this time, I do not think it is the correct option for control of a military to be within the purview of the Council."

Memory nodded encouragement to her sister.

"Very well," Hayes sighed. "Then that leaves us with marriage as the only recourse. The matches, of course, will have to be the most appropriate, so that we can establish the strongest channel of magic. You are the very last of Maellan blood, and it must be kept strong."

This Memory did know. Her reading of history texts revealed one scary thing — those of Maellan blood didn't live long lives. Accidents, illnesses, disappearances, it was like they were cursed. Memory and Eloryn were the last little twigs clinging to their family tree.

Memory rubbed her forehead. "So you think you need to match us up with someone who has lots of magic going on? I don't see the point. Thayl supposedly had little magic, but Eloryn and I seem powerful enough."

"You are a fool if you believe everything you hear, princess. It was just a vicious lie that died with your treacherous uncle," Hayes said.

"Why aren't I surprised that he's dead?" Memory said.

"Mem, what are you talking about?" Eloryn asked.

Epic face palm. Memory realized what she'd let slip. She hadn't told

Eloryn yet, hadn't told anyone. Didn't know if it was true enough to tell, only that it was too hard to tell.

"Our uncle, before he was *killed*," Memory threw a harsh look at Hayes, "told me that Loredanna never, you know, did it with the king."

Eloryn's voice was tiny. "And you think that means our father was Thayl?"

"I don't know if it was the truth. Even Thayl didn't know, but I'm leaning towards it." Memory paused. "I'm sorry. I didn't want you to find out this way."

"Hayes?" The way Eloryn looked to him for reassurance made Memory queasy.

"Lies, your majesty. A desperate man will say anything to survive," Hayes declared.

Memory stood up, slowly, firmly, in control. "I'm just trying to make the point that there are other ways to be powerful, rather than forcing people into relationships that ruin lives. Like Caliburn, both a metaphorical and physical tool of Maellan power."

Hayes stood, matching her. "You're speaking of things you know nothing about. Caliburn has been lost since the days of Arthur. An arranged marriage is the only way to solidify the support and strength of the people of Caermaellan."

Memory slammed her palm on the table. It rattled beneath her, flimsy, nothing like the ancient, sturdiness of the round table. She was about to continue her argument when Roen and his parents entered the room.

Eloryn stood up, a confused look on her face that bordered on hopeful. She greeted Roen's parents formally. "Your highnesses, so lovely to see you all."

Hayes met them with a bow, but his expression wasn't pleasant. "You're early, but never mind. If we could postpone what we were discussing, my ladies." He looked to Memory and Eloryn. Eloryn nodded.

There weren't any seats left at the table, so Bedevere offered his to Isabeth, and Brannon and Roen stood behind her. Roen's parents looked very much as they had when Memory first met them. Even in their falling-down cottage they dressed like royalty and held that bearing. And still Memory couldn't help but look at Brannon's missing arm, which made her think about Thayl even more.

Memory, Eloryn, and Hayes returned to their seats.

"How can we help you, Councilor Hayes?" Roen asked, awaiting the reply with a frown.

"It's more about how we can help you," Hayes began, opening his arms wide in a giving gesture. "I have arranged for those who took over your family's duchy to be relocated. As the estates of Sir Ewain have recently become available, those who had been occupying your family's lands have agreed to move and return your ancestral home to you."

Brannon put his only hand on his wife's shoulder and squeezed, and she reached up and took his hand in hers. She said, "We can go home? After all these years? We will have our home again?"

Hayes simply smiled, and so did Roen's parents. Roen's frown remained.

Does that mean he'll have to go, too? Memory turned to get a reading from Eloryn, but she looked like a statue, a polite smile frozen in place over a sickly white pallor.

"This is fine news indeed," Eloryn said, her voice almost robotic.

Brannon strode up to Hayes and shook his hand. "We are in your debt. We had thought our home was as lost to us as our other sons."

Hayes's eyes closed slightly and he smiled. "Come, we will adjourn this meeting so I can begin your arrangements to move. As the Lafaettes have occupied your estate for ten years, there will be some management required to organize the change. We will, of course, strive to have you home as soon as possible."

As if everything had been resolved, Hayes concluded the meeting, and everyone dispersed. Roen and his parents followed Hayes out. Memory sat stunned for a moment, then ran to catch up with Eloryn, who was exiting under the supervision of her guards.

"Lory, I'm so sorry. About, jeez, well, that whole meeting," Memory pleaded, trying to keep up with her. "Particularly about Thayl. I was going to tell you. I was just waiting for the right time. That *totally* wasn't the right time."

Eloryn stopped walking and looked at Memory. There were tears in her eyes, but her voice remained strong. "It's not that you didn't tell me. For all we know, it is only a lie. That is what upsets me. I don't understand how you could believe it. How could you accept him as a father after everything that he did to you?"

Because I'm not right, because my soul is broken, because I don't fit in anywhere with anyone else, because of all these reasons too painful to say.

Memory turned her face away. "We've all got something dark in us, Lory."

Roen met Memory at the entrance to his chambers. She flourished her hands around herself.

"Notice anything different?" she asked, her mouth edging into a smile. She looked much the same as usual, wearing a wide-skirted gown he'd never seen before, her pale hair pinned into a simple yet elegant style with a braid running across the front.

Roen looked Memory up and down and then laughed. "You've lost some weight."

"Boy did I," Memory said, looking over her shoulder. "About six men plus armor worth of weight."

Roen smiled and stepped out of his doorway. He'd been in a low mood since Hayes's announcement that his family could return home, but Memory always seemed to get a smile from him. The two of them began wandering along the corridor through to the main wing of the palace.

"Finally convinced them you don't need protecting?"

"Hayes has calmed down a bit, thank the god of all that is cute and fuzzy," Memory said. She opened a delicate silk purse that hung around her waist and pulled out a cream bun and started eating it. Roen laughed. Memory continued through a full mouth. "He's letting us go back to school again soon, and I get free run of the castle without getting trailed. Lory still has a few guards with her all the time though, being the all-important one, poor thing."

Roen wondered if those guards were also being ordered to keep an eye out for him.

Memory finished the bun and licked her fingers. "But the going back to school part is turning out to be a mess. I have to go to all my stupid etiquette classes now but have to restructure them to fit some time in to be tutored by Bedevere. Got to talk it through with the headmistress and see what will work, which is why I need this mirror whatsit."

"The Speaking Mirror," Roen said.

"Yeah, that. What's the story with it?"

Roen thought back to the fairy tales he'd known as a child that explained the magic of the mirrors. "The story is that a powerful Maellan queen created it. She was very vain and enchanted a mirror to compliment how she looked and talk back to her when she asked questions. Things

went bad for her, and the mirror was shattered into a number of pieces. A wizard discovered that the parts of the mirror could still communicate with each other, in a fashion. Alward had two, one from the Wizard's Council and another taken from Loredanna's estate the night after she died. Eloryn used one to speak with Lanval before we confronted Thayl."

Memory squinted, looking at the ceiling as she walked. "Gah, something there seems so familiar, but I can't pick it. Something from my past. I bet Will would know." She sighed. "You haven't seen him at all lately, have you?"

"No, not except his late night visits to my balcony every night," Roen said in a dreamy voice.

Memory punched him. "Has Clara been talking? I'm going to kill her!"

Memory looked across at Roen a couple of times then finally asked, "Do you think that you'll move back to your home, with your parents?"

Roen kept walking, chewing his lips, a deep frown over his eyes. It took a moment for him to answer. "No. I will stay at court. When Eloryn was dying I promised her I would never leave her, and I won't. Even if I hadn't promised, I couldn't leave her. Even if it hurts to be by her side, I won't leave her."

Memory seemed saddened by his response but reached out and squeezed his hand briefly. They passed through the main entrance hall and were about to climb the grand staircase when a man cried out.

"Stop! Thief!"

Roen froze. He shook off the fear and turned to see what was happening.

A very short, older man pointed his way and marched toward him and Memory. Roen's fear returned.

"Stop right there, thief."

Roen felt as though all blood had drained from his body. He smiled, but it didn't feel convincing. "Good sir, you must have me confused with someone else."

"Don't 'good sir' me, scoundrel. I recognize your face. You're the one who stole from the Guthrie estate just months ago. Jumped out the window with the mistress's finest gems." The man shook a finger as he spat out his words. He wore a servant's uniform bearing the Guthrie crest and was old, wrinkled, but his eyes were clear and sparkled with disgust.

The night I tore my shoulder from its socket. No, I was sure I got away clean. Roen's breath came hard like his chest was being crushed. He couldn't say anything. His worst nightmare was being enacted here, within the walls of Caermaellan palace.

A few other nobles in the entrance hall had stopped to see what was happening.

Memory stepped between the old man and Roen. "Chill out, mister, you've made a mistake."

The servant looked her up and down. "Your highness?" He bowed, spluttering, becoming flustered. "Your highness, I have made no mistake. We must call guards to protect you from this criminal. Guards!"

He looked about frantically and spotting some guards across the hall, started heading to them. Memory grabbed the back of his shirt, trying to slow him down.

Roen felt a hand on his shoulder and waited to be shackled and imprisoned. Instead, he heard Hayes's voice.

"You have a complaint?" he said. He had come down the stairs behind Roen and continued down toward the servant.

The servant clearly recognized Hayes, and looking triumphantly at Roen, opened his mouth to loose his accusations.

Hayes held up a hand and the man stayed quiet. Turning back to Roen and Memory, Hayes said, "I'll handle this."

Hayes led the servant away to a private chamber, speaking quietly to him.

Roen realized he'd been holding his breath, and let it out in a rush. Nobles around the room went about their way, and Roen tried to convince his legs to keep holding his weight.

Memory hovered around him. "Are you okay? I mean, you know, with the stuff, and things."

Roen looked at her and grinned, relief spreading through him. "I can't believe you tried to tackle an old man for me."

"I wouldn't call that a tackle, just a bit of shirt pulling." Memory smiled back at him, but frowned when she looked to where Hayes and the servant had exited. "Hayes better be looking after this properly. I'm not sure if I like the idea of how he handles things."

Roen leaned on the cold, marble banister, pushing his hair back from his face. "I'm just glad it's being handled. The fact it is something that has to be handled is too much of a shameful imposition already. Hayes has been more than kind."

Memory snorted. "Hayes? Kind? Doubt it. Everything he does gives me the squeams. Like the fact Hayes announces arranged marriages and tries to send you away on the same day. Co-incidence? I think not."

Roen shook his head. He was so grateful for having so narrowly avoided the shame of his crimes. He wouldn't question the man who had saved him. "Let's get you to the mirror."

CHAPTER NINETEEN

The rain and winds that shrouded Caermaellan for weeks had eased, and the sunlight had everyone outside. The ringlet-topped girl with too much enthusiasm from their classes had recommended they all spend their break sitting on the grass in the large courtyard of the finishing school. In an attempt to cultivate friends and some sort of normal life, Memory and Eloryn agreed.

A half-dozen other girls from their classes came along, and they all sat on the ground, the fluffy fabric of their skirts puffing around them, like a field of marshmallows.

Memory wriggled in hers, trying to sit comfortably on the grass in a corset and hooped skirt. She looked at the pagoda across from them longingly. "There are a bunch of benches, right there!" she whispered to Eloryn.

Eloryn rolled her eyes and smiled. "Hush, this is nice. And you've never been one to worry about the risk of staining your gown."

Laudine, with her ringlets, practically bounced in place as she stared at Eloryn, starry eyed. "How many suitors have you met with so far?"

Eloryn blushed. "Two." She didn't elaborate, but Memory knew her feelings about the dates without hearing more. Unfortunately, Eloryn's suitors and marriage were all the other girls wished to discuss.

Laudine sighed. "It must be so wonderful. You must have the pick of the best nobles in Avall."

Eloryn screwed up her mouth then dropped her shoulders as though giving up. She pulled a piece of paper from her binder of notes. "Here, you can see for yourself."

Laudine's eyes nearly popped from her head. "Is this *the list*?"

Eloryn nodded and Laudine reached for it reverentially, but another girl grabbed it first. A huddle of giggles and lace formed around the paper.

Memory frowned. That list becoming public could be a political disaster. "Should you really have given…" One look at Eloryn's expression, so distant and tired, and Memory's warning faded to nothing.

Memory sighed and lay back on the grass to watch the clouds and take some strain off her corseted chest. Clouds were building, and it seemed the sunshine they enjoyed would be brief. Beside her, Eloryn smiled, but Memory could easily see through her expression.

Eloryn glanced at Memory a couple of times then asked, "Have you spoken with Roen recently?"

"A bit. Not a lot, I mean." Memory swallowed. She still felt guilty for what had gone on between her and Roen. What little there was. "I haven't been seeing him as much since Tristan got expelled."

Beside them their classmates remained enthralled by the list of Eloryn's approved suitors, gasping their opinions at each selection.

"Ew. Too old, too old."

"Oh no, not him, frightfully dull witted."

Their commentary didn't fill Memory with confidence in the Council's choices.

Eloryn looped her finger around the necklace she wore and pulled her jade pendant from where it was hidden under the neckline of her dress. She rubbed it between her fingers in what seemed like an unconscious action. Memory knew where she had gotten the pendant from. She gave Eloryn a knowing look, and Eloryn tucked it away again.

"Did he say when he was leaving?" she asked.

Memory shook her head. "He's not going with his parents. He's going to stay here."

Memory could see Eloryn take a deep breath. Feeling mischievous, she said, "You know he's staying because of you."

Memory only had a moment to appreciate the look on Eloryn's face before they were interrupted by a few young men who joined the group, formally introducing themselves. Memory forgot each of their names instantly.

The huddle of girls broke up, passing the list between them when the guys showed interest in it, like a flirty game of keep-away.

Eloryn and Memory's guards watched the group carefully, but the male additions to their group kept a respectful distance from the royal pair anyway, except for one who came and sat close to Memory.

Memory stole a few side-long glances at him as he laughed at the escalating game with the list. He was gorgeous. His blue eyes reminded her of Will's, but he had wavy blonde hair that was tied back into a short nub of a ponytail. He was dressed formally, but didn't wear the puffy tie almost all other men wore, and the top buttons of his shirt were undone.

He caught her looking and smiled.

Damn it.

Memory tried to casually cover her ogling. "Sorry, I didn't catch your name."

"I'm Dylan."

"Memory," she said, and shook his hand.

He gave her a sly grin, then pulled her hand up and kissed it. "Your highness, I did recognize you."

The kiss made Memory's hand twitch. She wasn't sure if it was pleasant or unpleasant, but the situation was getting out of her comfort zone, so she began the process of standing up to leave. Doing so gracefully proved difficult. She managed to step on her own skirts in a way that meant she couldn't straighten her legs and fell back on her butt.

Dylan hopped to his feet and offered her a hand up.

"Thanks. Lory, I'm heading off," Memory said, then looked back to Dylan. His good looks caught her off guard, as though she didn't believe it until she saw him again. The slight pout to his bottom lip was a thing of beauty. "It was nice to meet you, Dylan. But I'm off to the library to do some research for the afternoon."

"Might I join you?" he suggested.

"I'm not sure you'd be interested. It's just econom-er-etiquette. Etiquettey things, girly stuff. Yep."

"Econom-er-etiquette is one of my specialties," Dylan said, his eyes sparkling.

Fine, you win this round.

Memory gave him the okay to follow her with a flick of her head.

Memory sat across the desk from Dylan in a small private room adjoining the school's library. Her ink pen splotched over her work, and Dylan laughed at her. She scrunched up the paper and threw it at him, causing him to chase her round the table. The librarian walked by the doorway and gave them a look. They both sat back in their seats with suppressed giggles.

The daylight shining through the broad window grew dull, and Memory wondered if she should head back to the palace soon. She had enjoyed her afternoon with Dylan so much she didn't want it to end.

Memory relished the chance to grill him about economics, law, and politics, and it turned out that he was very well studied. He was funny and had a deadpan world-weariness that appealed to Memory. He also made for a pleasant, if distracting, view across the table.

Roen appeared in the doorway and came in as though he were looking for her. Memory prepared to introduce him to Dylan, but it seemed like they already knew one another.

"How dare you show your face here?" Roen shouted. He ran at Dylan, grabbing him by the coat and pushing him into the bookshelf behind him, knocking books to the floor.

Memory had never seen him so angry. "Roen, stop it! What are you doing?"

"Do you have any idea what you did to our family?" Roen shook Dylan with each word, bashing him against the solid wooden shelving.

Dylan spoke behest words and light flared around Roen's face.

Roen gasped, letting go and backing away. He rubbed at his watering eyes, blinking. With a grunt he lunged back toward Dylan.

"I will use the behest again," Dylan warned.

Roen grunted and stepped back. He ran his hands up into his hair, pacing in front of Dylan like a lion penning in its prey.

Dylan reached a hand out to Roen. It was ignored. "What I did, was only to protect myself, Roen. All of our brothers were dead, and I didn't intend to end up the same way."

"You could have come with us! But instead you chose to serve yourself, and Thayl, over your family."

"You're making it sound like I supported him," Dylan said.

"You supported him by not opposing him."

"What would you do? Punish everyone in Avall who did not fight to the death against Thayl? Half the court would be included. You can't punish everyone who complied with a new ruler in order to survive."

Memory looked between the two of them. She should have seen the resemblance before. "Roen? This is your brother?"

Roen turned away. "He is no brother of mine. He is a wretched coward, and he's just leaving."

Dylan's jaw worked like he had more to say, but he bowed to Memory and left. Roen watched him until he was out of sight then turned to Memory.

"Are you all right? He didn't hurt you at all, do anything to you?" He ran his hands down her arms as though checking for injuries.

Memory shook her head, confused. "Of course I'm all right. We were just studying together."

Looking at Roen, Memory could see the similarities between the two brothers more now. Both so handsome, with strong jaws, and golden features.

"Be careful, Mem, he's not to be trusted. He's always been the most selfish person I've known. You shouldn't spend time with him," Roen warned.

Memory stepped back, his words hitting a sore spot. "I can spend time with whoever I want. Especially since your time is better spent uselessly pining over Lory."

The wild electricity in Roen's eyes scared Memory. He grunted. "Is this what you want?"

He grabbed her, pulling her in roughly and kissing her.

The kiss was full of passion and anger, his lips hard.

Memory cried out, pushing at Roen, his arms stronger than hers, imprisoning her. A sick feeling swelled in her, and books around them started rattling on the desks. The glass in one of the square window panes cracked.

Roen let go of Memory. His eyebrows were low, confused, appalled.

Memory backed away from him. Her chest ached, and she took a moment to gather herself.

"No," Memory said. "It's not because I know it's not what you want. Be with Eloryn," she said, looking into his eyes. "Stop letting anything get in your way."

"I'm… Memory, I'm so…" Roen put a hand to his mouth.

Memory knew that he hadn't been in control, that he had lost himself for a moment. She knew what that was like. But it didn't make her feel any better about it.

"You should go," Memory said.

And without saying a word, he did.

Memory flopped to the floor. Thin arms wrapped her from behind and held her tight. She held them back, clinging to the black and white striped sleeves.

"I know how horrible it feels," said Hope.

"Something specific, or just everything, always?" Memory asked with a dull laugh.

"The pain of having someone choose somebody else over you," Hope whispered in her ear.

"I don't even want Roen, I just—"

"It still cuts."

Memory nodded and put her head down on Hope's shoulder. "How do you know how it feels?"

Hope paused. "Just part of our life that you can't remember."

Had I been in love before?

"Tell me about it," Memory asked.

"All you need to know is that the people you care about will only hurt you. Love is a poison that has no antidote."

After receiving a note from Memory to meet with her, Roen waited in the private gardens of the palace, pacing near the entrance to the hedge maze. It had been freshly trimmed and the rich grassy smell of the cut leaves brought back memories of his early childhood in his family's estate, playing in the garden with his brothers. He didn't know why she'd ask to meet there, of all places, but his thoughts were too occupied to care. He ran through wordings for his apology in his mind over and over. He hated that Memory had seen him behave so venomously. Seeing his brother had unleashed years of pent-up rage. He couldn't believe that Dylan had the audacity to speak with the princess, after everything he had done. It made his blood boil, and he had projected some of that onto Memory. Words could never undo that, but he had to let her know how sorry he was.

Some staff arrived, putting out a table with placements for high tea. He approached, thinking it was for his meeting with Memory, when Eloryn and one of her suitors appeared, trailed by a procession of guards.

Roen ducked back behind a hedge as the couple made their way up the path and took seats at the table.

Memory… Roen knew that she must have set him up to see this. Was she punishing him, making him be a spectator to Eloryn's courtship?

Watching from within the entrance to the hedge maze, Roen wondered how he could get away without being seen. The maze itself only had a single entry and exit, and if he stepped out he'd surely be noticed. He had to stay, and he couldn't stop himself from spying.

Servants in formal dress and white gloves solemnly poured tea from silver teapots. Roen found small comfort that Eloryn didn't appear to be enjoying the other man's company. He was tall, and fairly good looking, but he controlled the conversation in a way that left few gaps for Eloryn to speak. His arms swung in grand gestures that came close to knocking over the tall tower of cakes, and he laughed frequently at his own jokes.

As Roen watched he saw Eloryn move from tolerance at the banality of her companion to pure boredom. Fake smiles of humor became commonplace and pained.

When her partner stood up to enact some anecdote, faux fencing and barely paying attention to Eloryn, she reached a hand to her chest. Her fingers grasped at something, and she looked longingly into her palm before squeezing her hand closed.

Around something small, green, a pendant the color of her eyes.

Is this what Memory meant for me to see?

Roen's heart split. He knew he owed Memory a heartfelt thank you along with his apology for what she had tried to do for him, but the outcome for him brought only pain.

Staying here in the palace, so he could at least be near Eloryn, if never being with her, had only been tolerable on the notion that it was merely him whom would suffer. He had assumed that Eloryn didn't have feelings for him. But having seen this, the hint that she may feel the same for him — he couldn't cope. He would have to leave.

CHAPTER TWENTY

Memory waited at the foot of the palace steps for a carriage to be prepared. Now they were being allowed out of the palace again, she was desperate to go and visit her shelter. Maeve had been sending her updates, but Memory hadn't been to see them since before the bombing.

It had taken her all morning to find a suitable dress to wear. She was nervous and all her fancy gowns seemed too over the top for visiting the homeless. Clara set out on the mission and had returned not long after lunch with a simple day gown of charcoal-colored linen, with only a modest bustle and long, fitted sleeves.

Memory wondered how Roen was enjoying her little trick with Eloryn. It made her nervous too, but she couldn't help meddling. The two of them were silly over each other. Eloryn had been dutifully, mournfully, working through her list of suitors, but Memory had flat out refused to go on any dates.

How long did it take for them to get a damn carriage out here? Are they building one from scratch? Memory rubbed her hands which felt shaky. Thick, low clouds were keeping the world blanketed and warm, so she couldn't blame the cold. It felt like everything that had happened recently kept building inside her, wringing her emotions. She needed some kind of emotional holiday, but wasn't sure how.

Memory heard someone walk down the stairway behind her. "Is standing on the steps your new pastime, your highness?"

She turned and saw Dylan. "Call me H… Mem, please."

She eyed him warily. The time they'd spent together in the library had been fun, but it was clear how Roen felt about him. Yet he kept showing up, and Memory couldn't say she hated that. "What are you doing here?"

Dylan gestured back at the palace. "I live here."

Memory raised her eyebrows and Dylan chuckled. "I've just moved into a guestroom, temporarily."

Memory's eyebrows rose further. "You're staying in the castle? Is that wise, with how Roen feels about you?"

Dylan hopped down two steps below her, so they were the same height. "It is my foolishness either way. I requested to be able to take a room here in order to reconcile with my family before they return to our lands. Once they're back home, I doubt they will open their doors to me."

A carriage rolled up in front of them. "Finally."

"It was lovely to speak with you again, Mem." Dylan bowed to her and began walking back up the steps.

"Do you," Memory started talking before she thought it through. *Too late now, spit it out.* "Do you want to come into the city with me?"

A handsome grin split across Dylan's face. "I thought you'd never ask."

Three guards had been waiting with Memory to escort her into town. Dylan lifted his chin at them, which they seemed to take as a signal they weren't needed anymore.

Typical, like I'm safe as long as I have a man around to look after me.

Dylan took her hand and helped her up into the carriage then sat beside her on the same seat.

"Where are we heading?" he asked.

The carriage started rolling, the gravel of the driveway grumbling beneath them. "I'm going in to visit my homeless shelter. Sorry, it probably won't be very interesting for you."

"If it's interesting for you, I'm sure it will also be for me. Although I don't for the life of me know what a homeless shelter is."

Memory rolled her eyes. People in Avall just didn't seem to understand dealing with poverty. Maybe it was their prosperous history that left them so unprepared. "Well, you take homeless people, and you shelter them. It's pretty simple really." Memory sighed and looked out the window at passing terrace houses. "Actually it's not that simple at all. I was so focused on these poor little orphans, right? I wanted to help the kids, but then I realized how many more people there were who needed help. So the shelter is turning into a bit of a training school as well. Not only does it give a home to the orphans, it's giving jobs to a lot of other people who've lost their way. There's so much to be done, from repairing the building, to cleaning and cooking, and if they don't know how to do it, I have to find people to teach them."

Dylan whistled like he was impressed. "Where do you get the funds for this?"

"Pawn shops mostly," Memory laughed. "Also asking a lot of favors. Most of my servants work there instead of in my chambers, and a few other people I know are helping out." Peirs was enlisted straight away after Hayes fired him. Memory trusted Peirs. She liked him from the moment he made a pun about how she defeated Thayl. His dismissal from captain of the guard came at a good time for her when she'd become torn about how to run the shelter. She wanted to let everyone in, to help everyone, but kept getting scared someone would abuse her trust somehow. She worried so much for the kids in her care. The amount of responsibility terrified her, so Peirs was there to make sure everyone was safe.

The carriage stopped, and Memory was about to jump out when Dylan moved first so he could help her down. She took his hand, but it felt odd when she could get out of the carriage fine herself.

The building Memory had purchased for her project was huge, if old and dilapidated. Four stories tall, it had once been an inn, so it had the perfect layout for her needs. Memory had bought it only seeing the plans and a sketch of the front, and seeing it now made her smile. Its architecture was of an older style than many buildings around it. Made of gray bricks with diamond shaped windows and pointy gothic features, it had an imposing presence. Stepping inside, Memory was pleased to see how the place was cleaning up.

A skinny girl with brown hair so long, curly, and thick it seemed larger than her body, jogged up to them, holding layers of old skirts out of the way of her legs.

Memory lifted her hand in a fist, and the girl bumped it with her own. "Yo, Maeve, this is Dylan."

"Good day to you," she said, holding up her fist.

Dylan lifted his up as well and laughed when she bumped it. "Is

this some kind of secret handshake?"

Maeve just winked at Memory. "Would you like the grand tour?"

"Why yes indeed," Memory said and linked her arm around Maeve's.

Dylan followed close behind as Maeve showed them the building. Lots of kids came out to watch them pass, and some ran up, just to touch Memory's hand briefly then run away again. Memory was pleased to see they were happy, their rooms clean, and some of them putting on weight.

"You're a hero to them," Dylan said.

"She's done a fantastic job, sir," Maeve agreed.

Memory blew a raspberry. "Nah, my money is the hero here."

"Not at all." Maeve directed them through the kitchens. A cook offered Memory some food, but for some reason she didn't feel hungry so she declined.

Maeve pointed out some women who were learning from one of the palace chefs. "It's more than just money. The way you're able to come up with ideas about how to help us. It's almost like you know this world, these troubles. Nobody else in Avall knows how to help us, but you seem to understand."

Dylan looked at Memory with pride. "She spends her time studying such matters."

Memory just shrugged. Their praise made her feel awkward. *Coming from a group home myself helps too. From what little I remember.*

Maeve slowed her pace and let go of Memory's arm. She gripped her hands together nervously. "I'm afraid I have some bad news for you, though. There have been some of the orphans leave us."

"Don't they like it here? Is something wrong?"

"No, it's more like… they just vanish. We aren't sure where. Peirs has men looking. Maybe they are leaving to go somewhere else, but I thought I'd bring it to your attention, especially since Edele is among them, and I know you were fond of her."

Memory reached for the bracelet she still wore. "Edele? Little Edele is gone?"

Maeve nodded. She looked far more worried than she was saying.

Memory spent the rest of the afternoon talking with the guests at her shelter, from youngest to oldest, to Peirs and the staff from the palace. No one seemed to know where people were going or why. No one had any idea where Edele had gone. She was only six, where could she have gone? Memory refused to consider all the alternatives. She

couldn't bear to lose a single person more from her life or discover those in her care weren't safe.

Dylan waited patiently as she made her rounds, but it was clear he'd become tired of the place. Memory also grew frustrated with the lack of information and the worry that lacking caused. It was dark by the time she gave up and apologetically told Dylan they could leave.

The carriage waited for them on the street just outside, but Dylan took Memory's hand, holding her back. "It's a beautiful night, let's walk a little. You look like you need to relax a bit."

"So obvious?" Memory let him lead her by the hand along the cobbled pavement. It had rained while they were inside, and the stones glistened in the light of the streetlamps. The lamps seemed to have wisp lights in them, and Memory wondered whose job it was to come along and behest them all each night.

"I hope it is not too forward of me to say, but on a night such as this, your skin is comparable to the moon," he said while keeping a straight face.

"Gray and full of craters?" Memory laughed. Dylan winced. *Aw, the poor boy was trying so hard.*

He stopped and twirled her around to face him.

"I picked this for you." Dylan revealed a single red rose bud, which he handed to Memory. She had no idea where he had been keeping it. Maybe he had some qualities in common with his brother.

"Nice trick," she said, sniffing the flower because she thought it was the polite thing to do. It didn't have any fragrance.

"Do you like magic?" he asked.

"Complicated question. Let's just say yes for now."

Dylan bent forward and Memory tensed, thinking he might kiss her. Instead, he whispered a few words of a behest to the rose and the bud spread and bloomed, its petals unfurling large and silky.

Memory gaped. "You're good with magic, aren't you? It's funny. I've never seen Roen do anything like what you can do."

Dylan seemed disheartened that his trick resulted in a discussion about his brother. "You don't know? My brother is the seventh son of a seventh son. It means that he has no Spark of Connection at all. My father, knowing rumors of the curse and that he was already a seventh son and had six of his own, never intended to have Roen. It's sad, really. The Faerbaird lineage is actually quite strong in magic."

Now she thought of it, not once had Memory ever seen Roen use magic, but she never realized that he outright couldn't. "He's never said."

"Well, he wouldn't. It is his most shameful secret."

Maybe not his most shameful, Memory thought, considering how Roen felt about his thieving skills. Memory felt a strange burst of pride for Roen with the way he lived and coped, without any magic at all, with the prejudice that must come with that. And to have known his parents never meant to have him for that reason, and be left as the last son they had, all their wanted children dead or gone. No wonder Roen was angry at Dylan for abandoning them. Memory shook her head internally at herself. *No, Roen's parents love him no matter what. I can see it.* They were proud of him for how he looked after them despite his handicap, just as she was. She wished Roen could feel that pride, too.

Dylan offered Memory his hand again, drawing her from her thoughts. "If comparisons to the moon do not please you, then let me compare you to that rose, although the rose will surely come off second best."

Memory rolled her eyes but couldn't fight the bashful smile that appeared. Over Dylan's shoulder, in a shadow of a building up ahead, Memory noticed Hope, watching. Memory caught her eye and tilted her head. *Should I?*

Hope gave a distinct nod.

Memory took Dylan's hand.

The shelter was near the center of town, and Dylan walked with her over a stone bridge into the bustling nightlife street. Revelers ambled by and cats stalked in the light fog that rolled along the ground. They came to Beyond the Veil, the pub Memory had been to before, where she and Will had made a scene when he'd come to her defense. Despite the trouble caused, Memory missed the days when he'd come to her defense. Times when he'd see her at all. She didn't even know if he was still around and the thought that he might have gone away made her stomach roll.

"Would you like to go in?" Dylan asked.

Memory realized she'd been staring at the pub for long enough to seem strange.

"Nah, I don't think I'm ready to show my face there again just yet." Having Will dominate her thoughts also left her in no mood for clubbing.

Dylan and Memory were about to walk away when Memory saw a face she recognized. One of the older orphans from her shelter was

beyond
the
veil

leaving the pub with a gangly man. Memory focused, and saw the man had the elongated, emaciated limbs of a corpse, and all black eyes. An unseelie fae.

The mousy haired boy with him - Memory searched her mind, his name was Bran - looked dazed as if he'd been drugged.

"Bran?" Memory called out. The boy didn't respond.

Memory headed toward them. "Bran, are you okay?"

The unseelie fae creature led him away completely under its spell.

Memory ran until she could stand in front of them, blocking their path. She waved her hand in front of Bran's eyes, but he seemed to stare straight through her.

She looked up at the fae. Its skin was pale gray, both wrinkly and stretched like pulled taffy. It wore a suit in the human style, but it was dusty and tattered.

"What do you think you're doing? Where are you taking Bran?"

"No concern of yours. He's mine. Get out of our way." Its voice surprised her. For a masculine creature, it sounded almost like an old woman.

Memory folded her arms. "Okay, now I'm really not letting you take him."

"Who do you think you are? Unnatural scum." The creature spat a glob of black goo at Memory's feet. "Think you can order anyone about? You're nothing but a power store created by my master, who'll come to collect soon, you mark my words."

Whoa, what? Those few words from the creature slammed Memory. So much meaning, but what did it mean? Who did it mean? Providence? Could Providence have been a fae?

Dylan caught up to Memory and pushed her behind him.

"How dare you speak that way to our princess?"

The fae leaned down, hissing at them through needle-like teeth.

Dylan reversed, running into Memory who held her ground. His voice was high pitched. "Back down. If you do anything I shall Brand you, unseelie fae."

A crowd of humans and fae emerged from the tavern to see what the commotion was about. Memory frowned at them, willing them to leave. *Great, caught up in another spectacle. I really can't come back to this pub again.*

"Do you think I care?" The unseelie fae howled, wild anger in its cry. "I can feel my life fading from me, ebbing away. Not long and it'll

all be gone. I wouldn't mind taking a few humans with me."

Memory gasped when the creature lashed out at them, swinging a long arm and backhanding Dylan across the jaw. It knocked him sideways, and he fell on the pavement hard.

The fae advanced on Memory, and she backed away. Some of the crowd moved in to try and pull her to safety.

Memory saw Dylan spit blood from his mouth. He looked up and spoke through red-tinted teeth. "Bronmarbh Aileadh."

The unseelie fae loosed a cry that drilled through Memory's body, aching her eyes. A rune symbol appeared on its forehead, as though burned into the gray flesh.

But the Brand didn't slow the creature down. The unseelie fae lunged at Memory. She managed to dodge, bumping into a large man who walked into the fray, smiling.

The mark on the creature's face changed everything.

The humans and seelie fae around her were no longer on the defensive. They moved forward, happily turning on the unseelie fae. The creature was seized, and the humans fell upon it, tearing into it.

Three men held down the unseelie fae who screeched and buckled in their hands. The large man she'd bumped walked up between them and started stomping on the creature's head.

Pixies darted about high above to get a good view. Dust and what looked like thick mud started pouring from the unseelie fae. It smelled of ocean winds and rotting mushrooms.

Bran watched blankly from right by its side. Memory ran over to him, unsure whether he was really seeing anything, but covered his eyes with her hand anyway.

She wanted to look away herself, but couldn't.

Some of the seelie fae swooped down at the creature like buzzing hornets. Cries of 'monster' grew in the crowd, cheering on the violence. The large man had succeeded in pulling off one of the unseelie fae's arms. He held it above his head on display.

Dylan stood beside Memory, wiping his mouth. "Stupid monster deserved it."

Memory just shook her head. "I want to go home."

Memory took Bran under her arm and walked him back to the shelter. On the carriage ride home to the palace, Dylan tried to lighten the mood again and failed at every attempt. The violence kept flashing

inside Memory's eyelids with each blink. She stared into the black night around them and tried to contain her lurching stomach.

By the time they arrived and hopped out of the carriage together, it had passed midnight. The very few guards patrolling the grounds who saw them eyed them scandalously.

Memory grunted. "Fantastic. More reasons for people to gossip about me."

Dylan paused and caught Memory in his arms. His lips lifted on one side in a wicked smile.

"You know, Memory, if people are going to talk, why don't we really give them something to talk about?"

Still smiling, Dylan leaned in and kissed her on the mouth.

The world spun.

Memory found herself in the Ivy Room.

Goddammit!

Memory gagged out the feeling of the Veil. She hadn't been expecting Dylan to do something so spontaneous, not after the night they'd had. And she certainly hadn't expected the result.

Memory turned slowly in a circle and found herself desperately disappointed she didn't discover Will sitting behind her amongst the vines.

"At least I've saved myself from the walk of shame," she muttered, making her way off the roof and down the stairs to her room. Her Veil door defense mechanism occupied her mind, and she was glad to let it take over after the earlier events she never wanted to think about again.

Was that twice now? Did the dream count? Or was it more? Memory thought back to when Thayl's magic had killed the wizard hunter with the scarred face, and she was pinned under his body. She didn't know what happened at the time, how she got free. Maybe his body had just been knocked off her, but maybe this uncontrollable Veil dooring had been happening since then. Either way, it was happening too often.

Memory reached her chambers and stepped inside with her shoulders drooped. She was about to close the door when Dylan bolted down the hall with an anxious expression.

"Thank the fae," he gasped. He took a moment to catch his breath then chuckled softly. "I kissed the princess and made her vanish. If I didn't find you, I would have been in trouble!"

Emotionally spent, Memory just mumbled. "Sorry about that. It's just this condition I'm dealing with at the moment."

Dylan held her chin in his hand. "If I do say so myself, it seems I had quite an effect."

Memory thought of the effect and her destination. She wasn't sure exactly who was having an effect on her.

With his mouth close to hers, Dylan whispered, "Would you begrudge me another attempt?"

Part of Memory wanted to pull away, not ready for physical contact, not now. But the lure of Dylan's persistence won out. As though being desired so much could make her feel better, make *her* better. Memory lifted her head and he pressed his lips against hers.

This time she stayed where she was. The kiss left a bitter taste in her mouth and a shiver low in her spine. But he liked her. He wanted her. That was all that mattered. Right now, she needed that.

Memory half smiled when Dylan pulled away. "I'm still here. Disappointed?"

"Not at all."

With a kiss of her hand, Dylan said goodbye and Memory shut the door, closed her eyes and leaned against it. Her head was a mess, and she just wanted to sleep.

After a few deep breaths, she was ready to drag herself to bed. When she opened her eyes, Will stood in front of her.

"Goddammit!" Memory choked. "Will, you scared the ass off me!"

Will stared down at her, breathing heavily, his expression dark. Half naked, ferocious, the way he used to look.

Memory's pulse pounded in her throat, and she felt sickened by the idea Will had watched Dylan kiss her. She spoke softly, knowing just next door Eloryn probably slept. "Did you see… Were you watching me?"

Will growled low in his throat. "You shouldn't be seeing him. He's only pretending to like you."

"Right, because it's so unbelievable someone could like me that way?" The thought that Will couldn't understand someone would like her burned like a scorching sun in her gut. Memory could feel her temper slipping again, but Will had a habit of bringing high emotions out of her. She continued, her voice rising to a yelled whisper. "Thanks so much for dropping round, spying on me and telling me I'm unlovable."

"That's not what I said. I'm trying to warn you. He's not good for you."

Memory folded her arms across her chest. Staring at his, she saw the scratches there almost healed. She softened her tone. "Is this me we're talking about or you? Why don't you tell me what your relationship

with Mina is really about?"

Will turned away, and Memory worried he would bolt. He looked over his shoulder, his blue eyes sparkling under strands of dark hair. He looked cute when he frowned that way, the same way he'd frown when he was a boy, as though his eyes held thoughts deeper than a boy should know.

"It's complicated," he said.

"Don't Facebook answer me. I want to know if you're okay, that she isn't…" *Hurting you. Hurting you. Hurting you.* The words ricocheted in her head, but her mouth was dry and wouldn't work.

Will spoke again, his voice shaky. "You said you've remembered some things. Have you remembered much about where we came from?"

Memory thought of their tattoo, her rules, how they met. It was her fault for letting the kid follow her everywhere, crush on her, making him do what she said. *He must hate me. He must blame me for bringing him here.*

"Is that what you want? To go back there?" Her tone was harsher than she meant, her pain biting into her voice.

Will's only reply was to growl and leave.

Memory collapsed into an armchair, not even enough strength left to make it to bed.

CHAPTER TWENTY-ONE

Memory pulled the curtains to her living room open, but the dim sky didn't offer much light. She'd been unable to sleep, so when the first hints of morning sun appeared she gave up trying and got up. Her mind wouldn't stop, filled with questions and theories and worries about the day before. And the day before that. And the day before that.

The things that fae creature had said haunted her. And Bran, being led away, to who knows where. Memory had already sent out a letter for Peirs, instructing him to investigate 'Beyond the Veil' and other fae hang-outs to stop more abductions. Memory kept imagining little Edele being taken as well and what might have become of her at the hands of a monster like that.

And then there was Will. Another life she'd destroyed.

Memory stretched and shook herself out. It was time to start finding answers. She stared at the spread of notes on the floor, all in Alward's handwriting. They'd been left in her room while she was out the night before. There was a note on top from Eloryn, apologizing that she hadn't had time to study them herself and how she thought Memory might like a look.

Hope picked up the note and scowled. "Didn't she give you every bit of help I told you she'd give you?"

"Lory is busy, that's all. And she could have kept all this, but she gave it to me instead. That's something."

"Like she could have given you the crown, but kept it instead?"

"Not even the same thing." Memory knelt down and shuffled through the papers. Alward's notes were rambling, but well annotated with clear subjects and headings. Memory focused in on his theories on the other world, and ways to travel there. *If Will really wants to go home, it's the least I owe him. I have to work out how.*

"Semi-permeable membrane," Memory read aloud.

Hope squatted down beside her, looking concerned. "Are you having a stroke?"

Memory pointed at the section of research that had caught her eye. "That's how Alward describes the Veil, as a membrane between dimensions, between the human world and the fairy world. He seems to think what the fae did when they separated Avall from the rest of the world was bring it into some kind of bubble within the Veil."

"Stop changing the subject. Eloryn isn't to be trusted, didn't I tell you?"

Memory didn't reply, too caught up in her epiphany. She considered the knowledge the dragon had left with her, the way she pinched and pulled at the Veil to open doors. Moving within Avall was like bending that membrane, skimming the surface of the bubble holding Avall. To get through to either the rest of the human world or the fairy world would require punching a hole right through.

"When I tried to open a door to the other world for Thayl, it felt like pushing against stretch fabric. I was trying to do the same thing I normally do, just skimming the membrane, and I just ended up pushing against it when I needed to pierce through."

Memory flicked to the next page. Alward had spent sixteen years trying to write a behest to get to the rest of the world, find her, and return them both safely to Avall. The return seemed to be the hardest part in his opinion.

But Memory didn't need a two-way door. She doubted Will would want to come back for visits. "I think I can do this. It's just a different mindset." Memory chewed her lips, reading and absorbing the information.

Hope stood back up and kicked at the papers, messing up the rough order Memory had laid them out in. "Why are you wasting your time on this stuff? You don't want to go back there. You don't remember what it was like. Your place is here. As queen. That's the way to solve your problems, not this stuff."

Memory slapped at Hope's foot. "Quit it. It's not my problems I'm

trying to solve here."

Hope blew a raspberry and dumped herself in an armchair across the room. "Then who is going to solve yours? It's not going to be Eloryn, too busy. Not Roen, he's only interested in her. Not Will, off with the fairies. There's just you and me. Don't think otherwise. Except maybe Dylan, but he's just a bit of fun. Why don't you go get some of that right now instead of this garbage?"

Memory ignored her. She was absorbed in Alward's curling handwriting, and the knowledge it contained. The idea of seeing Dylan again after last night also left her cold and uncomfortable.

You're nothing but a power store created by my master, who'll come to collect soon.

The dark fae's master. The fae were able to travel between worlds. They only didn't anymore because of all the cold iron in the rest of the world. Providence was able to open a doorway to the rest of the world. *Opened one and sent a human through to do her work for her,* Memory realized.

"Do you think Providence is a fae?" Memory asked aloud, even though she was already certain.

Hope stared at Memory for a long moment. "Makes sense. Let's face it, only a fairy could be that cruel, right? Should be exterminated, the lot of them, if you ask me."

Memory scooped up a few key papers then stood up. "I'm going to see Bedevere."

"Bedevere? Really?"

"What? He wasn't on your list of people who wouldn't help me. I trust him. He's been helping me so much in our private lessons."

Hope blew another raspberry and turned away to look out the window. Memory left her behind.

It was only when knocking on Bedevere's door that Memory noticed she was still in her night gown. She'd been up too early for Clara to have come and readied her for the day. In her mind a dress was a dress, but her appearance forced a crack in even Bedevere's stoic expression when he greeted her.

"Yeah, yeah, I know," Memory said. "What I want to show you is far more interesting, trust me."

Bedevere let her into his chambers, which were plain and immaculately kept. A tray on his desk had a steaming pot of tea and a plate with nothing but some crumbs. She was glad he seemed to be a morning person.

Bedevere pulled a seat out for her, but she remained standing.

"I want to open a Veil door to the rest of the world." Memory said.

"Straight to the point." Bedevere poured himself a fresh cup of tea, carefully straining the golden liquid with a strainer and putting three spoonfuls of sugar in. "Do you believe you are able to?"

Memory nodded and explained her new understanding of the Veil. "I want to try it, but I wanted someone around, you know, just in case."

"Wise. It hasn't been unheard of throughout history for wizards to attempt to travel between worlds. And a few have succeeded. At least we can assume so by their absence. Unfortunately, wherever they went, they never returned."

Memory nodded again. She was getting jittery, nervous of what she was about to attempt, and her head felt like it was bobbing up and down of its own accord. "Thayl said the same thing, that Providence said it's pretty much one way, unless someone is holding the door open, like she did for Thayl."

Bedevere put his tea down without having drunk any and leant against his desk, as though the enormity of what they discussed required some support. "If you succeed, is that what you would do for me? Hold the door open, so I can confirm what you have done?"

"Only if you want to go through. I know it could be dangerous, and I'm asking so much."

"Not at all. To even take a step into the other world would be an incredible experience. It would prove so much of what I've theorized. I trust you to help me return home again."

Memory wasn't sure she liked the answer. It meant she had no reason left not to try, and Bedevere's faith in her only made her feel worse. *What if something goes wrong?*

But she had to try. For Will. "No time like the now, I guess. Shall I?"

A single nod marked his approval, and Memory focused her thoughts. She considered locations, and picked the vacant lot from one of her returned memories. Instead of pinching the Veil she placed her hands palms together and jabbed them forward like a thrusting blade, then spread them, widening the hole, spilling the heat of her magic into it. Before her eyes, the Veil tore and opened, swirls of smoke whipping about.

Bedevere said nothing, just looked at her for approval and then stepped through.

Memory held her breath, and just a moment later, he returned. His face had turned an off-green tinge, and he walked straight to the lounge

across the room and sat down.

Memory let the doorway fade.

It worked. She could tell just by the look on his face. Memory sat down hard in the seat Bedevere had offered her before. She had opened a door to the rest of the world. Will could go home. He would go home. He would leave her.

Memory's hands shook, and her throat felt blocked. The pot of tea rattled violently beside her. Bedevere put his hands on it to keep it still and looked at her, concerned.

"Deep breaths, in, out, in. You have just achieved something incredible, but you have to keep calm. When your emotions overflow, so does the magic inside you. Like a pot boiling over." Bedevere spoke a few words in the magic language, and the pot bubbled and steamed, spilling tea from its spout. Memory sympathized with his demonstration. "I believe that's what is causing your accidental Veil door events also. The Veil is of magic, and like calls to like. The mass of magic within you is unstable, and when you aren't in control, that magic tries to flow through the Veil as well, taking you with it. You just need to keep calm."

"I just need to keep calm," Memory repeated like a mantra. Her inner voice laughed maniacally at the idea.

"The other world, the rest of the world, even the brief glimpse…" Bedevere's jaw shook. "I would love to go back, for longer, again, anytime you would let me. But of course we must learn if a way to return to Avall is possible, in case the door closes."

Travel between the worlds would change Avall forever. It would change the rest of the world forever as well, to discover Avall, to discover magic was real. It was too much to consider, too large of a responsibility. At least for now, as far as they knew it was one way only. Just enough for Will to go home.

"No one else can know. Not yet," Memory said, looking at Bedevere.

The pleading expression on her face must have been obvious.

"Of course. It is too early," he said.

"Thank you," Memory said and stood up. Bedevere stood as well and put a hand on her shoulder when her center of gravity failed and she almost fell. Still shaky, she thanked him and headed to the door.

"Memory?" Bedevere said.

She looked back.

"You are a wonder," he said with a bowed head.

She left.

Back in the hall to her chambers, she found Roen, pacing in front of her and Eloryn's doors.

"Hey you," Memory called to him as she approached.

Roen looked up, startled out of thoughts that had him frowning. Those frowns turned into a smirk at one look of her outfit.

"So sometimes I get distracted and forget what I'm wearing! Honestly, I am actually making an effort at my etiquette classes now. And still I end up like this." Memory tried to laugh casually, but wired nerves made it sound like a snort.

Roen chuckled silently and dropped his head, looking at the floor. When he looked back up his smile had faded slightly, and his eyebrows were twisted.

"I'm leaving," he said. "I'm going home with my parents, back to our duchy."

Memory stopped in her tracks. She had in no way prepared for any craziness today aside from her own. "Why? You said you'd stay? Is this, because of me, what I did sending you to see Lory?"

Roen shook his head but his lack of voice made Memory second guess his response.

He put his hands in the pockets of his coat and shrugged. His hair was a mess and gray smudges marked his bottom eyelids. "I wanted to tell you and El first, before letting my parents know. And then the Council, since they seem keen on my absence."

"Have you told her yet?" Memory asked, tilting her head at Eloryn's door.

Roen looked at the door for a long moment. "No. Soon."

Roen bent forward and kissed Memory softly on the cheek then walked away.

She watched him go then stood in the hallway, numb, for a long while after.

Hope is right. Soon I'll have no one left.

Roen felt sick and empty. A cold fear grew in his stomach, and he didn't really know what he was doing. He had the vague notion that he was leaving, but sometimes he found himself asking why. His whole self felt torn between surrendering to the truth he and Eloryn couldn't be together, and the desire to deny that, to fight it, to do anything to make it happen. But fighting could hurt more than just him. He would not follow Thayl's path. He had to leave.

It was hard telling Memory. He hoped he would survive telling Eloryn. He'd put it off long enough.

He knocked on the door of her office and exhaled slowly.

"Enter," called a man's voice. Roen opened the door and found Hayes working at the queen's desk, papers spread on every inch of the surface except a small plate of fruit in the corner.

"Councilor," Roen greeted him, confused. "I was hoping to see Eloryn."

"*Her Majesty* is busy, Roen, and I thought we had come to an agreement about your relationship with her?" Hayes's voice was calm, and he only barely glanced up from the documents on his desk.

"It is not a social meeting I seek," Roen said.

"Of course not. You won't be swayed will you?" Hayes put his pen down and looked up at Roen properly. His gaze wasn't aggressive, and he let out a loud sigh. "You're young, and for what it's worth I do understand. But never mind. You've come at an opportune time, as I have a favor you could assist me with. Could you run an errand in the city for me?"

"An errand?" Roen repeated, not fully understanding, but glad not to be on Hayes's bad side.

"We've discovered some rare magic works that survived Thayl's reign, and I need someone I trust to collect them so they can be safely stored in the Council's collection. I'd go myself, but I'm stuck here with this paperwork, and it really is quite urgent. "

"And you'd like me to collect them?"

Hayes eyed him critically. "I can trust you, can't I?"

"Of course. I can go right away."

"Very good," said Hayes, taking a slow bite from an apple. He scrawled an address on a scrap of paper and handed it to Roen. He already looked back at his documents and waved Roen off with a wiggle of his fingertips.

Roen felt odd doing a job for Hayes, but the distraction was welcome. A way to put off telling Eloryn for a little longer.

Or so he thought until he ran into Eloryn on the castle steps.

"Roen, are you on your way out?" she asked. She wore a more casual dress than usual, and her hair had been left loose and natural, tumbling down to her hips. The soft rose fabric of her dress played up the ever present flush in her cheeks. Roen swallowed and reminded himself how to speak.

"Just a quick errand in the city. And yourself?"

"I, well I wasn't feeling very well, so Hayes offered to let me have some time off today."

Roen bowed his head to her. "I'm sorry to hear you are unwell."

Eloryn shook her head and looked to her side. "It's something that has been troubling me for a while. But I feel I may find a remedy if I try harder to do so instead of avoiding the issue. I think a change of scenery would be nice to try. Could I join you on your errand?"

Roen took a deep breath and forced a return smile. "I would be honored to have you accompany me. As long as you are feeling well enough."

Eloryn's smile widened into her blushing cheeks. "I am. I'm feeling much better already."

A carriage took Roen and Eloryn into the city, with her bodyguards on horseback surrounding them. Roen looked across the cabin to her. The small bumps rattling the carriage made her hair dance and shimmer.

This might be the last time I ever spend with her, thought Roen. He planned to treasure it.

"Would you walk with me?"

She agreed with a quick nod and Roen stopped the carriage and helped Eloryn step down onto the street. Eloryn's guards dismounted and secured their horses then gave the approval for Eloryn to proceed. Erec, as usual, remained closest to Eloryn, just a few paces behind them. He smiled, unlike the other guards with their stern expressions, and Roen didn't like how attractive he was. He felt a pang of jealousy at how much time Erec must have with Eloryn and would continue to have when he was gone.

Roen extended his arm to Eloryn and she took it, walking by his side. He hoped she couldn't feel his trembling.

It was a dull day. The sky was a mass of low lilac clouds and a mist of rain curled up the fine strands of Eloryn's hair, making the edges glow like a halo in the filtered light.

Few other people were braving the damp, and the stone streets were eerily empty, with just a few city folk around to gawk at the queen and her handlers.

Roen led Eloryn into a small square filled with the cooing of pigeons. They lined every eave and sill on buildings around the square, sheltering from the wet. He smiled down at Eloryn. Looking at her, he could forget the weather, the trailing guards, or the fact he soon would be leaving. His nerves threatened to take over and he panicked about how to behave. Memory's voice came to him. *Just be yourself around her. Your flirtatious, sexy self.*

"Thank you for coming with me. It makes me look good, having a queen on my arm," Roen said in a mock haughty tone.

Eloryn raised her eyebrows slightly, her lips pursed. "It has been my greatest aspiration to become an attractive accessory," she replied with a straight face, followed quickly with a small smile and blush. Roen swallowed. He'd miss the way she blushed so easily.

"Well you do, make an attractive accessory. Not that I consider your beauty to be your only asset." Roen smiled wickedly at her. "You are also very rich. If only you weren't so terribly intelligent, you would be the perfect catch."

"Such a shame." Eloryn lifted her palm to her forehead dramatically. "A shame I had thought you a better man than to want for such a lady."

Roen slowed his pace and grew serious. He enjoyed these last few moments with Eloryn more than any other time he could recall, but their last day together couldn't be filled with jokes alone.

Sincerity made his voice rough. "If I may, I would have to admit that it is your mind, and your heart, which I value above any of your many other qualities."

Eloryn squeezed his arm in hers. He almost thought he could feel her trembling as well.

"I'm sorry I've not been able to spend more time with you, Roen," she said softly.

"You owe me no apology. I understand the demands of your position. In fact I should be the one apologizing. I have to tell you—"

Roen got cut off by a young girl with bushy, carrot-colored hair running to clutch at Eloryn's hand, sending her guards into a flurry.

The guards tried to push the wide-eyed waif away, and Eloryn raised her voice in a commanding tone.

"Step back, men. Can you not see she's but a child?"

The girl seemed confused and looked from Eloryn to the guards and back again, then gave Eloryn's hand a fluttering kiss.

"Thank you, m'lady," she said.

Another child ran up beside her, hair the same color, suggesting she was a sibling. Both wore scrappy, dirt-stained clothes.

"Thank you so much, your highness."

An older girl with rivers of brown hair followed the children, grinning widely. When she was closer to Eloryn, her grin failed, and she hassled the two children into deep bows, their chests lowered almost to the ground. She dropped herself into a curtsy.

"Forgive them, your majesty," she said. "They mistook you for Princess Memory."

"That's not their fault. We are twins after all. Although her hair is somewhat shorter than mine."

The girl stammered. "We've never seen her with her hair down before, majesty."

Eloryn gestured for the three of them to rise. "You know my sister well? What is your name?"

"Maeve, your majesty." Maeve stood back up but remained bent

slightly at the waist, her head down and eyes lowered. "Yes, your majesty, from her shelter she runs not far from here."

Maeve bobbed a small curtsey to Erec as well. He nodded in return, and Roen wondered how they knew each other.

Roen thought back to the clunky bracelet Memory wore all the time. "Is one of you little Edele?" he asked the two red-headed girls. They looked at each other nervously and then to Maeve, who frowned and shook her head.

Eloryn turned to Roen to continue on their way. Maeve took a step forward again, her mouth open, then lowered her gaze again.

Eloryn stopped. "You have something you wish to speak to me about? You can do so freely, please."

Maeve nodded seriously. She tried to talk, but it looked like her effort to overcome her nerves enough to speak with the queen would take a while.

Roen squeezed Eloryn's hand and let go. "If you'll excuse me, I will continue on. I'll only be a moment to pick up these items for Hayes and meet you back here."

Roen left them talking and checked Hayes's address again. It directed him down an alleyway just across the square. He glanced back at Eloryn and smiled before heading in. The gutter ran with grayed water and the tall stone buildings either side left the narrow alleyway heavily shadowed.

"Looking for something?" A burly man seemed to appear from nowhere. His nose looked like it had been broken more than once and his face was marred by scars, some which ran up onto his bald scalp.

Roen shook his head. The bruiser didn't look like the kind of person that would be the owner of magic documents. A second man stepped up behind the first. If possible he looked even rougher, wiry and wearing a makeshift eye-patch.

"We've been looking for something, haven't we?" the new man said.

He held up a crumpled sheet of paper. Even in the low light, Roen could read the word 'wanted,' and see the rough drawing of his own face.

Roen spun around, straight into the sights of another two men. They already held daggers in their hands, their intentions clear. The alleyway was only the width of one man and Roen could see no way past them, and no way back. A battle on two fronts.

On instinct Roen felt for his own blade in the seam of his pants, but he never carried it anymore. He held out his hands innocently and

smiled. "I really think you have the wrong person. I am friends with the queen."

"Yeah and I'm buddies with the lusty queen of the seelie fae." The bald man laughed, groping crudely at his crotch. His expression turned vicious as he drew a bronze sword. "We know exactly what you are. Go on, run. Run like the street rat you are."

Before the man even finished speaking, Roen kicked off against the grimy wall beside him, bounced off the other, launching himself higher in the narrow space between the buildings.

Reaching a point well above the men's reach, he suspended himself there with outstretched arms and legs, looking for a window or some other exit.

"They always run, but we always catch 'em," said the bald man, laughing. He picked up a block of wood from some refuse beside him and hurled it at Roen.

Roen twisted his torso and the block flew past, cracking on the bricks beside him.

A second object flew at him before he could recover from the first assault and a blinding sting in his thigh made his knee buckle. Just a scratch, but enough to make him lose the tension he needed to stay suspended between the walls. A dagger clattered on the ground behind him, and he slipped.

He hit the ground hard, landing with a splash in the gutter. The block of wood lay just near his head, and he snatched it up, knowing it would be his only weapon, his only defense.

The third man, missing an ear and most of his teeth, lunged at Roen before he had a chance to get on his feet. Roen swung the wood at him, blocking the dagger and with a second hit, knocking away a few more of the man's teeth. The man stumbled and slumped against a wall. There was only one man left on that side who'd already thrown his dagger. Roen rolled to his feet and ran at him, trying to break past.

Roen barged through and made a run for the end of the alleyway. Almost there, his leg gave out beneath him. It bled freely and hurt too much to keep his weight on. The wound was worse than he first thought.

Roen managed to turn around in time to block the sword aimed for his back. The three men were right behind him. The bald man walked leisurely, matching Roen's hobbled attempts to flee. He jabbed his short sword playfully at Roen. Roen blocked and parried with the piece of

wood, but every movement seemed to tug and tear at the cut in his thigh. Sweat ran onto his lips and he breathed hard to try and stay focused.

The bald man fumbled his sword. Roen took the chance to knock it away with the wood. He realized his error too late. The man had bluffed, letting his weapon go so Roen would over extend. The block of wood was snatched from Roen's hands and smashed into his face.

"We're going to enjoy this," was all he heard before he lost consciousness.

Eloryn knew nothing about the girl who stood in front of her, working up the courage to say something. Something important, it seemed.

"Maeve, really, it's okay," Eloryn encouraged.

The word, Memory's word, made Maeve smile and seemed to give her the courage to speak. "As you know, the princess has been doing so much for us. I don't know what we'd do without her and her shelter. So I wanted to ask, your majesty, respectfully, with apologies, whether it is true, the rumor I've heard?"

Eloryn was lost. "Rumor?"

Maeve looked distraught at being pressed to give details. She lowered her head some more. "That you and Master Hayes are going to shut down the shelter."

Eloryn shook her head. She'd heard nothing about it. She hadn't even known what Memory was doing in the city for these children, let alone anything about closing down the shelter.

She wanted to give her assurances that she'd want nothing of the kind to happen, but she didn't know enough, about what Memory had set up, or whether Hayes truly had some objection to it. She looked around to see if Roen was returning yet since he seemed to know at least a little more about it.

Her eyes found Roen at the entrance of an alley across the square, stumbling backwards. Her heart launched into a gallop when she saw he was fighting off a group of rough-looking men.

Eloryn tried to run to him. Her guards, seeing what she saw, held her back. Maeve gathered the younger girls to her side and rushed them away protectively.

Eloryn cried out in frustration at her guards, ordering them to release her.

"You must return to the castle, majesty. This is not safe," one said,

grabbing her around the wrist.

She knew they were only trying to protect her, that was their job, but she had to help Roen. He and the men had disappeared, back into the alleyway.

Erec, at the front of the group, tripped and fell, taking the other guards down with him. Eloryn took the chance to break free. She spoke a behest to weave the guards clothes together, one guard's to another's until they were caught tied in a mess. She swore she saw Erec wink at her as she lifted her skirts and dashed after Roen.

Reaching the alley, there was no sign left of him or his assailants. Words fell from her mouth, the same behest she'd used to track Memory when she went after Thayl. The wet ground glittered, a group of footsteps forming, leading away at walking pace.

"Deann-ruith," Eloryn said. *Faster.* The glowing steps increased their pace and Eloryn followed at a jog. "Deann-ruith!"

Eloryn ran through the streets, into the long shadows of a cluttered warehouse district. Ankle-deep mud covered the road, sliced into by cart tracks. Half of the buildings appeared disused, closed up and cold. The buildings backed the river and a moldering fishy smell tainted the air.

The footsteps led Eloryn to the side door of a smaller warehouse. She ended the behest there, to not alert those inside to her presence. Peeking through a crack in a boarded up window, she could see four men circling Roen.

They had him hanging by the wrists in the center of the room. He'd been stripped of his jacket, which one man held, searching through the pockets, and his shirt had been torn down so it hung about his waist.

The men laughed and mocked Roen. Eloryn heard every second thing they said.

"Let's see if he lasts till the money arrives."

"The bounty does say alive *or* dead."

The bald man lifted his arm, and the crack of a whip echoed.

I have to help him. How can I help him on my own? Eloryn put her palms on her forehead, trying to still her panic and think. *Memory would know what to do. I just have to think creatively, like she said. Then I can do anything.*

She assessed the room to see what could be used. Shafts of light from just a few high grimy windows broke the darkness. A desiccated pig corpse hung not far from Roen, and Eloryn guessed this must have once been a butcher's storehouse. On the sawdust strewn floor, rats

moved about without concern for the men. There was plenty throughout the space she could use. She hoped it wouldn't come to that. She was queen. That should be enough.

Eloryn pushed the door open without knocking and strode in with her chin raised. Sawdust stirred under her feet, tossing rancid odors and dust motes into the air. It took a while before they noticed her. Another strike with the whip, before they turned to take in her presence. Eloryn seethed.

"I am your queen, and I demand you free him," she announced.

Eloryn caught Roen's eye. He frowned hard but gave her a short nod which she returned. Red welts marked his chest and blood ran from one of his legs, dripping onto the floor at a speed that worried Eloryn.

The men stared at her then looked to a wiry man with an eye-patch for direction, whispering amongst themselves.

"He weren't joking about knowing the queen after all," said the man in the eye-patch.

One man tried to run, and the largest of them put a firm hand on his shoulder and said, "You think she's just going to leave us be after this? Think she and her kind won't hunt us down wherever we run?"

The men shot anxious glances around their group, gauging their options. Eloryn thought to tell them she'd let them be free if they left now but saw the bloody whip and knew it would be a lie. A place deep in her churning stomach wanted them to fight.

"Not matter what we do, they'll hunt us down," the skittish man said.

"She's here alone. I say we finish them both off before anyone else knows what's happened. Get rid of the bodies." The large bald man snapped the whip between his hands.

The man in the eye-patch nodded and drew a sword. "No one left that seen our faces. No one won't even know where to start looking."

The four men circled around her, penning her and closing in.

Eloryn narrowed her eyes. She breathed a deep breath then spoke her words of magic, behest running into behest, commanding help from her environment.

Her very first spell meant the men had time to draw closer, but it had to be made first before she dealt with them. Seeing it done, she turned her attention to the cruel bounty hunters.

The bald man struck the whip at Eloryn. It crumbled in the air, brittle as old bone.

Chains with hooked ends like the one Roen hung from grew long, catching up the man with the eye-patch and one other, wrapping them tight. Eloryn made no effort to make their bonds gentle.

The coward with missing teeth who thought to flee at the presence of the queen tried again. He found the hinges on the doors had fused shut. His terror multiplied as the floor beneath him became spongy, sucking him in up to his neck.

The dried pig carcass swung across the room and slammed Eloryn hard into her chest, winding her and knocking her down. Her words became useless gasps.

Someone wrenched her up to her feet. The large bald man dusted the remains of the whip from his hands menacingly. Eloryn's breath returned, but she barely managed a syllable before the man wrapped his hands around her throat and lifted her off her feet, crushing her neck. Eloryn's eyes watered.

A wet crunching sound was followed by a shudder that ran up the man's arms and into his hands around Eloryn's throat. His grip loosened and Eloryn landed back on her feet.

The man crashed to the ground.

Behind him stood Roen, half a brick bloodied in his hand.

Her first behest had been to free him. She had to free him first. No matter what happened to her, he had to be freed.

Roen took a step toward her around the fallen giant then crumpled to his knees. Eloryn dropped into the sawdust beside him and started checking his wounds.

Roen raised an arm slowly, stopping her, then put that arm around her waist and rested his head softly on her shoulder. He pulled her into his chest. She could feel his breath on her neck.

"El," he whispered. "You came for me."

"Of course," she whispered back.

"Of course," Roen repeated in reply, laughter in his voice. He winced then stilled again.

"You were amazing," he said.

"The fear of losing you proved to be great inspiration." Eloryn tried to chuckle lightly, but it sounded a little like a sob.

"It's okay, I'm not going anywhere." Roen gave her another squeeze. "Back at Elder's Bridge inn, when I'd been caught and called out, I had been ready to die. I told you and Mem what I really was because I wanted you to hate me like I hated myself. I wanted you to leave me there to my fate. At the time, I thought I deserved it."

Eloryn's head shook in fierce denial.

"Today, I could only think about how much I needed to live. Even if everyone knows the truth of my past. It seems as though at some point I have stopped hating myself. I don't know when, or how, but I suspect it has more than a little to do with you and your sister." Roen's mouth lifted into a half smile and he pulled back to look to her fully. Eloryn reached for his hands and he continued.

"There are things I've done I'm not proud of, things I must make amends for, but everything I have done has shaped who I am now, and I value that. I'm not just… a thief. I need to live long enough to show you who I really am."

Eloryn touched his cheek lightly. "I can already see."

Eloryn had seen the skills of Roen's criminal trade, she'd seen him play the flirt, and she'd seen him behind a formal polite façade. She'd seen his courage, his shame, and his passion. He was not any one of those things, but all of them and more. There was not one part of him that Eloryn didn't love.

Her head tilted back. She lifted her mouth to his. A look of confusion, relief, desperation, and desire, all rolled together, flashed across his features. He bent his face to meet hers.

Their lips didn't meet.

The sound of thudding footsteps and guards calling for their queen broke them apart.

Eloryn quickly got to her feet to meet her escort. "Take these men into custody, for hunting an illegal bounty and attempted regicide."

The men she'd caught were all watching her. She flushed, angered and embarrassed they had been present during her moment with Roen.

Erec tied a quick bandage to apply pressure to the gash in Roen's thigh until he could be healed magically, then pulled Roen to his feet and gave him his guard's jacket. Eloryn bit her tongue to try and slow her heart and remind herself there was more occurring of importance than Roen, shirtless, in uniform.

The other guards extracted the mercenaries from their bonds and dragged them from the building.

Erec ran his hand through his hair and laughed breathily. "It is a great relief to see how well you can handle yourself, your majesty. Otherwise

I might have been in real trouble. I am supposed to be protecting you, not hindering your protectors."

Eloryn smiled warmly at him. "Thank you, for your help. I won't forget it. Rest assured you would have been in no trouble from me or my sister if it came to that."

Erec smirked. "It's not you and yours I'm worried about. It's my brother that'd kill me if I let you come to harm."

Roen got Erec to help him across to the man with the eye-patch and took a piece of paper from the man's pocket. Eloryn followed and stared at the poster with the etching of Roen's face

"The bounty?" Eloryn asked. "Who set it?"

Roen scrunched the paper in his hands and dropped it to the floor. "People I have wronged. I was recognized not long ago by someone from an estate I once robbed. Only that was supposed to have been dealt with." Roen paused, putting his thumb against his lips and shaking his head. "Maybe the man who spoke with Hayes wasn't the only one to have seen me."

Eloryn bent and picked up the crumpled poster, squeezing it tight in her hands. She didn't want anyone else to find it. "I'll make sure they are appeased, anything to keep you safe."

Roen put his hand over hers. "No. It's time I faced my past."

CHAPTER TWENTY-TWO

Roen spoke well, when faced with the formal gathering of Avall's nobles, wizards, legal authorities, and his parents. Eloryn had never been more proud of him and nervous for him.

"Know that I am ashamed of my thieving. For myself, and for my family. But also know this. I would never change my past because without it I would never have had my path cross with that of the Maellan twins. They are a treasure in my life, as they are to all of Avall."

The confession was followed by his promises to try to repay those he wronged, then Eloryn took over and offered Roen an absolute and unconditional royal pardon. She spoke heartfelt words of how Roen had given himself to her cause. From the applause of the crowd, it seemed they agreed that everything Roen had done to help the Maellan twins and to defeat Thayl outweighed any crimes from his past. Memory cheered for him in a boisterous and decidedly unladylike manner, which made Eloryn grin wider than she knew was proper for her station.

When the meeting ended, Eloryn amazed herself that she held in her tears when Roen's parents both brought him into an embrace. She watched from a distance as the three of them held each other for a long moment.

Erec leaned in to whisper in her ear from his usual place by her side. "I've had a few men scouring the city, and all bills and mentions of the bounty on Roen have been removed."

"Thank you," Eloryn whispered back. She breathed out shakily. She'd been more scared than she wanted to admit. Crime of any kind was treated harshly in Avall. She could still see some of the guests gossiping amongst themselves, enjoying the scandal of it all. But now it was public and officially forgiven Roen should be safe from further reprisals.

Erec cleared his throat and spoke even softer. "Those from the estate named on the poster are denying having any knowledge of the bounty."

"Has there been any further information from the bounty hunters on who they were to meet with, or who tipped them off as to where to find Roen that day?"

Erec set his jaw and stepped back in line behind Eloryn.

Hayes appeared, looking stern and sympathetic. "Those cutthroats knew nothing more than what was on the bounty poster and have since been disposed of as they should be."

Hayes put an arm around Eloryn, directing her to a quiet corner of the room. "Your majesty, I know you had your qualms before, but when even a close friend of the queen can be attacked in broad daylight, surely now you have reason enough to grant me, as Legate of Civil Defence, the use of military force. The streets are filled with criminals such as those men. If you had given me control earlier, this entire, almost fatal mess could have been avoided."

Eloryn looked across the room to where Isabeth fussed over Roen. By the time they'd gotten him into a carriage and Eloryn had begun healing him, he'd lost a dangerous amount of blood. Now he had not a mark on him to reveal what he'd suffered, but Eloryn could almost still feel the wounds herself. Her hesitation had killed Waylan, and again her hesitation almost killed Roen.

Hayes paused to lick his lips. "Illegal bounties have become more commonplace with the increase in poverty. There simply isn't enough authority to deal with it all, and so a lot of the victims of crime will turn to illegal bounties and rough mercenaries for help. If we were granted a larger police force, or militia, we would be able to clean up the streets of those who would hang and whip a man for money."

Eloryn held her hand up to silence Hayes. "Yes. I've heard enough. Yes. Please do what you must to make our land safe."

Hayes bowed and then gave her a modest hug. "You are a wise ruler, my child. Sometimes the best thing someone in power can do is hand that duty over to someone who will be more capable in the role."

The kitchens of the shelter were smaller than those at the palace, but just as busy. The food being prepared was also much simpler fare, but Memory was amused to see that her hamburgers were becoming popular on the shelter menu. She knew she had Clara to thank for that. Workers in white aprons loaded trays for delivering lunch into the mess hall as Memory finished discussing the meal planning with the head chef.

Clara leaned on a bench next to Memory and scrutinized her. "I don't like this at all."

Memory wiped her forehead, the heat of the kitchen making her sweat. She was tired and feeling dazed at everything she'd taken on. She second guessed her every decision. "Do you think I'm budgeting for food wrong?"

"No. I don't like this, seeing all this food pass under your nose and you not taking a bite. Who are you and what have you done with my Hope?"

"I'm Memory, for starters. And I'm just not hungry."

"No, that doesn't sound like you at all. You've barely been eating anything lately. You're acting so differently, I may have to do some tests to make sure you've not been replaced with a changeling," Clara joked and picked up a small bowl of pudding.

Memory took a small bite out of some bread and choked it down. She didn't really feel like eating. Food had become tasteless for her. "Satisfied?"

"Only if you finish all of it, and then another, and maybe one more, then I'll be convinced you're really you. And you can let me know what's happening with you and that fine gentleman of yours while you're at it," Clara grinned and popped a spoonful of pudding in her mouth.

Memory's heart seemed to clamp shut. "I haven't seen Will for ages. And also, really? Will? A gentleman?"

Clara raised an eyebrow. "I meant Dylan."

"Oh." Memory felt her face grow hot. *Why did I think Clara was talking about Will?* He had been on her mind a lot since she managed to open a door back to their home world. But it should have been obvious she meant Dylan.

"I'm just studying with him. That's all."

Memory still wasn't sure how she felt about Dylan, but there had been more visits, and more kissing. He was the one person she could be around and feel completely wanted, but she didn't feel like their relationship was developing, despite Dylan's enthusiasm. Memory wondered if her inability to be enthusiastic back was due to her broken soul. She certainly blamed that for her allowing things to continue despite her lack of feelings. She was already broken, already a monster, and Dylan was the only person who seemed to want her anyway, so she'd take it.

A commotion broke their conversation, and Memory could hear Maeve yelling a stream of Avall curse words. She ran to the front door to see what was happening, Clara on her heels.

A squad of armed men had entered the shelter, facing off with Maeve and Peirs. The men wore guard uniforms marked with the symbol of the Wizard's Council that Memory had seen before.

On spotting Memory, the men stepped back and stood at attention.

"What's happening?" Memory asked, coming to stand beside Maeve.

Maeve swiped a punch through the air, directed at the men. "They are here to close us down, but I won't let them."

"Under whose authority? You know who I am, right?" Memory asked the men.

The men nodded. "Councilor Hayes has classified this building as a house of ill-repute, and a beacon for undesirables. He requires it be emptied and closed immediately for the betterment of the city."

"That's ridiculous. This is a solution to the problem, not the cause," Memory said.

The guard just shrugged. "Orders are orders."

I'm arguing with the wrong person. Memory stepped between her friends and the militia men. "You'll have to go back and say I wouldn't let you carry out your orders then, because unless your orders allow dragging me out of here kicking and screaming then you're getting nothing done here today."

The guards looked at each other as though assessing their options, then bowed and left hurriedly.

Memory rubbed her forehead with both of her palms. Everything she tried to do, everyone she grew close to, everything she wanted. She would lose all of it. The inevitability turned her blood to cold sludge.

When she turned around she saw that both Peirs and Maeve had their hands on hilts of daggers. Clara just looked stunned.

"They will be back," Peirs said grimly. "Hayes has been taking action all over the city to remove vagrants, but that's not all. I've also heard rumors that he's using his militia to gain control of the trade guilds through force."

"Why hasn't Eloryn done anything about all this?" Memory questioned.

"I doubt she even knows," Maeve said, her hands on her slim hips.

Clara spoke, her tone scandalous and low. "I see his control even at the palace. Since your uncle was arrested there has been a steady stream of prisoners coming into the castle. Anyone who questions the queen or the Council is arrested, and a lot of them don't come out again." Clara made a delicate swipe across her neck with one finger.

"You mean anyone who questions Hayes." Memory looked at the three of them before her. "Damn it. Guys, you can talk like this to me, but watch yourselves, okay?"

They nodded seriously. Memory looked around the shelter. From every doorway leading into to the entrance foyer, from between the bars of the stairway banister, little eyes watched. Memory couldn't let anything happen to them, but she couldn't be here all the time.

Memory was suddenly glad she'd let Clara dress her up with more accessories that day. Memory unclasped her necklace and started slipping rings off her fingers. She placed them down on a side table, along with her purse and the gold it contained. She stripped brooches and jeweled buttons off her dress and the ornate buckles off her shoes. She took off a heavy gold bangle, leaving just Edele's wooden bracelet on her wrist. Her hair had been pinned up using golden filigree combs which she removed, letting her hair fall free, still short above her neck at the back. Maeve put a hand to her mouth as though the sight of the cropped hair shocked her.

Memory pointed to the pile of valuables. "Maeve, Peirs, get all the kids together and find somewhere to lay low while Hayes is on his rampage. Use this stuff to get you through until I work something out. I'll try talking to him or Eloryn. They can't shut us down."

Memory said it but didn't believe it. *If I believed it I*'d be letting them stay.

Memory stared at the wealth on the table for a moment, then picked out the three most beautiful pieces and presented them to each of her friends. "I want you each to have something as well, to say thank you for being there for me, and to keep you safe."

Her companions were speechless as Memory made her goodbyes and beckoned Clara to begin their ride back to the palace.

Memory fidgeted with the bracelet from Edele. A symbol of one of the many lives taken from her. It was as though her broken self was a repellant to life, and anyone to come close would soon be lost, die, or be so repulsed they'd simply leave. She knew it wouldn't be long before another person she cared for would be gone from her world.

On their way out to the carriage, Memory said, "Clara, could you do me a favor?"

"Anything, Hope."

"Could you get me some hair dye?"

Memory took one step at a time, walking in slow motion. She ran her fingers along the rough wall as she circled up the tower stairs on her way to the ivy room. Her face ran with tears that she couldn't seem to stop. Her mouth trembled, but she made no sound.

Hope walked backward a couple of stairs ahead and stared at her. "Why with the waterworks?"

"I don't know." Memory hesitated through tears. The words collapsed on themselves, imploding, as if she didn't have the breath to utter them. "I'm… happy, for Roen and El, that they have finally started to sort their lives out, and I'm happy that Will can go back to where he belongs."

"Yeah, you look sooo happy."

Memory shook her head, and a tear flicked off her cheek. She'd put this off since she'd proven she could open a door to the other world, but she knew, no matter what, Will deserved to have the choice. She imagined that Will would probably just want to go back on his own, but she began to toy with the idea that they could go back together. Neither solution seemed right, but nothing seemed right to Memory anymore. Memory grew increasingly anxious about everything around her, her shelter, Hayes, her magic and lost soul, even Hope, and depression ached in her bones.

"Are you going to start believing me yet? That you're never going to just fit in, the way you are? That the only way to command respect is as queen?"

It made sense. She wasn't even a complete person. How could she hope to fit into a world full of people who were beginning to make sense of their lives?

"You shouldn't be crying," Hope continued. "You just need to fix things, that's all, become queen, and everything will be better."

Memory climbed out through the window and onto the roof, letting the light breeze dust away her concerns, trying to think clearly. "Being queen hasn't seemed very easy for Lory."

Hope kept in front of her, in her face. "If you were queen you could control everything. Eloryn just lets everything, and everyone control her instead. She's not right for the role. You are."

Memory shrugged. "That's too bad then, isn't it, because she's queen and I'm not, and I can't see any way that could change."

"There is a way, if you're strong enough. I can help you become queen, where you'll be loved and wanted and never treated badly, but when you are, you have to do something for me, okay?" Hope stopped and blocked the way, forcing Memory to pause and look at her. "It's simple. You would become queen if Eloryn wasn't around anymore."

Memory pushed passed her into the Ivy Room. Her head spun with dark words and pain and confusion. She barely noted the time on the clock tower or the bareness of the space around her.

"He's not here," she mumbled.

"When is he ever?" Hope said.

Memory nodded. She had expected this. She pulled an envelope

from her purse and propped it on one of the stone benches. It had taken her three hours to get the wording of the letter right. Eventually she left it simple.

I can send you home.

Hope followed Memory for a little of the way back to her chambers, but Memory was completely unresponsive, so Hope vanished. Memory was at a loss for what to think or do.

Sleep would be good. Sometimes she imagined that she could sleep forever. It seemed easier that way. She approached her chambers and could hear the crashing of a brawl inside. She swung the door open.

Dylan and Will were locked in a brutal fight. Will was on all fours with Dylan pinned underneath him on the floor, slugging him in the face.

Both were spattered with blood. Bruises already swelled on their skin.

"Stop." The word was barely a breath. Neither man heard her. Dylan tried to shield himself with an arm, and Will shook him against the ground.

Memory put both hands to her head and screamed, "Stop it!"

The room rumbled and Dylan and Will were thrown apart by the invisible force of her magic.

Dylan slid along the silk rug. Will hit the side of the fireplace. He immediately got back up and rushed Dylan.

Memory stepped in between them.

Will's fist froze a hairs-breadth from her face.

He bared his teeth and looked for a moment like he might vomit. With a roar he ran off, practically throwing himself from the balcony and disappearing.

"Will!" Memory stepped toward the windows and felt Dylan's hand close around hers, pulling her back. It was slick with blood and Memory shuddered. She looked down at him where he lay on the floor.

"Stay. I need your help," he said, his lips red and swollen.

Memory nodded slowly.

She knelt beside Dylan. The damage to him was brutal.

"That savage should be caged," he said, wiping his mouth.

Maybe he's right. Maybe the Council was right all along.

"How hurt are you, can you stand?"

He nodded and Memory put an arm around him, helping him into her bedroom and laying him down on the bed. She grabbed a hand towel and dampened it, and came back to wipe away some of the blood.

"It's insane, allowing a brute like that to run wild," Dylan said.

Will. Memory remembered the boy who sang so beautifully. She'd done this to him, turned him into what he was now. So much anger, so violent. He'd never seemed that way to her before, but maybe she'd just refused to see it. Dylan groaned and Memory wondered if she should try healing him with magic but was worried about hurting him even more. All she did was hurt people.

"It's lucky you showed up." Dylan grinned wryly in a way that reminded her of Roen.

"Dylan," Memory said. She sat back, holding the stained towel in her lap, frowning as her mind worked through events. "Why didn't you defend yourself with magic? Like with Roen?"

Dylan ran a finger down Memory's cheek. "I'm worried about you. Promise you'll keep your window locked from now on."

Memory twitched away from his touch. "Is my brain skipping? Did I not say that out loud? Why didn't you defend yourself? Will can't use magic, just like Roen can't."

"It doesn't matter. I'm all right, see?" Dylan sat up so he was closer to Memory. His voice was low, gravely, and he pushed his lips against hers. Memory tasted blood and her stomach churned.

Stop, stop, stop. "Stop." Her voice was lost under his mouth. He placed his hands over her shoulders, pulling her in closer.

A frantic shuddering built in her limbs, and Dylan flew off her and was pinned against the headboard of the bed. He cried out in pain. Memory fought to calm herself, letting him go.

Dylan slumped and looked at her fiercely.

"What are you doing?" he shouted. "You bring me into your bed after your creature beats me and then you carry on assaulting me? Do you have any idea how difficult it's been with you?"

"What do you mean?" Memory moved off the bed, stepping away from him. He stood up and followed her.

"I deserve better than this. Hayes should have given me the good twin, not you." Dylan spat blood on her floor. "You think I came into your life by accident? When you refused to even look at the suitors the Council offered you? I was chosen for you to keep you busy and out of trouble. And the lengths I've had to go to."

Memory's lips curled, her whole body jolting with disgust. The one reason she liked Dylan was that he desired her, to have someone

around that really wanted her, and it was all a lie. The truth was nobody wanted her. How could they?

Dylan made his voice gentle again and reached to touch her. "You should be grateful and just take what you've been given."

Memory felt the ground shaking under her feet. The whole world felt unstable and ready to topple. She had to get out of there.

Memory smacked his hand away from her and ran to the door. She bumped into Clara who was staring at the messed up room and sprays of violent crimson.

Clara gasped at Memory. "Hope, are you—"

"Call the guards," Memory said to her, not stopping. She pointed back to her bedchambers where Dylan followed. "Just get rid of him."

"Highness," Clara said in confirmation.

"Guards? Whose side do you think the guards are on?" Dylan called after her as she ran. She could hear his mocking laughter chase her all the way up the stairs.

CHAPTER TWENTY-THREE

Please be there, please be there.

Memory ran all the way to the Ivy Room. She didn't know what she was going to say to Will, but she needed to see him.

Memory burst through the screen of ivy, and the sight of Will in front of her almost stopped her heart. He stood still and tall. His reddened hands shook and his cheeks were marked with the tracks of tears, but he didn't move, didn't cry.

He looked her in the eyes, both staring at each other for a long moment, before he flinched and looked away.

"Did I hurt you?" he mumbled.

Memory mouthed the word "no," but no sound emerged.

Will started pacing, like a caged lion. His voice grew louder. "He just... you didn't hear the things he said. That he could tell you didn't like to be touched. That he'd force you anyway."

Memory just stood there watching, like she had no energy left to move or talk. Dylan provoked the fight, and let Will beat him, let Will be the animal. But why? Just to get Will out of her life? It was going to happen anyway. She looked over at her letter to Will and saw the envelope torn open. Bloody fingerprints marred the cream-colored paper.

Will saw her look and scowled. "You don't believe me."

"I do. I know Dylan was a fake, just like you said."

"But you still want me gone."

I just want you to be happy and safe.

Memory reached out for him. Will growled viciously at her.

Memory let out a soft cry, not from fear, but from the pain of Will turning on her. Her Will.

Breath tore through Memory like daggers, and she gritted her teeth and opened the Veil to the other world. She held the door open.

Will looked at her with those blue eyes, and a single tear ran down his cheek.

"Just go," she said.

Memory turned away to hide her own tears that ran, closing her eyes, unable to look.

No. She curled her hands into fists. *Look at him. It will be your last time.* She turned around and opened her eyes. "I… I'll miss you."

He was already gone.

"Will? WILL?" Memory screamed.

A rumbling built inside her. She clutched at her chest to hold it in, sobbing. The leaves of the ivy trembled, gusting like a strong wind took hold of them. Memory tried to grasp any scrap of calm within her, but it all flew away, anguish tearing her raw. It spilled out, burst from her. The vines around her were shredded, charred, every last leaf and tendril disintegrated. The ivy that hid and protected the room, that gave it its name, was gone. Memory's knees cracked as they hit the ground.

Will. My safe place. Everything is gone.

Memory wasn't sure when it had gotten so late. The moonlit courtyard was empty and through the windows of the palace she only saw the odd servant passing in the halls.

Her gown was marked with blood and ashes, and she just walked, wherever her aching feet would take her.

"Of course Will left you. What did you think he'd do given the choice?" Hope said.

Memory walked so slowly that Hope circled around her, doing laps.

"I'm sorry about Dylan though. Who could have known that would end badly?" Hope kicked at the pebbled path. They came to a large marble fountain, and Memory focused on the sound of the running water, trying to drown everything else out.

"But it was just like I said, wasn't it? No one can like you how you are. But if you were queen, things would be different. You could save your shelter. You could just get rid of Hayes. You could do anything you wanted."

Could I? "What about my sister?"

"Don't go getting sentimental. She's not your friend. Her and Hayes are working together, on everything they've done. Eloryn knew about Dylan, and about your shelter. Eloryn's seen inside you. They are cruel to you because they know you're barely human. I told you this would happen. They're not you real friends – I'm your only friend. The only one you can trust."

"I can't... do anything to Lory."

Hope grabbed Memory by the arms. "You can. You don't remember yourself, what you have in you, what you're capable of."

"Stop it, I don't want this." Memory tried to pry Hope's hands off her, but her grip was tight and Memory had lost all strength.

"We have to get rid of her," Hope hissed.

"Shut up! Shut up, shut up, shut up!"

Memory threw herself at Hope, pushing them both into the pond around the fountain. Hope disappeared out from underneath her as they splashed in. Memory sat staring into the water. The ripples stilled and she saw her reflection. With a snarl she smashed at her face on the water surface, hitting it over and over. The water was icy and she let it numb her.

"Mem?" Roen called her. She could hear him running over the pebbles. "What are you doing in there? I heard you screaming."

His arms wrapped around her and pulled her out of the water. "It's okay, calm down. Let's get you back to your room."

Memory pushed out of his arms, shaking her head roughly.

"No, not there, I can't go back there. Dylan could still be there. The blood."

"You're soaked through. We have to get you warm. Come on."

Roen put his arm around her again, and she let him lead her into his chambers nearby. Roen held up a blanket around her while she unclasped her dress with shaking fingers and let it drop. They left it in a puddle and Roen wrapped her in the blanket. His chambers were only a single room, unlike hers, and he sat with her on the bed, keeping her in his embrace, rubbing her arms. Memory could tell she was shivering

but felt nothing.

"Can you tell me what happened?"

"Dylan." Memory's breath came hard and she had difficulty expressing herself. "He was... working for Hayes."

"I'm sorry. Would you like me to break his knees for you?"

Memory's mouth twitched, lifting a little.

"You know I'd be more than happy to. Just say the word."

Memory frowned again. "I don't know what I want. I don't even know who I am anymore. So how can I know what I want? Everything about who I was got stripped away. Everything that was Hope: my memories, my clothes, my hair, even my piercings, all taken or lost until I was Memory. Memory, Hope, I don't feel like either of them anymore. I need a new name."

"How about Mope, it'd suit you the way you've been lately," Roen said.

"Har-dee-har-har."

"It's okay, to not know who you are. I don't know who I am, and I'm not facing half your obstacles. You have time. You'll work it out," Roen said.

She sat tucked right in under his shoulder, and she snuggled against his chest, seeking warmth and life. Roen gave her a small peck on the side of her head.

"You almost didn't flinch that time," Roen observed.

"What do you mean?" Memory asked.

"You flinch, you know, every time someone touches you. Even me. I see it. Maybe it's only a little, but I still see it. Actually, Will's the only one you don't flinch at."

"Yeah," Memory groaned, "but now he flinches at me. I think..." *He's gone.* "I think..." *He's left me. I'll never see him again.* "I..." Memory couldn't even get the words out.

They sat together in silence as Memory focused all her being on keeping calm. It was starting to come more easily to her now, like she had no energy left for her emotions.

"I'm sorry I'm such a mess. The worst thing is I keep having to see Eloryn, every day, being so bloody perfect. And it's like... she's everything I could have been. I hate her for that sometimes. That's terrible isn't it? I shouldn't. I shouldn't have even said..."

Roen just squeezed her tight.

Memory looked up at him and could see a distant look in his eyes,

a deep sadness.

She asked, "How are things, with you, and her? Is something wrong?"

Roen smiled but the sadness remained. "I asked the Council if I was allowed to court Eloryn and they vehemently refused, told me I shouldn't be seeing her at all. And I thought I could get by, hide my feelings, but I can't."

Memory thought of Will, and how she'd been told she shouldn't see him. She wondered how much of Dylan's provocation was his idea or how much was Hayes's. It didn't matter anymore. Memory squinted to hold in tears.

"What are you going to do?" she asked.

"The usual. Cry myself to sleep each night. But at least now I'll have someone to blame other than myself," he said, smiling wryly. "You don't want to try again, you and me? We could both do with some comfort."

Memory shook her head but stayed in his arms. "I know you don't really feel that way about me. I might look like her, but I'm not the girl you love. Besides, if she's too good for you, what are you saying about me?" Memory dug a thumb into Roen's ribs playfully. Although she spoke lightly, the words cut into her. Maybe Roen only ever wanted her around because she reminded him of Eloryn. Another person who didn't truly want her, or care for her. Not for who she really was. Memory tried to shake off the dark thoughts. *No. He's still my friend, maybe the only one I have left.*

A hectic banging at Roen's door startled them and before they could move the handle turned and Eloryn stepped in. "Roen, have you seen Memory? Something has happened in her chambers and she's—"

Eloryn froze when she saw them on the bed together. Her nose twitched and she lifted her chin.

Memory realized how it must look, with her in just undergarments and a blanket, wrapped up in Roen's arms.

"El, I can explain," Roen began. He got off the bed and walked to Eloryn.

Eloryn put her hand up and he stopped. "No, I want to hear it from Memory. Have you two been seeing one another? Can you deny you've never been intimate?"

Memory stuttered. "It's not how it looks. We kissed once, ages ago, but that's it."

"You kissed her?" Eloryn asked Roen.

"I kissed you first," Roen said.

"You what?" Memory blurted.

She and Eloryn spoke in unison. "How does that make it better?"

Eloryn pushed her hands against her stomach, her face twisted, staring at Memory. "I try my best, I try to do things correctly, stay positive, but you just wade in, not understanding anything and do whatever you want. Take whatever you want. I could almost have accepted this if you'd come to me. I could have been happy for you both. But you," Eloryn's voice wavered and she turned her face away from Memory. "You taunt me with tales of how Roen feels for me. You tell me to share my feelings, to risk everything to allow myself to care for him, only to take him for yourself?"

Eloryn ran from the room.

Roen ran after her, without even a glance back at Memory.

Every dark thought inside Memory felt confirmed. She felt completely, helplessly alone.

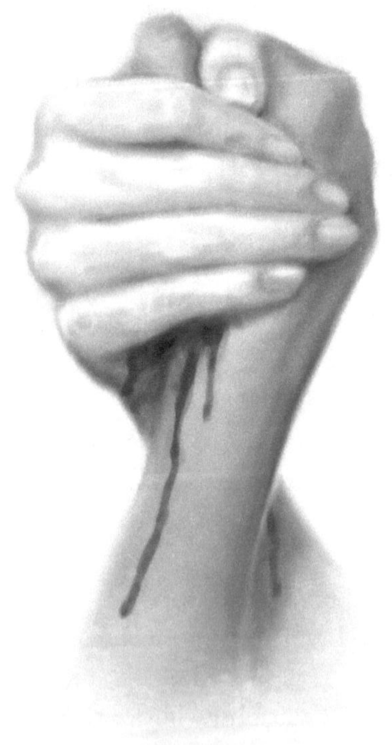

Memory let loose her churning emotions, opened herself to the Veil, daring it to take her away, somewhere, anywhere better than this. She found herself back in her room. Disappointed, Memory crawled into bed in her still damp underclothes.

"I've lost everyone," she whispered.

"You still have me," Hope said. She laid her head down on the pillow next to Memory.

Memory turned to face the other way. "It's your advice that keeps screwing everything up. I should never have messed around with Roen or Dylan."

Hope groaned pointedly. "No, it was my warning all along that everyone would reject you. It was you who wanted to play happy families like you're a real girl. It was my advice all along that the only way to make people treat you right was to be the queen, so they had no choice. Let me help you."

Memory rolled back over, face to face with her old self. "Can you help to stop everything from hurting?"

Hope smiled sympathetically. "I can help you become queen, and then it will be better, I promise. You can pay me back later. We just have to kill Eloryn."

A chill ran up Memory's back. "There has to be another way. I'm not a murderer."

Hope pursed her lips as though thinking. "Sit up. I want to give you something. Something that will give you the strength to do what needs to be done."

It took all her energy to sit up. The blankets felt like lead. "What?"

"Your memories. I've been learning too, and I think we can do it. And once we do, then you'll see. Then you'll know who you really are, what we're capable of."

Memory exhaled sharply. "My memories? What about my soul? Can you fix it? Make me better again?"

"Your soul is kind of *me* now. I don't know how to put that Humpty back together again. But I think I can share our memories so you have them too."

Memory stared at Hope, at who she used to be. If she could at least have all her memories back, would she feel more whole?

"What, you don't want them?" Hope's voice was teasing.

"Do it."

Hope grinned, and pulled a small, unfamiliar knife from her pocket.

She cut the palm of her own hand harshly, letting blood seep out. She took Memory's hand and did the same. Memory flinched but made no sound when the blade sliced her skin.

Hope took Memory's hand and pressed it into hers, their blood mingling, and began speaking words of magic.

The world faded as Memory fell into her past.

She ran out of the children's home, running blindly up an alley strewn with trash bags. Her body ached all over, and she felt sick in a way like she could never get better. A man in an old-fashioned suit stood there, reaching a hand out for her.

Thayl, Memory realized, her thoughts overlaying the memories. *This is the last moment, last memory, before he took them all from me.*

Time jumped backwards, and she stood in front of a charred body. A corpse. Nothing burnt so badly could be alive. A choking stench like burned rubber and pork fat filled the small space, murky with smoke. She bent to pick up her knife from the floor as though she still needed protection. Horror coiled inside her. *I was wrong. Make it stop. I don't want to see more.*

Back again and a wide-set man grinned at her as he unbuckled his belt. She wouldn't let it happen this time, enough was enough. She drew the knife she'd stolen the day before and told the man to back off. She'd always thought he wasn't quite all there, mentally, and the confusion on his face confirmed it for her then. As though he couldn't understand her defiance. As though he thought she wanted this and couldn't believe she'd turn on him. It angered him in a way she'd never seen before and he struck her. Her knife fell uselessly from her hand, and the man beat her and beat her until she thought he'd knock the life right out of her. She curled up on the floor, trying to shield herself. A bubbling pressure built inside her. She tried to hold it back. She knew how dangerous it could be. The man cracked her chin with his boot. She couldn't hold back. She exploded and the man burned.

Back again and she's drawing tattoo designs with Will in her room when the man comes to get her. Small, frail Will stood up like he wanted to do something, but didn't.

Back again. Each vision played faster than the next, hopping backwards in time, playing through her whole life, faster and faster, flooding her.

An entire life in rewind. Every scene scarred by the vision of the burned man. Every scene silenced by the repeating words, *I'm a murderer.*

CHAPTER TWENTY-FOUR

Eloryn felt surrounded by lies. She wanted to trust people, to give the world the benefit of the doubt, believe in the goodness of those around her, but she felt repaid with betrayal. Like Memory and Roen, together, behind her back, despite everything they said. At least they had made one part of her life easier, allowing her to reach one decision.

First thing the next morning, Eloryn went to find Hayes where he worked in her office. *Can I still trust him? What if he is all lies as well? No. I can't think like that or I'll have no one left to trust.*

Hayes scribbled notes down on a stack of pages bound in string.

"Your majesty?" He looked up, seeming surprised at her presence.

"Hayes," she said. "I'm sorry I have delayed progress on approved courtship and marriage plans. I wanted to let you know I'm now ready to do my duty as queen. I'll marry whomever the Council deems most appropriate."

Hayes put down his pen and rose to his feet. "That is wonderful news. I shall call a meeting this afternoon for the announcement." Hayes put his hands on her shoulders fondly. "Do you mind if I ask what prompted your decision?"

The image in her head was still too clear. Roen and Memory, holding each other on his bed, wrapped in each other's arms. "I would prefer you didn't."

Memory awoke. She last remembered it being late in the night, but now sunset shone through her window, the pink glow tinting the room. It had become a different day, and she had become a different person.

Her eyes closed again, but a knocking on her bedroom door made her sit up. She could hear Clara calling through it. "Hope, please, open the door."

I finally am Hope again. The thought didn't bring her much happiness. Memory looked around. The doorway was barricaded with furniture and Memory wondered who did it. The other Hope sat on a chair that blocked the way in.

"Welcome back," she said.

"How long have I been out?" Memory stood up and wavered a little before steadying herself.

"All of last night and today. How do you feel?"

Memory paused and looked at her hands. She needed some nail polish. "Like me."

Clara knocked and called, but Memory ignored her pleas. Memory went to her wardrobe and pulled out the box of her old clothes, taking the whole lot into the bathroom. Standing at the mirror, she worked on putting all of her piercings back into place. Some of the holes had started to close and she forced the jewelry through. The slash on her hand stung and bled as she screwed in the labret. Memory examined her face then tugged at her hair. It had grown an inch or two, trying to be more fitting for this place that no longer felt like home.

"It's all back?" Hope asked, trailing beside Memory as she returned to the bed and retrieved the knife Hope had used to cut their hands. Clara seemed to have given up and gone away. Memory went back to the bathroom.

"Yeah. Still a bit messed up. It's definitely there though. Everything makes a lot more sense now," Memory said. She sawed at her hair, cutting the back short again.

"Of course your head will be a bit busy at first. You've just had a life's worth of memories injected into your brain. I think we can forgive it a little."

A life's worth of memories. A life's worth of pain.

Her insides were raw, like a scab picked away to the mess underneath. Memory began to feel sick and the mirror rattled against the wall. She felt like an emotive proximity mine. *Keep calm. Keep busy.*

Memory threw her t-shirt and jeans on over the old fashioned bodice she wore.

"It's not right," she said, looking herself up and down in the mirror.

"I like it. You look like you," Hope said.

"No. I look like who I used to be." Memory started changing back out of her old clothes. She slipped on a plain underskirt. She meant to put a proper dress on over the top, but lost motivation half way, left in her t-shirt and the flowing layers of silk that dropped from her waist. *Still not right.* She picked up a make-up brush off the dressing table and started blackening around her eyes.

Hope groaned. "Enough dress up. Now you know what we're capable of. Are you ready to take what belongs to you, become queen?"

"You're asking if I'm ready to murder Eloryn?"

"You don't have to be so blunt about it, but yes. It's what needs to be done. Eloryn is heavily guarded. But you've got the best chance to get close to her. Remember it's got to look like an accident. The point is to get you to be queen, not executed for regicide."

Memory said nothing and continued lining her eyes. She wondered if she could go back to the other world. Maybe find Will again. The thought of the other world left a deep nausea in her bones. She couldn't go back, especially now she knew she was a murderer there. The floor shook, and the exposed pipes running to the bath and sink groaned like they could crack.

Memory centered herself, considering her options. She couldn't go back. What she had to do to stay here seemed impossible. What else could she do?

An eerie calm fell over her.

The room stilled.

Memory stared at herself in the mirror, then down at the cloth bag on the dresser filled with the coarsely ground powder that Clara assured her was hair dye. It looked worse than the cheap packet sachets Memory used to steal from the drugstore.

I'm calm. I'm in control.

Memory closed her eyes and breathed deeply, imagining the result she wanted, "Change it."

She opened her eyes. Her ivory blonde hair had become a rich royal purple, the bottom halves of the longer front sections tipped black.

Hope stared. A faint look of concern flashed on her features before she punched Memory in the shoulder and smiled. "Fancy stuff. Getting those emotions locked down, huh?"

"Something like that."

"Good. It's all forward from here, 'kay? And you know what the next step needs to be. I'll do what I can to help you, just give me the go ahead."

"No." Memory took the knife and headed for the door. "She's my sister."

Eloryn was passing time within the Round Room, waiting for the meeting Hayes had scheduled for later that day that would seal her fate. A messenger had told her that Roen's parents were preparing to leave and everyone was making their goodbyes. She wasn't able to bring herself somewhere she knew Roen would be.

She ran her hands up one of the pillars that stood around the room and found a crack in it still from the explosion. She spoke a behest to fix it. If only she could repair everything so easily.

"Eloryn?" A friendly voice came from around the corner.

"Isabeth," Eloryn greeted her with a smile. "What are you doing here?"

"I understand it might be asking a lot, but I came to see why the queen hadn't come to see us off."

Eloryn worked hard to keep the smile on her face.

Isabeth frowned. "My child, what's wrong?"

The obviousness of her emotions caused Eloryn to lose control, and she began weeping.

Isabeth took her in her arms, gently stroking her hair. "You surely can't be that upset to see me go," she joked softly.

Eloryn put her hand to her mouth in an attempt to hold back her grief.

"It's all right. Don't hold it in. Tell me everything."

Eloryn had never known the comfort of a mother's arms. She found every one of her doubts and worries falling from her mouth. "I feel I'm making so many mistakes. I owe the Council my trust and loyalty, but find my trust given to men with misogynistic, antiquated, hard-line

views. And even knowing that, I've handed so much power to them because I couldn't use that power myself. I'm just not a ruler. But I'm worried. So worried that I've done the wrong thing. I don't know if I can keep going along with their wishes, but don't know how to challenge them." Eloryn pulled back. She dried her face with a handkerchief but desperation still filled her voice. "What if you try your hardest to be strong, and do your duty, but it's simply not who you are?"

"Sweet child, let me tell you something," Isabeth put her hands on Eloryn's shoulders and looked at her straight. "Your mother had all the same complaints. And if she had stood up for herself, then things would never have gotten so bad for so long. I'm not blaming your mother, dear, I'm only saying... don't make the same mistakes that she did. Follow your heart."

But the one my heart wishes for has already chosen another. "I can't. I can't have what I want. Even if I could, would you still encourage me to follow my heart if it meant I would no longer be royalty? That I and the one I chose to be with would not hold this power?"

Isabeth laughed softly. "Power and duty be damned. You are sad to your core, and it makes me sad to see you so. You should do whatever makes you happy, and if that's serving your kingdom then so be it. But if it's not what you want, then why can't someone else do it? Shouldn't a prerequisite to rule be the passion and desire to do so?"

Eloryn had already given Hayes so much power, but the thought of handing over what remained gave her chills. "I cannot let Hayes rule. I... I just don't think he's right for it."

Isabeth looked at her like she was a dullard. "Of course he isn't. I said passion and desire, child. Not greed."

"I've been so foolish." Eloryn put her head on Isabeth's shoulder and held her tight. "Thank you. It feels like an age since someone has been so honest with me, Isabeth. I'm so used to lies and duplicity and spending wasted effort on making myself trust and believe. Even from family. Even my sister..."

"If there is one thing that I have learned you can trust, it is family." Isabeth said. "And I am no hypocrite to say so, despite having just learned how my son kept us fed and clothed all these years. His words were lies but in his actions, every coin he brought home, every sack of flour or new dress spoke clearly, 'I love you, I care for you, I would do anything to keep you safe.' And all those years I lied to myself, saying

the weight we placed on his shoulders was not too much, that he had not such a hard road."

Isabeth squeezed Eloryn tight. "For whatever has come between you and your sister, have you looked at the truth in her actions or just seen what you wanted to believe?"

To follow my heart, to be with Roen, has terrified me at every turn. I've sought every reason not to, and in Memory and Roen's intimacy I gave myself the ultimate excuse. Was it just what I wanted to believe?

Maybe she over-reacted. Maybe she should have trusted Memory more. Eloryn gave everyone else the benefit of the doubt. It was the least she owed her twin. In her heart, if nothing else, she desperately wanted to believe Memory's insistence that said she and Roen weren't in love.

CHAPTER TWENTY-FIVE

The entire Wizard's Council gathered in the Round Room. Fifteen of them. All that remained, who'd lived in fear of their lives for so long as all their brethren were hunted. Those who had lived in complete isolation from the world for sixteen years, even more than Eloryn had.

Eloryn's partner for the rest of her life would be decided by these men. It didn't seem right. She'd requested it, but her talk with Isabeth left her mind spinning, unsure. The meeting came upon her before she could clear her dizziness and find clarity.

Only the Council was in attendance, although Memory had been sent an invitation to the meeting. Her absence concerned Eloryn. There was more they should have said to each other. Apologies to be spoken and forgiveness to be given. To know for sure, before she recklessly sealed her fate.

Hayes stood and waited until he had everyone's attention, then sat and nodded to Bors. Hayes smiled in a way that unsettled Eloryn. Something greedy in his eyes twisted the expression. Did he always look that way and she was just seeing it now?

Bors cleared his throat. "Your majesty, we hear that you wish to expedite the arrangement of your marriage?"

Eloryn found she couldn't speak, so she nodded.

"In order to accommodate your request, we have been carefully reviewing the candidates for your partner. In light of recent events and

changes, we've reached a somewhat untraditional conclusion, but we feel it is now our best option."

A number of the Councilors were frowning, but nodded in agreement.

Could it be? Eloryn's heart beat like a voice, *Roen, Roen, Roen.*

Bors gestured to Hayes at the head of the table. "We have come to the agreement that the most suitable candidate is one of our own, Councilor Hayes."

"It is my most humble honor," Hayes said, bowing his head slightly.

Eloryn's jaw dropped. A few Councilors offered muted applause and congratulations.

"I don't understand," Eloryn said. "What about the list of other candidates?"

Madoc grumbled from next to Bors, "The list, unfortunately, somehow made its way into public hands. It has been trouble enough quieting the furor that entailed, with families demanding to know why their sons weren't selected, and those who were selected suddenly receiving proposals from across the land. I'm afraid every one of those candidates had to be removed from selection."

Eloryn felt the breath knocked out of her. She'd so flippantly handed the list to a group of giggling girls. She didn't even consider the consequences. She was thinking of nothing but the name that wasn't on the list.

"But a member of the Council?" she said.

Bedevere, who rarely spoke up, grumbled from beneath his frown. "Believe me, we debated this decision at length. We had very little choice. I'm sorry, your majesty."

Hayes left his position at the head of the long table and paced down to stand by Eloryn's side at the other end. He held his walking cane horizontally in both hands.

"My peers are all in agreement that I am the most magically powerful contender and thus the most obvious choice for king."

Eloryn felt sick to her gut. Should this go ahead Hayes would have more power than her. Not only would he be king, but should they have children - Eloryn swallowed rising stomach acid - his children would be heir to Avall's throne, before Memory, before anyone.

Is that what he was after all along? Every foothold of power she'd given him over the past weeks had been begged and manipulated from her, and now he would have it all.

Her own indecision and naivety had brought them to this juncture.

She couldn't let it continue.

"No, I can't. I won't," she said. Her words felt clumsy in the face of this man's arrogance.

Hayes frowned sympathetically, and put a hand on her shoulder. "This is the decision of the Council and we must go along with their wishes. Your majesty, we must do this for Avall."

"No, for Avall, for myself, I deny you." Eloryn tried to stand, but Hayes pushed her firmly into her chair under his grip. He bent a little and whispered in her ear.

"You cannot go against the council's decision, girl. Even if you would, here's something else to consider. I have full control of the military. Control of Avall's police and militia is in the hands of those loyal to me, and I have complete domination of the trade guilds. Should you refuse to marry me then I will simply cripple the economy of Avall, punishing her people, and force control through a coup."

Eloryn winced then set her face firm. She did this. She gave him the power to force her into this position. She had to find a way to undo it. Even if she stripped him of his power now, he had armed militia under control of his loyalists who would wage a war to take it back. But there had to be a way.

Hayes squeezed her shoulder as if consoling her, but his words were venomous. "Keep in mind, you're not the most popular monarch or figurehead at the moment. Even your dim-witted sister is more popular than you. You're much too young and weak willed to rule a kingdom on your own. I deserve this position." Hayes straightened back up and addressed the whole room again.

"The Council recognized the leadership I have displayed as we suffered and survived Thayl's rule, the cunning that saved us. I vow to devote that same ingenuity to my role as King. I vow to do anything required to save Avall." Hayes pounded his walking stick on the floor with each intonation. He moved away from Eloryn and she stood up, but made no move to run from the room despite it being her greatest desire.

Hayes bowed to her, but the look on his face remained cruel. "You must do this for your kingdom, your majesty. You cannot simply marry some Sparkless thief." Hayes rumbled a deep, mocking laugh that some of his allies echoed. "That fool had the audacity to come to us, the Wizard's Council, to ask for your hand. A seventh son of a seventh son asking for the hand of a Maellan?"

The pounding in Eloryn's chest seemed to wake her from the numbness of what was happening. *Roen formally asked to be with me.* It shouldn't have been the most important piece of information she'd taken in so far, but it was, to her. It was all she cared about, and that realization gave her the hunger to find a way to make it happen. And she would find a way to destroy every greedy goal of the man in front of her with the same act. *I know exactly what I can do.*

Eloryn spoke, making her voice loud and firm. "Very well. I will marry you, Hayes."

Hayes looked like a wolf who'd just had a lame goat cross its path. Eloryn smiled sweetly and spoke over him before he could say anything in reply. "On the condition that upon signing of a behest-bound pre-nuptial agreement, you hand all control of the militia and trade guilds to the ruler of Avall and to not use them against myself or our heirs."

Hayes smirked. "For what difference it will make, being as I shall be king."

"I want it drafted and signed now." Eloryn lowered her eyes and bobbed a short curtsey as though signaling he had won.

Bors unfurled a roll of parchment and began scrawling the words in large flourished script. As he worked, Eloryn heard a small scuffle from the corner of the room and saw Erec holding Roen back. The sight of him almost chased her resolve away. Eloryn caught Roen's eyes and warned him with the tiniest shake of her head. *Trust me*, she mouthed. He bared clenched teeth, but nodded.

"I am now binding the agreement with the required magic," Bors said, and uttered a few behest words. "It is ready to sign."

Without delay Hayes moved over to the contract and signed it.

Eloryn stepped over to the paper and also signed.

Eloryn turned to the Council, purposefully ignoring Hayes.

"Good sirs, I hereby formally announce my abdication as queen."

All around the table voices grumbled, outraged and confused at her announcement. She could hear Hayes breathing hard behind her.

She turned her head, barely looking over her shoulder at him. "Someone once told me, that sometimes the best thing someone in power can do is hand that duty over to someone who will be more capable in the role. I trust we will find my sister to be more capable."

"You can't do this," Hayes hissed. She knew he'd calculated what she'd done. Since they were not yet married, Memory was still the legal

heir and through abdicating Eloryn ensured Hayes would never be king through marriage to her. With the contract, she'd stripped him of any power he'd accumulated through control of his militia. They were now under Memory's control, and he was behest-bound to never use them against either of the twins.

"No one will support your halfwit sister in power," Hayes warned, salivating at the mouth with rage. He looked around the table, but all other voices remained silent. Bors kept shooting panicked looks at Hayes.

Eloryn still refused to turn and face him. She made her case to the rest of the Council. "Memory will make a better queen than I ever could. She has been diligently studying the laws of Avall and has consistently made better decisions than I have. She has always stood by her own instinct, rather than what I did, which was almost handing the kingdom over to a greed-driven warmonger. I was never made for this. It was never truly what I wanted." She flicked Hayes a sparkling glare. "Besides, I have recently heard that my sister was a more popular choice than me anyway."

The Council looked back and forward between themselves and her. They muttered to each other as though she were barely there.

Hayes snatched Eloryn's arm and spun her to face him. Bedevere and two other Councilors jumped to their feet. Erec and Roen appeared by her side, and Hayes snarled and let go.

"Is that all who would stand with me against this man, who would threaten our land with military might for his own ends?" Eloryn said, daring each man around the table. "I will no longer be queen, and he will not be king through me. He will be punished for what he has attempted, and do not doubt that any who stand with him will be as well."

Bors joined the other Councilors on their feet. He licked his lips, eyes darting. "I cannot remain silent any longer. Hayes's crimes exceed what any of you may imagine."

"Bors," Hayes growled.

Eloryn raised her hand to Hayes. "Not another word from you. Bors, please tell us everything. You are safe."

He nodded, his voice lifting with each word as though fearful excitement drove it louder. "The entire threat from your uncle was a fabrication. Hayes killed Waylan for challenging him too much. He dressed it up as an attack on you in order to also remove your uncle. And Hayes was the one who put the bounty on the Faerbaird boy. These were all things he

did to get what he wanted and to remove who he didn't."

As Bors continued, the words Eloryn heard behind her lifted the hairs on her neck.

"Guidhe beag lugha ob—"

Eloryn turned and slapped Hayes across the mouth, stunning him silent. He stumbled back a few steps, fury dripping from him.

There was chaos in the room. Every other Councilor got to their feet, calling accusations and demands to each other, to Hayes, Bors, and Eloryn.

Eloryn finally looked him in the eyes again. "I trusted you, Hayes. I freely gave you all my trust, and this is what you've done with it?"

Hayes yelled across the clamor in the room. Everyone drew quiet. "Everything I have done was for the kingdom, and I would continue to rule as I have begun, doing anything that needed to be done for our kingdom! You, foolish thing, should reconsider your abdication."

Hayes lifted his hands in an offensive manner.

Some of the people in the Round Room moved clear, anticipating danger. Roen remained near Eloryn, but she stepped away from him, toward Hayes.

"Strike me with what you have, Hayes. You cannot touch me." Eloryn stood defiant, ready for him. "I am Maellan. *You bred me for this.*"

In a roar of words, Hayes cried a behest as though each word would physically strike her.

Eloryn's voice, calm and focused, was lost under his shouts. She spoke with the world as though they were oldest friends, every element understanding her, knowing her intentions, on her side. She smiled and waited.

Hayes's spell echoed through the room. Everyone tensed. Nothing happened.

Hayes growled and repeated his behest.

"Give up, Hayes. You are done," Eloryn said.

Hayes stuttered and drew a scroll from his pocket to read from. Eloryn recognized the intention of the behest and watched as Hayes seemed surprised when the air did not solidify around her.

Desperation filled his words as he turned to his vilest spell. "Guidhe beag lugha ob ciorram greim-bàis eucail spad eug!"

Eloryn's body did not turn on itself. She did not retaliate. She watched silently and waited as every attempt Hayes made failed him.

"The world will not listen to you, Hayes. I have asked that all your behests be denied."

Hayes reached to his side again, and Eloryn shook her head at his stubbornness. He grabbed at his walking cane and twisted it apart in his hands, pulling the handle from the length. The zing of metal filled the room.

She barely realized what was happening as the concealed sword swung at her neck.

An inch from her beating veins the blade stopped, blocked by another. Erec held his sword firm, and Roen burst passed him. He grabbed Hayes's arm and wrenched the thin sword from his hand.

"I may have no Spark of Connection, but I believe we're now even in that regard."

With a second strike at the wizard's chest, Roen knocked him to his knees.

Roen lifted his chin, daring Hayes to keep fighting. Hayes remained on the ground.

Behind them, guards, Councilors, and servants all moved forward to defend Eloryn. Everyone stood with her, and she knew she'd made the right decision.

Eloryn had Erec and men he trusted take Hayes to the dungeons. He shouted curses and blasphemies as he was dragged away.

The room was in turmoil. With their leader gone, and their queen abdicated, the Council were at a loss, arguing amongst themselves. Bedevere's voice cut through the chaos, trying to get his bewildered companions in order.

Eloryn caught Roen's hand in hers and dragged him from the room. He followed without a word. The two of them slipped away silently, not missed by the crowd they left behind.

In the quiet hallway, Eloryn stopped and turned to him. She kept his hand tight in hers. He looked at her with the golden eyes she loved.

"I'm sorry, Roen, for not doing everything in my power to be with you sooner. I doubted how you felt, I doubted my place in this kingdom, but I never doubted how I felt for you, and I should have acted on that. I'm sorry I'm so bad at the relationship I have with you, and that I'm not impulsive like Memory. I won't object if you want to be with her, or leave, or do whatever you need to in order to be happy."

"El," Roen's forehead creased but a smile sat on his lips. "I have

tried to love others, but could only love you. I have tried to deny it, and only loved you more. I love you in a way that should make me a poet, but instead leaves me speechless. If you love me but a hundredth of how I love you, then I am happy."

Eloryn's hands reached for Roen's collar, but she couldn't feel the movement, could feel nothing but tingling nerves. Fingertips brushed his neck and sent a flush of warmth through her as she pulled him down to touch her mouth gently against hers.

She could feel his smile under her lips and kissed him again before letting go.

She blushed triumphantly as he looked down at her, shaking his head like he couldn't believe what was happening.

"I hope that felt like a little more than one hundredth," she said.

"Hard to say. I think I may just need to try..." His words became breath, disappearing to nothing as he walked into her, pressing his body against hers. Roen scooped the back of her head into both hands and kissed her cheek and neck.

Eloryn wrapped her hands around his shoulders, and he lifted her off her feet, spinning her in the air.

CHAPTER TWENTY-SIX

The knife had warmed to body temperature in her hands. Memory wasn't sure what she intended to do with it but couldn't let it go.

Servants gave her worried looks as they saw her walk by, but Memory barely noticed. People always stared at her wherever she went. It came with the hair colors and piercings. They made people judge her on first glance and that was how she liked it. It meant people left her alone. She felt shut off from the world, too busy struggling with herself. She'd already made her decision, but the options kept rattling around like loose change, tempting her. Would taking Eloryn's life solve her problems? No. Not even in her darkest fantasy. But she had to see her one more time.

Memory knew they would all be at the meeting Eloryn had called. The meeting didn't matter to her, but she was surprised that she had been invited at all, or that they even remembered she existed. She felt like she was already gone and couldn't understand that others didn't think the same.

Memory heard giggling and slowed down. At the end of the hall, she saw Eloryn and Roen. They looked utterly happy, wrapped in each other's arms, kissing again and again.

Memory looked away, squeezing her dry eyes closed, holding the image of them together like a snapshot in her mind.

Hope's familiar voice whispered from behind her. "If you want Roen, then you can have him once Eloryn is gone. You can have everything you want."

"No. I want Roen *and* Eloryn. I love them both. I love them and want them to be happy." Memory turned and headed back the way she'd come. The knife dropped on the floor, tumbling into a dark corner behind an ornamental suit of armor.

Memory didn't know if Hope still followed her, but she spoke aloud anyway. "I already know the problem that needs to be removed. It's not them. It's me."

"What a fun trick we played." Mina laughed, making a sound like tinkling chimes. She lay on top of Will in long, lush grass, spotted with wildflowers. The overwhelming fragrance of the blossoms added to the sick feeling in Will's gut.

She'll think I went home without her. I have to get back.

Mina had snatched Will away right at the worst moment. He'd been avoiding her, and this was how she punished him. He knew the more he wanted to go back, the less likely it would happen. He tried to seem relaxed, carefree.

Mina rolled over him into the grass, and the blades lit up from within where she touched them, glowing golden, and sprays of petals danced as she giggled. Even now, Will ached at her beauty, that dangerous beauty he wished he could deny, like being lured by poisoned honey.

Will stretched casually and carefully picked his words. "Wouldn't it be a good trick if you sent me back now? She must think I'm gone. She'll be surprised if I show up again."

"No." Mina flipped onto her stomach and put her elbows under her, lifting her chest up like a sphinx. "You'll go back when I'm bored of you."

It had already been all night and most of the day Mina had kept him with her. He wasn't sure where they were. Somewhere deep in the hunting grounds, but he wasn't as familiar with this forest as he was with his last home. The small meadow grew dim and shaded, and a pair of deer wandered in, grazing. Mina sprung up onto her knees, reached out a hand, and the deer cantered over to her.

Will shifted in the grass, off his back and into a crouch, eyeing the elegant creatures. Recognizing the look on his face, the form of his body, the deer changed course. He was a predator, and they knew it. They bounded off into the darkened woods.

Mina smacked her hands onto the ground, shrieking. "I wanted to play with them."

"They're gone now." Will shrugged and lay down again. He yawned and closed his eyes. "You could probably catch them if you want. But I'm tired."

Mina threw handfuls of torn-up grass at him. "Horrible boring boy."

She floated up into the air, shimmering dust falling from her, and zipped away through the trees.

Will remained still for a few moments more, waiting to make sure she had gone, then pushed up to his feet and started running. He ran west, following the setting sun until he started to see familiar ground, then ran until he reached the palace walls.

Will climbed the vines to Memory's bedroom. The window was locked, for the first time Will had ever known.

Will knocked hard on the paneled glass, and a figure rushed to open the doors for him.

The red-headed maid stood in front of him, worry all over her features.

"Where is Memory?" Will asked, stepping into the room. It was still a mess from his fight with Dylan.

"Will, I'm so glad you're here. I don't know what to do." Clara handed him an open letter, written on the same cream-colored paper as the one Memory had left for him in the Ivy Room.

Clara rambled, almost hysterical. "She locked herself in her room earlier. I could hear her talking to herself. And now this."

Will only needed to read the first word. *Goodbye.*

"How can we find her?" Will roared.

Clara squeaked, "Maybe her sister, or—"

"Take me. Now."

A fear Will hadn't known since he was a boy in the other world gripped him. Back there he'd often worried, often thought it could happen. But he hoped here Memory had found a new life, had escaped her past. Something must have changed.

Clara led Will at a run through the palace. Will didn't care what he wore or the looks he got. He only cared about reaching Memory in time.

They found both Eloryn and Roen together, smiling despite the turmoil of wizards and messengers rushing about them. Will didn't understand what was happening. The castle seemed to be in chaos.

"We have to help Memory," Will said.

"Where is she?" Eloryn asked, her expression of joy slipping away to concern.

"We hoped you could find her," Clara said. "She may be planning to do something awful."

"She has no one with her? No guards or servants?" Eloryn asked.

Roen shook his head. "You know what she's like. She'll be alone."

Clara nodded and began to cry. "She only has me, and I wasn't there for her. It's my fault. I shouldn't have left her like that. The things she was saying, things she was doing. I'm so worried."

"It wasn't just your responsibility. If she's in danger, it's all our faults," Roen said.

Will's breath grew rough, each exhalation a growl. "We have to hurry."

They started moving, and a handful of guards that had their eyes on Eloryn followed. Will stopped. "Just us. It has to just be us, no one else."

Eloryn gave the guards a signal. One in particular nodded.

The guards remained where they were and Will, Clara, Eloryn, and Roen ran to find Memory.

What am I doing?

Memory felt more broken than ever. Regaining her memories had made things worse, not better. She hurt in a way that she didn't know how things could ever be better again.

She found solitude in Thayl's old quarters. The whole wing was still closed up, and she could wander freely without anyone staring at her. Only Hope was with her, ever by her side, as Memory wound her way around the tower stairs, up and up.

Memory paused along the way, drifting through the piles of junk in storage in the tower. She ran her hands over the stack of mattresses and their moth-eaten covers. A rolled tapestry on the floor showed burn marks. Paintings with cracked frames were stacked haphazardly. Splintered pieces of the round table had been piled in a corner.

This is the place for broken things.

She didn't belong in Avall with Eloryn and Roen. Maybe they thought so at first, but as the jigsaw of their lives came together, it became clear that Memory was a spare, broken piece that didn't fit. No one really knew her. No one accepted her for who she really was. Not even herself.

Now she remembered her past, she knew she'd always been trying to be something she wasn't, someone different, running from herself.

Memory wondered whether Thayl felt like this as he made his way up this same tower, that there was no place in the puzzle for them.

Memory stood at the balcony and looked down.

Hope pulled her away by the arm. "What do you think you're doing? I've told you how to solve your problems. Why won't you believe me and just get it done?"

Memory looked out the window into the distance. "My own screwed-up brain is telling me to kill my sister. I don't deserve to live."

Hope shook her. "I'm not your brain. I'm real."

"Prove it."

"I knew things that you didn't. I knew you killed that guy before I showed it to you."

Memory snatched her arm from Hope's grasp. "Yeah, thanks for that."

"I just wanted to prove what you were capable of doing."

"And now I know." Memory headed again toward the edge.

Hope grabbed her roughly, dragging her back into the room and slamming the balcony doors closed behind her. "I'm sorry if your memories weren't all puppy dogs and picnics, but you have to snap out of it, we have things to do."

Memory faced Hope. She snarled and the room shook.

Hope smiled uneasily. "I thought you'd gotten yourself under control?"

"I have." The tower shook, and Hope was knocked to the floor.

Hope looked at Memory with genuine fear in her eyes. "I know it's a lot to ask, to kill your own sister, but it will work, I promise. If you want I can do it for you. Let me do it for you, and you can owe me a favor in return. Just give me the all clear."

Memory turned her back. "Shut up, Hope. Whatever you've got to say, whatever experience you think you're calling on for this advice you're giving me, it's all in me again now too. There's nothing anymore you can offer me. You've given me everything I needed to end up here."

Memory pulled the balcony doors open again, a soft breeze rushing in past her. The last sliver of orange sun kissed the horizon. She watched until it dropped from sight then stepped up onto the balustrade, balancing on the thin marble edge. "Later, Hope."

CHAPTER TWENTY-SEVEN

"Memory?" Eloryn's voice reached her. "What are you doing?"

Eloryn, Roen, Clara, and Will ran up into the room, and the sight of them almost made Memory slip and fall. Her heart thundered and feet tingled until she steadied herself.

What am I doing? What the hell am I doing?

Memory simply looked at Will, confused.

"Will?" Memory asked. She sounded inebriated and didn't know if it was her voice or hearing that was faulty. The whole world seemed to swim in her senses. "I thought you left me."

Will edged toward her. "Why would I leave?"

Because of all the horrible things I said, and do, and am.

Will shook his head as though she'd said the words aloud. *Did I?*

"Mina took me away. I didn't go through the door."

A small fire of jealousy lit in Memory, a spark of passion in a body she'd thought had already lost all life. "You stayed for her."

"Mem, please get down. What are you doing?" Eloryn pleaded.

Clara just watched with her hand over her mouth.

Memory couldn't look them in the eyes, so she looked down at the ground so far below. "I'm removing a problem."

"You're not a problem." Roen said, moving closer to her. "You've done so much good, inspired so much good, in me, in Eloryn, in Avall."

Clara nodded. "And the lives of the poor in the city. I've never seen such caring."

"You're both wrong. I'm a bad person. I don't belong – not here, not anywhere. Any good you've seen me do? Fake. I'm just trying to fit in but all that isn't the real me. The kids at the shelter only like me because I give them money. Why do you think you like me, Roen? It's because I look like Eloryn. Clara's only around because looking after me is her job. The Council just wants to study me. Dylan was just following orders." Memory ran her hands up through her hair, tugging at the purple strands. "The real me? I hurt people. I… kill people. *My soul is broken*. I might as well die. I know I murdered someone, and that was before Thayl's ritual stole my soul. How much of a monster does that make me now?"

Eloryn seemed confused. "Your soul isn't broken, Mem." She smiled like that solved everything. "If it were, I would have known when I joined spirits with you. How do you think that was even possible? Thayl was wrong – he never understood magic. He just assumed the power he stole was your soul. It was just magic he stole, just pure magic tangled with your memories. Not your soul."

Memory's shoulders fell. She felt thin as paper. "This is what I am *with* a soul?" *No.*

If this was all there was to her – the complete package – her actions were always hers. The way people reacted to her, the wrongness of her, she had nothing to blame but herself. There were no excuses, no get-out clauses. No getting better.

Memory's legs gave way beneath her. Her skirt billowing out behind her like a parachute trying to hold her in place. She could hear footsteps like thunder behind her as she fell into the wind.

Hands clutched at her, but she was already falling.

She could still feel arms around her and opened her eyes. The ground rushed up toward her, and dark brown hair blew into her face. Will tangled his limbs around her, trying to protect her from the fall, as though his own body would be shield enough to save her. His ice blue eyes remained fixed on her face.

Will. My Will.

Adrenaline flamed through Memory's limbs, making her gasp. The deadly ground flew at them. She ripped a hole into the Veil. The two of them fell through.

Will landed first, still holding Memory above him. They crashed down hard on the stack of old mattresses. The top three mattresses split and burst on impact, spraying dust and downy feathers into the air.

The stuffing fell around them like snow, and Memory cried out as she tried to sit up. Her hand stung like fingers were broken. Will lay still beneath her, and she put her good hand on his chest, trying to stir him. The second she touched him, he opened his eyes and pulled himself up, dragging her into his lap and holding so tight her bruised limbs ached more.

"You're an idiot to think I'd leave you. I would always be with you, if I could." Will's voice trembled, stopped and started, like each sentence was a struggle. "You make me so angry, but… but I could just die I love you so much. I've always wanted to be with you, when things are good or bad, no matter what color your hair is or where we are. My home is where you are."

Memory clung back to Will, sobbing. The only person who knew her, that knew Hope and Memory, before and after, good and bad, and still accepted her.

He whispered into her neck. "I know you're hurting. It would be insane if you weren't after everything you've been through. There's no quick fix, but I'll be there for you. And you will be there for me, too, like you always have. You can't take yourself away from me."

And if he could accept her as is, maybe someday she could too.

"Will, I got my memories back. I remember it all. Everything."

He shifted back to look into her eyes, searching. "Are you… okay?"

Memory giggled softly, shaking her head. She pointed to the balcony. "See exhibit A."

"You will be. You will be okay." Will brought her back into his arms.

Roen, Eloryn, and Clara stood watching them. Roen held Eloryn as she stared at Memory, crying. Memory tilted her head back as a welcoming gesture and they came to join the embrace.

Memory let the warmth of her friends bodies soak into her, bringing her back to life.

She'd failed them by refusing to believe they could care for her. She knew how wrong she'd been when she could feel it now in every tear that fell on her.

Even Hope, in her own way, cared so much.

Memory shook her head. *Hope.*

"Hope," she whispered then spoke louder through the muffle of her friend's embrace. "Then who is Hope?"

Eloryn, Will, Roen, and Clara let her go.

Memory wobbled her way off the mattresses, her legs shaky and sore. "Hope, come out. I know you're out there!"

Clara looked at the others, confused. "Aren't you Hope?"

"No, there's another me. I didn't tell you all because she said she was made from my broken soul, and I didn't want you to know. But if that's not true…" Memory looked around the circular room. "Then who are you? What are you?"

She didn't appear. Memory groaned in frustration.

"Is Hope who you've been talking to?" Roen asked. He and Eloryn looked at each other with clear concern.

"Don't tell me she isn't real, that I really have been crazy all along." Memory squeezed her hand into a fist. The cut across the palm still stung. "It can't be. A hallucination couldn't have cast the spell to bring my memories back. She knew things, about my past, before I did. Game's up, Hope, come out!"

A movement flashed in the corner of Memory's eye. Hope stepped out from behind the stack of paintings. Memory's friends gasped, and she sighed in relief that they were seeing her too.

"You spoiled everything," Hope pouted. "It was just meant to be you and me, but now they all know, things will have to change."

"You're not me, not made of my soul, so what are you?" Memory demanded.

Hope picked her way through the unwanted furniture in the room. She lifted her palms upward, the vision of innocence. "Hey, I only knew what you knew, right? Maybe I'm just made up of your memories after all?"

"Don't bullshit me. The things you told me to do, that isn't me. It never was."

"What, you really wouldn't do this?" Hope cocked her head to the side. "Cuir aerlaith, briseadh cloich, séid goath."

Hope's words of magic bent the air around them, flinging a gust of wind that pushed Eloryn toward the open balcony windows.

"What are you doing?" Memory screamed. Eloryn was yelling her own magic words, but nothing seemed to stop the gale forcing her to the edge. She looked to Memory for help.

"I'm doing what you should have done. Such a shame your sister

would die from a tragic accident." A few more words from Hope, and the balcony Eloryn slid toward crumbled away. Eloryn fell to her knees, clutching at the ground, trying to hold herself still. Roen ran to grab her and was caught in the rush of air himself.

"Ah yes, unfortunately this time, there are also witnesses that will have to go." With a look from Hope, the air seemed to wrap Clara and Will, pushing them the same way. Clara shrieked, crying.

The sound of the wind rushed through Memory like a river. Memory roared over it. "Stop it!" She let her magic loose, forcing a bolt to strike Hope.

The wind stilled. Memory's friends scrambled for stability.

Hope didn't even sound human when she screamed back. The whole tower rumbled, and the stones beneath Eloryn's feet fell away. Clara pulled her across onto a solid piece of ground then looked surprised at herself. She barely had a moment before the floor under them started breaking away.

Memory threw more magic at Hope. Even with the new control she'd found, it was all she could do. Each burst of magic knocked Hope back, disrupting her for just a moment. Memory wanted to Veil door her friends to safety but was worried if she let up her assault on Hope for even a second it would be too long.

Memory pummeled Hope back across the room, but it barely seemed to distract her.

Memory yelled. "Stop this!"

The floor kept crumbling on its own, too little left of its structure to stay intact. Furniture and old frames slid into the gaping pit. The stones under Memory dropped away. She almost fell backwards into the spreading hole. Will grabbed her and dragged her to solid ground at the edge of the room.

A wooden beam dislodged itself from a wall, throwing itself across at her friends. Memory managed to deflect it, but it still clipped Roen on the back when he stepped to block it from hitting the girls.

Memory gritted her teeth, staring at her twisted twin. "Why are you doing this? I didn't give you permission, I didn't..."

Hope had said she'd do it for her, if she'd just give the word. She should have known then, should have realized.

Hope only showed up after Thayl had died. Appearing at will, manipulating her, wanting debts and bargains and asking permission to harm those she loved. Just like Providence. Just like...

"Bronmer... Bron... Shit. Eloryn, I think she's a fae, Brand her!"

Eloryn cried, "BRONMARBH AIL-"

Hope was gone. Vanished in a flash, just the way a fairy would.

Memory breathed, liked it was the first time she had in weeks.

But the tower still roared like a crumbling stone dragon.

"The tower's coming down," Roen yelled over the sound.

"Can you try and hold it together?" Memory asked her sister.

Eloryn already spoke her words and nodded so as not to interrupt them with her reply. A sudden jolt shifted all of them a foot across the floor.

"Loreee?" Memory sang. "Whatcha doing? Can you hold this?"

Eloryn shrugged, shook her head, kept speaking words of magic anyway.

"Time to run, then."

Everyone nodded. Clara remained still, terrified, and Memory grabbed her hand and they ran first down the stairs. Eloryn, Roen, and Will followed close behind.

The roof of the tower flattened the room they had been standing in just as they hit the stairs. Memory let go of Clara who kept running and paused to check everyone was out and okay. Roen and Eloryn passed her on the stairs.

Dust and shattered slate pelted them from the destroyed roof. Eloryn stumbled her steps, and stumbled her words. The tower lurched, tipping to the side. They all slid with it and hit the wall of the stairwell.

An explosion of noise cracked around them and the stairwell split. Eloryn and Roen looked back at Memory, and she looked down at them from across the chasm where the stairs had been.

Will grabbed her hand, a question on his face.

Memory nodded.

He scooped her up, and at a run he jumped the gap, running along the wall and hitting the landing at the bottom on his feet. Memory bounced in his strong arms and tucked herself tight into his body.

Sprinting down the last flights of stairs, they slid out into the adjoining corridor atop an avalanche of crumbled masonry. All that was left of the tower.

They all sat there coughing, checking over each other with silent looks.

It was Eloryn who spoke first.

"Mem, are you okay?"

Memory wafted dust from her face. "Yeah, in one piece."

"I mean, really okay?"

Memory felt like laughing. She was full of relief and wanted to express it through that unstoppable sort of laughter that hurt your belly. But her sister stared at her so seriously, she worried her relief was misplaced. Maybe she had a metal pipe sticking through her chest and didn't know it yet, like those dumb chicks in gore flicks.

"Why?"

"Because you're going to need to be." Eloryn bit her lip and tried to smile. "I've abdicated. You're now the queen of Avall."

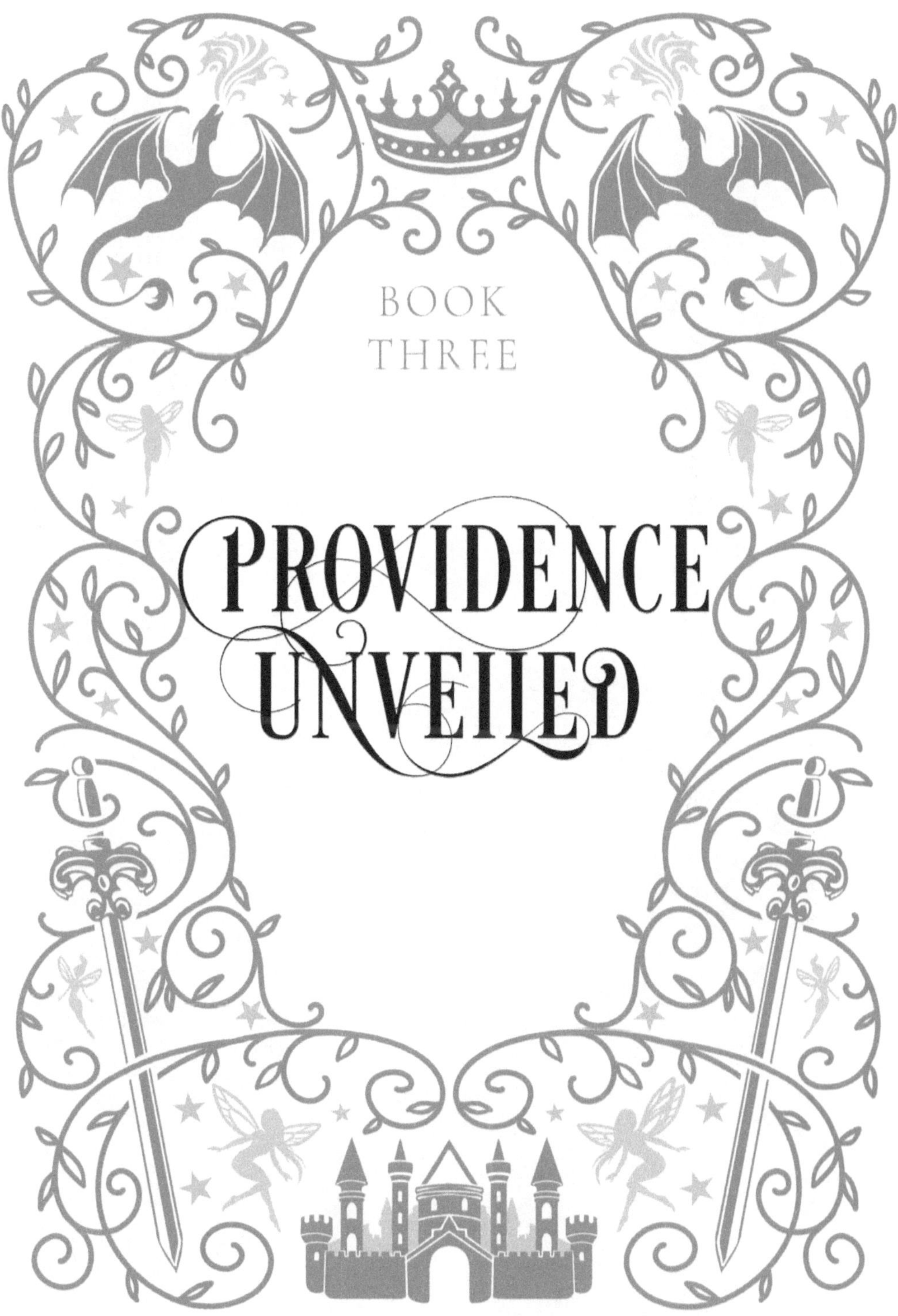

BOOK
THREE
PROVIDENCE
UNVEILED

Human World
Avall
Faerman Ogh

CHAPTER ONE

Memory laughed a strong, high-pitched laugh that made her sides ache. The surrounding cloud of dust was chalky on her tongue and the last small pieces of falling tiles and roof shingles clattered onto the debris that surrounded her and her friends. Eloryn, Roen, and Clara sat sprawled where they had tumbled out of the tower that had collapsed around them. Will was right beside Memory, close enough for her to feel his warmth and hear him still panting from their wild escape. They were all powdered with dirt, but safe and mostly uninjured. Memory was sure one of her fingers was broken. Everything was such a blur, she wasn't sure if it happened during the tower collapse, or earlier when she and Will hit the mattresses after their fall. But she was grateful for it. Grateful that was all they'd suffered, and that she was still alive. Will held her other hand.

Memory couldn't stop laughing.

Eloryn sighed. "It's not a joke. You are now the Queen of Avall."

Memory paused long enough to take a breath. "That's even funnier," she wheezed, and started laughing again. "I thought I was the crazy, irresponsible one, and then you go and make me queen!"

Memory wiped tears from her bottom eyelids and tried to breathe between her giggling. It didn't help. Trying to stop only made it worse and her whole body shook with uncontained laughter.

Roen grinned roguishly. "I have to admit, it is rather funny."

A chuckle burst from Eloryn as though she had been holding it in and was no longer able to contain it.

Small at first, her laughter built until it matched Memory's. She moved forward and wrapped her sister in a tight hug. Memory put one arm around her, the other hand still entwined with Will's.

They laughed together there in each other's arms, and Memory whispered, "What the hell happened? I'm really queen? What am I going to do?"

Eloryn whispered back, "You'll manage. You'll be great. I know you can do this."

"I'll try."

"I'll be there for you. Anything you need, anything I can do. You're my sister, and I love you."

Memory pressed her face into her twin's shoulder. "Can you fix my busted finger?"

"Of course." Eloryn tightened her hug. "I like your new hair color."

"Want me to do yours? You'd rock a fading pink."

Eloryn kissed Memory on the cheek. "Don't ever leave me."

They separated and stood up, smiling at each other. Will, Roen and Clara also stood by Memory, holding her hands and her shoulders, supporting her.

My family.

Memory still felt shaky and overwhelmed. In the last fifteen minutes of her life she'd tried to kill herself, had someone else try to kill her friends, then had everyone almost all die again from the fall of the destroyed tower. Her emotions were so high strung and confused she could barely think. She drew deep breaths, letting herself accept the support of her friends, accept that they were there for her now, and for whatever lay ahead.

I will manage. I will be great. For them.

Shocked servants and guards appeared at the end of the hall, gawking at the destruction. The entire north wing tower was now a pile of rubble, and the wall it had been attached to was all but gone, opening the corridor to the cold winds of night outside.

Memory felt guilty for having a part in knocking down one of the palace's towers. Not a great move for her first day as queen.

Acknowledging the arriving servants, Clara said, "I'll inform the staff to begin organizing the cleanup and bring help."

"Thank you. I think we're all okay though. Just make sure no one was injured outside," Memory said.

Clara nodded and took a step away, then with a puppy dog expression, turned back and gave Memory a firm hug. Then she hurried down the hall to speak with the other staff.

Roen moved in next and held Memory.

Memory giggled at the tag team. "I'm okay, really. Only current risk is being cuddled to death."

Roen let go and looked insulted. "Do I need a near death experience to embrace you now? Being queen is already going to your head."

Memory laughed again, then stopped abruptly. "Hang on. I'm the queen. That means Hope got what she–"

Swirling winds and gray smoke filled the room, interrupting Memory. Sparks of gold swam within the Veil mist like fireflies as it opened up in a round portal. The sound of distant rain dripping on bells came with a flood of warmth, and a crowd stood before them.

A crowd of fae royalty. The Seelie Queen, Aine, and her human consort Lugh were flanked by a dozen fairy knights. Each guard wore armor of woven silver with embedded mother of pearl and held a fairy gold spear twice his or her height. Behind the unearthly beauty of the queen and her companion, stood a group of sprites, including Mina, and Yvainne, the princess of the sprites with whom Eloryn had once made a bargain. Standing all together, the sheer beauty of them made tears well up in Memory's eyes. Pearlescent skin was contrasted with tangles of silky hair and the pretty tatters of their cobweb and feather dresses. Aine's dress was more whole, full of draping translucent folds that teased at the shape of her body, leading a viewer's eyes up to her face. Her long auburn hair that Memory had once seen trail on the ground behind her was bundled into a tall and intricately woven mass atop her head, stuck through with glass flowers and silver twigs. Her skin had a warm shimmer, like diamonds drenched in honey, but her expression was far from warm.

Aine's gaze swept across the rubble and settled on Memory's face. Her lips were stretched thin and eyebrows lowered. "So, the fickle humans have changed their ruler yet again."

Memory looked to Eloryn, who gave her an encouraging nod in return.

Memory lifted her chin. *Time to start being queen.* She curtseyed to Aine. "I only just found out myself. News travels fast."

"We have watchers for anything we consider important, or dangerous."

Yvainne and Mina stood proudly behind their queen. *They've still been keeping tabs on me after all.* Memory wondered just how much she'd been watched, and what they might know. Mina stared Memory down with her usual glare. With the malicious creature Hope now confirmed as being a fae, standing in front of this group of them made Memory's paranoia tie itself in anxious knots. *Hope could be Mina, or Yvainne, or Aine. Any of them.*

Memory calmed the shiver chasing up her spine and curtseyed a second time for good measure, then pointed with her thumb at the ruined building around them. "Your Majesty, you can probably see that this isn't the best time for a chat. Can we do the ruler meet and greet a bit later on if there's no urgent issue?"

Aine's eyes narrowed. "We take issue with you."

Mist from the torn Veil spilled into the corridor again, and a second group emerged from it. A raspy male voice hissed, "As do we."

The Unseelie King, Finvarra, and his daughter Nyneve became clear as the smoke faded, their own darkly armored guards following.

Memory noticed down the hallway a troop of palace guards led by Peirs rushing to the scene, and held up a hand to halt them. She turned back to the newly arrived fae royalty with what she hoped was a brave face.

Nyneve wore her usual shades of mourning, her hair even blacker, impossibly black, not a highlight showing in the nebulous masses swirling around her silver skin. Her father's gnarled body was clothed in a maroon color darker than night. Between them they presented a front of imposing darkness. Nyneve stood a step behind her father, head bowed slightly, as the black eyed king growled at Aine like a feral dog. "Trying to slip in and make decisions without us? We must have our say as well."

Memory cleared her throat. "Inside voices, please. I'd already noticed that the fae aren't very keen on me. You guys have always known I'm full up on magic. What's changed?"

Aine said, "Now you are monarch of the humans. We can't allow such power to be in the hands of a ruler. There must be restrictions."

Restrictions? Memory shook her head. "You let Thayl go about his business."

"You compare a candle to a forest fire," Aine said.

Finvarra's needle-like teeth ground against each other, scraping like chalk on a blackboard. "She's unnatural, stealing away the life of the earth, hoarding it within her. Restrictions aren't enough. She should not

be allowed to be queen. She should not be allowed to exist."

By her side, Will took a step forward, and Memory matched him, blocking his way. She said, "*She* is right here and doesn't appreciate threats to her existence. I am queen and you should treat me with some respect."

Nyneve raised a silver hand and put it on her father's shoulder. It seemed to calm him and he muttered what might have been an apology.

"Whatever magic is inside me, it's not there by my choice." Memory knew it had been given to her by Providence, whom she was sure was a fae. But now didn't seem the best time to be making wild accusations. There were still too many questions. *If I'm going to be queen, I need to be smarter, better. I need some answers first.* "There's not much I can do about it. It's in me now, part of me, for better or worse."

Aine tilted her head in a supplicating motion, but the slight sneer on her lips made the motion a lie. "We ask that you give an oath never to use your stolen magic again. For the safety of our worlds."

Eloryn spoke up. "Is that really necessary? Never before has a human ruler had such a restriction placed on them."

Nyneve added her voice, deep and concerned. "It does seem a great imposition."

"Never before has there been a human like her. We won't accept her as queen without it," Aine said. "Agreed, Winter King?"

Finvarra grumbled. Memory could see Nyneve's hand squeeze his shoulder.

"Father, no," she whispered.

Finvarra shook her hand from him. "No? It is barely enough as it is. It is agreed, this girl should use none of her stolen power."

Never use magic again? Memory wondered if that was even possible. One emotional slip up could change everything. She was more in control now but the risk was there. It would also mean she'd be stuck with purple hair for good, unless Eloryn could behest hair color as well. She whispered to Eloryn beside her, "Out of curiosity, what's the penalty for breaking a fairy oath?"

Eloryn replied in hushed tones, "Tantamount to a violation of the Pact, punishable by Branding and death."

"Serious like a pinky promise. Gotcha."

Memory addressed Aine and Finvarra again. "What if I don't agree? What if I think you should trust me to rule fairly despite the magic inside me?"

"Just as we trusted your double to rule?" Aine walked up to Eloryn

and stared down at her from at least three feet taller. "Maellan girl, we requested that you be the human ruler. We wanted you, not your volatile sister. You made an oath to rule with the sprite princess, Yvainne. You may not have technically broken your oath, as you did rule - briefly, barely - but we will be less inclined to trust you or your twin to persevere in her promises now."

Eloryn looked at her feet. "I'm sorry, Your Majesty. I did not intend to dishonor my oath."

"And yet you did, the moment ruling became difficult for you."

Something changed in Eloryn's expression. "Had I not ended my rule then, you may have found a new human ruler that would please you far less than my sister."

Aine turned her back and walked away, striding around the room. "You mortal creatures with your in-fighting displease us. We want stability for Avall, for all our peoples."

Finvarra spat into the debris. "Don't pretend you have a care for our kind. You prefer the human vermin over the unseelie fae, when we are your other halves, the dark to your light. We are your balance. You don't care that they treat us as monsters. You would not care if we were hunted clean from the world, when it is those parasites that should be removed!" He clawed a hand through the air toward Memory and her friends.

Aine rolled her eyes at his dramatics and addressed Memory. "Agreeing to the oath offers us some stability. A show of faith to allow our peoples to work together. Denying it can only lead to chaos for all."

Finvarra grinned and his all black eyes twinkled. "We welcome chaos. We are born of chaos."

"All right, enough! I'll make your oath," Memory said. "I agree. It *is* time for the fighting to stop. Between all of us."

"Mem, are you sure?" Eloryn said.

Memory looked to her friends, and found them all staring back at her. She nodded to Roen and Will. "It's not so bad. Some of the best people I know don't use magic."

Aine smiled and the simple expression seemed to light her from inside. "Then we make the oath. You shall not use the magic within you again from this moment forth."

"Not quite. I don't always have complete control over all this," Memory said, swirling a pointing finger at her chest. "I can't be held accountable if a bit spills out here or there against my will. But I do

swear I will not knowingly cast any behests with my magic."

Aine paused, assessing her, and then placed a hand over Memory's heart. "Agreed. This is our binding deal."

All the fae around her chanted, "The deal is binding."

Finvarra's ragged lips curled around his teeth. "And when you break this deal, I will relish enforcing the penalty."

Aine stared him down. "You will take no action. My hand bound the deal, my hand will enforce the penalty when the deal is broken."

"Guys. It's *if. If* the deal is broken. A little confidence, please." Memory tried not to feel shaken. She had as little confidence in her ability to keep the oath as they did. *Girls with impulse control issues shouldn't be agreeing to binding oaths.*

Aine simply nodded, and the creeping mist in the corridor began to build again. Mina, who had been giving Memory all kinds of filthy looks, turned to Will and flicked her chin up. Will looked toward Memory, unsure.

When Will didn't leave Memory's side, Mina stamped a foot on the ground. "Here, boy. Now."

Aine and Lugh, Finvarra and Nyneve, and the host of seelie and unseelie guards all turned their attention to Will, and Memory could see a defiant look in his eyes. He took a step forward and something tugged Memory's arm.

Will's hand was still around hers. It had never left it, not since they'd escaped the tower, as though they'd been fused together. He turned back to look at her, frowning deeply.

"It's okay. Go. You know where to find me," she said, offering him a supportive smile. Memory didn't like the idea of Will going anywhere with Mina. She didn't like the idea of letting go of his hand. But she could tell he needed to go. No matter how Memory felt about Mina, it was clear Will didn't want to make a scene in front of fairy royalty.

Will's hand slipped slowly from hers, fingertips trailing along her palm. Memory put her hand into her other one, so it didn't feel so empty.

Will stood beside Mina, and the seelie fae faded into the Veil, taking him with them. Finvarra turned his back on Memory and was simply gone. Nyneve gave Memory a sympathetic nod before following her father.

Memory waved goodbye to the empty space. "Good talk. No, no, thank *you*."

Eloryn and Roen remained with her.

Memory smiled at them wryly. "Onwards to our next crisis?"

CHAPTER TWO

"You did? And then he did that? Really? Wow. Just, wow."

Eloryn filled Memory in about the reason for her abdication while they rushed back toward the Round Room. She covered the horrible things Hayes had done, and saw something dark cross Memory's features when she explained it was Hayes who set off the bomb that killed Waylan, and sent the bounty hunters after Roen, all as part of his long campaign of manipulation.

"Hayes is all locked up, right? Lucky bastard. He'll be safer there." Memory scowled.

The forced marriage, and Eloryn's contract to ruin Hayes's plans came next. "Abdicating was the best solution I could see. It passed power to you, including power over Hayes's militia thanks to the pre-nuptial contract, and stripped all power and options from him."

Eloryn glanced at Roen, walking on the other side of Memory. She wanted to reach out and touch him. She knew, regardless of Hayes, she would have given up her throne for Roen. Her heart was not in ruling. Her heart was his. Her lips still tingled from their kiss. It felt like weeks ago, but her confrontation with Hayes had happened barely half an hour before. They were already encountering the aftermath of her abdication as they walked. Pages and guards ran about, spreading the news, dealing with the changes to rulership in the palace. Between

that and the collapsed tower, the castle was a chaotic hum of activity.

"Hayes really was one skeezy bastard." Memory put a hand on Eloryn's shoulder. "Can I get away with an I Told You So? Just a teeny one?"

"I think you could get away with a quite large one," Eloryn said.

Memory grinned. "Nah, I'll skip it. Sounds like you kicked his ass. I wish I'd been there to see it. And join in the kicking of said ass."

The Round Room came within sight, and was still filled with the remaining Wizards' Council, milling about, shouting at each other and arguing.

Memory slowed her pace. "We can't let them know I'm not allowed to use magic anymore. We can't let anyone know. It could be exploited too easily."

Roen nodded. "It's a secret worth keeping."

"Have your parents left yet? Can you go and check? Bring them back if you have to. And can you send after Erec and Peirs, too?" Memory asked him.

"Of course," Roen said. His gaze turned to meet Eloryn's and his lips curled into a tiny smile. She blushed, remembering what the curves of those lips felt like pressed against hers. With a nod, he hurried off back the way they'd come.

Memory stared at Eloryn with a toothy grin.

"What? Stop that. You're being dreadfully creepy," Eloryn said.

Memory tilted her head down, making her grin even more lecherous. "You and Roen, huh?"

"Me and Roen?" The innocent tone Eloryn aimed for was spoiled by a catch in her voice.

"She plays it coy! There's no fooling me, I saw you guys all smoochy before. It's about bloody time. I'm so happy for you both." Memory grabbed Eloryn in a quick hug.

Eloryn let out a deep breath and closed her eyes. Part of her had been worried about what Memory would think and feel about her relationship with Roen, that it would somehow hurt Memory. But her sister seemed truly happy, and that filled Eloryn with warmth.

Memory pulled back and looked down the hall at the room of squabbling old men. "Okay, it's wizard wrangling time."

Memory continued into the Round Room and Eloryn walked at her side. Returning to face these men felt surreal after she'd just abandoned her title and destroyed the plans and credibility of their leader in front

of them all. But she had to be there for Memory.

The two of them made their entrance.

Their arrival was barely noticed by the wizards. Their discussions were heated, and the small statures of the twins were lost in the room full of men.

"Shame I don't have a cattle prod on me. Could be handy right now," Memory muttered. She took Eloryn's hand for balance then climbed up onto a chair then up again onto the long table in the center of the room. She put her finger and thumb between her lips and let loose a piercing whistle. The Council silenced and all attention turned to her, skepticism clear on all faces.

"My sister tells me she's abdicated," Memory said. Her voice started out rocky, but grew in strength as she continued. "And now I have to stand in front of all of you and make you somehow believe in me as a leader. That's going to be hard, because I don't even believe in myself as a leader. And from what I've heard of Hayes's actions, I imagine you'll be struggling to have faith in any leader right now."

A grumble of agreement came from a few of the gray-haired men.

"But someone needs to rule this land and make things right. We owe it to the people to get our acts together and stop seeking revenge or grabbing for power or generally squabbling like idiots. I'm just a kid; I haven't been trained for this, not enough. One day I hope I can be the ruler Avall deserves, but right now I need all of you to step up. I need you all to do your job, and I want to be able to trust you to do it. But I'm not going to trust you blindly. I will be watching you all closely and if you intend to betray my trust, remember this- were you scared of Thayl? Well, he stole his magic from me, and only ever had a fraction of my power. Be scared of *me*."

Silence filled the room as Memory let those words sink in. "And if that's not enough, I think you also know what my sister is capable of. What do you all say? Are you ready to work together, work with me, to start making things right?"

Eloryn smiled up at her sister, filled with pride. Memory spoke forcefully, passionately, and without pretense. Memory was everything she was not when it came to ruling. *I made the right decision.*

"What are we to do?" Bors asked, more to the men around him than to Memory. He still seemed panicked by nearly meeting death at Hayes's behest. "Hayes went too far, too far, but he was our leader."

"We did not always have a leader." Madoc, the oldest of the Council, pushed his way to the front. His raspy voice made the white whiskers around his mouth quiver. "The Council is meant to be a body of equals. It was only during Thayl's rule that Hayes took control of us. We don't need a leader."

"You have to admit, having someone with overriding authority did expedite many decisions," a wizard behind Eloryn said.

She turned to face the crowd. "And where did that blind faith in him lead us? He even killed one of your own for challenging his authority."

Memory addressed the group again from her position on the table. "Whether or not you want a leader for the Council, and who that leader is, can be something you decide for yourselves. But for now, Bedevere will be the point of contact between me and the Council."

Bedevere, who had remained quiet through the bickering, nodded solemnly to Memory. The rest of the Council exploded again into turmoil. "Him? With his foolish notions of the other world and its artefacts?"

Memory's mouth set firmly and she raised her voice. "I've got my memories back now and can tell you his *notions* of the other world are correct. It did not become Hell."

Her statement only fueled the voices in the room, and wizards argued, demanding more information, or disputing her claims.

"All you know how to do is argue!" Memory grunted. "You've all been hidden away from the world too long. Consider this my first order for you all. It's time you did some real work in the real world." Memory waved her arms, pointing out wizards and sectioning off groups. "I need men to head to the city, to reopen my shelter and fix any damage Hayes's militia might have done. The militia itself needs bringing under control and there's also the matter of clearing up a tower that collapsed in the Northern wing. There is work to be done now. Prove yourselves as the great wizards I know you must be."

The crowd grew quiet. Madoc moved to the front, bowed to Memory and said, "Yes, Your Majesty."

By his side, Lambeth and Bors did the same. Soon the whole Council followed, bowing, then leaving to carry out their assigned tasks. Bedevere stepped in front of Memory and bowed low for a long moment.

"Bedevere, stay with me, please. We've got more to do," she said.

Eloryn reached up for her sister's hand and helped her down from the table. Memory's hand shook violently between Eloryn's fingers.

Memory's bottom lip pulled to the side and her eyebrows wrinkled. "Did I do okay?"

"Better than okay," Eloryn said.

"Ugh, that was hard! I put on my best grown up voice but felt like I just sounded ridonkadonk. They're going to think I'm an idiot."

Ridonkadonk? Eloryn smiled inwardly. Her sister often surprised her with strange new words. Eloryn saw the uncertainty in her sister, but only grew more confident that Memory was the natural ruler she never was. "The message will come through regardless of the words you use. Just be yourself, be sincere and open, as you always are, and people will respect you."

Memory seemed about to say something more, but was interrupted by Isabeth.

"Oh my dears, my dears!" she cried, as she rushed toward Memory and Eloryn with her arms outstretched. She gathered them both into an embrace, then looked over their damaged and dusty appearance with a scolding gaze. "Can't leave you two alone for a moment, can we?"

Roen and his father followed her in. Roen seemed out of breath and a flush of red highlighted his cheekbones that made him all the more beautiful. He smiled. "Duke and Duchess Faerbaird, as requested."

As Memory greeted them properly, Eloryn stepped across to Roen and took his hand. He gave her a small questioning look, and she smiled back in return.

It only took a moment before Isabeth, and then Brannon, noticed the pair. Isabeth put both hands to her mouth as though she were about to cry, then grabbed her son and Eloryn into her arms.

Memory sighed and put her fists on her hips. "Here I am, queen now, and look at my sister still hogging all the attention."

CHAPTER THREE

Memory stared at the group before her. People she trusted. Memory and Eloryn caught everyone up on what had happened with Hayes while they waited for Erec and Peirs to arrive, and for Bedevere to create a Veil door to bring Lanval in. Memory already regretted giving up her magic. The traditional Veil door behest was pages long, and Bedevere's droning of the words quickly became tedious when Memory knew how fast she could open one.

She turned her back on his progress so she could address the others. They had seated themselves along the temporary table in the Round Room and all faced her where she stood. She cleared her throat. "The very first thing we need to do is establish some proper leadership in Avall, the government Hayes neglected to set up. I know I'm queen and Maellan blood and whatever, but I'm only seventeen for chrissakes. It's time for some adults to be doing the adult things. But how am I supposed to choose who makes up that government? Who do I trust? As Lory pointed out, I don't know one Avall noble from another. But you do," Memory said, acknowledging Isabeth and Brannon. "Between you and Lanval, you know the bloodlines, the individuals, the who, what and where. I trust you to make the right decisions. Bedevere will have the Council start Veil-dooring people in ASAP, nobles from each region, heck, even non-nobles as far as I'm concerned as long as they

can do the job. I'm so sorry to hold you back from returning to your home, but could you do this for me?"

Isabeth looked to her husband. "We will do our best, although you know we've been removed from politics for many years. Still, in just the short time we've returned to court, it has been very easy to judge the character of those around us based on how they treat our return. Lanval has been well connected both within Thayl's circles and without, and will be valuable indeed in making these decisions. You are right to ask for him."

Memory nodded firmly and smiled at Erec and Peirs who waited at the entrance. She waved them in.

Peirs had a sly half grin on his face, stretching the sandy freckled skin, as he kneeled in front of Memory. "Your Majesty. The position suits you well. As does the new hair color."

"Quit it." Memory swung a foot playfully at him. "Can I make a no kneeling rule?"

Peirs remained kneeling and became solemn. "You are worth kneeling for even if it means breaking the rules. You will be a fine queen."

A swell of pride and worry clogged Memory's throat. She had so much to live up to. "Just a title so far. Speaking of titles, I want you back as captain of the guard. I need you, Erec, and the people you trust out there removing Hayes's loyalists from positions of power in the military. Right away, please. We need everyone to know things have changed before any more damage is done."

Peirs stood and he and his brother bowed and turned to leave. Memory grabbed him by the arm. "Any news of Maeve and the kids? How are they doing?"

Peirs shook his head. "I lost contact with them when they were found by the militia and forced to move again."

Memory frowned, but patted Peirs on the shoulder and let him leave. She turned back to the others. Beside her on the table was a small tray of her favorite foods. Memory knew they were from Clara, but hadn't even noticed her come in and leave them there. Her stomach grumbled. She smiled inside at how Clara mothered her and predicted her needs. Bedevere continued to read his behest and Isabeth and Brannon were already writing notes on who they wanted to see as candidates for the government.

Eloryn had a pained look on her face. "There's one more thing we will be required to do."

"What?" Memory asked. Her brain was starting to get fuzzy. She was too tired and had already put so much effort into trying to do things right and get everything under control. What had she missed?

"There will need to be a public announcement about the change in rule."

Memory winced. "But do we really have to? There's enough confusion and disrespect going around because of our age and how we came back, and now we go and play swapsies for who is queen. Can't we just, you know?" Memory mimed picking up a mat and sweeping under it. "I'll just pretend like I'm you and nothing has changed. No one will have to know, right?"

Eloryn fought a smile. "I somehow think people would notice, even if we change your hair again. There will be no harm from this announcement. The people of Avall love you. You are their hero. When they think of me, they think only of my connection to Hayes and everything he did. When they think of you they think of the person who defeated Thayl, who has shown such courage, compassion and ingenuity in helping the homeless and fighting for equality."

Memory groaned. "Fine. Okay. I'll make an announcement. Just enough with the compliments. And I'm not all that popular. I haven't been making any friends amongst the noble crowd with my efforts."

Roen leaned back in his chair and shrugged. "Some of your efforts challenge their traditions. But a tradition is only that until you don't do it anymore. People will learn, and grow, and it will be for the better."

The full impact of being who she was started settling on Memory. She had that power now, to make great changes to this world. She desperately wanted to use that power well, and realized how many plans and dreams she had to improve the land for the people she now ruled. A smile spread slowly on her lips. "Maybe it is time to break some traditions."

A faint glow of morning light had begun to show through the glass ceiling of the Round Room by the time Memory had reestablished enough stability to leave affairs in her advisors' hands.

Eloryn and Roen walked Memory back to her room, arms linked and shuffling along together. Clara had returned as well. Memory wasn't sure when. She blinked often, trying to keep her eyes open. Exhaustion had set in, aching in her temples and burning her muscles where adrenaline had been keeping her going since the tower collapse. Since she'd tried to take her own life. It all seemed like a distant dream.

Memory wanted to go to the Ivy Room, or what was left of it, to try and find Will, to see if he'd come back yet.

When she explained where she wanted to go, Eloryn just shook her head.

"He will come to you when he can," she said.

Will he? Memory still wasn't sure what their relationship was, or of how Will felt about her. He'd said he loved her, loved her so much he chased her off a balcony. *How could he? How could anyone love me that much?* Doubt settled like an uneasy sickness in her, its voice sounding like the voice of Hope. Not just the dark manipulations of the creature that had pretended to be her, but the voice of her past self, a self that was now part of her again. With her memories returned, Memory knew she used to be the kind of person who had no love for herself, and no concept that anyone could love her. Even she could see how much she had changed since coming to Avall, but the old, painful feelings remained. She was too tired then to process the discord of her past memories conflicting with her new identity. It wasn't long ago that her affection for herself was so low she'd almost ended her life, but the spark of life remained, and she could feel it now wanting to grow. She didn't want to doubt any more that anyone could love her. She wanted to allow herself to be loved and accept that she could be loved.

Memory's heart rushed and she bit her lip hard at the thought that overwhelmed her. *I don't just want anyone to love me. I want Will to love me.*

Eloryn and Roen had escorted Memory all the way to her bedroom before she blinked her vision clear again and saw where she was. Clara turned the bed down for her, fluffing the pillows more than a few times each as though she'd become stuck in some sort of loop.

Memory shook her head and her vision and speech blurred. "Can't sleep yet. Still have talking about to do, about Provi-Hope."

Roen locked Memory's bedroom bi-fold doors into their fully open position. Yawning, he undid his top shirt button and slumped down into an armchair in the adjoining sitting room. "You can't even talk straight anymore. You need to rest. Don't you think we've done enough for one day?"

Eloryn picked up a purple velvet cushion from the lounge and curled up in an armchair beside Roen's, cuddling the cushion under her chin like a teddy bear. "We'll be right here."

Memory was about to tell them to go back to their rooms and sleep themselves, but knew exactly why her friends were here, and why they weren't giving her any privacy.

I tried to kill myself. The thought now felt surreal to Memory. She ached when wondering how it made her friends feel, to have almost lost her that way.

She smiled at how protective they were. If they weren't a reason to keep living, she didn't know what was. So many of the negative thoughts she'd been having had been whispered to her by Hope, and now she knew that Hope was just an imposter, everything seemed different, and better. Sunrise had broken fully and the new day looked glorious through Memory's bedroom window. She kept smiling as her head hit the pillow and she instantly passed out.

When her eyelids rolled open again it was still daylight. Memory felt disoriented, with no idea how much time had passed. She was groggy, and so hungry it could have been a week later. At the end of her bed, Will sat cross-legged, staring through the diamond glass of the closed balcony windows.

He came back. Memory's heart back-flipped.

Will had found a shirt somewhere, warm grey with a wide poet's collar, but his feet were still bare. Memory moved to sit up and he turned to her. His eyebrows were low over his light blue eyes, his dark hair a wild mess the way she liked it.

He put a finger to his lips. Memory looked behind him. The doors between her bedroom and sitting room were still open, and she saw Roen and Eloryn, heads bowed, both fast asleep in their chairs.

"As much as I feel like I did, I'm guessing I haven't slept for a century. What time is it? What day is it?" Memory whispered. She sat up on her pillow, leaning against the headboard while she stretched her arms up and arched her back.

"Afternoon. Same day." Will's voice was also hushed. Even in a murmur it was a beautiful voice, always deep and strong, reminding Memory of how he used to sing when he was a boy. With all her past returned to her, the man that sat in front of her was now also so much the boy she used to know. Always ready to hide his fear to show off for her, take up her dares and challenges, and get into trouble with her.

She'd been unkind to him back then, in the way a big sister would be to a weakly younger brother. The way he used to look up to her, idolize her, made Memory blush now. She felt their roles had been reversed. Will was her constant point of reference, always patient and loyal. She wanted to be like him; be with him.

Will shifted uncomfortably and Memory realized she'd been staring at him for way too long.

"I'm sorry I left with Mina," he said.

"I'm sorry I tried to kill myself. Boom. I win the Sorry Game."

Will's smile was more of a frown.

"Too soon? Yeah, you're right. Sorry… and that's a Sorry Game DOUBLE VICTORY!" Memory whispered a crackling sound like applauding crowds.

Will gave her a patient look.

Memory gave him a cheesy grin in return. "Fine. Moving right along. What happened with Mina? I wasn't a big fan of her jealous girlfae act," Memory said.

"It's not as simple as that."

Swallowing away her embarrassment, Memory asked, "Do you… love her?"

Will remained quiet for some time, too long for the answer to be a clear no. "She saved my life, just like you did. But Mina doesn't do things selflessly."

Memory remembered the time he meant about her, when she'd saved him from a bad fight with some bullies. "I didn't really save your life, you know. I probably just saved a few baby teeth."

Will shrugged. "Either way, from then on, I was yours."

Memory blushed so hard all over she felt ready to self-combust. The recollection of that day was so clear to Memory now. She hadn't thought anything of the kid back then. Being honest with herself, she wasn't sure if she'd stepped in to help Will or just because she wanted to get into a fight. When she'd chased the bullies off, young Will had looked up at her with those startling blue eyes, wide and grateful, like she was a hero. He really did think she'd saved his life, and even at that age he had these romantic and childish notions of repaying that debt. He became her shadow. He had been hers, from that moment on.

Memory looked at Will now, grown and having lived and suffered through so much. She didn't know how she could ever repay Will, or live up to that. Maybe the only way was to become the hero he saw in her.

"Do you remember when Mr. Hindmarsh came out and found us together after the fight, after the others had run off?" Memory had a chuckle in her voice as she spoke. "He totally thought I was the one that whaled on you. When you denied it, he thought you were just embarrassed about getting thrashed by a girl."

Will smiled and dropped his head bashfully. "You saved me, and got detention for it." Looking up at her, his eyes searched her face. "You really have it back? All your memories?"

Memory tapped the side of her head. "Every last one. It's massively screwed up. It's not like just remembering a life normally. It's like I just watched my whole life again on fast forward. I can even remember being a baby in hospital, recovering from the cut on my chest from the ritual. So vividly. I can remember… All sorts of things." Memory put a hand to her chest, running her thumb over the ugly bumps of the old scar. "But I'm whole now. I feel like all of me again, the good and the bad. The only thing I need to do now is keep adding good into my life to balance the contents out a bit."

"I hope I can help add to the good," Will said.

"You already have."

The way Will smiled then filled Memory with happiness even more.

The entrance door opened and Clara walked in, balancing a silver tray full of food.

Clara placed the tray down on a table in the living room, and the sound of jostling plates piled in hamburgers woke Roen and Eloryn. Memory didn't ever remember discussing breakfast burgers with the chef, but there they were, neat little buns with bacon and eggs and a thick, chunky ketchup. She wondered whether it was the chef or Clara who'd been experimenting. Memory's hunger returned and she smiled at Clara gratefully.

Memory threw her legs out of bed, and caught a foot on the covers as she tried to stand up. Before she could wobble or fall, Will caught her wrist to balance her.

He let go quickly. "Sorry."

Memory reached out and squeezed his hand. "It's okay. Don't worry, it's all about breaking rules these days. Those rules were Hope's rules, anyway. Consider them gone."

Taking quick stock of her appearance, Memory realized she was still

in her old broken heart t-shirt and long skirt she'd changed into the day before. It felt like so long ago. She knew she probably stank, and was still covered in any dust that didn't rub off in bed, but she needed to talk things out with her friends and didn't want to take time out for a bath first. She also wanted to eat. Now.

She wandered into the living room. "Thanks for reading my mind, Clara."

"Well, I know it's well into the afternoon, but I thought you would all be in need of some comforting breakfast foods," Clara said, with a neat curtsey. She'd been somewhat more proper and formal since their ordeal, and Memory worried she'd offended her somehow. "I've also seen to re-assigning the queen's guard from Eloryn to yourself. Erec and his finest men are already outside."

Memory groaned and rolled her eyes in a wide dramatic loop. "You of all people should know I don't want guards trailing around behind me all the time."

Clara raised her chin, looking more at the ceiling than at Memory. "You will simply have to tolerate it as best you can, Majesty. Who knows what threats there are to you out there? Dylan is still unaccounted for. That Hope creature is who knows what or where. We can't have you wandering around unprotected. We can't have you—"

Clara's voice broke, and she turned away, but not fast enough to hide the tear on her cheek.

Memory dashed across the room and drew Clara into a tight hug. "I'm so sorry. You're right. I'll keep the guard. I won't let anything happen to me, okay?"

Clara sniffled. "You'd better not."

Roen stood up and stretched. "Indeed. I, for one, expect a written apology, and perhaps some form of ritualistic dance of penance."

Eloryn smirked at him from her chair then addressed Memory seriously. "You did give us all a fright. We only want for you to be happy and well. And to know you can talk to us, if you need to, about anything."

Memory tried to think of something absurd to talk to Eloryn about then and there, but knew it wasn't the time to be flippant. She paused a moment, gathering together how she really felt, right then in time, how she felt about what she'd almost done, and how she felt about the future.

"There's still a lot of pain inside me," she said. "Enough that I know it's going at be hard at times to keep going. But I'm not planning

on doing anything rash. I know now that I'm whole. I'm not missing my memories. I'm not missing any part of my soul. This is me. It's all I have to work with and for the first time in my life I want to work. I have so much in my life now to be grateful for. When I first got my old life back, I forgot all the good in my new life. It's my turn now to work hard and be better."

Memory looked around at all her friends. The pride she saw so clearly from them was everything she needed to stay strong. "So, let's eat already!"

Memory picked up a burger and handed it to Will before taking one for herself. She took a seat on the floor between Eloryn and Roen's armchairs. Clara began tidying the room, which was still in disarray after the fight between Will and Dylan, and Memory's magical tremors. Memory scolded Clara until she came and joined the picnic on the floor. They each chewed their food silently for a while, until a thought that had been plaguing Memory had to be voiced.

"Lory, is the Maellan family cursed at all? Have there ever been any mentions of a curse?" she asked.

"Not that I've heard of or read in my studies. Why?"

"It's just that I've seen our family tree, and it seems to me that all Maellan die young. A lot of them before they even have children, which is why we're pretty much the last of them, right? I mean, isn't that a bit weird?"

"It's true. I know some of the deaths have seemed suspicious, but there's never been evidence to prove more than simple ill-fate, I'm afraid. It's been that way since Arthur's time, maybe even before, but since Arthur was a commoner there is no record of our family tree before him."

"But what if there was something, or someone, out there, taking out some wicked huge grudge on all Maellan?"

"Only a fae could live long enough to be the sole cause. Which I admit isn't unlikely. There were many fae who were in opposition to the Pact, especially in opposition to Arthur when he pushed to include Branding into the agreement."

Memory nodded, her theories confirmed. "Providence. Providence was a fae, and I also think Providence was Hope. It was like everything she told me, everything she encouraged me to do was to punish me. She told me to be with Roen, which almost ruined our friendships. It was like she knew Dylan was using me and encouraged it to happen. She told me all the time that everyone hated me, and did everything

she could to prove it."

Eloryn reached out for Memory's hand. "She was just trying to separate us, drive you against us so you had nothing left but her."

Memory took her twin's hand. "I think it was more than that. She wanted things from me, wanted me to do things, horrible things. She…" Memory winced at her sister, but it had to be said. Everyone had to know the full story. "She wanted me to kill you so I could become queen."

"Queen, like you are now?" Roen asked. "Is that going to be a problem?"

"I don't know. Maybe she just wanted to screw with my life as much as possible. Maybe she's been doing it to all Maellan all this time."

"Providence's magic, and Hope's magic, is a very old form of magic," Eloryn said. "All fae have natural traits that seem like magic- their glamour, strength, and travelling through the Veil. But they don't have behests like humans do. Only a few fae have learned human magic. Nyneve is most famous for it, having learned the runes from Myrddin, who was her lover. But she's gone on to teach other unseelie fae."

"Like her father? If anyone was capable of this kind of cruelty, I'd put money on him. He's got them crazy eyes." Memory wriggled her eyebrows and jiggled her eyelids. "Nyneve has always seemed pretty tame to me. A bit emo, but I can't exactly talk."

"Working out what Providence wanted is the key." Roen finished his burger and leaned forward in his chair. "She may have used Maellan blood in her rituals, but it was Thayl she wanted something from."

Memory shook her head. "Yes and no. Whatever she wanted from Thayl, she wanted it bad. Their deal was that she would help him kill all the Wizards' Council, and then he would somehow repay his debt to her. But he never got his side of the bargain while there were members of the Council still alive, so she never got what she wanted in return. I think she was still trying to help him get rid of the last of the wizards. Remember those banshees in the wagon? They said they were hunting for wizards for their master, and the Council said that other unseelie fae were also hunting for them."

Memory stared down at the woven rug she sat on, seeing a small spray of blood there from Will and Dylan's fight. She shivered. "Hope first showed up right after Thayl died. She kept pushing me to become queen through any means possible. Kept saying she would help me if I owed her. That's what makes me think Hope and Providence are the same. The one thing they both were pushing for was to get a human

ruler, with iron magic, into their debt. Providence needed Thayl for something but when he died she turned to me as a backup. Whether or not that has anything to do with all Maellan or not is unknown, but I can't help feeling it does. It's a crazy idea, but I just keep going back to it like it's a bad boyfriend."

Clara had turned white. "The more powerful fae can glamour themselves to look however they wish, so Providence could be anyone."

"Do we think she'll try again?" Roen asked. "In a different form, or maybe a different target?"

"No idea," Memory said. "I'm just a hunter lost in the wilds of speculation. But we have some leads. Some creepy, gangly fae attacked Dylan and me out in town one night. It was one of the ones stealing people, and it sounded like he was connected to Providence. I've already got Peirs keeping a watch out for any more of them."

Will frowned, and Memory wasn't sure if it was at the mention of her being attacked, or of her being out with Dylan. "I could ask Mina. Fairies gossip," he said, simply.

Memory nodded reluctantly and got to her feet. "Any lead is worth looking into. There may be fairy intel that could help that humans aren't hearing. And speaking of our fluttery friends, I want all of us to start carrying iron, just in case."

"We can't," Eloryn said. "Even if we had your knife, that's all the iron there is."

"Oh, dear sister, have I got a surprise for you." Memory reached down and helped Eloryn up. "We've got somewhere to go. I want my knife back, especially now I can't use magic. I want it for protection and don't care what anyone thinks."

Roen stood quickly as well. "Mem, you still look tired. How about I take Eloryn? I know the way."

Memory pouted, wanting to give Eloryn the big reveal herself, but even the idea of walking all the way down into the cavernous depths and back left her feeling exhausted. "Fine. I absolutely trust you are doing this to let me rest and not to take my sister off into a dark and isolated area."

Roen just shrugged. "It appears that my deception skills are getting sloppy through misuse."

Eloryn blushed from head to toe.

CHAPTER FOUR

In the old servant runs, Roen smirked as he pushed a section of stone wall and it swung open to reveal a long tunnel, winding off into the darkness.

Cool air that tasted of mossy stone met Eloryn's tongue as she caught her breath. She thought she knew everything there was to know about Caermaellan castle. She was clearly mistaken. "I can't believe you and Memory kept this secret from me. This is of tremendous historical and societal importance. We should have been trying to discover where all the iron down there originated."

Roen shrugged, causing a lock of caramel brown hair to fall in front of his eyes. He pushed it away. "I bade Memory tell you. I think she was too worried about Hayes taking control of it at the time."

Eloryn sighed. "I suppose she was right there. What a fool I was."

Roen put his hand against Eloryn's cheek. "Do not think that. You are trusting and kind in the most beautiful way. If others misuse that, it is their offence, not yours."

Eloryn shivered as Roen turned away and lit the oil lamp he carried.

Roen had retrieved a lamp from his room while he explained to Eloryn where they were going. She understood why the lamp was required. She wouldn't be able to summon a wisp with a behest around so much iron. The living energy of the fae creature would refuse the behest. But she could still magically enhance the flame of the oil lamp, and they travelled down the ancient stone stairs in brightly lit comfort. Dripping

water in the distance kept a steady rhythm and the temperature dropped as they descended. The carved tunnel was narrow and steps slippery from a slick coating of mud, and Eloryn kept bumping against Roen as he walked beside her. The warmth of his body seemed contagious, and whenever she felt it, a flush of warmth spread through her as well. Roen slowed to help her down a steep section where a step had crumbled away and she brushed against him with half her body.

Roen let out a breathy groan. "Are you trying to drive me crazy on purpose?"

His tone was playful, but Eloryn could only blush and shake her head. "I'm sorry."

Roen frowned. "Don't be. I'm sorry. It's not proper for me to voice my desires so. It's just… to have you so near, knowing you feel for me how I do for you, it's all I can do not to take you and hold you and do all sorts of delicious things with you." Roen bit his bottom lip and his smile returned.

Eloryn didn't think she could blush any harder, but she did. Her body turned to fire just wondering what delicious things Roen could mean. She didn't know what they were, but she knew she wanted them, and wanted him. She also couldn't help but wonder whether there had been other women in the past that he'd done such things with.

"You know I've never…" Eloryn began, but choked up. When her words returned, they came at rambling speed. "My first kiss was yours, and I know little else of love apart from the simple romance in fairytales and one archaic text book on anatomy and reproduction. I fear that love may be an area in which you are more knowledgeable than I."

"Whatever experiences I've had, they weren't of love. You are my first experience of love." Roen took both her hands in one of his, and the warm light of the lamp he held beside them seemed to make them glow. "I don't expect you to act at all outside of your comfort, or of society's standards. I would never think to pressure you further. I simply want you to understand how desirable I find you. How strong, and brave, and kind you are."

Eloryn wanted Roen to kiss her then. She wanted it with every nerve in her body. But he only stood and looked at her with an expression that filled her with love. He was being so patient, so gentle with her. She knew he would wait for her as long as needed, and it was up to her to take the next step.

Her voice seemed very small when she asked, "May I try something?"

Roen tilted his head, confused, but nodded.

Pushing herself up on her tippy-toes, Eloryn very slowly placed her lips against Roen's, a soft brush against his skin. Her eyelids fluttered and she lowered herself back down, smiling widely. Light headed with emotions and pride, her foot slipped on the step and she wobbled backwards.

Roen caught her around the waist with one arm and the lamp clattered against the wall beside them. They gasped together, as though the movement had sucked the air from both their bodies, and time slowed as the sound of the lamp hitting stone echoed through the stairwell. Then Eloryn brought her mouth to Roen's again, her fingers running up his neck. His arm tightened around her, bringing her chest toward his, pressing them together. Their footing slipped again and they stumbled together down the stairs, ricocheting from one wall to the other, trying to stay on their feet, tangled in each other's arms, unwilling to let go. Eloryn's lips burned delightfully every time they met Roen's. Her hands sought his golden hair, his shoulders and muscles on his chest. Desire left her head spinning and when the stairs finally flattened onto a pebbly floor she felt just as dizzy. The two remained entwined, stumbling, gasping, until the both of them tumbled into the icy water of the underground lake.

Will had waited while Memory cleaned herself up and changed into the rust-red gown she often wore, the first dress he'd ever seen her wear. When she returned, she put her head down on a cushion on the floor beside him. She said she'd just rest her eyes for a moment while they waited for Roen and Eloryn, then promptly fell asleep. Clara cleared up the food and left, and Will remained sitting beside Memory.

A strand of her purple hair fell across her face and Will reached over to push it back behind her ear, then hesitated.

First rule - No touching.

He took a deep breath, then allowed his fingers to meet her flesh. The old rules were no more. Her skin was soft and warm as he brushed the hair off her cheek. His Hope had changed so much, and he knew shedding the old rules meant she had grown so much stronger. He was happy for her, but there were other rules he still lived by that left a deep sadness in him.

Memory said it was time to start breaking rules, and he agreed. No matter his situation with the fae, Memory was more important. He would no longer sneak in what time he could with her. He would outright defy Mina if he had to. Only, he didn't know how effective that would be. Denying Mina something only made her want it more. He considered keeping away from her amongst the iron in the secret cavern, but he wanted to be with Memory, not hiding underground. And he couldn't explain to Memory either. Not now, not yet. Memory had enough to deal with right now. And despite how he felt about his relationship to Mina, he still felt an obligation toward her. She had saved his life.

When he first arrived in Avall as a small boy, Will didn't know how long it had been before he first met Mina. He only knew he was starving to death and lost in an endless forest. He'd eaten berries despite knowing they could be poisonous. He'd even eaten grubs and insects he found, desperate for any sustenance. But it wasn't enough. He'd never been a strong child and he quickly grew weak, too weak to keep going. He had curled up on the leafy forest floor, unable to do anything but cling to the last scraps of life.

When Mina first appeared, he thought he had died and Mina was an angel. She was so beautiful his face ran with tears and his weak body crumpled at the sight.

"Little boy," she said, and the jingle of tiny bells seemed to carry after her words. "Are you hungry?"

Will tried to speak but couldn't. He barely managed to nod.

The beautiful creature reached out her cupped hands and a plump and luscious fruit appeared cradled there. Shaped like a pear and twice as large, it was a soft pink with a purple blush on one side. "Take it," she said, smiling.

He did without hesitation, biting in. Juice ran down his chin and strength, hunger and desire burst inside him. He tore into the fruit, consuming the whole thing in seconds. When he was done, the woman held another one for him, and giggled.

"My sweet pet," she sang, and twirled around him, dancing as he ate. She had delicate, tattered wings which trailed a stream of glittery light behind them.

Will ate and ate. Mina sang and smiled. He thought he'd received a miracle. He thought he was saved. He had no idea what had just happened. His life had become the property of the fairy before him.

"My little boy. Who saved you when you were too lost and hungry to survive?"

"You did," he said, grinning a juicy grin at his savior.

"Who will show you wonders greater than you could ever imagine?"

Will knew of fairies and magic from storybooks. He knew now what the woman before him was. "You."

"Who is the most beautiful thing you've ever seen?"

"You are." He knew it was true.

"Who do you love above all else, even your short mortal life?"

He hesitated, and Mina scowled. A deep fear of realization and regret filled him then. He was so far from home, so far from anything he knew, so far from the only family he had left, the one girl he would wait for forever. He would do whatever he had to do to stay alive and stay strong while he waited.

"You. I will love you."

The fairy smiled again, and Will swore a promise to himself that no matter what wonders he was shown, no matter where this creature took him, he would never forget Hope.

Beside him, Memory shuddered in her sleep and her eyes snapped open. Back in the group home she often had nightmares. She would always deny it, but Will knew it from the haunted look in her eyes. He had his own nightmares, of being trapped under rubble, so he knew that look well. He wondered which of many terrors tormented her dreams then. But when she looked up at him, she smiled. He smiled back down at her.

Roen and Eloryn returned then, looking as wet as they looked embarrassed.

"You two miss a step?" Memory said. She sat up, leaning against Will's shoulder.

Roen looked at Eloryn and chuckled. Eloryn looked mortified and excused herself to change into a dry gown in her room next door.

Memory grinned at Will. "Cough-cold-shower-cough."

Roen sat down and emptied his pockets onto the ground between the three of them. He handed Memory her flick knife and took a small dagger for himself as well.

"We tried to pick small things that we can always carry with us, concealed. El already has the arrowhead with her," he said. That left two items, a small hooked tool and a large button, one for Will and one for Clara.

Will shook his head. "I can't take one. Not if I'm trying to get info from Mina."

"I'll keep it for you for later." Memory nodded and picked up the hooked tool, slipping it into her bodice with her knife.

She picked up the button as well.

Clara rushed in through the door then.

Memory flicked the button across to her. "Good timing, this one's for you."

Clara caught it in almost a daze and clasped it in her hands. She frowned deeply. "There's news," she stuttered. "News from Hayes. He's still demanding to marry Eloryn."

Memory and Roen frowned at each other and got to their feet. The doorway between Memory and Eloryn's chambers clicked closed and Eloryn stood there, neatly dressed in a simple lace gown, her face almost as white as the fabric.

CHAPTER FIVE

"What do you mean he has the legal right? He's a scum-sucking criminal!" Memory paced up and down the long table in the Round Room.

Bedevere's expression remained stoic. "It is also legally within your rights to have Hayes executed for those crimes of treason, which would solve the matter."

Memory cringed visibly. "No more death. I don't want that to be the way I deal with problems. When something tough comes up, it's not right, just snuffing out a life so the issue disappears. We'll find another way."

Eloryn nodded, backing up her sister. It felt important that she support Memory's decisions as queen, since it was her actions that made Memory queen. And her actions that brought her now to this ordeal. Eloryn sat still in the center seat, with Roen on one side and Bedevere, Lanval and Roen's parents seated around them. She put her hands on the table and it felt so flimsy. She really had to get to work on repairing the table that belonged in this room, the true round table that had been there since Arthur's time. Memory would be able to pace much more effectively around the circle it formed than up and down this straight edge.

Curious, the things one ponders of at times like these. Eloryn wondered if she was in shock, or simply in denial. As soon as Clara shared the news, Eloryn realized what a fool she'd been. Her contract of marriage with Hayes had foiled his plans to become king, and had revealed the crimes

he'd committed. She thought she'd won then. She didn't consider that the contract still stood, or that he would take advantage of that. She should have known better. Hayes was the type to take any advantage he could.

He looked far too pleased with himself as he was marched into the meeting by the bailiff and two other guards. Eloryn recognized the shackles as the same that Thayl had used, that block magic on the wearer.

Roen's hand rested on the table beside her and she moved hers closer, so that their little fingers touched, seeking that smallest comfort. He locked gazes with hers and she took strength from him.

Hayes stood before the group and smiled at Eloryn in a way that crinkled his hooked nose. The spite within the expression made Eloryn's stomach churn.

He bowed a shallow and mocking bow. "My dear soon-to-be wife."

Eloryn stared back at him, keeping her voice and gaze level. "You are doing this only to punish me. Why must you be so cruel?"

"Oh, not only to punish you. It's your little trick that has turned to bite you. You may not let me be king, but I can still hope that your wild sister never bears an heir, and that one of our many, many children will come to rule."

Memory choked. "I just threw up in my mouth a little."

She stood right beside Hayes, although he completely ignored her. All his attention and venom was focused on Eloryn. Something wild and desperate filled him now, something darker than the simple greed he had within him before. Eloryn wished she never had to take an action again that would create such an enemy to her. The feeling that this man could have so much hatred for her left her drained to her core.

"Despite the brain bleaching I now need, the fact is, Hayes, that you'll be in jail," Memory said. "How can you make her be your wife while you're in jail?"

Hayes replied, but continued to look at Eloryn. "It doesn't matter where I am, or what I am. King or prisoner, Eloryn will be my wife. She is legally and magically bound by contract, and I intend to follow through."

Memory put her palms to her forehead as if she was trying to contain herself. "Gah! I hate you so much right now if someone doesn't get you out of this room I'm going to pull your eyeballs out and vomit in the empty sockets."

Half the room stared open mouthed at Memory as the guards led

Hayes away, but Hayes just glared at Eloryn the whole way out.

Memory pulled a chair out across from Eloryn and flopped into it. "I'm sorry, I guess that wasn't very queenly of me."

"Are you all right?" Eloryn asked.

"Am I all right? How are you not a living emotional explosion right now?"

Eloryn took a deep breath. She didn't know the answer. She just knew she had to believe they would find a solution, and believe that nobody could force her away from Roen. "I guess I'm simply putting all my energy into not vomiting in someone's eye sockets, which is a horrendous concept, by the way."

Roen laughed, but it was short and sharp with anger. "Although if anyone were to deserve it right now, Hayes would have my vote."

"Good luck to Hayes, thinking he's going to get a wife and family while he's in prison forever," Memory said.

Eloryn stared at the table again. "But he will. I must marry him, even if the wedding takes place in his cell. And a wife has certain duties under law."

Memory paused for a second, clearly trying to add up the meaning. "Women have to have babies as a legal duty? Hell no, not in my kingdom they don't. Bedevere, do I have a legal advisor? If I do or don't, bring me one. We're going to find a way out of this. Including starting right now, we're going to change the laws about what 'duties' women have in this land."

"Oh. My. God. That's it. I'm done. I quit being queen," Memory said. She dropped her forehead onto the stack of paperwork on the desk in front of her and pretended to drool incoherently.

"You never did like homework," Will said with a sly grin. "Made me do it for you half the time."

Memory let out a groan that went for as long as she could force breath out. Rubbing her eyes with one hand, she flicked through the stack of unfinished documents and compared it to what she'd completed so far. Her first day of paperwork as queen was not proving very productive.

The monarch's office was a dark room, filled with timber furniture in rich chocolate tones and a desk bigger than what Memory thought a

dining table should be. Going in there that morning had seemed fun, exploring all the quill pens, ink pots, shifting rulers and other gadgets around the desk. The room made her feel important, like a proper queen. Then the paperwork began.

At least the chair was comfortable, and she rocked back in it and stuck her tongue out at Will where he sat cross-legged on a sideboard. He was reading a copy of Shakespeare's complete works, which they were both amused to find on the shelves. It seemed the fae imported all sorts of things back when they still travelled between the worlds.

"Can I help?" Will offered.

Memory sighed and picked up her next piece of parchment. It was velvety and thicker than the modern paper she remembered. "Nah, I'm okay. I need to get through this. It's part of my job now. And to be honest all I'm really doing so far is sorting things into stuff I know what I want to do about but not how to do it, stuff I can sign and be done with, and things I'm completely clueless about."

There was a knock on the door and Memory pumped a fist into the air and whispered, "Distraction! Yes!"

"Do come in," she said formally.

Peirs opened the door and remained standing in the threshold. He was out of his guard uniform and wore a simple fawn colored suit that matched his graying sandy-blonde hair. He held his cap in his hands against his chest and weariness accentuated the fine wrinkles across his face.

"Your Majesty," he said. "I've been doing as you instructed, undoing the wrongs Hayes committed. While undergoing this task, I've been visiting a number of prisons Hayes established for the masses he deemed to be wrongdoers, troublemakers, or undesirables. At one such prison I have found someone I thought you might like to see."

Peirs extended his arm, and from behind the door Clara stepped out, bringing with her a young girl with wiry red hair. The child's eyes were full circles, wide with awe and fear, and although she was clean, in fresh clothes and with an additional blanket around her shoulders, Memory could see the girl was even skinner than she had been when under Maeve's care at the orphanage. Skinnier and shaking like a leaf.

Memory got to her feet, a deep frown aching her forehead. In a few steps she was around her desk and kneeling in front of the girl to look her eye to eye.

"Hey, Isa," she said softly. "Where's your sister?"

Isa shook her head.

"Do you know where Maeve and the others are?"

Isa's lips pulled in and she shook her head again.

Memory stood back up and gave Peirs a questioning look.

He leaned toward her and whispered so the girl couldn't here. "After we got her out of the prison, while we got her fed and cleaned up, she said she saw Maeve and the others get taken by gaunts. She was the only one left. Apparently she was trying to find you when she got caught by Hayes's militia."

How dare they? She's just a child. Memory felt the fires in her chest roaring. She closed her eyes and took a deep breath. "Clara, can you find Isa a room in the guest wing below my chambers, and a handmaiden to look after her?"

"Already sorted," Clara replied, her eyes watery and lips tight.

Memory bent back down to the girl. "We're going to find your sister and the others, and bring everyone back here, I promise. Won't it be fun, living in the palace together?"

Isa made no movement to respond.

"I was a bit scared of getting lost when I first started working here," Clara said, smiling at Isa. "But don't worry, I'll draw you a map, and soon you'll be running all over like you own the place." Clara scooped the girl up, and carried her away on her hip.

Memory waved to them, then headed out of her office as well, beckoning Peirs and Will to follow her. Will jumped silently from the cupboard he'd been perched on and walked at her side.

"Have you had any luck tracking those fae critters who work for Providence?" Memory asked as she took long strides down the polished marble hall.

Peirs shook his head. "We've checked through all known unseelie fae territories in Caermaellan, and even seelie ones, but found nothing. We've spotted gaunts trying to take people a few times, but haven't been able to follow them. As soon as they've noticed us they leave their victim and flee, or worse, turn and fight to the death, the crazed beasts. They seem to have no fear for being Branded, and are blatantly showing more hatred toward humans."

"I'd like to blatantly show my hatred right back again," Memory muttered. "Have things always been this bad?"

Peirs's grin was wry, stretching the skin on his cheeks. "Not like this, but there has always been tension between the unseelie fae and humans. They are monsters, and they see us as inferior animals. That's why the Pact was made to include Branding, to protect each side from the other. In the old times, we used to be free to hunt the monsters for sport. I figure that's the only reason the unseelie fae went along with the Pact because they were so under threat. But many in the unseelie court have outright stated they didn't want the Pact as it was, that humans should have been made subservient to the fae."

Subservient to the unseelie fae? Memory could just imagine the kind of horrors that would involve. Still, having seen a fae creature suffer the fate of a Branding, she was pretty sure it fell under the category of horror as well.

Peirs slowed his stride, and Memory turned to see why. He still held his cap clutched against his chest. "Your Majesty, it is my fault the children have been taken. I should have stayed to protect them."

"Shoulda, woulda, coulda, nonsense. This isn't your fault. This is the fault of the damned vampires."

Peirs raised an eyebrow. "There really is no such thing as vampires."

"Color me unconvinced." Memory started walking again and Peirs and Will matched her step.

"This is new, what we've been seeing, and targeted solely on Caermaellan," Peirs said. "Some unseelie fae, like trolls, have been known to eat humans, but never drain their blood in the way we've seen in the bodies we've found. It's almost medical precision. No teeth."

"But we know it's those rotted dark fae though," Memory said. "How were they able to take everyone without being Branded?"

Will spoke up then, although his voice was quiet. "Fae tricks. Lost children are easy targets. They're easy to seduce and trap with promises of riches or happiness, a home, or even a simple bite of food."

Peirs nodded. "And when they make the wrong deal, they lose any protection from the Pact."

Vampires or not, Memory knew she had to find and stop the fae doing this, and find out what their connection to Providence was. No matter what, Providence had taken enough blood.

Memory took the stairs up and headed into the Round Room. She found the room a mess, with piles of splintered wood in small stacks all over the marble floor. Eloryn sat amongst them, sorting the pieces out, holding them to her ear and whispering to them in turn. She'd managed to recreate almost a quarter of the round table from the shattered and charred timber that remained after the explosion. A makeshift desk sat in the corner, out of the way, where Roen, Roen's father and a mousey legal advisory sat bleary eyed. They looked over contracts and searched through legal precedents to find a way to prevent Eloryn's marriage to Hayes. Eloryn looked particularly worn. Memory was sure she hadn't slept for days.

Memory worried about her sister, how she'd become so focused on repairing the round table, but Eloryn had said it helped her to think, and to relax, and that it was her way of trying to find a solution.

"How is it going?" Memory asked.

Roen looked up from the desk, his eyes red rimmed with grey smudges beneath. "Going splendidly if we want to amend the marriage contract for requiring a dowry or we wish to allow the husband's family to inspect the bride before the wedding to approve of her or her virginal status. The more I look at the laws in detail, the more I'm beginning to agree with your sentiment, Mem."

"That Avall kind of sucks for women? Yep, worked that one out back in etiquette class."

Eloryn placed a finger length splinter of wood against the restored section of table and spoke a few words. The wood crackled softly as it melded and blended back together. "We'll find a way. We can fix this."

"I'm glad you're still feeling positive, sis, because I need to break up your team. I need Roen for something else. I want Roen to find the place the gaunts are taking people and draining their blood. We think they have Maeve and the kids."

Everyone around the room stopped their work and looked at Memory.

"I know you probably want to be here, finding a way to stop Hayes's crazy demands, but I need you out there. You've got mad ninja skills like no one else I know. Finding Providence's blood drinkers is important."

Roen looked at Eloryn for a long moment, then turned back to Memory. He nodded, his jaw tight. "I know. I'll do it."

Brannon stood up from the table and put his hand on Roen's shoulder, the look of pride on his face overwhelming.

Roen gave a small bashful chuckle. "To be honest it will be good to get out onto the streets again. The best luck to ever strike me has been when I've been working. Maybe I will find some luck again to

help us here as well. Different ways of dealing with problems work for different people."

Eloryn rose from the floor and scattered a stack of splintered wood when she rushed over to Roen and held him tight. "Don't worry, I'll find a solution to this before you get back."

Peirs bowed to Memory. "Let me accompany him. I need to help. I need to right this."

"Of course," Memory said. "I'd go too, but there's more I need to do here."

Will, who had been standing to one side during the conversation stepped forward. "Do you want me to look too?"

"Yes, if you can. But somewhere else. I need you talking with the fae to find out what they know. There has to be some gossip to be had, and Mina strikes me as the kind of girl to gossip."

Will flinched ever so slightly, making his icy blue eyes flash. "I will go to her."

He turned to leave, and Memory caught him by his hand. "Come back soon, 'kay?"

Will turned away, his expression hidden behind tangled hair. "I'll try."

CHAPTER SIX

Eloryn walked slowly through the halls of the castle toward Thayl's old quarters. She had grown so used to hearing many sets of footsteps walking with her wherever she went, that now she was without her guards she felt very alone. She knew there was only one person she truly missed, and made a silent wish that Roen would stay safe and return to her soon.

Her sister had summoned her, and when Eloryn reached the entrance to what had been Thayl's chambers, she nodded to the guards that used to be hers waiting outside, then stepped in to see Memory.

Eloryn gasped. "Mem, you look… Stunning."

Memory grinned bashfully and tugged at the short skirt of the new outfit she wore. "Not bad, right? This was Clara's newest mission. I gave her my old clothes and asked her to work with the seamstresses to come up with something that was more me. I kind of just wanted some new pants, but I think they saw the little skirt-belt-thing on my jeans and rolled with it."

Eloryn smiled. The outfit was traditional enough not to cause a scandal, but at the same time very much suited her sister. Fitted pants in grape purple had lace cuffs around Memory's ankles, and around her waist a full bustle hung from the back with a shorter frill of skirt at the front. The seamstress had incorporated pink lace onto the front of

the tight bodice, in a cascading collar reminiscent of the heart design on Memory's shirt from the other world. A black, ruffled shrug jacket kept the whole ensemble modest and practical.

Memory had also taken to wearing most of her old piercings again, except the one in her lip, and over the top of lace gloves, she wore the collection of bracelets, buckles and cuffs that she had worn the day Eloryn first met her.

Eloryn hid her smile and stuck her nose into the air. "First hamburgers, now this. You'll have everyone wanting fashion like yours."

Memory laughed. "Just wait until I introduce Avall to coffee."

Smiling back, Eloryn ran her finger over a layer of dust on the desk beside her. "So, where do we start?"

"I guess I'll have to import some coffee beans or trees from the other world somehow..."

"I meant with your search plan, here, now," Eloryn said.

"I was honestly hoping you'd walk in and be all bam, solved the mystery with superhuman senses of observation and deduction, Sherlock Holmes style." Memory turned on the spot, looking around the room. "But you didn't. So I guess we just poke around."

"You really do think far too much of me," Eloryn said.

The rooms had barely been touched since Thayl was deposed. Eloryn knew the Council had been through once, looking for clues to Thayl's powers, but left quickly when they found no magical documents. His chambers consisted of a single large room that served as bedroom, lounge and office, unlike the royal chambers Memory and Eloryn now occupied which had a separate bedroom and sitting room each. The room hadn't been on the cleaners' rounds for a while, and grime had settled across all surfaces. Thayl's old clothes, worn during his imprisonment, still lay on the floor in front of an open wardrobe.

Eloryn frowned at the bed, which was small, a single bed only. As though Thayl had never even imagined sharing his bed with another person again after Loredanna died.

Eloryn made her way to the bedside table and began flicking through the books stacked there, searching for a journal or some other clue.

Memory followed, and bent down next to the bed, feeling around its base for anything hidden. She glanced at Eloryn a few times as she did so. "How are you hanging in there, with that whole nasty forced marriage business?"

Eloryn paused for a moment, then continued to flick through the copy of *Troilus and Criseyde*, although she doubted it would be of much relevance to their search. "Hayes has set a date for the wedding, a week from today, to be held in his cell."

"He's being a right asshat about this, isn't he? I'm starting to rethink my position of anti-killing."

"Don't. I do not want his death on my hands or yours. We will find a solution. Anything broken can be fixed. Changing the laws about a woman's rights in marriage will help me a little, but unfortunately I will still be married, just with more rights." Eloryn closed the book and a puff of dust blew into her face, stinging eyes that already felt raw. She blinked them clear. "It would almost be funny if not so horrible. We fought Hayes for wanting to arrange marriages for us, and now I've locked myself into an arranged marriage with him."

"If it weren't for this damn fairy oath, I would whoosh him away to the rest of the world for you." Memory winced as she reached her arm full length under the bed, fumbling around.

"I would still be bound by contract to marry him, regardless of his location. And without your magic we are unable to get to the other world anyway, regardless of what miraculous wonders it may hold, be it coffee or a solution to my problem."

Memory stopped searching and sat on the side of the bed, looking up at Eloryn. "What if you do go through with the marriage, and then get a divorce right after? Would that satisfy the contract?"

"A divorce?"

Her sister explained the concept to her. Apparently it was more common in her world than marriages that lasted.

"Happily ever afters aren't really a thing where I come from," Memory said.

"That would be a very big change for Avall in order to solve my problem."

"Meh, it should be allowed anyway. Even in the rest of the world I'm pretty sure divorce becoming legal was always because of some king or another wanting to do it themselves."

Eloryn nodded, a small spark of hope lighting in her then extinguishing just as fast. "It may be a solution, but it's not the sort of law change we could rush through. Nor are the other changes regarding women's rights. I will still be married to Hayes for some time."

"And any amount of time is too much time, I know." Memory leant back on her elbows, staring around the room as though it held answers. She pointed at the wall behind Eloryn.

"That's Thayl's sister," she said. "I saw her once before, in a dream."

Eloryn turned and looked at the large portrait on the wall. The girl looked about twelve years old and her rose red lips were highlighted by her pale skin and thick, ebony hair. She smiled like she'd just seen a rainbow for the first time.

Eloryn's heart sank like a sack of stones into black water. Memory had explained what happened to the child at just sixteen years of age. She'd been lost to sacrifice in Providence's dark ritual.

"She was so pretty," Memory said, looking as grim as Eloryn felt. "I can almost see some of her in you. In us, I guess."

"We do not know for sure she is family," Eloryn said.

Memory opened her mouth but Eloryn spoke first. "If you want to know, if you truly feel the need to know for sure, there are magical ways we could use to discover whether Thayl was our father. But I don't feel the need. Since learning the rumor about Loredanna not consummating her marriage, I see more and more a resemblance to Thayl in our features. I know he was special to our mother, and I know he was to you, too, in a way. Knowing all I know now, I don't hate the thought of him being our father. But nor do I wish to embrace it. Alward was my father in all ways that mattered, and I cannot forget that it was Thayl who killed him."

Memory had turned away so Eloryn couldn't see her face. "I thought I was a fool for wanting a father figure in my life so desperately that I turned to Thayl. You had Alward, who sounds like he rocked the father role. I had no one. Either of the men who could have been our father is just as tragic really, Thayl or Edmund. I think I also prefer not to know for sure. I know Thayl made mistakes, but at least I knew him, for a while. It would hurt too much for both of us, I think, to know for sure he was our father, or to know he wasn't. Maybe sometimes it's best to just leave things at maybe."

With a shake of her head, Memory stood up and ran her hands around the gilt frame holding the life-sized portrait of Thayl's sister. "Help me lift this down."

Eloryn took hold of the other side, and together they hefted the thick framed canvas from the wall.

Eloryn looked at the space on the wall the painting came from.

"Nothing behind the painting."

Memory pried the backing board off the frame and then pouted. "Nothing, damn it. People always hide things in frames in the movies."

"Movies?"

Memory shook her head. "Oh sister dearest, I have *so* much to catch you up on."

Eloryn grinned and went over to the cluttered desk.

"What's this?" she said, lifting up a small box, wrapped like a present with a small envelope on top. She opened the note and read it.

More as requested. Use them well. I grow impatient.

Memory had come over to look over her shoulder. "See? You do have super detective powers."

Eloryn rolled her eyes as she pried at the lid. The box opened with a snap and revealed a row of neatly laid out darts inside.

Eloryn reached to her neck. "Those are the same sort of darts the Wizard Hunters used to block the Spark of Connection."

"That's weird." Memory pried one out and held it near her eye, examining it. "They look like iron. It makes no sense that iron would stop magic from working."

As though to demonstrate the point, Memory pulled out her knife from a neat pocket in the waist band of her new outfit that looked made just for it. The way it was concealed there made Eloryn think it had been inspired by how Roen used to carry his fine electrum sword.

When she held the two pieces of metal together, the small dart wriggled from Memory's fingers with a life of its own and flung itself at the nearby blade.

Eloryn gasped.

"Magnetized?" Memory said. "More sense being made now. Hey, can I try something?"

Memory got a wicked look in her eye, and before Eloryn could reply, Memory jabbed her in the shoulder with the dart. It pricked lightly through her skin and wooziness rushed through Eloryn as her Spark of Connection closed down.

"Mem!" Eloryn clutched her sister's arm for support and Memory helped ease her down to sit on the bed. "Some warning would have been nice. And you better have a good excuse for doing that."

"Warning takes away all the fun," Memory said, her eyebrows wriggling cheekily. "We are pretty sure normal iron draws magic into

humans. And it looks like magnetized iron draws it out, like the change in polarity affects the way it funnels magic. It's just drawing magic out of you, right? So maybe the Spark of Connection is just a small bit of magic that's been put inside each human."

"It matches existing theory on the subject, yes. And it's a small bit of magic I would like back now please." Eloryn reached to collect the arrow-head she now carried in her purse, but Memory grabbed her hand.

"Wait, we haven't gotten to what I want to try yet. We already know that holding iron can re-start the spark. I want to try giving you some of the magic in me. I won't be casting anything, just sharing."

Eloryn frowned. "It sounds a little too close for comfort to me. You must be mindful of your oath."

"Oh shush. There's no behest for this, and it's behests I'm not allowed to do. It's just a little involuntary overflow."

Memory held her palms up in front of Eloryn's chest. "Okay. Now make me angry."

Eloryn laughed. "How shall I make you angry?"

"Tell me more about Hayes's scumbucketry, or Avall's women's rights issues, or the vampires stealing my friends, or talk about Mina, or…"

A glow flashed between them and Eloryn felt her spark re-open.

"It worked," she said, a little breathless.

Memory's face was closed for a moment as she breathed out an angry pant, then she shrugged and smiled. "And no fairy army banging down the door demanding my head. So we're all good."

"You really aren't fond of Mina, are you?" Eloryn asked.

A frown reappeared quickly on Memory. "She's only the most awful girlfriend ever, or whatever she is or was to Will."

Eloryn hesitated. She had grown increasingly worried about Will's situation with the fae the more she got to know him. For all she'd read about how the fae can claim human children or partners, Will seemed to fit that description. It was only the amount of freedom she'd seen him have that made her believe it wasn't true. Most humans claimed by the fae are taken to their world and kept there, or so the stories went. Like Lugh. Perhaps Will was simply friends with Mina and the sprites, and until Eloryn knew better, she decided it wasn't worth worrying Memory about.

"Still, we've not found any more clues regarding Providence. These darts are made to target human wizards, not the fae," Eloryn said. She

held the dart up to the light of the nearby window to examine it. "Do you think magnetized iron would be safe for fae?"

"Clueless. Why?"

"Because these are also engraved with runes, the same old type of magic that Providence used on you and on Thayl's hand," Eloryn said, placing the dart back in the box and closing it up. "I'm guessing this little gift came from her, trying to hasten the death of the Wizards' Council so Thayl's debt would come due."

Memory rubbed her temples. "Makes sense. I just need to know what the hell Providence wanted."

Eloryn looked around the room again. Thayl hadn't been a well-organized man. Every surface and shelf was overcrowded and cluttered. *There must be more in here to help us, but where to start?*

"You told me once I needed to be more inventive with my magic. I need to start experimenting some more, correct?" Eloryn said.

"And I will live vicariously through you as you do," Memory agreed.

Eloryn nodded, and began speaking in the magic language. *"Reveal to me, anything of Providence. Anything of Thayl's relationship to Providence. Make yourself seen."*

The box of darts on the desk gave a small rattle and then glowed a rich golden light. Beside it, three books down in a stack, a thin ledger book shimmered briefly too.

Memory pulled the book from the stack, letting the rest of the tower collapse behind it. "I was wrong. Sherlock's got nothing on you."

Eloryn tsked and carefully picked the fallen books back up. She loved any books too dearly to see them dumped onto the floor.

Both girls stood shoulder to shoulder as Memory began flicking through the loosely bound documents. They appeared to be letters, from someone who signed only with a rough X, outlining expenses to be paid and the development of missions they were undergoing for Thayl.

"And this is?" Memory asked.

"Maybe my behest failed."

Memory stopped flicking, and started leafing back the pages. "No, I'd say you didn't fail at all." Memory pointed to a sketch of a long hooked tool.

"That's the same thingamabob Roen brought up from the iron stash."

"It's a leatherworker's awl," Eloryn said. She took the ledger and began flicking ahead again. They soon found details of other iron items

they'd seen in the depths of the castle. Eloryn skimmed the handwriting throughout, drawing in all the details she could.

"Thayl was hiring this person to collect iron for him. He even gave the hunter leads, told him to seek out wizards in hiding, or anyone seen as being powerful with magic. Thayl must have worked that part out when he first began hunting wizards. He also provided this hunter and his men with the spark-closing darts and... Oh."

Eloryn put the letters down on the desk and stared straight ahead, trying to calm the shudders that racked her frame.

"What is it?" Memory asked.

Eloryn took a deep breath. "It mentions the hunter's dragon. The last letter says the hunters were going to the mountains west of Maerranton following reports of a man seen there matching Alward's appearance. They were the ones who chased us. Led by the man with the lion's hair and scarred face. All this time I had believed I was the cause of our discovery, that it was my folly that brought the hunters to Alward and me." Eloryn shook her head.

Memory put an arm over Eloryn's shoulder and squeezed. "Why is it always the good people who blame themselves for what bad people do?"

Eloryn put an arm around her sister as well. After another deep breath, she felt lighter than she had for months. "So now we know they were hunting for iron as well as for wizards. And delivering it to Thayl, who hoarded the artifacts in the palace depths."

"Not all of the iron down there was from him, though," Memory said. "Will said the fae didn't go there even before Thayl. Hundreds of years at least. But there's the interesting thing. Even if Thayl didn't put all the iron down near the lake, we know for sure he added to what was there, and that he was actively seeking more iron. He might have done exactly what I did, find a place the fae didn't go in order to store more iron there. Even if he was using it to recharge his magic, he didn't need so much, and yet he kept seeking more and more." Like an unconscious action, Memory drew her own iron knife again. Her expression was chilling. "There's only one other value in hoarding iron that I can think of."

Eloryn looked at the knife in Memory's hand, remembering the searing effect it had on a banshee's skin. "Defense against the fae. But to want so much, it wouldn't have been just for himself. There's iron enough there to fight a battle."

Memory looked grimly at her sister. "What if Thayl knew what Providence was? What if he had some idea of what she was going to ask of him to repay his debt? What if the iron was to prepare for that?"

Eloryn's voice was quiet. "A war with the fae?"

Memory shrugged and pinched the bridge of her nose. "But if Providence is a fae, and presumably a dark fae, why would she want to make a human start a war? Why not just do it herself somehow?"

"You've said Hope was always trying to turn you against the unseelie fae."

Memory muttered an interruption. "Not that I need much turning."

Eloryn's head tilted. "There is some great animosity between the seelie and unseelie courts. Perhaps Providence was actually a seelie fae, planning to have humankind and unseelie set at war?"

"Maybe? I don't know. But why else? Unless for some reason Thayl thought he needed that much just to deal with Providence alone." Memory threw her hands up in the air. "Thanks for nothing, Thayl's room."

Eloryn collected up the ledger and box of darts. "We know more now than we did before. These were important clues. We will work it out."

Memory groaned. "Okay, okay. Trying to be optimistic. Will is still trying to get some more info about Providence from Mina and the sprites. He's got her interested in it now. Says she's keen to gossip about it, so we'll see what there is when he comes back."

"Roen and Peirs may find something also. I hope they will all be back soon."

Memory smiled in a way that did not disguise her worry. Eloryn knew that her own expression must be a mirror image.

CHAPTER SEVEN

The heavy rain from earlier in the day had ceased, but had left the ground thick with mud that clung greedily to each footstep. Clouds still covered the sky and the moon glowed through the mist like an ominous ghost of the sun.

Roen and Peirs stood together just outside of the pool of light cast by a streetlamp. They chatted quietly and casually, observing the people around them, before moving on to their next location. For three nights they had done the same thing, loitering outside of taverns and inns, wandering through the pebbled streets until the early hours of the morning. During the days they sought out Peirs's contacts and questioned people on the street for clues.

Peirs sighed and tilted his head, indicating to Roen it was time to move on. There were a few taverns around Caermaellan that the fae frequented, and they had been watching Myrddin's Cup that evening.

"We'll find something soon," Roen said.

Peirs snorted wryly. "We better."

They had the exact same exchange every time they moved on in their search. Roen could see the lines of stress etched around Peirs's eyes and tight lips, as though every day they didn't find the stolen children, Peirs felt another child die in his heart. Roen grabbed Peirs's arm and pulled him to a stop.

"We will find them," Roen said, putting every ounce of hope and

sincerity into his words that he could.

Peirs shrugged, gazing up and down the street as though looking for answers. "Should we be doing this differently? Should I be sending guards to knock down every door in the city? I'm open to all suggestions."

"If I learned anything in my time as a..." Roen still hesitated to say it, but forced the word though. "...thief, it's that when seeking something precious, it's often best to do it quietly."

Peirs ran a hand through his hair. "I just can't think straight. Don't know if any decision I'm making is the right one." He closed his roaming eyes for a moment then looked at Roen. "You know, I was probably the age you are now when Thayl first took the throne as he did. I was no noble, didn't have much of a say in the whole affair, but it still made me angry. Angry enough to act. I never meant to be the leader of the resistance, but it sort of just happened." Peirs sighed and his breath formed a cloud, hanging in the icy air between them. "It's funny how we end up where we end up. Now a slip of a girl is our queen, and made me captain of her guard. I know some don't believe in Memory, but I have from the start. I could see it right away, something special about her. By the fae, she's still a child, but she sure is an extraordinary one. I'm just some nobody desperately terrified of letting her down."

"I know you've made her proud so far. She thinks of you as family."

"As she does every one of the children we still need to find." Peirs hung his head, his face hidden in the shadow as he began walking again.

As Roen turned away to follow Peirs to their next tavern, he finally caught sight of their target. A pair of gaunts, tall and gangly, squelched through the mud toward the entrance of the inn. They walked boldly as though they had little care of being seen. The suits they wore were threadbare and grayed, the fabric of the pants shredded to the knees, but one had a new bright red handkerchief in its breast pocket that stood out like an open wound.

"There, see? What did I tell you?" Roen said, calling Peirs's attention back.

Peirs blinked as though not believing it. "Now I guess we wait and see if they try to take someone."

"Not at all." Roen grinned. "Now, we track them."

Roen quietly led Peirs across the street to where the gaunts had passed by, and pointed to their elongated footprints in the mud, each one a pool filled with murky water.

"We track them back to their origin from here," he said. "Much

better than trying to follow the gaunts themselves and having them flee or fight us."

Peirs checked over his shoulder to where the gaunts had disappeared into the tavern. "What if these gaunts aren't from the same group that's taking people, or if they've come from somewhere different to where they take their victims?"

Roen nodded. "All right then. One of us will follow the tracks, and one of us will follow the gaunts."

"I'm not as quiet as you for following after the unseelie beasts, but I probably have less chance of following their footprints well. That's our best shot, since we haven't tried it before. You track, I'll trail."

Peirs held out his hand and Roen shook it before they each headed their separate ways. Roen flicked up the hood of his long leather coat, and began tracking the creatures' steps.

His thoughts quickly turned to Eloryn and how she was able to follow a path by turning invisible footprints into pure light. He hadn't been back to the castle in days, but it felt like much longer since he'd seen her. He would have liked her to be by his side now, as he always would, but they needed to find a solution to stop Hayes. And he needed no magic to track the gaunts; it would be easy with the thick mud, as long as it didn't rain again.

Roen moved quickly, his eye on the creatures' marks, pausing only briefly when the path forked to spot the way to go. The gaunts had taken a circuitous route that led him under dank bridges and through empty parklands, until he reached the outskirts of the city where tight terraced housing made way for larger estates with mansions surrounded by vast walled in gardens.

The trail led to a building that sat on a small hill. It was hunched and crooked from disrepair. Weeping willows lined the property boundaries with draping leaves that whispered in the wind.

No one seemed to be around, and Roen crept closer to the house, ducking between overgrown blackberry brambles and tumbled stone walls.

A dozen steps from the front door, the movement of figures in the dark made Roen duck for cover behind a cracked marble fountain. A gaunt had appeared from around the other side of the house, heading to the entrance, dragging a dazed girl.

This is it then, the place they are bringing the stolen people.

Roen froze, listening. *Did someone just call my name?*

The gaunt had disappeared into the house, taking the girl with him, and the door slammed closed.

"Roen!"

It was Peirs calling him. But Peirs was meant to be following the other two gaunts.

The other two gaunts...

Roen spun around in his crouched position. A bright flash of red moved in the dark in front of him- a bright handkerchief against tattered clothes. Two gaunts towered over him, the ones they had seen at the tavern. As he had tracked the gaunts, the gaunts had tracked him. One slashed its arm through the air, smacking Roen across the jaw and knocking him onto his back. Roen tasted blood on his tongue, salty and metallic.

Peirs ran up from behind them, still too far away. "Brand them! Brand them!"

I can't.

Roen grabbed for the iron dagger he carried. The gaunt in front of him stretched its black maw wide and loosed a wailing cry. The cry was matched by others, more and more howling at the intruders.

Hands grasped Memory's shoulders, shaking her roughly, waking her from sleep.

She struggled one eyelid open and saw Eloryn standing there. She looked so upset that Memory made an effort to shake herself awake. Will also waited next to Eloryn, looking equally concerned. Memory hadn't seen him for a while. He must have just gotten back.

"What's going on?" she asked, her voice croaky from sleep. She rubbed her eyes.

"It's Peirs, he's returned. But Roen hasn't," Eloryn said.

Memory was out of bed and getting dressed in a worried, half asleep blur. Clara rushed in soon after, in her bedclothes, and helped lace Memory into a thick leather corset, designed to provide light protection for fencing. Eloryn had dressed already, and Memory wondered how much magic was used to speed her into the practical dark colored riding outfit she wore.

When she'd done helping Memory dress, Clara brought Peirs in on

Memory's request.

"You found it then?" Memory asked while pulling long leather boots on.

Peirs bowed. He looked ashen. "We did."

"What happened to Roen?"

"He was captured by the gaunts. They swarmed on him, too many for me to fight, so I fled, to bring help." Peirs took a knee. "Forgive me, Your Majesty."

"You did the right thing. If you'd both been taken you'd both be lost to us. At least we know where everyone is now." Memory helped Peirs stand again then said to Clara, "Get Erec, tell him what's going on."

Clara finished winding her wild mass of bed-tangled red hair into a knot at the back of her head, then nodded and left, her white night gown fluttering behind her.

Memory collected her iron knife from under her pillow and strapped it into a custom sheath on her new belt. She also pulled out the hooked awl and pushed it into Will's hands.

His hands didn't close around it. "I can't carry iron. The fae won't be happy."

"Things have changed. We know more about Providence. I want you carrying iron from now on. Please do that for me."

Will took the awl.

Memory looked from him to Eloryn, who stood like a deep breathing statue beside them, then to Peirs. "Peirs, what happened? Where are the gaunts hiding out?"

"They are in an old building, one the locals say is haunted, and is avoided by most. It's a human's property, but disused. That's why we hadn't been able to find them in any fae territory. It was surprisingly easy to track them there, almost as though they wanted to be found. Roen and I were separated and I was too far back to help when they took him."

Eloryn looked at Memory. "Could they be luring us in?"

"Does it even need to be said? But there's only one thing to do with a trap, and that's spring it. Besides, what else would we do? Leave Roen there? And all the other people they've taken? Shyeah right."

Clara returned, along with Erec. She cleared her throat as way of announcement, then helped Memory slip on the leather jacket that matched her corset.

Erec gave his brother a look that seemed they were speaking silently

together, then turned to address Memory. "You've found where the children have been taken?"

"We're going now," Memory said.

Erec cleared his throat. "If you intend to mount a rescue, Your Majesty, I have to advise against your personal involvement, or your sister's."

"You can advise my ass, Erec. I know it's important for the queen to stay alive, but this is more important. Not just for Roen, but to find out who is behind all these kidnappings, and maybe even more. Doesn't the king ride into battle alongside his army? Are you going to keep the two most powerful magical talents of Avall from assisting?"

Eloryn shot Memory a look.

I know, I know. No magic for me.

"I'm going," Memory said.

Erec looked to Eloryn as though for support.

She shook her head at him. "As I am also going."

"I'm afraid I'm with them, brother," said Peirs.

"I'm with Mem," said Will.

Clara stood beside Memory, her fingers on her lips. "I... I'm..."

Memory put a hand on her shoulder. "We need someone here to organize for incoming rescues, okay?"

Clara pouted her full lower lip. "I'm sorry that I'm not brave like you."

Memory laughed. "We're not brave. We're stupid. You're probably the smartest of us all."

Clara gave the smallest smile. "Just come back to me, and bring everyone home with you."

Erec said, "I suppose I'll have to go to keep you all safe then? I'll organize some of my men to join the party."

"And quick," Memory said. "It's time to get our raid on."

CHAPTER EIGHT

The carriage sped through the empty streets of Caermaellan. Over the clatter of the wheels and hooves on cobblestones, Memory heard a nearby clock tower ring for two in the morning. She could also hear the dozen or so guards on horseback escorting them. More empty coaches, larger and slower than the sleek model Memory rode in, were driven behind, in the hopes there would be survivors to bring home.

It had felt like a lifetime since Memory had driven these streets, distant days of going to school or visiting her homeless shelter, or her night with Dylan where he compared her to the moon. Memory wondered where he was now and wondered when her life would slow down enough to go back to school again, to continue her magic classes with Bedevere, to continue with her life.

When the lives of those I love are also safe. That's when.

"Everyone has iron?" Memory checked again.

Eloryn and Peirs across from her, and Will, beside her, all confirmed.

"Are we dumb to do this frontal assault style? Do we have any other more reasonable plan?" Memory asked everyone.

Eloryn looked out the window for a long moment. "The faster we're in, the better. If it's a trap, they are expecting us one way or another. But we've got iron, so we're at an advantage. The property they've been using doesn't belong to the fae, so it doesn't count as their territory. That means the second they try and attack us, we're in our rights to defend

ourselves and Brand them. Whether the gaunts seduced their victims or not, they are in the wrong by law and it's our right under the Pact to stop them."

Memory glanced at Will then back to Eloryn and Peirs. "Well, you two can Brand. Will and I will stick to iron."

Peirs frowned, but said nothing.

A knock came from the window through to the driver's seat- Erec signaling they were about to arrive.

Memory looked to each of her friends in turn as she buttoned up her coat, the polished brass slippery under her fingers. "It's important to find evidence of who is running this place, to find out who Providence is or any clue about what's going on here, but remember, first and foremost this is a rescue mission. Roen, Maeve, the kids, we get them all out alive."

They shared silent nods, and the carriage came to an abrupt stop.

Eloryn took a breath so deep her whole chest rose and fell. "I will use my behests to help make all of us faster and stronger when I am able, but my main focus will be on finding Roen, finding the captives."

Erec opened the carriage door and Peirs stepped out first, followed by Memory, Eloryn, and Will. The team of guards dismounted around them, their horses nickering and restless from the fast ride.

As Erec gestured orders to his men, Peirs stepped up beside Memory. "I know you want to save the little ones as much as I do, but don't let that lead you to do anything foolish. Stay close by me. Be careful."

Memory bumped her shoulder into his and droned, "Yes, Dad."

The house stood silent and grim before them, a shambling mess of grey timber webbed with dead ivy that hung like tattered shrouds. No sound, no movement, no light showed from within.

Memory led the march up the steps to the front door, Will close beside her.

She found herself nose to nose with Mina.

"You? What are you doing here?" Memory said. *Providence couldn't be Mina, no way.*

Mina flicked her chin away from Memory, ignoring her. "Will, come with me."

Will's jaw twitched, but he spoke calmly. "I'm staying with Memory."

"No, you come with me, now," Mina shrieked, and her fiery hair whipped to life. "You are not going in that place!"

Memory stared Mina down. "He said he's coming with me. Just give

him a break, would you?"

"You're not going in there. You're not, you're not," Mina said. She snatched Will by the wrists, shaking him. "Why are you being so awful? I don't want you to go in there. It's not safe. You can't."

Will pulled his hands free, stepping away from Mina and closer to Memory. "I'm going wherever she goes."

Mina's glow flared, anger shaking the fairy dust off her in tides as her breath caught in sobs. Memory had never seen her so flustered. There was something different, almost hectic about her. *Maybe she really does want to protect Will from something, something in that house. As much as I want to protect Will from her...*

Mina swiped her arm to grab Will again and Memory held her hands up to calm her. "Will, look, just go with her. It will be okay. I'll be okay."

Will looked hurt. "Mem?"

Memory leaned closer to him and whispered. "I don't want to see you hurt. It's okay, go. Go and find out what firefly has buzzed up this girl's butt. She clearly knows something we don't."

Will gave a single, slow nod, but his eyebrows were low and darkened his bright eyes.

Mina snatched his hand in hers, and the two of them vanished in a shower of fairy dust and swirl of Veil mist.

The confidence Memory had been feeling a moment before vanished with him.

More and more she wanted Will by her side. It felt right. It felt like home.

I'll just have to get through this so I can see him again soon.

Memory waved a signal to Erec, who took half of his men at a sprint ahead of her and barged through the splintered front door. Her heart started pounding as the door broke through. No turning back now.

Memory, Eloryn, and Peirs went next, the rest of the guards taking position behind them.

A dull, earthy odor like old mushrooms hung in the air inside. The entrance hall was narrow, and doors to each side had been barricaded off, leaving only one direction to travel. All who could cast the light behest did, and the darkness gave way, showing wallpaper hanging from the walls like sloughing skin and a carpet littered in dead leaves and rodent carcasses. Portraits of the past human residents still hung on the walls, their faces slashed away by claw marks.

"Onwards," Eloryn ordered, and the group moved forward down the long tunnel. The ceiling above them had collapsed, leaving a gaping hole to the second floor.

Memory looked behind them and found the front door almost out of sight. The hall continued on much farther than she thought it would, leading them deep into the cavernous house.

"We're being forced along. Can we break through any of these doors? Search the rest of the house?" she asked the guards.

One of the guards lifted a small battering ram from his back, and held it between him and another man. The first strike at the door beside them seemed to shake the whole house.

"We've rang the doorbell now," Memory muttered.

Peirs grunted, "Where are the blasted creatures?"

The guards struck the side door again, and the frame began to split, a crack of space showing into the next room.

"Up front!" Erec called.

With disjointed movements, a mass of gaunts stepped up into the light. Memory counted at least six before shadows hid any more that stood behind them. They hissed at Erec.

"And behind," a guard at the rear replied.

Whipping around, Memory saw her fears confirmed. More gaunts. They'd been blocked off on both sides in the narrow passageway.

Eloryn held her wisp light high and walked to the front to face the gaunts. "Back away. Let us through or be Branded."

A soft scraping sound echoed down the hall, like dry leaves blowing across dirt. As it built, Memory realized it was the gaunts, all of them, laughing at them.

The gaunt closest to Eloryn snatched for her. Erec pulled her back out of reach.

Eloryn gasped, and grabbed the iron arrow head she wore on a necklace. She tore the necklace free and held the iron out defensively.

Erec spoke in a tone cold and quiet. "Bronmarbh Aileadh."

The gaunt howled breathily as the mark appeared on its forehead. Its companions joined the cry and surged forward in attack. Long, wiry limbs flailed, swiping at any human within reach.

The guards at the back of the group rushed at the gaunts behind them, and those in front followed Eloryn forward, striking at the other assailants. The cries of dark fae and men, and the putrid smell of iron

burning fae flesh filled the space. The guards used their daggers, unable to draw their swords in the small space, and the gaunts struck back with sharp talons. The unseelie fae from behind had broken through the guards at the back and fought with them up and down the corridor.

Memory tried to move forward, but was pinned between the backs of men, fighting gaunts on either side. Peirs kept shifting backwards, keeping her behind him and against a wall. She could hear him grunting as he clashed with the slashing gray arms of the creatures.

Eloryn and Erec were pushing forward with the main group, making headway with the iron they wielded and Eloryn's behests.

Memory saw a gap in the fighting, and ran to join them, but the body of a guard flew through the air straight at her.

Peirs stepped in front of her, taking the full force, but the momentum knocked him into Memory and they both hit the door beside them.

Already weakened by the attempts with the battering ram, it smashed inwards, and they fell into the side room and into darkness.

Memory fell hard on her back and her head cracked onto the ground. Her vision darkened and blurred and she widened her eyes and tensed, trying to fight off the black pull of unconsciousness.

The sounds from the corridor grew quieter as the fight sprawled further away into the house.

Memory strained to sit up, pushing away the sharp broken wood and crumbling wall that fell around her. She couldn't get her bearings in the dark room. She almost called a light behest before stopping herself.

"Peirs, can you cast some light?"

He coughed, and spluttered a raspy, "Àlaich las."

The wisp lightened the room, hovering beside Peirs's hand which was limply draped on the ground. They were alone, everyone else had spread out into the rest of the house. The room they were in had been cleared, all its furniture stacked around the edges, blocking windows and other doors. On some walls, holes had been broken through, claw marks showing on the sides. Holes just large enough to squeeze a person, or fae, through.

Peirs groaned beside Memory, and the guard that hit them lay face down on her other side. She reached over to check on him, and felt no pulse at his neck. Memory took a deep breath to calm herself.

Peirs coughed again and Memory looked down at him where he still lay beside her.

His chest was bleeding and he held it clutched in one hand. He saw her looking. "How bad is it?" he asked.

"I could lie and say not bad at all. But you're a big boy and holy hamballs it looks bad. Super bad."

Memory scrambled across the floor, ducking out the door to see if anyone was still around. She needed Eloryn, needed anyone that could heal.

The hall was empty except for an equal mix of bodies of guards and gaunts, sprawled on the messy carpet. Too many bodies. Too many lost lives.

Back in the room, Memory tugged down the old lace curtain from the window and shook the dust from it.

She folded it into a wad and lifted Peirs's hands away from the wound. She could clearly see the spread of four claw marks torn through his clothes, slicing into his flesh.

Peirs smiled crookedly. "I Branded the bastard back at least."

Memory pressed the fabric against the wound and lifted his hands back over it.

"Hold onto this, press it on firmly to stop the bleeding. I'm going to get help."

His hands flopped down weakly, sliding away from the wound.

"Crap." Memory took his place, keeping her hands against the old curtain to slow the flow of blood. The cream cotton lace was already stained red through.

"I've heard Maellan excel at healing magic. I know you're busy, but I'm not wildly keen on pain, Your Majesty."

Memory winced. She hadn't been able to heal anyone other than her sister before. And even if she could, she'd made the oath to not use her magic. *Damn fairies and their damn oath!* "My sister, she's the one that's good at that stuff."

Peirs's eyes rolled back and Memory squeezed his shoulder. "Stay awake, you'll be all right. The bleeding is already stopping."

"Probably means I just ran out of blood."

"Don't sass me. You're going to be fine."

Peirs blinked and seemed to have trouble opening his eyes again. "You always did have too much faith in me."

"Maybe putting lots of faith in people is what helps them rise to great things."

He smiled, but his lips were stained with blood, burbling from his mouth.

That is a very bad thing. Memory gritted her teeth. She should try, she had to at least try and heal him. Maybe she would be able to do it now. Screw her deal with the fae.

"Peirs, I'm going to have a go at healing you, 'kay? I'm not great at it like Lory, so keep your fingers crossed."

Peirs just stared at her. He was too still.

"Peirs?"

Memory squeezed his shoulder but he didn't reply. She shook him and he did nothing.

Peirs's wisp behest began fading.

Memory clutched for Peirs's wrist and found it quiet, no pulse tapping away under the skin.

A single, rasping sob tore up through Memory's throat and she covered her face with her hands, sitting still and quiet.

Sorrow swelled inside Memory and settled, large and heavy in her chest. She gave it a home there, alongside the weight of everyone else she had lost. She would carry them always, every one of them, even if she had to grow stronger to bear that weight.

The light faded out entirely and she held Peirs's hand in the dark, a dead man on either side.

She heard the crunch of feet crushing dry leaves behind her. No light of a wisp behest came with it. It was not another human. Memory reached for the knife at her belt. Before her fingers closed around it, a heavy hand slammed into the back of her head and she collapsed.

CHAPTER NINE

Erec kept in front of Eloryn, so she could barely see past his torso. She spoke her behest to enchant the bodies of those around her to be faster and stronger, and with her iron as well they were making headway into the crowd of gaunts.

"Some are running for it," Erec yelled over the fighting. He looked at Eloryn, urgency in his features.

Eloryn shared his concern. If the gaunts' plan to corner and capture them failed, they might turn on the captives. They needed to chase down the runners and stop them from getting to their prisoners first.

"Quickly," Eloryn ordered, waving the guards around her forward. "*Quickly*," she said again in the magical language. They surged onwards, chasing the remaining gaunts through the dark house, sped faster by Eloryn's behest.

The floorboards strained and crackled under the charging footsteps. Eloryn pushed to the front of the group, leading the charge. *I have to get to Roen before the dark fae do. Please don't let it be too late.*

Eloryn took a face full of cobwebs and wiped it away. The corridor came to a dead end, blocked by half a dozen armoires piled atop each other in a splintered mess. A hole had been clawed in the walls on both sides and one above in the ceiling.

"They've made this house a maze. Which way?" Erec said.

Eloryn changed the meaning of the behests she spoke, and the creatures' path was revealed to her in shining footsteps. "Two went right, one went up."

Erec signaled his men, splitting them off to the right and boosting some up through the hole in the ceiling.

As the space cleared of guards, Eloryn gasped. "Where is Mem, and Peirs?"

"They were right behind us," Erec said, looking back down the empty corridor. "Your Highness, it's my fault. It's my responsibility to protect the queen."

Eloryn looked back the way they'd come, then forward through the holes the guards had gone. Memory was behind and in danger, Roen and others were forward, and in danger. Memory was still with Peirs and some of the other guards. Eloryn hoped that meant she was fine. "Go back and find her, I'll continue on for the abductees."

"Your Highness, you'll be alone, are you sure?" Erec asked.

Eloryn hesitated. *No. I want to find my sister. She's too vulnerable without her magic.*

In the silent moment, Eloryn heard a soft sound that made her heart race. "Go and help Memory," she ordered Erec.

Erec nodded and ran.

Eloryn stood still, alone in the quiet, straining to listen. She stepped toward the mass of furniture in the corridor.

"Eloryn?"

It was like Roen's voice, but weaker, rougher. It seemed to come from within the barricade.

"Roen, where are you?" she called out.

Eloryn climbed carefully up onto the first armoire. It lay on its back on the floor and the doors bent inwards, creaking when they took her weight. Some of the other furniture on top of it shifted.

The glint of eyes shone from a dark gap between the cupboards. A low growl hissed, "Eloryn…"

It wasn't Roen's voice at all.

The creature launched itself out from the jumble of wardrobes, claws first.

Eloryn inhaled sharply and stumbled away. She turned to dodge the sickle-like claws and they caught in her hair, pulling it loose from its pins. She cried out as tearing hair made her eyes water. The gaunt swiped at her again. It was smaller than all the others had been, small

enough to conceal itself in that slim shadowed crack, preparing its ambush, but it was no less strong.

Its fingers tangled in her loose hair, grabbing on and tugging her head down so her face turned up toward the hole in the ceiling. The gaunt's other hand was above her, claws splayed and slashing down at her exposed neck.

She had to say the Brand, while she still had a throat to say it, but she knew there was no time left. "Bronma–"

The gaunt froze, eyes wide. It gurgled a harsh cry as its arms went limp, releasing Eloryn. Black smoke and slime spilled from its mouth and it fell to the floor, revealing Roen standing behind it.

Roen held his iron dagger, and it was slick with gray blood. Squinting at Eloryn and the bright light from her wisp around her, he said, "You look like an angel, my love." He grunted softly, winced, and wobbled on his feet.

Eloryn blinked, letting herself believe her eyes. Her heartbeat grew strong. "You've sustained a blow to your head," she said gently, wrapping her arm around Roen's waist to support him.

Roen nodded. One side of his face had a trail of blood running from his hair line to his jaw and he waved at it weakly. "I escaped the beasts, but this left me too weak to get out of the house. I've mostly been hiding and waiting for my princess to come save me."

Eloryn smiled and sighed at the same time. "I think we're one for one on that count. Thank you," she said, placing a hand to her still intact throat.

Roen smiled in return, but his eyes were vague, haunted.

Eloryn pulled a dressing from the collection she brought with her for treating wounds until she had time to perform proper healing behests. She pressed the wadded cloth to the gash on Roen's forehead. "How do you feel? I can heal you now but it could take some time and we've yet to reach the captives. We've also lost track of Memory and Peirs."

Roen just stared at her. "Come here."

He wrapped her in his arms, burying his head into her neck.

Eloryn felt tears aching for release in her eyes. "I worried I'd lost you. I shouldn't have let you go."

"Let's never lose each other, no matter what. Nothing will part us again."

Eloryn's tears burst free. "I promised I would solve Hayes's demands

before I saw you again, and I haven't."

"Never mind. Let's just run off to sea together and be pirates."

A breathy, rich laugh of relief escaped from Eloryn. She squeezed Roen tightly, but could tell his grip was loose, looser than the strong embrace she knew him to have. "I can heal you now," she offered again.

Roen let her go and smiled. "I will keep. And I know where the gaunts are holding everyone. Let's go."

Roen led Eloryn through the hole in the wall the two gaunts had gone before.

They soon came across the guards who'd gone that way, who had managed to dispatch the last of the gaunts. Their gray bodies and black blood mixed into the gloom and grime on the floor.

"This way," Roen said, and the guards followed. They squeezed through a narrow gap between two walls and around into a large ruined sitting room.

"It's down under there." Roen pointed to the center of the room where a round carpet lay underneath broken armchairs and a tipped over piano.

The guards began to roll back the rug. Roen shook his head and pointed again. "There. The piano."

The guards seemed confused at first, but together put their shoulders against the piano and slid it out of the way. A hole dropped into black beneath it.

Roen looked grim. Eloryn's body refused to move, to go and see what would be found in that dark pit. She forced it to, leaning over the edge and calling the names of children who'd gone missing, names Memory had told her.

The small, weak voice of a child made everyone move for the hole at once.

The guards dropped through first, helping to catch Eloryn as she followed. Eloryn strengthened her light behest to clear all shadows from the space.

The enormous basement had the tang of blood on the cool air. Clean cut stone walls had chains bolted into it at regular intervals, where the bodies of humans, pale and drained, hung like a butcher's shop window.

Many were adults, but some were children. Eloryn sharpened her senses, and could see the faintest rise and fall of breath on their chests.

"They live." *Some of them,* a mournful voice amended internally. "Help them down."

The guards acted quickly, breaking the shackles and cradling the prisoners as they dropped free.

Across the other side of the room, a ragged group of captives shied away from the light. Most had blank faces, compelled or dazed or too traumatized for thought. Eloryn approached them slowly. "Be still, we are here to help. You are safe now."

Hidden behind the front row, a huddle of dirty limbs and rags in the corner began to move. A pale face turned to blink at Eloryn.

"Mem?" The girl with the mountain of messy dark hair was familiar to Eloryn.

"No, Maeve, but she's nearby." *I hope.*

Maeve unwrapped herself from the clutch of other children she was hiding beneath her skirts and small body. She moved stiffly, as though she'd been fixed in that protective posture for weeks.

Eloryn stared, dumbfounded with grief and fury at what she saw in that cold stone room. Then she shook some sense back into herself. These people needed her to act, they needed her help. She began speaking words of magic. She could not heal everyone at once, or rid them of the horrors they'd experienced, but she could give them enough strength to move, to escape this prison.

Eloryn put on a friendly smile and took Maeve's hand, helping her get the other children to their feet.

Maeve mumbled, "It's lucky Mem's not here. This would break her heart."

"Or very seriously enrage her," Eloryn added.

Maeve coughed out a sobbing laugh.

Roen called to them from the hole above. "I've found a ladder to help bring people out. And Erec has returned."

Eloryn called back, "And my sister?"

Roen grimaced. "Peirs is dead. And Memory is gone."

CHAPTER TEN

Light flickered through Memory's eyelids. Her head ached and she forced her eyes open. Two gaunts carried her slung between them, one holding her wrists and one holding her feet. They were going down stairs. Her vision faded again.

She wavered in and out of consciousness. She saw snatches of her surroundings — tunnels, darker tunnels, dirtier tunnels — but had completely lost her bearings. Each time her eyes twitched open it took moments to even remember where she was and what was happening. She'd been captured. She was being taken somewhere. She had to fight back. And then darkness would steal her away again.

A slamming jolt shook her whole body, waking her up. She'd been dumped onto a stone alter on her back. Her body still quivered from the impact. She took quick stock of her surroundings, but all she could see were close, dark, stone walls, and cobwebs. She wished for light. The fae had much better night vision than her and moved without any. The only light was a glow coming from the opening to the room, the color of early sunrise, but dim and distant. Still, it gave Memory hope. Maybe there was a window somewhere nearby, a door, some exit she could escape to outside.

"It's awake," said one gaunt. A splash of black blood on its cheek shone wet in the dark.

"Keep it still," the other replied. Its voice was strangely high pitched

and gurgling despite its masculine appearance. "Remember what the master told us to do."

The creatures held her pinned, one at her arms, and the other pushing her thighs down. She may as well have been bound by metal bars for all she could move. Their sharp claws dug cruelly into her. Panic burbled aggressively in her chest.

The panic had a voice in her head, screaming, *Let go of me, let go, don't touch me!* Memory squinted her eyes, about to loose her magic on them.

She clenched her jaw so hard it made her aching head throb. *I can't. Calm down. I still have my knife. There has to be another chance to escape.*

Across her temple and down to her ear was a sore area that felt wet and sticky. Consciousness was a wild bird, struggling to fly off and leave her at any moment.

The gaunt holding her arms leaned close to her and sniffed at her head. "Can you smell that?" it asked the other dark fae.

The gaunt holding Memory's legs down, the one with black blood on its face, growled a warning. "Leave it. This one is the master's. All the blood is the master's."

"That blood is mine. Keep off me, monster," Memory said. Both creatures ignored her.

"So full of magic." The dark fae sniffing Memory leaned closer, dragging a long, raspy tongue across her forehead. It scratched on her skin like a cat's. Memory cringed in disgust.

"Full, full, full of magic." Excitement rose in the gaunt's voice as it licked her a second time, sharp teeth grazing her skin. Its clawed hands closed tight on her arms, tearing into her skin. Memory cried out and wrestled against it, trying to break free.

"Stop it!" Memory said. The gaunt kept licking, getting more and more excited, more ravenous each time. Memory yelled at the other one. "Stop him, he's going to get you both in trouble with your master!"

The gaunt holding Memory's legs down hissed in frustration. It hesitated, then let go, rushed forward and pushed the bloodthirsty gaunt away. In return it howled in the face of the other, a berserk fury in its cry.

Out of their grasp, Memory wasted no time to take her advantage. She whipped her knife from her belt and slipped off the side of the altar onto her feet.

Both gaunts heard her move and turned on her. One roared so loudly it made Memory's chest reverberate and hair fly around her face.

"Just stay back and let me go," Memory said, holding her knife up in front of her as a warning. Her vision still swam and she worried she'd simply drop like a stone into unconsciousness again at any moment. "Just let me go. I don't want to have to use this. I don't want to hurt you."

Both gaunts now had bloodied faces, the one with black dark fae blood, and the one with Memory's blood red around its mouth. The one with black blood grinned. "That's your mistake."

It grabbed the bloodthirsty fae beside it and pushed it toward Memory. The gaunt flew at her so fast it was impaled on Memory's knife to the hilt before she could pull back. Dark blood spattered, warm and sticky like molasses onto Memory's hand. She recoiled, yanking her knife out of the fae. The knife had already done its damage. The wound foamed and hissed, smelling like burning hair. Thick smoke that sparkled gold within as if sparks from a fire poured from the hole.

Memory stared horrified as the gaunt collapsed in on itself. She stared too long, and the remaining gaunt lunged at her, knocking the knife from her hands.

The gaunt grabbed for her, snatching her around the waist and throwing her over its shoulder. Memory kicked at it and scraped her fingernails on its back but it had no effect. The gaunt's musty jacket hung loose on its bony shoulders, and Memory reached down its back and grabbed the bottom hem. Curling her legs up, she wedged her feet against the gaunt's chest and pushed off as hard as she could. She launched herself backwards, off the gaunt's shoulder, and pulled its coat up and over its head as she went.

Memory landed against the wall with a crack and yelled in pain. The gaunt stumbled blindly, trying to free itself from the fabric covering its face.

Got to get up, get away. Memory's feet slipped as she tried to get them under her. Her body ached all over. A hand closed over her arm. Warm. Human.

She looked up.

Will.

He looked angrier than she'd ever seen him. He helped her to her feet then turned on the gaunt. "You hurt her."

The gaunt got its claws into the coat material and tore itself free.

Will held the iron hook, pointing it at eye level at the gaunt. Memory bent down with a groan and reclaimed her knife.

The gaunt stared at them both for a long moment. *Don't you dare kamikaze yourself at us you crazy creature,* Memory begged silently.

"Doesn't matter. My master will have you anyway, soon." The gaunt threw the remains of its coat on the floor and vanished away through the Veil.

"Holy crapoly," Memory said with a big sigh. "I do NOT like those guys."

"You're bleeding," Will said.

"And apparently it's tasty, tasty blood. Thanks for coming to the rescue. How did you get away from Mina so quick?"

Will didn't say anything, just held up the iron hook in his hands.

Memory raised an eyebrow. "You didn't hurt her, did you?" *Am I entirely sure if that would be a bad thing?*

"No. Just threatened. Made her send me back, once she told me why she didn't want me to go into the house. And who these creatures' master is."

Memory and Will found their way back out of the labyrinthine underground tunnel system and out into the cool morning wind through a wooden hatch around the back of the house.

Memory stood for a moment, breathing the freshness of that air. She felt exhausted, and not just emotionally. She was certain she was concussed. She just wanted to sleep and sleep, as soon as she knew everyone was safe. Everyone but Peirs and all the men who'd already died tonight. Memory started imagining how many families would wake up this morning without a father. She slumped, leaning into Will's chest in an effort to stay upright. Will took initiative from there, and in a smooth scoop she was up in his arms, carried there in a strong embrace. Memory let her eyes close for a short moment as she listened to his heartbeat and tried to forget everything else.

Reaching the front of the house, a guard who had just helped a young girl into one of the carriages saw Memory and Will, and raced back into the house. Soon Eloryn, Roen, and Erec came rushing back out.

Memory's chest warmed and tightened at the sight of them. "Roen, you're okay. You're alive."

Will placed Memory softly down on her feet. She managed a few

wobbly steps to greet the others and Roen met her in a just as wobbly embrace.

Eloryn quickly joined them, holding her sister strongly. "Thank the fae, you're all right. We were just about to track where the creatures had taken you."

"You found the captives, you saved them. Is Maeve out? Edele?"

"Maeve is fine." Eloryn hesitated, and stepped back. "We're still checking for everyone else."

Memory broke away as well. She turned to watch the first coach of captives rolling off toward the castle, and more people being directed by guards into another. Erec stood by the door, his face gray and eyes red.

"Erec. I'm so sorry about Peirs. He saved my life, and I... I couldn't save his."

Erec turned his head to Memory, and pulled himself into stance of attention. "I know if my brother had to give his life for anyone, he would have chosen you. He believes, believed greatly in you."

Memory just nodded, and watched as Erec returned to his duties.

Memory stared at the carriage in front of her, the smaller, faster one she'd arrived in and it felt suddenly so unfamiliar, as though it were years since they'd first arrived there that night, or that she expected to see a car there instead. She blinked, her eyes blurry.

"Let's go home," Eloryn said, putting an arm around Memory's waist and leading her forward. "There's lots of healing to be done, after tonight. But it is over now."

Tears flooded Memory's eyes and she blinked them away, refusing to let them fall. "No. It's only just beginning. This place, it was Finvarra's."

Eloryn stopped mid step. "How do you know?"

Will looked over his shoulder at the steps of the building. "Mina let it slip when she took me away. That's why she didn't want me to go in. Way too dangerous, out of bounds because it was the unseelie king's. She's been listening for gossip and that's what she heard."

Eloryn's eyes sought from side to side, the questions in her mind clear on her face. "Why? Some think him mad, but to do this? Why?"

Memory's voice was hard and low. "Mina heard that Finvarra believes drinking human blood will prolong his life."

Memory watched as guards brought out the last of the survivors. There weren't many. The driver climbed onto the carriage, ready to go. The few survivors Memory saw looked in pretty bad shape, mentally

as much as physically. She wondered what horrors they'd endured, all just to keep one twisted old king alive. Memory kept hearing how the fae were dying, but this was absolutely not the right way to stay alive.

"Now we know it was Finvarra who was Providence, and Hope," Memory said. "And me and Thayl, we were just some other experiment of his, turning us into a battery to steal the magic from to charge himself up with new life."

Roen frowned. "You think that's what Providence would have asked of Thayl after his bargain was complete? To take all that power for himself?"

"Sure. Think about it. Finvarra couldn't go to the human world himself to gather up all that magic. He had to send a human to do it for him. And he found just the right sucker with Thayl."

Erec joined their group and notified them that the house had been cleared. Another troop of guards was on the way from the castle for a more thorough sweep, and to remove the dead for burial, but it was time for them to leave.

As they climbed up into their own carriage, Memory said, "The only thing I can't work out is why he wanted me to be queen. Why was that so important? It wouldn't have anything to do with nabbing my magic to keep his ticker going."

Eloryn stepped into the carriage next, taking the seat beside her. "If anything, you being queen would make it harder for Finvarra to harvest the magic from you. Far more protections and politics in place. But that is our problem now as well. Finvarra is the king of the Unseelie Fae. There is not a move we can make against him for justice for this that wouldn't risk war, or risk the Pact itself."

CHAPTER ELEVEN

All living captives from Finvarra's blood lair were brought back to the palace for medical care. Both Eloryn and the wizards of the Council worked without sleep for two days to heal the survivors. Once well enough, they were also questioned on any further insight into what Finvarra had been doing. Most knew nothing, too dazed, compelled, or simply traumatized to remember anything other than an overwhelming sense of horror. Most remembered very little beyond being taken by a handsome man or woman who then turned out to be a gaunt. Those that remembered more never saw any fae except the gaunts, who would bleed the victims and take the blood away.

Memory had searched the survivors for one person in particular; a little girl called Edele. She wasn't there. It had been so long since Edele had been taken that her fate was clear. Eloryn could see the ferocity of emotions that discovery caused within her sister. Eloryn was proud to see Memory keep her sadness and rage reined in, but even a couple of days later, the teapots and crockery on their morning tea setting rattled just by being within proximity to Memory.

Eloryn had arranged for them to have some time with just the two of them, while Roen and Will spent some time together as well, and the sisters sat at a neatly set up table on the emerald lawn of the palace's private gardens. Eloryn poured out some chamomile tea for her sister. "All of Finvarra's captives have made a full recovery, physically at least,

and there have been no further reports of people going missing from Caermaellan since."

Memory rubbed her forehead with the palm of her hand. "But we still have to deal with him. Somehow. And Hayes, somehow. Your wedding is meant to be in just two days and all we have are somehows."

"We'll find something. We have to."

"You know what I want to do? I want to get both Finvarra and Hayes in front of me, then take a crap on my fist and punch them both in the mouth."

Eloryn coughed up her tea. "That was the singularly most graphic, disgusting and violent thing I've ever heard."

"You've led a very sheltered life."

"And yet I can't help agreeing with the sentiment." Eloryn sat back in her chair and looked up at the sky. The clouds hung so low and dark, barely any daylight shone through and the temperature was dropping tangibly. A hawk circled high above. She wondered what she must look like in its eyes. What their problems would seem like to that animal, so wild and free. "I've almost finished rebuilding the Round Table. I wish all problems could be solved by fixing, rebuilding, or creating. Violence and conflict lead only to more of the same. If only there were some way I could heal Hayes's heart, to take away his greed or ambition or any grudges he holds against me for my actions."

Memory leaned forward. "Can you? You are so good with your magic, and you can heal bodies so well. What about minds?"

Eloryn paused. *Could I?* She wasn't sure at all if it was within her power, but she saw the possibility there, and the hope. "If I could, wouldn't it be wrong for me to change a person's thoughts and feelings without permission, for my own gain?"

"Pfft. Always having to bring logic and ethics into the argument. Okay, think of it this way- would it be wrong to cure someone of blindness without permission?" Memory's mouth twisted and she made a smacking sound with her tongue. "Without permission. Yuck. Yeah, those words just taste bad together. I guess even good things done without permission turn bad, don't they?"

Eloryn placed her teacup carefully back onto the saucer and regarded her sister for a moment. "You've suffered more hurt than many. Even with permission, is this something you would seek out? To have your hurts healed, taken away, or forgotten?"

Memory looked down, the tiniest smile on her mouth, so small it looked sad.

"A week or two ago I might have said yes. But no. I wouldn't. If it meant forgetting those I've lost, then no. I never want to lose them."

Eloryn bowed her head. A small service had been held for Peirs just the day before. Memory wanted a grand event, to honor him, but Erec requested it be kept simple. Even still, the small graveyard overflowed with people coming to say goodbye. Erec was Peirs's only blood family, but there were the members of the resistance Peirs led, every guard from the castle, and every child from Memory and Maeve's orphanage mourning for him.

Afterwards, when everyone had gone and Memory thought she was alone, Eloryn saw her placing out a small marker in the graveyard for Edele as well.

As though sharing thoughts with her twin, Memory touched the corner of her eye to clear away a tear. "If it meant not being the person I am now, I would not. I'm the person I am now because of the hurt and the happiness I've lived through. I've lost parts of me before. I never want to lose anything again."

Eloryn's smile grew as her sister spoke, and grew so wide it almost forced tears from her eyes.

Memory kicked her under the table. "Quit it. You're making this all awkward now."

"I don't mind. You make me feel that somehow, everything will turn out fine."

Memory leaned to the side, looking past Eloryn. "This doesn't look very fine. Check it out. What's going on?"

Eloryn turned around to see Roen being escorted to them by Bedevere and a rank of guards. Will followed a small way behind.

She stood to greet them.

Bedevere looked deeply troubled, and Roen's expression matched.

Bedevere bowed to Memory and Eloryn in turn. "Your Majesty, Your Highness, I'm sorry to interrupt you but Hayes has been found dead in his cell."

Memory got to her feet too as Will came to stand beside her. "No way. You mean, naturally? Or..."

Eloryn looked at the guards again, keeping close rank around Roen. "You can't believe Roen had something to do with this."

Bedevere bowed his head. "It seems as though Hayes was poisoned. There is a witness that has reported seeing Sir Roen near Hayes's cell. Or someone that looked like him," Bedevere amended. "Given that he also has motivation, he will be considered a suspect until the investigation is complete."

"How long will that take?" Memory asked.

"Not long. We will be utilizing all techniques available to the Council. There are no secrets to magic. I wish I could oversee the investigation myself, but I'm afraid I also am considered to have conflict of interest, if not motivation, myself."

Eloryn nodded. She still missed his brother, Waylan, as well. "Is there nothing further we can do other than wait?"

"I fear not," Bedevere said.

Roen tilted his head, seeming more embarrassed than anything. "They want to confine me to quarters for now. Apparently I'm considered of little risk of escape due to my lack of spark. I asked to be taken to you. If I must be confined to quarters, your quarters are much more accommodating than my own."

Eloryn's lips twitched into a small smile. She already knew it couldn't be him who murdered Hayes. She just had to trust the investigation would also prove his innocence. Taking him by the hand, she began leading the way back to her chambers. The guards parted, making way for them and Memory and Will following.

Bedevere stood back and watched them leave. "At least this has solved the dilemma of the marriage contract."

Eloryn turned back, answering over her shoulder. "We never wanted it solved this way."

Bedevere bowed low. "I know. For all Hayes did to my family as well, I am not happy to see him ended this way. There is no honor in this."

Memory pulled the thick, fur-lined cloak tight around her shoulders. Her teeth rattled as she puffed out a breath, watching it form mist on the air and mingling with the delicate snowflakes falling around her.

"Come back inside. You'll get cold," Will said from behind her.

"Like you can talk," Memory responded, shaking her head. Will still only wore a single layer of clothing, just one thin, button down

shirt and pants. No shoes. She swore he didn't feel the cold at all. Snow fell all around them, soft and gentle, as they watched from Memory's balcony. Enough had fallen to start giving the trees and ground of the palace gardens a light blanket of white. "It's so beautiful. They say this is the first snow to fall in Avall since before the Pact."

"I've never seen it snow here before," Will agreed.

"The Pact and the fae in Avall changed its whole climate from a cold wasteland to temperate paradise. Clara says people are taking the snow as a bad omen, that too many fae are dying or gone, and Avall is reverting to the harsh land it used to be." Memory paused to try and catch a snowflake on her tongue.

Will stared out into the hunting grounds where he used to spend more time. Memory wondered if he was thinking about Mina, or the other fae he knew. She wondered whether they were slowly dying as well.

"I think it's the iron," Will finally said.

Memory nodded slowly, frowning. "I've been thinking that too. The rest of the world is so rich with iron, and Avall has barely any now, not even raw iron ore. They had to get rid of iron for the fae, but they've screwed themselves over by doing it. It's like the rest of the world is one huge magnet and Avall is a tiny magnet and the huge magnet is sucking away and hogging all that hippy earth blood life force magic the fae live on. I've been hoping that I'm wrong, because what could we possibly do about it? We can't take on the whole rest of the world. 'Hey rest of the world, stop making steel and stealing our magic!' Can you see that working? Nope."

Will turned his back on the forest and looked at Memory. "Think about how fast industrialization is happening. It's going to get worse. Faster and faster."

"I've seen the flow of magic in the Veil. It's like a tide, flowing out of Avall." Memory stared at Will's eyes, icy blue and rimmed in dark lashes, they seemed to belong in this weather, like a black branch covered in snow. He reached out and brushed a thumb across her mouth.

Memory drew in a shaky breath.

"Your lips are turning blue," he said.

"I'm fine."

"You always say that."

"It's always true."

"Always?"

Did Will just step closer to me, or does he just suddenly feel a lot closer? Memory had to tilt her head up to look at him. A snowflake hung in his earth-brown hair right beside his cheek. His gaze on her was intense. "Are you really okay, after losing Peirs, after almost losing Maeve? After those gaunts caught you?"

Memory shivered, and not due to the cold. Will knew her too well. She'd been telling herself she was fine, but the whole event had left her shaken. To be held down against her will was nearly more than she could bear. It brought back too much pain.

She began shaking her head, ready to say the words again. *I'm fine.*

Will did step closer then and wrapped his arms around her shoulders, pulling her toward him. Memory gasped and hot tears flooded her eyes. They poured over her eyelids unchecked, darkening the thin fabric on Will's chest where she pressed her face.

"Damn it," Memory mumbled between sobs.

"I'm sorry I wasn't there. That I couldn't stop them touching you." Will's breath warmed through her hair as he spoke.

"I don't expect you to protect me all the time. I need to be able to look after myself."

"I know. But I want to protect you."

Memory clenched her fist around the cloth on Will's back.

He squeezed her tighter as well. "I want to be there for you when you need me most."

"You are," Memory said, sniffling away her sobs. "You're here with me now."

Will held her like that as the snow fell on them. After a few moments, Memory stood back, wiped her nose and took a deep breath. "I need to fess a few things to Lory and Roen. Will you come with me? Moral support?"

Will simply nodded. Memory held out her hand to him and led him back inside to the joining door between the sisters' chambers. She paused there for a moment.

"What will I do if it was Roen who murdered Hayes?" she asked in a small voice.

"Do you think it was?"

"Most of me says no. No way. But part of me knows that we weren't finding any other way out of the marriage contract. Roen and Eloryn had to be getting desperate." Memory looked at the wall between her

room and the corridor as though she could see straight through it. She knew if she could, she would see a troop of guards out there, keeping Roen confined in Eloryn's quarters until the investigation was complete.

"I'm Roen's friend. He's like a brother to me. But I'm also queen and I have to be fair and treat any crime as it should be. Ugh. If this isn't just the shittiest shit-tastic shit storm ever." Memory wiped her face again and puffed out a long breath. "Okay, let's do this."

Memory opened the adjoining door without knocking, and found Eloryn and Roen holding each other in the middle of the room.

"Aw, come on! I was hoping to catch you guys up to something much naughtier," Memory said, waggling her eyebrows at them.

Roen smirked. "What's happened? Have you heard anything about the investigation?"

"Not yet. I actually have something else I wanted to talk to you both about."

Memory panicked as everyone quieted to listen to her. She prolonged the task by getting everyone to sit down, and asking if anyone needed something to drink or eat, or more cushions, until Will gave her a stern look. Memory stopped fussing and stood still in front of her friends.

Then she told them everything about her past in the other world. Her time in the group home. The abuse she suffered there. She glossed over most of the details, until she got to the time right before she was brought back to Avall. The time she was beaten, and her magic killed the man who had been abusing her.

Memory shifted on her feet. They felt numb underneath her and she stared at them instead of looking at her friends. Anyway, I had to tell you. You might have already known, or guessed, but I had to say it out loud. I know it's the big cliché thing. Poor girl sexually abused in her past. But that's because it happens all the time. Happens too much. When it shouldn't happen at all. Never. Ever. *Ever.* And if I could do anything to stop it happening again, to anyone, I would. And now I'm a ruler maybe I can."

With a deep sigh, Memory dared to look her friends in the eyes again. "Now here I am, meant to be a ruler, someone who decides right and wrong, creates laws and defends justice. How can I do that when I'm a murderer?"

Eloryn had been sitting very quietly, staring at her hands in her lap. A long teardrop wound down one of her cheeks. She looked up at

Memory with enormous sadness in her eyes. "I saw it happen. When I shared spirits with you, I saw flashes of your past. I didn't know for sure, then, because it was all so horrifying and confusing, but now you've explained the details it makes more sense. It wasn't murder, not hardly. It was self-preservation only. You did nothing wrong."

"I believe Eloryn. I saw how you looked when you first came to Avall. Beaten all over." Roen stood up and took her hands. "You've got an amazing heart, Memory. A quality many rulers overlook. I trust you to make just decisions."

A knock at the door startled all of them.

Memory answered quickly and found a page waiting there. He announced that the investigation had been completed, and they were all required in the Round Room immediately.

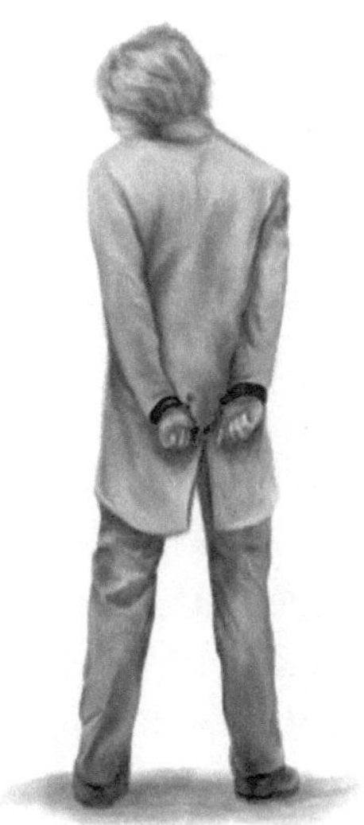

CHAPTER TWELVE

The troop of guards, including those escorting Roen and Memory's normal bodyguards, led them to the Round Room where Bedevere and a number of other wizards waited for them.

Memory saw another young man standing in the center of the room, bound in shackles. From a distance, the shade of his hair and angle of his jaw made him look just like Roen.

"Dylan?" she said.

He turned to look at her. His eyes were wide and eyebrows low, a combination of terrified and furious.

Bedevere gestured to an older wizard beside him "Madoc has completed the investigation and proof has been found of Sir Dylan Faerbaird's guilt in the matter of Hayes's murder. The fugitive was then captured whilst trying to steal from Hayes's chambers and flee."

Memory glanced at Roen beside her, worried about what reaction he'd have to seeing his brother like this. Roen seemed more confused than anything.

His voice was low and sharp when he asked, "Dylan, why have you done this? Are you trying to hurt our parents even more?"

Dylan's head bowed, but with a shake he lifted it again, staring furiously at Memory. "Hayes ruined my chances at having a comfortable life by his scheming to set me up with her. A life for which I'd already

sacrificed a lot in order to keep." Dylan's glance flicked briefly to Roen before he turned on Memory again. "It was all Hayes's idea, he forced me into relations with you, Your Majesty. I was trying to get him to clear my name but he refused. He spoiled my future. He had to pay."

Memory gaped. "You killed him for revenge?" Her brain ached, trying and yet unable to comprehend. *Can any desire be so destructive as vengeance?*

"I don't care whose idea it was to pair the two of us up. But what you've done now, there's no coming back from that." Memory walked forward to stand in front of Dylan. "Even after what you did to me, I could have forgiven you. Truly. I'm really into forgiveness these days. You had a chance to reconcile with your family. *Your family*, Dylan. But now I must sentence you for this terrible crime."

Dylan rasped out a rough laugh, his eyes growing wider, wilder. "Why? I did you a favor! I know the old man was trying to marry the princess. I removed your problem. I was trying to help you."

Roen spoke from beside Memory. "You were only trying to help yourself. It's all you know how to do."

Memory turned to look at Roen and thought about how he would have to deliver this news to his parents and her heart broke for him. Five of his brothers had been lost in battles, and Dylan had left them by choice, wanting riches and comfort over a life in hiding with his family. And now he was more of a criminal than Roen ever had been. She wished she could simply remove all the anger and greed from within Dylan, and return him to his parents as a beloved son, and no one would have to suffer. But she knew in her heart no magic could do that. But maybe time could.

She sighed. "Would I be right in assuming the standard punishment for murder in Avall is some sort of execution?"

Bedevere nodded solemnly.

"Not any more. Dylan, your crime is one of the worst, but you will learn nothing from dying and teach nothing to others. And I couldn't live with myself if I took another of Isabeth and Brannon's sons away from them. You will be imprisoned, and you will work to help make Avall a better place. We're going to introduce Avall to some things called community service and rehabilitation."

Memory called the guards to take Dylan away. He craned his neck as he was taken, watching Memory. The look on his face was confused, possibly even relieved. She hoped he would take her mercy and use it well.

Roen put a hand on her shoulder. "Thank you. For all that he is, he is still my brother."

Memory still watched the empty doorway. "I know. But I didn't save him for that reason. I believe people deserve a chance to right their wrongs."

"I hope he lives up to your expectations. Even as a child, he was always selfish, deceitful, and even cruel. What if some people are born that way and can never change?"

"I have to hope that they aren't. To bring myself away from the darkness inside me, the darkness that almost killed me, I have to try and always see the best in people. Maybe if I can see it, I can reflect it back for them, to let them see what they could be. Maybe that is all they need to change."

Roen squeezed Memory's shoulder and then strode across the room into Eloryn's waiting arms. He lifted her off her feet and she giggled in utter joy and relief.

"Are you sure this is a good idea?" Clara asked.

Memory shifted the skirts she'd gathered into her hands to get a better grip on them and clear them away from her legs. She picked up her pace, her friends following along. They were already more than fashionably late. "Good idea? No. It's more the kind of idea that would make a bad idea feel good about itself."

"It is a good idea," Will said. "Just be careful."

"It would be better if I weren't running late," Memory said. Roen had been giving her sword fighting classes, and the two of them got too caught up in training, forgetting the time. Changing from the fencing uniform into a formal gown wasn't a short procedure either. Clara was still adding accessories and finishing Memory's look as she chased her along the corridor.

Memory stopped outside of the Round Room and wriggled her gown back into place. Eloryn helped brush some crumbs off her shoulder from the last minute snack Memory had scoffed down on the way.

Memory peeked around through the entrance and saw the King of the Unseelie Fae, the Queen of the Seelie Fae, and the room full of their followers, seated inside. The circular table, which Eloryn had

finally completed repairing, was laid out in a range of the castle's finest delicacies, fruits, candies, and treats that both human and fae could eat, interspersed with tall, happy floral arrangements overflowing with multicolored roses from the palace gardens. Memory could already hear the larger party started downstairs in the grand ballroom, and wondered how it looked at that moment, filled with humans and fae mingling under shining chandeliers.

She sighed. "There are these movies back in our world with this super-secret agent who always meets his nemesis face to face and sizes him up at some big fancy do. I figure holding a big mixer like this, having a bit of a formal meet and greet with the fairy nobility in a friendly and diplomatic environment is a good way to get our eyes on Finvarra and maybe even get some info out of him."

"Do these meetings normally work well for this, *super-secret agent*?" Eloryn asked, her head tilted in a curious, if long-suffering, expression.

Memory cleared her throat. "Yeah. Uh. All the time."

Will frowned at her. "I'll be right here if you need me."

Memory felt the urge to throw her arms around him, to kiss him or do something that showed him how grateful she was of his presence, both there now and in her life as a whole. She swallowed hard and thanked him awkwardly before turning away and entering the Round Room.

Aine and her companion Lugh both stood as Memory and Eloryn strode into the room. Nyneve matched them on their feet, but it took a few longer moments for Finvarra to get off his chair, groaning and struggling at the effort to stand for the entrance of the human ruler.

"Thank you all for coming," Memory said, trying to sound confident and warm. "It's my intention to build better relationships between our races, and have asked Your Majesties here tonight to help me in that cause."

Memory took her seat around the table from the fae rulers so she could face them both. Aine smiled graciously as she took her seat.

Finvarra grumbled as he returned to his. "Words. Just words. Heard them all before from your predecessors. What are you going to do that's different? You've already got unseelie blood all over your hands."

Memory bristled and clenched her jaw to keep her mouth shut.

"Father, please," Nyneve gripped his wrist and he grumbled more beneath his breath, but soon quieted.

Aine folded her elongated golden fingers on the table in front of

her and looked across at Finvarra. "It is true, that more fae blood has been spilled recently than for a long time before. But the fault is not human alone, that is obvious."

Memory paused for a long moment, letting the fae watch her and wait. "The Pact is being violated more and more often. I've seen fae who don't give a damn about it or whether they are Branded. Humans are defending themselves more violently because they are seeing the fae becoming more threatening. If we're going to fix this, I need to understand why. Why are so many fae now willing to break Avall's laws?"

Finvarra and Aine both stared, mouths closed into thin lines.

"Because we are dying," Nyneve said. Her voice was deep and hard edged with pain.

Memory bowed her head to her. "I've heard the rumors, and seen evidence. It's all the iron, isn't it? Out in the rest of the world, drawing all the magic away from Avall."

Nyneve's eyes narrowed slightly and she nodded. "Avall is meant to be our sanctuary. Our own world, the lands of Tearnan Ogh, are a timeless place. Eternal, but lifeless, it has long ago lost the natural magics of life needed to sustain us. That's why the fae needed Avall and why we formed the Pact. But as this land too is sapped of all its life force, we will surely die."

Aine waved her hand dismissively. "Great human civilizations have come and gone before. The expansion and progress of the other human lands that is causing this imbalance may end at any time now, burnt out in war or plague or any other form of human weakness. This will not be the end of the fae, despite what those who are behaving rashly believe."

"We'd cling on a lot longer if the humans of Avall weren't using up what little magic is left," Finvarra said, spattering out the words.

"What do you mean?" Memory asked.

He eyed her up and down, distaste curling his lips. "Humans and their magic, their *behests*, using up what we need to stay alive on their frivolities. And you, the worst of them, all that magic stored within you. It's an atrocity."

Like you can talk. You made me this way. Memory glared back at him until Eloryn cleared her throat and Memory tried to form a more diplomatic expression.

Eloryn said, "Have the fae truly known all along that the rest of the world did not become a hell?"

"It did become a hell," Finvarra replied with a fierce wave of his clawed hand.

"Maybe to the fae, but not to humans." Eloryn shook her head. "You openly misled the people of Avall all along."

Aine shrugged her delicate shoulders in a graceful roll. "Have the people of Avall suffered in some way? I am sure Avall is much better off now than it would have been without the Pact. You've lost nothing from being disconnected from the iron hell."

Memory watched wisp light fall onto the glittering cheekbones of the fairy queen and wondered how something so beautiful could be so empty of heart and reason.

"That shouldn't have been your decision to make," Memory said. She felt like banging her head on the table in front of her. Any chance of uniting the races had been lost the minute they started talking, and she'd learned little other than just how selfish and oblivious the fae could be. "If you'd told humans earlier, let them know all along what was happening, we could have worked with you in finding some sort of solution."

Memory stood up and ducked a very small curtsey. "I think that's about enough for this meeting. I still wish to help if I can, but assistance only comes with honesty. We can't hope to help each other out with lies and secrets still hanging between us."

She directed her words straight at Finvarra, but received only a vague grumble in return.

Memory waited at the door as the fae left the room, heading downstairs to the larger party. As Nyneve walked past at the end of the line, she touched Memory's hand softly. Memory looked up and was struck by the deep black of her eyes, lined in bright silver eyelashes. The serpentine scales on her silver flesh seemed to form swirling patterns down her cheeks and neck.

Nyneve leaned close and whispered, "I still have hope the humans will be able to help the fae, too."

She smiled a small, soft smile at Memory before following her father.

CHAPTER THIRTEEN

Will leaned on the wall, waiting for Memory to finish in her meeting. He felt far too visible standing in the open, well lit corridor like this. After so long in the woods, adjusting to life indoors again with other people was taking longer than he liked. Even being in a room just with Memory's new friends all at once felt crowded and uncomfortable.

He could hear someone walking up behind him. The man's scent, like soap and the spiciness of cloves, and soft fall of his feet, told Will instantly it was Roen.

"Are they done yet?"

Will listened, and heard Memory stand up and end the meeting. "Almost."

Roen glanced sidelong at Will as they waited, his hands plunged deep into his pockets and shoulders pulled in. Eloryn had left Will and Roen together for a while once, but they hadn't really talked. Will wondered just what Memory's new friends thought of him. He knew he was different now, that his life with the fae had made him different, much like Aine's consort, the human man Lugh, had been made different.

But he knew he had to make an effort to fit into this new life, for Memory. And he wanted to for himself as well. Deep inside, he knew it wasn't long ago he'd all but given up on his own life. He was Mina's and lost all hope that the girl he waited for would ever come back to him. But now she had, now Memory was in his life again, he wanted to

take his life back, to make his own decisions again and see where that life could take him.

And while ever he still carried iron, Mina wouldn't be able to do anything about it.

Memory walked out of the Round Room then and smiled at him, and his heart's rhythm sped. Her rich purple hair was so at odds with the misty green formal gown she wore, but she looked so confident that it worked for her. In the past, her hair color and piercings always seemed to be a mask to hide behind. Now, she owned them. She was herself, and also someone new, someone better.

Memory bumped her shoulder against his as he stepped into place beside her and they continued with Eloryn and Roen down to the ball downstairs.

"How did it go?" Will asked.

"We all made it out of the room alive, so I'd call it a success," Memory said.

A herald announced the entrance of the queen, princess, and their partners as they reached the grand ballroom, and Will tensed as the crowd paused to stare at them and applaud. Clara had helped him dress as formally as any of the other human men out in the room, but it didn't help. If anything, the layers of shirt, overcoat, jacket and silky scarf left him feeling breathless, strangled.

Memory glanced at him. With a clearly fake yawn, she gestured to some seating in the corner, partially obscured by a draping curtain. "Want to sit down with me for a while? I'm exhausted from the fury hamster in my chest."

Will crooked an eyebrow.

Memory gestured to her chest, her hand going round and round. "Like my insides are an insane angry rodent, running like crazy on its wheel of fury all day. So let's grab a seat."

Will glanced out at the crowd again, then nodded, his mouth gone dry. *So much for taking my life back. A room full of people and I feel like running away.* He followed Memory around the edges of the busy room, and noticed she kept looking back at him, checking he was okay. By the time they sat down he was smiling again.

Memory kicked her crystal encrusted slippers off and put her feet up on a chair. She wriggled toes covered in sheer lace stocking and slouched against the backrest.

Eloryn and Roen had gone together straight out onto the dance floor and were already spinning joyfully between the other dancers. Wide hooped skirts gusted and twirled to the rhythm of the chamber orchestra. In between the humans in their suits and silk gowns, sprites and other fae creatures did their own, less structured dances. Most were seelie fae. While the unseelie had been openly invited, few seemed to accept the invitation, although Memory did identify one banshee in the mix. Tiny pixies flittered above the crowd, creating streaks of light and glitter in their path. A group of sprites at human size danced together in a ring in the center of the room, shimmering like fireworks.

Memory watched Eloryn and Roen dancing with a deep, wistful expression. Will almost asked her if she'd like to dance, but panic rose in him again, followed by a deep self-loathing that he was too scared to be the fun and sociable partner Memory deserved.

The fae royalty had already arrived and been announced into the gathering, and Will watched as they took their seats on a raised side section, reserved for royalty, above the general crowd.

The party-goers who were not dancing were cooing and fawning over the children serving food at the event. Memory and Clara had arranged for Maeve and the orphans to learn how to waiter the event, as another chance to build some bridge between the nobles and the poor of Avall. Mostly the party guests just seemed to think the little outfits the children wore were cute.

"Look at him," Memory said in a whisper just loud enough for Will to hear over the noise of the ball. She flicked her chin across the room at Finvarra, currently being served by the two redheaded orphan girls, Isa and her sister. "He's looking at them like they are the food."

While watching, someone else caught Will's eye. He frowned. Mina stood across the way, just standing, glaring, and fuming at him.

He felt for the small iron tool he carried in his coat's breast pocket, reassuring himself it was still there. Regardless, he doubted Mina would act out in a setting like this. The very fact she couldn't seemed to be making her even angrier.

When Memory leaned across from her chair and put a hand on Will's knee, laughing at a young man trying to hit on Clara, Mina stomped a foot and took a few steps toward him.

The midnight haired daughter of the unseelie king, Nyneve, interrupted Mina's path. They seemed to exchange a few words, and with one last

look at Will, Mina followed Nyneve away.

Memory was giving two thumbs up and a lewd grin to Clara across the room. She turned back to Will, gasping with laughter.

"Hey, do you want to…" Memory paused, a slight frown over her smile. She glanced at the dance floor, then again at Will. "You want to get out of here?"

Will bowed his head. "Yeah."

Will and Memory talked long into the night, reminiscing and laughing at how strange it was that Memory now recalled their past more clearly than Will did. They dragged cushions and blankets out onto Memory's balcony and sat there together, wrapped up in a huddle, watching the stars and a new, light fall of snow, until they fell asleep in each other's arms.

Memory woke up in her bed the next morning. Inside her chest the fire of the stored magic still burned as usual, and a warm happiness sat beside it.

Looking around, she wondered where Will had gone. Since raiding Finvarra's lair, Will had been nearly constantly by her side. It felt like that was how it should be, and even though she couldn't see him now, Memory was confident that Will would be close by.

Smiling, Memory climbed out of bed, greeting Clara who had come to help her prepare for the day. She was meant to be meeting Eloryn, Roen, Maeve, and a handful of other people their age who stayed at the palace, for a brunch in the palace gardens. It had been Eloryn's idea, in order to make some new friendships, to normalize their lives a little. Memory had invited Will, but he seemed reluctant. It was clear he still had trouble being in crowded situations, which made Memory sad for him, but she knew he would need time to adjust to the changes in his life. She was happy to give him as much time as he needed. He had waited so long for her, after all.

Memory dressed in one of her new outfits, which were much faster to get on without help than the gowns in her wardrobe. The tailor had managed to create a new pair of jeans for her, although the denim wasn't really denim, but rather a soft canvas dyed gray-blue. She pulled them on. Over a collared cream shirt, she clipped a royal purple and cream striped corset closed then sat down to put on a little make up.

"Have you seen Will this morning?" Memory asked Clara.

Clara worked on brushing Memory's hair and pinning it into a braided up do. She had bobby pins between her teeth as she said, "He's already out in the grounds with the others."

Memory jerked her head in surprise and Clara scolded her, taking out a few pins and redoing the section again.

"Will? My Will?" Memory asked.

"Yes, *your* Will." Looking above her head in the dressing table mirror, Memory could see Clara smirking.

Memory tried to stand up, and Clara pushed her back onto the seat.

"Is my hair done?" Memory asked.

"Almost. What's the hurry? You're the one who slept in. Overcome with a sudden jealousy that *your* Will might be interacting with other people?" Clara was downright grinning now.

"No, just..." *Just what? Worried? Proud? Or Jealous?* Memory wasn't sure. She just knew she wanted to be there with Will. "Can I go?"

Memory stood up as Clara tried to hold her head still to slide in one last pin. "All done."

"Ouch," Memory grunted, then placed a quick kiss on Clara's cheek. "Thanks, Clara."

Memory was already dashing out of the room as Clara giggled. "You're welcome."

Pulse tapping in her throat, Memory ran all the way through the palace. Breathless, she dashed out into the private grounds at the back of the castle, near the hedge maze. The air was chilled and dry and made her throat ache. The sky was clear blue, and a light fall of snow remained from the night before, making topiary hedges and shrubs look like cakes dusted in icing.

On the large area of mosaic pebble paving, a long table had been brought out and spread with tiered food stands. A dozen people sat around it, including Eloryn. Maeve was standing aside with Erec who seemed to be on guard duty, but paying more attention to her. Memory also recognized Laudine and another girl from the finishing school.

They all watched a fast, dangerous looking swordfight taking place between Roen and Will. Everyone smiled and clapped when one of the two fighters made an impressive move.

Boys, Memory thought.

Will hadn't noticed her yet, and she watched quietly from the side of the yard.

A small hollowness of jealousy opened in Memory. She didn't want or expect it, but seeing Will interacting with other people so openly brought it anyway. He had been something that was hers, just hers, and that was changing. Only a moment after, happiness filled that space, flowing into her like taking a deep breath. It rushed inside her with the realization that Will had stopped being *hers*, and started being *his*. Seeing him adjusting to his new life, embracing his new life, made Memory swallow back a happy sob.

Will had Roen on his toes. They each had a fencing sword, and Will mimicked the formal style Roen used, but his height and reach had him at an advantage. One or two times Roen made a show of shaking out his sword hand after a particularly strong blow from Will clattered their blades.

Then with a wicked grin, Roen stepped up his performance. He smiled like he'd been so clever to trick Will into thinking he had an easy win, until Will flicked out his other hand and the small hooked tool he held in it, and with one twist, disarmed Roen and left him knocked flat on his back in a flurry of snow.

Memory was running again. She ran so she didn't have time to hold herself back.

Will saw her coming only a second before she jumped up into his arms. She pressed her lips against his, her hands threading their way into the wild hair she loved so much.

Memory heard the dull thunk-thunk of Will's two weapons fall on the ground behind them as Will brought his arms up around her and pulled her close to him. A low growl came from the back of his throat and he kissed her back, lips pressing hard on hers.

A round of polite applause from the bystanders brought Memory back to reality. She dropped down with a bashful smile and rose-flushed cheeks.

Memory giggled at their audience, then smiled up at Will.

He still had his eyes closed, smiling and panting deep breaths.

When he opened his eyes and looked at her, again it was as if they were the only people there. His lips shivered a little as he said, "I wanted to dance with you at the ball. I should have but I was scared. I don't want to be scared anymore. For you, and for me, I don't want to be scared to live my life. And I want to live my life with you. Whatever the rules,

whatever might happen, I don't ever want to be apart from you again."

"Worlds couldn't keep us apart," Memory replied. "Tried and failed already."

Will laughed.

Memory turned and noticed the sword and Will's iron hook lying on the pavement a few paces behind them. She moved back to pick them up for him.

Only one step away, a rush of air filled the space between Memory and Will. In a burst of whipping winds and the ember filled gray smoke of the Veil, Mina appeared.

Her eyes were wide and gleaming as they looked down at Memory, frozen in shock there where she bent to pick up the weapons.

Will has no iron on him. Memory's heart pounded. *He has no protection.*

Mina's hair whipped around her as though she were caught in gale force winds. "No! You cannot have him. He is mine. He ate food from my hands. I saved him and his life is the debt he owes to me. I own him and will keep him far from you forever!"

Memory grabbed up the iron hook near her fingertips and swung it back at Mina.

But she was already gone.

And so was Will.

CHAPTER FOURTEEN

Memory's knees hit the ground.

Eloryn, Roen, Maeve, and Erec were all standing around her. She wasn't sure when they had come over. Had they tried to stop Mina too? They were all too slow.

Will is gone.

Everyone was talking but Memory couldn't hear. A dense humming filled her head and her magic boiled, ready to explode. Eloryn put an arm around her shoulder.

Memory realized she was holding her breath and gasped air in. It struck like a knife in her chest and she bit back a cry. The world came back into focus.

Her voice came out as a harsh whisper. "I was wrong before."

Will.

Her hands formed fists, pressed against the crushed grass. "This is what having your soul broken feels like."

"Oh, Mem," Eloryn said.

Clenching her teeth, Memory took a deep breath and stood up. "I'm going to get him back."

Erec watched her for a moment, then hurried away. The other guests at their brunch were standing back, faces white and fearful. The iron awl hook that had been Will's protection was still held in Memory's hand,

her fingers rigid around it.

"She must have been watching, waiting for a chance to get to him," Memory said. "The minute he didn't have iron on him... How could she even do that? It can't be allowed. She said she owned him. She doesn't own him. No one *owns* him."

"I'm so sorry," Eloryn said. "But she could own him. Under fae law, if she saved his life, if he ate fairy food, she could own him. Everyone in Avall knows to be careful not to lose themselves to the fae like that, but coming from your world, he would have been easy for Mina to claim."

"You're telling me this now?" Memory grunted.

Eloryn looked at the ground. "I didn't know. All I know are fairytales of humans being claimed, stories parents tell at night to stop children going near the fae. Or stories of those who go willingly, like Lugh. Will seemed to have so much freedom, living in the forests in Avall. In the fairytales, the fae always steal the child away to Tearnan Ogh, the fairy realm."

Memory's face ached with unspent tears, tears she refused to shed until Will was back by her side again. She looked up at her sister. "No. That's not it. You didn't doubt what was happening, you just didn't think I could cope with knowing."

"I..." Eloryn stuttered then looked at her feet. "I'm sorry."

Memory couldn't blame her. She wished her friends, her family, would trust her more. She felt she'd showed them time and again that she could be strong. But she'd also shown them how very weak she could be. They'd seen her at her darkest and she knew it would take a long time to gain their confidence again.

I will show them how strong I can be.

After a deep breath, Memory said, "Tearnan Ogh... Is that where Mina has taken Will now?"

"That would be my guess," Eloryn said.

Memory saw Erec return. He'd brought Bedevere back with him.

Memory eyed them. "You're worried I'm going to run off and do something cuckoo banana pants, aren't you?"

"Well, I wouldn't necessarily use the term cuckoo banana pants..." Bedevere said in his dry voice.

Memory forced another deep breath into her tight chest that seemed to have forgotten how to breathe on its own. "Don't worry. I'm not going to be *that girl*. I'm not going to dump everything else in the world

for one person, for a boy, for… love."

Bedevere just bowed his head, waiting.

"What do we need to do, to make sure everything is in order here in Avall? I can't leave Avall in chaos again, so that's our first job, to do everything we must to make sure it won't be. I want things stable here in case I'm gone for a while."

"Your Majesty, if you travel to Tearnan Ogh to recover Sir Will, you may not come back at all," Bedevere said.

Memory held up a hand. "I'm getting Will, and we're coming back. That's happening. I need you to help me make sure everything is set right here before I go. Can you do that for me?"

Bedevere simply nodded.

"Then let's get started." Memory marched back toward the castle, and everyone fell in line behind her.

"Mem, stop and think about what you're saying," Eloryn protested. "I know you want Will back, we all do, but going into the fae lands is beyond dangerous, it's…"

"Stupid?" Memory asked.

"Suicidal," Eloryn finished, her tone cold.

"We've dealt with nasty fae tactics before."

Eloryn's chin tensed and she grabbed Memory by the arm. "Travelling into the fae realm is entirely different to dealing with the fae within Avall. It is one hundred percent their territory. One false move and a human can be Branded, but has no power to Brand in return. You would be vulnerable to their every whim and trick. Humans simply do not travel into the fae realm unless they are taken by the fae. Even royalty and dignitaries are not safe. That's why all official meetings between our races are held here in Avall."

Memory pulled her arm free and continued up the stairs into the palace. "I'm not leaving Will as a prisoner to that crazy sprite."

"Then we will go with you."

Memory stopped her march. "You just told me it was suicidal. Why the hell would I let you come with me?"

Eloryn stopped too, eye to eye with her sister. "Because if you don't I won't tell you how to get into Tearnan Ogh."

Memory matched her sister's look. "Bedevere will tell me."

Eloryn held a hand up to the wizard but held her sister's gaze. "Don't you even dare."

Bedevere made no sound or move.

Memory huffed. "Then I'll work it out on my own."

"And how much longer will that take?"

Every second Will was gone scratched a sharp tally mark on Memory's heart. Would Mina punish Will for choosing Memory over her? What would she force upon him or make him do? The thought of Will as a slave to that sprite twisted Memory's guts.

Memory was torn; she didn't want to put her friends in danger but she knew she would need help.

Roen spoke from behind Memory, breaking the staring battle between the twins. "You may find this hard to imagine, but I think we've all become fond of the fellow. Will's our friend too. We all want to do what we can to bring him home."

Memory whimpered a little then steadied herself. "We're all going then. And we'll keep each other alive, just like we've always done."

Erec cleared his throat, breaking the intense look the three friends were sharing. "Your Majesty, you say you're going, so you are, and I'll spare my objections. But you must also spare your objections to my coming with you. I failed to protect you in the gaunts' lair, and I plan not to fail again."

Memory shook her head. "If you come with us, you could die, and I can't have your death on my hands. Not after Peirs."

Erec, who had been standing at attention, relaxed his posture. The move somehow seemed to give him more authority. "Travelling into Tearnan Ogh, you could all die. I will go and I will do everything I can to keep us all alive. That is my decision, and should I die it would not be at your doing."

Memory smiled and gave him a small nod. "Anybody else? Anybody?" She looked around with a wide grin, caught Bedevere's gaze and pointed him down. "No. Not you. I need someone to keep the rest of the wizards under control."

Bedevere bowed. "The realm of the fae is not the one I wish to explore, so I am happy to stay, if saddened to see you leave. You are our queen. We would send a legion of men with you if you wished it. But I know you do not."

"Then you know me well. Saving Roen, Maeve and the others, that was different. We had to stop the kidnappings, find out who was behind them. This is personal. So we settle what needs to be settled here in

Avall, we work out a plan, then we go and get Will." Memory started forward again, climbing the steps into the palace two at a time. "We've got a lot to get done, so let's get it done. I don't even know how we get to fairyland yet. Do we eat magic cake till we're shrunk all itty bitty and wash ourselves down a drain with our own tears or what?"

Reaching the halls of the palace, both Bedevere and Erec called staff over to them, sending messages off in different directions before taking their leave and heading another way themselves. Roen and Eloryn continued beside Memory.

"You have some strange ideas of magic," Eloryn said. Her slippers made hushed sounds pressing into the long carpet runners that had been brought out to cover the cold marble floors when the snowy weather hit Avall. "The fae have doorways similar to Veil doors, spotted throughout Avall wherever they hold territory, such as within fairy rings. They use these doorways to travel between Avall and Tearnan Ogh. Fae can generally traverse through the Veil as they wish within Avall, much as you could, but to travel between worlds they use the established doorways. Mina would not have taken Will directly to Tearnan Ogh when she vanished with him, but to a doorway first and then through that."

Memory thought back to her trouble with trying to force a doorway through to the rest of the human world, how much harder it was to break through than skimming within the Veil in Avall. "These doorways, do they stay in the same place?" she asked.

"Not exactly, but close. They shift very slightly, as though there is an ebb and flow displacing the join between the worlds."

Memory took a deep breath and her pace grew more confident, faster. As much as she declared unwaveringly that she would bring Will back, she was terrified she couldn't, that she had no idea where to start. Not anymore. "I know where to start looking."

CHAPTER FIFTEEN

The woods were cut through with the horizontal orange beams of the setting sun. The light cast long shadows and created sharp contrast against a black and white ground of sludgy leaves and spots of melting snow. The cold air was scented with wood-smoke, and the trees above Memory and her friends leafless, showing the darkening sky above.

Eloryn, Roen, Erec, and Clara trailed after Memory silently as she led them on through the forest. They were all dressed and prepared for a long journey. Even Eloryn had chosen pants, and brought the satchel that had once belonged to Alward, which curiously seemed to fit more food and supplies than expected. Memory refused even the suggestion of a skirt, and instead wore tough leather riding pants and knee-high boots that buckled tight three times up the sides. The deep purple coat she wore matched her pinned-back hair, and had its own mini-skirt length bustle at the back and double breasted buttons of brass.

She had left off the corset, breathing would be fairly important today after all, and had been hard enough to do since Will had been stolen away. Six days it had taken to wrap up her affairs as queen so Avall could continue on while she was gone, or if she never came back. Six breathless days.

The new government Memory had been working toward was already close to complete. Between them, and Lanval, who she'd left as her

replacement, if she never came back, she felt confident Avall was in good hands. Honestly, she was more confident in the adults she'd put in charge than she was in herself as a ruler anyway. She felt good that the people of Avall had someone as their leader other than a seventeen year old girl with possible mental health issues. She had found a desire in herself to lead, and a desire to lead changes and progress in Avall, but knew she wasn't ready. She was little more than the Maellan-blooded figurehead and knew it, but those desires had become one more reason she wanted to live- to grow old and wise enough to rule well, one day.

And she wanted to grow old and wise with Will by her side. *Worlds couldn't keep us apart.* She would get him back. And then she could breathe again.

That morning, Memory had said her goodbyes to Maeve and the children. Maeve had wanted to come with Memory, to help however she could, but Memory needed her to stay and look after the other kids. She couldn't bear for something to happen to them again.

Saying goodbye was hard, especially when Isa clung to Memory's leg and had to be pried off, crying and screaming, by Maeve.

Clara, on the other hand, had flatly refused to say goodbye. "I'll say goodbye when it's time to say goodbye, and then I will say see you soon."

"It might be a long way out into the woods," Memory objected weakly. She didn't want to say goodbye either, but knew a foray into the fairy realm was no place for Clara.

"I'm perfectly capable of walking. It's just the hunting grounds anyway."

Memory watched her now, tripping over more sticks than she managed successfully to step over. Erec kept close beside her to keep her upright, a gentle smile on his face when he caught her arm each time. Memory started to wonder if the damsel in distress act was for his benefit. It worried Memory to be leaving Clara out here alone after saying goodbye, she would have arranged an escort to take her home again if she'd had more notice, but she felt better knowing she had a way to call home and check on her.

That had been the last thing Memory did before leaving. On their way out of the palace, Memory took her friends to the chamber that kept the Speaking Mirror.

The piece of magic mirror in Caermaellan castle was a long, thin sliver, shaped almost like a scimitar and about that size. Memory reached

up and reverentially placed her hands on either side of the frame that held it, and lifted it from the wall.

She could see Eloryn's eyes pop wide as she brought the frame over her head then threw it on the floor.

The frame broke apart and the Speaking Mirror shattered into pieces.

Eloryn cried, "Are you insane? That is priceless! Irreplaceable!"

"So are you." Memory crouched down in front of the wreckage, and collected out the five largest pieces. One for her, and one for Eloryn, Roen, Erec, and Clara. That left a few small pieces for those remaining in the palace as well. She stood back up and passed them around to her friends, careful to not let the razor edges slice their hands.

"When magically connected, each part of this mirror can see and hear the other parts, right? I didn't break the magic, I just made more pieces. One each, so we won't be out of contact."

Eloryn stared at the triangular shard in her hand. The mirror glinted and sent sparks dancing up onto her cheekbones. She choked on words that she couldn't quite get out. "But… it's…"

Memory shrugged. "If you guys had mobile phones or walkie-talkies I would have used them instead, but we use what we've got."

"Only Erec, Clara, and I can use them anyway," Eloryn said. "You know you and Roen can't without someone to make the magical connection."

Memory nodded slow and deadpan. "I did realize that. I figure it's still worth it for you guys and was hoping you could set it up now and keep the line open. Connect yours to Roen's, and mine back here to Clara and the Palace. That way we're always connected to someone if we are separated, and if we're together then all is good anyway."

Eloryn hesitated, still pouty at the destruction of a precious magical artefact. Then she sighed and spoke her behest words to connect the mirror pieces. Memory held hers up, and could see part of Clara's red hair in the icicle shaped mirror. There was barely enough mirror to see a complete eye when Clara also held hers close to her face, but when she spoke into the mirror, her voice came through clear and loud to Memory's piece.

Roen and Eloryn tested theirs as well, and Erec flipped his around in his hands. "I sure feel left out," he said.

"You can connect yours to anyone whenever you want," Memory said.

He grinned and tucked it away in a pocket on his vest. "Details."

Memory put hers away as well in a pouch on her belt. "We all have

iron. We all have a speaking mirror. We have a plan. I think we're ready."

In the hunting grounds, Memory stared at the small ring of red and white spotted toadstools in front of her. It sat within lush green, needle-thin winter grass and a spray of white wildflowers.

They were ready, they had a plan, but the next step, literally, was a scary one.

Eloryn stared as well. "Do you think this will really work?"

Memory shrugged. "Only one way to find out."

"Why must you be so flippant? If this doesn't work, you will be lost."

Erec, Roen, and Clara stood across the ring from them, and all looked up at Memory for her reply. She didn't want to lose herself, or lose them. But she'd already lost someone and that had to be fixed.

"It works, or it doesn't. I'm doing it anyway, so why ask?"

Eloryn turned from the fairy ring to stare at Memory, her green eyes squinting, assessing her. "I just want to know if you are doing this because you truly care for Will or just because your pride is hurt."

Memory felt the verbal slap in those words. She took a deep breath to let the stinging fade. There was no question anymore what the truth was. "I care for him," she said. "As deeply as you care for Roen. Don't ever question that again, Lory."

Eloryn grinned a little slyly. "I was just waiting for you to finally admit it."

"You little trickster!" Memory shoved her sister's shoulders with both hands, laughter in her words. Pointing at the other three who were all grinning as well she said, "Go on, get. Time for you lot to hide."

Roen and Erec patted Memory on the shoulder as they walked past, and Clara kissed her on the cheek. Eloryn just nodded to her, her expression serious again. Memory returned the nod and tried to wear a hopeful smile. She watched them disappear behind thick tree trunks, the echo of Eloryn's behest words settling in the cool air as her magic concealed them further.

Letting out one long, deep breath, Memory clenched her jaw. *Life as a flower couldn't be too terrible, could it?*

She stepped forward and instantly she felt the tug and pull of the fae magic there, enclosing her within the small ringed space. Reaching out her hands, she ran them around the edges of her confines, feeling the firmness of the air there. Memory leaned her whole body into it, pushing as though to escape. She wondered if this was how being in a

padded room might feel.

After ten minutes of pushing and prodding and waiting, Memory started to get anxious.

Clearing her throat, she called as loudly as she could, "Oh bother, I seem to be trapped."

The sun had fallen low, and shone directly into Memory's eyes. A rustle of leaves had Memory squinting into the light and a silhouetted shape crept toward her, haloed by the golden glow of the sunset behind.

"Hello human." A soft whinny shook the words as the fae creature spoke. The faun stepped close to the fairy ring, the white fur around her cloven hooves muddy and spotted with wet leaves.

"Hello... furry thing."

The faun regarded Memory with all black eyes, spiked with silvery lashes. "Stumbled in again, did you? This time, you are mine for reals. Isn't that how you said it? For reals? You belong to me now." Lips covered in a soft white down pulled up into a satisfied smile.

"Oh no, oh dear, alas, you've got me now," Memory said, the back of her hand against her forehead.

"You are mocking me?" The faun shifted, her legs coming up and her hooves pawing at the ground. Silvery dust fell from her eyelashes as she snorted. "I think I will turn you into a flower this time. Let the bees have you."

Memory barked a laugh. "You're such a bluffer! You got me with your lies last time, but I know what fairies can and can't do now. Got myself an education."

The faun gazed at her, body rigid with what looked like anger, or confusion. "You know nothing."

Memory began ticking off items on her fingers. "I know you guys are all strong and nearly immortal, can glamour appearances, and travel through the Veil, but unless you learn human magic there is very little else you can actually do."

The faun showed its teeth in a truly cheeky grin. "Maybe I hoped I could just glamour you to look like a flower, and you'd be so shocked you'd fall down dead from fright."

Memory raised an eyebrow at the faun's honesty.

The faun's grin widened. "Flower or not, I still own you now."

"So are you going to keep me as your pet, or what? Take me back to Tearnan Ogh? Can you even do that with your puny fairy magic?"

Memory folded her arms, unimpressed.

"Of course I can! Don't know if I will though." Her long nose wrinkled and trembled as she sniffed the air. "You still stink of iron."

Memory nodded out into the trees. "Actually, this time it's not me."

As if sensing what was about to happen, the faun jumped and turned to run but was too slow.

Memory could hear Eloryn's behest words as she sprang the trap. A thin, web-like iron cage encircled the faun, trapping her within its toxic framework. Every piece of iron they carried had been given to Eloryn, and she used her magic to stretch and spread the mass of them large enough to hold the creature.

Erec, Clara, Roen, and Eloryn stepped out from hiding and into a circle around the cage.

The faun shrieked and her body started to swirl with Veil mist, trying to escape through the Veil. But it was obvious she had no strength surrounded by iron, and the wispy smoke evaporated uselessly. In panic she lashed out, kicking at the cage and her hoof sizzled at contact.

Clara gasped and turned away. Memory's stomach clenched violently, watching the little thing buck and shudder. "Just stay off the bars, calm down!"

The faun's eyes widened to completely round black orbs and her goat-like ears hung down. She shrank herself small, desperately trying to keep clear of the iron web. "Let me out!"

Memory made calming gestures with her hands. "Make a deal with me and I will. You will take me and my friends into Tearnan Ogh. You will be our guide there, will not harm us or knowingly lead us to harm, and you will return us to Avall. And then you will be free again."

"Free?" The faun sagged against the ground, her body shuddering and heaving with sobs. Perspiration foamed and curdled on her snowy coat. "Taking you there, it will be death for me. The members of the court will kill me for taking you to our lands."

Memory stepped back, knocked by the words. Would her quest mean death for this creature no matter what? Was that a price she was ready to pay? She stared at the creature's black eyes, unseelie eyes, trying to feel only hatred for it. She couldn't. "I will make sure you are safe."

The faun huffed. "That is a pretty lie."

Erec stared down spitefully at the creature. It was clearly easier for him to hate the white beast. "My queen does not lie. Make the deal, beast."

"I don't want to die!" the faun cried, scaring a flock of black birds from the branches above. They fled into the darkening mauve sky.

Memory had worried that the faun, after being trapped, would simply welcome death as the gaunt she'd once faced did. But her behavior seemed like that of a child. A small terrified child. It looked young, but that was no indicator for an immortal creature like the fae. Still, Memory wondered if maybe it wasn't as old as other fae she'd known. It trembled as Memory moved closed to the cage. The faun really was afraid of death, and Memory knew it. She wished she did not know it, because it gave her the leverage she wished she didn't have to use.

She tried to speak kindly. "Agree to the deal, and maybe you will die, later, at some time. Or maybe you won't. Maybe you will live. But if you do not agree to our deal you will die now."

"I will Brand you." The faun's voice was a desperate whisper.

Eloryn frowned, clearly troubled by everything. "You can't. We have not touched you and not attacked you. We're offering to free you, not hurt you."

Erec sniffed and lifted his chin. "Say the words if you must."

The faun gasped, and stuttered, its eyelids screwed shut. "Bronmarbh Aileadh."

Memory tensed, scared that maybe it would work, that they hadn't followed the law thoroughly, that their loophole wouldn't protect them. But it did. Not one of them was marked with the Brand.

"Monsters. You are monsters," the faun whimpered.

Looking down at the huddle of white fur, shivering on the muddy ground, the faun seemed so small and childlike that Memory did feel like a monster then. But she knew the fae were tricksters and would change how they looked for their own benefit. She remembered the banshee who looked like a child before it transformed and attacked. She remembered Hope, looking the mirror image of herself before she brought the tower down around her and her friends. Her lips grew tight. *Monsters? The unseelie fae are the monsters.*

Memory's voice turned cold. "Do we have a deal?"

The faun gathered herself up onto her knees. "So be it. I agree to your bargain. May it be everything you desire. This is our binding deal."

"Our deal is binding," Memory finished, sealing their agreement under fairy law.

Memory signaled Eloryn who spoke her behest words. The behest

was long, and Memory knew it was a complicated one, that even Eloryn, who normally could create new behests on the fly, had to plan and run past Bedevere for confirmation. The iron webbing retracted, forming back into molten lumps, and then finally into their original forms. Memory's knife, Eloryn's arrowhead, Clara's button, Roen's dagger, and a spearhead for Erec. They collected their pieces off the ground.

The faun staggered to her feet, her eyes still wide with pain and body coated with sweat and a smell that reminded Memory of nickels rubbed together in a hot palm.

Memory worried the faun would flee, vanish into the Veil, and everything would have been for nothing, but the creature remained. Sullen, she stared at them with frightened eyes, standing back a few feet and wrinkling her nose as they put their iron away.

"This is goodbye then," Memory said, looking at Clara.

Clara fidgeted with her fingers, her face pale already from watching the caged faun. "I could... I could come with you."

Memory dropped her head and raised her eyebrow in an 'oh really?' expression.

Clara smiled a small, embarrassed smile. "To be honest, I'm not sure right now if I'm more scared to go with you or stay behind without you. Oh I wish you didn't have to go. I cannot stand to see you all walk away knowing you may not come back. You are heroes, every one of you, and I'm just..."

Clara blinked back the tears that stood in her eyes but one fell anyway, leaving a long gleaming trail down her cheek, highlighting her freckles.

Memory blinked back tears of her own. Clara was like the mom Memory never had. A young mom who did outrageous things with her daughter, but a mom nonetheless. Would she ever see Clara again? Would any of them?

Yes, she told herself. *We will all return, safe and sound and with Will.*

Memory gave Clara a quick hug. "Go back to the palace and make me some of those delicious pastries with the custard and hot caramel inside. We'll be back before they get cold."

The faun snorted, her velvety nose pointed into the air. "If you are ready to go we need to go now." *Before I lose my nerve and break a binding oath,* went unsaid but Memory heard those words anyway. Maybe they were the faun's, or maybe her own.

None of them spoke for a long moment, inhospitable glares passing between the humans and the faun.

Eloryn moved to stand beside the white fae, slowly, as though approaching a feral cat. "What's your name?"

"Shonae," the fae replied, huffing and backing a step away. "What does it matter to you?"

"I'm Eloryn, that's Roen and Erec and Clara. Memory you already know."

"I wish I did not."

Memory felt her top lip twitch into a sneer. "We all wish a lot of things." Eloryn gave her a look but Memory ignored it. Will was more and more lost with each passing second and she had no time to make their guide feel better.

"We are ready to go," she said.

"To our deaths, then," Shonae said and turned around. Her white tail flicked up as she waved a swirling Veil door into existence in the middle of the fairy ring and trotted through.

Erec took the lead, one hand on the spearhead sheathed in his belt. Eloryn looked at Memory and then Roen. Roen stepped forward and Memory felt a twinge of envy at the protective arm he put around Eloryn's waist. It was overcome by worry though, worry she really was taking them all to their deaths. Her friends she loved the most, who had just claimed the love between them, who were so happy together, about to start a life together.

They stepped through the Veil door one at a time. Memory went last, waving to Clara as she left the human world.

CHAPTER SIXTEEN

Small strands of loose purple hair tickled Memory's cheeks and lips, brought to life by the wild winds within the Veil. Pressure built and popped in her ears and she stepped clear, out into the land of the fae.

She took a deep breath to clear her lungs of the tightness of Veil travel and the air tasted rancid and dry on her tongue, like mud and burned sugar. Her stomach curdled. Blinking, Memory shivered at what lay before her.

The world of the fae. Tearnan Ogh.

In her mind she'd imagined rainbows and sparkling streams where unicorns frolicked around pots of gold, or some other fairytale images. But the world she saw was bleak and lifeless. A shadowed husk of a world.

She'd heard the fae speak of how their world held none of the natural life force that the human world did, the life force they needed to survive, but to see it in reality shook Memory. It disturbed something deep within her and scared her in a primal way. What could have caused their world to become like this? Did the fae pay for their immortality with the death of their world, or did they kill it carelessly the same way humans seemed to be doing with their own?

Murky ink-black puddles and pools made a patchwork pattern across dead, cracked ground. The water rippled occasionally as some loathsome creature turned below the black surface. Angular, broken trees with immense, hollowed trunks, turned gray with petrification, crowded

around them. Their buttressed roots forked out into the water in woven cages. Memory touched the nearest tree to her and it was cold like stone.

No one in her group moved, frozen, as they stared at the world before them.

Shonae watched them in return, the corner of her furred lips turned up in a small smirk. "The wilds of the Unseelie Court. My... home." The smirk faded.

Memory frowned. *This wasn't the deal, not where we needed to go.*

But Eloryn nodded slowly. "Your home. We would have needed a seelie fae to be able to take us directly to the realm of the Seelie Court."

"Then how to we get from here to the Seelie Court? How long will it take?" Memory asked.

"Don't fret human, I want to be free of you as fast as possible. We will travel the briar path. It won't take long." Shonae sniffed the air and tucked her shoulders up close to her neck. "This way. Keep quiet."

Shonae broke away from them, leading off across the rough ground. Her hooves beat swiftly along the dirt and the group of humans had to walk fast to keep up with her but she always kept well ahead, just within sight. Memory knew Shonae did not want to be too near them because of the iron they were carrying. It would sap her strength, which was the last thing either of them wanted. Memory needed Shonae up and moving. She needed to get to Will. Yesterday.

Under Memory's feet, the path sparkled lightly, as though the dirt was made of crushed glass. The hazy mist filled the air and pooled on the ground in thicker swirls.

Memory felt a strange surge of relief as she passed by a small tuft of flowers, growing in an odd arrangement along the top of a fallen log. Maybe there was some life left in the world. The flowers were star-shaped translucent bells, hanging from long stems, and tinkled sweetly in the light breeze. Memory reached to touch one. It slid gracefully over her fingertip so smoothly that it took a few seconds for the pain to register. Memory cried out and clutched her finger, staring in shock at the thin razor cut the flower had sliced there.

From the front of the group, Memory heard Shonae chuckle.

Eloryn dashed over beside Memory and clutched her hand as well, working swiftly to wrap the finger in a bandage. "Don't let your blood drop on them. And don't touch anything else."

Memory just nodded, staring at the plants. She could see now that

they weren't real flowers at all, but finely spun glass and fairy gold, made sharp as a knife. Raising her head, she looked out behind the log and saw a wide field of the faux-flowers, spreading out into the stone forest. "This place officially receives my stamp of creepability. I don't even want to know what would happen if my blood dropped."

"At least we don't seem to be headed that way," Roen said over Eloryn's shoulder.

"No, instead we get to travel through the hopscotch of deadly black swamps," Erec said cheerfully from behind him.

"Fantastic," Memory said, and they all moved along after Shonae again.

The farther they walked, the closer the dark waters seemed to close in around them, until soon they walked along a thin pathway between the growing swamp.

Along the curved roots of one massive tree, white shapes fluttered like butterflies, then blew away. Just ash on the wind.

From the tops of the poisoned pools rose a dense mist that coalesced into shapes as they passed them. Faces leered at them, and voices rang out from visages whose mouths vanished long before the wails that came from them did.

There was something so terrible and sad about the sounds that Memory wanted to stop walking, lie down and weep tears into the lifeless ground. She could feel her pace slowing, her breath catching.

This is just fairy tricks, horrible monster tricks. Her resolve hardened and she ignored the mist, staring ahead at Shonae only, keeping her eyes on her guide.

In front of her, Eloryn gasped. "Alward."

Memory had never known Alward alive, only seen his dead body briefly, but she still recognized him there in the swamp. Grayed blonde hair tied back in a ponytail and round glasses balanced on his nose, he seemed real, solid, as he struggled against a sea of ghostly faces surrounding him.

"Ellie!" he cried.

"Steady," Roen murmured.

Eloryn winced and looked away. "I know. It's not real. It's an obvious trick." She spat her accusation out at the world around them. "As if we'd fall for something so simple."

Memory nodded, proud at Eloryn's strength. But still she could see her

sister's mouth move, as though saying silent spells to keep herself strong.

"It wasn't him," Memory said in a low voice.

"I know that, Mem."

"It still hurt though."

Eloryn's eyes closed for a short moment. "Terribly."

"I'm sorry."

Eloryn gave her sister a small smile. "They won't take us so easily."

There was an echo of evil laughter and a plump raven with a white streak from beak to tail soared overhead. It landed, tangling its wings in a skeletal tree branch before uttering hoarse caws at them.

"Ellie!" the raven cried, its voice a mix between bird and human. "Ellie!" The caws came faster, harsher, sounding like the laughter.

Eloryn's face drew still. "Come on, we're moving too slow. We stick together with all our iron and they can't touch us."

Memory knew she was right but she also knew that the fae were hardly finished. They would throw whatever they could at them in the attempt to get them to split up. The iron had unsettled them. They were desperate to divide the iron's strength, and the group's as well.

Patches of grass along the path rustled as they walked along. Shonae seemed to avoid it, bounding and hopping around it as she led. Memory tried to do the same, but missed a step, and the black grass she placed her foot down on shattered and crumbled, as though it had been burnt to a crisp so fast it had kept its shape perfectly until touched.

Ahead across the black swamp and through the trees, a huge patch of vines reared up in a wide screen that curled around on itself in a way that made Memory's stomach do the same.

Shonae stopped, sniffing the air, her wide nose twitching.

"Is that the briar pathway?" Eloryn asked.

"No. Beyond there."

Shonae craned her neck, looking off to either side. The vines seemed to spread as far as they could see in each direction.

"Let's just go through then," Erec said, drawing his iron spearhead into one hand, and larger bronze sword into his other.

"Wait!" A voice rang out from behind them.

"Clara?" Memory squinted, and saw a figure running up the path behind them, a shadow within the mists.

"Could she have followed us here?" Roen asked warily.

"It's probably not her. It's probably another trap," Eloryn said.

A small shriek reached them and the figure stopped moving.

"What if it's not?" Erec growled. He took a few steps toward Clara. "We shouldn't have left her behind. She's come after us."

"Erec!" Clara cried out. "Help me, I'm stuck. Something… something is holding me." Her voice was broken with sobs.

"It's probably not her," Eloryn said again, but she didn't sound sure anymore.

Erec seemed sure, and began running.

Roen's arms shot out, gripping Erec around his waist. He wrenched side to side, trying to break free.

Memory's heart jumped into overdrive and she began fumbling for her pocket.

"Please! It's hurting me!" Clara's cries ripped through the air and the shadowed shape down the pathway writhed and crumpled.

Eloryn came and stood in front of Erec, still bound in Roen's arms, staring him down, trying to talk him down. He began to still.

"It is not her," Roen whispered.

Down the pathway, the mist thinned, clearing a view straight to the person there.

"It is her!" Erec roared, ripping at Roen's hold again.

It did seem to be her. Clara, just as they'd last seen her. Her feet had sunk into a boggy spot and a heavy figure made of fog and black water shot up from below her. Dark tentacles wrapped her body and grabbed her by the throat, squeezing so hard that her friends could see her flesh pinching closed.

"Clara," Memory called out. "CLARA!"

The small piece of mirror in her hands flashed and the image shifted. It spoke back to her.

Erec's arm flailed out and cracked against Roen's face. Blood trickled from a split in Roen's lip. Erec broke free, stumbling down the path to Clara.

Memory ran in front of him, holding the speaking mirror up in front of his face. "It's not her. Clara is safe, back in Avall. Look. LOOK."

Erec stopped in place, panting heavily.

Clara's voice came through clear from the broken glass. "Mem? I'm so sorry, it took me a moment to realize why my pocket was yelling at me. Is something wrong?"

Erec met Mem's eyes. He looked away again, down to the ground.

"I'm sorry. I'm sorry, I was foolish."

"It's okay," Memory said to him. Then to the glass she said. "We're all okay."

"Well, don't scare me like that then!" Clara scolded.

Down the pathway, the imposter Clara giggled in a sharp, high pitch. She merged with the larger monster behind her, coalescing into a single immense scaly form that slunk away back into the dark waters. The disturbing giggle continued to echo around them.

"Sounds like you're having a wonderful time," Clara said, the edges of her freckled nose filling the small mirror.

Erec had walked back and muttered a few manly mumbles to Roen and they shook hands. Both of them were covered with sweat and the blood coming from Roen's lip had already begun to dry. "Let's keep together," Roen said. "The fae are not going to stop trying to trap us until we are out of here so let's get out of here."

"Agreed," Memory said.

Eloryn already had her eye on the next hurdle, the thick tangle of vines ahead. She'd approached them, and started speaking her words of behest.

Shonae eyed them all carefully.

Memory took a deep breath. They were all still together, so far.

"Hello! Hello? Are you still there? Is this thing broken? Oh, of course it is broken…"

Memory grinned. "Sorry Clara, just wanted to check you got back to the palace okay."

"I'm just sitting on my bottom while you're all off in Tearnan Ogh, and you call back to see if I'm fine? Other than being worried to death about you all, everything is just splendid."

Memory laughed at Clara's tone. "We're doing great. Fairy tricks at nil points. See you again soon. More than just your nose that is."

The mirror filled with Clara's poking out tongue, and Memory chuckled as she put it back in her pocket.

CHAPTER SEVENTEEN

Roen rubbed his jaw, where Erec had landed his elbow a moment ago. His mouth still tasted of blood, but he couldn't be angry at Erec. He'd almost run to help Clara too. If it had been Eloryn instead, he knew he'd have gone.

He clapped his hand onto Erec's shoulder. "We're not doing too badly."

Roen wasn't sure he believed it. They'd barely made any progress, and had only just survived the fae lures so far. They had to do better than this or none of them would get home, just as his parents feared. When he'd explained to them where they were going and why, they'd asked him not to go, ordered him, begged him. He was their last son, and he knew they thought him travelling into the land of the fae meant he was lost to them forever as well. But he had to do it. For Memory. He owed her so much already, and deep down, he really believed Memory would get them all home safe again, somehow.

The mist had closed in on them again, as though taunting them, and Roen suppressed a shiver.

Eloryn stood in front of the wall of vines, and when Roen went to join her, he felt another tremor in his belly. The dense undergrowth seemed to be alive; it quivered and vibrated as Eloryn studied it.

"These vines do not look normal," Roen said.

Eloryn looked back at him, her forehead creased into her cute frown of concentration. "I'm certain they are an enchantment. They are not a living plant, but some kind of fae magic. I might be able to clear them away though."

She began casting, the air around the vines turned slightly blue, icy crystals forming like a spray of lichen across the twirling tendrils. The vines crumbled and turned to dust, and then they regrew as fast as they had died. Eloryn paused and shook her head. "Something else then," she said and tried a different spell.

"Aren't you going to help us get through here?" Roen asked Shonae.

"No," she replied, watching Eloryn intently.

The battle between Eloryn and the vines went on for long minutes. The vines would wither only to spring back to life. They made a groaning cry with every death and shrill scream with every rebirth. The air stank of fetid sap and dead leaves. The ground gave off a boiling black oil every time the vines landed on it, dead and tangled.

Memory clapped her hands to her ears. She spat her words at Shonae. "You're supposed to be our guide to get us to the Unseelie Court. Can't you help us through this?"

Shonae just raised an eyebrow and brushed her wooly hair from her cheek. "I know what I'm meant to be doing."

"I got it, I think!" Eloryn was panting but she was also smiling. There in front of her was a cleared section, a long tunnel leading into the vines. She headed for it. "I am going through."

Roen's breath caught.

I know what I'm meant to be doing.

His heart pounded so hard he felt his ribs could crack.

You will be our guide there, will not harm us or knowingly lead us to harm.

"El, no! Stop!" Roen yelled.

Vines that had appeared dead and fallen near her feet sprang to life, snatching Eloryn up into them. She turned, trying to escape and Roen saw her face, just long enough to see her eyes bulging in fear and her arms pinned helplessly to her side. Her face had gone a dusky red color, all breath squeezed from her body. She was pulled to the ground and dragged off into vines which closed up tightly around her.

Memory screamed.

Roen found his iron dagger in his hand, and hacked blindly at the vines. His hair whipped around his face as he screamed. Erec was there

beside him, slashing with his sword, alternating with the iron spearhead.

Roen felt the ground tremble beneath him.

A wild fury filled Memory's face and her breathing came in harsh snorts.

"Mem, calm yourself. The iron is working. El is smart. She has iron too. She'll look after herself till we get her back." He made his words sound strong, despite the part of himself that hoped Memory would explode, scorching this land till nothing remained, to punish it for taking Eloryn.

Hold on, El.

Memory screamed again, a rough, frustrated scream, and launched herself at the vines as well, slicing with her iron blade.

At each touch of iron, the vines burned and shriveled and stayed that way.

The vines dropped away and Roen pushed through. On through the thick wall of vines they all crashed, tripping where the creeping tendrils lashed around their ankles. One thick vine caught Memory around the waist, slithering and tightening its grip like a serpent. Smaller ones came to join it, twirling like whips. Erec cut her free just as they began hoisting her up into the vines overhead.

They broke through the final tangled screen and tumbled out the other side.

Eloryn was there, wide eyed and panting. In her hand she held her arrowhead, still pointed defensively at the vines, her arm coated in ash and black slime up to the elbow. Her coat had been lost and her ivory shirt was now gray and blood-stained, ripped apart off one shoulder. Long blonde hair had come loose of its ties and fell in tangles.

Roen fell to his knees beside her, scooping her up into his lap and burying his face into her neck. She clung back fiercely.

"Tell me you are safe, that I've not lost you and gone mad with grief," he whispered.

"I'm here," she whispered back. "But we are not safe."

Roen realized then that they weren't alone. The glassy clinking of metal and shifting of heavy feet in the crackling, dead grass told him all he needed to know before he looked up.

They were surrounded.

Memory stood protectively between where Roen held Eloryn on the ground, and the ring of huge creatures on horseback staring down at them. *No, those really aren't horses.* Certainly not like any horse Memory could recall having seen before. They were tall and shaggy, shaped like black lions with clawed paws and whip-like tails, and heads like a horse but covered in hard, shiny scales and sharp beaks. It was hard to tell because they were folded away behind the riders' legs, but Memory thought they might even have wings.

The knights themselves were all in heavy armor of black lacquered leather which gleamed and sparked in the dimness, covering whatever their true form was beneath.

Some carried spears and others had bows, arrows nocked, all tipped with the translucent yellow of fairy gold. All aimed their weapons at the humans.

Shonae crept forward out of the vines, keeping her distance from the humans and their iron. She bowed deeply, groveling to the ground in front of the mounted fae men.

Her head turned to the side and she hissed across at Memory, "Bow, fools. These are King Finvarra's soldiers. Bow and at least your death may be quick."

Memory shook her head. She would not bow and have her life taken. "Let us pass. We are just travelers. Our business is with the Seelie Fae, not with you or your master."

Not yet, anyway, Memory amended internally.

"We know who you are," one of the knights said. Its voice was deep, gravelly, and monotonous, like someone fighting throat cancer.

"Then you know attacking the queen of the humans of Avall is probably a big deal and shouldn't be done."

"Do you think we would be here without orders? You are nothing here." The knight who spoke drew closer, leading his steed up in front of Memory. Foam spilled around the creature's lips, and it snorted hot breath and spittle across Memory's cheeks. She turned her face to the side but held her ground.

Roen got to his feet as well, helping Eloryn up beside him. They stood defiantly beside Memory, with Erec on her other side.

Memory wanted to whisper to Eloryn. She needed advice, she needed some brilliant magic plan to get through this, but the knight stood too close to them, staring down. She was sure he was smirking at them

beneath his helmet. The knights weren't making a move yet, as though they were waiting for something, but there was a fight coming, Memory was certain of it.

Memory might have softened a little, but the girl she used to be never shied away from a fight. She lifted her iron knife, holding it against the thigh of the dark fae knight right in front of her.

Led by her action, each of her friends held out their iron as well.

"Let us pass and no one has to die," Memory said. *Wow, I even managed to sound like I'm not about to pee my pants.*

The white streaked raven from the swamp flew overhead, cawing in long taunting notes.

The knight in front of Memory lifted the visor of his helmet and glared at her. His eyes, fully black, were set in ghostly white wrinkled skin that seemed to drip like old wax across his face, revealing long, yellowed teeth in a protruding jaw. "Humans, walking in our territory, in the Unseelie Court, bearing iron against us. Well…"

The fae knight's all black eyes shifted. Without pupils it was hard to tell where he was looking, until he reached out a gauntleted finger and pointed crookedly at Roen. His lips curled into a vicious grin and he said, "Bronmarbh Aileadh."

Memory's heart stopped. Her chest tightened until her breaths came in tiny, short gasps as she waited, hoping, wishing it wouldn't work. Then she heard Roen howl in agony.

"Roen, no, no!" Eloryn was screaming as loud as him.

He had crumpled to the ground clutching at his forehead, his shoulders shaking violently.

When he turned his face up and screamed into the sky, Memory could see the rune-like mark of the Brand there, burnt into his skin.

Memory's eyes were wild, searching for answers, screaming for Eloryn. Her sister must be able to fix this, there had to be a way to fix this.

The knight in front of her was swaying his finger between the rest of them as though playing a cruel game of eeny-meeny-miny-mo.

Eloryn was lost in her own grief. She stood beside Roen, his hand gripped in hers, and began turning her magic against the fae before them. There were no plants, no animals, no life force of magic left in the world to help her. But she did have her iron arrowhead.

"Mem," Roen croaked from beside her. "Just take El away. Get her to safety. Please."

Memory nodded, all the while knowing that Eloryn would go nowhere without Roen.

It only took a moment, and two more words, for it to be too late anyway.

The knight's finger came to rest pointing at Eloryn, and he spoke the words of Branding again.

"Bronmarbh Aileadh," he crackled.

Eloryn cried out, and kept speaking the words of her behest through gritted teeth as the Brand burned itself onto her forehead.

The arrowhead in her hand began to melt, spreading and spinning and stretching into a long filament. As she fell onto one knee, Eloryn flicked her arm, sending the thin iron wire whipping out at the knights in front of her. It lashed across three of them, skimming uselessly over their armor. Their steeds weren't as lucky, and toppled so fast Memory was sure she was hallucinating.

A roar went up from all the knights and their beasts.

Memory knew there was nothing left to do. It was time to fight.

Lory. Roen. Memory's chest flamed and she roared at the useless magic inside her, magic that couldn't free her friends from their Brands.

She ran forward, plunging her iron knife into the gap between the knee guard and thigh armor on a knight in front of her. Sizzling smoke and gray ooze spilled around her blade as she pulled it back, whirling to find her next target.

Memory tried to make sense of the erupting chaos of death and battle around her. Did they have a chance to run? Was there a leader she could take down?

Erec had downed another lion-horse and its knight fell below the beast, his armor stained with dark thick blood.

Memory could see Shonae, scrambling away across the ground, the ashy dirt staining her pure white fur.

Roen and Eloryn were fighting back to back. Some of the knights had dismounted, beating them with the blunt ends of spears, knocking them to the ground.

Memory saw then that the fae men carried ropes, black and slick like the vines they'd just passed through.

Eloryn struck out again with her thin whip of iron, and screamed more words of behest as she did so. The iron danced and twitched in the air, striking into the vulnerable joints between the knight's armor.

Some fell, but more came. More and more. Too many.

The knights had not been there to kill them; if they had been they would have been dead already. They were so outnumbered, despite how many fell to the iron the humans wielded. The knights were there to capture them, no matter what the cost, but that revelation didn't help Memory.

The words of Branding were croaked out again, barely audible over the screams of battle.

Erec. Memory felt her eyes burn with tears.

One of the steeds bucked in panic through the fray, knocking Memory away from her friends. She tried to push back, fight her way back to Roen, Eloryn and Erec, but arrows rained down. One pricked her upper shoulder and blood bloomed quickly, dripping down her sleeve. Her left arm drooped, pain making it useless to her. Another barrage came from the air and Memory ducked and rolled away, taking cover behind one of the fallen animals.

Roen and Eloryn were screaming, lashed with rope and being dragged away from each other.

"Mem!" Eloryn's cry shattered through the air. She struggled against the knight holding her. His hands were like claws and they yanked her up onto his steed which twirled, paws digging into the dry earth.

Memory could see Erec, fighting still within a crowd of unseelie fae, drawing all their attention as he refused to fall.

Memory stood from behind her cover, ready to run and help him, or Roen, or Eloryn. One of them, somehow. She wasn't sure where she was going, only that her mind burned to *help them. Save them. Fight.*

A strong hand wrapped around her arm, cold fingers digging in firmly.

Memory tried to yank free, and turned to see a cloaked figure.

"You can't save them now. Run, fight later," silver lips said, shimmering under the shadow of the hood.

Nyneve? Memory stared into the black cowl, wanting to argue, but she was given little choice. Nyneve ran, dragging Memory behind her with unbreakable strength. She ran straight for the dark vines. They shrank away from them, clearing the way as Memory remembered the trees cleared their way from Eloryn the first time they met.

Shonae appeared, running frantically beside them, arms hugged around her chest and eyes wide. The vines gave off a low-pitched moaning, the sound hungry children made at the sight of food, and Memory had to hold her breath to keep from throwing up.

The three ran along the length of the wall of vines until Memory was out of breath, and when her legs failed her, Nyneve let go of her arm and Memory fell with a crack onto her knees, gulping air.

The moment she was able to stand, Memory turned back the way they had come, but hands wrapped around her wrists and held her tight.

Memory screamed and fought the cloaked figure, determined to go back and save her friends.

"Quiet, before you get us all killed."

Nyneve loosened her hold, and Memory pushed free, looking up at the unseelie princess. Her hood had fallen back while holding Memory still, and her midnight hair tumbled around her silver snake-skin face like inky shadows.

Her black eyes swept the area around them, silver eyelashes shining in the thin rays of light coming from the western edge of the sky.

"What are you doing here?" Memory coughed out.

"Trying to save your life." Nyneve placed the cowl back over her face. "I have little time, I cannot be seen with you and it cannot come to light that I helped you. If we are caught there will be no hope for your friends."

Did that mean there was some hope? Memory blinked back tears. "I'm covered in the blood of creatures I killed and just lost the people I love the most in the world so maybe you should talk real plain. How, how can we save my friends?"

Nyneve looked down her straight nose at Memory. Her face held little expression, like a fine silver statue. "Finvarra has captured your friends to get to you. He will keep them alive until he does."

That's why the fae Branded them first. Hatred made Memory's insides flame.

Nyneve's face softened then, and eyelids fluttered down slowly. "I want to help you. Branding is a horrible death. An unfair thing. I saw it happen to someone I loved, once, long ago." Her twig-like fingers rested on her heart. "I know what has been done to you by my father. Finvarra is… evil. He's grown old and twisted and I fear for his mind. I want to help you and your friends, but he is still my father, and still my ruler."

"I'm sorry you had to watch someone you loved die from Branding." Memory was, and what was more she was pretty sure she was about to understand that particular pain very well soon.

"Let's not let it happen again." Nyneve turned to the side, away from Memory. With her face obscured by the cowl Memory couldn't see her expression, but she sounded choked, as if she was crying, or maybe laughing. It was funny how alike the two could sound.

"Only the monarch of the offended race can lift a Brand once made. You can challenge Finvarra for the lives of your friends. You have one turn of the sun and moon to get to the Unseelie Court and fight for them before the Brand takes its toll. I will help you as much as I can when you get to the court but I have to go now." Nyneve looked over at Shonae, and Shonae shivered visibly under her gaze, making her body small as though to hide in plain sight. Pointing behind the small faun, Nyneve showed Memory a tunnel of twisted sticks and dry brambles, woven into neat and intricate patterns and filled with a golden glow. "There is the briar path. You must take it. Listen to me, and listen well- do not tarry. Finvarra wants you, but he is unpredictable in his insanity. He could kill your friends at any time. That's why I have to go back now. I

will try to keep them safe from him, but I cannot keep them safe from the Brand. Twenty-four human hours and it will kill them."

"Twenty-four hours," Memory repeated. The words tasted like blood in her mouth.

Nyneve nodded. Just like that she was gone, only a faint ripple of air left where she had been standing.

Memory stared around her, unable to think or even want to.

All she wanted was to crumple, to let the weight that had built inside her finally break her down and let her become nothing, to become more dirt and ash on the ground. To become something that didn't feel pain.

She felt utterly alone.

A soft scratching on the ground beside her reminded her she wasn't.

"Will we keep going?" Shonae's voice was a soft whinny. She had shuffled over close to Memory, but leaned back as though she could be struck at any moment.

"You're still here?" Memory mumbled. "What happened? Did you forget which direction you were running in?"

"We made a binding oath."

Stupid oaths, Memory cursed. She'd held back her magic, not knowing how to use it, not wanting to break her oath to the fae. Maybe with it, she could have taken the upper hand in the fight, but not before Roen was Branded, or Eloryn. She might have saved them from being captured, but they'd still be Branded, and Memory would too be Branded, hunted, or killed by the seelie fae for breaking her oath.

"Stupid snot-licking, hatred-vomiting, kitten-killing, ass on backwards OATHS!" Memory roared, cursing the sky and kicking at the dirt.

Tears blurred her vision and that time she could not stop them from falling. Warm wetness spilled down her cheeks, ran across the bridge of her nose, down her neck.

Shonae's voice was soft. "Keeping our oaths is what keeps the peace."

"Do you think this is peace?" Memory bellowed. "Everyone is fighting! People are dying, fae are dying! Finvarra is a raging lunatic and I saw my friends get Branded and dragged away!"

She turned on the faun, bearing down on her as the fae backed skittishly away. "And you, you KNEW about the vines, didn't you? I trusted you!"

The faun squealed. "I am not allowed to tell humans of such things. It is forbidden. I tried to keep my part of the oath. I did not lead you

into the vines, into the danger. I am here because I am still trying…"

"They were BRANDED!" Memory screamed. "Do you know what that means?"

Shonae's dark eyes flared with warning and her floppy goat ears stood straight up. "Yes, I do. Do you?"

"Yes!"

"Then why do you just stand there screaming?"

Memory's jaw dropped. "Because I… am venting and… totally freaking out… Because this is all my fault." She took a step back from the cowering white faun. "And I don't know if I can fix it."

Shonae said nothing. From the distance came the sickly rustling and whimpers of the vines, as though they were still trying to reach them. Memory wiped her eyes and took a long breath. Her whole body ached and her spirit was crushed, but not gone.

I'm going to save them all.

She dried her eyes on her sleeve. "Let's go, the clock is ticking."

Still holding her shoulders up defensively around her neck, Shonae asked softly, "Where would you have me take you first?"

It was a hard decision. Who did she love more? Was that the question? Would answering cost any of them their lives?

They were at the briar pathway. Beyond it would be the Seelie Court.

Will was there. Memory could get him back first, and then together they would be able to save Eloryn, Roen and Erec.

"Same as before. To get Will from the Seelie Court. I will need his help to save the others, and… and I need him." Tears pricked her eyes again and she swiped them away with the back of her hand, angry at her inability to control her emotions.

She turned her sodden eyes to the path before her. The briar path. Having just battled through the disgusting tangle of black whipping vines, travelling into another pathway of sticks and thorns seemed greatly unappealing. But at least the briar path was actually shaped like a path. Thick trunk-like vines that looked eons old, dry and lifeless, wrapped in spirals, forming a tunnel just wide enough for two to walk side by side. Dry silver sticks were layered and woven, twirling like fractals into a misty infinity. A smooth sandy floor shimmered like diamonds in the low light.

With a small nod from Shonae, Memory followed the faun into the briars.

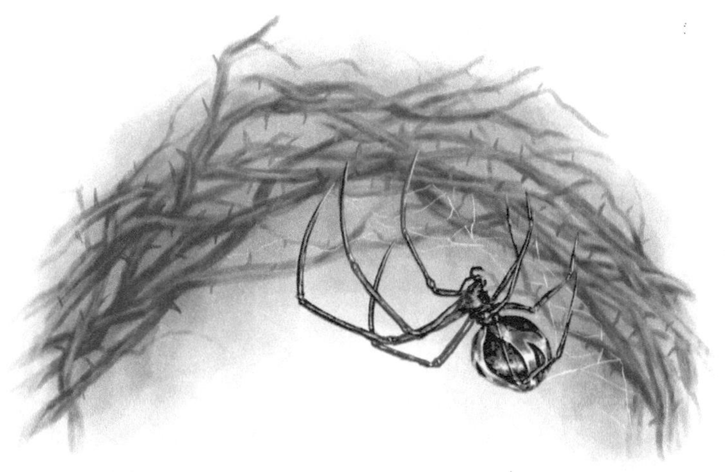

CHAPTER EIGHTEEN

How long have I been here?

Will shook his head, trying to clear his eyes and thoughts. Both were blurry, drunk with the bitter-sweet passion of fairy foods. In his years knowing Mina, she mostly left him in the forests of Avall, the neglected pet she came to toy with on a whim, but she had brought him to Tearnan Ogh on occasions, mostly to show off her human to the other fae. He was a status symbol to her. Few fae had their own humans anymore. He was Mina's, Lugh was Aine's, and he knew of only one other. Mina would bring Will here, flaunt him around the Seelie Court, and then banish him back to solitude in Avall when he seemed too needy. It wasn't his fault humans needed to eat regularly.

In all that time, he never worked out where fairy food came from. He never saw anything growing in the fae world, no real trees to grow those incredible fruits. The fae themselves didn't really eat, or if they did it was purely for pleasure, not for sustenance. He suspected the food Mina used to lure him as a boy, the food she now kept him drunk on, was created from pure magic. Maybe created from a fae's life force itself. Maybe that was why if you ate it you became bonded to them.

He didn't really care. He just wanted the strength to fight it.

He barely had the strength to sit up. He lay on his back in the softest of downs. Something white and so fluffy it was barely there under his fingers, cushioned around him like a cloud. Overhead was a ceiling

of branches with silver and gold leaves woven into seven-pointed star shapes. Colors shifted and flashed, reflecting off the metallic screen like living rainbows. He couldn't see anything else. His eyelids fluttered, falling closed.

He tried to gather his thoughts one at a time, lining them up, creating a wall of lucidity to protect himself.

I am Will.

I will find Memory again.

Worlds can't keep us apart.

Something tickled his lips.

"My sweet pet. You seem hungry."

Will could feel Mina snuggle in beside him. He growled, trying to push her away.

"Aw," Mina simpered, her voice sickly sweet. "Don't be like that."

Will forced his eyes open. Mina's face was right beside his, her amber eyes flickering with sparks of gold, lighting them from within as she smiled.

"Let me go back. Send me back to Avall," he said, as it felt he had done a hundred times.

"No," she said simply. "I don't think we'll ever go back there again."

Mina ran a fingertip around Will's lips. He lifted a leaden arm and brushed her away.

Mina pounced, landing across Will's chest. He could feel the skin of her thighs pressing into his bare stomach, and she dangled a blue cherry-like fruit over his mouth.

He tried to turn his face away, but she turned it back.

Mina hissed. "Behave, boy! Or I will cage you!"

As weak as he felt now, Mina was easily stronger. Her fingernails dug into his cheeks as she clawed at his jaw, pulling his mouth open, and the fruit dropped in.

Will roared, summoning every scrap of resistance he had. The fruit already melted into his mouth like chocolate in the sun. He wrenched himself up, throwing Mina off him.

She shrieked, cursing him.

He tried to find a way out, but his vision grew milky, fading.

He landed on the floor, and everything he knew fell away.

The tears helped Memory keep going. Some of her anger and fear ran out of her along with the salty wetness, splashing on the powdery path. All the emotions she had not dealt with came to the surface and she let them run.

Inside the briar pathway, the darkness was lit by giant webs strung across the floors and walls, shining gold with their own luminescence.

Shonae reached out with her downy fingers, and tugged at one long thread. It twanged softly as it pulled free of the rest and she began winding it around her narrow waist.

Memory watched, curiosity overriding her sadness. "What are you doing?"

"The web of Rump of Steel-skin spiders is valuable. I can trade this well, if I live through my obligation to you." Shonae flicked a look at Memory and flicked her tail at the same time.

"Rump of Steel-" *Rumpelstiltskin, spinning hay into gold… Everything is so connected.* Memory examined the webbing, spotted like glowing nightlights through the gloomy tunnel. "Is it actually real gold?"

Shonae snorted. "Not human gold. This is what fairy gold is made from."

Shonae tugged the webbing again, and a spider the size of Memory's face fell free of the tangled twigs, slipping down the thread into Shonae's hands. Memory gasped, but Shonae just gently brushed the iridescent gold arachnid away. It fell on its back onto the sandy ground, spindly legs twitching, until it righted itself and disappeared again into the briars.

Memory watched the thorny walls around her with a new level of paranoia.

Overhead, the branches looked dangerous and thick with thorns, safely just out of reach. Shonae warned Memory that would not always be the case. Neutral territory or not, the pathway demanded its price from those who travelled it.

"Everything has a price," Memory said. She'd learned that long ago, a world away. There, the prices were different and the rules were too but everything cost something.

Shonae eyed her for a moment. "I have an obligation to you and I will fulfill it. You want to save your friends? Yes? Then let go of all that anger and that greed because that will be what gets them killed, and me too."

"Greed? I don't want anything for myself!"

Shonae huffed. "Then why are you here?"

The question was a good one. It cut to the very heart of Memory's anger. They were there because she had wanted Will back by her side and her friends were all suffering because of her actions, because of her greedy determination to have what was hers.

But was Will hers? She loved him. She knew it deep down in the bottom of her soul. But Will, he belonged to no one. He was a human being, not an object.

From that moment on, I was yours.

She knew that Will had given himself to her, as the greatest gift she could ever desire, but a gift she could not keep. She may have come here for the wrong reasons, but she would make them right. "I'm here to free my friend, not to take him for myself. Any claim I have to Will when I take on firefly-face Mina, I will give up to give him his freedom."

And when he is truly free, would Will still choose me?

"Hmm." Shonae snuffled, still winding thin strands of web, creating a neat spool like a belt around her middle. "I've only known humans to be greedy."

Memory barked a sharp laugh. Talking with Shonae, as odd as it was, had improved her mood. She wondered why the creature was giving her breath to the conversation. She was under no obligation to talk to Memory. That was not part of their deal. Although the faun had been challenging with her words, they were never spoken unkindly.

"And I've only known unseelie fae to be evil monsters," Memory shot back.

Shonae tilted her head. "Would you call a snake or spider evil? They are creatures of nature, same as the unseelie, same as all fae, same as humans. We are as we are and all have our place in the balance."

Memory eyed the skittering shapes of elongated legs creeping above her through the briars. "Snakes and spiders generally only bite when threatened, and only some of them are outright aggressive. Most of the time they are more scared of us than we are of them."

Shonae tilted her head back the other way.

Oh... Memory frowned.

Shonae's furred lips seemed to have the smallest of smiles on them.

Memory knew that she was right on some levels. She thought she hated all the unseelie fae, but what did she really know about them? She

hated them based on her own limited experience, but were her reasons all personal and did they have any truth to them? And what about her experiences with the seelie fae? With Mina, or Aine?

A Rump of Steel-skin spider skittered across the ground beneath Memory's feet and with a clenched jaw she made an effort not to stamp down and squish it. It seemed to hesitate, angling its many eyes toward her, before rushing off again.

Memory watched Shonae walk in front of her for a while, the slight sparkle to her wild mane of wooly white hair, the long, black claws protruding from her furry paws. "What is the difference? Between seelie and unseelie fae, I mean. Both courts have all different kinds, and as far as I've seen you're all just as tricksy as each other."

Shonae lifted one shoulder. "Unseelie fae, we were born of the night, which gives us the shadows in our eyes. Seelie were born of day."

"So you don't get to choose?"

"Choose what?"

"Whether you are seelie or unseelie."

"No."

"So you are born good or evil and you get no say in the matter?"

Shonae's lips split, showing her teeth as she nickered loudly. "Would being born on one day or the other force a man to behave a certain way? Humans are just as capable of dark and light, of choosing their own way. We are not as different as you would like to think. The night gave me black eyes. That is all."

That is all. The cold nausea of confusion and uncertainty had started to spread in Memory's stomach. It was so much easier to hate the unseelie fae, to hate all of them, to think of them as monsters. But she'd hate even more to do so and be wrong. "That is really the only difference between seelie and unseelie fae? Your eye color?"

Shonae's grin vanished. The web she'd been winding came to an end, and she snapped it from where it was anchored to the curling tunnel. "I know your kind find the seelie fae more fitting to your ideas of beauty."

Memory paused. Was it really that simple? Did humans make the unseelie into monsters with just their thoughts and imagination, a prejudice that made the unseelie fight back and become the monsters they were perceived to be? Could it be as simple as visual bias?

Memory hopped forward a few steps so she was within Shonae's field of vision. "What do I look like to you?"

"Like a human."

"Do we all look different?"

Shonae wrinkled her nose as she often did when Memory came close. "Of course, but none of you is very pretty."

"Thanks a lot." Memory chuckled. "You look like a white deer-girl to me. Not as scary as some other unseelie I've seen."

"I am still young."

"Yikes." Memory's first reaction was to imagine the hideous transformations this deer-girl's body could take as she aged. But she had to stop and think- even if Shonae changed, if she looked like a troll or a banshee or some other monstrous fae she'd seen before, inside, wouldn't she still be the same being who spoke with her so thoughtfully now? It was only appearance. That was all.

"I'm sorry," Memory said. "For trapping you like we did. I realized then that you were young. You were just as scared to die as I am."

Shonae's black eyes opened wide. "I did not know you were afraid to die."

"Of course I am. Most people are. I think it's why we're so stupid all the time."

"I never knew humans feared death. You always seem to court it."

"Court it?"

Shonae rolled her hands in the air, as though that would help her explanation. "You always do things to put yourselves near death. Things that make no sense. Like jumping off the castle walls with just the gust of your skirts to protect you from a fall to the earth."

"You... saw that?" Mem said. The recollection of the deep sadness she'd felt in that moment, when she was ready to give everything up, filled her eyes with tears again. "That was... that was something else. I get what you mean though. In the other world people jump out of airplanes—big flying machines that go across the sky."

"That is a myth."

Memory wanted to laugh but she could see by Shonae's face that she believed that something like an airplane was simply a myth. "In that world fairies and magic are myths."

"We will be a myth in this world too, soon enough."

Just that morning, Memory might have said good riddance. She wasn't so sure now.

A loop of thin, dry wood hung low, spotted with thorns. Engaged

in the conversation with Shonae, Memory ducked away too slow and a small sting flared on Memory's cheek. She covered the cut with her palm. The tunnel walls felt closer than they did before, and again she had to dodge away from a branch extending close to her face.

"The path is getting smaller," she said.

"And it will get smaller again," Shonae nodded.

"And, why?"

"To start a journey is always easier than to finish one."

Memory shot a glare at Shonae. When did fairy riddles start making so much sense?

"Frotz," Memory swore as a thorny stick caught on her sleeve, pricking through to her skin beneath. "Is all the plant-life in Tearnan Ogh this bloodthirsty?"

"There is no plant-life in Tearnan Ogh. It is enchanted to move like it still lives, but it is all dead. The briar pathway is but a ghost. A ghost who takes payment in life to sustain itself." Shonae folded her hands across her waist, protecting her Rump of Steel-skin web, but made no other attempt to protect herself from the thorns closing in on them. "It will take what it demands. Don't fight it, and don't use your iron to cut through. This is the price we pay."

"No wonder this highway is so bare," Memory grumbled.

"It once was full of life. Fae would travel the briar pathway all across our world and others. Now those who are left remain in Avall and their own courts only. All others have turned to dust." Shonae kicked at the diamond sand on which they walked.

Memory's stomach turned. *Please be speaking metaphorically, pretty please.*

The tunnel had closed in until Memory and Shonae had to walk in single file. With every step, hooked thorns caught in Memory's hair and clothes, ripping thin razor cuts where it met flesh.

Memory stopped trying to avoid them. There was no way to. This was the price she would pay.

The briars rustled, a mix of dry wood crackling and a low slurping, licking sound that Memory was sure was going to drive her crazy.

The briars dipped lower, closing in completely. Shonae pushed through, grabbing onto Memory's wrist and dragging her behind. Scratches covered Memory's face and hands, her red blood dripping into the ground. She thought she heard a contented sigh coming from the briars.

With a final push, Shonae and Memory broke through the thicket.

Memory turned back to see the mess they had just fought through and saw instead a wide tunnel, looking just like the open mouth of the briar pathway they had entered on the other side.

"Typical," she muttered. "Still, we made it."

They had arrived at the court of the seelie fae.

CHAPTER NINETEEN

Memory picked a thorn from the back of her hand as she took in the landscape before her.

Neatly shaped trees of silver and gold were spotted in careful arrangements across a smooth, level ground, entirely paved in polished gold-streaked marble as far as Memory could see. The trees held no leaves, only blossoms studded along the bare branches. The flowers ranged from lilies to roses, all crystalline and glittering. Everything was too vivid, and the scent drifting down from the blossoms too strong, unnatural. A sprite zoomed through some of the branches, which tinkled and sang in its wake as it vanished again.

Up ahead, a palace loomed. A confection of milky quartz and twisting silver created a series of pointed dome shapes and towers which combined into a massive structure, reaching higher into the sky than Memory could see.

Although she couldn't see a sun in the mauve tinted sky, everything shone brightly, casting flares of light off every surface. Memory shaded her eyes with a hand. "I guess there's a reason they call this the Summer Court."

Shonae was squinting, her eyes barely open. She hunched, cowering away from the light. "I will wait for you here," she said. "I cannot go

any further."

Memory could see the fear held in her black eyes and hear it in the break of her voice. Even if Shonae had been allowed into the seelie court, she was terrified, and with good reason. Shonae had brought an interloper smelling of iron into her opposing realm.

"Stay safe. I'll be back soon," Memory promised, and began her march to the palace.

The paved ground felt slick under Memory's boots, and the warmth of light around her dried the cuts on her skin, making them pucker and sting.

She kept a close eye on her surroundings, worried a troop of seelie soldiers would rush out and capture her. The trees she walked by really did seem not just silver and gold colored, but actually made of silver and gold. Just one branch would have been enough to retire on in the other world. But she knew enough now to know not to touch them. More than anything, the precious trees made her sad. There was nothing real here, nothing alive. No wonder the fae were so keen to trick the humans of Avall into sharing their land.

Memory reached the wavy glass walls of the palace and found the gate, formed from what looked like a single slice of a massive geode. It was open and she walked through into the grounds and there she started to see some life.

A range of seelie fae spotted the bright courtyard. Sprites, dryads, a couple of gnomes- Memory was starting to know the different types by name. She thought she even spotted what looked like a small horse shaped creature with a long curved horn on its forehead.

UNICORN! Memory gave herself a mental high five.

All the creatures kept their distance, watching her warily. Some even turned to flee, shocked by her presence. Memory watched them warily in return. They were all beautiful in her eyes, but she couldn't help wondering now what they really meant.

The courtyard itself was also beautiful, filled with a forest of columns that opened at their tops into more artificial trees. The sweet sound of running water and birdsong filled the space, and Memory saw the pristine fountains and caged earth birds those sounds came from. Small staircases and raised pathways disappeared in all directions around the courtyard, leading up and down and off into tunnels filled with light.

Memory kept on, straight up the largest, main path into the palace.

She knew where she had to go, she had to find Aine.

Eloryn had explained that was the way to get Will back. Through the seelie queen, Memory could challenge Mina for ownership of Will.

Memory was glad of that. The palace was huge, and Will might not even be in it. He could be anywhere, but a queen should be in a fairly obvious place.

Memory climbed the steps and headed into the walls of the castle. Crystals in the shape of flowers were set within the ceiling, lit from within and showering down fine sparkles of fairy dust. Silver, gold, and emerald streaks ran in rich veins down the stone walls. The light glittered and danced off those precious trails, and bounced back into her eyes, blinding her slightly.

"Where's a pair of sunnies when you need them?" Her voice echoed back to her and she shivered. The bravado was lost in the echo and her voice sounded as frightened as she felt.

It struck her that she missed having Shonae at her side. No matter what the faun was, she was company. Now, Memory was truly alone.

Not for long.

Memory's feet twitched, impatient, the countdown to her friends' deaths filling them with panic. Walking was too hard. She broke into a jog.

Chambers flashed by, some filled with fae, some empty. Will was nowhere to be seen.

Huge double doors ahead of her were carved in swirling patterns, pulsing with magic that made Memory dizzy. They opened as she approached.

Memory skidded to a stop along the silky floor.

The room she'd reached put any of the ballrooms at Caermaellan to shame. The chamber's ceiling was so high Memory couldn't see it, or maybe it had no ceiling, opening up to the bare lilac sky above. But there must have been something there, because chandeliers of diamond dewdrops hung down from impossibly long golden threads. The room spun with pearly colors and iridescent metallic glows, caused by the swirl and dance of the fairy-kind who filled the space. Though no music played, they moved together like an ocean, a surging tide of giggling, glittering bodies.

Memory faced the members of the Seelie Court. They peered back at her and whispers broke out around the room and the waving motion stopped.

Moving slowly, Memory walked in, and the fae separated around

her as though she were a ship breaking through sparkling ice.

In the center of the room, on a throne atop a high pillar, sat Aine.

Memory's pulse thundered and her breathing was too fast. She took a long slow breath and held it, willing herself to be calm, and then approached.

Although Aine's face was turned to the side, Memory could see the seelie queen's eyes tracking her as she crossed the floor to stand below the throne. The fairy's long hair tumbled like living bronze down from her high perch, all the way to the floor, and swished when she shifted position to address Memory. Her gown seemed to be made of the same type of cobwebs Shonae had been collecting, woven into a tight fitting, barely-there slip that dangled around her, the tattered tips ringing with small bells. She was impossibly beautiful.

Memory knew her own hair had been torn loose from its ties and fell in ragged, tangled clumps, and that her coat and plain pants were stained with bloods, unseelie black and human red, and the soot, slime and dirt of her journey.

She steadied her stance and raised her chin to meet the seelie queen's gaze.

"The human…" Aine let her eyes roam up and down Memory's appearance, "*queen* has come into my realm? What an honor this is. What, no gifts for your host?"

"I am sorry for coming unannounced, and the gift I will give you is my quick departure, after I have what I came for."

The fae around the room gathered closer, all eager to watch how their monarch dealt with the strange new human queen.

Aine's eyelids drifted closed and opened slowly as though bored. "And tell me, Your Majesty, what have you come for?"

"A fairy from your court has stolen what doesn't belong to her, and I've come to claim him back."

Aine settled into her throne, arching her back like a cat waking from a long nap. "I know the boy you mean. You speak nonsense. The human has long belonged to Mina. I saw her bring him here myself, long before you walked this world."

"But I have owned him since before he came to this world." The words tasted wrong on Memory's mouth. But she had to say it. The only way to free Will was to claim ownership of him.

A buzz of gossip spread through the assembly of fae.

Aine straightened up into a formal position. "A challenge it is then. Mina? Would you bring your pet here?" Aine called sweetly, the grin on her face dripping with venom.

Memory straightened to attention as well. Will was already here, and Mina too, in this room? Her eyes darted through the crowd, trying to spot him. Some movement to her right caught her attention, and the other fae parted to allow Mina to come forward, Will at her side.

Memory bit her tongue to keep her expression neutral and hold back her gasp. Will wore barely any clothing, his skin covered with rich gold paint, smeared in finger-painted patterns across his chest and shoulders. His eyelids were low, hooded, and looked only at Mina with a warmth that made Memory shiver.

Mina flared when she saw Memory, lips curling cruelly.

"Why is *she* here?" Mina asked. Her wings jittered, sending rainbow colored splashes across the faces of the onlookers.

Memory stared at Will, daring him to look up at her, to see her and remember her. To remember himself. His face was slack and his eyes held no emotion. His mouth hung open slightly, lips glossy and an aching color of red like they had been kissed hard and long.

Memory turned her attention to Mina. "I have come for my possession."

"Yours?" Mina's eyebrow raised high. She ran a fingertip up Will's thigh, smearing the gold paint there. Will's shoulders rolled with pleasure. "Will is mine. He ate food from my hands and is pledged to me forever."

"Too bad. He was mine before that, so any claim you have to him doesn't count." Seeing Will like this, so vacantly lustful, threw Memory. Her voice trembled and she realized she was close to tears.

Lock it down, girl.

Aine sounded greatly amused when she said, "If he is yours, it will be proved."

"I have proof." Memory began to speak, telling the court of the time that she and Will had shared in the other world, how she had saved his life and the promise he had made to her that day.

"Will owes me a life-debt, he is mine until I release him. I have proof Will promised to be mine—forever."

Memory walked close to Will and lifted his arm. It was heavy and warm and he barely reacted to her touch. Memory held his arm high, to show his wrist and the tattoo that was on it to the crowd around them, putting her wrist and matching tattoo beside it.

The gossip and murmuring in the crowd quietened.

"A story and a marking. That means nothing," Mina scoffed. She wiped her finger across Will's lips, the paint she'd smeared off his thigh leaving them tinted gold. Then she swiped cross-hatched scratches along Will's chest. "I have marked the boy too."

Mina turned, her eyes daring Memory to respond. Memory almost responded with her fist.

Mina leaned back, purring softly as she nuzzled into Will's chest. He brought his arms up around her, spreading his palms on her belly and dipping his face to her neck. "I think everyone here can see that this boy is mine."

He. Is. Not. Yours! Memory screamed inside herself, but she knew she had run out of ideas.

"Will? Will, look at me. Please just look at me!" Memory yelled, starting to panic.

He lifted his eyes lazily, barely passing them over her before burying his head back into Mina's fiery hair. Those eyes were cobalt blue, deep and rich and dark.

Memory blinked. Her lips curled. "You think you own him? You don't even know what color his eyes are. Will's eyes flash bright, like lightning in a snow storm." Memory backed away from the man. "I don't know who this is, but it isn't *my Will.*"

Mina reared back, fairy dust shooting like sparks from her skin.

The fairy queen clapped slowly. "How entertaining! Seems you do own the boy, human queen."

The glamour dropped like a curtain. Will, the imposter Will, vanished.

Memory looked around desperately. "It was a test? Where is he? Where is Will?"

Aine flicked a limp wrist toward the nearby wall, and there, Memory saw a cage that wasn't there before. Or more like a box, with thick silver walls checkered with small clover-shaped holes. Those walls clattered and shook as though something struck them.

"Will?" Memory tried to push through but Mina blocked her way.

"Don't even," Memory spat. In a swift movement, Memory clutched a fistful of the sprite's hair in one hand, yanking her down as she kicked out her feet from under her.

The seelie queen shrieked with laughter, clapping her hands faster.

Mina crumpled, her wings flashing and fluttering as she hit the

floor and stayed there. When she looked up her face was devoid of expression but there was still rage in her voice. "You take him from me and you will pay!"

"Mina! Your ploy didn't work. You've lost your pet. Let them free," Aine said sharply. "We honor our laws, here."

Mina argued back, but Memory wasn't listening anymore. She ran to the cage as it thudded again from inside.

"Open it!" Memory screamed.

No longer amused by the proceedings, Aine's voice was hard and deep, barely human. "Take him and go."

The cage opened, and Will was there, his bloodied fists still pressed against the wall.

Memory reached in for him, and he growled at her touch. His shirt was shredded down the front, hanging in strips off his arms and shoulders. His eyes, the brilliant blue she knew so well, flickered and roamed, not settling on her.

"It's me, Will. It's Mem. Can't you see me?"

He winced, shaking his head, gaze still not focused. "Mem?"

"Come on. You're free." Memory reached again for his hand, and took it in hers. His hand shook as she helped him up and out of the tight, dark space, and then tightened around hers.

"What have you done to him?" Memory yelled at Mina, who skulked below Aine's throne.

Mina hissed, and with a flick of her chin, vanished away.

Memory turned to Aine for answers.

The look on the seelie queen's face said she would get none. "I said take him and GO!"

The roar was so loud the floor shook beneath Memory.

Memory squeezed Will's hand and he followed her blindly as she led him through the silent crowd of fae around them.

No matter what, I have him again. Memory's heartbeat accelerated in relief but she dared not show it, or allow the smile that was tugging at her mouth to crease her face. She was seriously outnumbered and things could change at the queen's whim.

Just as Memory and Will reached the doorway, a deep voice spoke softly. "Water from the well down the stairs in the courtyard will clear his eyes."

Memory looked and saw Lugh standing before her; Aine's human consort, said to have been with her for decades, maybe centuries. He was like a golden god of a man, strong, tall, with shimmering silver-blonde hair. His expression seemed almost bored, but his eyes glittered with sadness.

Memory stopped and looked up at him, her heart swallowing itself. "What about... what about you? Is there anything I can do?"

Lugh looked as though he could laugh, but his smile quickly became small and sad. "Child, strange as it may seem, I am here of my own choice. But thank you, and good luck."

"Thank you," Will said.

Out through the doors, Memory wanted to run. It was only Will's blindness that kept her pace slow and steady down the long glimmering corridor and out into the courtyard.

Across to her side, Memory could see a wide section of steps leading down into the earth in a V-shape, starting wide and becoming narrower as they descended.

"This better not be like the briar path again," she grumbled, and supported Will as she took him carefully a step at a time.

He said nothing, just let her guide him. The warmth of his chest leaning on Memory made her feel safe and sad at the same time.

Memory recognized the pants he wore as the same he had on when Mina stole him, but they were tattered and torn, worse than her own clothes. In a fit of self-consciousness, she suddenly remembered what she looked like, and what Will would see when his eyes worked again.

He won't care if I'm a mess. It's one of the reasons I love him.

The steps were level and smooth, as were the walls beside them. Fist-sized gems of brilliant aqua, set into the walls, cast a fresh light into the stairwell as they reached a depth the brightness of the world above didn't touch. There was no roof, just a cut in the earth that seemed to go forever, deeper and deeper into the earth.

Just when the sky above was nothing more than a thin ribbon, they finally reached the bottom. A small pool opened up before them, glowing with the same aqua light as the gemstones. Memory dipped her hands in to scoop up some water, and the scratches on her fingers washed away as though they were nothing but splashes of paint. She was desperate to wash her face in the magical pool, but reached her hands up to Will first.

"Tip your face back," Memory said softly. "And maybe duck down

a bit. You're a freaking giant you know."

Will did as instructed, kneeling down and turning his face up to the sky, and Memory dripped the water into his eyes.

He blinked three times fast, then one slow, then looked straight up into Memory's eyes.

"You're okay?" Memory's voice was barely a breath.

"You saved me." He looked at her with wonder. "I owe you all over again."

Will got to his feet and reached for her.

Memory frowned, stepping away. There wasn't much space, and her back hit the wall.

"You owe me nothing. Will, you are free, of Mina, and of me. I release you of any ownership or any debt. You don't belong to me, or anyone, not ever again."

The wavering light from the water lit aqua lines across Will's face as his expression changed through shock, relief, confusion, and sadness.

He looked down at his bare feet. "Don't you want... can I still be by your side?"

Memory drew a trembling breath. She felt all of her seventeen years old, staring up at the most beautiful boy in the world. "I do. I mean, if it's what you want. Not for anything you feel you owe me. Only if you want to. Only if you want... me."

Will's gaze stole straight into her soul as he bent his face to hers. "I want you."

The kiss Will placed on Memory's lips then was one that burned with the truth of what he just said. And as her lips parted to meet his again, they burned with love in return.

"I love you," Will gasped between kisses. "I have loved you so long. Since the day you saved me until this day. I've fallen in love with you over and over. I loved who you were. I loved who I remembered you were. Then I loved who you became."

"I love you too," Memory whispered, tangling her fingers into the dark twists of Will's hair. Will clutched at Memory, pulling her tight against his body.

Tears came to Memory and she let them run, tasting the salt of them between her mouth and Will's.

Gently, he let her go. "What's wrong?"

Memory brushed her hand down Will's cheek, wiping away a tear

there. *Mine or his?* "You're free. That's the good news."

"I'm free," Will murmured, smile wide on his face and eyes closed. He opened them again and looked around and up the stairwell behind them.

His dark brows dropped low. "Where are your friends? Did you come alone?"

Memory sighed. "That's the bad news…"

CHAPTER TWENTY

As Memory explained to Will her journey through the fairy realm so far, and what had happened to the others, she pulled Will's iron awl from a loop in her belt and handed it over to him. His hand wrapped around hers as he took it, and he lingered there, feeling the fragile coolness of Memory's slim fingers in his. There was also a tremble there that made Will want to pull Memory into his arms and hold her again.

Memory had lost her friends because of him. She'd risked everything to save him, they all had. And he couldn't be upset because he knew he would have done the same if the situation was reversed. And he knew that together they would risk everything again to save Eloryn, Roen, and Erec.

Will dabbed the healing well water across Memory's face and his jaw grew tight. He knew Memory planned to save her friends at the Unseelie Court. And he knew he would go with her, anywhere. But he still wished that they could simply go home, be safe, where nothing more could hurt the girl he loved. He wished it with every aching nerve in his body.

But he knew a quiet, safe life was never the destiny of this girl. Maybe he'd always known it. She always had the fire of a hero burning within her. He could see her great and terrible fate on her as clearly as the scratches that marred her skin. He couldn't stop whatever was to

come, but he would do everything in his power to protect the body and the heart of the young woman before him.

Will bent to collect some more well water and Memory held him back.

"That's enough," she said. "As nice as it feels right now, we're only going to get scratched up again. Plus we're on the clock."

Will nodded, and they strode up the deep stairwell and out of the Seelie Court.

A light breeze seemed to chase them from the court, out through the tinkling metal trees and over the tiled ground, so polished it reflected like a mirror. They found the briar pathway quickly, and a petite white creature emerged shyly from where she had been crouched in the shadows.

"Got him back, then?" she bleated, one long ear twitching.

Memory nodded. "Will, this is our guide, Shonae. She's… well… She's been helpful."

Shonae grunted, spat, and turned her back, taking the lead into the briar tunnel.

"Mostly," Memory muttered.

A giant spider skittered past along the twigs overhead, its shadow sending chills down Will's spine. Although he knew of the spiders and the briar path, this was all new to him. He'd never been through here before, because he'd never travelled outside of the Seelie Court. He'd never been free.

The concept still staggered him. For sixteen years he had been a pet to Mina. Neglected, toyed with, put on display, or put in a cage. He'd felt free, at times, when Mina had left him alone in Avall's forests for long stretches, but the choke of an invisible collar had always remained.

The girl he loved had freed him, and if he didn't think he could love her any more, maybe he could, for that.

They continued down the twisting briar tunnel until the entrance disappeared behind them. Just as Will took a deep, free, breath of relief, a familiar twinkle caught his eye.

"Stop!"

In a sparking explosion of fairy dust, Mina appeared before them, blocking their way down the narrow path. Fury lit her eyes like a fire within.

"I won't. I won't let you go." Mina stomped a foot on the ground. Her wings sent sparkling drops of red light into the air and Will had to squint to protect his eyes from the brightness.

"Mina, let us pass." Will's voice was firm and strong. "Go home. Don't make this difficult."

Mina came towards them.

Will saw Memory's fingers tightening on the handle of her blade. "You don't own him anymore, Mina. No one does."

Will put a hand on her slim shoulder, wanting her to back off—to let him handle this. She seemed to receive the silent message and stilled.

Mina flew right in front of Will, clutching at the tattered remains of his shirt with both hands. There was desperation in her eyes as they stared deep into his. "You love me. I know you do. Say it and stay with me. Stay here. Be mine."

Will kept his gaze steady, locking eyes with Mina. "You saved my life. I will always thank you for that. But I am free now. I choose to leave."

Her eyes filled with tears. The glitter falling from her wings turned to dust, black and heavy. "Are you really leaving me? I love you, I need you. Please don't go."

"Mina, you don't love me. You don't know what that even means. You just know you want me, you want your pet. Love is not the same thing as thinking you should have what you want just because you want it. It's not keeping someone with you when they want to go. It's not spells or tricks or keeping someone in a cage. That is not love, Mina, and until you know that you are never going to know love in return."

"You don't know how I feel!" Mina's face twisted, anger tightening her lips until they spread, baring thin teeth. "I will not let you just walk away from me. You're mine!"

"He was released by your queen," Shonae said. She shook her head at the sprite, a small warning, fae to fae.

Memory had a look on her face Will did not like. She was testing the edge of the blade with one finger and eyeballing Mina as though she was trying to get a bead on where to stick that sharp weapon. "Stop being the bad ex and just go home."

The light in the tunnel grew as Mina hissed, her firelight glow raging under her skin. "You. Everything was fine before you stumbled out of the Veil. Stealing my boy." Mina's snarl became a wicked grin. "Well, you have won Will, but you lost all your other friends to the Unseelie Court, haven't you? They won't be so easy to get back."

Memory said nothing. Her shoulders were rigid and her mouth pressed down into a thin line that told Will exactly how afraid she was

that what Mina had just said was true. Will pushed Mina's hands off his shirt and walked back to stand beside Memory, his love for her like a magnet, drawing him in. "It's going to be okay. We'll get everyone home safe. Come on, let's go."

Will brushed the back of one finger lightly across Memory's cheek.

"No! You can't choose her over me," Mina shrieked. "I don't care what the queen said. You might be free, but that doesn't mean you're protected. If I can't have you, no one can."

Mina ran at him, screaming. A bright gold light flashed in her hand, her inner light reflecting off the wide fairy gold dagger she held there. It took a moment for Will to believe it was real, that Mina would really try to kill him. She was many things, but he didn't believe her truly capable of such violence. That moment of confusion brought the dagger to his chest, the razor edge of it cutting through the remains of his once fine shirt. Distantly he heard Memory cry out as though far away, despite being right beside him.

Will sidestepped, sliding with the thrust of the weapon, rolling away from it before it broke his skin. Will grabbed Mina as she passed him, his fingers slipping over her arm and her hair smacking him in the face as they spun together.

He grabbed her small wrist, applying pressure. The fae were strong but brittle, much like their gold.

Mina screamed again. "You are hurting me!"

"I'll break you if you don't drop the blade."

The dagger clattered to the ground.

Will let go of Mina and picked it up, holding it defensively against her.

Mina backed away, her face glowing with rage.

"Do you honestly think you are going to get away from here without a fight? I have more friends here than you do!"

A hum built in the air, and the light brightened until the glare made Will wince. Memory raised her arm to shade her eyes. "What's happening?"

Shonae nickered a gasping high pitched sound. "We're for it now."

Will's breath caught in his throat. "We have to run."

Sprites flew up the tunnel behind them, like swarms of fireflies. In their smaller form, they seemed no more threatening than a tangle of Christmas lights, but Will knew better.

He grabbed Memory's hand and dragged her along the briar path.

Shonae ran beside them squealing as the flying creatures harried and tormented her.

Sharp stabs of pain marked Will's arms, his neck, and cheeks. The sprites buzzed about him, their tiny faces puckered with unholy mischief, their hands holding needle-like blades that sliced like paper cuts.

Laughter rang out from every corner. The buzzing of wings beat all the way inside his head. Memory fell, pulled to her feet by a mass of the tiny beasts in her hair. She shrieked in anger and pain.

Will hauled her to her feet, swatting at the fairies with his iron hook that Memory had returned to him. He kept a tight grip of her hand.

They ran, beating their way blindly through the cloud of sprites. The sting of the fae's attacks blended with the scratching of stick and thorn as they crashed against the walls of the briar path.

"Don't stray," Shonae cried out. "Don't stray!"

Her warning came too late. In a burst of dry and broken twigs, Memory and Will stumbled out and clear of the briar pathway, with Shonae falling behind them.

Will blinked in the sudden darkness, trying to adjust. The sprites were gone, the attack was over. He closed his eyes to fight away the trails of light burned into his retinas. Opening them again he saw black trees hanging over their heads and dead grass below his feet. Behind them there was no sight of the briar pathway, no entrance, no thorny walls, nothing. "Where are we?"

"Lost." Shonae grunted. Her shoulders were hunched and she licked at a bleeding cut on her forearm. "We strayed from the path, and now we're lost far from where we should be and I'll never be rid of you."

Memory sat on the ground, catching her breath. "Mina and her buzz-buddies are gone at least. They forced us out here but didn't follow us. This looks like the unseelie lands. Is that why they didn't keep chasing us? How far could we be from the court?"

Shonae huffed. "How far could it be from one side of your world to the other?"

Memory scrambled to her feet. "No, don't be with your riddles now. Are you saying we're not going to make it in time?"

"We got shoved out of the briars mid pathway. We could have come out anywhere." Shonae slouched and turned away.

Memory looked to Will with crushing fear in her eyes.

Will moved to stand in front of Shonae. "Please, can you try and

tell where we are? Is there anything you can see?"

Shonae sighed, and turned her face up to the empty gray sky. She tilted her head side to side, her goat-like ears angling around independently.

"There's nothing up there. What do you see?" Memory asked, looking at the sky herself.

"Our sun is dim, nearly dead, but she is there."

Memory turned back to Will. "We're not going to make it in time."

Will didn't answer. He just wrapped his arms around Memory and drew her close.

She murmured into his chest, "I don't know how long I've been here, how long since Eloryn, Roen, and Erec were Branded. I have no clock to know when their Brands will kill them. Nyneve said a turn of the sun and the moon but I can't even see them in this awful world!"

Shonae sniffed, then leaped up onto an outcrop of rocks that formed a small peak, hopping up them like a mountain goat.

When she reached the top, she looked all the way around, and then extended one arm. "That's the way we need to go." She pointed with her long white finger. "But it will take at least three days to walk there without the briar path."

"Three days." Memory's voice was a harsh breath.

"Let's go then," Will said. He knew it was hopeless, but what else could they do?

"We could Veil door there. Maybe. I don't know if I can do it in Tearnan Ogh or where we are going but I can try." Memory was babbling. Her face was pale and tired, and Will wondered how long it had been since she'd eaten or slept.

"You made an unbreakable oath not to use your magic. We only just escaped the Seelie Court. Let's not provoke them again." Will tried to smile, to win a smile from Memory, but it was a lost attempt.

"I have to do something."

"You will. I don't know how, but you will save them. You'll save everyone. You've always been my hero, and heroes always win."

He was rewarded with a small smile then. "We must have at least twelve hours left, right? So let's walk. We can walk for eleven hours, and then you can try your magic."

Memory nodded, and her whole body swayed. If it had been anyone else, Will wouldn't believe she'd last that long. But he knew Memory could.

"Deal," she said. "No backsies."

With a deadly serious shared look, they both spat in their hands and shook on it. And then they started walking.

Every step on the crackling, dead ground counted like a second ticking on a clock in Memory's mind. When they started out she'd tried to count in her head, count the seconds, minutes, to get some idea of how long they had walked, of how much time they had left. But there were too many seconds, and minutes, and her thoughts were too addled with panic and exhaustion.

We'll make it there in time, somehow. That became the new mantra Memory repeated over and over instead of counting as the three of them walked in silence. Maybe Nyneve could do something for her, extend the deadline. Something. Memory kept hope alive within the burning magic in her chest. The walking was easy enough, great flat plains of hard-packed, shimmering dirt with just a few twisted trees reaching high into the air like giant beanstalks. Memory cast concerned glances at Will as they went, seeking support. The determination and courage on his face when he looked back at her hurt almost as much as it helped.

Shonae told Memory to relax. This was daytime apparently, and there would be a night. They had at least until then.

Memory stared skeptically at the dull gray sky and wondered how they would tell the difference. She couldn't see the sun Shonae spoke of at all, only a slowly churning mass of monochrome clouds. There wasn't even enough light to cast shadows, but Memory supposed it could get darker. *Things can always get worse*, she reminded herself.

Something in the sky moved on the horizon, and Memory swallowed hard. *Say the famous last words? Of course I did.*

The wind picked up and there was a low whomping sound, ominous and drawing nearer. They all looked up, the small shreds of hope that had begun to settle on them shattering like thin ice on a lake.

There it was. The dragon.

CHAPTER TWENTY-ONE

"Just what we need," Memory sighed, reaching for her knife.

In the dim light his black scales had no shine, making the dragon look like a shadow or silhouette in the sky rather than a real creature. He was flying low, a loping, tumbling flight that lacked the grace Memory had once seen him possess.

Even still, he flew fast and would reach them in seconds. Memory's stomach clenched with fear at the thought of being bitten in half by those huge teeth, or set on fire by dragon breath. How badly would that hurt?

Memory knew they could not run or hide. She doubted they could fight. All they could do was wait. Will put his shoulder beside hers and they watched the dragon come to them. Shonae crumbled to the ground, her face down in the dirt in a deep kneeling bow.

The dragon landed in front of them. His feet hit the earth hard and skidded, sending puffs of dust flying up into their faces. Memory covered her eyes with her sleeve and Will coughed.

The dragon came to a stop lying on his side. Memory could see his wings were tattered. When the creature raised his head to look at the small group, it seemed to be with great effort.

Without moving his tooth-filled mouth, the dragon's words rattled into Memory's mind. "Hello human."

The massive serpentine beast made no threatening move or sign

that it would hurt them. He just waited.

"Hello dragon," Memory replied, eyeing him with a confused frown. "Been a while."

The dragon blinked huge verdant eyes. "I have been watching you since you came to our realm."

Memory winced, both for the power of the dragon's voice in her head, and for her failures the dragon must have observed.

Will spoke, obviously hearing everything Memory heard. "Why? What do you want?"

"I am trying to decide what it is you are doing. If you mean to harm or help the fae as we draw to our end."

"I'm just here to save my friends. Standard search and rescue then we're going home. I wasn't even thinking about..." *I wasn't even thinking about anyone else.* Memory let out a breath like she'd taken a baseball bat to the chest. *My friends are in trouble, and I wasn't even thinking about anyone else.*

Memory took a step closer to the dragon. His scales were patchy, missing in places, moldering. "Dragon, are you dying?"

"We are all dying. You already know that." The words held no bitterness. He extended a claw so carefully toward Shonae, scooping her arms onto it and raising her back to her feet.

Shonae shivered slightly, staring with round black eyes at the dragon, but she kept her fingers wrapped around his claw as though holding hands. Shonae looked so healthy, so alive, that it was hard to understand for Memory that she could be dying. Much like most of the fae. But seeing the dragon like this made the truth suddenly sink in.

The dragon tilted his head and Memory wondered how many of her thoughts he had access to. "My time is less due to my size. I need more magic to sustain me than the little ones. But eventually all of this will end."

"I've been so selfish." Memory shook her head, staring at her feet. "I am doing everything I can to save my friends but there are so many who need help. I should be doing more."

The dragon shifted, making a soft hushing sound in the shifting, glittered sand. "What does the fate of the fae matter to you? If you wish you can take your friends and go to the other lands. You can live there with the rest of the humans and never worry for the fate of Tearnan Ogh or Avall."

For a brief moment, Memory tried to imagine Eloryn and Roen

adjusting to life in the modern world. Eloryn would probably love the internet. Could they live there happily? What about Erec, or Clara? Then there were Roen's parents and Lanval. Maeve, and the orphans. Bedevere and the Wizards' Council. The rest of the castle guards and staff. Memory's thoughts spiraled out, larger and larger, reaching farther. The teachers and students at the university and finishing school. The people she saw on the streets of Caermaellan, Maerranton markets or Elder's Bridge Inn. All the humans of Avall. Shonae… Aine, Nyneve, Lugh. All the shimmering sprites of the Seelie Court. The banshees and trolls and gaunts of the Unseelie Court. The dragon. Every creature in Avall and Tearnan Ogh. How could she abandon any of them? How could she pick and choose who would live?

This entire world of the fae was passing into the shadows, and would take Avall with it. Avall had been created as a haven, but the constant drain of magic away to the rest of the world had wrought devastation on the fae, and it was only the fae that kept Avall habitable for the humans.

"What can I do?" Memory's words were a mere whisper.

"I think you already know."

Magic. Life. Like a bonfire, burning me away from the inside.

Memory nodded. Everywhere things and people were dying from a lack of magic. Could she give them hers? She took a deep breath, and reached to place a hand on the dragon's cheek.

"Dragon, would you let me gift you with some of my magic? I have more than I can ever use and it could save you."

His lips split, showing rows of razor tipped teeth, and a harsh gust of hot air rushed out along with a rumbling chuckle. "Oh you little human. No. I would not take your magic. It is too compressed into you, tangled up inside. Who knows what other *human* things I might get along with it?"

The dragon leaned slightly into Memory's touch, and Memory could feel the slow pulse of his life beneath his scales.

"Besides, I am old. Older than you can imagine, human, and I am the last of my kind. Life is just a series of lonely days and nights. There is no joy in it, no thrill. My mate is now dead and without her there is no love, no way to ease the stifling boredom that is centuries piling on top of one another. I am better off dying, then I could fly free again with my mate and the others of my kind who have gone before me."

Having grown up believing dragons only to be a myth, the idea that

Memory would discover they were real only to lose them again seemed too much to bear. It hurt to speak but she did. "Dragon, our worlds will not be the same without you."

"I agree." The sly humor in the dragon's voice was clear as it reverberated in Memory's head. She smiled at the dragon as tears streamed down her cheeks. Will took and squeezed her hand and put his other on the dragon's neck.

"Be strong, small ones. The worlds need you. And you need help now, so let me help you. I will fly you to the Unseelie Court."

"You are not a beast of burden," Memory said, reminding him of what he had once told her when she had a boon to request of him.

"No, but the time for old rules has past. The good fight for themselves and their friends. The great fight for everyone."

Memory bowed her head.

"I think you are worthy of a ride, or at least, one day, you will be," the dragon quipped. His words were light, but Memory thought she saw something on his wizened face, some emotion so close to human sorrow that it cut her to the very core.

Memory did not even bother to wipe away the tears that rolled down her cheeks. "I cannot thank you enough, Dragon."

The dragon laid himself low and Will helped boost Memory and Shonae up, then climbed up behind them. The dragon's back was smooth despite the scales and scars. Shonae took the webbing she had collected from the spiders and wrapped it carefully around the three of them and then around the dragon's neck. They sat in a row with Memory up front, Will behind her and Shonae clinging tightly at the rear.

"For all the risk and danger you put me through on your journey," Shonae snuffled, "perhaps it is worth it all, to fly on the back of a dragon."

Memory brushed her hands across the metallic black scales she sat on. *Perhaps it is worth it all.*

The dragon shifted under her, and as he raised himself up Memory gasped at how high she was, there on his back. The tattered wings spread, lifted, and pushed downwards, creating mini-tornadoes of sparkling dust as they lifted off the ground. Memory had to close her eyes when they took off and her fear mounted as they soared over treetops and higher, until the ground had vanished below the clouds they rode through.

Memory wasn't sure the dragon would even have enough life left in him to get them safely to the Unseelie Court, but if he trusted her

enough to let her ride, then she trusted him enough to try. Each dip and glide of the dragon's wings sent her stomach swirling, and she had to crouch low against the scaly back to shelter from the rushing winds. The Rump of Steel-skin web that she clung to felt too silky and delicate to be her tether on this creature so far above the world. She knew too well what it felt like to fall.

The warmth of Will's body behind her was reassuring, and after a while her thoughts took her mind away from her fear of falling off the dragon's back. Tearnan Ogh was dying, the creatures and people within it were dying, and there seemed to be no way to stop all of it. She could go back to the rest of the world if need be, and take her friends with her but what about all the other humans of Avall?

How would any of the citizens of Avall survive in a world they had so long been separated from? Time had passed, and the old ways that stayed with Avall long gone. Cars and nuclear weapons had replaced swords and horses; people ate food from paper wrappers and flew in steel tubes across the sky. Would the people of Avall be able to withstand those changes without going mad?

Maybe I should have helped educate people on the modern world, she thought tiredly. *I should have done... anything. I should have... Crudmonkeys! What is the use in thinking of what I should have done when it is obvious I need to do something right now?*

But what?

Memory knew even if she could take every human from Avall into the modern world, she couldn't take any of the fae. They couldn't stand the abundance of iron and steel there. *What can I do to save this land and the fae and the dragon? How could one person save an entire world?*

She wanted to save it. As strange and weird and terrifying as Tearnan Ogh was, it hurt her to think of it disappearing forever.

Memory wiped a tear away on her shoulder so it wouldn't fly back and splash on Will or Shonae behind her, alerting them to her uncontrollable emotions.

Will seemed to understand anyway. "Stop worrying. Just rest. You need it." His breath tickled her ear and his hand stroked her back.

He was right. She was beyond exhausted. They all were. Even the dragon swooped lower, floating on the updrafts and saving his waning energy.

Memory's head sagged to one side and her body relaxing into Will's.

His heart beat below his skin and she felt it echoing into hers as she fell asleep.

"We are here," Shonae said and Memory wished she did not hear the terror in her voice, wished she didn't hear her at all, that she could have slept one hundred years and given up all her worries and responsibilities.

But she knew no one else could do what needed to be done. And she was starting to understand what that was.

Since Memory had slept, the world had grown darker, black like the mottled scales of the dragon they rode.

The Unseelie Court came into view, a beacon of red fire light reflecting off dark crystal under the ebony dome of the sky.

Please. Memory said a silent prayer to anything that would listen. *Please just let my friends still be alive.*

CHAPTER TWENTY-TWO

The dragon dipped suddenly and Memory felt her stomach float up into her throat.

"How are you holding up?" she asked the dragon, hoping her voice, or at least thoughts, carried over the rushing winds for him to hear. "Are we okay for a landing?"

"Tired." The single word reply held a depth of emotion, the weariness of centuries.

Memory placed her hand on the dragon's neck, wishing she could do more for him. They soared toward the ground, lurching roughly through the air, and Memory tightened her thighs to steady herself.

The dragon skimmed over a vast boundary wall, a shimmering fence of glistening black crystal woven like tangled tree roots. It seemed to sing as the air from their flight trailed through it. Reaching the inner courtyard of the castle, the dragon spiraled, slowing his descent as the unseelie fae in the area dashed for cover.

They landed hard but stable. As the disturbed dust cleared, all around them Memory could see black-eyed faces peering up in awe.

"You've made a big entrance, that's for sure," Will whispered into Memory's ear.

"Nice way to make an impression," Memory agreed. "I only wish we had some kind of plan from this point on. I'm basically walking

right into a trap. As usual."

"Just be yourself. Save your friends. It will work out."

Memory grunted an unsure agreement then threw her leg over the side and slid down off the dragon in what she thought was a remarkable display of not falling on her face.

The dragon's head was close by her as she turned back to see Will and Shonae follow her off its back. She smiled softly to the huge beast. "Thank you."

The dragon's head dipped ever so slightly, and he poised to take flight again.

His wings were even more tattered than before. They were riddled with tears and holes, his scales were dulled and flaking and she knew he had cost himself much of his life by flying them through the night the way he had. Sorrow filled her, but before she could say anything else the dragon pushed down his wings and lifted into the sky.

Whispers blended with the sound of the dragon's flight. Hushed words buzzed around Memory and her friends as they stood in the middle of the grand courtyard, right on the steps of the Unseelie Court's castle, surrounded by curious onlookers. Two humans had come to the court on the back of a dragon, accompanied by a young unseelie fae. Strange things were afoot and everyone wanted to know what they meant.

Memory looked up at the castle and tried to draw on her well of courage and found it almost dry, already consumed from constant use. *Shouldn't it get easier, being brave? Why do I always have to dig deeper?*

The castle itself was similar to the Seelie Court, if anything more organic and flowing in its lines and design. Darker colors were used, but they made a rich, warm impression rather than the haunted house of terror Memory had been expecting. But she knew that the terror lay inside.

She forced her feet to move, and to the main entrance they went.

Guards met them. The tallest of them stood in their path, a fairy gold spear held firmly in his hand. He, and the dozen guards behind, all wore the same high gloss black armor as the soldiers who had stolen her friends away, but this lot wore no helmets. The leader's long white hair fell to his waist, and his skin was gray as ash.

The knight narrowed his eyes, his silver tipped lashes veiling the pools of black below his eyelids. "We've been expecting you."

"Then where is the red carpet?" Memory said.

The smugness dropped from the knight's face as he tried to interpret her reaction and phrasing.

Memory squared up her fingers to frame the dark fae's face and squinted through at him. "And that look on your face is exactly why I love saying stuff like that. So, are you going to let us in?"

The knight hesitated. Not in a way that seemed confused, but a way that seemed torn, and troubled, and made Memory's stomach bubble. "Human queen," he said in a hushed voice. "You should return home."

"Let them pass!" The deep, regal voice called from behind the crowd of guards.

Nyneve appeared, and the men parted to make way for her. She strode through them, wearing a dress encrusted with thousands of diamonds, as though she were glistening sea-foam on top of deep black water. The shimmer of her dress and the shimmer of her lightly scaled, silver skin blended perfectly so it was hard to tell where the close fitted bodice ended and her flesh began. The skirts, though, billowed around her strong frame and trailed in a long train behind her. With her hair like nighttime flowing all round, she seemed to be the very embodiment of the starry sky.

"Your Highness," the men muttered in rough unison, all taking a knee.

Nyneve looked darkly at the head guard who had showed hesitation at allowing Memory and her friends to enter the court.

"They are here by invitation of one of our own, or so it would appear." Nyneve's eyes raked over Shonae, who trembled and tried to press herself into a corner. "They are to be allowed entry."

"They tricked me into compliance. They carried iron," Shonae stuttered.

"Iron," a knight said, disgust written on his face.

Nyneve raised her chin slightly. "Yes. The iron. You cannot be allowed to bear it into the court, you must understand."

Memory reached instinctively for her knife in her belt. Without iron, they would have no protection at all, but what good was it to her now, truly? She could not fight her way with iron through every dark fae in the land to save her friends. It didn't protect them the first time.

Memory gave a single nod.

Nyneve waved for them to follow, and they walked into the long entry hall and to a small room to the side. "Leave your iron here. You can rest your thoughts, knowing no fae will be able to touch it, move

or steal it, lest they be burned."

Memory and Will placed their iron artefacts onto the table. They met gazes, shared a worried look, and turned away.

"Hurry now," Nyneve said softly. "Your friends live, but they suffer. You must act quickly. You have the right to declare or accept a challenge from the monarch, to prove the innocence of your friends and remove their Brand." She waved them back out of the room, then followed, gown flaring around her.

Out in the long arched hall, Nyneve took the lead again. The walls were like dark mirrors, reflecting her, Memory, Will and Shonae as they sped along the corridor.

"A challenge? What kind of challenge?" Memory half jogged to keep up with the long stride of the Amazonian unseelie princess.

Nyneve slowed as they reached a wider section of hallway which met a huge door, or more like gate, made of woven silver vines and elegant heart-shaped leaves. She touched it softly and it began swinging open. "Trial by combat," she said.

Memory's heart lurched into her throat. The gate opened into a gargantuan domed room, filled with monsters of every form and shape. It felt as though someone had opened up a compendium of fairytale monsters and let the beasts spill from the pages into real life. Minotaurs and trolls, gaunts and green skinned crones, banshees and crooked, twisted, dark winged harpies. Memory tried to see them with fresh eyes, tried to see beyond their physical appearance and judge them without bias, but all she could see was monsters. Monsters, every one of them. Because they were here in Finvarra's court.

The chamber was formed of the same mirrored dark crystals as the rest of the castle, but within them sparkling shapes and clouds of color moved, like nebulae in space, adding color and light to the darkness. In the center of everything was a raised dais where grand seats were formed from crystalline tree roots that met in a thick, twisted trunk that held the largest throne of all—Finvarra's. He sat there, within the hollow of the sparkling tree whose branches spread up, up, twirling into the high ceiling as though it was what held aloft the very roof.

The creatures in the room squabbled and gossiped, argued and drank. The race of news was already spreading through the room and Memory heard whispers of her name, and "dragon" in the chatter.

As the gates swung into their fully open position they clanged against

the wall, and then all eyes in the room were upon Memory.

Finvarra sat in his throne like a tumble of fallen branches, his body a mess of wiry limbs, sharp angles, and rough, ancient skin. He looked down at Memory and extended his arm, curling a sharp clawed finger at her to beckon her to him.

Shonae tugged at Memory's sleeve, cowering by her side. "As Finvarra has grown more cruel and twisted, so has he attracted the worst of the fae into his court. I fear we will not walk free from here again."

Memory walked in anyway. The dark fae moved apart, creating a path for her. She could see something in their all black eyes as they watched her. Hatred? Or could it be fear?

As the crowd cleared, backing to the edges of the room, Memory saw something far worse.

Eloryn. Roen. Erec.

Memory went cold and stiff all over, as though she'd died many hours ago and rigor mortis had suddenly set in.

Her friends were all bound in heavy webbing that wrapped around them and held them in place, dangling from the branches of the throne tree like living piñatas. Live sport for the amusement of Finvarra and the wider audience.

Memory knew better than to look at them for too long but she couldn't look away. Eloryn's body shuddered with small, sharp breaths, her skin a ghostly gray. Roen had blood crusted along his upper lip and chin, matching the dull red of the Brand on his forehead, and Erec sagged toward the ground, apparently lifeless. All of them had anguish written large in their expressions.

Is it the Brand torturing them, or has it been Finvarra and his court?

Memory wasn't sure, but she could see Finvarra was using them as an amusement, hung there on display. The crooked smirk as he watched her approach built hatred inside her she almost couldn't contain. Every terrible thing he had done to her, to her friends, to the people of Avall, made the magic inside her burn like a white-hot star. The magic he had put inside her. The scar he, as Providence, had cut into her chest as a baby itched and stung. She felt the pain she could see on her sister's face.

The ground trembled beneath her at each step she took. The room fell into total silence and for a moment, the smirk fell from Finvarra's face. She wanted to run at him, screaming and clawing and slicing with the iron blade she no longer had.

Will slipped his hand into Memory's and squeezed tight.

"Deep breaths. Stay in control."

"Thank you," Memory whispered to Will.

Side by side, they reached the base of Finvarra's throne. Nyneve, who had escorted them in, broke off from them and stood on the dais at her father's feet.

Memory swallowed, trying to wet her dry mouth, then spoke. "Finvarra, as queen of the humans, I come to seek the release of my people and the removal of their Brands."

"Hrm, only a small request then?" he grumbled, half a smile on his lips, baring the sharp teeth behind. A few unseelie fae around the room chuckled along with him. "These humans were a surprise gift to me from my people. They were found wandering uninvited in my lands, and attacked my men with iron."

Surprise gift? Your men ambushed us!

Finvarra continued, his words mixed with a mad chortling sound. "The Brand on their faces is proof of their crimes. I have every right to do with them what I will. Why would I ever release them?"

Memory fumed, but she also knew they had walked into the fae's homelands carrying iron. There was too much violence and it was only leading to more. There had to be another way.

"Because I am pleading with you to do so. I'm pleading with you to show kindness." Memory held so much hope within her at that moment, hope that there was any kindness within Finvarra that she could reason with, that maybe if he could show kindness in that one moment, she could work with him, help him and his people, maybe even forgive him.

But the look in his eyes told her it would not be. He hated her, she could see it. He hated all humans, hated the magic that resided within them, that he thought they stole from the fae.

"Kindness? You ask for kindness?" He spat a huge glob of smoky gray liquid down at Memory's feet. "I will relish watching the Brand leach the life from these few humans as small compensation for the crimes of all your kind against the unseelie race."

"You are not innocent either, Finvarra. I know your crimes." Memory glared harshly at the unseelie king, telling him with her expression that she knew exactly who he was and what he'd done.

Finvarra rose to his feet, back hunched from age. "You dare offend me so in my own court? Crimes? I have committed no crimes!"

The anger Memory had kept contained was seeping out like a poison. "I do dare because I have seen the damage your crimes have done. I've seen the pain on children's faces and the bodies drained of blood. I feel the fire of your crimes inside me every day!"

Whispers ran through the court. Prickles ran up and down Memory's spine.

Finvarra's black eyes held contempt and he steepled his long fingers together, tapping them on his chin. "I think you have gone insane. If you think I have committed crimes against you, then speak the Branding words. Try to Brand me, and the magic will prove my innocence."

"You know I can't! You know I'm forbidden to speak behests. You're trying to trick me into breaking my oath." Rage seized Memory. She was unable to stop seeing the faces of her friends, distorted and distended with agony. Things had spun totally out of control. Finvarra talked her round in circles, confusing her, and getting her no closer to freeing her friends. She didn't want to have to challenge him, but she was running out of ideas.

"I just want my friends back," she sighed, more to herself than as a plea to the monster before her.

Finvarra took his seat again on the throne. He lowered himself slowly, shakily, like an old man. It was an almost human movement, apart from the mad, scary grin on his face. "That is the problem with you humans. You *want* and you believe that your wanting entitles you to taking."

"Says the king who wanted Avall for the fae and lied to every human there about the rest of the world becoming a hell."

"The iron hell is just that," Finvarra snapped. "It is killing my people as we speak. Are we to just sit around and wait for the people in that world to finish destroying it? We have to protect ourselves!"

"By sucking the life from people, blood drinker?"

Finvarra seemed confused. He glanced over at Memory's three friends, hanging beside him.

Scowling at Memory he flicked his hand at her. "You disgusting creature, I've not touched the filthy blood of your companions. Queen of the humans, if you were not who you are, you would be mounted on my walls right alongside the others! I'll take no more offense from you. Get out of my court before I change my mind."

Memory frowned. There was something wrong. She couldn't put

her finger on it but it was there, right under the surface. If bringing her friends here was Finvarra's trap for Memory, then why was he telling her to leave?

Memory looked across at Eloryn, who was watching with dull, hooded eyes. Her blonde hair was a straggly mess across her face and she was gagged, unable to speak or use behests.

"I won't leave without my friends. Finvarra, I challenge you to a trial by combat for their freedom."

A wave of gasps spread throughout the chamber. Finvarra shifted in his chair, twitching upright and eyeing Memory. Then he laughed, small at first, then building, growing more maniacal and chaotic in its tones. "Little human girl challenges the King Under the Hill to combat? Do you even know what it is you challenge?"

Memory glanced across at Nyneve, who dipped her head in a small, encouraging nod. That gesture was familiar and more prickles ran along her scalp and skin. "If I win, the Brand will be removed from my friends. I'm also asking that if I win, you release us all from your court."

"Sweetening the gamble for yourself? What for me then, if I win?" Finvarra asked, then answered for himself. "Yes, if I win, I keep you all. What a fine trophy a human queen will be! Let the humans see the proof of unseelie dominance in this world. You will be my toy for eternity, or whatever is left of it for us."

And there it is. Memory sneered. He did want her after all. This must have been his plan, trying to lure her into this challenge so he could claim her legitimately. But did he really think he could beat her? He was a fae, so she knew he would be faster and stronger than her, but he seemed so fragile and old, and at least partly mad. Memory had her fair share of fights, and could now remember many times she'd taken on more than a few larger bullies at a time. With the extra sword training she'd had from Roen, maybe she could take Finvarra in a fair fight. If that was what this would be.

"There can be no magic," Memory said. She had seen the magic Providence possessed, using behests as freely and powerfully as Eloryn. She couldn't allow Finvarra to turn that on her now, while she had no magic of her own she could use.

"Of course not!" Finvarra growled. "I know the laws of the challenge. Do you?"

Well, no, actually.

Nyneve stepped forward then, speaking up before Memory had to embarrass herself. "The trial by combat to prove the innocence of the Branded is a duel to first blood. One on one armed combat with no magic."

Will squeezed Memory's hand. "Let me take your place."

Finvarra snarled. "I will only fight the queen. I am being *kind* to even give her this chance."

"It's all right Will, I can do this." Memory squeezed his hand again in return then let go, stepping up onto the dais.

Finvarra bent forward off his throne again, walking to meet Memory at the front of the raised floor. His smile was sinister and her scalp prickled again, a warning that something was still off—things were falling into place a little too neatly. He reached out an arm, and within moments a guard rushed forward, knelt, and presented Finvarra with a grand sword of fairy gold, almost as long as Memory was tall.

Holy fuuuuuuuuuuuuuu… Whoa, just keep it together. You only have to nick the old goat.

"You've taken away my weapon," Memory said. "I need something to fight with."

"You fight with what you have," Finvarra scoffed.

Memory held up her fingers, showing off the blunt, chewed on nails. "I don't have the same manicurist as you. How am I meant to draw blood?"

"You were the fool to challenge me without a weapon so that is how you will fight. Unless anyone here would lend you theirs?" Finvarra cast a glance out over the sea of unseelie fae, and Memory knew by the look on their faces that no one would help her. Even Nyneve looked away, unable to risk helping her openly.

Will came to her side. "It's not much, but we have this." He handed her the fairy gold dagger he had taken from Mina. It was barely bigger than her own knife, and she looked from it to the sword Finvarra held.

"I guess it will have to do," Memory said, letting her hands close around Will's as she took the blade, hoping it wouldn't be the last time she felt his touch.

"You and your toothpick ready?" Finvarra chuckled, showing rows of gleaming, pointed teeth. He wanted to humiliate her, take away the magic he'd filled her with. He wanted everyone to watch her being beaten and her friends dying. The unfairness, the utter cruelty of it made her

stomach churn. Still, she didn't want to fight him. He was weak, dying from the absence of magic, and it showed. He hated her, and she was disgusted by him and his ways, but did it have to come to this?

It was too late though, it *had* come to this. Memory gave him a tight smile. "Bring it, old man."

Any confidence in her cocky statement fell apart as Finvarra's sword swung at her with ferocious speed. A shriek escaped from Memory as she jumped backwards.

The fairy gold knife felt heavy and slippery in her hand. It was hard to hold onto, and its unfamiliar weight and curve made it difficult for her to concentrate, although it became clear at once that she needed to.

Finvarra moved like a different creature. No longer crippled and slow, though still with an arched back, he dashed and spun. His hands were a blur as he came after Memory, twisting the sword like a propeller. His laughter hung around the room as she back-stepped, skirting and circling around the dais. She tried to get a grip on her knife and fight back, but could barely regain her footing as she stumbled away from Finvarra's onslaught.

Why did I think I could do this? It's all I can do to stay alive.

Memory gasped again as the sword slashed the air in front of her face, and she felt the rush of air over her cheeks.

He wanted to cut her face! That made her angrier. He not only wanted to beat her, he wanted to scar her and give her an eternal reminder of what she had lost. She heard Roen groan in pain and her resolve hardened, wiping away the fear taking over her.

Think, think.

Finvarra thrust and feinted. The sharp edge cut through Memory's jacket but missed her flesh. She slipped to the right, her feet sliding on the cool floor.

He's fast, but the sword is still big, and heavy. It's taking him a while to swing it, and he seems to be tiring.

The pale gold blade swung to her left, lifted again, swung to her right.

It's also fragile. My knife is small, but maybe being more compact will mean it's stronger.

Memory stepped toward him, ducking under his arms as they came down so she could get behind him. His elbow clipped her shoulder, crushing hard against her skin and knocking her across to the throne.

To her side, Memory could see Shonae pleading with Will and trying

to hold him in place. Memory knew if Will stepped in, the fight would be over, and she could see in the pain on his face that he knew it to. He stayed where he was, every muscle in his body visibly taut and strained. Memory tightened her grip on her fairy gold dagger.

Finvarra grunted with anger, turning around and coming after her again.

As he raised his sword to strike, Memory widened her stance, steadying herself, then met his blade with hers.

The sound of their weapons meeting clashed through the air, a high pitched jangle of breaking glass, and Memory's arms ached from wrist to shoulder. Shards of sword rained down around her, barely missing her as they fell. The impact knocked her own knife from her hand and it spun away, out of sight under the throne.

Finvarra roared and Memory looked up wildly. She'd been only half successful, with the bottom third of Finvarra's sword still intact and dangerously jagged. And she'd lost her own weapon.

I've lost.

Finvarra lunged, and Memory moved close, blocking his arm with hers. Memory gritted her teeth and grabbed the throne for support, but as she pushed Finvarra's arm away her feet went out from under her and she could not prevent the fall.

Her head hit one of the crystal tree roots with a neck jarring crack. She managed to flip over on her belly and away from his next blow, which would have cut her deeply from shoulder to hip.

Memory scrambled to her feet, blindly stumbling across the dais and crashing into Nyneve where she had remained, watching the combat.

Nyneve clutched at her arm, painfully hard, steadying her. "Take it," she whispered, and held a knife between them, obscured by the sleeve of her dress.

Memory snatched it instantly, and Nyneve let her go, pushing her back into the fray. A warmth and strength of adrenaline filled Memory. Maybe she still had a chance.

She spun faster than she ever had before, trying to catch Finvarra off guard before he realized she had her knife back. She swung her arm in a wide arc and the blade in her hand sang through the air.

She felt it meet his flesh.

The barest of cuts, but that was all she needed.

I did it. Memory's heartbeat pounded through her, ringing in her ears as she finally stilled.

Finvarra froze in place, arms still lifted, broken sword in the air. A deep howl built in his throat, echoing across the room.

The line near his neck where Memory had cut him smoked and fizzed. Black blood gushed out from his flesh and his face went the color of dead ashes.

"What's wrong?" Memory gasped.

Finvarra crumpled, his knees cracking onto the floor, face twisted in pain. He screeched and groaned, clawing at the floor as the life poured out of him.

"What have you done?" Around the room, the unseelie fae cried and wailed.

The blade felt warm in Memory's hand, and her heart turned cold. In the midst of combat, she thought it was just the adrenaline, just the ache in her beaten hand, that made it feel warm. She thought the blade she held, the blade Nyneve gave her, was the fairy gold knife she'd dropped on the floor.

Memory looked at the blade in her hand, feeling dazed.

It was her own iron flick knife.

Memory pleaded, "I didn't know…"

Her words were lost in the furor.

CHAPTER TWENTY-THREE

Finvarra began to thrash about, his face growing grayer and his body shriveling. Horror filled Memory. A black cloud rose from the fallen unseelie king, twisting and writhing.

The fae around the room closed in, jostling against each other as they crowded the dais.

Where they hung from their webbed bonds, her friends also watched. Roen struggled weakly to free himself, and Memory could see the glint of a small blade working. He spoke to Eloryn, but she only looked at Memory, heartbreak all over her pale face.

Memory looked to Nyneve for help, hoping she would come to her defense, or do something to save her dying father. Nyneve crouched over the body of the king that now lay still.

"He is dead!"

"Murderer!"

"She used iron on our king!"

The unseelie turned toward Memory, Will, and Shonae.

"I did not help her. I was forced," Shonae bleated, being pulled away from Will and into the crowd. The fae battered at her body with their fists and claws, shoving her further into the enraged mass.

Memory jumped off the dais, wading into the fray, dodging as many blows as she could and warding fae away with her blade. Will fought his

way through too and together they managed to drag Shonae out from under the bodies piling up on her. They bolted back to the throne, keeping their backs to the grand tree structure. Memory looked across to Eloryn again, separated from her by a sea of enraged black-eyed monsters.

The white faun's hair had been torn and her lip bloodied. Her eyes were wide with terror and she hobbled, clutching at Will for support. A harsh, gasping sound rasped through her lips and Memory realized she was crying.

And with good reason. She had brought them there, brought the humans into her kind's court, and now Finvarra was dead, by iron.

Memory's eyes went back to her weapon in her hand. How was this even possible?

Nyneve...

Nyneve had handed her the knife, the knife she'd left on the table at the entrance to the castle. Nyneve held it, and hadn't been burned. How? A slow comprehension began to dawn, tingling in Memory's bones like frostbite.

All she had wanted to do was save her friends and she had done exactly what Nyneve had told her to do.

She had been tricked. Every step of the way.

Nyneve was looking at her with hatred on her beautiful face and she was smiling too, a hard and terrifying smile as she bent to her father and seized the crown from his head.

Her cry echoed throughout the room. "I am queen now! Be still, my people!"

Memory knew Nyneve wasn't calming her people for the humans' safety, that she wouldn't help Memory in any way again. Her tone was too triumphant. That was the only word to describe her. Nyneve was triumphant, reveling in her father's demise, in the way she had used Memory.

The creatures of the Unseelie Court quieted to a muffled level of hostility. They looked up at their new queen, waiting.

"The human queen has come into our lands-"

Lured here, Memory thought.

"And used the forbidden iron-"

You gave to me.

"To murder my father, the king!"

Your plan all along. But why?

"They have committed an act of war against the unseelie fae!" Nyneve cried, her deep, regal voice echoing through the crystalline chamber. Clamors of assent rose and Will moved closer to Memory, his body trying to shield hers while Shonae ducked below her arm, hiding her face.

An act of war. Memory almost buckled over to be sick on the ground. The final pieces of the puzzle were fitting in, and what had just happened, what she had done, and what that meant nearly ruined her. Only the knowledge that her friends were still in grave danger kept her on her feet. There had to be a way to fix this, but how? She could not bring Finvarra back to life... It was too late.

"You must pay for what you have done. All humans must pay for what they have done. We are tired of being treated as monsters when it is humans who deserve that title. When humans rule our world—OUR world!—and dare to rise above their original stations! Humans were meant to be slaves and slaves is exactly what they shall be!"

Nyneve's voice dropped to a quiet and deadly tone, and silence filled the room as all strained to hear her. "As monarch of the unseelie fae, as a response to the human's act of war against us, I declare the Pact null."

A pulse of magic burst through the room. The Pact was broken. They all felt it. There was a lurch and the world actually moved below their feet. The Pact, which separated Avall from the rest of the world it had been plucked from, the Pact that protected race against race, that allowed Branding, that put the Spark of Connection inside humans, had ended.

A faint cry came from Eloryn's gagged mouth. It was weak, and quickly lost as the unseelie fae roared, cheering their queen. Still, not all cheered. Some looked up in fear, and a few even fled. Shonae wept silvery tears down her white cheeks.

Memory stood muted by shock.

Will's fingers twisted on her arm as Nyneve advanced upon them.

Memory stuttered, "Why? Nyneve, without Avall, your people will die. All fae will die without an iron free sanctuary."

Nyneve smiled. "I won't die, and neither will those loyal to me. There is a way to save ourselves. You should know that by now."

She held my iron knife without being burned... Memory's thoughts raced.

Nyneve spoke just for Memory's ears. "If only you had followed my little clues and gone after Finvarra when I let you find my blood farm. Maybe then I wouldn't have had to capture your friends to lure

you here. But you always did make things difficult, and now you can watch them be the first to die."

Memory spun to see her friends. Roen had managed to slip his bonds, and cut the webbing from Eloryn's mouth. But Memory knew it was no good. The Pact had ended, and with it, so had ended any connection to magic within Eloryn. Within all humans. The ending of the Pact had also cleared the Brands from her friends. She could already see the life returning to them, but it barely mattered since Nyneve was screaming for the fae to kill all of them, and to make it painful.

Roen sliced desperately into Eloryn's bonds with a tiny blade, but it was too slow. Erec was beginning to regain consciousness, but was still completely bound. Memory heard Roen cry out as the first of the fae to reach them, a ghastly bird-like woman, slashed down his shoulder with its talons.

There was only one way to save them. Memory did not need the Pact to connect to magic. It was within her—a vast and undiminishing store. All bets were off. The Pact was gone. It was time to break all the rules.

Memory reached deep down inside herself, feeling that furnace of magic within. She opened a Veil door, across the room, right beside her friends. Bellowing at the rush of magic flaming through her that she hadn't felt for so long, she hurled that magic at the fae, clearing them away as she flung her friends, webbing and all, through the Veil door.

"Memory!" Eloryn screamed but Memory's magic carried her along with it on a tide that couldn't be fought.

Memory closed the portal behind them, then prepared to create an escape for herself, Will, and Shonae.

But another door opened, spilling Veil smoke into the room along with golden sparks and amber light. All stopped and stared as Aine appeared.

Her regal figure was surrounded by the guards and followers of her own court, all armed and in a defensive array around their queen.

"What is this?" Aine demanded. "The Pact is broken, we felt it!"

Nyneve met her fellow queen with a mocking bow. "The human queen committed an act of war against us, and as a result I have ended that damnable Pact as I had every right to."

Aine's fury made the wildflowers in her auburn hair burn to crisp ash as she faced Memory.

Memory shrank back, scrambling for the answers and courage to

face the chaos before her. "I was set up. I never meant to kill him. I was handed iron, I did not go into the fight with it!"

Nyneve laughed. "Handed iron? By whom? No fae could touch it, so it could only be the fault of a human. Don't believe this child. She is a liar, as all humans are."

Aine turned a distasteful glance to Nyneve. "So pleased, aren't you? You never did agree with the Pact, angered that your lover chose the humans over you."

Nyneve bristled. "Myrddin allowed the humans to include Branding into our Pact, and what did he get for it? Branded and killed by the very humans he loved too much! It's time to put all humans in their place, starting with her." Nyneve crooked a finger, pointing at Memory. "She broke her oath, and she must be punished."

Aine nodded, turning on Memory. She seemed almost sad, too tired for her usual arrogance. "You used magic when you swore an unbreakable oath not to. For this act alone, the penalty is death. For all else you've done, may the stars forgive you."

Memory shook her head, the unfairness of it all making her feel like a helpless child. "I had to save my friends."

Aine's beautiful face pulled into a grimace. "You chose to use your magic to save your friends. There is a difference. Every action you've taken, you chose, for your own selfish means. You came into our lands, fighting and taking what you please, and look where it has brought us. It will be the end of us all."

Aine drew a long, fine sword from the decorative scabbard at her waist. The sword, however, didn't seem decorative. It looked deadly.

"Kneel and I will make this quick. Fight, and you fight against every fae creature both seelie and unseelie."

It would have been easy then, to drop to her knees and have it end. There would be nowhere safe in Tearnan Ogh or Avall for her anymore. There would be nowhere safe for anyone soon.

But there was still one way out.

Staring into the seelie queen's eyes, Memory said, "I will fix this."

Then she punched a hole straight through the Veil.

Wind whipped, bringing the smell of exhaust and the sound of car horns and sirens. And iron; the wind reeked of its bloodlike scent. The fae screamed, many of them shielded their faces and ran to hide behind the throne.

Not Nyneve though. She stood there smiling that nasty smile and holding her father's crown firmly in her crooked fingers.

Memory took a deep breath, grabbed Shonae by one hand and Will by the other and jumped back into the other world.

The last thing she saw was Nyneve's gloating smile.

CHAPTER TWENTY-FOUR

The tunnel through the Veil was dark, roiling with clouds. It was rougher than Memory recalled, tossing and tumbling her like a wild surf. Memory could see again the golden flow of magic, rushing out like a tide, drawn from Avall and Tearnan Ogh into the rest of the world.

The wind rose, slow but intense. Memory could feel herself being pulled along with it and the urge to fight it was strong, but she did not.

In a huff of air, she landed hard on asphalt. Will and Shonae thudded down beside her, and the Veil door closed.

"Where have you brought me?" Shonae coughed.

Memory looked around to be sure. They'd been dumped out into an alley. The same alleyway near the children's home where she'd first been confronted by Thayl. Where she'd first fallen through into Avall.

Will stared around him, his jaw set. "We're home."

A rough whimper came from Shonae and she buckled over. She curled in a heap beside a torn trash bag, unable to move. Her entire body shook and Memory knew it was more than just the injuries she had received in the Unseelie Court. It was the world full of iron she had been dragged into.

Shonae looked up at Memory, her black eyes turning milky and gray and her white fur charring to ash. Blood dripped from her soft muzzle. "I don't want to die in this place."

Memory knelt beside her. "I know, I'm sorry."

"You should have left me behind."

"You would have been killed. I couldn't leave you there to die. And you are not going to die now. Don't worry. I have a plan. Well, an idea, at least. A theory. Shut up. Let's just try it." Memory still had her iron knife clutched tight in one hand, and pressed the blade against her palm of the other. It trembled there right on her flesh, the point pressing in but not cutting. It was harder than she thought it would be, cutting her own skin.

"This is seriously giving me the squeams. Ew, ew, ew!" Memory shrieked, then squinted her eyes and pierced the skin. Blood rushed up from the wound.

"Ugh. Done. Right, you. Drink," Memory said, thrusting her bleeding palm at the faun's mouth.

Shonae turned her head weakly, disgust twisting her furry features.

"Drink it, Shonae. It will keep you alive." *Or at least I hope it will. Otherwise things will be pretty awkward.*

Shonae let out a soft sigh that sounded so sad it made tears prickle in Memory's eyes. Then the young dark fae put her tongue out and licked the blood away. Her eyes closed and she began to drink faster, her mouth pulling at the thin flesh there on Memory's palm.

Pain lanced into Memory but she ignored it. She could see and feel Shonae growing stronger.

The faun broke away, gasping for air and staring up at Memory with glossy black eyes.

"I feel… better. Still weak, but I do not think now I will die," Shonae said, her voice hushed and husky.

"How?" Will asked as he helped the unseelie fae to her feet. "How did you know that would work?"

"It was Nyneve that handed me my iron knife. And it was her that was behind the blood lair after all. Her that was behind everything after all. I thought that maybe the real reason she was drinking human blood was as an antidote against iron."

"And now we know it's true." Will looked at Shonae, worry furrowing his brow. "Why did she need so many people, so much blood? Shonae got better so fast."

"I think that's because I have a lot magic inside me, so Shonae got better faster. I am not sure how many normal people Nyneve would have to drink to stay immune but it could be a lot. How she could stand to do that is beyond me."

"She could do it," Shonae said. "Nyneve has harbored her hatred for centuries. The only thing that kept her in check was Finvarra and the Pact, and now he's dead and the Pact is broken."

A low rumble shivered up Memory's legs from the pavement.

"Was that you?" Will asked.

"No. I think that was Avall." Memory groaned.

Shonae shook her head and her wooly hair jiggled around her goat ears. "With the Pact broken, the magic that held Avall within the Veil is ending. It will come back into this world."

Will raised an eyebrow. "Reasonably large land mass, just showing back up in an ocean somewhere... that is going to be bad."

The ground grumbled again in agreement.

Memory ran both hands through her purple hair, tugging at it in frustration. She slouched against the wall. "This is what Nyneve wanted. Think about it, with no haven free of iron, any fae who are against her will be dead soon. If she is immune—think how powerful she would be. Think how much damage she could do over here. Humans wouldn't have a chance against her, her magic, and the other fae that would follow her. She would enslave everyone and use their blood as an antidote against the iron. She wasn't lying when she said she thought humans should be slaves, but she didn't mean just the ones in Avall, she meant *all* humans."

There was a shout from the mouth of the alley and they turned to see a woman standing there.

"You kids! What are you doing down there?"

"Ham biscuits," Memory whispered. "Shonae, time to glamour yourself up, girl."

Shonae nodded, and her figure started fading and blurring. Memory and Will blocked the fae from view as she shifted form.

When they didn't reply, the woman took a few steps closer to them.

Memory squinted. "Doesn't she work at the group home?"

"Hope? Hope, is that you?"

"Time to go," Memory said.

Shonae finished taking on a human form, and the three of them broke into a run, ducking down the rubbished lane and through a maze-like path of graffiti covered alleyways. They quickly left the woman behind, and came out onto a wider street. Memory looked around, getting her bearings. The area was so familiar to her, yet at the same time felt so foreign. They stood right beside the twenty-four hour convenience store she and Will regularly

raided for cherry gum. Down the street was their favorite coffee shop and internet café. The group home was only three blocks south of here. It was hard to reconcile the fact it had only been a few months that she'd first been lost from this world. For Will it had been much longer. She looked up at him, but his expression was closed as he took in his surroundings.

Shonae stared openly, her jaw slack. Memory took in the fae's appearance, checking she was passable to be in public. Her clothes, like Memory's and Wills, were like something from a period drama, but she was so beautiful Memory doubted people would care much what she wore. Her body was proportioned like a supermodel, but petite in stature, and her wooly hair was now glossy blonde with streaks of pure white running through it right at the front, as though she weren't able to fully glamour color into herself. Her black eyes were now a brilliant blue, one Memory suspected was inspired by Will's and her mouth was as ripe and red as a berry. Memory had hoped for something a little less conspicuous, but despite her looking like a Hollywood starlet just off a historical romance shoot, most people weren't paying attention to her. Or Memory and Will in their shredded, bloodstained clothes. The continuing earth tremors kept everyone busy and distracted. Everyone was on their cellphones, dashing this way or that, cowering each time the ground shook. A larger quake hit, lurching the ground, and a few people screamed. One woman grabbed a baby from a stroller and sprinted down the street.

This could be the end. Of everything. And it's my fault.

Memory was too shell-shocked, nearly hysterical, to cry. She wondered whether Eloryn and Roen and the rest of her friends back at Caermaellan were safe— at least for now. She wondered how Eloryn must be feeling, her magic stripped away for good. The same as everyone else in Avall. *Helpless. They must feel so helpless.*

The smell of noodles and fish hung over everything, wafting in from the small Chinatown down the road, and Memory's stomach gave out a loud gurgle.

It's not over yet. I'm still here. I still have my magic.

"The Net Nest is just down the road. We need to regroup, refuel, and re-plan."

The sky above them darkened, the light of early morning shifting unnaturally into a blue twilight haze.

Memory shook off a shiver that tried to take control. "If I'm going to save the worlds, I'm going to do it on a full stomach."

CHAPTER TWENTY-FIVE

Eloryn landed hard.

Her back hit the ground and air expelled from her lungs with a giant whooshing sound. She clutched at her chest and gasped small breaths. She felt so empty inside.

She had experienced this before, when she'd been hit by the wizard hunter's anti-magic darts, but this time she knew her Spark of Connection would never come back.

Roen had landed right beside her. He grabbed her and pulled her to him across the floor, his eyes dark with concern. "Are you still in pain?"

"No." She blinked back tears. Watching him suffer the Brand had hurt her far worse than the pain her own Brand had inflicted. She knew he had felt the same. Finvarra had been amused by that, and had laughed at their anguish, as had the other members of his court. But now he was gone, and with him the Pact.

Eloryn knew that her sister hated Finvarra for all he had done, but to kill him, when the consequences were so great, was an action she couldn't understand.

Watching through pain blurred eyes, the whole ordeal felt like a bad dream and Eloryn was patchy on the details, but she knew the Pact was ended. She felt it inside.

"I feel so empty," she whispered into Roen's hair as he cradled her. "How do you bear it? Having no spark within you?"

"I've never known any different. I am too full of love for you to ever feel empty," Roen whispered back, planting a soft kiss on her cheek.

Eloryn warmed, her own love for him spreading through the emptiness.

"I love you, too," she sobbed.

Erec groaned from nearby. "Lovebirds, would one of you be kind enough to come and untie me shortly?"

Eloryn sighed and rolled away from Roen. Getting to her feet, she saw that they were back in Memory's chambers.

"Memory didn't make it through," Eloryn said, a harsh shiver making her hug herself.

"Not Will or Shonae either," Roen said, as he crouched down beside Erec and started cutting him free with his slim electrum blade. They had all lost their iron during their fighting and capture. "She used her magic to send us back here, to save us. She's broken her oath and there will be no safe place for her from the fae now."

"There is one," Eloryn said. "She could go home."

Eloryn hoped her sister had escaped the chaos of the Unseelie Court, but there was nothing she could do now to find out, or to help her. Besides, she had other work to do here in Avall.

The world trembled, and through the window the sky was a thick gray, blocking the sun. Jagged streaks of electricity webbed through the clouds and smote the ground, setting trees alight and crisping the fields and grasses around the castle.

The day was darkened like night, and Eloryn could see the Veil, ripped and torn, fluttering like ragged mist across the sky. The lightning turned red, green and violently purple before going back to silver as it arched across the sky.

Roen cut the last of the webbing off Erec and helped him to his feet. For a moment, they all stood in silence and watched the destructive light show through the window.

"Come now. We must hurry," Eloryn said.

Candles flickered here and there through the palace, but a bitter wind blew windows open and rushed through the corridors, putting them out quickly. Servants and guards ran by, as other guests of the castle called for assistance. A maid recognized Eloryn amongst the crowds and ran to her, asking for help, but she could not give it. There was no magic left for her, or anyone. Even when Thayl was in power, banning all but the most basic of magic, the people still had light, and warmth. Now,

the land felt dead and flat, missing its very heart, and Eloryn knew time was running terribly short. War was coming, and with it death.

"Where is the Council?" Eloryn asked.

"The Round Room, Your Highness," the maid replied, her eyes wide and voice shaking.

"Keep calm, and head to the throne room," Eloryn said, and sped up her pace. "Erec, I need you back on duty. I need information about what is happening out in the city, and I need the guards organized and helping the civilians. I need them moving everyone into the throne room and old keep."

Erec nodded, and split off from them. Eloryn and Roen reached the Round Room and found all of the Wizards' Council there, for once in silence. They stood in a circle, faces grave and gray as their hair, bodies bent like a ring of ancient stones.

Bedevere was the first to see Eloryn, and his back straightened. "Your Highness, by the fae, you are safe. But what of your sister?"

Eloryn shook her head. "I don't know."

"What happened?" Madoc spluttered, coming to life as well. "The Pact has ended, we all feel it, as we can feel Avall tumbling back through the Veil into the world of hell we left behind."

"It's true," Eloryn said. "Finvarra is dead. Nyneve has taken the unseelie crown, ended the Pact, and declared war upon humans." She stopped there. Memory's actions, all of their actions that had led to this point poisoned her with guilt.

"What can we do? We are powerless," Madoc sighed, dropping into a seat beside him.

The room brightened slightly, and out from the darkness, Yvainne appeared. The sprite princess's face was as solemn as the humans around her. Her normal glowing presence was dulled, her gossamer dress more like rags, and her hair hanging lifeless.

"Maellan Princess," she said, turning to Eloryn. "You should have remained the one to rule the humans. Now we all face destruction."

"Is this Memory's doing?" one of the Wizards' Council blustered, and a murmur of gossip spread through the group.

"She played a part," Eloryn admitted.

Yvainne hissed, "She killed Finvarra with iron! And broke her oath not to use her magic, then fled to the human hell to avoid her punishment."

So she did escape. Eloryn took a shaking breath, trying to inhale hope

back into her. "Yvainne, will the seelie fae stand beside humans for what is to come?"

For a moment, Eloryn thought she saw a look of sympathy on the normally aloof face of the sprite princess. "We will not. I was sent here to tell you as much."

"We have no magic left," Madoc cried, standing up and grasping for Yvainne. "If the unseelie fae come for us, we will be slaughtered!"

The sprite shook him off in a shower of fairy dust. "We shall all die if Avall smashes back into the human world unchecked. The seelie fae will be doing what we can to stabilize our refuge as it returns through the Veil. That is all we can do, for the humans and for ourselves."

"Can you not stop it returning?" Eloryn asked.

"It took the combined power of the seelie and unseelie fae together to draw Avall into the Veil when the Pact began. Without the help of the unseelie monarch, without Nyneve, all we can do is stem the damage as we prepare for the end of the fae." Yvainne turned away. "I am sorry."

Eloryn lowered her head as the sprite faded away. "Me too."

"We are to face the unseelie armies alone then," Roen said, his voice empty of emotion.

A dramatic gasp broke the deathlike silence, and Clara ran into the room, her face covered with tears and her red hair loose and streaming across her shoulders.

She huffed and pounded softly on Eloryn's arm with a fist. "The pastries went cold and none of you came back and I've been so scared for you all and I've been hearing all sorts of terrible things through the speaking mirror and NOT ONE OF YOU SPOKE THROUGH THE MIRROR AND TOLD ME WHAT WAS HAPPENING!"

"Oh Clara, I'm sorry," Eloryn said, and pulled her in for a hug.

"I... I couldn't do anything. I know I am not a hero but I wish there was something I could have done. Now the Pact is gone and everyone is totally freaking out."

"Totally freaking out? You have been spending far too much time with Mem," Eloryn's smile felt false and wobbly. "I think you will be able to help Clara. Tell me, are you still hearing anything through your piece of mirror?"

CHAPTER TWENTY-SIX

The Net Nest was jam packed. People were staring down at their laptops, tablets and the few desktop computers around the room, glued to the news as it came in from around the world. Another small tremor shook the ground. A few people shrieked or stared white faced at the shuddering walls of the internet café then turned back to their screens to type in new search codes or status updates.

Memory spotted a table where some empty coffee mugs hadn't been cleared away. The staff seemed too busy gossiping and looking at their own screens to be servicing the tables. Walking past, Memory swiped two cups in a casual movement, and took them to where a dripolator sat beside a sign reading "Free Refills." She poured herself and Will a healthy dose of coffee that she liberally doctored with milk and sugar.

A desktop PC became free as a man took a call on his cellphone and left in a rush. Memory indicated to Will across the room, and met him and Shonae there, handing him his coffee.

"Sorry Shonae, only two hands. Also I figured you wouldn't be interested."

Shonae sniffed. "Quite right."

Memory and Will each took a sip and sighed deeply.

"Oh, bad internet café coffee, I've missed you so much," Memory said to her mug, stroking it tenderly. That first sip helped steady Memory, but her stomach still ached. A sandwich lying on a table, uneaten while

its owner stared at his laptop, drew her eye. She looked from it to Will and nodded, hoping he'd remember their old tricks.

Stretching his arms in a wide yawn, Will shielded Memory with his body while her hand snaked out and grabbed the sandwich. She split it, handing Will his share of the booty. She offered some to Shonae who turned up her now human nose at it. By the time the owner of the sandwich looked at the plate again, Memory and Will had bellies filled with rare roast beef, mayo, and rye bread.

"Remind me I hate rye," Memory said tilting her cup toward her mouth.

"Shame there are no cakes unguarded." Will grunted.

Memory looked at the glassed in display counter with a twinge of greedy regret. "I know, that pumpkin cheesecake looks good."

"I was thinking the scone."

"Go get it then," Memory challenged. "Bring me back the cheesecake."

Will surveyed the room and ducked his head, muttering something about not being a cake commando. That made Memory laugh and she squeezed his hand. The warmth of his flesh below hers strengthened her more than the coffee and food ever could.

Memory poked the keyboard in front of her but the screen only showed a login gate. "Forget the cakes. What we need is cash. I want to check on something online, but we have to buy the minutes."

"The usual way?" Will asked, dark eyebrows lowered. Memory frowned back. He never was happy about her thieving ways, but he always went along with her, even when he was so much younger. *Wow, I really took that kid's innocence didn't I?*

"Don't worry, I won't make you do it this time." Even Memory wasn't too happy anymore about stealing. It used to be a rush, the thrill of the risk and the joy of new possessions drove her to fill her pockets in every store. She didn't need those thrills and superficial joys anymore. She'd found true happiness, and known true danger, and somehow developed a conscience amongst it all. If they weren't in real need of food and information, she wouldn't be up to her old tricks.

Squeezing through the crowd to the counter, Memory smiled to the assistant there who glanced up at her from his own screen.

"If you're after more coffee you're out of luck. The water is off," he mumbled.

"Can I get the bathroom key?" she asked.

"I said the water is off." The scrawny young man looked at her over his thick brimmed glasses.

Of course it has to be difficult, Memory grumbled in her head.

"That's okay, I just need a private place for a moment, you know, for lady things," she said.

With a small humph, the man turned to grab the key off the wall. While he did, Memory leaned over the counter, her hands a blur as she plucked a few bills from the shallow tip jar. By the time the key had been handed to her she had almost twenty bucks up her jacket sleeve. The assistant went straight back to his screen before Memory could say thank you.

A noise distracted Memory as she turned away from the counter. A sound like her own voice, calling out quietly amongst the chatter and clamor of the busy room.

"No way," Memory said under her breath. She plunged her hand into her pocket so fast she sliced her finger on the mirror shard there. Swearing softly, she pulled the mirror out and held it up to see what looked like her own eye, but shadowed by thick ivory bangs.

Her heart thudded. The speaking mirror was still connected to Avall, and her sister was there.

Speeding back across the room, Memory slapped the money on the desk beside Will.

"Get online, I'll be right back. Gotta take a call," she said, angling the mirror so Will could see the tiny view of Eloryn there.

Memory's hands shook as she tried to fit the key in the lock and get into the customers only bathroom. On the third try, the key slipped in and she pushed the heavy door open.

The bathroom was tiny, and a strong smell of lemon disinfectant overpowered the room. Memory put her hands on the cold sink and took a deep breath to steady herself, then looked at the speaking mirror. She could see only the ornate ceiling of Caermaellan palace now.

Her heart sank, and with it her body. She slouched against the tiled wall, sliding down to sit on the floor, wedged between the toilet door and basin pipes.

"Eloryn?" Memory called out, holding the mirror close to her face.

Her voice caught and tears prickled under her eyelids. Part of her almost hoped Eloryn wouldn't answer. As though talking to her sister would somehow make the grand weight of her failure more real. *I've screwed up everything.*

Nyneve's betrayal stung and confused Memory. It was all so obvious now, too obvious. She should have been smarter, she should have wondered why Nyneve was trying to help her, instead she had simply assumed she had a kind heart and wanted to see peace restored to the lands. But it was clear now Nyneve had no love for humans. Something in her past, something to do with her relationship with Myrddin, Memory thought, had twisted her into a creature of hate and vengeance.

"Mem! Please, Memory is that you?"

"Lory?" Seeing her sister looking back through the mirror at her made the fresh tears building in Memory's eyes spill out. "I'm so sorry. I've really pooched things."

Eloryn was silent for a moment. "Are you well? Are you safe?"

"For now. How bad is it? Over there?"

Memory heard Roen and Erec's voices in the background, then Eloryn spoke. "There is a lot of panic. The Spark of Connection has left every human in Avall. It is dark, and everyone is scared."

"Lory, listen. Nyneve was Providence all along, not Finvarra. It was her that gave me my iron knife."

"How—?"

Memory kept talking. "She's resistant to iron. It was her drinking human blood and that was why. And I think she will use the people of Avall as a blood farm to make her unseelie fae army also resistant to iron as Avall shifts back into the rest of the world."

Memory heard Eloryn draw a long breath. "We always knew Providence wanted a human monarch with great power in her debt, and this was why. She wanted to use them to kill Finvarra, bringing her into power and letting her break the Pact and start a war."

"When Hope couldn't get a deal out of me, Nyneve started messing with my head, working me into killing Finvarra in a different way, making me think he was Providence, was the one who had done everything bad to me." Memory leaned her head back against the cold tiles. "She knew I would be angry. She counted on it. She had to make me angry enough to want to kill him. Nyneve let us find the blood lair and set it up to make us think Finvarra ran it."

Eloryn followed on, the two of them thinking in harmony. "As Princess of the Unseelie Court she had control over the knights who captured and branded us, to drive you to Finvarra."

"She told me to challenge him then slipped me the iron knife mid-fight so that Finvarra would die in front of the entire court at my hand."

They both fell silent.

From outside the door, Memory heard sirens wailing and a thick scent of blood was building in the air, overpowering even the lemon disinfectant around her.

"You have to come home. You can explain to the seelie fae what happened. There has to be a way we can repair this."

"I did this, so I will fix it. I just have to work out how. Until I do, just please try to keep everything from… from…" She squeezed her eyes shut. What could she say? Everything had already fallen apart.

Eloryn's voice was small. "I don't have my magic anymore. I don't know what I can do."

"You can kick ass is what you can do. Sis, you're the smartest person I know. Trust yourself, believe in yourself. I know you will work something out."

The mirror shifted and Memory saw the hint of a smile on her sister's lips. "Okay. I'll do what I can here in Caermaellan to keep everyone safe while you save the world."

"No pressure," Memory giggled.

"Dear sister, I hope you know how much I love you."

"I love you too," Memory said, wiping tears from her cheeks. "See you soon."

The mirror went dark.

CHAPTER TWENTY-SEVEN

Eloryn tucked the shard of speaking mirror away into a pocket. Her clothes were still stained with the black ichor of the vines they had fought through in Tearnan Ogh, and with her own blood. Her hair was loose, tumbling down to her hips in long tangled falls, and her scalp tingled as though the air was filled with static. She picked up the ends of her locks and rolled them into a knot at the back of her head, pushing damp strands clear of her face. *Memory is right. I can do this.* There were people who needed help, and she knew she could offer it.

Erec had returned a while ago and brought her news from the city. Unseelie fae were already in the streets, and there were reports that they were snatching any human they could find. Eloryn shivered. *The people must be so scared, without light, without magic, being hunted in the dark.*

Erec remained in the room, silent and at attention with a small group of guards. Awaiting orders, but also there to protect her, Eloryn knew. Without Memory here, Eloryn was the only Maellan blood left to protect, not that she had any magic to show for it anymore.

Eloryn called order in the room and had the Council members take seats. Placing her hands on the repaired round table there hardened her resolve. She knew she had done that, repaired the ancient table from the splinters it had become after the explosion. If it could be fixed, maybe the shattered Pact, the breaking worlds, could also.

Eloryn sent Clara to fetch a book for her, then addressed the aged men. "I think you all heard what Memory said. I trust that she has a way to save us, but we must protect ourselves in the meantime however we can."

One of the wizards cleared his throat. "We are helpless without magic. We know what happened, and we know it was not Memory's fault, but what can we do against the fae? We're nothing but old men now."

"It is hopeless," another muttered.

"You are not defined by your magic alone," Eloryn said. "I am sure you have wisdom that can help us. When in hiding, Providence, or Nyneve rather, was sending unseelie fae to hunt down wizards as well, and yet you remained hidden from them for years. The fae see through glamour more easily than humans. How did you remain unfound?"

Bedevere's eyes sparkled despite the dull expression on his face. "Clever child. You're right, we used some of the old ways to ward against the fae, methods from before the Pact, methods that don't require magic."

Another councillor perked up, straightening his crumpled black and purple suit. "They were indeed effective. Kenth was chosen because there were only few fae there already but it was our wards that cleared them from the area entirely."

"Could they work again here? Do we have what we need to create them?"

"I'm sure," Bedevere said. "All we need is refined salt, and common herbs and branches wreathed into the right patterns."

Roen called a guard beside the door over to them. "Get down to the kitchens and stores and see what we have on hand. Madoc, please go with him to provide a list."

The wizard left, shuffling along at a hurry with the guard. Roen nodded at Eloryn again to continue, confidence in his eyes. It was contagious, and Eloryn felt it straighten her back and strengthen her voice.

"With these wards, we could make some safe areas, or even perhaps force the fae in the direction we wish," she said.

Eloryn closed her eyes, trying to think tactically. If she were Nyneve, she would be using small armies across Avall to herd people up and imprison them in the long term, but would hit the city of Caermaellan first, it being the largest city and the largest concentration of people. They already knew that attack had begun.

Eloryn called Erec over. "Put out the word to arrange for all civilians in the city to either flee into the countryside or come here to the palace.

Anyone who can fight, we want here. Every horse and carriage in the castle, send it out to help. We're not going to let it be easy for Nyneve, just snatching up people off the streets. If she wants human blood, she will have to come to us. And we will fight her for it."

Roen stood up beside them. "The militia that Hayes instituted could actually do some good. Send them a call to arms, too."

Bedevere scratched the corner of his eye, his ever dour face solemn. "Even if we find many to fight with us, we have little hope against the fae without magic. Our weapons are but nuisances to them."

Eloryn, however, was on a roll, enthusiasm building as she developed her strategy. "We have iron."

Bedevere merely raised a bushy eyebrow.

"Quite a reasonable amount, which strangely enough you can thank Thayl for." Eloryn raised her voice over the shocked whispers around the table. "We are facing a war against the unseelie fae, with no Pact and no Brandings. Iron is one of our only defenses. Erec, take some men to retrieve it. Roen can show you the way."

Bedevere's eyes were wide, a crooked smile on his mouth. "Full of surprises, you and your sister are. Just how much iron is there?"

"Not enough. Thirty, forty pieces at most but not any more than that. We might be able to split some larger pieces to spread it around more."

"Forty pieces of iron is at least forty dead fae," Erec replied, then turned to gather his men, delegating a range of orders through the group.

While he waited, Roen grinned largely up at Eloryn from his chair. "What?" she asked.

"Just you. Don't mind me, keep going, you're doing splendidly."

Eloryn grinned back, and Clara trotted into the room, holding a thick tome cradled against her chest.

"I hope this is the right book," she said, and placed it on the table in front of Eloryn.

Eloryn ran her fingers over the worn blue-gray fabric of the spine and the embossed gold letters on the cover.

The Principles and History of Infantry Warfare.

The pages riffled below her fingers and her heart ached as she thought about the times that Alward had read this and other books with her. She spoke a silent thank you in her heart for all that Alward taught her.

The pages were a blur, the dim lighting too weak to see any detail on them.

Eloryn blinked and muttered, "Àlaich las."

The words came to her from habit but her behest fell on deaf ears. Eloryn winced. It was so easy to forget her magic was gone, so natural to try and call light to her with a behest.

Roen chuckled. "Now you know what my life has been like. Still, I got by. Perhaps everyone might have to learn some tricks from me."

Extending an arm, Roen flourished his fingers toward an unlit candle in front of him. The harsh whisper of them rubbing against his palm was followed by a loud burst of flame appearing and setting the wick quickly alight.

Eloryn gasped in surprise and delight, and then her eyes narrowed. "I don't suppose you could reproduce that effect on a larger scale?"

"Planning to hire me as the official palace candle lighter? Because you should know my rates are costly."

"Actually, I was thinking of something much bigger." Eloryn smiled, and pulled the newly lit candle close to her book.

Finding the section she'd been seeking, she spun the book sideways so Bedevere could see the diagrams there. "Here. This is the strategy I think we should use."

"Look at this," Will said as Memory made it back to the computer.

Shonae's eyes were wide, leaning back in her chair away from the screen as though it were a poisonous snake. The café was now almost deserted. Everyone had gone out on the sidewalks, staring up at the tumultuous skies. Some were openly weeping, holding onto their loved ones. The air was filled with the scent of blood and tingle of static, as if the air was charged with iron magic.

A few people snapped pictures on their digital devices, or just stood there, staring, faces caught in an expression of complete confusion.

Shonae said in a frightened whisper, "This is bad magic."

Memory snorted. "A centuries old agreement between the humans and the fae being torn apart? Yeah. It's bad magic all right… Oh, wait… You mean the computers, don't you?"

Memory snorted and rolled another chair over, straddling it backwards. She looked over Will's shoulder at the screen which showed current news. Half the world seemed to be experiencing the tremors, which were

increasing in frequency and strength. Wild electrical storms, tornadoes and rising tides were striking all over, all apparently caused by a strange landmass appearing and disappearing in the middle of the Atlantic Ocean. Avall.

"I saw Nyneve talk to Mina at the palace. I bet she had something to do with persuading Mina to take me away to Tearnan Ogh. I was just a distraction for you, a tool to lure you there. I'm so sorry," Will said. "We have to get back to Avall and stop Nyneve."

"You mean kill her," Shonae said. "The only way to stop this is to kill her and hope her successor will want to restore the Pact and Avall's place in the Veil."

"I don't want to kill her," Memory said. "Killing can't be the only option. I want peace and you don't get to peace by walking over the bodies of people you kill."

"Good luck with that," Shonae said, sounding as human as she looked. "We are all going to die."

Memory stared at the people on the street. What could she do to fix this? The flicker of an idea kept taunting her, but nothing was locking into place. She needed to know more.

Memory rolled her office style chair forward, bumping into Will. "Squidge over. I've got to check something."

He slid across and she took control of the keyboard, tapping in her search string.

She talked as she typed and skimmed text on the pages that came up. "We already know that legends of King Arthur tie into Avall. Well, I've been thinking a lot about Caliburn, or Excalibur. I think it could help us."

Memory pointed at the screen to an image of a man throwing a sword into a lake. "And I think I know where it is."

Will only frowned. "Isn't that a bit like saying you know where to find a talking harp based on reading *Jack and the Beanstalk*? I mean, how did the stories of Arthur continue on over here after Avall was separated off? How would anyone know?"

"Because some people crossed over. The fae kept doing their little import and export thing until the amount of iron over here became too much for them, and some wizards toying with Veil door magic tried to come through as well. People like…." Memory rolled the scroll button on the mouse, scanning her eyes over the words on the screen. "This guy. Galfridus Arturus. I know his name from my Avall history book.

He's a wizard who went missing maybe a century or two after Avall was pocketed away into the Veil."

"And he stayed here, in this horrible place? Why didn't he return to Avall?" Shonae asked.

"Unlike Thayl, nobody kept a door open for him," Memory said.

"We don't have anyone keeping a door open for us either," Will pointed out. "And if I'm thinking what you're thinking, Caliburn is back in Avall."

"Yeah, it would have been almost impossible to get back before. With all the magic running out of Avall to here, trying to go back to Avall is like swimming against the tide. But since Avall is shifting through the Veil back into this world already, I don't have to punch all the way through the Veil by myself. We might be able to just slip through."

"Then we get Caliburn, and then what?"

"I... don't know," Memory admitted.

Memory turned back to the screen, but the words were blurring in her eyes. She turned away, staring down the city street as she took deep breaths.

Will took over on the computer again. She could hear his fingers gingerly pressing the keys, one slowly after another. Sixteen years was a long time away from technology after all.

I owe him so much. Now I owe everyone so much. What can I do?

The thought of the dire hatred Nyneve must hold against humans made Memory's stomach contract into a tight ball. Memory couldn't stop asking *why*. Why was she doing all of this? Did she hate humans so much she would do something so destructive, or was she truly insane? Inside her mind, Memory laughed wryly. No, Nyneve wasn't insane. She had planned so carefully and so cleverly for so long. She never seemed insane. If anything she just seemed deeply sad, and hurt.

Memory closed her eyes to the chaos around her, trying to think.

"I know how horrible it feels," said Hope. "The pain of having someone choose somebody else over you."

"You never did agree with the Pact, angered that your lover chose the humans over you."

"Myrddin allowed the humans to include Branding into our Pact, and what did he get for it? Branded and killed by the very humans he loved too much!"

Myrddin. His name was different here, and so was Nyneve's. Merlin and Nimue, she'd seen these names reading over the Arthurian legends just now.

In those legends, Merlin disappeared, and from the play she saw in the pub on her night out with Clara, as far as those in Avall knew he'd just disappeared as well. But Nyneve had definitely said Branded and killed. She loved him, but he chose Arthur and the humans over her, and then was Branded and killed. It hurt in Memory's heart just thinking about it. That could be the kind of pain to twist someone forever.

Across the street, a man stood on top of a truck whose bed held a round tank. A water reservoir. People lined up down the side walk, holding metal cooking pots, buckets, and jugs. One woman came out of her house holding a tall glass vase.

The water is off, Memory recalled. Such a simple thing, but something humans couldn't live without. Memory wondered if living without magic for the fae was like humans living without water.

The man on the truck took a long hose and dipped it into the tank, filling the length of the hose with water. Keeping one end twisted closed in a tight grip, he pulled the hose back out of the water, with the other end still in the tank and lowered the closed end down to the waiting vessels.

When he released his grip and opened the hose, the water started to flow, rushing through the hose, starting a syphon, bringing more water with it.

This world, filled with iron, is draining away all the magic from Avall. I've seen it in the Veil, rushing out like a tide, taking with it the life of all the fae. Without that magic, without the spark of connection within humans they need to defend themselves against the unseelie fae, they will all die. And yet I have so much magic inside me, so much it burns me up.

"I can be the hose," Memory said in a whisper.

"What? Mem, are you okay?" Will asked.

Memory just nodded silently. A plan was forming in her mind and with it, peace was settling on her. The feeling was like what she'd experienced when she'd once decided to end her own life, that same sense of calm and closure, but this one came with a sense of determination. She would fix this, no matter the cost.

Memory turned around and looked at Will and Shonae. Shonae still had her human appearance, but her eyes had shifted back to all black, her glamour fading along with her strength in this world of iron. "It's okay. We're going back to Avall," Memory told her, and then looked into Will's

eyes, her newfound calm almost breaking under their cool blue gaze.

"I have a plan," she said.

Will looked back at her for a long moment, a frown growing deeper as the moment dragged on. "Your mouth is saying you have a plan, so why am I hearing you say goodbye?"

Memory's mouth smiled, but her eyes were sad. Will always did know her too well. She didn't want to say it, but everything told her that it was goodbye. Goodbye to everything good she had found in her life, in herself. Goodbye to Will and their love for each other. Goodbye to her sister, and Roen, and all her new friends. Goodbye to everything she knew.

I don't want to go, not again, a tiny voice cried inside her.

Memory closed the voice away. She didn't have the luxury of selfishness or weakness anymore. "I have a plan," she said again, studying Will's features, the earthy shade of his tangled hair and the way his dark brows made his blue eyes flash like lightning, trying to capture and lock them in her mind forever. "And I know you won't like it. I know it might be goodbye. But I have the power to do this so I have to do it. I can save the humans, the fae, and Avall."

Will reached for her and held both of her hands in his. He spoke slowly, his voice crackly with emotion. "I don't want to lose you, but I understand. You've always been my hero, but as much as I want to, I can't keep you for myself. I know it's time for you to be a hero to the whole world."

Memory leaned forward in her chair, wrapping her arms up around Will's neck and shoulders, holding him tight.

He kissed her once on the space between her cheek and ear, then whispered, "Just know, no matter what happens, you'll never lose me. I'll always be there for you. I'll always wait for you. Always."

The lights began to flicker off and on and more tremors hit. The floor buckled, splitting the linoleum, and every computer screen went black.

"I think that's our cue to go," Memory said. "If my plan doesn't work we'll need a backup. Plan B is using Caliburn to stop Nyneve. The sword should be powerful enough to work against her even with her iron resistance, since it's made of magically dense iron. Fingers crossed, anyway."

Memory cast the man on top of the water tank one last glance. Her fingers tingled with adrenaline as she stood up and said, "It's time this vessel spilled."

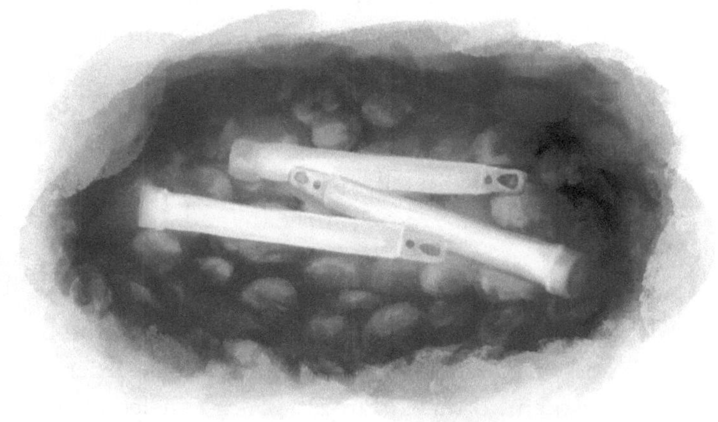

CHAPTER TWENTY-EIGHT

Only half of the horses and carriages sent out into the city to bring back civilians returned. The last horse that returned, returned without a rider, followed by a sea of monsters. Unseelie knights led them, mounted on their huge black griffons.

Eloryn watched from the grand balcony that fronted the palace, her hands clutching at the icy marble balustrade, a cold wind blowing in her face.

The plan was simple, force the larger unseelie numbers into a small space so that their best fighters could take them on armed with iron. Alward's book had spoken of three hundred men holding off an army of thousands by doing that and she was hoping to make that work for them too. It had to work. If it did not they were lost and Eloryn knew it.

Even if it did work, it was only a short term solution.

The throne room would be their battle ground. The balcony stood at the front of it and Eloryn looked behind her, assessing the preparations. The space was part of the old inner keep, directly below the Round Room, built of solid stone that had lasted a millennium. The two back entrances had been blocked off, hiding and protecting the people of Caermaellan where they sheltered in the servant quarters within the ancient fortified walls. Wards against the fae had been carefully placed out of sight through the large entry hall in a way to channel the fae without being too obvious. The wards would not hold forever, and once

the fae worked out what they were doing, the wards could be found and destroyed. The fae could only move in a certain direction thanks to those wards, blocking all other entries and leading them straight to the fighters with iron. Erec stood there, shoulder to shoulder with his best men. Behind the first row of fighters stood more soldiers, prepared to take up the iron of any who fell, and keep fighting. Behind that were doctors and wizards, ready to care for the injured.

Roen placed his hand over Eloryn's. "It's ready. We only had time for one, but it is ready to go when you are."

Eloryn nodded. She looked down at the people in the hall. They were all ready and willing, but could she really give the order that would send so many of them to their deaths? Eloryn exhaled slowly, feeling the breath warm her cold lips. She had to.

She faced the army of unseelie fae before her. A mix of twisted creatures filled the palace courtyard, giants standing out between them, looming over the rest. Higher still, those that could fly hovered and swooped in the air, ready to attack. Eloryn glanced at the window beside her, double checking the glazing of salt that had been applied.

The unseelie knight that had captured them in the lands of Tearnan Ogh came to a stop just below the balcony and looked up at Eloryn. His lion-like steed roared through its sharp beak.

"Leave here now," Eloryn called down, making her voice as strong as she could over the wind and thunder and shuffling of the monstrous army. "We still have our magic and will defend ourselves with it!"

"Human lies!" the fae knight roared to his troops.

Eloryn nodded to Roen. As she lifted her arms to the sky, Roen set off the flash bomb he'd created above the balcony. A huge fireball swirled through the air above Eloryn's fingertips, lighting the courtyard and raining orange sparks over all of them.

The unseelie fae shrank back, but the knight in command reared his steed. "Magic or none, we will fight! Our queen commands it."

Eloryn's hope that her ruse might turn the army back without any more deaths dissipated into the air along with the smell of black powder. Her hearing was already humming with the sound of her pounding heart when the knight called the order to attack.

She stood still, numbed. A fairy gold tipped arrow streaked past Eloryn's face. Roen grabbed her arm, shocking her back into action.

Together they ran down the stairs and through the entry hall to the

first line of fighters.

The fae crashed through the front doors, crowding into the hall behind them.

A semicircle of steps led up from the hall to the throne room. Eloryn's legs pumped and her breath came in hard gasps as she ran up them. She had never been so frightened. Everything seemed sharper, clearer. Every breath was one she drew purposefully, nothing was unconscious. She might die, and every breath seemed incredibly precious.

When she and Roen reached Erec, he nodded to one of his men beside him. The man was huge, and when he grabbed Eloryn around her shoulders and lifted her from her feet, she knew there was nothing she could do. She raged against him anyway. "What are you doing? Stop this!"

Roen's face twisted in on itself, anger and sadness and guilt all there as he looked at Eloryn and did nothing. "I'm sorry. Without your magic you can't be on the front line, and we knew you would insist anyway."

Tears filled Eloryn's eyes like hot acid. "Of course I insist! I can't leave you here. How dare you do this to me?"

Roen stood by Erec and drew the iron bar he'd been armed with, facing the oncoming horde. "Take her to safety, quickly," he told the large man. The soldier did as he said, carrying Eloryn swiftly through a cleared path between the human army to the back of the throne room.

Eloryn sobbed and screamed, betrayal firing off every emotion in her. And even then, she knew Roen was right. She could do nothing at the front line. She could not fight with a sword or blade as Roen or Erec could. She would only get in the way. Her own uselessness hurt her even deeper than the fact that Roen and Erec had to force her to accept it.

But if that was the last time she ever saw Roen, she wasn't sure she could take the pain.

Reaching the back wall of the throne room, the large soldier put her feet back on the ground, but kept her wrists held tightly in his. Around them, the wizards of the Council had laid out blankets and cots, pots of boiling water, liquor, bandages, every non-magical healing supply they could collect from around the palace. Bedevere and Bors flicked through the pages of an ancient book on herbalism. They stood there ready, looking in understanding at Eloryn and the man who held her.

"You can let me go," Eloryn said, trying to calm her ragged voice. "I will stay here, but I need to help tend to the wounded as they come back to us. It's something I can do. Please let me."

The crash of metal sounded from behind them as the first unseelie fae met the front line. Some tried to fly through to get behind them, but the wards blocked them midway along the room, holding them back like an invisible barrier.

One harpy got brave and tried to fly low through the front line of soldiers. She swooped, and Eloryn saw an iron blade clip her as she tumbled past the soldiers. She continued to tumble through into the back of the room, not far from Eloryn. The fae died screaming on the floor, writhing and twisting, her feathered wings burning crisply and sending the scent of burning flesh into the air.

The soldier let go of Eloryn's wrists, running back up to the front line to fight. Eloryn took out the iron button Clara had handed over, and for a moment thought to join him. Then the first of the injured came back to her, dragged out of the fray by one of the supporting guards. Every nerve ending in her body cried out as she forced herself to calm her breathing, and knelt by the injured soldier. Bedevere met her there, and together they worked to bandage the large gashes in the man's neck, trying to save his life. Everywhere hung the stink of battle, the sizzle and smoke of iron meeting fae flesh, the sweat and fear and blood of humans.

She would not be useless in this fight. While others took lives, she would do everything she could to save them.

Opening the Veil door back to Avall was easier than Memory hoped. Stepping back through the Veil was harder. Shonae went first, eager to leave the iron filled human "hell", and Memory and Will followed hand in hand. Memory could feel the strength in his hand, and knew he wouldn't let go.

They stepped out of the Veil into the darkness of the underground lake, deep beneath the palace of Caermaellan.

"Can you just imagine if I had been able to use Veil doors when we were younger? The trouble we could have gotten out of, or into." Memory sighed as she cracked some super-sized glow sticks they stole from a sporting goods shop before leaving the other world. Will had also grabbed a fitted black t-shirt from the store, discarded the last shreds of the old shirt he wore and put it on. By the time they left, they weren't the only people looting shops, but having the Veil door escape plan still made it easier.

Memory shook the glow stick, and the bright radioactive-yellow color it shed gave the cavern an eerie feeling. It sparkled over the black water in front of them, and the white fur of Shonae's natural form.

"There is iron here," the faun said.

Memory looked at the now empty crates left scattered on the loose sand and rocks. All the iron Thayl had hoarded there was gone, so her theory about Caliburn must be right. "Will, do you remember how you told me that the fae never came down here, for a long time, even before the other iron was here? The legends of King Arthur have these vague references to Excalibur coming from a lake, and being returned to a lake after Arthur's death."

Will said, "I thought the sword came from the stone."

"For something that is in the realm of myth and hearsay, passed down by word of mouth from the original source and changing every time, we have to work with what we've got. And what we've got, is this lake."

"Definitely worth a shot," Will agreed.

They unwrapped the rest of the glow sticks, and the sound of them cracking echoed in the quiet cave.

Memory stripped off her top layer of clothes, dropping her mostly shredded jacket on the ground beside her boots.

"Shonae, I need you to be our sensor."

The fae looked her up and down, mouth open in offence. "Your what?"

"I need you to come with us and feel out where Caliburn is."

The faun blinked, shivered, and stepped back. "Do you know what you are asking of me?"

"Yes," Memory said. "And I'm sorry. But there is more at stake here than just us."

"I am free of my debt to you now. I would leave, but the strength of the iron here saps my magic." Shonae sighed. The dark water whispered over the pebbled shoreline like hushed words, and Shonae's black eyes held Memory's in a level gaze. "If I had not been so afraid to die in your trap, none of this would have happened to me. I will accept my fate now. So be it."

Shonae began to walk out through the water. Her cloven hooves clacked and slipped on the pebbles, and Memory extended a hand to

help her.

The water was so cold it burned Memory's toes as she stepped in. She gasped, trying to get her balance and keep both of them up. Will had left his new t-shirt on the shore and waded into the lake in front of them as though he didn't feel the cold at all.

They left a few glow sticks on the shore, and each held a couple as they moved with hurried caution into the vast black body of water.

Shonae clutched tight to Memory's arm, leaning heavier and heavier to support herself. It was obvious that the fae was weakening fast. Caliburn had to be near. Just how near was the question. Would Shonae die before they even got close?

The water became too deep to walk. The three swam together, marking a rough grid pattern through the lake, Will and Memory working together to keep the faun afloat.

Shonae went limp and cried softly. Her head went under the water and Memory grabbed for her, holding her up.

The faun's eyelids hung heavy over her black eyes, water beading over her furred muzzle. "It's here… very near. I cannot go farther."

"No, you can't," Memory agreed.

Memory dropped her glow sticks into the water, watching then float down until they were like a small, pale stars in the depths. Will nodded, and with a deep breath, he dived down.

Shonae fell again, her body sliding under the water and her eyes slipping closed. Memory grabbed the faun, pulling her close and forcing her face to the air. She leaned back, floating with the faun on top of her, kicking slowly to the shore. Shonae was a dead weight in her arms and almost pulled her under as well, but Memory held tight, handfuls of the fae's soft white fur held tight in her fists.

Arms and lungs aching, Memory's feet finally touched ground again, and she walked the fae out of the water until the two of them fell with a splash in the shallows.

Panting and choking, Shonae looked up at Memory from where she lay in the water, her white woolly hair floating around her face like a halo. "Why did you save me? Before in the other world, and again now? Why bring me back away from Caliburn? I thought you would leave me to drift away alone in the water. I'm just a monster after all, aren't I?"

Memory blinked the water from her eyes and gave the faun a sharp look. "You really think I would have just left you there to die? No. You're

not a monster. I get it now, really. Things aren't just black and white, seelie and unseelie, human and monster. That's why what I'm going to do is to stop all the fae from dying. Save all the fae from the lack of magic that is killing them. All of them, seelie *and* unseelie."

"You would really save us all?"

Memory sat on the pebbles and watched as Will's head emerged from the water to take a breath, then dive down again.

"That's my plan," Memory said, almost a whisper. "I just hope that will be enough to stop a war."

Shonae pushed herself out of the water, sitting on her knees. She reached out, placing her palm against Memory's chest for a short moment in a gesture that seemed strange to Memory. *Must be a fae thing.*

"If that is truly your plan, if you think you can save us all, I want to help you. I will stay with you."

Memory saw the glint of something beneath the water.

"Thanks, Shonae, but it looks like you will have to stay at least a few steps away from me."

Will's face came up from under the black water again, close to shore. He stood up out of the water, rivulets running down his hair and over his chest. In one hand he clutched a bright steel sword, shining with the yellow of the glow stick in his other hand.

He strode into the shallows and knelt in the water before Memory, his chest panting with the effort of diving deep in the lake. He placed the sword across her lap.

"I believe this is yours," he said. "The sword of King Arthur."

He shook his head, staring at it with a small smile on his mouth. The sword was beautiful, just as it had been illustrated in Memory's history books. A huge amethyst was embedded in the hilt and the blade still sharp and untarnished, no rust or damage from its centuries underwater.

Shonae skittered backwards quickly until she reached what must have been a comfortable distance, about three body lengths away.

Memory wrapped her hand carefully around the hilt and stood up, lifting the sword with her. It felt perfect in her hand, made for her. It made the magic inside her *sing*.

"We have to get back to the castle, get Caliburn to Eloryn and the human army," Memory said.

Memory held up the sword, staring at her reflection in the shining metal. "I just hope we don't have to use it."

CHAPTER TWENTY-NINE

Memory's breath hitched in and out, and there was stitch stabbing at her ribcage. The sprint up the narrow stairs into the palace left her dizzy. Her adrenaline was up and her nerves were stretched thin. But she had to keep moving.

Will followed close behind, and Shonae a little behind that, as Memory led them through the old keep section of the castle, trying to follow the sounds of battle that seemed to echo from every direction. The tunnel from the lake emerged behind a wall on the second floor and the halls were devoid of life, not a human or fae to be seen.

Following the sounds of fighting, Memory took a shortcut into the Round Room to find an entrance down to the front of the palace.

Memory was first through the door. Momentum carried her forward even after she saw Nyneve appear before her. She was simply going too fast to stop.

Memory's bare feet skidded on the slick marble floor, wet from her dripping clothes. She slid straight toward the unseelie queen. Nyneve laughed a husky chuckle that sent shivers down Memory's spine.

Nyneve's fairy gold sword flashed in the dimness.

Pain shot through Mem's entire body.

The clang of dropped metal battered her eardrums.

She went hot, then cold. Something was wrong. Very wrong.

She tried to raise Caliburn but the sword was on the floor, skidding

away from her, still clutched in her fingers.

Her mind spun.

My hand is on the floor. She couldn't comprehend. *My hand is on the floor.*

Memory screamed, clutching at where Nyneve's blade had severed her at the wrist. She fell, her legs sprawling underneath her.

Everyone was screaming around her, for her. Nyneve was laughing still, louder now.

"Thought you could come back and kill me with damned Arthur's sword?" she said.

"That's not why I came back." Memory gasped the words out, pain making everything difficult. Blood oozed from her wrist in small spurts timed to the beat of her heart.

She couldn't even move as Nyneve swung for her again.

Will had gone after Caliburn. He ran back to her, sword in hand, but was too far away.

The sword meant for Memory struck into something soft in front of her eyes. The soft white body of Shonae.

Nyneve's sword took her in the chest, slicing right through. Dark blood sprayed across the unseelie queen's diamond gown as she wrenched her weapon out of the faun. Her gaze was cold and distant, as though the young faun was nothing but a nuisance to her.

Shonae slumped to the floor, her dark eyes going pale.

"No!" Memory cried out.

Shonae had jumped in to save Memory, had died for her. Memory could still hear in her head the fae's desperate cries from when they had first trapped her, so scared for her life. Now that life was gone. An animalistic scream of pain and rage sounded from her lips.

Nyneve didn't even hesitate to thrust her sword again. This time, Will stepped between Nyneve and Memory, blocking with Caliburn. The fairy queen scowled, adjusting her swing and sweeping her sword away before it made contact with the iron.

"You don't have to do this," Memory said. "There's another way, a way to save all the fae."

"Do you really think I would agree to a new pact with humans?"

"No, that's not—" Mem protested but Nyneve was not finished, her venomous words continued to tumble out in a calm, calculating tone.

"You've treated the unseelie fae as monsters for too long. The humans will be my slaves. The blood of the people of Avall will save the fae.

It will protect me and my followers as I take over the rest of the world too, destroying every last human. Then, then the fae will be saved."

"No... Work with me. Can save everyone. Humans, fae, don't have to die." Memory's eyes were losing focus and she was struggling to stay conscious. Her own blood formed a growing pool on the ground around her, mixing with the blood of the faun. She managed to get her belt off and used it to tourniquet her wrist.

Nyneve kept her eyes on Caliburn, where Will held it steady in front of her face. She swayed slightly, sidestepping casually, testing him, but he kept the point aimed strong. The unseelie queen's own sword wavered close by, threatening, but not daring to meet the iron.

"You do have to die, every one of you. Humans have always been a scourge. It's past time you were finally removed for good."

Memory tried to reason. "Myrddin was half human, you loved him."

Fire flashed in Nyneve's eyes at the mention of that name. "And he betrayed me. He chose humans over his dominant unseelie side, chose Arthur instead of me. Even though Arthur never loved him in the same way." Nyneve's deep voice was low, the hurt in it clear. She edged forward as she spat the words, but Will kept her in check, forcing her away until she backed up into the wall. "I still loved him anyway, and when he went missing it took a millennium of study and sacrifices to find he'd lost himself in the Veil. When I finally found him, and pulled him out, I discovered he'd gone into the Veil to save himself from a Branding. A Branding from his precious humans, a Branding he got defending Arthur from his own poisonous family."

The words floated around Memory, her mind drifting in a haze of pain. She stared from Shonae's crumpled body, to her hand where it lay, just an inanimate object, nothing but dead flesh.

Poetic justice perhaps, Memory thought. *To lose the hand that once cut off the hand of another.*

"Once I'd found him, we barely had time to say goodbye before the Brand took Myrddin. He let humans sway his heart and he is forever gone because of it. I made sure Maellans have paid for their treachery over and over again throughout the years and now I will finish the last of them."

Will growled, a ferocity in him bringing out his animal side. He had backed Nyneve into a corner, and he was going to kill her, Memory knew it. Part of her wanted him to kill her, to cut her as deeply as possible, to claim vengeance for Shonae and so many others. The rest of her never

wanted to see death again.

Will chanced a glance back at Memory, and the fury and worry in his eyes scared her. He placed the tip of Caliburn against Nyneve's neck. Memory saw a small bead of blood well up there, dark against her silver flesh. She heard Nyneve's hiss of pain as the wound sizzled. She transformed right in front of their eyes, becoming Hope.

"Go on, little boy," she taunted, looking just like Memory, wearing the black broken-heart t-shirt. "Where's your guts, you little pet? You animal."

The glamour flickered and faded, the strength of the iron in Caliburn too strong for Nyneve to hold onto her magic. She frowned at that, a scowl that twisted her serpentine skin. Her dark hair flew out behind her as she roared.

Her sword flashed in her hand, moving faster than a normal human could dodge.

She struck out at Will's chest, but he was no normal human, Memory knew. Not anymore. His time with the fae had changed him, made him stronger. He jumped backwards, twirling and striking back. Nyneve cried furiously at him, dodging away around the round table, holding her weapon away from Will's.

"Beirsinn fair nalldomh!" she yelled, reaching her arm toward Memory. Memory knew those words, but the realization came too late as her own iron knife weakly wriggled free and clattered across the floor toward Nyneve. She scooped it up, angered by the weakness of her magic. She faced Will again, fairy gold sword in one hand and iron blade in the other.

Will's next swing was met with iron against iron. Nyneve swept the smaller blade upwards, channeling the motion of Will's strength away in a smooth movement. Sparks flew.

Will grunted with effort and Nyneve faded back into her form as Hope, taunting him as he followed her across the floor, their eyes locked on one another's as the battle between them began in earnest.

Memory knew that Nyneve was taunting him on purpose, baiting him into anger so he would not think, only react.

Memory knew that was what she had to do now. She had no time left to think. She was unsteady on her feet, her reflexes were slowing and she could barely see past the thin gray darkness seeping in at the edges of her vision.

Kneeling there on the floor in the sticky blood, she knew she had to act now, before she fell, and all was lost.

CHAPTER THIRTY

Memory's entire body ached with the strain of raising her magic. She fumbled, trying at first to use the hand that was no longer there, and the pain of that injury and loss almost broke her. Gritting her teeth, she changed her posture, working only with her remaining hand. She pinched the Veil, tearing it the way she had learned from the dragon, then created a larger hole, punching a Veil door that led from right there in Avall back to the rest of the human world. She brought herself to her feet and stepped within it, half in and half out, feeling the magic trickling from the Veil into her, drawn there by the store of magic inside her, like calling to like.

Memory hesitated. In the periphery of her consciousness she knew that Will was still fighting Nyneve, but she didn't know where they were. She knew she could not wait for the outcome. The whole world felt like it was tilting on its ear, and she could barely stay on her feet. She had to do this now. If it worked, she might be able to level the battlefield for the humans, and save the fae too. She did believe that they needed saving, they all needed saving, and she was the only one who could do it. She had hoped to sway Nyneve to her side, that if she knew there was another way, she would stop her war and help keep Avall in the Veil, but Memory knew now that wouldn't happen.

Memory summoned together all of the magic within her. The vast stores of magic that had been drawn into her through her years within the Veil, that felt like a fire in her chest. She said a silent goodbye to Will, to Eloryn, to Roen, to Avall, and to herself, and then expelled all of that magic out into the world.

The magic flowed out of her like a river, churning smoothly and spreading, rippling like water. She felt it going. It was like letting go of a rope she had been holding for too long, a rope that had a huge weight hanging at the other end.

She sent some of her magic into every human of the land, re-creating their Sparks of Connection. The rest of the magic went out into Avall, filling it again with the magic that had been drained away, saving the fae who had been starving without it.

Her expulsion of magic created a movement, a flow through her. It was like creating a siphon, a two-sided funnel which would bring the magic through from the rest of the world into Avall. As the iron in the rest of the world drew magic away, her siphon would draw it back in, never leaving Avall or the fae without magic, as long as she remained the hose through which it could travel.

The magic throbbed and flowed through her, coming in from the other world and out into Avall. The flow was intense, golden-edged and flaming. It lifted her from her feet, holding her in the air, burning out of her skin.

The first burst of energy ended and when it went there was blankness. A darkness in her mind came through, burning through her memories, taking them away and her with them. Panic built within her as her identity fled her body. All the moments and memories that made her were so tied and tangled with the magic she cast out, that they all went with it.

I chose this. I accept this. It's what had to be done.

She repeated it over and over, reminding herself while the emptiness built inside her and the fear came with it.

There was a white static in her head. Sleepiness overtook her even as she was more awake than she had ever been in her life. A man and a strange woman blurred through her vision. Who were they? Why were they fighting?

Remember who you are. You chose this... She tried to hold onto just one memory, just the one that told her what she was doing, and why she was doing it, but soon it too was gone.

There was only pain and confusion.

What's happening? Where am I?

Everything hurts.

She tried to break free, to see, to understand. Her vision was a blur of golden light.

I can't move.

She couldn't feel the ground, could feel nothing but pain. Nothing made sense.

She was nowhere. She was nobody. There was nothing to hold onto to. She had nothing left. All she knew was nothingness.

Who am I?

She didn't know. She was stuck, trapped in this vortex of pain and confusion. Trapped forever.

Magic slammed into Eloryn like a wave. It flowed over her, leaving a small spark behind, warming her, filling the empty place inside.

She gasped, straightening up from where she bent over tending an injured soldier. She saw the effects of the invisible wave ripple through the chaotic room. Wizards rose from their patients, gasping as she had gasped, clutching their chests.

Eloryn's sleeves were rolled up and her hands bloody. There was barely enough floor space to hold the dead and injured being pulled back from the front line. Eloryn had desperately tended one after another, doing whatever she could for them. There hadn't even been enough time for Eloryn to see whether one of those dead or injured was Roen.

But now things had changed. Now she had her magic again.

Eloryn knew that this was Memory's doing. The magic, it tasted of her, of her consciousness, just as she had known it once before. Somehow, her sister had returned the Spark of Connection to her, and for what she could see and guess, to all humans in Avall.

Eloryn didn't know how. But she was determined to use it.

Getting to her feet, she cried, "Briseadh cassahn deannil dom es."

In a line from where she stood to the front line of the battle, the floor began to buckle. It split, breaking a pathway between the melee as it went, pushing away standing or fallen bodies. Eloryn strode down it in long steps, drawing her iron button into her hand as she went.

She could see the heart of the fighting now. Some of the soldiers

had also realized their Spark of Connection was returned, and cast minor offensive spells into the fray to blind or stun their enemies. The unseelie fae seemed even more intent on killing the humans now that they had their magic returned to them. The magic their queen had told them was stolen from the fae. They were in the madness of rage and bloodlust and fear, driven by the lies of their hateful queen.

Eloryn spoke to the iron in her hand, and it shattered, turning into small deadly drops like fine mist. She reached the front line and stopped there.

Bellowing out her words of behest in a way to make herself known to all around her, she held out her small, white hand, and let those droplets of iron spray out into the oncoming fae.

The effect was instant and devastating. Unseelie fae fell screaming, twisting in pain from the iron raining upon them, burrowing and burning into their skin. Five or six creatures deep from the front line were hit, falling like wet autumn leaves to the ground. The creatures behind them cowered, unsure.

"Stop now!" Eloryn yelled. "Stop fighting now. Please do not force me to do that again."

She grabbed an iron spearhead from a bloodied soldier beside her. She turned it into deadly droplets as well, letting them float in a threatening cloud above her hands.

CHAPTER THIRTY-ONE

Nyneve's fairy gold sword sliced a shallow streak diagonally from Will's ribcage to shoulder. Blood spilled out, sticking the fabric of the t-shirt to his skin.

His arm ached with every thrust of the magical sword he wielded and his mind burned with fury.

No matter what he was feeling, he knew Memory was suffering more.

Her hand. His lips curled in a snarl.

It was too late to save her hand. No healing magic available. Maybe, maybe if he could stop Nyneve soon enough, they could get back to the other world and get to a hospital. If Memory was still conscious, still strong enough to get them there. Either way, he had to stop Nyneve now or there would be no rest of the world to go to. He had to stop Nyneve, and keep Memory safe until then.

Will struck fast and fiercely at the unseelie queen, driving her around the large circular table and away from where Memory had fallen. His pants were still wet and tugged at his skin, restricting his movement. Strangely, Nyneve in her long shimmering gown seemed to have no such trouble. She feinted and parried, slipping the crystalline sword always out of reach of Caliburn, brushing the iron away with Memory's small steel knife instead. Will knew if he could only get the angle right, that small knife would also break under the strength of Caliburn, but

Nyneve's movements were fluid, redirecting each blow. She spun her arms and torso like a dancer, always in movement, a blur of dark hair and sparkling blades.

Will had still managed to land a few blows, small nicks and slashes. The stomach of Nyneve's gown was sliced open, black blood oozing around the diamond encrusted fabric, smoking slightly.

But no matter how often he struck, Nyneve didn't slow. Her dark magic healed her far too quickly. Will started to wonder whether her iron immunity was enough to protect her even from Caliburn.

Nyneve's sword swiped right in front of his eyes and he back-flipped to escape the blade. His vision blurred and the muscles of his calves tightened, burned and itched as he fought to keep his footing on the slick, bloodied floor.

A strong wind filled the room, swirling in the round space like a vortex. In the corner of his eye he saw a flurry of mist spill into the room as Memory opened a Veil door and stepped within it. Was she leaving him? He wished he knew what her plan was, all of it, any of it. All he had now was trust.

But he knew he could not spare more thought for Memory if he were going to help her. He had to keep Nyneve from getting to her, and to do that he had to concentrate, forget what Memory was doing, might be suffering, or sacrificing.

The room filled with a golden glow, and Nyneve's eyes widened.

Will didn't miss his chance, and lunged at the distracted fae. He grunted, yelling strength into his swing, and Caliburn struck Nyneve's shoulder, cutting in the width of the blade itself. For a moment she swayed, her eyes losing some of their dark sparkle.

Will hesitated. He drew Caliburn back away, and could see strength already returning to Nyneve. He could swing again, and end it now. But he knew that wasn't what Memory wanted. She was doing something, something that she hoped would end the killing. He just had to buy her more time.

Will chanced a glance behind him and saw Memory suspended in the air, radiating amber light. He didn't know what it meant, but the expression on Nyneve's face suggested she did, as did the renewed vigor in which she turned again on Will, trying to slice through him to get to Memory. He knew then he shouldn't have hesitated. Everything on Nyneve's face said that she would not stop, she would never stop.

Will worked fast to readjust, but Nyneve's new fury had him on the back-foot. She threw a chair into his path, and when he twisted to dodge it, she kicked him hard in the chest, her gown swirling up past his face in a spray of stars.

The force of the blow knocked him onto his back, sliding across the room until he hit a column.

His skull met the marble and pain shot down the length of his body. Caliburn was no longer in his hand.

In his swaying vision he saw Nyneve standing over him, her sword raised high.

Her gold weapon flashed in the air, aimed at his vulnerable neck and Will knew, in that tiny split second of time; he knew he was going to die.

He had let Memory down. He wanted to spend the rest of his life with her, and in a way he had, but it was too short.

Nyneve's sword sang a high, thin song made by the air being cut into halves by the razor edge, but just before it came down on his throat it met another weapon.

A shattering sound filled the room, as though the world had been made of glass and been hit by a sledgehammer.

Will blinked, sure he was dead, sure his head was bouncing along the bloodied ground somewhere, but instead Mina stood in front of him. Her glittering wings hung like broken cobwebs and her face and hair had gone the color of spoiling milk, white with a greenish tinge.

Her lips were set in a determined expression as she held Caliburn pointed at the unseelie queen. The hilt was wrapped in a thick layer of fabric, protecting her hands, but she clearly suffered to be that close to the magical iron.

Nyneve's fairy gold sword lay all around them, a spread of broken, glittering shards. Her composure also broke. This sprite's presence clearly wasn't part of her plans. "What are you doing?"

Mina hissed. "I won't let you hurt my boy."

The words echoed through Will's ears. *My boy.* The fear the sprite could take him away again got him scrambling to his feet, using the column as support.

"I lost him and it is your fault. You told me to steal him away! You promised if I took him to Tearnan Ogh he would be mine forever and you lied!" The tip of Caliburn sank from where it threatened Nyneve, down to touch the floor, and Mina's shoulders slumped. She was weakening

too fast. The sword dropped from her grip.

Will acted fast, scooping the sword into his hands.

Mina cried out as Nyneve sliced her across the cheek with Memory's knife. She fell to the ground, a crumpled heap of fairy dust and long trailing hair.

Before Nyneve had even finished swinging at the sprite, Will drove Caliburn up and through the unseelie queen's rib cage.

Nyneve looked down at the blade protruding from her chest, dull confusion marring her brow. All of her glamour twitched around her, shifting between Hope, Providence, and her true, midnight-haired form. Memory's knife fell from her hand and clinked on the floor.

Will pushed forward again, driving Caliburn in deep, running the fae through. A thin ooze of blood swelled, crystalizing and crackling across the dress's fine fabric. Nyneve's face went still, her mouth open but silent.

The blood around Caliburn sizzled and dried, crumbling. Dark veins ran from the wound outward across Nyneve's body. A low grinding sound began, and her chest changed, turning from silver to a mix of dull gray and rust red, hardening and disintegrating at the same time. The rusty tide spread through her, down her legs and along her arms before encasing her face and hair. She stood there still, like a tarnished, powdery statue.

Will grimaced as he stared at the where the sword he held entered Nyneve's body.

He jerked Caliburn back, and the iron ore that had been the unseelie queen crumbled into bits, and blew away in the wind that rushed around the room.

Will exhaled slowly, letting his sword arm relax. The wind in the room blew his dark hair around his face and smelled of blood. He heard a whimper at his feet.

Mina lay crumpled there, ill from even the presence of the magical sword clenched in his fist. Adrenaline still rushed through Will. He knew he could kill her so quickly, so easily. Part of him wanted to. She had tried to kill him. She had kept him as a pet for so long, and the fear she could somehow claim him again made his sword arm twitch. He could finish it now and never fear being owned again.

It's not what Memory would do.

The girl he loved believed in second chances, in finding another

way, in trusting people to learn and do better. Will knew he had to do the same.

"Mina," he said. He knelt beside the sprite where she curled in a tight ball. She shuddered.

Will placed Caliburn on the ground and pushed it across the room, away from the fae girl. She turned slowly to look up at him, a long gash still sizzling across her cheek.

She was losing some of the blue tint to her face but she was weak and it showed. He helped her to sit up, his hands lingering on her shoulders.

He remembered then how she had first found him, alone, cold, and starving. Weak and dying. She had done him a great wrong, but she had cared about him in her own way too. She risked everything to hold Caliburn and fight Nyneve.

Will bent his head and looked her in the eyes. "You saved my life, again. Thank you."

Mina pouted. "Does that mean you aren't mad at me, that you will be mine again?"

He dropped his forehead onto hers. "You saved me when I was too lost and hungry to survive. You have shown me wonders greater than I could have ever imagined. You are the most beautiful thing I've ever seen."

He felt Mina shiver. She whispered, "Who do you love above all else, even your short mortal life?"

"Memory."

Mina pushed Will away. She stood up, swaying slightly, but her color returned with her stubbornness. She humphed, and Will sighed, a small smile stealing onto his lips at the childish behavior he knew so well.

"I do care about you," he said. "But I am not your pet. I will never be a pet again. Not anyone's. But maybe, one day, we could be friends."

She looked at her feet. "You do not need or want me any longer, Will. I know it. A pet that is determined to roam will, and if you keep it chained all you will get is bitten."

"Still not a pet." Will rolled his eyes.

"But maybe friends?" Mina fluttered her eyelids as she looked up at him again.

Will nodded shallowly. His gaze was already back on Memory, still held in the glowing rush of magic within the Veil door, suspended in the light, a heartbreaking expression of pain and confusion on her face.

"Friends help each other. Will you help me now?"

Mina shrugged one shoulder in a non-committal way.

"Go to Eloryn. Bring her back here for me. For Memory. Please," he asked.

The look Mina gave him was a sad one, but with a small nod she vanished before his eyes.

An eerie stillness had fallen.

Inside the throne room, the unseelie fae army had halted their attack. Outside the throne room, Eloryn could hear the storm still raging through the sky and the Veil, a sky that swirled from blue to red to black to a low hanging indigo-purple. Whatever Memory had done had given the humans back their magic, had stopped the war, but hadn't stopped Avall from crashing back through to the rest of the world.

There were murmurs through the unseelie fae, a change to the emotion in the room. Just as the humans had been given back their Spark of Connection, Eloryn sensed something was now different for the fae as well.

Still, she held her cloud of iron at the ready, a warning to the enemy who were paused in confusion.

At her feet, the dead lay in piles. Bodies sprawled with open eyes staring up, both human and the fading black of lifeless unseelie fae.

Eloryn squinted her eyes closed away from the sight, terrified then that she might see the caramel eyes of Roen there.

There was a light touch on her waist and she opened her eyes. There he was, standing – leaning – beside her. Alive. Roen was alive.

"You're hurt," Eloryn choked out, her words crushed under mixing relief and sadness.

"I'm so sorry. I'm sorry I sent you away. Can you forgive me?" he said, looking up at her from under a mess of tawny hair and blood splatter. He held a broken flagpole tucked under one arm, supporting his weight on it like a crutch.

"I would not have forgiven you if you had died," Eloryn sniffed. "Is Erec—?"

Roen lifted his chin, and through a small crowd of soldiers, she saw Erec sitting on the steps, catching his breath.

She smiled and swallowed away a sob.

In the small gap of space between the recovering humans and unseelie fae, a darkness roiled up from the ground. Eloryn readied her iron, her nerves taut and her mouth moving as she began the spell to release that iron, but she stopped as the thick fog of the Veil took shape.

The unseelie fae staring at her was a regal looking woman she had never seen before. Long, slender hands of smooth silver-white were held up in a human gesture of surrender. Her black hair hung almost to the ground, and her resemblance to Nyneve was unsettling. Unnaturally tall and thin with a smooth, almost featureless face, she turned to the unlight forces gathered behind her and it was clear they all knew who she was.

Her voice echoed as she said, "Nyneve is dead. I am Oonah, wife to Finvarra, and I claim the unseelie throne."

There was a shuffle of movement as the unseelie fae bowed before her. Oonah lowered her arms, her silver and gray robes drifting in the powerful gales of wind. "We have been saved. Magic is returned to us, and to Avall. This war is over, leave this place!"

The unseelie fae were quick to act. Some fled on foot, others vanished through the Veil. Each movement caused a wary reaction from the human soldiers, their eyes wild from the strain and carnage. The short silence in the room became noisy turmoil again, men running to aid others, bring them to the wizards once again able to use healing behests. A blur of movement surrounded Eloryn and the new unseelie queen. Eloryn let her arm down. It shook from the effort of holding the iron cloud in check. The iron spearhead reformed, falling to the ground.

Oonah turned to Eloryn. She peered down at her from twice the height. Her black eyes were large and wide, no eyelashes or brows. An intricate wreath-like silver circlet created a boundary between her nebulous ebony hair and her moon-like face.

"Human queen, we will speak soon. I must leave now for the seelie court and work with Aine to keep Avall from leaving the Veil."

"Thank you." Eloryn nodded slowly, then shook her head, confused. "I'm not the queen."

"Are you not the next in line? You are the last of Maellan blood."

A chill spread slowly across Eloryn's body. "What do you mean? What's happened to Memory?"

The ground shifted under her feet and she wondered if it was real, or her own grief making the world seem to tumble. Roen grabbed for

her, steadying her, and Oonah looked out the front of the palace at the violent sky, urgent concern on her thin lips. She left without another word.

Eloryn's mind raced. *What happened to Memory? Where is my sister?*

There was confusion everywhere. Eloryn stared about at the snarl of bodies and living and waved for Erec. He finished giving commands to the men around him then began walking over.

Bedevere and the Council were hard at work on the injured, and Eloryn could see Clara, face white and looking away from the bodies, picking through the crowd toward her as well. Eloryn waved to her. Maybe Clara had news from Memory. *I hope she does.*

Eloryn turned her back away from where the battle had been and faced Roen "We need to find Memory. Do you need me to heal you now, or will you—"

"For Nyneve!" A harsh voice cried over Eloryn's words.

"El! Roen screamed.

Something hard hit her, knocking her to the ground. A strange and almost inarticulate scream split the air and hot red fluid seeped along her back. She could feel it sinking into her shirt. A soft weight pressed her down onto the floor. A freckled hand and strands of bright red hair flopped down in front of Eloryn's eyes. Everyone screamed around her and she heard the clashing of blades again. She tried to scramble out from under the weight. Roen knelt beside her and helped.

Rolling free, Eloryn saw with horror what the weight was. Clara lay there, her eyes open and lifeless as blood still spread from the fairy gold dagger in her heart.

Beside her on the ground was the body of the unseelie knight that had led Nyneve's army. Erec stood over him, his eyes wild.

"Clara?" Eloryn called, but it was too late. Too late for words or tears or magic to bring back the life that was gone.

Roen placed his hands on her cheeks and turned her face away from the body of their friend. "Don't look."

Tears burned tracks down Eloryn's face and Roen's fingers. "How? How did this happen?"

"She saved you," Erec said, kneeling on the ground beside her. "That wasn't her job. It should have been mine. She shouldn't have—" His voice broke and he looked away.

Clara had always said she felt like a coward compared to the rest of them. But this shouldn't have been the way she proved she wasn't. It was all too much. The only thing holding Eloryn together was Roen's hands on her face, his gaze holding hers.

"Memory will be devastated," Eloryn said in a hush. "If she's… If…"

In a sparkle of fairy dust, Mina appeared beside Eloryn. She looked around the room, her normally mischievous face solemn. "Your sister needs you." Her expression changed quickly to impatient. "Are you coming then?"

Eloryn looked to Clara again. Erec brushed her red hair from her face and closed her eyelids. Eloryn wanted to stay, to cry hot tears for Clara and all the dead around her until the earth was soaked in that salt water.

But grieving had to wait.

"Erec, stay with Clara for me," she said.

He nodded, face hard and closed.

Roen took Eloryn's hand and she wiped her face.

Her voice was commanding when she told the sprite, "Take me to my sister."

CHAPTER THIRTY-TWO

Rushing air from the Veil door tore like claws at Memory's purple hair and tattered clothes.

Will stood before her, terrified and helpless, staring at her vacant eyes.

He wanted to pull her free, use brute force to save the girl he loved, but he was too scared he might do more harm. So he stood there, where Memory could see him, and hoped his presence was a small comfort to her, if nothing else.

Memory's blank face gave no indication she knew he was there at all.

In a flash of light, Mina returned, bringing Eloryn and Roen with her.

That they were exhausted and wounded was clear. Eloryn's hair was hanging around her wan face and her hands were stained with drying blood. Roen's shirtfront was liberally smattered with gore, and he leaned heavily into a makeshift crutch.

Eloryn ran straight to Memory and raised a hand that hovered tentatively just away from the golden glow of magic.

"Oh, Mem," she gasped. "You stupid, clever girl."

"What's happening? What did she do?" Roen asked.

"This is how she gave us all back the Spark of Connection, how she brought magic back for the fae. She turned herself into a doorway. The flow of magic she started, she's part of it now, tied into it."

"For how long?" Will growled.

"Forever," Eloryn whispered.

Will clenched his teeth and spoke through them. "No. I don't accept that."

I can't. I can't lose her now.

Roen hobbled over. "Can't we just pull her out?"

Eloryn's head shook. Her voice caught. "You don't understand. She's not stuck in the doorway. She *is* the doorway. She *is* the flow."

Roen wobbled slightly, then slumped to the ground, covering his eyes with his hand.

Will's breath came in ragged gasps. Memory really had been saying goodbye. She knew this would happen, that once she started this, she would be giving herself to her plan forever.

Why did she have to sacrifice herself? Will knew why, he knew the hero Memory was, but it still hurt. Too much. It just didn't seem fair.

Will picked up a chair from beside the round table and flung it at a wall.

Eloryn's watery eyes followed the flying furniture, flinching when it smashed and clattered to the ground. Will saw her expression change from hopeless to curious.

"Is that...?"

She strode across the room to where Caliburn lay discarded beside a column.

She crouched down, brushing a fingertip along the blade.

Her head shot back up fast and she spoke breathlessly. "Caliburn."

Roen looked up, his eyes red-rimmed. He struggled back to his feet, supporting himself on his crutch. "You're thinking something. What are you thinking? Please, if anyone can save Memory, it's you."

Eloryn grinned wryly. She ran her hands into her hair, holding her head as her eyes looked about as if seeking answers. "Maybe we could... It might... We might be able to swap them. We might be able to exchange Caliburn for Memory."

"We can save her?" Will asked in a whisper. Whether they heard or not, no one replied.

Eloryn clutched the sword and strode back to the Veil door and Memory. "If anything were ever a stronger channel for magic than Memory, it is Caliburn."

She thrust the hilt into Roen's hands. "You will put Caliburn into the flow."

Looking Will in the eye, she said, "You will pull Memory out. I will be doing what I can with my magic to redirect the flow and bind Caliburn into Memory's place as the doorway."

"What about me?" Mina's voice was small. She stood away from them, arms cuddling herself and face confused.

Will tilted his head. Maybe she really was trying to change.

Eloryn said, "Go back to the seelie court. Oonah said she is going to work with Aine to stop Avall breaking back through to the rest of the world. Keep us updated on their progress."

Mina cast a sidelong glance to Will, then nodded and left.

"We have to time this just right," Eloryn said breathlessly. "On my mark."

The three of them stood in a semi-circle before Memory and the Veil door she had merged with. Magic blasted their faces as they drew closer.

Eloryn began chanting, speaking her behest words, talking with the earth and the Veil and the very magic of life. The glow surrounding Memory built, crackling like electricity.

Without a break in her words, Eloryn flung her arms out, gesturing to Roen and Will.

With both hands, Roen lifted Caliburn high, then plunged it downwards into the Veil door beside Memory. The point sliced into the marble there. Digging deep, it held, propped up in the stone.

Will stepped into the gushing stream of magic, shielding his face and eyes to the brightness. He pushed through, each step a battle against the tide.

With one final grunt of effort he reached Memory and wrapped his arms around her waist. Her purple hair whipped in his face. He cried out as it took all of his strength to pull her free.

They tumbled out of the Veil door together, rolling across the floor, with Memory cradled in Will's arms.

Will could hear Eloryn continue to cast, binding Caliburn into the doorway, allowing the flow of magic through, keeping all the fae renewed and the magic life force circulating properly the way Memory had sacrificed herself to achieve.

But all Will cared about then was the tiny, limp body in his arms.

"Memory," he said, brushing his hand down her cheek.

Her eyes were still open but unaware. He laid her carefully flat on the floor.

"Eloryn, I need you here now. I need you to heal her. Something is still wrong."

She was there immediately, Roen by her side.

Memory moved slightly, her eyes blinking, looking all around, blinking again.

Roen grinned wide. "There, she's okay. You're okay," he said, smiling down at Memory.

She shied away. "Who are you?"

At those words, Will's hand tightened into a fist and he almost broke.

A dismal gasp came from Eloryn. "No, please no."

Memory brought herself up into a sitting position, becoming frantic as she looked around the room. She tried to put down her hand that wasn't there anymore and cried out in pain as the stump scraped the ground and she slipped back down to her back. She brought the limb in front of her face and screamed.

"What have you done to me?" she sobbed. "Why can't I remember anything? Not anything!"

That sentence broke Will's heart. Memory had accomplished what she had set out to do but she had paid a high price. Her mind was gone again, all of her memories wiped clean. How could that be fair? How could that be fair at all? For what she had given she deserved so much more.

He wrapped his arms around her, bringing her up onto his lap. At first she struggled, but then she curled into him, weeping.

"There is nothing to be scared of. You're safe now. I'm Will," he whispered to her. "This is Eloryn, and Roen. We're here for you. We're your family."

CHAPTER THIRTY-THREE

They tell me my name is Memory.

They tell me that I did amazing things.

They tell me all about this land I'm in and the changes that are happening here.

Avall was experiencing a wary peace.

Oonah was proving to be a kind and intelligent ruler of the unseelie fae. She was Finvarra's wife, Nyneve's mother, whom Nyneve had exiled for being too sympathetic to humans. She and Aine worked together with the forces of seelie and unseelie fae to stop Avall shifting back to the rest of the world, stabilizing it within the Veil, separated again from the world it had once been part of. But the doorway that Memory had opened between the worlds, whose opening was smack in the middle of the Round Room of the palace of Caermaellan, remained open. At least, on Avall's end.

The Wizards' Council had used their magic to hide the opening at the other end. They did not think Avall was ready to be rediscovered by the rest of the world yet. Most were afraid of that world and its technology, but some were excited by it, thrilled at the prospect of being able to share again, to import new things and to allow Avall to move forward. It had been stuck in its time rut long enough, and it had outlived the antiquated ideals and principles that had once ruled the land. Bedevere had already made a number of trips into the other world.

The world they told Memory she was also part of.

I try to understand, but the hole inside me feels so big that it could never be filled.

Will looked across at Memory, his face the normal mix of small smile and small frown she had grown to know. He was always by her side, as long as she wanted him to be. There were times when she needed to be alone and he would let her be, but mostly she appreciated his presence, and his answers. They sat together on the balcony of her bedroom, staring out at the springtime flowers in the courtyard below, legs dangling over the balustrade, feet tickled by the ivy leaves that grew there. Memory smiled back at Will. He had become a good friend.

She had a sister here, too. Eloryn. And Eloryn's boyfriend, Roen, seemed to treat Memory like family as well. They were around often, but also had responsibilities that kept them busy. And there were many other friends she was learning the names of. There were also a lot of names that were spoken of friends who were gone.

Alward, Thayl, Waylan, Peirs, Edele, Shonae, Clara. Memory recited the names often, although she couldn't remember the people themselves. It hurt her, to know that maybe she would never remember them, that these people had died and she would never now have a chance to know them.

Eloryn had tried to explain Memory's complicated relationship with Thayl. At times it made Memory too sad and she had to stop her sister, taking the story in small installments only.

A warm breeze blew past the balcony and Memory sighed. "So many terrible things," she whispered quietly to herself.

Will's normally small frown deepened and Memory had to remind herself again how good his hearing was.

"Lots of terrible thing have happened. To this world, to you, and to me," he said, staring over the courtyard to the forest beyond. He turned back and met her gaze. The icy blue of his eyes made her heart jump. "But know you're the best thing to happen to me, and to this world."

Memory looked down at her right hand, or what used to be her right hand, and sighed. A finely crafted silver prosthetic hand was now attached there. Eloryn had spent days planning an intricate behest which imbued the replica hand with a sort of life. It responded to Memory's thoughts and moved just as a real hand would, however while it could touch, it could not feel. Sometimes she could have sworn she still felt the tingle of real flesh, then when she looked down and saw the cold metal at the end of her arm it confused and scared her beyond anything

she wanted to admit.

Losing her hand, losing her memories and herself, were the sacrifices she had apparently chosen to make. Everyone said she had changed everything, and talked about the differences, but she did not remember what it had been like before.

There was no Pact anymore, no forced peace treaty, and no threat of Branding. There was just an implicit agreement to treat everyone, seelie and unseelie and human alike, as equals. So far everyone had managed to behave. Nobody knew if that would or could last, though they all hoped that it did. The fae had been given life again due to Memory's actions, and there was a grand sense of gratitude for that. The numbers of fae spending more time in Avall had grown and it was rare to spend a day without seeing a fae of one kind or another. And with the return of the fae, the weather had also improved. The bitter snows ended and a mild sun shone across a flourishing land.

The Kingdom of Avall was being managed by the people Memory had put in place, but they had yet to crown a new ruler. Memory was still queen, at least in name, and everyone seemed to be waiting for her, hoping that she would regain her memories or learn enough again to step back into that role. In the meantime Eloryn was acting in her place.

There was a quiet knock on the door, and Eloryn and Roen came in together. The happiness Memory could see in them always made her happy as well, and somehow sad.

They didn't say a word, just came over and joined Will and Memory on the balcony. The sun had just begun to dip toward the horizon, warming the clouds around it to a blazing gold.

Eloryn rested her head on Memory's shoulder, and Roen put a hand on hers, and together they watched the sunset.

Memory found the whole thing strange, the way people treated her, and talked about what she did. She felt like they were talking about someone else. In a way, they were. She didn't recall doing those things, didn't know the people who spoke to her, and she never knew what was exaggerated. It all sounded like an exaggeration to her. Could anyone really have had that much magic? How had she have survived it? It seemed like she would have just exploded, or imploded, something oded, just to get rid of it at some point. It had to have hurt.

When things became too confusing, Will was always there for her, always ready to comfort her and to talk to her and to tell her about their

shared past. Guilt swamped her on a daily basis. He loved her. It was obvious, despite how he tried to hide it, how he tried to put no pressure on her to feel the same. Her heart was as empty and hollow as the spot in her head where her memories had once resided. She apologised daily that she wasn't the person he remembered. He said he could wait, and that he would wait forever for her if he had to. She believed him. He treated her with nothing but the utmost patience and love.

Everyone treated her like a hero even though she remembered nothing of what she had done. But she knew one thing— that person they all saw in her, that was who she wanted to be.

EPILOGUE

The wedding between Eloryn and Roen was a sumptuous affair.

It was a celebration of their love, but also a celebration of the new peace and prosperity Avall and all its inhabitants had found. Seelie and unseelie fae and people of all walks of life were in attendance. The ballroom was filled with sprites dancing, their wings shedding bright colors onto the fur of black-eyed fauns and satyrs around them. People in rich velvets and homespun cottons, women in tightly laced corsets and fae in wispy gossamer gowns filled the chamber and overflowed into the gardens and grounds of the palace.

The feast was huge and many of the people who had been going hungry in the land were at the groaning tables, stuffing intricately iced cakes into their mouths and laughing joyfully. There was plenty for everyone. The fae were no longer in danger of leaving the world forever and so Avall was no longer at risk of becoming a barren wasteland again. The land was healing, and the races along with it.

Music swirled and the dancers clapped their hands. Gaiety was everywhere, or almost everywhere. Some people remained still, looking around with the sad expression of a person searching for someone who will never come in the door again.

Memory leaned against a pillar, watching Eloryn dance with Roen. It was tradition in Avall for the bride to receive a gift of some form from

a fae, and so Eloryn's gown was a gift from the seelie queen. It was a blend of gauzy, lighter than air fabric and gems like dewdrops that fell in smooth lines from her waist, spilling onto the floor like a shining pool at her feet. The golden tones mirrored her hair, which was pinned up in a mass of curls, highlighting her delicate face, made more beautiful by the flush of happiness it held. Roen wrapped his finger around one loose curl of hair, his eyes only for Eloryn's as they spun in slow circles around the room.

Leaning on the other side of the pillar, Will asked, "Do you want to know how they fell in love?"

"No," Memory answered. "It's enough to see that they are."

Memory swallowed, mustering up the courage to ask something she hadn't yet been able to. She'd pieced some of it together herself, from how Will and her other friends behaved and talked, and at first it made her only feel sad. But something had been stirring inside her, and she felt she was ready. "If you could though, if it's not too hard… maybe sometime could you tell me about how we fell in love?"

Will had a guilty look of being caught out. "You know?"

Memory grinned mockingly. "Sheesh, give a girl some credit! You can't look at me with those eyes without me seeing all the feels."

Will looked at his feet. "I didn't want to force anything by having you know."

"I know. Thank you. But I want to know. I'm not saying I'm ready to be in a relationship with you again or whatever it was we were. I'm not sure that is the path I want for myself now. Not that I don't like you, I mean, I do like you, I mean…" Memory took a deep breath and looked away from Will's blue eyes and mess of dark hair and strong shoulders. "Yeah, so. Ahem. Maybe we can have that chat sometime."

Will nodded and looked away, sparing Memory from him seeing the growing redness in her cheeks.

Across the room, Memory saw Oonah giving Eloryn a gift, some kind of large book. The two turned in unison and looked straight at Memory. She felt strange under the Unseelie Queen's inhuman stare, and the mix of emotions on her sister's face confused her. She didn't know either of them well enough to understand what it meant.

But she didn't have to think about it for long.

"Dance with me?" Will asked, his voice so slightly shaky.

"I don't know how to dance," Memory said.

Will chuckled. "Do you think I do?"

Memory grinned, and took his extended hand. They shuffled out into the crowd, awkwardly trying to copy the moves of those around them. Soon they let joy and silliness and the beat of the music take over, moving any which way they liked, laughing and panting and swinging about the room.

As one lively song ended and a slow waltz began, Memory found herself in Will's arms. They stood mostly still, swaying together on the spot.

Will bent down, tentatively, and gave her a soft kiss on her forehead. She smiled at him and her heart swelled, as though growing to love him again was the most natural thing in the world.

"It's late," Roen said, silhouetted in the doorway.

Eloryn looked up at him from where she was hunched over the desk in the queen's office. "Is it?"

Then she frowned at him, seeing him standing there in the darkness. "Where is your wisp light? You've been getting good at that behest, but you do still need practice."

"Thanks, teacher," he said, and Eloryn imagined the grin on his face despite not being able to see it. She did see him shrug. "I guess I'm just not used to being able to do that yet. I've always been comfortable in the dark. Àlaich las." A small glow appeared in his hand, shining up and making his caramel features turn to gold.

Eloryn smiled. He had been getting much better. When Memory replaced the Spark of Connection in the humans of Avall, it entered everyone. Even Roen. Even Will. Eloryn had been teaching them how to use their new connection to magic. Just one of her current projects.

Roen walked in and sat on the arm of her chair, putting his hands to .work on the tight muscles at her neck. She closed her eyes, enjoying his touch.

His words were quiet. "I know what you are trying to do, and I want it as much as you do, but please don't lose yourself to this."

Eloryn looked back at the desk where Nyneve's journal lay open. Oonah had proved a kind ruler in many ways, and this wedding gift to Eloryn had been just one. Somewhere in these pages they hoped would be a way to help Memory.

The book was bound in leather that still held a stickiness like wet blood. The pages had been created out of thin linen and the ink was clear and legible even when the hand that had written the words within had shaken from grief or rage or jealousy.

The book felt wrong. The cover and pages had a weight to them that made Eloryn want to wipe her fingers on her skirts after each leaf turned.

"There are things in here I would be better off not seeing or knowing. Nyneve was beyond the darkness, she was headed into lightless territory," Eloryn said.

"I will try to keep you in the light," Roen replied.

A smile took the shadows from Eloryn's face.

She had to admit it, reading Nyneve's journal had taken a toll on her.

It started out innocent enough. Then Myrddin began to appear often in the text, and soon Nyneve's love turned to poison, to hatred. She refused to see what she was doing to him and their relationship, with her jealousy over Arthur and the humans that Myrddin loved so much.

The emotions in those words were so raw and powerful that Eloryn could feel them tangle her insides. They battered at her heart and she had to stop reading those passages. But the next passages, once Myrddin had gone missing, were worse. Dark spells, sacrifices, and blood pacts, anything to bring Myrddin back to her. Her first body sacrificed was Myrddin's father, using his blood to make like call to like, drawing Myrddin free of the Veil. It was much as Alward's failed Veil door and Eloryn had accidentally drawn Memory back out of the Veil when she had been lost.

Once Nyneve learned that Myrddin had attacked Mordred, seeking revenge on the man for killing Arthur and was then Branded by the human, things really turned dark.

That's when the blood drinking began.

Eloryn learned that while Nyneve had been building her resistance to iron by drinking human blood, she had also been testing her resistance to iron by being in contact with it. When Memory's past was freed into the world after beating Thayl, Nyneve had been able to experience some of Memory's past, filtering the memories into her through the iron.

Nyneve could not possess Memory's past, but she could learn enough from it to act as Hope. But there was something there, something in her methods that started connections firing in Eloryn's mind. Eloryn knew that holding iron had returned some memories to her sister in the past, but magic came with it, and she didn't want her sister suffering from

an overflow of that again.

The Wizards' Council had collected and locked away all remaining iron artifacts after the battle, understanding now its connection to magic and what too much contact with it could do. They did small and highly monitored tests, and in their own way were trying to help Memory too. But they hadn't yet discovered a way to return Memory to herself.

The rest of the pages of Nyneve's journal were filled with darker magic than any before. Blood sacrifices, runes cut into flesh, and spells with hearts the color of coal. The journal needed to be destroyed, or taken somewhere and hidden for all time so that nobody else could use the evil magic and spells inside. The lure of that power was too tempting, even to Eloryn.

"No, I won't lose myself." Eloryn shuddered and closed the book, no longer wanting to see those words, to feel the residual magic, twisted and sickening, that lingered there.

She moved out of Roen's grasp and turned to look at him face to face.

"I found something, in Nyneve's mad words. The way she returned Memory's past to her the first time, it might be a way to bring our Memory back to us."

"But without any sort of sacrifice, of course?" Roen asked, one eyebrow raised.

Eloryn frowned. It was a sacrifice of sorts, for Memory. Eloryn closed her eyes, picturing how she saw her sister earlier that day. She was laughing, rough-housing with Maeve on the palace lawn, green grass clinging to her dress and a daisy tucked behind her ear. She seemed so happy. None of the weight and pain of a terrible past, the suffering she had lived through.

Would it be better if she remained free of that suffering forever?

It's not your decision.

The words bounced around in her head and she wished they were not true, but they were. It was up to Memory whether or not she wanted them back.

Roen's eyebrow rose further. "You're worrying me here."

"No, no sacrifices," Eloryn said.

"Do you think she will be okay?" Roen asked, echoing Eloryn's fears. "The last time she got her memories back, she tried to kill herself."

Eloryn stood up and put her arms around Roen. "I know. I'm scared too. But this time, we'll be there for her."

Memory, Eloryn, Roen and Will, stood staring at the open Veil door that sat in the center of the Round Room. Wispy gray smoke circled the blurry window to the rest of the world, and in the middle stood Caliburn, wedged into the floor and glowing golden, spilling light and magic out into Avall.

The room had been cleared of everything except the round table itself, and a crystal display case holding Memory's iron knife. A mural had been painted on the wall that wrapped the space. On one side it showed Arthur and his knights, riding through flowered fields. Fae of all shapes and sizes fluttered around them or spied from the surrounding trees. On the other side of the room was an artist's impression of the Veil door they stood before. Caliburn was shown illustrated within, stylized curling flames surrounding it, and behind that, a small, feminine silhouette, aglow with magic.

Memory wondered if it was meant to be her. She looked down at her silver hand and the stump it concealed. "Will I remember... everything?"

Eloryn tilted her head. "Yes."

"But you don't really remember pain, do you? I mean, I'll see what happened, but I won't feel it?" Memory grunted and stuck her tongue out. "Gah, I sound like such a coward. But seriously guys. Hand cut off. I don't want to feel that again. Or anything... else."

"The memories may be painful in themselves. But this time it will be just the memories returned, not the magic. Caliburn is the key, using it as a filter as it channels magic through the worlds. We can filter just your memories back to you." Eloryn held her sister's remaining hand. "Mem, I made a promise to you long ago that I would restore your memories to you. It's a promise long overdue in its keeping. I think it's time."

"Yeah." Memory exhaled the word. "You're right. Let's do this. I know I am going to see and remember stuff I don't want to, but I do want to remember you, all of you. I want to remember me. I want to be whole again."

They all clasped hands as they gathered around the doorway and the magical sword within. Memory took a long moment to look at each of her friends' faces, the faces she didn't really know anymore, but had and would, she hoped, know again soon.

"See you on the other side guys." Her voice faded as Eloryn spoke her magic to the Veil door and the wind began to howl out a mournful tune. The flow of magic from Caliburn was directed through Memory, filtering through her, rushing through like burning ice.

"We should wake her up."

Everything was warm, slow, and dark. The words drifted around Memory in her haze of sleep.

"No, we can't. She has to recover on her own. Getting her memories back is going to be traumatic."

"It's been days. What if... what if she doesn't wake up?"

"She has already relived her memories once, now she has to start all over and what is more, now there are new horrible memories. What if you had to recall every single detail about your life? The bad stuff, the stuff you don't want to talk about, the things that cut you the most? What if she doesn't want to wake up?"

"She wants to."

"Then why doesn't she?"

It's okay. I'm here.

Her mouth and eyes didn't want to work yet. But her mind was waking up. It was giving names to the voices. And faces. And pasts. The exact shade of Will's eyes and the bad haircut he got when he was eight. The color Eloryn's cheeks turned at regular intervals. The corner of Roen's mouth that twitched up when he was doing something charming. Erec's sandy complexion that was so much like his brother, Peirs's. Peirs, who died to save her. Clara, who died to save her sister, and had lived to flirt with every soldier in the palace.

"If I had to live the worst again, I might never get out of bed," she heard Erec say, and she knew he was thinking about Clara. It had only become clear after Clara was gone, the love he'd been harboring for her. Only clear to Memory now, now she remembered everything again.

Will spoke, his voice low and hoarse. "There used to be a story about a prince who kisses the sleeping princess and brings her back to life. Just a fairy tale, but I wish I had that magic, some way to help her."

"Maybe I've been waiting for you to give it a try?" Memory croaked, her voice rough from sleep. She peeled dry eyes open and looked up at Will and her friends, standing around her bed. Daylight streamed through the window, making dust motes spark like pixies in the air.

"Memory?"

"Yes. It's me. All of me."

Will fell on top of her on the bed, scooping her up.

She could feel his heartbeat against her chest, then more arms wrapped them, and she heard the small, squeaking sobs of her sister and Roen's relieved laughter. She took a moment to know them, really know them, to recall exactly who they were. Some of her memories were awful. She had done things and suffered things she almost couldn't live with, but there were so many good moments too, memories of these people, her family.

"I love my cuddle fests," she sighed, nuzzling against her friends. Then she pushed them away. "But I smell food. Get me to the food, I'm starving! How long have I been sleeping here, a hundred years?"

"Felt like it to me," Will said.

"It was barely two days," Roen scoffed. "How you ever waited those sixteen years I'll never know. This fellow is the most impatient person I've ever known."

"I'm so happy you're home," Eloryn said.

She helped Memory out of bed, holding her hand and supporting her by the elbow on the other side. Memory noticed she was wearing her old broken heart t-shirt, and what seemed to be brand new sweat pants. She quirked an eyebrow, wondering where they came from, but was happy to be in their fleecy embrace regardless.

In Memory's living room, every surface was filled with bouquets and garlands of flowers, and mountains of cakes and pastries. Rainbow colored roses from Loredanna's rose garden filled the room with a sweet scent, and... was that a cake shaped like a hamburger? *No way.*

The thought of Clara, missing this, being gone from their lives, drilled a deep hole of pain in Memory's heart. *Alward, Thayl, Waylan, Peirs, Edele, Shonae, Clara.* She remembered them all. She would never forget them again.

Memory swiped the first delicacy that was within reach and bit through the flakey crust to the custard cream inside.

Maeve entered the room, wearing a palace maid's uniform and balancing another tray of food. Her wild mass of brown hair was bundled neatly atop her head and she looked stronger and healthier than ever.

She stopped abruptly when she saw Memory awake and eating.

"It is you!" she yelled, dropping the tray onto a table, and running in.

Memory was enveloped in a huge and almost smothering hug and she laughed, "Yes, it is me. Sorry I was gone for so long. How are the kids?"

"They are amazing, thanks to you and your friends. Some of them still have nightmares though, and might for a while yet."

"I'm sorry I didn't ask about them sooner."

"How could you have?" Maeve said. She held up a fist, and Memory punched it three times then they both mimed an explosion.

Memory laughed. "You were totally just testing if I really remembered, weren't you?"

"Maybe," Maeve grinned. With Clara gone, Maeve had fought other servants off almost physically to be the one to take over her position as Memory's only assistant. Maeve had known, even when Memory couldn't, that it was what she would have wanted. Memory pulled the feisty girl back into a hug again as a silent thank you for that.

They all sat down together, relaxing on the floor and chairs. Not talking, just eating in silence, knowing they were all together again and that that was enough.

The friends that were missing weren't completely gone. Memory closed her eyes for a moment, feeling the weight of them, their loss, their lives, in her chest. Holding onto every precious memory.

She still felt fragile, brittle like fairy gold, from the return of her old memories. But she also felt stronger from the return of her newer ones.

She no longer burned inside with all the excess magic she had felt her whole life. All that was left was just the normal, small Spark of Connection. No missing soul, no missing past, no longing for a family she didn't know.

She had everything she always wanted.

She finally felt whole and complete.

The rest of the day was spent much the same, just enjoying each other's company within the small space of Memory's chambers. After a while Erec and Maeve left together, and then Roen and Eloryn as well.

Will hugged Memory close, and she leaned up to kiss him. His lips were warm and soft and she let herself melt into him. Memory closed her eyes, a smile blooming on her face. Finally, she was home.

ABOUT SELINA A. FENECH

Whether it's painting artworks or writing novels, creating fantasy works is Selina's biggest passion. She lives in Australia with her daughter and cats, and loves food, gardening, geekery, and all things fantasy.

Find out more about Selina at her official website-
www.selinafenech.com

9 780648 026952